REJUVENATING COUNTRY THROUGH INNOVATION

INNOVATION

INNOVATION MANAGEMENT AND THE RISE AND FALL OF A NATION

Zhou Jizhong

SCIENCE PRESS
Beijing

Responsible Editors: Lin Jian   Liu Chao

Brief Introduction

This book defines innovation management in broad sense from three dimensions, i. e. , institutional design, innovation management and innovation culture, providing a perspective to observe the national strength of a country. Innovation management, in narrow sense, only refers to the management of scientific and technological innovation.

Focusing on China as well as some other influential countries in the world, including developed countries, such as the United States, the UK, Germany, France, Japan and Italy, and emerging economies including Russia, India and Brazil, the book discusses extensively the relationship between innovation and national strength from the perspective of innovation management in broad and narrow senses, highlighting the dominant role of innovation in development in the 21st century.

This book is intended for employees of businesses, teachers and students in institutions of higher education as well as civil servants and cadres at all levels.

ISBN 978-7-03-032556-3

Preface

It has been eight years since the publication of *Management of Scientific and Technological Innovation* (Economic Science Press, 2002) , during the period I have thought about republishing the book, so as to update some information. Nevertheless, in exploring the diversity of research approaches, I came up with the idea of publishing this book *Rejuvenating Country through Innovation—Innovation Management and the Rise and Fall of a Nation* in cooperation with Science Press.

Since I majored in physical chemistry of metallurgy first and then turned to management of technology (MOT) in university, the first research project I took charge of was about the "Scale and Composition of China's Science and Technology Investment", funded by National Natural Science Foundation of China (Department of Management Sciences) in 1987. I went to the United States in the September of the same year, as a visiting scholar in the field of "science and technology policy and management" in the Science, Technology and Society (STS) center, Massachusetts Institute of Technology (MIT). After returning to China, I published *Science and Technology Trends in the United States: Policy Trends of a Scientific and Technological Power* (Science Press, 1991), and later *On Scientific and Technological Education* (Science Press, 1993), *International Scientific, Technological and Economic Cooperation* (Science Press, 1993), and *The Ultimate Choice: Science and Technology and Education* (Shaanxi People's Education Press, 1997). *Management of Scientific and Technological Innovation*, published by Economic Science Press in 2002, is organized and written in a quite systematically manner and has been used as the textbook for my graduate course "Management of Scientific and Technological Innovation" in the Graduate School of the Chinese Academy of Sciences for years. As my research interest gradually turned from the macro to micro management of technology, I published R&D *and Services for Innovation Systems Engineering* (Economic Science Press) and *Linkage of Technological*

Innovation and Intellectual Property Rights (Science Press) in 2009. Like my previous works, the two books were also fruits of the research projects funded by National Natural Science Foundation of China (Department of Management Sciences) and National Social Science Foundation, but what's different is that they were the co-works by me and my students. The two books are about our studies on the management of technological innovation and intellectual property rights in telecommunications, pharmaceutical and financial industries as well as businesses in these industries, highlighting that "enterprises are the main practitioners of independent innovation".

As *Management of Scientific and Technological Innovation* has also been used asa textbook by some other universities, in 2009, some teachers from other universities asked me to update some information when republishing the book, because great changes have taken place in this field in recent years. Unexpectedly, I suffered from a serious illness shortly after I decided to republish the book at the end of 2009. Recovered from this illness and inspired by the works regarding "the rise of China" (especially Martin Jacques' *When China Rules the World: The Rise of the Middle Kingdom and the End of the Western World*), I came up with an idea of "grafting" "innovation management" into "prosperity of a nation", and thus wrote the book *Rejuvenating Country through Innovation—Innovation Management and the Rise and Fall of a Nation.*

Among management disciplines, policy design in public administration and management of scientific and technological innovation in innovation management are both related to national strength, design of innovation policy, innovation culture and innovation management. Therefore, this book can be considered as the continuity and development of my thoughts, a confluence of my works including *Management of Scientific and Technological Innovation* (Economic Science Press, 2002), *R&D and Services for Innovation Systems Engineering* (Economic Science Press, 2009), *Linkage of Technological Innovation and Intellectual Property Rights* (Science Press, 2009), *Science and Technology Trends in the United States: Policy Trends of a Scientific and Technological Power* (Science Press, 1991), and *International Scientific,*

Technological and Economic Cooperation (Science Press, 1993) . It is, hereby, noted that there are many quotes from those books in the first three chapters of this book, i. e. , " China in a Century" , " The United States in Crisis" , and " The Conservative UK".

"Innovation management" or "rise and fall of a nation", particularly the latter, is an extremely large topic and broad field of research. It is impossible for a single person to expound these two issues in details in a single book. Therefore, the book is written in a style of "extremely rough sketch" to set up a three-pillared framework of "institutional design", "innovation management" and "innovation culture" and briefly illustrates the changes of a country's national strength. Compared with "complicated descriptions", "sketchy simplicity" is not detailed enough and far from being completed; however, it impresses readers with being simple and clear. Finally I had to choose "a simple style", due to my limited energy and knowledge. With the "simple" exposition, however, I often felt the book's limit in its depth and scope. Thus, it is never modest remarks that "there must be many errors and mistakes in the book and I earnestly expect your understanding".

In the end, I want to extend sincere thanks to my three students for their contribution to this book. Xu Zhi, a post-doctoral student back then, co-authored two parts in Section Two, Chapter One, i. e. , " Bottlenecks in the allocation of resources for basic research" and " Service innovation in China's commercial banks"; Hou Liang, a doctoral student back then, co-authored one part in Section Two, Chapter One, i. e. , " Innovation management of China's telecom enterprises"; and Zhao Yuanliang, a doctoral student back then, co-authored four parts in Section Two, Chapter One, i. e. , " Innovation management of China's pharmaceutical industry" and three cases of pharmaceutical enterprises.

I also want to express my heartfelt gratitude toward the Department of Management Sciences, National Natural Science Foundation of China for their 20-years support for me. Since my first research project funded by the Foundation in 1987, it has been giving financial support to my research work. The writing and publication of this book has also been directly supported by the project of "comparative study of 'services- R&D linkage model' in China's enterprises" (project No. : 70773110) of the Department of Management Sciences.

I would like to extend especial thanks to the Science Press for its support all along. Since the publication of *Science and Technology Trends in the United States: Policy Trends of a Scientific and Technological Power* in 1991, seven books of mine have been published by the Press. My thanks also go to Lin Jian, managing editor and also the first reader of the book, who has offered me many valuable suggestions on the contents and style of this book.

Zhou Jizhong

December 2010

Beijing

Contents

Introduction

Rejuvenating Country through Innovation

"Innovation is the soul of progress of a nation, and it is the inexhaustible impetus for the prosperity of a country. The essence of science is innovation, which entails ceaseless discovery and innovation." "The decisive factor of today's worldwide economic, scientific and technological competition lies in the capacity of innovation." "Scientific and technological innovation has increasingly become an important foundation and mark of the emancipation and development of social productive forces, and decides more than ever the development process of a country or nation. Unable to innovate, a nation could hardly be prosperous, and could hardly stand towering in the international community. To this problem, not only leaders and cadres at various levels, but also the society, as a whole, should have very strong political awareness." "Innovation comprises theoretical innovation, institutional innovation, scientific and technological innovation, and other innovation. Emancipation of the mind, and theoretical innovation, are mighty forces driving the advancement of a society." (Jiang Zemin, 2006)

Then, how did innovation become the soul of a nation's progress, and how did it become the inexhaustible impetus for the prosperity of a country? Why do we say that "The decisive factor of today's worldwide economic, scientific and technological competition lies in the capacity of innovation?" How did emancipation of the mind and theoretical innovation become the mighty forces driving the advancement of a society? Why do we say that innovation mainly comprises theoretical innovation, institutional innovation, and scientific and technological innovation? All these questions have continually been discussed in theoretical studies and social practices both at home and abroad. This book attempts to deal with these questions from the perspective of "Innovation Management and Rise and Fall of a Nation".

Management is an activity, and it is also a science. Innovation management is a branch of the management science. Management can be divided into four functions, i. e. , planning (including making systems, strategies and decisions), organizing, assuming leadership, and controlling (Jones et al. , 2005). Innovation management, therefore, may briefly be defined as an extension of the aforesaid management functions: planning innovation (including institutional innovation, strategic innovation or decision-making innovation), organizing innovation, leading innovation (including mind innovation and theoretical innovation), and controlling innovation. Here, innovation is in its broad sense.

In the academia, innovation management largely refers to the management of technological innovation or the management of scientific and technological innovation. This is because in the management science community, the management of technological innovation or the management of scientific and technological innovation, as an area of knowledge, became an established subject early, and was later conventionally called innovation management for short. Innovation management is a secondary discipline in management schools of some universities. Therefore, innovation management books currently published are largely about the management of technological innovation or the management of scientific and technological innovation. Examples include, among many others, *Innovation Management and New Product Development* by Paul Trott (2005), *Managing Innovation: Integrating Technological, Market, and Organizational Change* by Joe Tidd et al. (2008), *Managing Innovation: New Technology, New Products, and New Services in a Global Economy* by John E. Ettlie (2008), *Overall Innovation Management: Theory and Practice* by Xu Qingrui (2007), and *Innovation Management* by Chen Jin et al. (2009). The so-called "innovation" here is in its narrow sense. Of course, even though in its narrow sense, innovation management touches on the issue of national development to a certain degree.

"Innovation management" in the title of this book, which integrated the above-described two connotations, is innovation management in its broad sense, including not only institutional innovation and innovation culture, but also the management of scientific and technological innovation (namely innovation management in its narrow sense). The organic fusion of institutional design, innovation management and innovation culture, i. e. integration, ought to lead to advanced productive forces, improved competitiveness and ultimately national prosperity. Therefore, there is an essential relationship between "innovation management" in its broad sense and "rise and fall of a nation", and that is the core view of this book.

Prof. Michael E. Porter (2007), of Harvard Business School, says in his book *The Competitive Advantage of Nations* that "The new theory on the competitive advantages of nations must include 'technological advancement' and 'innovation' as major aspects to be considered. We must explain what role nations play in the course of technological innovation. Technological innovation entails the continual investment in tangible assets, human resources and research and development, so we must also explain why some nations are enthusiastic about research and development while some are not. The problem is how a nation provides an industrial environment that allows its enterprises to make innovation and progress faster than their rivals. From the broad point of view, the advancement of technology drives economic growth, and that is also one of the major reasons for economic progress of nations. "

Thus, there have been adequate studies by linking innovation to the prosperity of a nation. In his book (Chinese edition, about 940,000 characters), Porter mainly used his "diamond model", which consists of factor conditions, demand conditions, firm strategy, structure and rivalry, and related and supporting industries, to measure the competitive advantage of a nation from specific industries, while this book (about 900,000characters) discusses the rise and fall of a nation in a much broader way from three aspects, namely "institutional design", "innovation management" and "innovation culture". As to the relationship among these three aspects, "innovation culture" has a subtle influence on "institutional design" and "innovation management"; "institutional design" acts directly on "innovation management" and reacts on "innovation culture", making them both "keeping abreast of the times"; and "innovation management" enriches and changes "innovation culture" and "institutional design" both in content and form. The full linkage between them (not merely interaction between two of them) will result in spiral growth on the whole.

The "rise and fall of a nation" in this book is not only a relative but also dynamic concept. From the quantity and quality point of view, the "rise and fall of a nation" happens within relative space-time; from the historical point of view, the development of a nation might "rise and then fall", or "fall and then rise", or "rise, fall and again rise", or "fall, rise and again fall". In China, for example, in a history of over 3,000 years from the Zhou Dynasty to the present, if we say that it was rise during the Spring and Autumn Period as well as the Tang and Song Dynasties, and fall during the late Qing Dynasty and the Republic of China, then, from the end of the 1970s when China began reform and opening up to the present day of the 21st century, it is a new period of "rise again". Other countries in the world may also be looked at this way.

As per above accounts of "Innovation Management" and "Rise and Fall of a Nation", this book is structured as follows. Ten countries are chosen, and each is discussed in terms of the relationship between "Innovation Management" and "Rise and Fall of a Nation". One four-section chapter is arranged for each of the countries, dealing with its "Institutional Design", "Innovation Management" and "Innovation Culture", followed by "Innovation Management and National Strength", a summary of the entire chapter. "Innovation Management" in the book title is in its broad sense, comprising three aspects, namely "Institutional Design", "Innovation Management" in its narrow govern the interrelationship of human beings; they are reflections of various relations in human society. There are both broad and narrow institutions, large and small, for example, national institutions, legal systems, policies made by central and local governments, rules and regulations made by departments and organizations, and so on. To be specific, there are also wage systems, employment systems, distribution systems, promotion systems, etc.

Within the range of the management of scientific and technological innovation, there are laws and regulations on scientific and technological, scientific and technological policies, industrial innovation policies, methods for evaluation and appraisal of scientific and technological achievements, intellectual property systems, scientific and technological rules and regulations formulated by enterprises, universities and scientific research institutions, and so on.

Apparently, innovation of above-mentioned institutions is revolutionary at national, departmental, local and enterprise level.

This book uses "institutional design" instead of "institutional innovation", because the word "design" can reflect more distinctively the core connotations of the activity of institutional innovation.

(3) Innovation Management

The activity of management is a process of designing an environment that allows people to achieve their established objectives (Weihrich et al. , 2004). And this process comprises four basic management functions, namely planning (designing an environment and setting an objective), organizing (arrangement of people working in the environment), assuming leadership (directing and encouraging the organization to complete the objective), and controlling (testing the organization objective and the efficiency and effectiveness of completion thereof).

Therefore, in brief, innovation management in broad sense is designing new environments, institutions and policies, making new arrangements for people working in the environments, making new directions and designing new incentives for completion of tasks, and designing new methods, measures and means to test organizational objectives and the efficiency of completion thereof.

While innovation management in narrow sense is-by limiting the above-described activities to the scope of technological innovation management or scientific and technological innovation management, including making strategies, plans and policies for scientific and technological development-designing a particular environment such as

sense and "Innovation Culture"; the second section of each chapter, "Innovation Management", because of being in its narrow sense, deals only with the country's scientific and technological innovation or innovation in management approach.

In order to avoid repetition in the accounts of the countries (namely, the second section of each chapter, "Innovation Management"), the book gives a systematical description of the main aspects of "Innovation Management" in its narrow sense in Section 2 of Chapter 1, "Innovation Management" in China, mainly the main process of the management of scientific and technological innovation, including innovation strategy and research and development (R&D) (organization of innovation, pilot production and marketing of newly-developed products, risk of technological innovation, and marketing of technological goods), resource allocation and enterprise innovation. "Innovation Management" regarding other countries is treated by only choosing typical aspects.

In the book *The Competitive Advantage of Nations* Porter wrote in 1990, the ten countries chosen are the United States, the UK, Germany, Italy, Japan, Republic of Korea, Singapore, Sweden, Switzerland and Denmark, because the first five countries were the most competitive developed powers then, the middle two were Asian countries with outstanding competitive performance and the last three were small European countries with excellent competitive performance. This book, however, was written 20 years later, in 2010, when great changes had happened to the international competition situation: China, India, Brazil and Russia were hailed as the "BRICs", while the United States, the UK, Germany, Italy, Japan and France were 6 of "G-7", a group of seven industrialized countries. A comparison of the two groups of big countries gives a great sense of the times, and is more realistic when looking into the international competition situation in decades to come. The ten countries chosen are all big powers, which compared to small countries, have a bigger influence on the world and have a greater value of reference to China as a big country. Why did the book choose these ten countries? The United States, the UK, Germany, France and Italy are, so far, still the examples of developed countries (also including Canada, Australia, etc.). What's more, Italy, the UK, Germany and France served as the science center of the world at some point in history and the United States is still the world's center of science and technology up to now. As to Japan, it is not only an economic power and a science and technology power in the world, but also geographically close to China. China, India, Brazil and Russia, the so-called "BRICs", can be used as the examples of emerging countries (also including Indonesia, Mexico, South Africa, Turkey and Vietnam), and they are very likely to become the leading forces in future world economy. Small countries, such as Finland and Singapore, are also worth discussing with respect to "innovation management and the rise and fall of a nation", but considering worldwide influence, big countries have a much greater influence, and a bigger reference value, especially to China.

In geological terms, of the ten countries, two are in America (one in North America and the other in South America), five are in Europe (three in Western Europe, one in Eastern Europe and one in Southern Europe), and three are in Asia (two in East Asia and one in South Asia).

The main thread running through this book is "innovation management" in China- the country which was even not mentioned in Porter's *The Competitive Advantage of Nations* 20 years ago.

Corresponding to the definition of "innovation management" in its broad sense, the book also uses the broad definition of "innovation"-the act and process of creating new things. Such new things can be on physical or mental level; they can be new ideas, concepts, theories, institutions and culture, and they can also be new technologies, products, equipment, industries and systems.

As to how to define and measure a country's rise and fall, the book didn't give a precise definition, not did it make calculations like the "national power equations" of German scholar Withelm Fucks and American scholar Ray S. Cline or the "dynamic equation of comprehensive national power" of a deceased Chinese scholar Huang Shuofeng (2006). It only conducted analysis and comparison in an extensive manner that combines broad elucidation (by using others' research findings for reference) and quantitative index data (borrowed from other authoritative organizations' data). This is because "national power" could hardly be measured by merely using a single approach; of course, attention should also be paid to avoid being trapped in the "fog of comprehensive national power" (Wang Zhongyu, 2009) because of excessive index complexity.

Below is a brief description of the connotations of "mind innovation", "institutional innovation", "innovation management", "scientific and technological innovation" and "cultural innovation", and of why these five aspects of innovation are integrated into "institutional design", "management innovation" and "innovation culture" in this book.

(1) Mind Innovation

Mind innovation is the creation of new thoughts and ideas. Dare to think, speak and act; above all, dare to think (Lu Xun). Therefore, the emancipation of the mind and innovation is the precursor of reform and opening up, and of course it is the precursor of national prosperity. This has been widely illustrated in countries throughout the world.

The notion that "Practice is the sole criterion for testing truth", raised in 1978, could be said to be the first example of mind innovation during China's "period of rise". This thought, as a matter of fact, had appeared as early as in Chairman Mao Zedong's article, "*On Practice*". But it was used to smash the "two whatevers" (which refers to the statements that "we will resolutely uphold whatever policy decisions Chairman Mao made, and unswervingly follow whatever instructions Chairman Mao gave"), which was quite creative. In that special age, much courage was needed to do that.

That was followed by Deng Xiaoping's thought, for example, his 1979 idea of building "special economic zones", his 1980 talk of "contracting production quotas to individual households", his 1988 discussion of "Science and technology are the primary productive forces" and his statements in his "south talks" in January ~ February, 1992, such as "The essence of socialism is liberating the productive forces" and "on capitalism and socialism", all revealing mind innovation. Deng Xiaoping is recognized as the chief architect of China's reform and opening up, which is, first of all, manifested in above mind innovation. The mind innovation of "top-level design" would give rise to a wide variety of new concepts, ideas and even slogans. Among others in that period, the idea of "leasing out land in exchange for cash" in Shenzhen and the slogan of "Time is money, efficiency is life" in the Shekou Industrial Zone were specific reflections.

Mind innovation is the precursor not only of institutional innovation, but also innovation management and innovation culture. Institutional innovation is a reflection of mind innovation in policies, laws and rules. When treating each country in the parts-"Institutional Design", "Innovation Management" and "Innovation Culture", therefore, this book, in fact, is guided by "Mind Innovation" and fuses it into the parts. To streamline the book in structure and avoid unwanted duplication, the didn't make "Mind Innovation" a single section.

(2) Institutional Innovation

Institutions are a series of rules and regulations, and systems they form, desi a new-and high-tech development zone or a technological innovation project, arranging different working groups involved in scientific and technological activities, directing and encouraging the completion of scientific and technological plans, and evaluating and testing the efficiency and effectiveness of scientific and technological activities.

(4) Scientific and Technological Innovation

Science is a system of knowledge about the laws of the natural and physical world and human spiritual activities, and it is also the spiritual activity that human beings conduct to know the objective laws of the world. Technology is the experience and knowledge that human beings have accumulated in the course of utilizing and transforming nature and shown in their productive labor. Technology is the concrete and practical application of scientific knowledge. Any technology uses scientific knowledge to some extent. And at the same time, technology is the scientific summarization of practical experience. Technology, in its narrow sense, means engineering technology, which refers to various technical operating methods and skills formed by scientific knowledge and practical production experience. Generally speaking, scientific and technological innovation is the act of innovation for aforesaid scientific and technological activities. Because research and development as a creative and innovation activity is at the core of science and technology, in a way scientific and technological innovation refers to creative activities of basic research, applied research and experimental development. Basic research is the activity of increasing knowledge about the objective world and of seeking and discovering new facts and laws and searching for the essential relationships between phenomena. Applied research is the creative activity carried out to obtain new knowledge about principles (laws and mechanisms) and new knowledge about technology. Experimental development is the substantial improvement and systematic work done to produce new materials, products, devices, new processes, systems and services by using aforesaid research findings.

Since this book, rather than dealing with specific scientific and technological research activities, treats innovation at scientific and technological management level of these activities, i. e. innovation in such aspects as scientific and technological planning (institution, strategy and policy), scientific and technological organization, and scientific and technological encouragement and evaluation, contents regarding "scientific and technological innovation" were incorporated into "innovation management" in its narrow sense.

(5) Innovation Culture

In its broad sense, the concept of culture refers to the summation of human activities carried out to transform the objective world and subjective world, and achievements thereof, including two categories: material culture, human culture reflected by material activities and achievements thereof; and spiritual culture, human culture reflected by human spiritual activities and achievements thereof, including ethics and scientific culture. In this book, "innovation culture" mainly means the "values" relating to the above-described "institutional innovation" and "innovation management", including "free exploration", "democratic management", "tolerance for failure" and "open-minded cooperation". Because "national power" and the "rise and fall of a nation" are touched on in this book, there are also contents about "soft power" in "innovation culture".

If this book were stylistically too much structured, there would be repetition and overlap in content, given that the book, with a length of some 450,000 characters, is to treat the relationship between innovation management and national development in ten countries. Therefore, the above-described five aspects were merged into three sections, namely "Institutional Innovation", "Innovation Management" and "Innovation Culture", and integrated into the theme of the book-- *Rejuvenating Country Through Innovation*.

Chapter 1

China in a Century

"The rise of China" currently talked of at home and abroad, in temporal terms, refers to the historical period from 1978, when China began implementing its national policy of reform and opening up to the present, a period of only more than 30 years. In China's 5,000-year history of civilization, it is, indeed, as short as in the twinkling of an eye. But whether in Chinese history or world history, it is a historical period that deserves to be particularized, and what's more, this period is still ongoing, rather than being over.

"A Century" in the title of this chapter"China in a Century"refers particularly to the one hundred years from 1978 to 2078. A century is too long for me to see the end of it, but at the same time it is very short, only one eighth of the period of the Zhou Dynasty and slightly longer than one fourth of the period of the Qing Dynasty. This one century, however, has great and far-reaching significance for the development and history of China.

In the past 17th ~ 20th centuries, a historical period of some 400 years from the late Ming Dynasty through the Qing Dynasty and the Republic of China until the founding of the People's Republic of China, the national power of China, in contrast to the increasing national power of such countries as the United Kingdom, the United States, Germany, France and Japan, increasingly went downhill. The Cultural Revolution that lasted during the 1960s and 1970s, once again brought New China attempting resurgence to a sudden standstill. The ensuing national policy of "reform and opening up", which was begun in 1978, boosted the country's national power as rapidly and strongly as unexpectedly, which was acclaimed as "the rise of China" or "China Model. " Some people are so humble that they are reluctant to accept the title of "China Model. " As a matter of fact, a model is nothing but a pattern of things. As far as Asia is concerned, since there can be "Japan Model", "South Korea Model", "India Model" and "Singapore Model", of course there can be "China Model. "

But it is only in the 21st century that China can really go far. In the first 10 years of the 21st century, China overtook Germany and Japan in GDP to become the world's second biggest economy. By the mid-21st century, namely around the year 2050, China will surpass the United States (optimistically, 17 years later, namely in 2027) to become the world's biggest economy at the centennial of the People's Republic of China. And nearly 30 years from there, estimated at the end of the 2070s, namely around the year 2078, not only will China become a world power in both GDP and national power, but it also will truly stand towering in the international community as

Chinese Taiwan returns to China (there's no doubt about this). That is how the century from 1978 to 2078 is special to China.

Over 60 years has passed since the People's Republic of China was founded in 1949, but it is only one eightieth of China's 5,000-year history of civilization. China is one of the two big nations (the other is India), among the world's four great ancient civilizations, which have risen once again today. On technological innovation, in addition to the "Four Great Inventions" (papermaking, compass, printing and gunpowder) of ancient China, which greatly boosted the advancement of the world, the "Dujiangyan Irrigation System", the unique traditional Chinese medicine, the technological developments in shipbuilding and in seafaring during the voyages of Zheng He to the "Western Oceans", and *Bencao Gangmu* (*Compendium of Materia Medica*) were all shining pearls in world history of science and technology.

China has a territorial area of about 9,600,000 sq kilometers, and a population of 1,321 million (by the end of 2007), which is estimated soon to reach 1,400 million, one fifth of the world's total. China abounds with natural resources; its proven reserves of such mineral resources as rare earths, tungsten, antimony, molybdenum, vanadium and titanium rank first in the world; its reserves of such mineral resources as coal, iron, lead, zinc, copper, silver, mercury, tin, nickel, apatite and asbestos rank among the world's largest each; its hydropower resources amount to 680 million kilowatts, ranking first in the world; its land resources are characterized by a large absolute amount, a small per capita possession, complex and diverse types, and a small farmland proportion. In terms of the per capita ownership of natural resources, China is inferior to such countries as the United States, Russia and Brazil.

China has 56 nationalities, with the Han Chinese constituting about 91% of the total population. There is a multiplicity of religions in China, dominantly Christianity, Buddhism, Islam and Catholicism, with followers of various religions exceeding 100 million altogether, 8% ~9% of the country's total population. According to the 2008 ~ 2009 survey data on Christians in 31 provinces (autonomous regions and municipalities directly under the Central Government) across China by the Institute of World Religions under the Chinese Academy of Social Sciences, there are about 23,050,000 Christians in China, about 1.8% of the total population. But the majority of the country's total population believe in no religions, which is rare among the world's big countries.

Much experience deserves to be summed up from the "Rise of China" or "China

Model. " This chapter only looks at it from the perspective of "institutional design, innovation management and innovation culture", and compares it with some representative countries described in later chapters, in the hope of finding out some internal correlations between "innovation management and rise and fall of a nation. "

1. Institutional Design

The fundamental institutional design of a country is the enactment of its constitution. Following the founding of the People's Republic of China, four constitutions were enacted by the National People's Congress in 1954,1975,1978 and 1982,respectively. The current version was adopted in 1982 with further revisions in 2004 (revisions were made three times before).

The "Rise of China" began with mind innovation as the precursor and with institutional innovation as the framework. From the analysis of the institution given in "Introduction",during the whole period of the "Rise of China" (called the "rising period" or "new period" for short in this book), the Communist Party of China (CPC) and its government established and introduced systems,laws and regulations, and policies at various levels,largely the results of institutional innovation. Given the length of the book,only a brief description is given to the promulgation of the following two types of important systems,laws and regulations,and policies.

The "*Several Guidelines on Intra-party Political Life*", which was formulated under the guidance of Comrade Chen Yun in 1979 and was promulgated in 1980, played a momentous,creative role in toppling the fetishism of the "Two Whatevers" and in redressing the unjust,framed-up and wrong cases. Not only did these Guidelines lead to the "*Decision on the Rehabilitation of Comrade Liu Shaoqi*". which redressed the most unjust case of the Cultural Revolution,but they also,along with other important systems,laws and regulations and policies,redressed the cases involving unjust false and wrong charges with more than 3 million cadres,reinstated over 470, 000 CPC members in Party membership,and set millions of innocent cadres and masses free (Chen Yanbing et al. ,2008).

In the meanwhile,Comrade Deng Xiaoping's use of what Chairman Mao Zedong advocated "Seek truth from facts" to demolish the fetishism of the "Two Whatevers" showed great wisdom,and was a mind innovation which would initiate numerous institutional innovations later.

The economic restructuring wave, during the "rising period", was first started by Chinese rural farmers, and that was the implementation of the household contract responsibility system with remuneration linked to output (or household responsibility system)-a living example demonstrating that social practice precedes institutional innovation. This reform, which was first carried out by farmers in Anhui and Sichuan at the end of 1978 and the beginning of 1979, was soon embodied in the minutes of a symposium held in September 1980 by the CPC Central Committee, "*Several Issues concerning Further Strengthening and Improvement of the Agricultural Production Responsibility System*". On January 1, 1982, the CPC Central Committee approved and distri- buted the "*Minutes of the National Rural Work Conference*", recognizing that the various responsibility systems then being carried out in rural China-including the specialized contract responsibility system of linking payment to output and the system of fixed output quotas to rural households-all belonged to production responsibility systems of socialist collective economy. In 1983, the CPC Central Committee issued a document stating that the contract system with remuneration linked to output was a great creation of Chinese farmers under the leadership of the Party. The Eighth Plenary Session of the Thirteenth CPC Central Committee, held during November 25 ~ 29th, 1991, adopted the "*Decision of the CPC Central Committee on Further Strengthening the Agricultural and Rural Work*", proposing that the responsibility systems, primarily the household responsibility system, be long stabilized as a basic system for collective economic organization in rural China, and continuously enriched and improved in practice.

Above-mentioned minutes, decisions and annual "No. 1 Documents" of the CPC Central Committee were a series of institutional innovations preceded by mind innovations in China's rural reform. The agricultural development laid a solid foundation for the development of Chinese national economy and, more important, the institutional innovations in agriculture led the fashion for the later irreversible trend of "reform and opening up. "

The " Shenzhen Special Economic Zone (SEZ)", another achievement of Comrade Deng Xiaoping's "institutional design", is 30 years old now. When it was initially set up, its economic development mode relied primarily on the three types of processing plus compensation trades. By the 1990s, the industrial capital of the Shenzhen SEZ began transferring to hi-tech industries. In 1994, it surpassed 10 billion yuan in output value of hi-tech products. In 1998, it introduced the well-known "22

Articles", namely " *Several Regulations on Further Support of the Development of High-and New-tech Industries.* " From the beginning of the 21st century, the Shenzhen SEZ began developing towards the field of information technology, with per capita GDP already over $7,000. In September 2008, it formulated the " *Overall Plan of Shenzhen as a National Innovation-oriented City* " , China's first regional plan on independent innovation. In 2009, the city's R&D expenditure stood at 29,656 million yuan, 3.62% of its GDP—equivalent to Sweden's level in 2007 (3.60%), which ranked second in the world (Liu Chuanshu,2010).

In recent years, on the one hand, China decided to carry out new reform measures in the Shenzhen SEZ; on the other, it designed and planned a number of new SEZs, such as the Binhai New Area, the Haixi SEZ and the Liangjiang New Area. This is because the socialist market economy system, as a type of experiment, entails continuous exploration, continuous experimentation, emancipation of the mind, and everlasting innovation.

1.1 Whole-Nation Regime

The " *Opinions of the National Development and Reform Commission (NDRC) about Major Aspects of the Work on Further Carrying Out Economic Restructuring in 2010*" , approved and forwarded by the State Council on May 27, 2010, proposed "exploring and improving the whole-nation regime for scientific and technological innovation in the socialist market economy to fully promote national innovation system building. " Then, what is a "whole-nation regime?"

After mind innovation evolves into institutional innovation in respect of policies, laws and regulations, to carry out new systems, policies, and laws and regulations throughout the country and, with the strength of the whole nation, to seek overall development or solve local problems hence form a system of rules and regulations. And this system is a "whole-nation regime. "

Then, what connection is there between regimes and institutions? Institutions can, according to nature and scope, be divided into basic systems such as political, political party, economic, military, educational, scientific and technological, cultural, diplomatic and financial systems, and rules and regulations, such as employment system, distribution system, examination system, managerial system and wage system.

Regimes, also known as regime institutions, are systems of rules and regulations that are used to manage affairs in various aspects of social life, such as economy, politics and culture. Examples include state leadership system, economic system, military system, educational system and scientific and technological system. Institutions determine the contents of regimes and restrict their formation and development. An institution may be embodied in different regimes. For example, a market economy system may adopt the practice of either a free-competition market economy system, or a planned market economy system with relatively centralized management by the government.

The "whole-nation regime" that China has established during the "rising period" can be viewed as a type of institutional innovation. From the Three Gorges Dam, the Qinghai-Tibet Railway to the ongoing South-to-North Water Diversion Project, from the Beijing Olympics 2008 to Expo 2010 Shanghai China, from the special economic zones to hi-tech development areas, the Yangtze River Delta, the Pearl River Delta and other regional plans, from the partner assistance to quake-stricken Wenchuan to the partner assistance to Xinjiang…, all of these could not separate from the "whole-nation regime."

1.2　One-Party Rule

What force has long sustained such "whole-nation regime?" Or, to put it another way, in more essential terms, it is just because of the long-standing one-party rule of the CPC that China has developed rapidly during the "rising period." This point, which has been criticized by some Western experts, scholars and politicians, is the very reason responsible for the rise of China. Of course this is also the stiking point that makes them unable to understand why China could rise rapidly and enjoy lasting peace and stability. Therefore, the book attempted to give a brief analysis below.

There have been three monumental turning points in the development process of the CPC: the founding of the People's Republic of China in 1949 following its defeating the Kuomintang's regime, suggesting the CPC's daring, resolution and ability to resist old forces; the conclusion in 1976 of the Cultural Revolution, which lasted ten years, suggesting its courage and determination to rid itself of cancers within; and the steering of the "reform and opening up", which has lasted from 1978 to the present, revealing its farsightedness and mindset of carrying forward the cause and forging ahead into the future.

An article titled "How is China's political system superior to Western ones", published at the website of the Singapore-based *Lianhe Zaobao*, thinks that compared to the Western multi-party system, China's one-party system has six advantages: "(it) can make long-term national development plans and keep policy stability without being affected by different stances, different ideologies and the replacement of parties; respond in time and effectively to emerging challenges and opportunities, especially disaster emergencies; effectively curb the spread of corruption during the special period of social transition; build a more responsible government; set up talent training and promotion mechanisms and avoid the waste of talent; truly represent the whole people" (Song Luzheng,2010). That is positive justification.

We may also look at it from another aspect. Suppose that China practiced the Western "multi-party system" or "two-party system" from the very beginning of its "reform and opening up" in 1978, what would China be like? The simple picture might be like this: the voters who oppose "reform and opening up" or whose interests are affected in "reform and opening up" form one or more opposition parties which would, driven by their campaigning strategies and tactics, go on strike or demonstrate, leading to economic stagnation and even the split of the nation and finally to national chaos. Not only did this repeat during the 10-year Cultural Revolution between "conservatives" and "insurrectionists" and teach bitter lessons to us, but this also is the shackles which some countries and regions in the world could hardly break away with, as well as one of main root causes of trouble, which, as yet, they still are paying a high price for.

The Western "multi-party system" or "two-party system" seems to be the important institutional guarantee of national prosperity that developed countries firmly believe in, is also imitated by some less-developed countries. As a matter of fact, some problems have to be dealt with. For example, the voters act independently and defiantly according to which political party they support, and, to come to power, during election campaigns the two or more parties would attack each other's administrative program or performance. As a result, when in power the ruling party could hardly represent the whole people. Because of a limited time being in power, 8 years, 4 years, or even shorter, it is difficult for the two-or multi-party system to make long-term development objectives for the country, and all systems, policies, laws and regulations are designed during the reign of the ruling party. Though the "multi-party system" or "two-party system" is advantageous with respect to supervision of each other, it is disadvantageous in that the two or more parties denounced and hold down each other. And legislative disputes, therefore, involved are protracted, which makes the efficiency of legislative administration low and substantially affects national development. The major projects enumerated in 1. 1 "Whole-nation Regime", "from the Three Gorges Dam, the Qinghai-Tibet Railway to the ongoing South-to-North Water Diversion Project, from the Beijing 2008 Olympics to Expo 2010 Shanghai China, from the special economic zones to hi-tech development areas, the Yangtze River Delta, the Pearl River Delta and other regional plans, from the partner assistance to quake-stricken Wenchuan to the partner assistance to Xinjiang", all involved a high-efficiency process from design to completion. Just think of it, if the legislative and administrative bodies debate these projects ceaselessly and the ruling party also has to consider votes, the result would be much less desirable for sure, and even null and void.

Less-developed countries are much more affected by the two-or multi-party political system than developed countries. "Money-for-vote deals" are ubiquitous during electioneering for the ruling party, which is bound to worsen into "power-for-money deals" during the reign of the ruling party. Therefore, corruption and division are side effects not only during electioneering but also during the reign of the ruling party. By the same token, this affects less-developed countries much more than developed ones. Some believe that the Western electoral system leads to "rigid corruption", and that is justifiable.

The CPC has been able to be in power as the only one party, not only because of its convincing past-overthrowing the old regime and correcting the errors of the Cultural Revolution, but also because it ensures that "government decrees are clear and well-understood" by mustering the wisdom of the whole people in a style of "coming from the masses and going back to the masses" and perseveres in doing so. For example, the mind innovation of "Crossing the river by feeling the stones" gave rise to the development strategy of "progressive reform," which was entirely different from the then globally fashionable "leaping reform" of "shock therapy" and led to totally different results.

Of course, one-party rule also faces some problems. For example, there is the problem of effective supervision of the ruling party and its officials and members, namely, how to be "truly representative of the people" in a political environment, in which there is no rivalry, or how, under long-term one-party rule, to give the people more right to supervise, to know and to vote. For another example, although "ensuring stability as a principle of overriding importance" builds an ideal environment for lasting peace and stability of the nation, a price has to be paid for this, giving rise to the new problem of how to reduce this price as much as possible to achieve both good efficiency and results.

Therefore, the development connotations of the long-term reign of the CPC, especially in the "new period" from 1978 to the present, are the institutional guarantee during the rise of a large nation, and they are of fundamentally institutional innovation.

To make this institutional innovation long vigorous, the CPC has already made the following arrangements in terms of ideological and theoretical building and institutional reform: Party principles and goals should keep abreast of the times; there should be new ideas about the systems and methods for the development, selection and supervision of Party and government cadres at all levels; there should be innovations in the building of electoral systems under one-party rule of various types and at various levels; every effort should be made to ensure the harmonious development of the government and the people including ethnic minorities, and so on. To combat corruption, for example, China has introduced such systems as the "shuang gui (double rule)" system (under which officers detain suspects for questioning in a secret place for an unlimited time), offence reporting system, officials proclamation system and officials' property declaration system, showing that the CPC is stepping up its building of systems regarding supervision of Party and government cadres. We believe, with reason, that these efforts will inaugurate a situation of institution innovation.

1.3 Institutional Design Cases

Case 1: Western China Development

In his address, titled "*On Twelve Major Relationships*", at the closing ceremony of the Fifth Plenary Session of the Fourteenth CPC Central Committee held in September 1992, Comrade Jiang Zemin, the then General Secretary of the CPC Central Committee, talked of "the relationship between eastern and western China", pointing out that "solving the development gaps between regions and persevering in the coordinated development of regional economies are a strategic task for future reform and development." In December 1995, in his inspection tour to Shaanxi and Gansu provinces, Comrade Jiang Zemin indicated that the CPC Central Committee's policy on the development of western China was that "by the early 21st century, (western China will) begin advancing in the direction of gradually narrowing the gaps between eastern and western China, and by the 2050s, basically realize modernization like other regions across the country." In March 1999, at the Party leaders conference of the Second

Session of the Ninth National People's Congress (NPC) and the Second Session of the Ninth National Committee of the Chinese People's Political Consultative Conference (CPPCC), Comrade Jiang Zemin officially raised the strategic idea of "Western China Development."

Afterwards, the related departments of the State Council convened a series of "Western China Development" symposia, hearing opinions from various departments and local governments and from experts in economy, agriculture, forestry, water conservation and environmental protection, and carrying out feasibility studies. At the Fourth Plenary Session of the Fifteenth CPC Central Committee held in September 1999, "Western China Development" was made into the meeting resolution.

Such a massive national development project should be implemented by a cross-department leading group set up by the State Council, as per the system operation requirement of China. In January 2000, the State Council printed and distributed the *"Decision to Set up the Western China Development Leading Group of the State Council"*—appointing the Prime Minister as group leader under the leadership of whom were directors from 19 departments under the State Council (later increased to 23 departments under the CPC Central Committee and the State Council), marking the official start of the "Western China Development" strategy. Although the national leaders were reelected twice, in March 2003 and March 2008, it is the Prime Minister that took up the post of the group leader.

Including 12 provinces (autonomous regions, and municipalities directly under the Central Government)—Shaanxi, Gansu, Qinghai, Ningxia, Xinjiang, Sichuan, Chongqing, Yunnan, Guizhou, Tibet, Inner Mongolia and Guangxi—as well as three minority autonomous prefectures—Xiangxi in Hunan, Enshi in Hubei, and Yanbian in Jilin, "Western China Development" covers 6,850,000 square kilometers—71.4% of the national territory, with a population of 368 million (at the end of 2002)—28.8% of the country's total population. By 1999, counted as per the poverty line of 625 yuan per capita, of the rural poor population of 34 million across the country, 60% were in western China; and of 592 impoverished counties across the country, 307 were in western China. By the end of the 20th century, 9 of 12 western provinces (autonomous regions, and municipalities directly under the Central Government) failed to make ends meet; of over 3,600,000 square kilometers of soil erosion across the country, 80% happened in western China; and of over 2,400 square kilometers of desertification increment each year, 90% happened in western China. It is no exaggeration to say that without thriving and powerful western China, there will be no prosperous and strong China.

The grand objectives of "Western China Development" are: improving the living standards of people in western China; returning farmland to forestry while exploiting petroleum, natural gas, hydraulic power and mineral resources in western China, with a view of gradually improving the ecological environment there; strengthening the unity of the Han nationality with 52 ethnic minorities living in western China, and resisting attempts at splitting the nation; developing the bilateral relations with more than 10 countries bordering on western China (80% of the national terrestrial frontier lie in western China), for the purpose of combating terrorism together and, thus, ensuring national security. China has favorable conditions to implement "Western China Development": the economic and political safeguards stemming from the rise of China; the economic scale of industry, agriculture and service sectors, and abundant materials of great varieties; the initial establishment of the market economy system; the mechanism of partner assistance by eastern China to western China; and particularly, the country's stable political environment and consistent national policy environment, which provides the condition for long-term, sustaining operation of the Western China Development strategy.

"Western China Development" has also received international support. Russia and the five Central Asian countries (Kazakhstan, Kyrgyzstan, Tajikistan, Uzbekistan and Turkmenistan) signed a number of cooperation agreements with China in such fields as petroleum, natural gas, environmental protection and electric power; Japan also provided financial aid used for development in Sichuan, Qinghai and Tibet.

By 2005, a large number of major infrastructure projects regarding water conservancy, transportation, communications and so forth had been put into service or commenced. Afterwards, with the "Western China Development" being gradually defined, a range of measures were raised in succession, including "improving people's livelihood as the top objective", "stressing the equalization of basic public services" and "giving equal importance to environmental protection and development." On regional layout, regional economic development plans were formulated, for example, for "Western Longhai-Lanxin Economic Belt", "Upstream Yangtze Economic Belt", "Nanning-Guiyang-Kunming Economic Area" and "Tibet and Xinjiang Ethnic Minority Regions."

In July 2006, the Qinghai-Tibet Railway was open to traffic. The success of this "project of the century" is attributed to China's mastery of the world leading permafrost engineering technology. The Tibet-inbound trains are equipped with oxygen-supply devices which China developed independently, keeping oxygen concentration inside at 23% ~25%, which is enough for passengers traveling on the plateau.

By the end of 2008, ten years after the project of returning farmland to forestry began in western China, farmland-returned forestry had amounted to 139 million mu; forestation of barren hills and wasteland had amounted to 237 million mu; and forest reservation had amounted to 27 million mu.

By 2009, the "West-East Power Transmission" project had put into operation power plants with a combined installed capacity of 51 million kilowatts, along with those in progress with a combined installed capacity of 52 million kilowatts; the "West-East Gas Transmission" project had also provided immense energy sources to central and eastern China. By the end of 2009, the 16,000km-long trunk roads of the "Five Vertical and Seven Horizontal Routes" project in western China had all been linked up, with a combined traffic mileage of 1, 477, 000 kilometers, and the expressways had amounted to 18, 600 kilometers in length; western China had completed over 800 hi-tech industrial projects, and planned to build 16 hi-tech industrial bases, including the Xi'an Yanliang National Aviation Hi-tech Industrial Base and the Yangling Agricultural Hi-tech Industrial Base; "Six Categories of Small Projects for Rural Areas", designed to improve the well-being of people living in western China, had been constructed, which included water-efficient irrigation, potable water supplies, methane gas production, hydroelectric plants, roads, and pasture enclosures; and forestation in western China accounted for 57% of the country's total.

From 2000 to 2009, the total output value of western China rose from 1, 670 billion yuan to 6, 690 billion yuan, an average annual increase of 12%—higher than that of both central and eastern China; the per capita regional GDP increased from 4, 624 yuan to 18, 257 yuan, up 11. 4% each year on average; the local fiscal revenue increased from 112. 7 billion yuan in 2000 to 605. 5 billion yuan in 2009, up 20% each year on average and, as the country increased transfer payments to western China, the local fiscal expenditure increased from 260. 1 billion yuan to 1, 754. 9 billion yuan, rising 23. 3% each year on average; and a total of 120 key projects were initiated, with an investment size of over 2 trillion yuan.

On education, science, culture and healthcare in western China, China formulated *"The plan to make nine-year compulsory education basically available throughout the western region and basically eliminate illiteracy among the adults* (2004 ~ 2007)". By

2007, this plan covered a 99. 5% population, with an 87% rate of compulsory education fulfillment. In 10 years 6 million people were rid of illiteracy, and the rate of illiteracy among young and middle-aged people lowered to below 5% . In 2009, there were 6,772,000common high school students, 4,574,000 more than 1998; about 4,740,000 common college and university students; 1, 272, 000 adult college and university students; and 294, 000 postgraduates. The TV and radio coverage rates in western China reached 97% and 96% , respectively. In 2008, hospital beds and medical personnel in western China amounted to 1,080,000 and 1,500,000, respectively, up 32. 1% and 6. 4% from 1999; 16,440 town healthcare centers and nearly 180,000 village clinics were built.

In western China, the per capita disposable income of urban residents reached 14,213 yuan, up 168% from 1999 and growing 10. 4% each year on average; the per capita net income of rural residents reached 3,817 yuan, up 133% from 1999 and growing 8. 9% each year on average (Zeng Peiyan, 2010).

On May 17 ~ 19, 2010, the CPC Central Committee and the State Council held a Xinjiang symposium in Beijing. President Hu Jintao pointed out that, the tasks of Xinjiang under the new situation were to: stick to the development path with Chinese characteristics and in accordance with current conditions of Xinjiang; advance economic, political, cultural, social and ecological civilization development as well as Party building; by 2015, make the per capita regional GDP up to the national average, and make urban and rural resident income and basic public service capacity per capita up to western China's average level. The CPC Central Committee decided that a resource tax reform would be carried out first in Xinjiang, changing the levy of resource tax on crude oil and natural gas from specific duty to ad valorem, and that financial resources increased from the reform would be mainly used to improve people's well-being and resource development would benefit Xinjiang people more directly. There are 19 provinces (and municipalities directly under the Central Government), which provide partner assistance to Xinjiang, for example, Beijing to Hotan Prefecture and Agricultural No. 14 Division of XPCC; Guangdong to Shufu and Peyziwat Counties in Kashgar Prefecture and Agricultural No. 3 Division of XPCC, and Shenzhen to Tumxuk City, Kashgar City and Taxkorgan Tajik Autonomous County; Liaoning to Tacheng Prefecture; and Zhejiang to Aksu Prefecture. This is another application of the institutional design of "Whole-nation Regime. "

"Western China Development" also has some potential development values. One of them is that western China is very likely to become another granary of the country. Research has shown that water resources in northwestern China are no less than those in northern and northeastern China. Although northwestern China is largely dry and short of water, water resources abound; although the utilization rate of water is not high, there is abundant cross-border water. According to a national water resource distribution survey in 2003, Qinghai's water resources per capita were 11,940.9 cubic meters and Xinjiang's were 4,793.6 cubic meters, ranking first and second in the country, respectively. Some experts, therefore, believe that Inner Mongolia, Xinjiang and Ningxia are very much likely to become the new grain-productive areas of the country. Take Ningxia as an example. Among China's 31 provinces (autonomous regions, and municipalities directly under the Central Government), Ningxia is only a small province with small amount of water resources, land area and population. But under institutional design and innovation management by leaders at various levels and through efforts of the people there. In 1984, it was the first in northwestern China to have realized self-sufficiency in grains, and even transferred surplus gains to other places. Currently, the province farmland, only 29% of the region's total land area, produces 74% grains of the entire region, making it one of the major commodity grain producing areas in western China and even in China as a whole (Zhang Zhengbin and Duan Ziyuan, 2010).

Ten years have passed since the start of "Western China Development", and it is estimated that four decades more is needed to crown it with success. Without "long-term one-party rule" and the institutional design of "Whole-nation Regime", such a major project would almost be unimaginable.

Case 2: 15-year Anti-corruption Institutional Design

On July 11, 2010, the General Offices of the CPC Central Committee and the State Council printed and distributed the "*Regulations on Personal Information Reporting of Leaders and Cadres*" ("2010 *Regulations*" below). That is an important institutional design, which concerns not only the ruling party's prestige and possibility of long-term ruling, how it ensures the availability of cadres having both ability and political integrity as successors, but also the people's trust in and support of the ruling party and, thus, the nation's lasting peace and stability. Fifteen years has passed since the inception of this institutional design; if there were no "long-term one-party rule" but "alternate two-or multi-party ruling" that changes policy frequently, there would be no survival of this system today.

In 1995, the General Offices of the CPC Central Committee and the State Council printed and distributed the *"Regulations on Income Declaration of Party and Government Leaders and Cadres at the County (Division) Level and above."* This document, in which declarers were cadres and income was only limited to their own income, is far inferior to the 2010 *Regulations*, whether in the scope of declarers or in detailed requirements on property to be declared. In June 2001, the CPC Central Commission for Discipline Inspection and the Organization Department of the CPC Central Committee jointly issued the *"Regulations on Family Property Declaration of In-service Provincial and Ministerial-level Leaders and Cadres (Trial)"*, which extended declarers from cadres to include their family members and added such items as cash deposit, marketable securities, house property, calligraphic and painting works and antique to the income to be declared. The *Regulations on Personal Information Reporting of Party Leaders and Cadres*, which was formulated in 2006, expanded the scope of leaders and cadres to include Party leaders and cadres at public institutions and state-owned enterprises, and added such items to be declared as marital status, going abroad on private business, as well as opinions on dealing with false reporting.

Leaders and cadres designated in the 2010 *Regulations* include not only cadres at country-division level and above in all levels of Party organs, NPC organs, administrative organs, CPPCC organs, judicial organs, procuratorial organs and democratic party organs, as well as cadres at country-division level and above in mass organizations and public institutions, but also leaders at middle level and above in large and ultra-large solely state-funded enterprises and state-controlled enterprises (including solely state-funded financial enterprises and state-controlled financial enterprises), and leadership members in medium-sized solely state-funded enterprises and state-controlled enterprises (including solely state-funded financial enterprises and state-controlled financial enterprises). The 2010 *Regulations* also gave local Party and government organs the authority of deciding whether or not to include sectional-level cadres as declarers. Not only did it require the declarer to report on his/her going abroad on private business, migration of his/her spouse and child (or children) to other country, their professions, including their professions and positions overseas and investigation into their criminal responsibility, but it also required the declarer to report on his/her wage and bonuses, allowances and subsidies, and earnings for such services as giving lectures, writing, consultancy, proofreading, and painting and calligraphy, house property of his/hers, spouse and child (or children) living with them, investments or marketable securities, shares (including equity incentives), futures, funds, investment insurance and other financial products otherwise held by he/she, spouse and child (or children) living with them, investments of his/her spouse and child (children) living with them into unlisted companies and enterprises, and their registration of private businesses, sole proprietorship enterprise or partnership business, etc.

In addition to the specification of the time and way to submit declarations, the 2010 Regulations also provides that the declarer will, if in violation of any of the regulations, be criticized and educated, ordered to correct within a definite time or to conduct self-criticism, given an admonitory talk, criticized by circulating a notice, or changed to other post of duty, or removed from office, depending on circumstances; in the case of breaching the principle, be given a disciplinary punishment in accordance with relevant regulations; and in the case of failure to report on time or as things really are without proper reasons, or to do as per the organization's opinion, be treated correspondingly.

Of course, the 2010 Regulations is by no means the end of China's anti-corruption institutional design, but only an interim achievement in this regard. Whether or not this achievement can change into effective action from provisions on paper still relies on resolute execution by Party and government organs and departments at various levels. The society's effective supervision is a powerful device. On the other hand, how to turn the 2010 Regulations to law and how to put reporting contents under legal supervision as per procedure are the task of reform in the next stage. Some scholars argue that there still is "a lack of proclamation provisions" in the 2010 Regulations, but in my opinion, this should be carefully treated, as 2010 Regulations may be hardly executed effectively due to such a large number and the high level of objects and the possibility of exposing cadres' privacy. Effective measures taken by foreign countries can be used as reference for proclamation. Of course, returning the excessive resources from the Party and government organs and departments to the market is essential for anti-corruption. In the present state, we'd better place emphasis on how to execute the 2010 *Regulations* effectively and resolutely. In a word, the anti-corruption institutional design will be conducted in a more scientific way as the nation's economy and national power grow and the process of democratization progresses.

1.4　System Design of Scientific and Technological Innovation

China's scientific and technological innovation since the start of "reform and opening up" began with Deng Xiaoping's mind innovation that "Science and technology are the primary productive forces." This guiding principle was the essential mastery and abstraction of the relationship between science and technology and the productive forces and then the national power and contemporary progress in the second half of the 20th century. Undoubtedly regarded a scientific assertion today though, this assertion was proposed 20 years ago with not only courage and determination but also full preparation to overcome formidable obstacles in practice. And the difficulties and obstacles it encountered were no easier than a harsh campaign. When we take delight in the countrywide "independent innovation" today and think back to Deng's farsightedness and insight when he formulated this thought, it would be not difficult to understand the intrinsically dependence between mind innovation and the institutional and scientific and technological innovation.

The power of institutional innovation and policy design can be understood simply by giving a brief account of China's development strategies, plans, policies, laws and regulations regarding scientific and technological innovation since 1978 and enumerating the key points.

In March 1978, China called the National Science Conference, bringing about "the spring of science." Because China was still in an era of planned economy then, people had a burgeoning awareness of what role scientists and their scientific research would play in social development, and their knowledge of the function of technical experts and their experimentation and development was still rather shallow. This was because the integration of technology and economy could only be fully manifested under the market economy system.

In March 1984, the Standing Committee of the Sixth National People's Congress adopted the *Patent Law of the People's Republic of China*, which was amended three times, in 1992, 2000 and 2008, respectively. Its 2008 version included "enhancing innovation capacity" in the purpose of its enactment.

In March 1985, following the economic restructuring, "*Decision on the Reform of the Science and Technology Management System*" was introduced, with the aim to: on operational mechanism, reform the appropriation system and develop the technology market; on organizational structure, change the irrational situation in which research institutions and enterprises separated from each other, and promote the translation of technological achievements into productive forces; and on personnel system, facilitate the rational flow of talent.

In March 1986, four Chinese scientists, Wang Daheng, Wang Gancheng, Yang Jiachi and Chen Fangyun, jointly wrote to the CPC Central Committee a letter, titled *"Suggestions on Tracking the World's Hi-tech Developments. "* Approved by Deng Xiaoping, the National Hi-tech R&D Program (namely the "863 Program") was officially launched at the end of the same year. Taking the policy of "limited objectives, placing focus on key technologies", with the aim of narrowing the gaps to the advanced levels of developed countries, the 863 Program initially chose seven hi-tech fields for research: biology, aviation, information, laser, automation, energy and new material, which were viewed as of great influence on the country's development. The program would be continuously expanded in the "10th Five-Year" and "11th Five-Year" Plans of the country.

On July 2, 1993, the *Law of the People's Republic of China on Science and Technology Progress* ("Science and Technology Progress Law") was promulgated, becoming China's fundamental law on science and technology. In 2007, it was amended according to the Constitution, and On December 29 of the same year, the amended version was adopted by the NPC Standing Committee, and went into effect as of July 1, 2008, which comprises 75 articles under eight chapters, including "General Provisions", "Scientific Research, Technological Development and Application of Science and Technology", "Technological Progress of Enterprises", "Scientific Research and Technological Development Institutions", "Scientists and Technicians Personnel", "Guarantee Measures", "Legal Liability" and "Supplementary Provisions. " The amended version stresses four major aspects: the leading role of enterprises in technological innovation, support of basic research on agricultural science and technology, increasing input in agricultural innovation, ownership of intellectual property rights in state-funded scientific research projects, and the principle of "tolerance for failure" in scientific researches.

In November 1993, the *"Decision of the CPC Central Committee on Several Issues of Establishing the Socialist Market Economy System"* was adopted, proposing that the scientific and technological system reform is targeted for facilitating the development of market economy and the integration of science, technology and economy. By sheer coincidence, in November 1993 too, *Technology for Economic Growth: President's Progress Report*, of the United States, was published, which stressed the important roles of advanced manufacturing technologies, particularly information technology, in economic development, and made overall arrangements for national information infrastructure.

In May 1995, "*Decision of the CPC Central Committee and the State Council on Stepping up Scientific and Technological Progress*" came up with the strategy of "invigorating the country through science and education" for the first time, and specifically raised the scientific and technological input objective of "increasing R&D spending of the whole society to 1.5% of GDP by 2000."

In May 1996, the NPC Standing Committee adopted the *Law of the People's Republic of China on Promoting the Transformation of scientific and Technological Achievements.* The phrase "transformation of scientific and technological achievements" as used in this Law means the entire process of the follow-up tests, development, application and widespread use of the applicable scientific and technological achievements, made as a result of scientific research and technological development, through to the final creation of new products, new techniques, new materials and new industries—all for the purpose of enhancing the productive forces. Article 29 of this law states that "When transferring a scientific or technological achievement made by employees while holding positions in a unit, the unit shall take not less than 20 percent of the net income, obtained from transfer of the achievement, to award persons who made important contributions to the achievement or to its transformation."

From late 1997 to early 1998, the policymakers of the Chinese Academy of Sciences (CAS) drafted a report titled "*The National Innovation System Oriented towards the Knowledge Economy Era*" according to their experience learned from years of practice in the process of reform and opening up and by making reference to the OECD study report "*The Knowledge-based Economy*". This report raised the concept of "Knowledge Innovation Program" and its framework and contents, and proposed to experiment with it in CAS. After the approval of this report by leaders of the CPC Central Committee and the State Council, the CAS started the "Knowledge Innovation Program" in June 1998. Phase I of the experimentation lasted from 1998 to 2000, and upon evaluation by relevant departments, Phase II started in 2002 the "Knowledge Innovation Program" and was carried out across the CAS. The program saw great improvements in 2005 ~ 2010. As a key scientific and technological development program, the 13-year-long Program comprises the following elements. Its overall objective is to "by around 2010, form the national knowledge innovation system and operational mechanism which is in keeping with the laws of socialist market economy and scientific and technological development, able to support the sustainable development of national economy and efficiently operates; build a group of world-famous national knowledge innovation bases (national scientific research institutions and research universities), continuously obtain major scientific and technological achievements of international influence, and develop large numbers of high-quality talent in science and technology who have innovation awareness and capacity; strive to lift the country's knowledge innovation strength to the level of moderately developed countries" (Lu Yongxiang, 1998). Its innovation framework comprises: one center—the world-famous National Knowledge Innovation Center; two component parts—the academic part composed of academicians and the world-famous scientific institutions; three major functions—knowledge production, knowledge diffusion and knowledge transfer; and four strategic priorities—implementing basic research, conducting strategic research, undertaking national key scientific and technological tasks, and providing scientific and technological consultancy and services. Its institutional building aims to establish the "modern system for national scientific research institutions", and establish and improve the "annual budget appropriation system for national scientific research institutions", "research council system for scientific research academies and institutes" and "scientific research personnel appointment system. " Its structural readjustment is aimed to: build a group of world-famous national knowledge innovation bases; create a cultural environment which is conducive to knowledge innovation; develop high-quality talent of innovation awareness and capacity; promote cooperation between scientific research bases and universities and enterprises; and enhance the international exchange and cooperation in science and technology. By 2002, the CAS had, through over four years of practice, fixed the overall arrangement in disciplinary system for 9 key development fields and 7 fundamental disciplines. On operational mechanism, it practiced a personnel system which is featured by "setting posts according to need, open recruitment, choosing the best through competition, and dynamic updating" and distribution of a triple structure (consisting of base pay, job allowance, and mainly performance-based incentive). And for this purpose, it designed and introduced a research institution evaluation system. In 2010, the CAS finished the experiment. From 2011 to 2020, it will continue to further implement the Knowledge Innovation Project, with a view to meeting the challenges posed by the new scientific and technical revolution and boosting the sustainable socioeconomic development. For the decade to come, the program's new objectives are to: define the strategic priorities of scientific and technological innovation; organize the implementation of projects regarding scientific and technical precursors and form institutional mechanisms that help encourage innovation; foster talents for innovation, perfect competition-based recruitment mechanisms and distribution incentive and restrain mechanisms, and improve the education system in close connection with scientific and technological innovation; enhance scientific and technological cooperation with enterprises, industrial sectors, local authorities, universities and other scientific research institutions, as well as foreign countries and international organizations, bring in international innovation resources, promote the translation of scientific and technological achievements into practical production.

In August 1999, the "*Decision of the CPC Central Committee and the State Council on Enhancing Technological Innovation, Developing High Technologies and Achieving Industrialization*" was announced at the National Technological Innovation Conference, giving prominence to the thought that "Innovation is the soul of progress of a nation. " Also in this year, supported by government financial appropriations, 242 scientific research academies and institutes were restructured, merging into enterprises, or becoming science and technology enterprises, or intermediary agencies.

Between 2003 and 2005, the "*National Medium-and Long-Term Program for Science and Technology Development* (2006 ~ 2020)" was formulated under the leadership of the National Scientific and Technological Program Leading Group. It clearly states that building an innovation-oriented country is a national strategy for future development of China, placing emphasis on the following four aspects: implement a group of momentous hi-tech product and engineering projects by which to promote the leapfrog development of productive forces; identify key technologies in main fields and improve the country's overall competitiveness; get a firm grip of fundamental sciences and technology fronts and improve the capacity for sustained innovation; and deepen the reform on the management system of science and technology and build the national innovation system.

In December 2005, the Ministry of Science and Technology (MOST), the State-owned Assets Supervision and Administration Commission of the State Council (SASAC) and the All-China Federation of Trade Unions (ACFTU) began jointly implementing the Technological Innovation Guiding Project. In July 2009, the Technological Innovation Guiding Project was renamed the National Technological Innovation Project. The MOST, Ministry of Finance (MOF), Ministry of Education (MOE), SASAC, ACFTU and China Development Bank (CDB) jointly issued the

"Overall Scheme for Implementation of the National Technological Innovation Project", with the aim of enhancing enterprises' capacity for independent innovation, improving the core competitiveness of industries, accelerating the building of the technological innovation system and setting up the national innovation system.

On January 9, 2006, at the National Science and Technology Conference, President Hu Jintao made a speech titled *"Stick to the Path of Independent Innovation with Chinese Characteristics and Work Hard to Build an Innovation-based Country"*, in which he pointed out that "To take the path of independent innovation with Chinese characteristics, the core is keeping to the guideline of carrying out independent innovation, developing with priorities, sustaining development and leading the future. Independent innovation is, starting from national capacity for innovation, to enhance original innovation, integrated innovation, and introduction, absorption and then innovation. The objective is to move China to be among the world's innovation-based countries in 15 years" (Hu Jintao, 2006).

In June, 2010, the *"Outline of National Medium-and Long-term Program for Talent Development (2010~2020)"* (Table 1-1) was announced.

Table 1-1　Key Indicators of National Talent Development (2008~2020)

Indicator	Unit	2008	2015	2020
Aggregate talent resources	10,000 persons	11,385	15,625	18,025
Research personnel per 10,000 workers	Person year/10,000 persons	24.8	33	43
Ratio of hi-tech talent to technical workers	%	24.4	27	28
Ratio of highly-educated population at job ages	%	9.2	15	20
Ratio of investment in human capital to GDP	%	10.75	13	15
Contribution rate of talent	%	18.9	32	35

Note: "Contribution rate of talent" is the mean value over a span of years. 2008 data is the mean value for years from 1978 to 2008; 2015 data is the mean value for years between 2008 and 2015; and 2020 data is the mean value for years from 2008 to 2020.

From 1978 till now, Chinese "government, enterprises, academic circles and research institutes" have never relaxed determination and execution of scientific and technological innovation, from the formulation of "Science and technology are the primary productive forces", through the *"Decision on the Reform of the Science and Technology Management System"* of 1985, the strategy of "invigorating the country through science and education" raised in the *"Decision of the CPC Central Committee and the State Council on Stepping up Scientific and Technological Progress"* of 1995, the "Knowledge Innovation Program" started in 1998 and the "Technological Innovation Project" started in 2005, until the goal of "Stick to the Path of Independent Innovation with Chinese Characteristics and Work Hard to Build an Innovation-oriented Country" set in 2006. Securing continuous strategies and policies is the best example proving that the long CPC ruling supports national development. If two or more parties had reigned in rotation and different parties' strategies, policies, laws and regulations had changed repeatedly in over 30 years, all circles would have no idea of what they should work for.

1.5　Room for Improvement of Institutional Design：The Second Reform

Since the national policy of reform and opening up was implemented in 1978, China has been reforming and constructing various systems, including the political system, as the reform of the political system is the basis for that of economic and scientific and technological systems. Examples include intra-party democratic system building, reform of the electoral system, and the ongoing experiments in the electoral system reform regarding rural grass-root Party and government organizations and regarding urban Party and government leaders and cadres. A great many institutional innovations have been introduced, for example, leadership learning system (helpful to enhance and broaden knowledge of leaders at different levels) , "*shuang gui*" against corruption, "real name-based offense reporting system", "leadership proclamation" and recently introduced "leadership property declaration. " Below is a brief analysis of efforts in innovation management and institutional design.

From the point of view of the "Theory of two points", one-party rule and whole-nation regime, as two innovations in China's institutional design, should also be thoroughly reformed to avoid possible failure of them, as one-party rule for a long time may give rise to such maladies stemming from inadequate effective supervision as autocracy and dictatorship, and the whole-nation regime may also bring about such weaknesses as waste of resources as a result of failure to act on the laws of market economy. We have learned bitter lessons in the first 30 years (from 1949 to 1976) following the founding of the People's Republic of China. For "one-party rule" treated in the section "Institutional Innovation" above, particularly, there still is much room for improvement in institutional design on Party and government. The CPC will still reign in the foreseeable future, working miracles in world history of politics and political parties. There are many ways for future reform in China. The recently published "*Suggestions on the 12th Five-year Plan*" once again raised the need for "transformation of the economic growth mode. " This is undoubtedly correct. But why is there still no fundamental change 28 years after the need was raised? In fact, the former Soviet Union had raised such "transformation" earlier, which, however, died on the vine for infeasibility. The key to the problem lies in the fact that "transformation of the economic growth mode" involves a series of difficulties, for example, in resource allocation by government, monopoly enterprise restructuring, restructuring of state-owned enterprises, investment-to-consumption proportion, and income distribution. All these are related to government restructuring. Though proposed many times, government restructuring has gained little effect, because government departments can hardly transfer powers to lower levels and carry out self-supervision. Therefore, government restructuring must be one of the main aspects of the political system reform. And for this purpose, we may call this reform as "the second reform" in relation to "the first reform" started in 1978 focusing on "reform and opening up". "The second reform" of course also gives an eye to opening, but it is by no means easier than "the first reform", as it focuses mainly on government restructuring, a self-revolution. In the meanwhile, it at least comprises the following five aspects.

The first is the reform on the generation, training and promotion system of Party and government cadres at various levels. Currently there already is a relatively mature and effective set of systems. From the institutional innovation perspective, there is still the need to place special emphasis on procedural democracy reform on system building in terms of the generation, training and promotion of Party and government cadres. For example, in the process of "generation of Party and government cadres", nominees for candidates may include, at a certain percentage, those nominated by higher-level organizations and leaders and by grass-root Party organizations, Party members and masses, to enter one or two rounds of screening voting. And the process of voting should comprise voters' receiving votes, secret voting (not monitored), scrutinizing voting and calling out the names voted. The "appraisal of Party and government cadres" should practice the system and mechanism that make known to the public the results of appraisal during and at the expiry of their term of office. Different from "property proclamation of leaders and cadres", "proclamation of appraisal results" involves nothing about personal privacy, and currently there are conditions for immediate implementation. It is important that what is proclaimed shall give consideration to increasing the people's "right to know" in the democratic reform. The current "nominee proclamation" system still has room for improvement. For example, institutionally provide for what to be proclaimed, or introduce "proclamation regulations" specifying what the masses have the "right to know;" during proclamation, higher-level organs organize symposia or one-on-one conversations intended to seek opinions, and announce as appropriate what is discussed, to prevent "proclamation" from becoming formalistic. More importantly, all these measures shall be institutionalized.

The second is the system reform on full-time deputies to the People's Congress at various levels. China once made a portion of deputies to the NPC Standing Committee full-time. It should be recognized that if there were no full-time deputies, their capability of discussing political affairs and representation of the populace would be lowered, and they would have no time and energy to communicate with both higher-level organs and the masses. In fact, quite a number of local grass-root problems and petitioned problems, and even conflicts between officials and ordinary people, could be solved through consultation between Party and government cadres and people's deputies, especially full-time ones. This helps enhance the Party's leadership and core position, build the authority of People's Congresses at various levels, enhance the cohesion of the Party and nation and promote social harmony. At People's Congresses at various levels, there can be certain percentages of full-time and part-time deputies through different electoral methods. Full-time deputies should have more power to supervise government departments, for example, the power to inquire between sessions into the accountability of government departments and their administrative authorities. For this purpose, full-time deputies in principle may not be officials dismissed by or retired from the government; or it would be difficult to conduct effective supervision. And this also should be institutionalized.

The third is the system reform on "third-party supervision." The difficulty that "one-party rule" has in supervision system building is how to conduct "self-supervision." On the basis of the existing system, innovation should be made in "third-party supervision" system building. This "third party" can be an intra-party agency of power that operates independently (for example, the CPC Central Commission for Discipline Inspection), or a task force formed by government agencies free of administrative subordination, or an authoritative website and real-name and anonymous offense reporters. "Third-party supervision" can also be reflected in "inquiry system building". This includes such forms as people's deputies inquiring government department heads at "People's Congress" meetings and the deputies elected as per legitimate procedure by the masses inquiring relevant Party and government cadres. It is important to have supervision institutionalized and made it known to the public. Currently, there is only the *"Law of People's Republic of China on Supervision by the Standing Committees of the People's Congresses at All Levels"*. In this regard, so it is necessary to prepare a supervision law appropriate to the masses, while broadening their right of supervision.

The fourth is the reform to weaken government agencies' role in resource allocation. At the core of this reform is to define the main function of government departments as making policies, laws and regulations and coordinating the operation thereof, with a view of weakening their function of resource allocation. A "strong government" should not manifest itself in "strong domination of resource allocation", but in its ability to organize, coordinate, and make policies. In this regard, India is worth reflection. It is widely recognized that Indian governments at various levels have to be considerably improved in terms of leadership and execution. But private enterprises in India are not lifeless and, to the contrary, outstand among many enterprises in the world for their international experience in business operation. Of course, that does not mean to blindly imitate Indian government departments, but that if China's government departments at various levels relax their control as appropriate, better results will be achieved. Years' efforts on "weakening government agencies' function of resource allocation" yield effects far less desirable, because its fundamental significance to root out corruption is not recognized. It is just the excessive power of government departments in resource domination that gives rise to varied "rend-seeking" corruption and hence endangers the core of market economy. Therefore, "weakening government agencies' function of resource allocation" itself is a revolution, requiring much more "institutional design" with great wisdom. One example is about the relationship between government functions and the reform of state-owned enterprises. In recent years, a portion of government officials were sent to assume leadership of state-owned enterprises, rather than choosing talent from "professional managers. " This doesn't accord with market economy laws, leading to poor performance of the enterprises and even corruption (this has been proved by statistical data) . Similar problems also exist in the field of education: university presidents are assumed by officials at the department/bureau level, rather than selected from educational experts and scholars. Without corresponding laws or regulations, the reform of "weakening government agencies' function of resource allocation" is likely to go through the motions.

The fifth is to strengthen the design of "procedural democratic systems. " This requires further improvement of the operational modes and methods of some democratic systems, so that they operate in a more standard, transparent and scientific way. And particularly, it is necessary to build "procedural democratic systems", for example, for various levels and types of electoral systems, hearing systems, and systems regarding publication and verification of all kinds of statistical data. Efforts should be made to procedurally provide for ways of operation and contents to be followed, and finalize them in corresponding laws and regulations. The right to vote, right to know and right to supervise (three rights) necessary to build a democratic society in China should be under their own "procedural democratic systems" as guarantees, which are still insufficient now. Therefore, laws for this purpose shall be prepared. Before such laws are enacted, procedural democratic systems concerning the three rights can be experimented as part of the political system reform, to gradually realize the "unity of the three rights. "

"Unity" means "sustainable development"—the sole criterion for testing the democratic systems of all countries. Therefore, China's building of a democratic society may consider such institutional arrangement: gradually expand the people's right to vote, right to know and right to supervise and seek sustainable development of the country and society, within the framework of "one-party rule. " As a matter of fact, when the people have sufficient right to vote, right to know and right to supervise, they also are performing their right to participate. In other words, to what extent the people participate in democratic life depends on to what extent they have the right to vote, right to know and right to supervise. And, not only is such "extent" a gradual measure, but it also needs to be stipulated in law; that is, democratic development and legal system building should go abreast. For example, an electoral law, a right-to-know law and a supervisory law suitable for the public can be enacted, rather than only such laws for the People's Congress, because "three rights" of people are not implemented in the same way as those of the deputies. Among others, what leaders to be elected, how they are elected, to what extent and how people know about them, and how the people exercise their right to supervise, should be definitely stipulated in laws and regulations.

China's "unity of three rights", independent of the Western "separation of powers", adds a new model to the world's political development. And if effective, it will also become part of China's "soft power" and will strengthen the country's overall national strength for sure.

The political system reform including the contents described above is a gradual process and a holistic systematic project. It relates to the country's economic development and the people's education and literacy, and the so-called "shock therapy" doesn't work. But as the country has already risen to the world's second biggest economy, which means our political system reform has entered a critical stage, there should be a timetable for the reform, for example, by 2020 as an affluent society is built in all aspects, what objectives the corresponding political system reform should achieve, and by 2050 when the country's economic strength overtakes that of the United States, what achievements the corresponding democratic system building should make. A "five-year plan for political system reform" formulated every five years and made known to the whole country and the world is a manifestation of confidence of a big power.

Improvement of Party and government institutional design also implies "much room for learning" from both developed and other developing countries. In spite of disagreement with some foreign experience and views, there may be some others suitable for China. For example, renowned economist Joseph Stiglit raised the following points of view in his article *How Should China Build Its Innovation System*: the returns delivered by the patent system fail to bring corresponding social benefits; the patent system not only restricts the application of knowledge, but also gives a party the exclusive right to use the knowledge, leading to a man-made monopoly which distorts the allocation of resources; a poorly-designed intellectual property system can even suppress innovation; each country must have an intellectual property system appropriate to its own situation which must strike a balance between costs and profits; and China needs an innovation system, which should pay more attention to incentives and to government-funded research and pay less attention to patents than other countries such as the United States (Joseph Stiglitz, 2010). Venturing to differ from Stiglitz's view about an intellectual property system, I really admire him for his wish and motive to give advice on China's innovation system building, and agree on his opinion that each country's institutional design should be conducted according to its own national conditions. And he is correct in admitting that a patent system indeed is monopolistic, to which China should pay attention during its institutional design. However, while giving the patentee the monopoly right, a patent system requires patentee to announce the contents of the patent, giving the patented knowledge some attributes of public goods. The payment for the use of a patent is the reward, encouragement and protection of the inventor's innovation.

In the final analysis, there is much room for institutional building and reform under the regime of "long-term one-party rule. " The institutional reform is called as the "second reform" to show the toughness and significance of the reform, and that China's reform has already entered a critical stage. It is anticipated that the reform will greatly improve the China's survival and development environment, enhance its "hard power" and "soft power" for sure, and contribute much to the world as to how to build a democratic society and promote human civilization.

2. Innovation Management

As described in "Introduction" to this book, in order to avoid unwanted repetition in the contents (namely, the second section of each chapter, "Innovation Management") of each chapter (country), the book, while describing China's innovation management, gives a systematical description of "Innovation Management" in its narrow sense, namely the main contents of scientific and technological innovation, including scientific and technological innovation strategy, research and development (R&D) management (organization innovation, pilot production and marketing of new products developed, risk of technological innovation, and marketing of technological goods), resource allocation and enterprise innovation.

2. 1　Scientific and Technological Innovation Strategies

To a big developing country, the separate formulation of a " technology introduction and assimilation strategy" and a "technology leapfrogging strategy" in the process of scientific and technological innovation seems some paradoxical, but in specific circumstances, is rational. And, the two seemingly conflicting strategies are also likely to be unified: adopt the "technology introduction and assimilation strategy" in the earlier stages and implement the "technology leapfrogging strategy in the later stages. This is a strategic mix.

2. 1. 1　Technology Import and Assimilation Strategy

Among present-day countries with plentiful achievements of scientific and technological innovation, Japan in the 1950s and 1960s, South Korea in the 1960s and 1970s, and China in 1980s and 1990s, all placed more emphasis on a "technology import and assimilation strategy. "

"Import" means to introduce technologies and related equipment into China. Technologies to be imported also include "soft technologies" such as know-how, patents, technical drawings, and paid technology transfer, and "hard technologies" such as key equipment, equipment complex and production lines. "Assimilation" means that the importer's R&D team studies the imported technology or equipment and, after having mastery of the technology, carry out "second innovation", for example, technological transformation or technical inventions.

The two strategies essentially purport to develop one's own "second innovation" ability: the ability to choose, disintegrate and re-create technologies.

In 1984, Guangdong Fotao Group Co. Ltd. imported a color-glazed tile production line, and soon its R&D team tackled two key projects-large-sized ball mill and roller kiln (tunnel kiln was used in China then). In June 1984 as the imported production line was not put into production, the "semi-muffle fuel firing roller kiln" developed by the R&D team was successfully put into operation. Particularly, the rollers of fine ceramics developed in 1987, the core component of a roller kiln, not only saved import costs of tens of millions of dollars each year, but were also recognized as the world's then most advanced technology, leading Germany, Japan and other countries to negotiation over transfer or cooperative production of the technology (Wu Guisheng, 2000).

China's technology import and assimilation strategy mainly has three problems: repeated import without being constrained by economic levers; inappropriate selection of technologies to be imported; and attaching more importance to import than to assimilation. To solve the "repeated import" problem, the establishment of market economy system and mechanism is of course fundamental, but the government's control and coordination are also quite important. As early as 1951, the Ministry of International Trade and Industry (MITI) of Japan formulated specific measures for protection of its auto industry, imposing strict measures on the import of foreign autos and the foreign direct investment in the auto industry. It was not until 21 years later, in 1972, that the Japanese government permitted the import of auto engines. This 21-year period marked a precious time for Japanese enterprises to assimilate imported technologies and carry out "second innovation. "

On selection of technologies to be imported, the motivation should be market demand and the needs for technologies, mainly the former one. To China, a big developing country, what the market needs are not necessarily all high technologies; perhaps more "intermediate technologies" and "appropriate technologies." Considering the economic globalization today, the import of technologies should also give consideration to such issues as international economic division of work and worldwide industrial restructuring.

As to the problem of "attaching more importance to import than to assimilation", according to 2004 statistics on Chinese enterprises, the ratio of technology import costs to assimilation costs stood at about 100 : 15 (MOST,2007); that is, for every 100 yuan paid to import technologies, only 15 yuan were used for assimilation of them. Although recent years have seen some improvement in this regard, there is still a big gap to such countries as Japan and South Korea where resources several times import costs are used to assimilate technologies imported. To solve this problem, in addition to strengthening the government's function of coordination and increasing the input (including human and financial resources) into technology assimilation, the strengthening of "anti-corruption bid" among government departments and enterprises (especially state-owned enterprises) with respect to technology import cannot be neglected.

2. 1. 2　Technology Leapfrogging Strategy

Leapfrogging means a late mover jumping over certain stages to catch up with or surpassing a first mover. Technology leapfrogging is a technological leapfrogging development strategy, which the late mover, after having analyzed the technological development path of a first mover, formulates as per its own strength (for example, available technological reserve, resource integration ability, and specific technology selection ability), to catch up with or surpass the first mover.

The possibility of implementing a technology leapfrogging strategy is, in fact, a result of necessity in the cause-and-effect chain of scientific and technological development. Scientific and technological development leads to scientific and technological advances, the consequence of which is that the latecomers surpass the formers. It is probable that a late-developing country or region can achieve technological leapfrogging, but of course there are conditions.

Not only developed countries but also developing ones may implement a technology leapfrogging strategy, as it is an ideal strategy for late-developing countries to catch up with advanced ones. For example, South Korea-based Samsung's technology leapfrogging strategy for "semiconductor RAM chip" during the 1980s and

1990s was very successful. As a matter of fact, it is technology import and assimilation that should be done in early stages of a technology leapfrogging strategy. The said example is Samsung assimilating the semiconductor technology imported from the United States. Since China started its independent innovation strategy in 2006, enterprises with favorable conditions have developed and implemented the strategic combination of "technology import and assimilation + technology leapfrogging. "

2.1.3　Strategy of Cooperation among "Government, Enterprises, Universities and Research Institutes"

China has implemented the strategy of "cooperation among enterprises, universities and research institutes" for many years. In fact, this strategy should be renamed the strategy of "cooperation among government, enterprises, universities and research institutes", or of "cooperation among government, enterprises and universities (now that universities also engage in research), considering the important role of government. In Beijing, for example, Beijing Municipal Science & Technology Commission (BMSTC) has developed—in its effort to find out the so-called "Beijing Model for transformation of scientific and technological achievements"—a model of "all chains, all elements and all the society. " "All chains" refer to the whole process of scientific and technological achievement transformation from basic research and applied research to experimental development, intermediate test and finally to commercialization and industrialization. "All elements" refer to the achievements, funds, talent, information, management, policy, infrastructure, preproduction elements, etc. involved in the process of scientific and technological achievement transformation. "All the society" means the inclusion of enterprises, government, universities, research institutes, financial institutions, intermediaries, etc. as players in the transformation. Take the "industrialization of green printmaking technology" as an example. It involves such chains as printmaking consumables, printmaking software, printmaking equipment and market applications. BMSTC has a R&D team to cooperate with Peking University Founder Group in printmaking software development and marketing network building, and with Beiren Printing Machinery Holdings Limited in printmaking equipment, and with some other powerful printing works in Beijing. As for "all elements", BMSTC has taken active measures for the industrialization of green printmaking technology, such as providing scientific and technological funds and taking shares in the form of scientific and technological achievements, and partnered with Lenovo to form a new entity, so that the project has adequate financial input. At the same time, the government also provides logistics support in such aspects as high technology certification, talent settlement and intellectual property protection. From the perspective of "all the society", coordinated by the government, Nano Think was co-founded as the enterprise for "industrialization of green printmaking technology" by Legend Capital, Legend Holdings, Founder, Beiren, *Beijing Daily* Printing Works etc. (Yan Aoshuang, 2010)

In addition, there are also other strategies such as "Technology leadership Strategy".

2.2　R&D Management

Examining scientific and technological innovation by viewing management as a process (namely dividing management into four functions or processes: planning, organizing, leading and controlling) can help us analyze in time and space the features of scientific and technological innovation. From logical forms, the process of scientific and technological innovation covers basic research, applied research, experimental development, and commercialization of scientific and technological achievement; generally speaking, mere technological innovation does not involve the basic research. Practically, the process of scientific and technological innovation can be viewed as a "linkage network" of science, technology and economy, in which all kinds of activities interact with each other, rather than the aforesaid "linear process" of logical forms. Concepts concerned such as R&D are explained below in 2.2.1, for better understanding about the process of technological innovation.

In 1989, when writing the report "The Size and Composition of Scientific and Technological Investment in China", a program funded by the National Natural Science Foundation of China (NSFC), the author applied to the research on China's scientific and technological input the R&D (research and experimental development) indicator system I had learned as a visiting scholar in the Program in Science, Technology, and Society at the Massachusetts Institute of Technology, and concluded that "China's scientific and technological financial input is low and on the decline", proposing that "expenditure on R&D funds should be 50% of national scientific and technological funds." The report's conclusions and suggestions drew attention at a scientists symposium held by the CPC Central Committee in May 1990. Jiang Zemin, the then General Secretary of the CPC Central Committee, instructed at the meeting that a program be initiated to further research into statistical criteria for scientific and technological input (Cheng Zhendeng et al. , 1992), in which the author has participated. Through concerted efforts, the program members for the first time measured and calculated the indicator data on China's R&D spending (China only had the indicator of "scientific and technological funds" in general terms before, making it impossible to make an international comparison), which was officially published in 1992 by the National Bureau of Statistics of China (NBS). The research also led to the conclusion that scientific and technological activities in China were comprised of three parts, namely R&D, transformation and application of scientific and technological achievements, and scientific and technological services (Cheng Zhendeng et al. ,1992) . These findings not only provide available statistics for international comparison in terms of scientific and technological input, but also helped domestic and foreign experts and scholars to conduct in-depth research into China's R&D activities and international comparison in this regard.

2.2.1   The Concept, Process and Internal Logic of Scientific and Technological Innovation

(1) Three Types of Scientific and Technological Activities

Because scientific and technological statistics are highly quantitatively prescriptive on the classification of scientific and technological activities, we may have an understanding of the concept and classification of scientific and technological activities and scientific and technological innovation from the world's authoritative statistics and indicator systems thereof.

In its *Manual for Statistics on Scientific and Technological Activities*, the United Nations Educational, Scientific and Cultural Organization (UNESCO) divides scientific and technological activities into three types: R&D (including basic research, applied research and experimental development) ; scientific and technological education and training at broadly the third level (including education from junior college education to postgraduate education, and lifelong training organized for scientists and engineers) ; and scientific and technological services (including information services, consulting services, and dissemination services; geological, hydrological, astronomic and meteorological surveying and observations; scientific and technological standardization, testing, metrology and quality control; and activities relating to patents and licenses) (UNESCO, 1990). Among others, R&D activities are innovative and creative, and that is why most countries only have R&D statistics in their scientific and technological statistics.

The first efforts to standardize R&D definition and statistics were made by the Organization for Economic Cooperation and Development (OECD), which, in June 1963, convened a conference in Frascati, Italy, where the *Proposed Standard Practice for Surveys on Research and Development* ("Frascati Manual") was discussed and accepted by experts of member countries. As OECD comprised member countries with the most advanced science, technology and economy in the then world, the R&D indicator definitions and data statistics given in the *Frascati Manual* became the standards for other countries. As a matter of fact, UNESCO, according to the specific conditions of developing countries, developed the *Manual for Statistics on Scientific and Technological Activities* in the 1970s, on the basis of making reference to the *Frascati Manual*.

Through studies and surveys, China, by applying UNESCO definitions and classifications to its national conditions, stipulated in the early 1990s that, its scientific and tech-nological activities comprise three groups of activities: R&D, application of R&D achievements, and scientific and technological services, for the purpose of statistics. The NBS has begun publishing China's R&D statistical data since 1992, to be aligned with international classification standards.

The definitions of scientific and technological indicators by an authoritative statistical department are standards in that only as per their statistical results, is it possible to make international comparisons, for decision makers at various levels to have a quantitative decision-making basis and for management personnel at various levels to have uniform management standards.

(2) Three Types of R&D Activities

R&D is "any systematic and creative work undertaken, in order to increase the stock of knowledge, and the use of this knowledge to devise new applications". The basic research is "any experimental or theoretical work undertaken primarily to acquire new knowledge of the underlying foundations of phenomena and observable facts, without any particular or specific application or use in view", and applied research is "any original investigation undertaken in order to acquire new knowledge, directed primarily towards a specific practical aim or objective. " In some Chinese works and practice, applied research is divided into applied basic research and applied technology research; the former falls under scientific research (also known as "strategic research" or "directional basic research" abroad), and the latter falls under technological research. Experimental development is "any systematic work, drawing on existing knowledge gained from research and/or practical experience that is directed to producing new materials, products and devices, to installing new processes, systems and services, and to improving substantially those already produced or installed" (UNESCO, 1990). For example, the theory of relativity and its mass-energy relation in physics are results of basic research, the research on nuclear fission conducted on the basis of this is applied research, and the work on nuclear electric power gene-ration or atomic bombs undertaken on the basis of the preceding research results is experimental develop-ment. Besides, the research on the double-helix model in biology is basic research, the genetic engineering research on the basis of this is applied research, and the research on transgenic food carried out on the basis of the preceding results is experimental development. Today's scientific and tech-nological development has made not that clear-cut the boundaries between basic research and applied research, and between applied research and experimental development, in some fields of knowledge, so it is not necessary to mechanically divide each research into above-mentioned three groups.

In the *Frascati Manual* (1993), the indicator of basic research is divided into "pure basic research" and "oriented basic research. " The former is carried out "for the advancement of knowledge, without seeking long-term economic or social benefits or making any effort to apply the results to practical problems or to transfer the results to sectors responsible for their application", and the latter is carried out "with the expectation that it will produce a broad base of knowledge likely to form the basis of the solution to recognized or expected, current or future problems or possibilities" (OECD, 1994).

On some particular research or statistical occasions, basic research is sometimes divided into "pure basic research" and "oriented basic research", and applied research into "applied basic research" and "applied technology research. "

(3) Technological Innovation

If analyzed merely from the linear process, "technological innovation" is a process that begins with partially applied research (namely applied technology research) in R&D, and, then, lasts from experimental development to trial sale and marketing of new products and finally to their becoming of goods, not including basic research in R&D and applied basic research. In short, in the R&D stage, there is technological innovation, excluding the scientific research. Therefore, technological innovation is the interaction between technological and economic activities. Most Chinese writings view technological innovation as the entire process from new technological conception, via applied research, experimental development or technological combination, to the formation of new products or processes and their commercialization (Wu Guisheng, 2000).

Therefore, successful technological innovation means not only innovation in technology, but also in related organization, management and institution.

Since technological innovation culminates in commercialization of technological results, it is different from technological invention, which is only a stage in the process of technological innovation.

(4) Scientific and Technological Innovation

To sum up, scientific innovation covers innovation in basic research and applied basic research, while technological innovation includes applied technology research, experimental development, and commercialization of technological results. Scientific and technological innovation is the sum total (not simple addition) of the two. From the simple logic of linear process, scientific and technological innovation is the entire process from basic research, applied research, experimental development to commercialization of R&D results, which, of course, is much more complex actually. It is the process of interaction or the linkage process between all the aforesaid elements. For example, customer opinions about new products are fed via salespersons back to an enterprise's R&D division, which is, thus, impelled to introduce improved products; an enterprise's the R&D division is inspired by, for example, other enterprises' products or advertisements, to produce new creative ideas or concepts; in the fields of information technology and biology, new products or technologies are developed directly from oriented basic research results; and new ideas and creative thoughts emerge from "reverse engineering"; and so on.

(5) Classification of Technological Innovation

As scientific innovation only refers to innovation in basic research and applied basic research, the process is relatively simple. Technological innovation, however, not only includes applied technology research, experimental development (including pilot plant test and partial trial production), trial production, marketing and commercialization of new products, but also involves scientific and technological personnel, marketing personnel, suppliers, customers and financial service personnel, who, in the process of innovation, interact in multi-directional ways (which can be called "linkage"; to be explained below) to form a complex innovation network. In most cases, therefore, scientific and technological innovation is not further divided, and research is only conducted on classification of technological innovation.

Technological innovation can be classified according to degree, object and mode of innovation, etc.

1) Technological innovation can be divided into original innovation and incremental innovation according to its degree. Original innovation, or alternatively "destructive innovation", involves substantial overall breakthroughs. For example, both the invention of mobile phone in relation to that of fixed phone and the invention of CDMA (Code Division Multiple Access) mobile phone in relation to that of GPS (Global Positioning System) mobile phone fall under this category.

Incremental innovation means partial improvement of functions or components, such as the addition of hand-free function to the fixed telephone and the redialing function.

2) According to its objects, technological innovation can be divided into product innovation and process innovation. The result of product innovation is the generation of a new product, which involves a new principle, conception or design, adopts a new material, offers a new performance or function, or has a new purpose or meets the market demand. Process innovation refers to innovation in operating procedure, modes or methods, or system reformation in production and application of technologies. If we say that the object embodied by product innovation is its result, then that embodied by process innovation is its process. Of course, both of them have their own original innovation and incremental innovation. Product innovation is easily understood, for example, in telephone, TV and washing machine. Examples of process innovation include the thermometallurgy, hydrometallurgy or electrolytic smelting in the field of metal smelting. Generally, as far as the same industrial sector, process innovation takes place as product innovation develops to a certain extent.

The above are main types of technologi-cal innovation. Classification according to innovation mode is not discussed here.

(6) Process of Technological Innovation

The process of technological innovation can be analyzed from interaction between innovation elements.

Currently, it is generally recognized in the academia that the process of technological innovation has experienced five development models: ① technology push in a linear process; ② market pull in a linear process; ③ interaction between market and technology (Fig. 1-1); ④ coupling of multiple innovation elements; and ⑤ integration of innovation elements.

The flows of the technology push and market pull models are as follows:

1) Technology push model: New technology—R&D—Manufacturing—Marketing and commercialization;

2) Market pull model: Market demand—R&D—Manufacturing—Marketing and commercialization

Fig. 1-1　Model of Interaction between Market and Technology

Source: Zhou Jizhong, 2002

In fact, both the 4th-generation "coupling of multiple innovation elements" and the 5th-generation "integration of innovation elements" are an extension of the 3rd-generation model. Innovators recognize that technological innovation in fact is not merely the linearity of innovation elements, but an interaction and linkage. When innovation elements are extended to a linkage of multiple innovation elements beyond market pull and technology push, this "linkage" interaction is the model of coupling of multiple innovation elements. When the idea of integration are brought into the 4th-generation model, it is the model of integration of innovation elements.

The process of technological innovation can also be analyzed from the life cycle of a product, which comprises four stages: introduction stage, growth stage, maturity stage and decline stage.

Introduction stage: Product innovation begins with the conception and development of a new product. In this stage, the initial communication between the new product and the market leads to improvement directed towards R&D, but with high risks due to small production scale and high cost.

Growth stage: product innovation tends to be steady, process innovation begins and the sales volume of the product increases gradually, making it likely to lower costs. Because mass production has already begun or is about to start, design has to be finalized and specialized equipment adopted, giving much prominence to process innovation. In this stage, cost recovering begins and the risk gradually lowers.

Maturity stage: The sales volume is stable, both product innovation and process innovation enter a new development stage, and innovation reduces in quantity. Price and service become the focus of competition, and imitators gradually increase.

Decline stage: the marketing strategy becomes vital in the competition, including lower prices, product service or seeking new markets. At the same time, a new round of product innovation begins until the old product is washed out. In the meanwhile, "second development" can be undertaken to prolong the life cycle of the product.

(7) Secondary Innovation

In the maturity or decline stage, secondary innovation or "secondary development" can be undertaken as a response to competition or market feedback, with the aim to prolong the growth and maturity stages of the new product. This is a valuable sort of innovation.

There are many ways of secondary innovation, for example, in-depth assimilation of imported technologies, getting inspirations from customers' feedbacks, learning from and imitating competing products, and undertaking logical improvement and re-creation on one's own product innovation. Enabling full exertion of innovation ability, secondary innovation features continuity, time effectiveness and economical efficiency, which is particularly valuable for developing countries.

(8) Basic Research, Applied Research and Experimental Development

As mentioned above, scientific and technological innovation covers the entire process of R&D. But between technological innovation and R&D there is an intersection—the process of applied technology research and experimental development. From the perspective of the coupling and integration of innovation elements, the actual process of technological innovation probably begins with customer or market feedback and goes on with experimental development or a process of partial second innovation, rather than begin with applied research, not to mention basic research.

Therefore, the R&D process discussed in this book is the unity of logic and reality. That does not mean all technological innovation goes through the applied research and experimental development in the R&D process.

Theoretically and practically, the three R&D stages—basic research, applied research and experimental development, are not only in linear development (namely basic research—applied research—experimental development), but also interact with each other, which is manifested, for example, in the reverse impact of applied research or experimental development on basic research and the reverse action of experimental development on applied research.

1) Basic research. Since basic research is conducted to know about the objective world, it is largely undertaken out of curiosity of researchers for new facts, laws, and intrinsic relations between phenomena. Generally speaking, such research is not directly in connection with markets. Its results are published papers and writings, and their priority is determined in order of their publication. And the appraisal of these results is subject to recognition by an academic community or to peer review. Therefore, it is obvious that researchers in this regard are less than those engaged in applied research and experimental development, but they are of higher quality. Although aggregate spending on basic research is less than that on applied research or experimental development, research spending per capita is higher, because basic research personnel have higher academic levels. The feature of being "curiosity driven" also requires a flexibly structured organization with more democratic management and environment, which enables freer work.

According to OECD's statistical standards, basic research is further divided in the *Frascati Manual* into pure basic research and oriented basic research.

As far as basic research organizations are concerned, all research universities generally are bases for basic research. Among government research institutions, the Chinese Academy of Sciences (CAS), the United States government laboratories, the Russian Academy of Sciences (Росс йская акад емия на ук, РАН), the National Center for Scientific Research (Centre National de la Recherche Scientifique, CNRS) of France, the Max Planck Society of Germany, the Commonwealth Scientific and Industrial Research Organisation (CSIRO) of Australia, and the RIKEN of Japan are all world famous institutions primarily engaged in basic research.

Such institutions are mainly funded by government departments, plus semi-official national science foundations. Some large businesses, such as US-based IBM and Germany-based Siemens, also finance or get engaged in basic research.

In China, research academies and institutes of the CAS, national key laboratories at main universities, and laboratories at some enterprises get engaged in basic research. The National Basic Research Program (973 Program) and the National Natural Science Foundation of China financially aid basic research projects.

2) Applied research. Because applied research comprises parts of both scientific research and technological research, to make the boundaries clear, it is sometimes

further divided into applied basic research and applied technology research, the former of which is creative research undertaken to acquire new theoretical knowledge (laws and principles), with specific actual objectives, and the latter is creative research undertaken to acquire new technological knowledge, also with specific actual objectives (UNESCO, 1990). Table 1-2 gives examples illustrating the concepts of basic research, applied basic research, applied technology research and experimental development.

　　In China, the scientific research institutions, universities and enterprises, including national engineering research centers, all undertake a considerable part of applied research.

Table 1-2　Examples Illustrating the Concepts of Basic Research, Applied Basic Research, Applied Technology Research and Experimental Development

Project	Basic Research	Applied Basic Research	Applied Technology Research	Experimental Development
Study of rayon application	Study of the spatial structure of rayon by using the X-ray technology	Study of molecular condensation (into long-chain molecule) of amido and carboxyl with a view to demonstrating the long-chain structure of macromolecule	Development of long staples of polyamide (that is, the 66 polymer can be pulled into staples like silk) through substantial experimental research	Experiments on the full range of processes from raw material production to polymerization, throwing, cooled drawing and pilot plant test
Study of countercurrent extraction theory and application	Study of extraction chemistry with a view to founding the countercurrent extraction theory on the basis of Alders' theory of liquid-liquid extraction	Application of the countercurrent extraction theory to the separation of rare earth element with a view to seeking basic laws governing the extraction of rare earth elements	Formulation of the countercurrent start model and of the optimized design principles and methods for "three-exit" extraction processes, and the foundation of the computational procedure used to simulate small-scale countercurrent extraction experiments	Use of theoretical design to seek new rare earth extraction processes with better separation effects and lower production costs

Continued

Project	Basic Research	Applied Basic Research	Applied Technology Research	Experimental Development
Study of polymer blend theory and application	Study of phase separation thermodynamics and dynamics	Study of the mechanism of plastic toughening and of the synergistic effect in performance of polymer blend	Study of blending processes and technologies for plastic toughening with a view to obtaining optimal plastic toughening	Full-range experiments on plastic and rubber blending, processing and shaping processes, including pilot plant test

Source: Zou Shangang et al. ,1993; quoted from Zhou Jizhong, 2002.

3) Experimental development. Experimental development is any systematic work, drawing on existing knowledge gained from research and/or practical experience that is directed to producing new materials, products and devices, to installing new processes, systems and services, and to improving substantially those already produced or installed. Therefore, it outstrips basic research and applied research in scale, complexity and resource allocation.

Experimental development activities are carried out in what is called pilot plant, where lab results are scaled up and trial manufacturing and selling is carried out. They are followed by trial production of new products and new processes and then by marketing operation for commercialization—the end of the entire technological innovation process.

Therefore, the technological, management and marketing personnel have increasing contacts with the market and customers in this stage. Some market or customers' feedbacks leads to creation of new products through improvements by experimental development personnel. Hence, from the perspective of commercialization of technological results, experimental development is a stage of great importance.

This stage requires considerable financial input, which generally stands at 60% ~ 70% of the total R&D expenditure.

In China, experimental development expenditure is largely over 70% of the total for R&D, and paid mainly by enterprises.

2.2.2　Creativity of R&D

Due to differences and connection among its three stages, R&D has multi-faceted functions. In short, basic research focuses primarily on knowing the world, while applied research and experimental development focuses on transforming the world.

　　Science is a system of knowledge about the laws of the objective world and human spiritual activities, and it is also a creative activity that human beings conduct to know the objective laws of the world. Technology is the experience and knowledge that human beings have accumulated in the course of utilizing and transforming nature and apply in their practice production, and is the concrete and practical application of scientific knowledge. It is also the scientific summarization of practical experience. Technology, in its narrow sense, means engineering technology, which refers to various technical methods and skills based on scientific knowledge and practical production experience. The development of science and technology follows its intrinsic laws. Therefore, R&D development is the intrinsic impetus for scientific and technological advancement.

　　Considering the purpose of transforming the world, R&D is the primary impetus for commercialization of scientific and technological results, the main path for enterprises to obtain technological capability and the basis to get economic benefits, the powerhouse of competitiveness of enterprises and even countries, and of course the foundation for survival and development of enterprises.

　　Epistemologically, R&D is the most powerful tool available for mankind to know the world (including the spiritual world), and one of the main forms of improving the spiritual and physical activities of human beings.

　　The creativity of R&D begins with creative thinking. There are several typical views on creative thinking, namely, creative thinking as imagination, a synthesis of intellect and analytical ability, and the unity of intellect and imagination, with the former manifested in formal logic and the latter in visual logic. Some, typically Einstein, view creative thinking as intuitive. The author is more inclined to viewing creative thinking as the connection of imagination and intuition (or insight). Imagination is the ability to connect phenomena, which are seemingly irrelevant but virtually may be relevant, while intuition is the insight into essential connection of phenomena. To produce imagination and intuition, you must concentrate on what you study to the extent that you are almost saturated in thought, and the ensuing mental and physical relaxation will bring you "creative results." The richer and broader your knowledge is, the bigger the room and possibility for producing imagination and association is.

　　Creative methods, such as brainstorming, thought experiments, permutation and combination, and analogy analysis, have been discussed in many treatises. But these methods perhaps are only rudimental, and the key still is "lasting concentration on study plus short mental and physical relaxation", along with exchange and communication with persons of the same trade.

2.2.3   Organizational Innovation of R&D: Demonstration Zones of Independent Innovation

R&D is creative, so its organizational forms also can be innovative, for example, high-tech development zones, incubators, and strategic alliances for technological innovation. Below is a brief description of China's high-tech development zones ("HTZs" below) and Zhongguancun National Innovation Demonstration Zone.

China's HTZ model was born out of the "Science Park" model that appeared in the United States after the World War II.

Since 1988, China has set up 83 national-level HTZs. In 1991, the State Council promulgated a 48-article policy on HTZs, which gave great support to start-up HTZs. Geographically, these HTZs are concentrated along the coastal areas, in Liaoning, Beijing, Tianjin, Shandong, Jiangsu, Shanghai, Zhejiang, Fujian and Guangdong, more in southern China than in northern China. On development models, 83 HTZs can be divided into three groups: innovation incubation HTZs, R&D HTZs and export processing HTZs. As per the management system, they are managed either by head offices, governments of tier-1 administrative regions, or by park committees.

On organizational management of enterprises in HTZs, there are high-tech limited companies, scientific and technological trust and investment companies, high-tech venture capital companies, multinational companies, technological diffusion networks, etc.

Currently, HTZs, as an important form of organization for technological innovation in China, has become pilot zones for fostering new economic growth points. And this R&D organizational innovation is continuing, for example, the "Zhongguancun National Independent Innovation Demonstration Zone."

(1) Zhongguancun National Independent Innovation Demonstration Zone

Zhongguancun High-tech Development Zone, the earliest and largest among national HTZs since China began its institutional design of science and technology for developing emerging industries of strategic importance, was approved in 2009 by the State Council to found the Zhongguancun National Independent Innovation Demonstration Zone, with the aim of building Zhongguancun the world's most influential scientific and technological innovation center that focuses on seven strategic emerging industries—new energy, energy conservation and environmental protection, electric automobiles, new materials, new pharmaceuticals, biological breeding and information industry.

The Zhongguan National Independent Innovation Demonstration Zone should carry out the following pilot work in terms of institutional reform: ①equity incentive reform: carry out an equity and profit-sharing incentive reform among colleges and universities, scientific research institutes, institute-turned enterprises and state-owned high-tech enterprises; ②financial reform on science and technology: support the cluster development of "angel investment", venture capital investment and equity investment, bring into playing the role of investment funds, gradually perfect the financial service system covering the entire process of technological innovation, make experiments on non-listed companies in Zhongguancun enter the agency share transfer system for price quotation and transfer of shares, and introduce such supportive policies as secured loans, credit loans and intellectual property collateral loans; ③engage new-industry enterprises and R&D organizations in national key scientific and technological programs: encourage new industrial innovation organizations such as strategic alliances for industrial technology innovation as well as private scientific and technological enterprises in Zhongguancun to participate in the country's major projects, scientific and technological infrastructure construction and relevant scientific and technological programs and projects; ④ implement the government procurement plan: make experiments on government procurement of independent innovation products, and extend the use of independent innovation products through such measures as first purchasing or ordering major technical equipment from Zhongguancun and carrying out first equipment experiments and demonstration projects in Zhongguancun, with a view to supporting enterprises' independent innovation; ⑤promote the high-level talent plan: implement the "Zhongguancun top-level talent gathering project", attract overseas high-level talent, innovate talent systems and mechanisms, and build the world's first-class new research organizations; ⑥build the intellectual property park: build the Zhongguancun National Intellectual Property Demonstration Park and the Zhongguancun National High-tech Industry Standardization Demonstration Zone, and implement the "Patent Engine" plan; ⑦ implement the plan on integration of "enterprises, universities, research institutes and users": implement the Zhongguancun Science Park Open Lab project, develop strategic alliances for industrial technology innovation, and deepen the reform on administrative examination and approval system; and ⑧improve government services: achieve convenient and high-efficiency "one-stop" government services, "one-website" examination and approval and "full-range agent service. "

The Zhongguancun National Independent Innovation Demonstration Zone covers Haidian Park, Fengtai Park, Changping Park, Electronic Town, Yizhuang Park, Desheng Park, Yonghe Park, Shijingshan Park, Tongzhou Park and Daxing CBP, among which, Haidian Park is at the core of the demonstration zone (Information Office of the Administrative Committee of Zhongguancun Science Park, 2010).

(2) Development of HTZs in China

When China founded the first HTZ—the Zhongguancun High-tech Industrial Development Zone in Beijing—in 1988, the country's economic, scientific and technological development, especiallyt high technologies and high-tech industries, were at a rather low level. Through over 20 years' effort, not only national-level HTZs amounted to 83 (in 2010), but they also promoted the countrywide development of high technologies and high-tech industries. In 2008, the 53 HTZs countrywide housed 52,683 enterprises employing 7. 165 million people, which, by types of registration, included 22,533 limited liability companies, 8,536 foreign-invested enterprises and 1, 361 state-owned enterprises; their total operating revenues amounted to 6, 598. 57 billion yuan, profits to 330. 42 billion yuan, tax payments to 319. 87 billion yuan, and exports to $ 201. 52 billion; there were 670 incubators with a combined area of 23. 155 million square meters, 44, 346 enterprises being incubated, and 31, 764 incubated enterprises (China High-tech Industry Data, 2009)

China has made the following achievements in its development of HTZs ① introduce the organizational innovation model of integrated development of science, technology and economy; ② developed rapidly—in over 20 years 83 national-level HTZs were built in such a big developing country; besides, a technological innovation system appropriate to a developing country was found, representing a miracle in HTZ development across the world; ③ provide scientific and technological personnel, entrepreneurs and private scientific and technological enterprises with an innovation environment, for example for the application of the venture capital mechanism; ④ one feature of China's HTZs is that governments, both central and local, have made quite favorable policies and shoulder the functions of administration and coordination; and ⑤ stress the combination of regional and industrial policies, for example in the establishment of the industrial development zones around the Bohai Sea, in the Pearl River Delta and in the regions of Beijing and Tianjin.

Compared to some well-known science parks abroad, China's HTZ development still faces the following problems: ①favorable policies, if less influential in relation to market economy, are liable to produce dependency of HTZs and enterprises therein on these policies, making some high-tech enterprises "technologically low"; ②in some HTZs, technological innovation and institutional and market innovation failed to supplement each other and, thus, failed to considerably promote economic development, a big problem facing not only some HTZs but also the entire process of scientific, technological and economic integration; and ③the 83 national-level HTZs seem to "converge" in industrial structure and technology priority, mostly engaged in electronic communications, bioengineering or new materials, with no distinctive characteristics.

2.2.4　Trial Production and Marketing of New Products

The experimental development stage begins with development of new products and new processes, which is followed by trial production and marketing of them. New products can be with completely new functions (such as 3G mobile phones), improved functions (such as improved auto parts), added functions (such as the heat preservation function of cups, and the calendar function of watches), new look (different design of the appearance, for example, difference patterns), and so forth.

(1) New Product Development Strategy—Choose New Products to Be Developed

The new product development strategy, to an enterprise, is subordinated to its development strategy and technological innovation strategy. From the perspective of the technological innovation and development strategies, the enterprise's leading strategy, technology import and assimilation strategy and technology leapfrogging strategy can all be viewed as prior to the new product development strategy.

First of all, new product development should comply with the enterprise's market positioning. Second, it should be based on the enterprise's R&D strength, core competitiveness and resource allocation ability. Here, market positioning not only means the enterprise's position in markets, especially in segment markets, but also relates to such factors as market feedback, market demand, and relevant information on domestic and foreign markets.

Viewed from market objectives, there are such strategies as developing markets, and increasing or reducing market share.

As for types of products, the trial production and marketing of consumer goods and industrial products also has different development strategies (Table 1-3).

Table 1-3   Features of an Enterprise's Strategies at Various Levels

Strategy Features	Corporate Strategy	Business Strategy	Marketing Strategy	New Product Strategy
Scope	Business operations Corporate develop-ment strategy	Product-market devel-opment strategy	Depth, breadth and expansion of targetma-rket and product line	Strategic competing fields: product-use-customer-technolo-gy
Objective	Overall objective Income growth, prof-it, return on invest-ment	Subject to corporate ob-jective Productmarket objectives	Subject to corporate business objective Particular product-market objectives	Development ob-jective Market objective Special objective
Resource alloca-tion	Allocation by business	Allocation by product-market and by func-tional departments of business units	Allocation by particu-lar product-market marketing mixes	Allocation by com-peting fields of new products and by development pro-jects
Competitive strength	Financial and man-power strength More R&D High or-ganizational synergy	High relevance of competition strategy High ability of busi-ness units	Effective product po-sitioning Powerful marketing mix	Product differentia-tion advantage
Synergy	Resources and tech-nologies shared among business operations	Resources shared among different prod-uct-market operations	Marketing resources and activities shared among product-market opera-tions	Share relevant technological, marketing and hu-man resources

Source: Liu Qiusheng, 2001.

(2) Development Process of the New Product

The development process of a new product covers the generation of the creative idea or concept and the production of its prototype and products for trial production and marketing. The development process should consider not only whether the new product is technologically advanced, but also the possibility of cooperation with a university, research institute or other enterprise so as to lower risks and costs, as well as economical efficiency issues, such as conversion costs.

The progressive development of new products covers generation of creative ideas and concepts, technical and commercial analysis of new products, lab development and prototype scaling-up, technical and market testing of new products, and pilot marketing as well as other links. It features low risk, but low adaptability and slow response to the market.

The concurrent development of new products, which employs the CE (concurrent engineering) approach, carries out such activities as new product design, market survey and trial production in a concurrent manner, and considers marketing and other issues during the conceptual design. It is advantageous in that it gives overall consideration to all links of the development process and implements them in an integrated way, which leads to high possibilities of commercializing the new product and lowering the real cost, while its weakness lies in difficulty in management and information communication (Liu Qiusheng, 2001).

New product development can be carried out independently or cooperatively. In case of cooperative development, the enterprise can control core technologies and components and has products assembled by other enterprise; it can also outsource some components to other enterprise and controls all product production and distribution; or the two parties to the contract cooperate by equal division of work.

The constraint for economical efficiency of new product development is manifested mainly in the conversion cost expressed in the formula below:

$$C = (P - D) - V$$

Where, C is the conversion cost; P is the original value of equipment; D is the accumulated depreciation of equipment when replaced; and V is cash realizable value of equipment when replaced, i. e. selling price. $(P - D)$ is depreciated value of equipment. Apparently, if the accelerated depreciation method is adopted-that is, $(P - D)$ diminishes, the value of C, namely conversion cost, diminishes. In addition, the longer the equipment is used, the smaller the conversion cost becomes. Therefore, the government's "accelerated depreciation" policy is to lower enterprises' costs for new product development, encouraging them to carry out technological innovation.

New product development is closely related to the overall environment of trial production and ensuing production. For example, advanced manufacturing technology systems and their management systems will provides new methods and ways for development of new products. Advanced manufacturing technology systems include, among others, computer integrated manufacturing system (CIMS), flexible manufacturing system (FMS), agile manufacturing, just in time (JIT) and lean production (LP).

The trial production of new products is carried out on a small-lot basis, and the country has favorable policies on R&D organizations' trial production of new products. Adjustments have been made in these favorable policies following China's access to WTO.

Trial marketing following trial production is vital. In the entire process of technological innovation, trial marketing marks the shift in focus of technological innovation from technology to economy.

Problems to be addressed for trial marketing of new products are: identifying users and potential users, defining segment markets for new products, estimating the market size and market growth, estimating the response of rivals, and so on.

rial marketing methods for consumer goods include sales wave experiment, simulated store test, and actual market testing; trial marketing methods for industrial products include trial use of products, participating in or holding trade fairs, and product testing in showcases in distributors' or dealers' stores (Wu Guisheng, 2000).

In addition, when going to market, new products are likely to give rise to interest conflict with such stakeholders as potential buyers, rivals and suppliers, to which attention should be given during trial marketing. Of course, solving this problem entails a longer time after new products go to market.

To sum up, the commercialization of technological innovation can be divided into five steps—conception, incubation, demonstration, promotion and extension—for a comparison of the process' linear model and step model (Table 1-4).

Table 1-4 Comparison between Linear Model and Step Model of the Commercialization of Technological Innovation

Linear View on Innovation	Basic research	Applied research and development	Product development and engineering	Production and distribution	Further research and development
Five-step view	Conception	Incubation	Demonstration	Promotion	Extension
Expected results	Ideas which are based on unique technologies and in combination with market demand	Plans on technological feasibility of ideas, their commercialization potentials and further development	Combine technologies with products and/or pro- cesses appealing to the market	Make products or processes rapidly received by various market elements	Create long-term value by cementing and expanding the application of technologies and keeping lea-dership

Continued

Linear View on Innovation	Basic research	Applied research and development	Product development and engineering	Production and distribution	Further research and development
Points of achievement	Theoretically demonstration of technologies, obtaining patents and preliminary projections	Prepare commercialization plans, and build a technological or product platform to be tested together with customers	Publish business projections of products or technologies	Rapidly acquire a profitable market share	Obtain returns on investment in technologies and infrastructure
Main risk participants	Persons of the same trade, colleagues, research partners and media	Venture investors, development partners and potential c-ustomers	Potential customers, providers of supporting technologies, and colleagues and business partners in other fields	Customers, end users, opinion leaders and salespersons	Corporate management departments, changing customer groups, and commercialization partners

Source: Jolly V K, 2001.

Though this section mainly deals with product innovation, process innovation is equally important. Here is an example. Three decades ago, the combustion of sulfur gave off SO_2 in a large smelting plant in China. The part with concentration at 3% and above was made into sulfuric acid through the contact process, while the part with concentration below 1% could only be discharged into air via a chimney taller than 100 meters, which, thus, polluted the air. It is theoretically simple and also not hard in lab experiment to neutralize and absorb SO_2 by an alkaline solution, but cost high in field operation. The plant formed a task force to tackle the problem, and the author as a member participated in the design of the following scheme, which could be seen as a process innovation in the 1970s: ammonia water, the raw material for fertilizer, was used to absorb SO_2, the ammonium sulfite solution produced was sent to a paper mill as a solvent to erode raw materials for paper making, and the waste liquid produced from paper making had no pollution to farmland and proved to be of good fertilizer efficiency. This process, which solved the pollution caused by SO_2 in the smelting plant and by waste liquid in the paper mill, was an integrated process innovation and accorded with "recycling economy" advocated today.

2. 2. 5　Risk and Opportunity of Technological Innovation

Risk can be understood in the following way. On one hand, high yield and high risk are significant features of technological innovation; higher degrees of innovation give rise to greater uncertainty and risk. Therefore, the scientific, systematic management of risk involved in technological innovation allows enterprises to acquire maximum security at minimum costs, which has great significance for enterprises' innovation management. On the other hand, opportunity comes along with risk. The core competitiveness of outstanding executives lies in their ability to turn risk into opportunity. We should identify risks and turn them into opportunities, rather than fear them.

The US-based Project Management Institute (PMI) defines a risk as "an uncertain event or condition that, if it occurs, has a positive or negative effect on a project's objectives" (PMI, 2000). A technological innovation risk means an uncertain event or condition in the process of technological innovation that may have positive or negative effect on a technological innovation project's objectives. An event with a positive effect is called an opportunity, otherwise a threat (or crisis). If unable to identify uncertain events or conditions, an enterprise couldn't conduct follow-up analysis on and take measures against risks. Therefore, risk identification is the first step of the risk management; and more comprehensive risk identification plays a bigger role in risk management, thereby avoiding losses or seeking bigger profits as much as possible.

Also a challenging task, risk identification means to predict future uncertainties, and it is impossible for any enterprise to identify all risks. Nevertheless, an enterprise may use various methods to identify risks as many as possible, for example, expert interviews, brainstorming, analogy comparisons, checklist, and top-level risk matrix. Below is the further classification of technological innovation risks according to the hierarchical classification approach similar to the top-level risk matrix, which can effectively help enterprises to conduct deeper-level risk identification. In Fig. 1-2, technological innovation risks are classified into eight categories at three levels. These risks, if dealt with appropriately, mean opportunities.

(1) Risk and Opportunity at the Strategic Level

Risk at strategic level refers to decision-making risk. Affecting the overall situation, technological innovation poses very high requirements on the decision

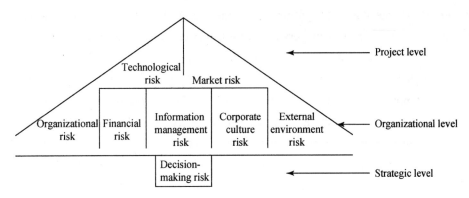

Fig. 1-2   Tree Diagram of Classification of Technological Innovation Risks
Source: Zhou Jizhong, 2002.

maker, who, if lacking a far-sighted vision and global perspective, is likely to make a false decision on technological innovation, for example, a false type of strategy, a technological innovation project not fitting the organization's strategic positioning, failure to grasp the strategic opportunity, or withdrawal from the market at the wrong time and, thus, missing possible huge profits. Risks at the strategic level can affect the whole situation. Whether a danger or an opportunity, results in amplified losses or profits. As risk sometimes implies opportunity, decision-making risk changes into "opportunity decision making" under certain conditions.

(2) Risk and Opportunity at the Organizational Level

1) Organization risk and innovation. Risk at organizational level varies as organizations arc different from each other in structure, scale, environment they operate in, and maturity degree of management. Such risks can be divided into organizational risk, financial risk, information management risk, corporate culture risk and external environment risk. A proper organizational structure allows appropriate combination of various resources required for innovation and moves innovation activities ahead smoothly, while a chaotic one results in ambiguous duties and gross internal consumption, and, thus, causes the lack of necessary resources, finally leading to failure in technological innovation. After an enterprise's new products or services enter the stage of rapid growth, its size of business probably expands fast, demanding more personnel, equipment, raw materials and distribution channels. If the rigid organizational structure fails to meet the requirement of rapid development and makes the entire supporting framework overloaded, that may lead to excessive costs, decline in the quality of personnel, substandard quality, and losing financial control. In addition,

during or after the stage of rapid growth, if the senior management for limited time or energy gives lower-level managers the excessive decision making power and are only concerned about such issues as resource allocation, objective setting and performance evaluation, it is very likely that the lower-level managers act in an isolated way due to lack of a panoramic view and of coordination, thus bringing about tremendous risk to the whole enterprise. What's more, addressing organizational risk sometimes can give rise to organizational innovation, for example, the founding of an organization of cooperation among industries, universities and research institutes and of R&D team.

2) Financial risk and financing innovation. An enterprise may be unable to provide funds in time in all stages of technological innovation due to financial inability or improper planning. During the planning of a technological innovation project, inadequate supply of funds may make it impossible to initiate the project, or cause a rush initiate a project, which may make irremediable losses if the initiated project is improper. During the implementation of a technological innovation project, the short supply of funds leads to inadequacy of equipment and raw materials and even an outflow of key technological personnel, making the project come to nothing and making it impossible to recover early investments. When a new product or service is put into operation, inadequate funds may cause the shortage of production equipment, raw materials and personnel or the disproportion of processes, leading to inadequacy in production scale, increase of per unit costs, or lowered product quality. When the innovation results are introduced to the market, inadequate fund is likely to make it impossible to open and expand the market, thus making it impossible to acquire profits and even unable to recover innovation costs. On the other hand, methods of solving financial risk sometimes give rise to innovation in financing, for example, seeking venture capital or applying for innovation fund support.

3) Information management risk and innovation. Information management risk is manifested in the inadequate external information collected by an enterprise. If lack of professional staff or organization or their incapability to collect and analyze external information like customers' demand and scientific and techological advance, the enterprise will be unable to initiate innovation projects, or initiate improper projects, which lead to severe consequences. In the process of innovation, all kinds of information recurs increasingly and spreads increasingly fast, and any link in the market—R&D— production—market cycle, if without smooth communication of information, is likely to lead to innovation failure. If an enterprise grows rapidly due to introducing its innovation

achievements to the market, but fails to reform its information management system, this information management system would be overloaded and give rise to business risk. On the other hand, the process of solving information management risk sometimes brings about innovation in information management, for example, introducing new software management into the organization.

4) Corporate culture risk and corporate innovation culture. In some enterprises, both leaders and employees perhaps don't like change, unwilling to give up original technologies and equipment and learn new technologies. And leaders of some other enterprises believe in survival of the fittest through competition, but excessively tense internal competition is bound to produce pressure on employees, who may no longer share information with each other due to the competition between them, which hinders internal information circulation and leads to failure of innovation projects. Some successful leaders unconsciously turn deaf ears to bad news, viewing those speaking bluntly of project difficulties and potential crisis as pessimists without courage. And in such cases, the employees probably no longer pass to the top leaders the possible risks for the project, and thus cannot obtain correct decisions as well as support from the top management, leading to failure of the innovation project. On the other hand, the process of addressing corporate culture risk sometimes imperceptibly creates an innovation culture, for example, blending different corporate cultures during mergers and acquisitions (M&A).

5) External environment risk and opportunity. This includes the change of macro-political and economic environments and even of the natural environment. For example, the change of inflation and financial policies may arouse corresponding financial risk; following its access to WTO, China needs to adjust and revise its original laws and regulations, and the enactment of new laws and regulations—for example, on quality and environmental protection—probably makes it impossible to continue to produce new products or use new processes, leading to failure of entire innovation projects; force majeure events such as earthquake, flood and war may cause unavoidable risks to technological innovation projects. On the other hand, the process of overcoming external environment risk sometimes may give rise to development opportunities in external environments; for example, enterprises have to develop "low-carbon technologies or products" for environment protection.

(3) Risk and Opportunity at the Project Level

Risks at the project level mainly refer to technological risks and market risks, meaning the degree of maturity of the technology and market.

1) Technological risk and innovation. The adoption of new materials and/or new processes, inadequate demonstration of new technologies, or the unavailability of product standards required for new technologies will increase uncertainty and risk. The innovation project may be stopped or postponed, if the technological personnel are less competent, or the enterprise is unable to finish all operational processes required for new technologies. Some enterprises make up their weakness of inadequate technological abilities or shorten innovation periods by brining in new technologies, but the technology transfer may, fail due to the immaturity of technologies or the inadequate supply abilities of the providers. High technologies are developing rapidly, and are very likely to be imitated by rivals, or replaced or eliminated by newer ones if not advanced enough. If a new technology differs greatly from the current one, the production equipment, processes and production capacity probably cannot meet the requirements of the new technology, entailing high conversion costs, which make it difficult to put the new technology into service. If the raw materials or new components required by a new technology are unavailable on the market or cannot be provided in required time period, bulk production would be impossible. If the enterprise is incapable of sustained development, the new technology cannot be further improved. On the other hand, the process of preventing technological risk sometimes gives rise to technological innovation.

2) Market risk and opportunity. When being introduced into the market, a new product or service might be doubted by customers due to inadequate market promotion or publicity. Even if there is adequate market promotion, there will be a time lag between the introduction of the product or service and the effective demand, which, if unduly long, will make it difficult to recover R&D funds. Moreover, although an enterprise is sure that there is need for its new product or service, it cannot identify exactly who and where the customers are in a short time, which makes it impossible to set its marketing strategy and gain profits as soon as possible.

Sometimes the market demand for new products or services has already manifested itself, but because it is impossible to predict the size of the market demand, a false production or marketing strategy might be made.

During the introductory stage of the life cycle of a new product, an enterprise can hardly predict when and how fast the market grows. The growth and maturity periods, if shorter than anticipated, are likely to make it impossible to obtain due profits and make an innovation project at a loss. An enterprise, sometimes, can hardly predict what competition means the rivals will adopt to compete with its own new products or services. If the competition is so fierce that prices fall short of the anticipated level, the enterprise can hardly realize anticipated profits. On the other hand, in the process of preventing market risk, market opportunities sometimes can be identified.

(4) Risk Matrix Formed by Technology and Market

The combined technology and market of different maturity degree forms a project risk matrix (Fig. 1-3). Overall project risk changes along with the technology and market risks.

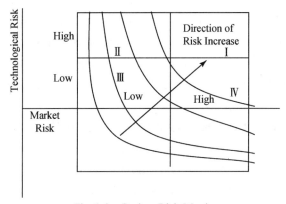

Fig. 1-3   Project Risk Matrix

Note: Quadrant I: Highest risk, which probably gives rise to huge profits if the market is large enough.

Quadrant II: Higher risk, which occurs when technological replacement takes place on the existing market.

Quadrant III: Lowest risk, which also usually means limited commercial opportunity.

Quadrant IV: High risk. To a multinational company, opportunity is generally regional.

Source: Hartmann G C and Myers B M, 2000

(5) Case of Organizational Design That Turns Risk into Opportunity: Innovation Relay Center

Sometimes risks coexist with opportunities. There is an interactive relationship between different risks, and the occurrence of one risk may cause many other risks to happen. Therefore, such possible correlations should be considered in risk identification. On the basis of analysis on possible risks during technological innovation described above, an enterprise can, according to its actual situation, prioritize risks qualitatively and quantitatively. It had better quit the project, or avoid risks, in case of both high possibility and severe destructiveness of risks as well as the probability of failing to obtain expected profits. Otherwise, it should take measures to deal with risks with higher priority and prepare technological prevention and control schemes to prevent, control, keep or transfer the risks to minimize the losses that may caused by risks, so as to get maximum profits. Innovation is an activity pregnant with uncertainty, and it therefore is an activity involving great risks. But the enterprise ought not to avoid risks by simply rejecting innovations, because the biggest risk is making no innovations.

Risk can be converted into opportunity under certain conditions. In 2010, the Torch High Technology Industrial Development Center of the MOST established 11 provinces (autonomous regions and municipalities directly under the central government) including Beijing, Shanghai, Anhui and Hubei as the pilot units for China Innovation Relay Network (CIRN). That is an institutional design to turn innovation risk into opportunity. The CIRN borrowed the idea of the European institutional design of the Innovation Relay Center (IRC) Network aiming to promote technology transfer among European SMEs, universities and research institutes and provide a platform for technology transfer of European SMEs.

Before that, the CIRN Hubei had already become the first Chinese branch of the Enterprise Europe Network (EEN), the Enterprise Europe Network in Central China (EEN-CC), and, in 2008, was included by the MOST in the list of China's first "National Technology Transfer Demonstration Organizations. " CIRN Hubei is designed as an open technology transfer center depending upon the Wuhan Science and Technology Exchange Center, which, coupled with the Wuhan Optics Valley United Property Rights Exchange and the Hubei High Technology Development Promotion Center as two platforms, is geared to the East Lake Independent Innovation Demonstration Zone, major industrial clusters throughout the province and the Wuhan City Cluster. In 2009, the Wuhan Science and Technology Exchange Center identified more than 250 enterprise needs, helped form over 200 partnerships, conducted an in-depth analysis of 106 European needs, passed over 80 pieces of information to enterprises and research institutes, and helped form over 50 partnerships between European and local enterprises and research institutes. The CIRN Shanghai also drew on IRC institutional design and experience to have formed a technological innovation network that links the Shanghai Technology Transfer & Exchange to the local districts and countries, science parks and research institutes. The CIRN Anhui and other branches also have basic conditions.

Currently, the CIRN has to address the following issues: cross-region and cross-field flow of technological elements; shift of the technology transfer system from the supply system to the market price basis, giving SMEs have equal access to public scientific and technological resources; and strengthening of the coordination and services for technology transfer. Services provided by the CIRN include: screening of technologies developed under national science and technology programs, pilot scale experiments and incubation, integration, market-based development, investment and financing services, policy consultancy, technical consultancy, intellectual property consultancy, foreign-related technologies, and negotiation services.

The government will support the CIRN in terms of funds, organizational coordination and policy, which will greatly help increase the country's technology transfer and transformation (according to statistics, in 2009, only 26,104 items of technologies developed under national science and technology programs were transferred and transformed in China, which only accounted for 12.2% of the country's total number of technology deals) (Han Shide,2010).

The statistics just mentioned above indicates that technological innovation involves risk, but through the institutional design of CIRN and the innovation management during implementation thereof, it is possible to change risk to opportunity.

2.2.6　Marketing of High-tech Goods

The commercialization of high-tech results is the last part of the entire technological innovation process. The marketing of such goods is not merely a process; to customers, it is the whole of transaction. Considering the connotations of modern product marketing, products are not only tangible goods that can meet particular needs of consumers, but also intangible services. To put it another way, goods consist of three levels: core products with the most essential functions; tangible products with features of quality, function, feature, pattern and package; and additional products comprising transportation and installation, repair and debugging and after-sales services.

(1) Features of High-tech Products and Factors for Successful Marketing

A high-tech product has the following features: being developed with high technology and high intellect; with a higher rate of renewal; marking an innovation for the market; requiring higher R&D costs; and able to satisfy the demand in some particular markets.

Factors for successful marketing of such goods are: grasping information on future needs of consumers; closely cooperating with the marketing and R&D departments;

possessing necessary resources; introducing high-tech products with a relatively short life cycle; and fast responding to customers. For example, aside from some shared objectives such as making profits for the enterprise, the R&D department and the marketing department have different focuses in their work. The former pays more attention to applied research and internal quality and functions of products, while the latter care more about the experimental development, external quality of products, and marketing features of products.

(2) Factors Affecting High-tech Product Buyers

Factors affecting the high-tech product buyers comprise cultural factors, social factors, psychological factors and personal factors. Cultural factors include ethic background, religion and regional traditions and customs; social factors include buyers' social status, social life and working environment; psychological factors include mental satisfaction the buyers have about high-tech products (identity with social classes, feeling consolation, etc.); personal factors relates to buyers' ages, occupations, economic conditions and lifestyles.

(3) Competitors and Distributions Channels of High-tech Products

In Prof. Michael E. Porter's "Five Forces Analysis", there are rivalry among competitors, threat of new entrants and threat of substitutes, with the latter two worth more attention. For example, a pharmaceutical company, if the new medicine it has developed with huge investments is substituted by a latecomer soon after introduced to the market, would suffer great losses. Of course, whether or not potential competitors can successfully make inroads into a market depends on these entry barrier factors: capital investment, economy of scale, government approval, distribution channels, established brands, etc.

(4) Particularities of Marketing of High-tech Enterprises

Compared to enterprises in traditional industries, high-tech enterprises frequently encounter some particular problems in the market.

1) Market demand is not easy to predict. This is mainly because many commonly-used market demand prediction techniques, which were designed according to the characteristics of traditional products, are usually not suitable for high-tech products. The questioning approach that is most commonly used in market research, for example, has one precondition to be effective: the interviewee is able to understand the future development trend in technology of the product, as well as his/her future needs for the product. However, interviewees usually don't have such ability, because: ①a

high-tech product is fairly complex, while customers as nonprofessionals usually lack adequate knowledge of the product and can hardly accurately predict its possible development; ② the short life cycle and the high rate of updating of the high-tech product make it harder to predict its development; ③customers can hardly understand the value the innovation of a high-tech product brings about, making it almost impossible for them to predict their needs for the product; ④as the target market of a new product is usually different from that of a current product, market research can hardly accurately choose the audience to be surveyed; ⑤ the depth of product development can hardly coincide with customer needs, and a high-tech enterprise can hardly predict the real market demand, i. e. at what level of technology a product can be widely received by the target customers. When publicizing their products, some enterprises can only introduce their technological advantage, and consider little customers' expectations and their degrees of acceptance; in particular, enterprises with venture capitals, which are eager to obtain customer commitments under all-round pressure, develop product functions, regardless of costs, and usually ignore customers' real needs and their affordability.

2) Product life cycle is irregular. The life cycle of traditional products typically consists of a short product development stage and short introduction and growth stages, but a longer maturity stage, and a decline stage with a lower rate. Compared to traditional products, high-tech products have fairly special life cycle. First, the R&D stage is relatively long, mainly because of high complexity and high content of technology. In case of original innovation, the R&D period will be much longer. Second, both the introduction and growth stages are relatively long, mainly because products are so complex that it takes customers and potential consumers a long "silence stage" to recognize and accept the uses or benefits of the new products. Third, both the maturity and decline stages are relatively short, mainly because of the high speed of scientific and technological advancement, the extensive dissemination of high-tech products and the spillover effect of technologies, which always allow high-tech enterprises to continuously introduce new products. The introduction of new products causes tremendous impacts on existing ones, forcing them to enter the decline stage soon. Besides, some high-tech enterprises which have established a technological monopoly give an active impetus for eliminating existing products and introducing new ones, attempting to maximally tap market potentials. Therefore, high-tech products are quite liable to become outdated, whose life

cycle is shortened much more than that of traditional products.

2.3 Resource Allocation

Resource allocation to R&D covers the allocation of financial resources, human resources, material resources and information resources. Financial resources shall be allocated to basic research, applied research and experimental development. Below is a discussion of China's resource allocation to basic research only. This issue is of course not the whole of resource allocation, but it involves how to crack the "Needham Question" and the "Qian Xuesen's Question", and is of key importance to solve the issues on human resources, the mutual convertibility between financial and human resources under certain conditions.

As far as financial resources are concerned, China's current R&D funds are already not low in terms of its proportion in GDP; in 2008 the R&D/GDP ratio reached 1.54%, far ahead of that of other developing countries, and even higher than that of some developed countries, such as Italy. The problem now is about the efficiency of R&D funds. Generally, enterprises, especially private ones such as Huawei, BYD and Geely, have higher efficiency of R&D funds; but the input-output efficiency of universities and research institutes, especially in large scientific research projects, is worth attention. Some scholars questioned whether the procedure of application for research projects with R&D funds of up to tens and even hundreds of millions yuan was scientific and whether the "Matthew Effect" and "government-university collusion" worked. Therefore, "how much R&D funds are" and "how efficiently they are used" are two different concepts.

Analyzed from channels for R&D financial resource allocation, main channels for the government include: national science and technology programs (for example, the National Basic Research Program "973" Program, "863" Program, National Key Technology R&D Program, China Torch Program, China Spark Program, Knowledge Innovation Program, and National Technological Innovation Program) and national foundations (such as the NSFC, National Social Science Foundation of China, and Innovation Fund For Technology Based Firms), as well as scientific and technological funds appropriated by the central ministries and commissions and provinces (autonomous regions, and municipalities directly under the central government). Resource allocation by enterprises is mainly in two ways: self-financing (mainly for large enterprises), and financing by intermediaries.

Given the length of the book, this section mainly deals with resource allocation for basic research and with financing by scientific and technological intermediaries, because they are both ends of the long chain of R&D.

2. 3. 1   Difficulties in Resource Allocation for Basic Research

Since the scientific and technological system reform in 1985, China's financial input into basic research grew rapidly, which increased from 450 million yuan in 1987 to 14. 8 billion yuan in 2006, or if calculated with constant prices, twelve-fold[1], with an annual average growth rate of 13. 32% —far higher than macro-economic growth (9. 81%) and financial revenue growth (9. 93%) in the same period.

There are two types of basic research. One is directed towards national objectives, with a view of addressing the major needs of social development, economic development and national defense, namely "strategic basic research" (or "country-oriented research"). The other is a sort of free exploration, which is driven of personnel interest, features more uncertain subject, process and result that entail no consensus, and thus more possibly produce original research results.

The two types are generally financed by two systems of the government: the "science foundation system" (generally referred to the system of free application, mainly the NSFC and the National Social Science Foundation of China), which finances "free-exploration" research (also known as "pure basic research"), and the "national science and technology programs", which finances country-oriented research (strategic basic research) (Fig. 1-4).

(1) Case Study about Resource Allocation to Basic Research: Basic Medicine

This section is a case study about "basic medicine", a discipline of natural science. First, we use the National Natural Science Award—winning projects in the field of basic medicine during 2000 ~ 2006 to analyze the impacts of China's basic research funding model (consisting of two basic research funding systems, namely science foundations and science programs) on basic medicine and discuss the role that the coordination between the two systems plays in major original innovation.

Below is an analysis on the correlation between original innovation in basic medicine and the two funding systems. The National Natural Science Award is the supreme award the Chinese government provides in the field of natural science, which is

---

① Basic research funds grew 33-fold nominally in 20 years.

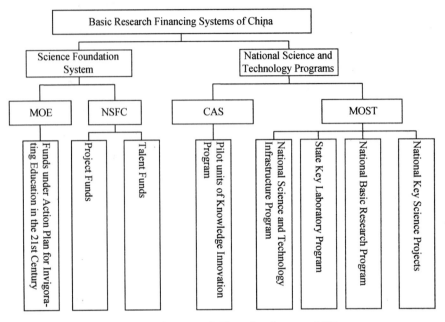

Fig. 1-4 Basic Research Financing System of China

given to Chinese citizens, who have made momentous scientific discoveries in basic research and applied basic research in explaining the characters and laws of natural phenomena[1]. Since China's regulations on science and technology awards were revised in 1999, the National Natural Science Award has comprised the first prize and the second prize, covering the areas of knowledge of mathematics and mechanics, physics and astronomy, chemistry, geoscience, biology, basic medicine, material science, engineering science and information science. It is recognized that project results that have won the National Natural Science Award represent the country's highest level in their respective fields of knowledge, and they also are momentous original innovations in related fields.

In 2000 ~ 2006, 92 person-times involved in 20 projects in basic medicine won the second prizes of the National Natural Science Award. These award-winning projects, which represent the country's highest research level in the field of basic medicine, are original results of great scientific discovery significance and of great international influence. For example, the award-winning project "Research on Nosogenesis of

---

① According to the Review Scope and Criteria of National Science and Technology Awards, a major scientific discovery should meet the following three conditions at a time: i) not discovered or explained by any predecessor; ii) of great scientific value; and iii) recognized by natural science communities both at home and abroad.

Brachydactyly Type A-1" made momentous breakthroughs in gene mapping and clone research through in-depth probe into the inherited diseases of human brachydactyly. A milestone in genetics history, the project for the first time discovered that the IHH gene in the human body and the three mutation positions in this gene are directly responsible for Brachydactyly Type A-1, and for the first time in a century unveiled Gregor Johann Mendel's puzzle about autosomal dominant genetic diseases, and extended to human beings the knowledge that IHH—the focal gene of biological research on animal development—plays a significant role in skeletal development, discovering the connection between the IHH gene and height formation. The research findings of the project have produced a great influence in the international academia.

Currently, in China, funds for basic medicine research come mainly from the "973" Program for Population and Health[①], the NSFC Department of Life Sciences (and recently established Department of Health Sciences), as well as relevant departments of the Ministry of Health (MOH), MOE, CAS and Academy of Military Medicinal Sciences (AMMS). Restricted by data availability, this section only gives an account of projects funded by the NSFC Department of Life Sciences and the "973" Program for Population and Health.

Of the 20 award-winning projects, except for two Hong Kong scholars, the rest 18 projects all received NSFC funds, each on average receiving NSFC funds under 11 items; 10 projects were also funded by the "973" Program. Of the 92 award winners, 36 received NSFC funds, 28 received both NSFC funds and "937" Program funds, one only received "973" Program funds, and 27 receive no funds from the two sources (Fig. 1-5).

Basic medicine research usually takes fairly long time. For example, an R&D project from a new vaccine until a new pharmaceutical at least takes 5 ~ 10 years before success, while to articulate some mechanism of a basic research in life science requires a long time alike. This is because any one problem in life science cannot be solved through one or two experiments. In this context, the continuous support by a multiplicity of scientific funds (or funding channels) can provide researchers with a material guarantee necessary for their long-term creative work; at the same time, as different funds (or organizations) have their respective emphases, the level of basic research can

---

① Currently, the 973 Program comprises seven fields of study: agriculture, energy, information, resource and environment, population and health, materials, and synthesis and frontier science. Administered by the MOST Department of Basic Research, it is China's most important national program to support basic research.

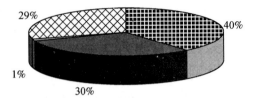

Received NSFC funds, but undertook no project supported by the "973" Program

Funded by both NSFC and the "973" Program

Funded by either NSFC nor the "973" Program

Undertake a project supported by the "973" Program, but received NSFC funds

Fig. 1-5   Statistics on Financial Support to National Natural Science Award Winners in Basic Medicine

Source: Zhou Jizhong et al. ,2009.

be gradually improved in a "upward spiral" process of "discovering new phenomena, verifying new hypotheses, proposing new theories and bringing about new problems. "

Representative of momentous original innovation in the country's field of basic medicine, the National Natural Science Award projects have also revealed that the continuous support by science foundations and national science programs are conducive to great innovation. In 2000 ~ 2006, all the 18 chief researchers of the award projects were continuously supported by the NSFC to a different degree; of them, 14 were also in charge of projects under the "973" Program and 4 served as chief scientist for relevant projects under the "973" Program.

The NSFC and the "973" Program are important entities funding basic research in China, but they differ in funding scope and the selection of projects to be funded. The NSFC has a broad scope of funding, and it selects projects by depending more on expert peer review. The "973" Program, as a government-supported science program directed towards key basic research fields, gives more consideration to the country's medium and long-term development objectives, requiring that projects be concerned with national development strategies and aim to solve key scientific issues that meet the needs of national strategies, to provide a scientific foundation for sustainable socioeconomic development and to provide innovations at source for future formation of high technologies. Although the establishment of projects under the "973" Program is also subject to peer review, its authorities have more power to make decisions than the NSFC[1]. Because the NSFC and the "973" Program differ in funding scope and the

---

[1]   Projects under the 973 Program are determined by the MOST according to expert review conclusions and national scientific and technological priorities.

selection of projects, they have different funding mechanisms which, to achievement of key original innovation results, are supplementary.

Of the 14 chief researchers who received funds from both the NSFC and the "973" Program, except one who received funds from the "973" Program after winning the award, the remainder had been continuously funded by the NSFC and the "973" Program before they won awards, who obtained 3. 21 NSFC projects and 1. 22 projects under the "973" Program on average and spent averagely 9. 1 years from the time they obtained NSFC projects to the time they won awards. The NSFC primarily funds free-inquiry basic research, which helps to inspire "imagination", obtain unexpected results and find the sources of scientific and technological innovation. But no matter how novel a concept is at the beginning, a real systematic field of innovation value deriving from the concept can, by no means, be completed through one or two short-term research projects. This entails lasting, stable support to these research projects from science foundations and programs, so that they can obtain new results on a continual basis. National science programs have provided much more funds than science foundations. For example, in 2006 the NSFC Department of Life Sciences funded general projects and key projects for 249,400 yuan and 1,447,400 yuan on average, and the National Science Fund for Distinguished Young Scholars funded each of its projects for 2 million yuan on average; in 2001 ~ 2005, the "973" Program funded 29 population and health projects for 705 million yuan, 24. 3103 million yuan per project on average. The national science programs' aid of science foundation projects helps transform free-inquiry innovative ideas into original innovations of great influence. In fact, the 14 award winners had obtained 2. 43 NSFC-funded projects each on average, before they shouldered the relevant projects under the "973" Program.

Take the 2000 National Natural Science Award second prize-winning project, "Research on molecular mechanism of treating malignant blood disease with all-trans retinoic acid (ATRA) and arsenic trioxide (As_2O_3), as an example. The project team obtained 23 NSFC tasks in the field of leukemia treatment and 3 tasks under the "973" Program. As early as the late 1980s, the project team had successfully applied ATRA to treat acute promyelocytic leukemia (APL). At the time, the problem of how to illustrate its mechanism at molecular level aroused great controversy among many research teams in the world. From 1990 onwards, this project team received NSFC funds to conduct theoretical research into ATRA-induced differentiation mechanism, and when it made vital breakthroughs in APL research, the NSFC engaged the team to research into leukemia differentiation and apoptosis and gave it great support. From the mid-and late-1990s, financially supported by the NSFC, the project team completed the research on the targeted therapy of APL induced differentiation and apoptosis. It was just the "enzymatic" action of the NSFC that the key members of the project team obtained the "relayed" support from the "973" Program. The adequate financial support greatly improved the experimental conditions of the project team. In a period of over 10 years, continuously supported by the NSFC and the "973" Program, the project team illustrated systematically and in an in-depth way the vital role that the fusion gene caused by chromosome translocation and its protein product play in APL pathogenesis, and succeeded in applying ATRA and As_2O_3 to conduct the induced differentiation of APL, which was recognized by international colleagues as likely to make APL the first curable acute myeloid leukemia (AML) in human history. The research findings received the second prize of the National Natural Science Award in 2000. The research process of the research team also suggested that despite the difference in positioning, funding mechanism and intensity, the close cooperation and contact of the NSFC and the "973" Program in some key issues and major projects is one of effective ways for national foundations to fund life science research, as shown in Fig. 1-6, the model in which the NSFC produces "free-inquiry" results while the "973" Program produces strategic research results (Zhou Jizhong, 2009).

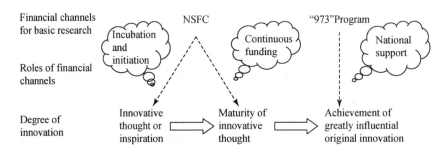

Fig. 1-6   Coordination between NSFC and "973" Program in Key Original Innovation

Source: Zhou Jizhong et al. , 2009.

(2) Problems about Current Basic Research Funding Models

1) Lack of fair competition in application for projects under national science programs. The science history of the 19th and 20th centuries suggested that if there were no government support and science could not become a state-supported cause, basic research would be no more than a personal interest that elite have to satisfy their

curiosity. But if we overemphasize that basic research should be subordinate to national strategic programs, especially when some oriented basic research programs formulated go against the development logic of basic science itself, the result is usually getting half the result with twice the effort. Moreover, when there are possibilities of manipulation or semi-manipulation behind the scenes when introducing administrative decisions, phenomena that scientific and technological resources are allocated and acquired in a noncompetitive manner and by power and status would exist extensively, and vested interests would through dilution distort national objectives during implementation of policies (Yang Zhenyin et al. ,2003).

Under the dual constraint of a scientific research environment, in which "strategic basic research" has an absolute advantage to acquire financial resources and during the transition *guanbenwei* (official-centeredness; that is, schools are not managed by professors and research institutes are not managed by scholars) prevails, the allocation of scientific and technological resources in a noncompetitive way and by power and status will produce the effects of "deteriorated allocation of resources" and low efficiency of resource allocation. This will, in turn, aggravate the Matthew Effect", so that more precious resources concentrate in the hands of "scholars having close relations with officials in charge" and "disadvantaged" scholars have to use more time and energy to better their relations with the vested interests for the purpose of seeking projects and funds.

In the long run, the emphasis of the country-oriented basic research programs should shift from the current focus on science direction and project selection to creating an environment that introduces competition into project application and result evaluation. At the same time, the share of the science foundations in the current funding pattern should be increased. Although further improvement is still needed in many aspects, the management of scientific funds by foundations is more rational, efficient and cost-efficient than the government's scientific and technological administration departments, whose management costs are lower than those of the latter.

On the current government-led national science programs, though the selection of projects is also subject to peer review, the government departments in charge have more power to make decision than the science foundations. In the review of large projects organized by government departments, scientists' "networking standards" is likely to replace academic standards. If precious resources are allowed to concentrate more in the hands of "scholars having close relations with officials in charge", the consequences will be "resource waste, mind corruption, and innovation obstruction" (Shi Yigong and Rao Yi, 2010).

2) Excessive input into national scientific and technological programs. As the national department in charge of scientific and technological development, the MOST each year allocates scientific and technological funds of over 30 billion yuan, primarily used to support the country's current four major science and technology programs ("863" Program, "973" Program, National Key Technology R&D Program, and National Science and Technology Infrastructure Program), which are far higher than the aggregate funding size of the country's national foundation system. As described above, the average funding intensity of population and health projects under the "973" Program reached 24.31 million yuan, sub-projects of which had also an average funding intensity of 3.69 million yuan, while in 2006 the NSFC Department of Life Sciences' general projects and key projects had an average funding intensity of 249,400 yuan and 1.4474 million yuan, respectively, and the average funding intensity of the National Science Fund for Distinguished Young Scholars stood at two million yuan. The oriented national science programs far exceeded in funding intensity the free-inquiry science foundations (Table 1-5). Of course this accords with the funding principle of the "973" Program, "taking the whole situation into consideration, giving prominence to priorities, and conducting researches on a selective basis."

It is formulated in the "*Outline of the National Medium-and Long-Term Program for Science and Technology Development*" published in 2006 that intensive efforts should be made to develop four major scientific research programs (all of which are national science programs), striving to make key breakthroughs in scientific front fields like protein science, quantum science, nano science and technology, and developmental and reproductive biology, and making them rise up to internationally leading level. It is estimated that in 15 years to come China will invest nearly 10 billion yuan into each of the programs[1]. But to the NSFC, the main player of the foundation system in the basic research funding pattern, its funds have fluctuated at around 24% of the country's total for basic research since its inception (Fig. 1-7); in nearly 20 years from 1987 to 2005 the country invested an aggregate sum of 18 billion yuan into it. Luckily, in recent years the country considerably increased funds to the NSFC; in 2009 the NSFC funds

---

[1] In 2006 alone, the MOST invested 1,120million yuan in the "China Human Liver Proteome Project"; 10 projects were established under the National Key Scientific Research Program (Protein Project), which were funded for 127.1 million yuan.

reached 7 billion yuan, which greatly increased its funding of projects.

Table 1-5　Funding Statistics of the"973"Program (Population and Health) and the NSFC Department of Life Sciences (1998 ~ 2005)

Year	973 Program (Population and Health)		NSFC Department of Life Sciences	
	Funding/million yuan	Projects Established	Funding/million yuan	Projects Established
1998	72.9318	3	261.76	1,413
1999	170.1742	7	257.97	1,398
2000	48.6212	2	304.32	1,792
2001	121.553	5	404.1	2,021
2002	97.2424	4	578.99	2,772
2003	72.9318	3	669.4	2,989
2004	97.2424	4	839.74	3,780
2005	243.106	10	1,104	4,122
Total	923.8	38	4,420.28	20,287

Note: NSFC projects included general projects, youth-led projects, key projects and major projects.

Source: NSFC data came from *Chinese Bulletin of Life Sciences* (Issues 6, 1998 ~ 2005), and 973 Program data came from the website of National Basic Research Program (http://www.973.gov.cn/).

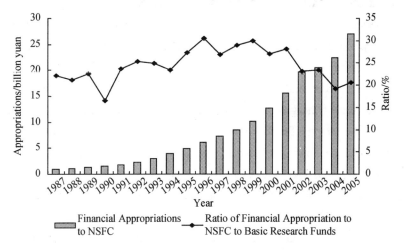

Fig. 1-7　Financial Appropriations to NSFC and Their Ratios to Basic Research Funds (1987 ~ 2005)

Source: Zhou Jizhong et al., 2009

As a developing country, it is reasonable for China to emphasize in its basic research funding pattern the "strategic basic research", but if investment in it is much greater than that in "pure basic research", it is likely to lead to no resolution of the "Needham Question" and the "Qian Xuesen's Question." This is because "free inquiry" is vital for the generation of scientists and excellent achievements. Overemphasizing the role of national development strategies and programs in improving the level of basic research and attempting to "muster forces to fight a war of annihilation" in scientific research don't accord with the intrinsic laws of modern scientific development. Present-day fundamental science research has come to a fairly fine degree, bringing about large quantities of branches of science. Basic research comprises countless research subjects, which are intersected with each other and extremely professional. Choosing a few key fields and concentrating substantial resources on them is, on the one hand, at great risk, and on the other likely to ignore more research subjects of equal importance. Scientifically and technologically developed countries also have many government-led scientific and technological programs in the field of basic research; on the protein scientific front, for example, the United States has a "Protein Structure Initiative (PSI)", and Japan has a "Protein 3000 Project." But these projects were proposed by scientists, academically debated and finally proposed to governments, rather than being guided by scientific and technological authorities.

3) Inadequate funds or low efficiency? There was a phenomenon worth attention as the country was considerably increasing financial input into basic research. Although basic research funds increased year by year, the proportion of expenditure of them to that of aggregate R&D funds kept low, at 5%. The problem is that from 1998 when the prime minister of the government announced the implementation of the strategy of "invigorating the country through science and education" as the main task of the then government, China's funds for science, technology and education grew considerably. In 1998 ~ 2000, massive investment was made in science and education projects relating to basic research: in 1998 the CAS initiated the Knowledge Innovation Program, into the phase I program (1998 ~ 2000), of which the government finance invested over 5 billion yuan; almost in the same period, the government finance (central and local) invested over 10 billion yuan into 10 key universities. It is estimated according to the uses of funds that a fairly large portion of these funds were used for basic research. After that, nearly all universities, out of consideration for their own development, followed the above-mentioned model to raise funds from

government finance and various other channels, which considerably increased their funds. If the appropriations to the "973" Program founded in the same period and to the NSFC committed to fund basic research (actual appropriations to the NSFC in 2009 reached 7 billion yuan) are added in, it is justifiable to say that the years 1998 ~ 2009 marked a peak of the country's funding of basic research. It is baffling why the country's statistics on R&D funds failed to reflect the change. The proportion of basic research funds to aggregate R&D funds in 1999 and 2000 was almost no difference from that in 1995 and 1996, and even lower than that in 1997.

Currently, the proportion of basic research funds to total R&D funds in developed countries has already reached 12% ~ 20%, but in China it is 4.70% (2007). China's intensity of input into basic research (proportion of basic research funds to R&D funds) is far lower than that of innovative countries and even lower than some developing countries (Zhou Jizhong et al. ,2009).

On the evidence that China's proportion of basic research funds to R&D funds is low, only at about 5%, some attributes the country's low level of basic research to shortage of adequate funds. The 5% proportion, in my opinion, was caused by statistical problems, because this indicator varies between 10% and 25% in developed countries and is greatly higher than 10% even in developing countries.

This indicator is largely over 20% even in non-developed countries, as shown in Table 1-6 below. Unimaginably, in such developing countries as Czech Republic, Hungary, Poland and South Africa, which have no national key programs in support of basic research like China's Knowledge Innovation Program and "973" Program, this indicator is unexpectedly five to six times that of China. This is unimaginably queer.

Table 1-6   Gross Expenditure on Research and Development (GERD) and Composition in Non-developed Countries (Unit: $ 100 million)

Country	GERD	Expenditure on Basic Research		Expenditure on Applied Research		Expenditure on Experimental Development	
		Amt.	% of GERD	Amt.	% of GERD	Amt.	% of GERD
Czech Republic (2002)	9.03	3.38	37.40	3.21	33.50	2.44	27.02
Hungary (2002)	5.20	1.64	31.50	1.69	32.50	1.87	35.96
Poland (2001)	9.51	3.60	37.90	2.45	25.76	3.46	36.38
Portugal (2001)	7.56	2.10	27.80	3.25	42.98	2.21	29.23
Spain (2001)	44.11	8.93	20.20	17.10	38.77	18.08	40.99

Continued

Country	GERD	Expenditure on Basic Research		Expenditure on Applied Research		Expenditure on Experimental Development	
		Amt.	% of GERD	Amt.	% of GERD	Amt.	% of GERD
Russia (2002)	40.03	6.29	14.60	6.85	17.11	29.89	74.67
Mexico (1997)			23.20				
Slovakia (2001)			25.70				
South Africa (2005)			18.60		38.80		42.60

Source: *China Science and Technology Indicators 2004* of the MOST; *OECD Science, Technology and Industry Scoreboard 2003*; "*National Survey of Research and Experimental Development (2004/2005)*" of Minister of Science and Technology of the Republic of South Africa.

So, what gives rise to the statistical problems? First, China's statistical scope of "basic research" is relatively narrow, which probably doesn't cover all "strategic basic research." Second, statistics on compensation for basic research are relative low. And, third, the division by flexible experimental development funds of rigid basic research funds leads to a lower proportion. The country's basic research funds are financial appropriations on the whole, which are of great rigidity, while experimental development funds come largely from enterprises, which have grown rapidly in recent years and are likely virtually flexible. This also is responsible for the low proportion of basic research funds.

China's expenditure on basic research is at least higher than that of India, but from the efficiency point of view, India outperforms China in terms of research results, whether in citation by the world's three major index journals (SCI, EI and ISTP) of papers published or in winning of Nobel Prizes. There are both institutional and cultural reasons. On scientific and technological institution, the government's management on science and technology is too specific and aggressive; scientific and technological affairs should be a field the government feels most relaxed about, while basic research is "at the extremity." On academic institution, government departments at various levels, universities and research institutes should transfer power to scientists and professors, letting them "manage schools and institutes." As to culture, this book will discuss the values of Indian intellectuals in 9.3.

2.3.2　Financing by Scientific and Technological Intermediaries

Different from government finance-supported basic research, channels for enterprises' R&D resource allocation comprise self-financing, and financing by intermediaries. The former is mainly appropriate to large enterprises, which is not treated in this section; the latter mainly serves small and medium-sized enterprises (SMEs), which is the focus of this section. Financing by intermediaries is divided into two types: financing for SMEs by scientific and technological intermediaries co-founded by governments and financial institutions, and financing by venture capital.

(1) Scientific and Technological Financing Platforms Co-founded by Governments and Financial Institutions

Relevant data suggests that scientific and technological SMEs account in quantity for about 3% of all SMEs in China, but they have produced more than a half of patents and new products. However, the difficulty in getting financing has long been a main problem confronting the development of most scientific and technological SMEs in China. If there are ideal financing channels, these SMES can perform much better.

The building of scientific and technological financing platforms through cooperation between governments and financial institutions is a financing channel, which China has been exploring. On September 30, 2005, the China Development Bank (CDB) Tianjin Branch and the Tianjin Municipal Science and Technology Commission (TMSTC) entered into an "Agreement on Cooperation in Providing Loans to Scientific and Technological SMEs", to co-build a loan platform and a guaranty platform. In accordance with the agreement, the TMSTC designated the Tianjin High Technology Transformation Center as the loan platform by which to borrow and repay loans, and Tianjin Capital Investment & Guaranty Co. , Ltd. as the guaranty platform which is responsible for implementing counter-guaranty measures for the borrowing entity. The Tianjin High Technology Transformation Center is responsible for the credit gathering and evaluation of scientific and technological SMEs, the receipt and review of loan projects, loaning by mandate, post-loan management, and collection of loan principal and interest. This center conducts the evaluation in industry, finance, law, credit etc. of loan application projects as per the commercial loan model, has these loan projects examined and verified by related professional organizations, and then submit them to the CDB which will engage a specialized bank to make loans, subject to its approval. The borrowers as end loan users use and repay loan principal and interest. This center is dually directed by the Tianjin Technology and Intellectual Property Exchange Management Commission and the Tianjin Capital Investment Joint Committee.

In accordance with the agreement, in 2005 the CDB Tianjin Branch provided a volume of credits of 100 million yuan for scientific and technological SMEs in Tianjin, with a view of promoting the development of Tianjin's high-tech industries and strengthening the building of the SMEs credit system. In recent years, more than 200 scientific and technological SMEs in Tianjin have applied to the loan platform for an aggregate amount of 100 million yuan. Following its cooperate with the CDB, the Tianjin High Technology Transformation Center went on to cooperate with such financial institutions as the China Bohai Bank and the Agricultural Development Bank of China, seeking resolution of the problem about providing unsecured petty loans to SMEs. By building the loan platform and establishing the specialized expert evaluation system, the Tianjin High Technology Transformation Center lowered the threshold for scientific and technological SMEs to obtain commercial loans, and has supported a large group of SMEs with strong innovation abilities and growth potentials.

Different from previous technology appraisal teams largely consisting of university experts and scholars, this center's experts come from various professional fields like finance, marketing and management, particularly including experts from enterprises. The loan platform's preliminary examination primarily targets market prospects, to help the banks minimize risk.

As the most effective and most difficult part of the reform, this center, considering that fact that most scientific and technological SMEs don't have adequate realty as collateral and there is no mature evaluation system for such intangible assets as copyright and patent rights, relies on government credit and coordinates the commercial banks' credit service divisions for SMEs to implement credit policies different from those regarding large enterprises and give scientific and technological SMEs preferential treatments in terms of line of credit, mode of credit extension, term of loan, guaranty and examination and approval procedure. At the same time, according to industrial development policies issued by related government departments, it actively coordinates the commercial banks to adjust the direction to which credits go, expand the scope of loaning to scientific and technological SMEs and actively probe into varieties of credits appropriate for development of these SMEs.

Targeting such problems as management extensiveness of scientific and technological SMEs, the center also actively builds SMEs credit information gathering, evaluation and informatization platforms, providing them with credit evaluation reports. When conditions permit, it will provide credit guaranty for enterprises to lower their financing costs. The Tianjin High Technology Transformation

Center has begun exploring ways of further development. The TMSTC will, on the basis of this center, set up an investment company, which takes out loans from banks and sets foot in development of some scientific and technological SMEs.

In September 2006, Benefituser (Tianjin) Technology Development Co., Ltd. obtained a loan of 200,000 yuan from the China Bohai Bank, initiating the practice in Tianjin of using intangible assets as collateral for loans. In June 2006, Tianjin-based Senhao Technology Development Co., Ltd. obtained a loan of 30 million yuan from the CDB, which was the first to obtain a fix loan as a scientific and technological SME. In September 2006, together with other companies, Tianjin Jinyu Biotechnology Co., Ltd., Tianjin Polytechnic University Textile Auxiliary Company and Tianjin Guowei Feeding & Drainage Equipment Manufacturing Co., Ltd. acquired a bank loan of seven million yuan, marking the success in providing bundled loans to scientific and technological SMEs.

For excellent projects, the Tianjin High Technology Transformation Center will help to publicize them, to guide them to apply for innovation funds and for scientific and technological projects under the China Torch Program, and to obtain financial support from other central and local channels. Each year the center receives about 2,000 scientific and technological projects, more than 20% of which may enter the industrialization stage of pilot-scale production and volume production. At the same time, it financially supports the establishment of scientific and technological projects applied for, with a view to the borrowers' product technology levels, market competitiveness and responsiveness, as well as abilities to repay loans.

Although the Tianjin High Technology Transformation Center has made certain achievements in the loan platform's information communication and project evaluation, its mechanisms for loan package and loan platform operations need to be further improved, so that it can bear greater risk.

(2) Venture capital should become the main channel of financing for small enterprises' innovation

Different from both the mode of financing described above and both loans, venture capital (VC) is a mode of financing, in which a private venture capitalist through a contract links a creative project to a willing investor (either an investment institutions or an angel investor), venture capital owns equity in the venture business it invests in, and the venture capitalist and the venture business co-develop the business and eventually realize high returns through retreat (or listing or M&A). Because of quite appealing incentive to venture capital and of clear-cut responsibilities, rights and interests, the venture capitalist and the venture entrepreneur usually can bring about innovation in technology, products, business, talent and market.

(3) Venture capitalists and innovation inventors: collision and fusion of two types of cultural values

The field of venture capital is a fairly professional field, and venture capitalists and innovation inventors (in most cases, though not all, innovation inventors grow into venture capitalists) are the key talent of the field. Why are they viewed as the key talent for the development of high-tech industries too? If the industrialization of a high technology is viewed as a process, then the entire process comprise the stages of R&D, commercialization (including pilot production, pilot marketing, advertising and marketing of products) of R&D results, and industrialization. The level of R&D determines the value of the high technology, and the commercialization degree of R&D results determines the market value of them. Both two aspects are related to the number and quality of venture capitalists and innovation inventors and are more concerned with the degree to which they are combined. The higher level a venture capitalist has, the earlier he/she is able to take part in industrialization of a high technology, and the earlier a venture capitalist and an innovation inventor combine, the greater their returns on high-tech results are likely to be. This nature of venture capital investment requires them to be professionally and culturally proficient.

On cultural values, innovation inventors uphold free inquiry and are unwilling to come under administrative interference from government and economic interference from market and investors, while venture capitalists concentrate on the commercial value of innovation projects and attach great importance to management and corporate culture of businesses they invest in. There is no doubt that the cooperation between professionals of these two types will give rise to the collision of ideas. It is no exaggeration to say that the failure of a portion of venture capital investment activities was related to this. Moreover, the less developed a country's or region's market economy is, the more likely the aforesaid collision of values leads to failure.

Thus, although practice itself has fostered venture capitalists, venture entrepreneurs and innovation inventors one generation after another, it is an important task for human resource management in the new economic period to actively develop such professionals as per the requirement on their high standards and cultural values. And this task falls upon universities and enterprises.

To enable China's venture capital to bring about new products, new technologies and renowned enterprises, the following problems have to be solved. On institutionally design, related policies should be introduced as legal provisions ruling venture capital. This include how to attract private saving deposits (even a small percentage, for example, 5%) into venture capital, which, if successful, will greatly surmount the country's current venture capital size of only over 30 billion yuan a year. Efforts should be made to foster venture capitalists. Most important, what are desired are private or government-aided private venture capital firms, rather than government-run ones.

To know about well-known venture capital firms in China, please see Appendix 1 "2009 China's Top 50 Venture Capital companies. " Hope fully, there soon will be "China Top 100 Venture Capital companies. "

2.4　Enterprise Innovation

China's enterprise innovation, from the industrial point of view, can be divided into two types, i. e. manufacturing enterprise innovation and service industry enterprise innovation. Given the length of the book, only the pharmaceutical and telecom manufacturing sectors of the manufacturing industry and the telecom service and banking sectors of the service industry were chose as cases for discussion, because these sectors are representative of China's "rising period. "

Considering the fact that enterprise innovation is carried out in an innovation system with multiple subjects and objects, this section will use the concept of "linkage" to help explain many other concepts, and give particular attention to "linkage between R&D and services. "

2.4.1　Linkage between elements in the innovation system

The so-called " linkage " here refers to a process of continuous dynamic development, in which system elements act reciprocally and then react on other elements after learning from the feedback generated by such reciprocal action. The characteristics of linkage include:

1) Spatial systematicness. Different from interaction, reciprocal action between elements in linkage adopts the mode of "one-to-many" or "many-to-many" instead of "one-to-one".

2) Temporal continuity. Elements react on mutual feedback and learning, which leads to temporally continuous development.

3) Learning spontaniety. It is the cognition of the feedbacks generated by reciprocal action between other elements, a precondition of maintaining a process of continuous dynamic development.

Therefore, the linkage methodology is a systematic and dynamic argument that, applying linkage and methods, analyzes reciprocal action and continuous feedback and learning between elements in a system. The linkage between elements can be summed up as knowledge, learning and motivation. The content of linkage is knowledge, the channel is learning, the guarantee is motivation, and the result is gradual optimization of the innovation system.

The occurrence and continuance of linkage relies on some particular mechanisms. To put it another way, the "linkage between R&D and services" is a type of systematic engineering of system elements under some mechanisms, for example, feedback mechanism, non-linear mechanism and coupling mechanism. Feedback means the relationship between a system's information output and an external environment's information input. Feedback is the basic attribute of a system. The so-called "linkage perspective" is an analysis of the complex feedback loop that exists in a system. A feedback loop is a loop consisting of a series of causes and effects and interactions, or a path composed by information and actions. A positive feedback loop produces the behavior of self-growth, while a negative one produces the behavior seeking a particular objective and is of self-regulating.

The linkage between the elements of an innovation system refers to the relations and interactions that effect the continuous change of the innovation system. The linkage analyzed from the system theory point of view can be divided into two levels: linkage between subsystems and the system, and linkage inside subsystems. The two types of linkage together determine the generation and evolvement of an innovation system, and they operate according to mechanisms, the nonlinear mechanism and the coupling mechanism.

The nonlinear mechanism is about the generation of the relationship between elements. This relationship is not the unilateral one from A to B, but includes not only the bidirectional relationship between A and B but also the multi-directional relationship between A, B, C, D, E and so forth. Mutation and branching are the most essential and obvious manifestations of the action of the nonlinear mechanism. This mechanism is linking various elements together through nonlinear action to form varied and diverse pictures of evolvement.

The coupling mechanism is also known as coordination mechanism. The coupling mechanism for linkage between the elements of an innovation system means the elements of an innovation system are not independent from each other, but are an organic whole of products (logistics), funds, information, technology, talent, knowledge and other facts which are coupled together (Zhou Jizhong et al. , 2009a).

2.4.2   Innovation Management in China's Pharmaceutical Industry

The pharmaceutical industry is a high-tech sector of the real economy of manufacturing, whose products concern people's well-being. It is a priority industry to all countries. At the same time, it is an industry where technological innovation and intellectual property interact with each other. And because the traditional Chinese medicine is a complete system outside the Western medicine, there is the problem of how to achieve internationalization of the Chinese pharmaceutical industry. Therefore, the technological innovation in the Chinese pharmaceutical industry is worthy of study.

(1) Technological innovation and intellectual property: The pressure on and impetus to Chinese pharmaceutical enterprises

In the 21st century, of nearly 8, 010 types of pharmaceutical raw materials that Chinese pharmaceutical enterprises produce, about 97% are modeled on foreign old varieties; there are only about 3, 500 types of preparations, only one third of those produced by pharmaceutical enterprises in a developed country, and most of them are traditional old varieties.

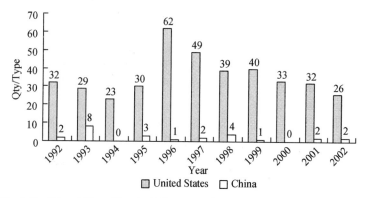

Fig. 1-8   Class I New Chemical Pharmaceuticals Approved by China and the
United States in 1992 ~ 2002
Source: Zhuang Wu, 2006; Keneth I Kaitin, 2004.

According to statistics, China has approved a total of 38 varieties of Class I

chemical pharmaceuticals, which were independently developed (Zhuang Wu, 2006),
but only two of them really gained international recognition—Artemether and Sodium
Dimercaptosuccinate. The gap is obvious between Chin and the United Stated when
they are compared in Class I chemical pharmaceuticals approved in 1992 ~ 2002 (Fig.
1-8). According to statistics by the State Intellectual Property Office of China
(SIPO), in the pharmaceutical field, the United States owns 51% of the world's
patents, Europe owns 33% , Japan owns 12% , and other countries together own only
4% ; in the human gene field, the United States owns 40% of the world's patents,
Europe owns 24% , Japan owns 33% , and other countries together own only 3% [①]. In
the aspect of pharmaceutical patents, although China's quantity of pharmaceutical
patents has increased greatly (Fig. 1-9), of these over 10, 000 pharmaceutical
patents, 80% were obtained in China by foreign research organizations and
multinational corporations, and more than 90% are patents for invention (Shi Wenjun
and Zhu Chenghui, 2007). For the remaining 20% of patents owned by domestic
pharmaceutical enterprises, a big gap exists in technology to foreign countries, and
most of them are technologically-low preparation process patents or preparation patents
(Yuan Hongmei and Yu Shuangli, 2007)

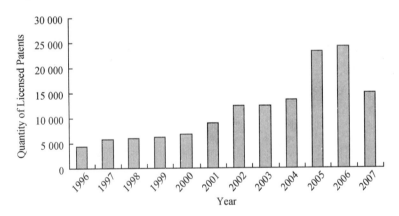

Fig. 1-9   Licenses Patents Owned by Chinese Pharmaceutical Enterprises in 1996 ~ 2007
Source: Calculated according to IPC classification standards and as well as data from the website
http://www. sipo. gov. cn/sipo/zljs/.

One of the main reasons responsible for the above-mentioned situation is that
Chinese pharmaceutical enterprises' R&D investments are small and their technological

---

① 2004 *Report on Biotechnology Development in China*, China Agriculture Press, September 2005.

innovation capacity is weak on the whole. Related data shows that the ratio of R&D spending to sales (namely R&D intensity) of the pharmaceutical companies among the world's Top 500 businesses is about 20% on the average, but this indicator is only about 2% for Chinese pharmaceutical enterprises. Moreover, because most of Chinese pharmaceutical enterprises have a weak awareness of intellectual property, the drain of intellectual property in traditional Chinese medicine is quite severe. For example, eight patents on mint, a Chinese herb in Jiangsu, have fallen into American hands. According to statistics, of the patents applied for Chinese medicine in the United States between 1995 and 2000, China accounted only for 3.5%, unexpectedly ranked behind Japan, South Korea and Germany (Shi Wenjun and Zhu Changhui, 2007). Many foreign pharmaceutical enterprises came to China searching for traditional, clinically proven ancient prescriptions proved recipes and, after obtaining them, revised and applied for patent protection of them and, in return, restricted Chinese pharmaceutical enterprises' R&D and distribution. In human resource terms, in foreign large multinational pharmaceutical corporations, R&D personnel account for about one fourth of the total employees, but in domestic large pharmaceutical corporations this indicator was below 10%. After China's access to WTO, it is no longer impossible for pharmaceutical enterprises' replication of pharmaceuticals as they are subjected to intellectual property protection clauses. ① If an enterprise had continued to copy a foreign new drug, it would be fined $ 400 million to 1 billion as damages; even a buyout of a patented drug would cost $ 5 million to $ 6 million②. Moreover, the world's top 20 foreign pharmaceutical multinational corporations, all of which have already entered the Chinese market, is forming an increasing pressure on Chinese pharmaceuticals as China is increasingly integrating with the world economy. To contend with their foreign counterparts, Chinese pharmaceutical enterprises must foster strong capacity for pharmaceutical innovation and develop effective, side effects-free new drugs with independent intellectual property.

The above shows that the Chinese pharmaceutical industry, which also has

---

① Five commitments China made to its access to WTO: protecting intellectual property in pharmaceuticals; lowering import taxes on pharmaceuticals; removing control over the import of large – sized medical appliances; opening up pharmaceutical distribution services; and opening up the medical treatment sector. From these commitments, the enhanced intellectual property protection of pharmaceuticals would bring about great difficulties to Chinese pharmaceutical enterprises producing generic drugs, while foreign pharmaceutical enterprises' entry into the domestic market would intensify competition on the domestic pharmaceutical market; both are likely to put Chinese pharmaceutical enterprises in a plight.

② *WTO and China's Pharmaceutical Industry*, Jiangsu Information Network Center, *Pharmaceuticals Edition*.

traditional Chinese medicine as part of it, should have higher priority than other industries in terms of awareness of and demand for technological innovation and intellectual property. This is also the reason this book chose the pharmaceutical industry to be first discussed at great length.

（2）Weaknesses that Chinese pharmaceutical enterprises have in intellectual property management

The pharmaceutical industry is an industry built on R&D, which, featured by high investment, high risk, long period and high profit, is typical of high-tech manufacturing. However, it is just because it depends substantially on technological innovation entailing enormous early investments and innovation results are easy to be replicated that whether intellectual property after innovation can be used to monopolize innovation profits becomes vital for sustainable development of pharmaceutical enterprises. But because China's intellectual property law has been implemented for a relatively short period, many enterprises have not yet been aware of that intellectual property is an important competitive resource to them and that intellectual property management has strategic significance for technological innovation and improving their core competitiveness. First of all, many pharmaceutical enterprises still rely on monetary investment, marketing and hype competing on the market for short-term profits, and they have not yet shifted to relying on innovation and intellectual property for winning a long-term competitive edge. This is not only adverse to the protection of their intellectual property, but also liable to infringement, leading to ceaseless disputes on pharmaceutical patents. For example, because there was no systematic patent protection of "Xiaokechuan" —a best-seller anti-asthma drug developed by HPGC Second Chinese Medicine Factory, in less than two years more than 20 enterprises throughout the country offered products the same as the aforesaid one, causing the originally undersupplied drug to be kept long in stock and suffer great losses. Second, only a very few Chinese pharmaceutical enterprises have set up a specialized intellectual property management department (Table 1-7), and many others have not yet had such department as well as relevant systems and policies. Once their patents are infringed, these enterprises, which fear complicated proceedings and high costs, are willing to bring an action against such infringement, ending with suffering their due rights and interests. Finally, Chinese pharmaceutical enterprises lack talent in intellectual property management. Intellectual property management requires all-round talents, who have both expertise and knowledge about intellectual property laws and management. But currently such talents are rare in these enterprises, nowhere near enough to meet the needs of intellectual property management.

Table 1-7　Intellectual Property Management Department Setup of Pharmaceutical Enterprises

Type of Enterprise	No. of Enterprises Surveyed	Patent Management Department			Patent Lawyers	Patent Agents
		Full-time	Part-time	Total		
State-owned	54	13	49	13	13	7
Private	99	31	77	30	30	24
Total	153	44	126	43	43	31

Source: Zhou Yawei, 2007.

(3) The present situation of and difficulties in Chinese pharmaceutical enterprises' implementation of "two major strategies"

So-called two major strategies refer to the technological innovation strategy and intellectual property strategy already viewed as national strategies.

The pharmaceutical industry is very "flexible" in both intension and extension. From the industry chain, it comprises such fields as pharmaceutical R&D, production, marketing and distribution; from the types of pharmaceuticals, it includes such pharmaceutical fields as Chinese medicinal plants, traditional Chinese medicines prepared in ready-to-use forms, pharmaceutical raw materials and preparations, antibiotics, biochemical pharmaceuticals, radiopharmaceuticals, blood serum, vaccines, blood products and diagnostic pharmaceuticals. It can also be divided, by production processes, into pharmaceutical raw materials, intermediates and preparations; by use requirements, into prescription drugs and over-the-counter (OTC) drugs; and by availability of patent protection, into patented drugs and generic drugs. The industry can also be divided according to similarity of production technologies and processes for pharmaceutical products (Wang Yumei, 2007). According to the *Guiding Opinions about Development of the Pharmaceutical Industry during the 11th Five-Year Plan Period* issued in 2006 by the NDRC, the Chinese pharmaceutical industry comprises five sectors: chemical pharmaceuticals, Chinese traditional medicines, biopharmaceuticals, vaccine production and medical appliances. This section only deals with chemical pharmaceuticals, Chinese traditional medicines and biopharmaceuticals as the output value of the three sectors together accounts for about 80% of the entire industry's total[1].

---

① Guiding Opinions about Development of the Pharmaceutical Industry during the 11th Five-Year Plan Period (2006), the NDRC.

Over 50 years of development, China has formed a pharmaceutical industry system that is able to produce the complete range of products. In recent years, the Chinese pharmaceutical industry has kept a good development momentum (Fig. 1-10) and has become one of the fastest growing industries in the national economy, with an average year-on-year growth rate of 16.1% (Wang Weigang, 2007), which is far higher than the growth of national economy in the same period. From Fig. 1-10, the ratio of the industry's output value to GDP kept rising considerably on the whole, which was at around 2.08% in 2003 and 2004, rose to 2.41% in 2006 and reached 2.82% in 2007. As the Chinese economy is fast growing, the people's living standards are improving; urbanization is accelerating; and population aging is intensifying. The pharmaceutical industry will continue to grow rapidly and its position in the national economy will continue to rise.

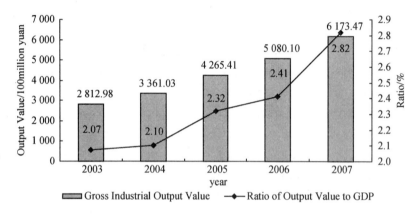

Fig. 1-10　Changes in Ratio of Gross Output Value of the Chinese Pharmaceutical Industry to GDP

Source: 2008 Risk Analysis Report on China Pharmaceutical Industry, *China Economic Herald*, the NDRC, June 2008.

According to an 17 August 2010 report by *Medicine Economic News*, in the period from January to May 2010, the Chinese pharmaceutical industry saw a gross industrial output value of 460.890 billion yuan, up 26.04% over the same period in 2009, 8.01 percentage points higher than the growth for the same period in 2009. During the period, the industry's profit margin on sales stood at 10.42%, up 0.71 percentage point from the same period in 2009, and up 0.2 percentage point from the period from January to February 2010. And the profit margin on sales of pharmaceutical raw materials, chemical preparations, biological preparations, and traditional Chinese medicines prepared in ready-to-use forms, compared to the same period in 2009, rose 1.41, 0.72, 2.31 and 0.95 percentage points, respectively.

Nevertheless, compared with the rapid development of the world pharmaceutical industry and with the world's noted pharmaceutical companies, China has a big gap to be bridged whether in R&D capacity, product structure and market share or in degree of enterprise extensiveness and internationalization. The rapid-like growth of the Chinese pharmaceutical industry cannot enshroud the phenomena which Chinese pharmaceutical enterprises manifest themselves in: small in size, large in number, severe homogenized competition and low efficiency (Cheng Liru, 2007). The key reason responsible for these phenomena lies in the fact that Chinese pharmaceutical enterprises' innovation abilities are seriously inadequate—97.4% of the pharmaceuticals produced by more than 5,000 pharmaceutical enterprises across the country are modeled on others' products and innovative pharmaceuticals with intellectual property are less than 3% (Yao Weibao, 2005). These enterprises have long been in a low-end position in the global pharmaceutical industry chain. A typical example of severe homogenized competition is: there are 1,640, 1,500 and 1,380 official approval documents for metamizole sodium, acetyl aminophenol and cephalexin tablets or injections of different specifications, respectively, and even the phenomenon that hundreds of pharmaceutical factories produce the same one product exists substantially (Zhuang Guangzhou, 2007). As shown in Table 1-8, the average quantity of patents for invention granted to Chinese pharmaceutical enterprises is below 0.3, revealing that most of Chinese pharmaceutical enterprises lack R&D motive power and capacity. This is where the "difficulty" lies. Why does this "difficulty" exist? The superficial reason is that pharmaceutical enterprises' technological innovation is not only long in period but also complex in process, and the deep-seated reason is that the "two major strategies" have not yet really become their development strategies.

Table 1-8　Patent Output of the Chinese Pharmaceutical Industry

Year	Patent Application		Patent for Invention	
	Patent Applications	Avg. Patent Applications of Enterprises	Patents for Invention	Avg. Patents for Invention of Enterprises
2000	574	0.17	414	0.13
2001	735	0.21	308	0.09
2002	999	0.27	484	0.13
2003	1 305	0.32	459	0.11
2004	1 696	0.36	902	0.19
2005	2 708	0.54	1 134	0.23

Source: Calculated based on data provided in *China Statistics Yearbook on High Technology Industry*.

(4) The technological innovation processes and features of pharmaceutical enterprises

1) Technological innovation processes of pharmaceutical enterprises. The pharmaceutical industry is a knowledge-intensive industry, and the optimization and efficiency of industrial resource allocation depends mainly on R&D activities for technological advancement, product innovation and processes improvement. Technological innovation has great significance to pharmaceutical enterprises for the formation and improvement of competitiveness. A pharmaceutical enterprise's technological innovation comprises new drug conception, applied research, experimental development and commercialization. Because the pharmaceutical industry is a scientific research-based industry and closely linked to human health, its innovation process is more complex than those of other industries. But as far as new product development and processes innovation are concerned, a pharmaceutical enterprise' innovation is typical linear innovation (Tait and Williams, 1999). Scientific discovery is the foundation of pharmaceutical innovation, and as long as it has substantive breakthroughs, a spate of important innovations arises. In this sense, pharmaceutical enterprises' innovation is technology-push innovation. Because of the social responsibility that falls upon the pharmaceutical industry, more and more development of new drugs is geared directly to meet market needs; particularly, the emergence of some drugs treating infectious diseases, such as AIDS, is more market-pulled. Therefore, innovation in pharmaceutical technologies is also demand-pull innovation.

The primary innovation process of the pharmaceutical industry comprises four stages—basic research, preclinical trials, clinical trials and application for approval, production and marketing (Fig. 1-11). The central part of this process is to seek new complex molecules of therapeutic value. This stage entails the selection and screening of vast similar molecular compounds, as well as preclinical pharmacological research, preclinical safety research, clinical pharmacological and safety research, etc. , with very little possibility of success. Generally speaking, patent protection is applied for in this stage. This stage is followed by preclinical and clinical stages. The clinical stage lasts some 5 ~ 8 years on average. Phase I clinical trials are conducted to assess preliminary clinical pharmacology, safety, tolerability and pharmacokinetics of a new drug, providing the basis on which the dosage regimen is formulated; this stage requires participation of some 20 ~80 healthy volunteers. Phase II clinical trials are conducted to preliminarily assess the efficacy and safety of the new drug and recommend the clinical

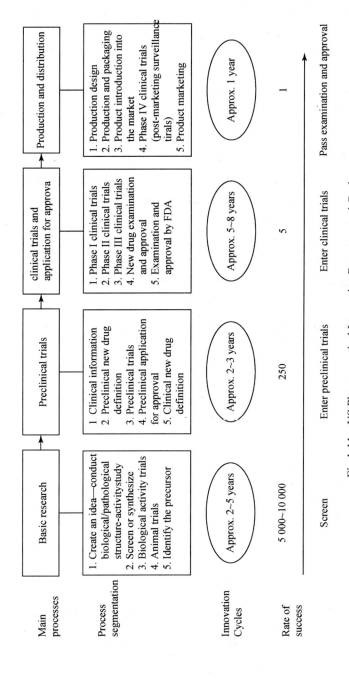

Fig 1-11　US Pharmaceutical Innovation Processes and Cycles

dosage, with involvement of $10 \sim 300$ voluntary patents. Phase III clinical trials, with involvement of $1,000 \sim 3,000$ volunteers, are conducted to examine the long-term curative effects of and untoward reactions to the new drug, through which efficacy and safety are further assessed. New drugs that have passed preclinical and clinical trials must be approved by drug authorities before coming into the market. In the United States, it takes about 33 months on average for the Food and Drug Administration (FDA) to examine and approve a new drug (Dimasi, 1995). After a new drug has been introduced to the market, Phase IV clinical trials have to be conducted to examine efficacy and untoward reactions on the basis of the extensive use of the drug (particular attention is paid to rare untoward reactions); if severe untoward reactions happen or its efficacy is indefinite, the production, distribution and use of the drug must be halted, and the manufacturer have to withdraw the new drug on sale and compensate for damage caused by the drug. In the late 20th century and early 21st century, a large group of drugs were removed from the market, including: Bayer's Baycol, a drug used to lower cholesterol; Pfizer's Rezulin, an anti-diabetic drug; and Janssen Pharmaceutica's Cisapride, a drug used to ease the symptoms of severe heartburn.

The above processes are appropriate for innovation of "wholly-innovative drugs"[①](Me-only drugs) and of Class I original drugs. China's drug administrative

---

① Innovative drugs are primarily divided into three groups, namely wholly – innovative drugs, partially – innovative drugs, and innovative drugs with altered forms of application. Wholly – innovative drugs generally involve a big investment, a long period, high risk and great many difficulties; average enterprises usually have no financial power enough to carry out R&D of this group of drugs. Partially – innovative drugs are new drugs developed based on known pharmaceutical information (for example, functioning mechanisms, chemical structures of compounds, pharmacology and clinical efficacy); internationally they fall under patent drugs, but they are more of extension or optimization on the basis of original R&D, rather than being of originality; this group of drugs have a higher rate of R&D success because of their definite development purposes and relatively mature technologies and processes. Innovative drugs with altered forms of application can be further divided into standard replicas (replicas of drugs on which there are already national standards), altered replicas (drugs with altered routes of administration or acid radicals or bases, if they have come into the market abroad; or drugs with altered forms, if they have come into the market at home); rush replicas (drugs first modeled on or following the drugs whose patents have expired), exclusive replicas (drugs produced by importing the patents of or through compulsory license for foreign patent drugs, which have come into the market), and creative replicas (Class I drugs, which, though unavailable on foreign markets, are mature to some degree) (Chen Chuanhong, 2002).

law provides for the classification of new drugs[1]; different classes of new drugs have different R&D requirements and difficulties. On the whole, the initial R&D stage of new drugs from Class I to Class V shortens in the said order, whether they are traditional Chinese medicines or chemical medicines; that is, only Class I[2] new drugs are likely to involve R&D activities in the discovery/lead compound synthesis and screening stages. From Classes I to IV, innovation decreases by degrees and the research period and difficulty also decrease on the whole, resulting in decreasing requirements on R&D expertise and resources (Liu Xue and Ma Hongjian, 2004). On the other hand, China is somewhat different from the United States in examination and approval of new drugs. According to China's State Food and Drug Administration (SFDA), a product, which has passed Phase II clinical trials may obtain a new drug certificate, be sold on a restricted basis after a registered number of approval for pilot production has been obtained, and must finish Phase III clinical trials and go through examination in two years before this number is changed to a license number for production of the drug. But there are generally no Phase IV trials in China. In the United States, after a new drug has come into the market, the FDA will also conduct market research on the drug, including its safety, efficacy, sample testing and social response, which is known as Phase IV clinical trials (Ma Yan, 2007).

2) Characteristic of pharmaceutical enterprises' technological innovation. The first difficulty confronting pharmaceutical enterprises is high investment. From synthesis of a new compound to introduction of a new drug into the market, if calculated by constant prices, it would only take $ 50 million in the 1960s and 1970s, but in recent years it has increased $ 800 million on average (Fig. 1-12). In 2002, the world's top

---

[1] China's current definition of new drugs adopts what the 15 September 2002 *Regulations on the Implementation of the Drug Administration Law* defines in Article 83 as "drugs that have not been sold within China." The 1 December 2002 *Drug Registration Administration Measures* defines in Article 8 the application for new drugs as "application for registration of drugs which have not been sold within China. Drugs available on the market, if altered in form or route of administration, shall be administered as new drugs."

[2] According to the *Drug Registration Administration Measures* implemented as of October 1, 2007, Class I new drugs refer to the drugs, which have not been sold at home and abroad; they are representative of radical innovation in the pharmaceutical industry. Class I new chemical drugs include: a) bulk drugs produced through synthesis and semi – synthesis, as well as their preparations; b) effective monomers extracted from natural substances or through fermentation, as well as their preparations; c) optimal isomers produced from known drugs through resolution or synthesis, as well as their preparations; d) drugs with fewer components produced from multi – component drugs available on the market; e) new compound recipes; and f) preparations already available on the domestic market, to which new indications not approved both at home and abroad are added.

50 pharmaceutical enterprises had a combined R&D budget of 55, 500 million dollars, with R&D expenditure greater than their expenditure on market promotion. Statistical data show that the US pharmaceutical industry has an R&D intensity of 16. 7% ~ 20%, ranked first among various industries, five times and twice that of the defense and spaceflight industry and the computer industry, respectively (Zhou Jizhong, 2002). Though much lower than foreign R&D expenditure on new drugs, China's expenditure on new drug innovation is vast; for example, the innovation (from R&D to production to introduction into the market) of Class I new drugs Butylphthalide and Bicyclol cost 350 million yuan and over 100 million yuan, respectively.

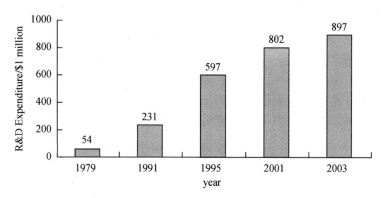

Fig. 1-12   Multinational Companies' R&D Expenditure on New Drugs
Source: Tufts CSDD and Lehman Brothers, 2004.

The development period of a new drug refers to the span of time from the patent application for a new compound to its approval as a new drug to come into the market. It has prolonged to present-day 12 ~ 16 years from average 6 ~ 8 years in the 1960s (Fig. 1-11). For example, the R&D process of China's Class I new drugs Butylphthalide and Bicyclol took 32 and 24 years respectively from R&D to production, and finally introduction to the market.

(5) Institutional Design on Pharmaceutical Intellectual Property

China's pharmaceutical protection comprises intellectual property protection, administrative protection and new drug protection.

1) Intellectual property system. China's *Patent Law* implemented as of 1 April 1985 provided in paragraph three under Article 23 that no patent shall be granted to "drugs as well as substances obtained by using chemical methods." This means that medicine-related drugs as well as substances obtained by using chemical methods, namely pharmaceutical products themselves, enjoyed no protection by the *Patent Law*,

but pharmaceutical preparation methods and medical appliance inventions could apply for patent. The then *Patent Law* provided so primarily in consideration of the domestic pharmaceutical industry's weak and backward R&D and innovation capabilities, which entailed particular protection. But in the negotiations in 1992 over China's access to WTO, intellectual property protection became a major issue. For this purpose, the NPC Standing Committee reviewed and adopted the *Decision about the Revisions in the Patent Law of the People's Republic of China*, which was implemented as of January 1, 1993; one of the most important revisions was the inclusion of drugs and chemical substances in the scope of patent protection and the prolongation of the term of protection of patents for invention from 15 years to 20 years. In 2000, China joined WTO and the TRIPS (Agreement on Trade-Related Aspects of Intellectual Property Rights), and, to better comply with international standards, once again revised the Patent Law in 2001, strengthening the protection of patent and adding pre-litigation provisional measures as well as provisions prohibiting "offer to sell" from patent infringement. Hence, China's intellectual property protection of drugs was basically aligned with international standards.

On trade secrets, China enacted the *Anti-Unfair Competition Law* on December 1, 1993, Article 10 of which defines a trade secret as "technical and operational information which is not known to the public, which is capable of bringing economic benefits to the owner of rights, which has practical applicability and which the owner of rights has taken measures to keep secret." To pharmaceutical enterprises, technical and operational information encompasses such information as know-how, produce recipes, manufacturing processes and methods.

On trademark protection, in 1983 China enacted the *Regulation for the Implementation of the Trademark Law*, providing that "any drug must use a registered trademark" and that an application for registration of a drug trademark should also be enclosed with "a certificate approving production obtained from a health department or beauty at provincial, autonomous region or municipal level." In 1993, the Trademark Law was revised by increasing the provisions on protection of well-known trademarks (Article 25 of the *Regulation for the Implementation of the Trademark Law*). The *Detailed Rules for the Implementation of the Trademark Law* which went into effect in September 2002 annulled the provision for compulsory registration of drug trademarks, permitting voluntary registration of drug trademarks. In March 2006, the SFDA issued the *Notice on Further Standardizing Drug Name Administration*, explicitly providing that except drugs with new chemical structures or new active constituents as well as drugs for which compound patent is kept, any other drugs may not use a trade name. Thus, only through independent innovation can a pharmaceutical enterprise set the stage for founding a brand on the market in the future, and generic drugs can only promote their sales on the strength of enterprise brands.

2) Administrative protection. Since the introduction of the reform and opening up policy, China's protection of new drugs has been gradually legally institutionalized. *The Methods for Examination and Approval of New Drugs*, which came into force on July 1, 1985, defined new drugs as "drugs never produced within China" and divided both traditional Chinese medicine and Western medicine into five categories. Chinese pharmaceutical enterprises, thus, could copy foreign patent drugs, but their copy behavior encountered objections from foreign pharmaceutical enterprises. To avoid direct friction with Western countries, on January 17, 1992, China signed the *Memorandum of Understanding (MOU) on the Protection of Intellectual Property Rights* ("the MOU" below) with the United States. Article Two of the MOU was about the administrative protection of drugs and agricultural chemicals, giving the 7.5-year-long administrative protection to the United States' eligible patent drugs and agricultural chemicals developed between 1986 and 1992. That was complementary to China's patent law, which before 1993 gave no protection to drugs. Afterwards, China also entered into bilateral agreements on the administrative protection of drugs and agricultural chemicals with the EU and with such countries as Japan, Switzerland, Sweden and Norway.

To execute the MOU, China formulated the *Regulations on Administrative Protection of Pharmaceuticals* ("the Regulations" below), which was approved by the State Council on December 12, 1992, promulgated by the former State Drug Administration, and entered into force on January 1, 1993. Drugs given administrative protection enjoyed exclusive rights nearly equal to patent, but were not subject to compulsory license. Most of the drugs covered by the Regulations were those which had come into the market in foreign countries or were being developed in China, and, by around 2007, about 163 types of drugs had been given administrative protection, but for most of them, the term of protection had expired; only 36 types still enjoyed protection (Chang Wenzuo, 2007). After 1993, foreign drugs started to enjoy patent protection in China, so the administrative protection of drugs is only a transitional arrangement.

On the protection of traditional Chinese medicine, the State Council promulgated the *Regulations on Protection of Traditional Chinese Medicines* in 1992, providing that any traditional Chinese medicine up to national pharmaceutical standards or the standards of provinces, autonomous regions and municipalities directly under the Central Government was entitled to such protection. The term of protection for first-class varieties may be 30 years, 20 years or 10 years, according to the degree of innovation, and that of second-class varieties is seven years. During the term of protection, the protected traditional Chinese medicines can only be produced by enterprises, which have obtained a *Certificate of Protected Traditional Chinese Medicines*. In conclusion, China practices the administrative protection of drugs through the implementation of such regulations as the *Regulations on Administrative Protection of Pharmaceuticals*, the *Regulations on Administrative Protection of Agricultural Chemicals* and the *Measures for the Administration of Drug Registration*.

　　3) Protection of New Drugs. To help Chinese pharmaceutical enterprises to master foreign advanced technologies as soon as possible and promote pharmaceutical R&D, the Ministry of Health (MOH) launched the *Regulations on Protection of and Technology Transfer Concerning New Drugs* in May 1999, which provided the terms of protection of new drugs: 12 years for Category I drugs, eight years for Categories II and III drugs, and six years for Categories VI and V drugs. It also provided that for any new drug within its term of protection, without technology transfer by the owner of the New Drug Certificate (original copy), it can neither be replicated by any organization or individual, nor be approved by any drug administration authority. Since the Patent Law had already put new drugs under patent protection, the *Measures for the Administration of Drug Registration* introduced in December 2002 annulled the new drug protection system, established a technical monitoring system on drugs, and provided a monitoring period of no longer than five years for new drugs produced by Chinese enterprises or entering the Chinese market for the first time, with a view to preventing pharmaceutical enterprises from capitalizing on the administrative protection of new drugs to prolong their production monopoly. After that, the SFDA revised the *Measures for the Administration of Drug Registration* in 2005 by introducing clauses concerning patent protection and the protection of undisclosed information. In 2007, the *Measures* were revised once again. The new version provided more stringent criteria of new drugs to narrow down the scope of new drugs, strengthened incentives to drug innovation and increased restrictions on generic drugs. Three measures in this Measures are conducive to innovation: i) changing "fast-track examination and approval" to

"special examination and approval", providing special channels for innovative drugs and, through early intervention, giving innovation enterprises the opportunity to modify, add or improve information; ii) the narrowing down the scope of new drugs, only allowing real new drugs to obtain new drug certificates; and iii) separating new drug certificates and new drug production approval documents, encouraging research institutes to engage in technology cooperation and transfer when a new product is developed, so that they can concentrate on R&D and thus increase returns.

(6) Case: Innovation Processes of a Category I New Drug Butylphthalide

Butylphthalide (trade name: NBP)[1] is a brand-new chemical medicine with the primary indication of ischemic apoplexy. It's China's first innovative drug with independent intellectual property after its access to WTO. The successful development of the drug marked that China's research on cardiovascular and cerebrovascular drugs reached an internationally advanced level. This drug was originally developed by the Chinese Academy of Medical Sciences (CAMS), which extracted the chemical monomer-L-3-n-butylphthalide—from the seeds of celery in 1978 and synthesized butylphthalide in 1980. The pharmacological trials then proved that butylphthalide was obviously anticonvulsant and center-sedative, and research findings also showed that it was effective to multiple epilepsy models. In 1986, after finding that apoplexy and epilepsy shared some features pathologically and cerebral ischemia and epilepsy had a similar mechanism for brain damage, the researchers began research into the therapy of ischemic apoplexy with butylphthalide. In 1993, great breakthroughs were made and a series of patents were applied for, and, in 1999, these patents were approved one after

---

[1] Here, butylphthalide is the generic name, and NBP is the trade name. A drug generally has three names: a chemical name, a generic name and a trade name. The chemical name of a drug is the scientific name given to the drug according to its chemical constituents. The generic name of a drug is its official name ratified by a state drug administration, which should be the same as its international nonproprietary name and that used in China Pharmacopoeia and standards issued by drug authorities; it is a nonproprietary name within a country or worldwide, which is nonexclusive. The trade name of a drug is a product name designated by the producer and approved by drug authorities. Under a generic name, there can be several trade names given by different producers. A trade name is a distinctive and novel name, which an enterprise gives to a drug it produces, in order to distinguish its new drug products from others' similar products. A trade name can be registered as a trademark. The relationships between generic name, trade name and patent are as follows: a generic name may have several trade names, and a trade name may correspond to several patents; after the expiry of the term of protection, a patent drug can be produced by other manufacturers, which may give different trade names to it; if a manufacturer has made innovation on the basis of the original drug and applied for patent, a trade name may also correspond to several patents. The determination, protection, positioning, dissemination, promotion and maintenance of the trade name of a drug are all important parts of brand management.

another.

In 1999, the CAMS transferred to China Shijiazhuang Pharmaceutical Group Co., Ltd. (CSPC) the butylphthalide for 50 million yuan; CSPC would conduct Phases II and III clinical trials, and both parties would cooperate in follow-up product innovation. Considering the important role of intellectual property rights in drug innovation, CSPC, from the very beginning of both parties' cooperation, made plans for patent application and protection regarding the R&D, production, and marketing of NBP. Findings of the two-year clinical trials showed that butylphthalide had an overall efficacy of 70.3% and no severe adverse reaction was incurred. In September 2002, CSPC obtained the new drug certificate and pilot production approval for the raw materials and soft capsules of butylphthalide. During the ensuing Phase IV clinical trials, the efficacy of butylphthalide reached 78.2%; led by Peking Union Medical College Hospital, these trials were carried out at 94 hospitals in 11 cities, involving 2, 050 cases of ischemic cerebrovascular patients. In 2005, an official production approval was obtained (Zhu Min and Sun Ruihua, 2007). To expedite the industrialization and commercialization of butylphthalide, in 2003, CSPC founded NBP Pharmaceutical Co., Ltd. with an investment of 120 million yuan, and developed NBP soft capsules for apoplexy. In the follow-up asymptotic innovation, CSPC applied for 15 domestic patents and entered eight international PCTs (Patent Cooperation Treaties). NBP enjoys patent protection in 23 countries and regions including Europe, the United States, Japan and South Asia.

The R&D and industrialization of butylphthalide obtained policy and financial support from multiple ministries and commissions such as the NDRC, MOST, SFDA and MOH, and received financial aid from the funds for key programs under the NSFC, Key Science and Technology Programs for the 8th and 9th Five-Year Plans, "863" Program and "1035" Program①. The project of butylphthalide industrialization was also appraised as a national "Demonstration Project on the Application of High Technologies in the Pharmaceutical Industry" (Wu Hongyue, 2007).

After obtaining the new drug certificate in 2002, NBP gradually underwent large-

---

① To promote the R&D of new drugs, during the 9th Five – Year Plan period, the former State Scientific and Technological Commission developed the "1035" Program, where "10" referred to developing 10 types of innovative drugs, 10 drugs introduced into the market for the first time, and 10 drugs from genetic engineering, and "35" referred to building 5 new drug screening centers, 5 lab quality standardization centers and 5 clinical trial quality standardization centers.

scale production and commercialization, with sales climbing year on year; its sales in 2006 grew by nearly five times over 2005, which was undoubtedly very encouraging to the development of a new drug. To further expand overseas markets, CSPC with multiple patents in NBP established partnerships with multinational companies through licensing. In 2006, it signed a letter of intent with a US multinational company for cooperation in the patent and market licensing of NBP soft capsules in European and American markets, making NBP the first drug in China's chemical pharmaceutical field, whose patents were licensed in foreign countries. At the end of 2006, as the first installment on patent transfer fees from the United States was put into CSPC's account, the clinical trials on NBP in the United States entered the implementation stage (Ma Yousong and Wang Na, 2007). In 2007, CSPC once again signed a patent licensing agreement with South Korea-based Kyung Dong Pharmaceutical Co. , Ltd. , marking another great leap forward CSPC made in developing international markets through patent licensing.

The development of butylphthalide reflects the difficult innovation process of Category I new drugs. The process costs large sums of money, involves great risk and takes a long time, which can hardly be afforded by average pharmaceutical enterprises. Therefore, real new drug innovation can only be completed by capitalizing on the strength of the pharmaceutical innovation system. In this process, research is conducted primarily by research institutes or universities; enterprises usually participate in the follow-up processes of applying research results in industrial production and marketing; the government supports the R&D and marketing of new drugs by introducing relevant policies and programs. According to the theory on the linkage between elements of the innovation system, the innovation process of new drugs is just a process of adequate linkage between "the government, enterprises, universities and research institutes" in the pharmaceutical innovation system and, at the same time, a process of linkage between technological innovation (R&D and marketing) and intellectual property rights (patents, trademarks and brands) in the innovation system of pharmaceutical enterprises. Moreover, in the innovation process of new drugs, intellectual property rights play a crucial role throughout the process of technological innovation. Butylphthalide could successfully make inroads into international markets in the later stage of commercialization, becoming a paragon in this regard, just because CSPC was aware of the importance of intellectual property rights, made intellectual property strategies in cooperation, applied for peripheral protective patents on the basis of basic patents, and obtained international patents according to its market development strategy.

Below are the case studies about China's technology-leader pharmaceutical enterprise (Tasly Group), technology-follower pharmaceutical enterprise (Xiuzheng Pharmaceutical Group) and large state-owned pharmaceutical enterprise (North China Pharmaceutical Company Ltd. , NCPC)

2. 4. 3   Tasly Group, Forerunner in the Internationalization of Traditional Chinese Medicine

(1) Linkage between Tasly's "Two Major Strategies"

Tasly was founded in 1994 as a small enterprise with fixed assets worth only 14 million yuan. Over ten years of rapid development (Fig. 1-13) with Great Health industry as guideline and pharmaceutical industry as its center, it has developed into a hi-tech group whose scope of business includes modern TCM, chemical medicine, and biological medicine, covering the fields of research and development, planting, manufacturing and distribution. In 2009, its total assets reached 9. 4 billion yuan and sales income registered 8. 6 billion yuan; the sales of its main product Compound Danshen Dripping Pill ("CDDP" below) exceeded one billion yuan for the ninth consecutive year, reaching 1. 46 billion yuan (Feng Guowu, 2010). Tasly was among *Fortune's* Top 500 Listed Chinese Companies in 2010.

In its course of development, Tasly developed a modern TCM product cluster, which comprises more than 50 varieties such as CDDP, Nourishing Blood & Cleaning Brain Granule and Bupleuri Dripping Pill. Its main product, CDDP, has obtained 72 PCT patents, registered as a trademark in 34 countries and regions, and made inroads into the main medicine markets in 16 countries and regions. Its sales exceeded noe billion yuan for the seventh consecutive year in 2007, registering more than two billion yuan, also the best performance in the industry. In 2005, Tasly was recognized as a "Chinese Well-Known Trademark"[1], becoming the veritable top modern TCM brand in the international market, and thus built a brand image of modern TCM worldwide.

---

[1]   "Chinese Well-Known Trademark", designed to measure a brand's popularity and reputation, is China's only brand mark protected by international laws. China began the "Chinese Well-Known Mark" certification following its access to the Paris Convention for The Protection of Industrial Property in 1985, with view to implementing a famous-brand strategy, encouraging independent innovation and revitalizing the national industry. Because the appraisal criteria are extremely rigorous, only more than 700 brands have been recognized as Chinese Well-Known Trademarks over the past 20 years; among them, only 72 are drug brands.

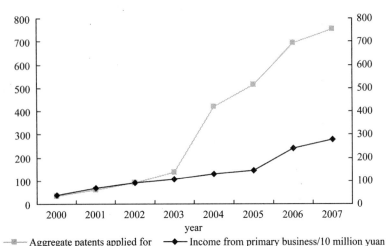

──▓── Aggregate patents applied for　──◆── Income from primary business/10 million yuan

Fig. 1-13　Tasly Group's Aggregate Patents Applied for and Income from Primary Business

Source: Based on related data on Tasly from Sina Financial Network and State Intellectual Property Office of China①

http://money. finance. sina. com. cn/corp/go. php/vCI_CorpInfo/stockid/600535. phtml.

The fast development of Tasly over the past decade is attributed to the co-action of a great many external and internal factors, such as the policy environment of reform and opening up, the initial establishment and perfection of market economy, entrepreneurship of the founder, timely development strategy, effective internal management and continuous technological innovation. But two main factors, technological innovation (R&D, production and marketing) and intellectual property rights (patent, trademark and brand), have played a vital role in Tasly's development, whatever the perspective is. As a typical technology-leader enterprise, Tasly developed the innovative product CDDP tailored to market needs, established a marketing network and opened up markets through the protection of intellectual property rights, brought about a brand effect to the initial trademark and built it a well-known brand. The follow-up innovation in return brought about more intellectual property rights (patented technology, know-how and trademark), which cemented and enhanced its intangible assets, such as brand and reputation. During the process, Tasly's technological innovation (R&D, production and marketing) and intellectual property rights (patent, trademark and brand) formed a close linkage effect (Fig. 1-14).

---

① See the material at http://money. finance. sina. com. cn/corp/go. php/vCI_CorpInfo/stockid/600535. phtml.

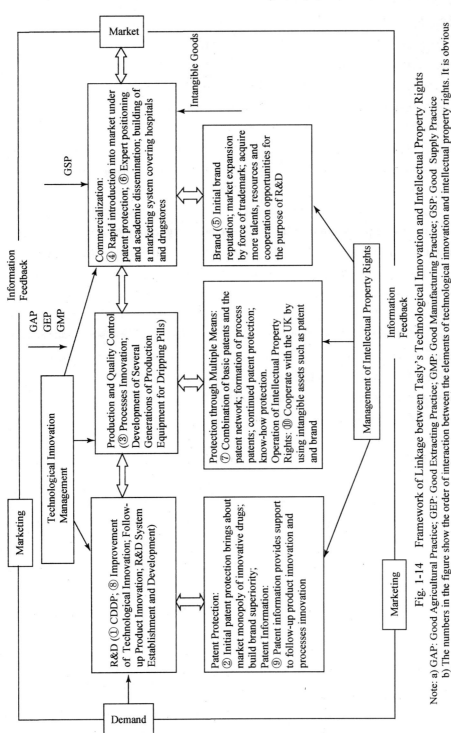

Fig. 1-14　Framework of Linkage between Tasly's Technological Innovation and Intellectual Property Rights

Note: a) GAP: Good Agricultural Practice; GEP: Good Extracting Practice; GMP: Good Manufacturing Practice; GSP: Good Supply Practice

b) The numbers in the figure show the order of interaction between the elements of technological innovation and intellectual property rights. It is obvious from the figure that this interaction has no particular pattern and is nonlinear.

Source: Li Wenjian and Li Chuncheng, 2008.

(2) Initial Development of Technological Innovation and Intellectual Property Rights System

Ten years ago, realizing in research practice that such diseases as coronary heart disease and angina pectoris had already become "top health killers" as population aging was gaining momentum, Yan Xijun and his wife, co-founders of Tasly, began aiming at research into drugs for cardiovascular and cerebrovascular diseases. They singled out Compound Danshen Tablet—a common drug used for therapy of cardiovascular and cerebrovascular diseases, separated the effective constituent by using modern scientific and technological means and combined them anew[1]. But a good medicine must have a good form for its administration; otherwise, it could only be made into traditional "pills, powders, extracts and pellets" or simple compound preparations as before, which is not only hard to market and popularize but could hardly be recognized by foreign consumers, who had been accustomed to Western medicine. Facing the situation, the two co-founders focused their attention on the form of dripping pills which take effect fast and are easily absorbed, in expectation of making it a modern drug featuring "three smalls, three effectives and three conveniences."[2] After countless tests, they finally succeeded in 1993 in bringing out the innovative product, CDDP.

After CDDP had successfully passed appraisal, what the inventor did first and foremost was applying for and obtaining the patent for invention. By force of the legal monopoly of patent and of the technical barriers brought by unique technological processes, Tasly became the exclusive producer of CDDP, and CDDP captured the market rapidly thanks to its healing effects. This first-mover advantage impelled consumers to gradually accept the "Tasly" brand, and brought about the initial brand effect. On marketing strategy, Tasly adopted the marketing model of "expert positioning and academic dissemination", and set up a capable sales and management team for prescription drugs to recommend the new drug to doctors and rapidly open the market. In 1995 alone, CDDP was sold for over 32 million yuan; in 1997, it became the first TCM preparation in the world to enter in its capacity as a drug the Phases II and III clinical trials under the FDA's IND (Investigational New Drug) program; and

---

① According to the traditional experience of TCM, the recipe of CDDP encompasses only three types of traditional Chinese medicine. Tasly's innovation lies in its extraction through modern research means of 14 monomer effective constituents, formulation of the proportioning between these constituents, and formation of its own intellectual property rights, including recipe, monomer effective constituents, processes and quality control.

② Three smalls: small volume, small dosage and small side effects; three effectives: quickly effective, highly effective and long effective; five conveniences: convenient for carrying, taking, making, storing and transporting.

in 1999, it won the third prize of the National Science and Technology Progress Award. The FDA's certification further proved the novelty and quality of CDDP, which also brought a vital opportunity for Tasly to increase the influence of the brand and improve its corporate reputation. Over the past decade, with a vast investment (nearly 7% of its sales income) in the R&D of new products and technologies, Tasly has developed a modern TCM product cluster comprising more than 50 varieties, such as Cleaning Brain & Nourishing Blood Granule, Bupleuri Dripping Pill, Andrographolide Dripping Pill and Polyvalent Virosomal Influenza Vaccine. All patent-protected, these new drugs have become a new competitive edge of Tasly.

On equipment innovation, Tasly itself developed two-generation manual and automatic pill-dripping machines to reduce the impurity and pollution in production, and, in cooperation with Tianjin University, developed an automatic packaging assembly line. So far, it has developed the third-generation computer-controlled, self-contained large production equipment, installed the China's largest, state-of-the-art production lines that feature total computer control, intelligent process combination, online testing of key technological parameters, and continuous acquisition programming, and passed the certification by Good Agricultural Practice for Chinese Crude Drugs and ISO 9001-2000 Quality Management System. These helped Tasly solve the difficulty in standardizing the production of traditional Chinese medicine.

On R&D organizational innovation, Tasly has built an open-style technological innovation system centered around Tasly Institute, comprising the Modern TCM Department, Chemical Medicine Department, Biotechnology and Biological Product R&D Center, International TCM Registration Research Center and Food Department (Yao Wenping et al., 2005). By recruiting high-level researchers from different regions, countries and fields, Tasly Institute has built a domestically top-notch postdoctoral workstation that maximizes the sharing of knowledge. All these have become important resources necessary for Tasly to expand foreign markets and cooperate with foreign companies[1].

On marketing innovation, Tasly has not only secured a leading position in R&D

----

[1]　By force of its technologies, brand strength and intangible assets, Tasly founded Tianjin Tasly Sants Pharmaceutical Co., Ltd. in cooperation with the UK-based COOPER Group Ltd. Different from Chinese enterprises' practice of attracting foreign capital with tangible assets like land and factory plants in the past, what Tasly invest in the joint venture were intangible assets including its brand, new product development technologies with intellectual property rights, and new forms of prepared drugs. The COOPER Group Ltd. invested 200 million yuan in cash into the joint venture. Source: He Jiankun and Meng Jie. March 5, 2008. Promoting Great Health Industry and Helping to Build a Harmonious Society. *Science and Technology Daily*, 10.

of the innovation value chain, but also capitalized on its CDDP patent to establish a marketing system of its own and changed the original situation of "incomplete autonomy" that could only develop and produce drugs, but could not sell them without the aid of agents. This "incomplete autonomy" was adverse to the linkage between technological innovation and intellectual property rights, making it difficult to bring about the brand effect. Through its efforts made in network building since CDDP came into the market in 1994, Tasly has built a countrywide three-level marketing network which, consisting of five tier-one incorporated companies, six tier-two incorporated companies, 21 greater regions and 185 representative offices, interconnects the three major channels, namely hospitals, drugstores as well as urban and rural markets, making Tasly one of the few Chinese pharmaceutical enterprises that have a distribution advantage at both ends—hospitals and drugstores—and take a firm footing in urban and rural drug distribution markets (Zhang Jing, 2005).

(3) Linkage between Technological Innovation and Intellectual Property Rights in Innovation Processes

1) Linkage at the R&D stage. Tasly introduced the management of intellectual property rights early in the R&D stage. Considering that patent protection is region-dependent, when developing new drugs, Tasly retrieved information on TCM protection, patent application and granting on the target markets in different regions and then adjusted its R&D routes and patent application schemes (Li Wenjian and Chen Yang, 2007). In the meantime, it began considering the patent design of new drugs, including recipe, constituent proportioning, processing technology, active extracts, Chinese materia medica preparation, preparation methods and new medical uses (Liu Yuexuan, 2006). It is, therefore, apparent that intellectual property rights are not only, where R&D begins but also where it ends, playing an important role in regulating and guiding R&D.

It is just by force of strong capacity for technological innovation that Tasly has created a large quantity of signature high-tech fruits, which form exclusive core technologies. By 2008, Tasly had filed 863 patent applications and obtained 247 international patents (Bao Guozhi and Li Xian, 2008). CDDP has obtained 72 international patents in 30 countries; in South Korea, it has a 20-year term of patent protection. These patents, as the core competitiveness of Tasly, enable the young company to complete in the TCM market with those century-old brands[1].

---

① http://www.tasly.com/news.aspx.

To protect the core technologies it has developed, Tasly has built a patent protection system consisting of "core patents, competitive patents and defensive patents", which forms a powerful patent network providing overall protection to its products. It applies for patents for all of the products its has developed, including TCM products, chemical medicines and biological medicines; it protects strategic manufacturing processes as trade secrets and conducts secrecy education to technicians and skilled workers, who have access to its major plants; and it files no patent application for technologies to be made public as required. At present, there are 189 CDDP-related patents, nearly covering all aspects that may require protection; other products usually have several patents each.

Surrounding CDDP, Tasly has formed a tight patent network, with the aim of providing a broader protection for core technologies, so that it has a technologically long-term, broad market monopoly on the product. Built from the technological route perspective, this patent network covers almost all currently foreseeable directions of invention and creation, such as various variations of CDDP constituents, compound preparation methods, preparation of active extracts, compound preparations, new uses of compounds, appraisal methods and content determination methods, as well as extract preparation processes, form studies, new pharmacological functions of active extracts and even the extraction of monomeric active constitutent in Chinese patent medicine. By overcoming the barriers to the all-round protection via single patent of complex TCM technologies, this network also widened the scope of technological protection for Chinese patent medicines as well as the room for technological application (Liu Wei and Dong Xiaohui, 2007).

Given the characteristic of the TCM industry, patent protection may not be completely effective, and, thus, must be aided by other forms of protection. While protecting its products through patent, Tasly actively sought the registration of trademarks. From the corporate logo and name to the trade names of products, from tangible products to intangible services, it not only had its trademarks within its business registered, but also paid attention to the all-class and reverse registration of trademarks; at the same time, it applied for reserve trademarks. In recent years, Tasly has registerd more than 250 domestic trademarks and nearly 30 international trademarks (Li Wenjian et al. , 2007).

In addition to patent application and trademark registration, the management of intellectual property rights in a market strategy should also focus more on the monitoring of intellectual property right infringement. For example, in March 2005 when Guangdong-based Dongguan Super Success Pharmaceutical Co. , Ltd. was discovered attending pharmaceutical fairs with Cleaning Brain & Nourishing Blood Granule modeled on Tasly's, Tasly immediately brought an action to the local court against this firm for its infringement of the patent for invention of Tasly's Nourishing Blood & Cleaning Brain Granule. Based on the evidence Tasly had gather in nearly two years that followed, the court ruled that the defendant had infringed on Tasly's patent and should immediately stop producing and offering to sell the patented product of Tasly and assume corresponding civil liabilities (Yang Shizhang, 2007).

2) Linkage between raw materials and manufacturing. Because of the particularities in recipes and preparation processes, TCM drugs have such defects as vagueness about effective constituents, unclear toxicological and pharmacodynamical mechanisms and nonstandard quality monitoring indicators, making it difficult for them to be recognized by international authoritative organizations and patent application restricted to a certain degree. This is an obstacle to TCM internationalization. To guarantee the quality of TCM drugs, therefore, importance must be given to the cropping of medicinal herbs at source. Considering that no relevant cropping standards were available in China, Tasly founded a GAP (Good Agricultural Practice) medicinal herb base by referring to European herb cropping directives, with the aim of ensuring that medicinal herbs are of high quality, pollution-free, have a high content of effective constituents and are up to intensive and standard cropping requirements. Tasly viewed obtaining the FDA certification as a long-term strategic task, which made it possible for the company to be the first TCM enterprise certified by FDA and entering the North American market.

On recipe, preparation and process inspection, Tasly applied advanced extraction, condensation and drying technologies for innovation in pharmaceutical technologies, processes and forms, leading to the stable qualitative and quantitative control of effective constituents of TCM, which accords with the modern preparation requirement of "small volume, small dosage and small side effects" and "high effectiveness, quick effectiveness and long-term effectiveness."[1] Moreover, its enhanced innovation in technological processes led to the independent development of a large digital dripping pill production line and a large automatic packaging production line, both up to an internationally advanced level; it adopted the state-of-the-art

---

[1] http:/www. tasly. com/news. aspx.

multiple fingerprinting technology for total quality control, established a national GMP (Good Manufacturing Practice) certified modern TCM production base, and applied for the patent protection of its multiple fingerprinting technology, which is not only protected its quality control technology but also restricted the emergence of counterfeits.

(4) Organizational and Institutional Guarantees for Promoting the Linkage between Technological Innovation and Intellectual Property Rights

1) Integration and linkage at organizational level. Tasly's technological innovation activities are primarily carried out by Tasly Institute. In 2003, Tasly set up a Legal Affairs Center, under which there is an Intellectual Property Department in charge of intellectual property rights regarding the group and its subsidiaries (including Tasly Institute) (Fig. 1-15). This governing body is at the group's core management level, so that intellectual property work is incorporated into the group's business activities. The Legal Affairs Center is staffed by 11 persons—five masters and six bachelors, and

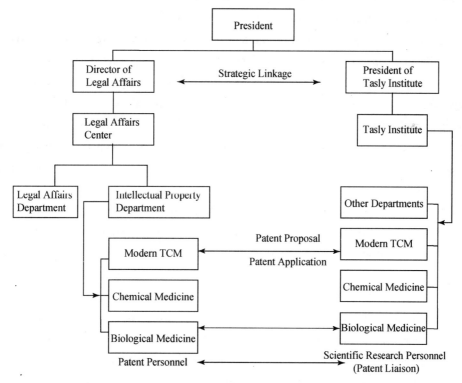

Fig. 1-15　Organizational Linkage between Tasly's Intellectual Property Rights and
Technological Innovation
Source: Zhou Jizhong et al. , 2009b.

five of them hold a certificate of patent agent or lawyer, forming a well-structured force of intellectual property talents.

The full-time patent workers who staff the Intellectual Property Department, and the intellectual property directors and liaisons at the departments under Tasly Institutes and at the subsidiaries, together with the group's intellectual property governing body, form an intellectual property management network, an intellectual property management system, which, with the group's patent management body at the heart, is supported by Tasly Institute and the subsidiaries' patent management departments. Tasly's intellectual property management system is in the shape of a pyramid: the top encompasses highly qualified specialists in intellectual property rights; the body consists of the Legal Affairs Department and Intellectual Property Department under the Legal Affairs Center, both of which cooperate with each other and yet have different duties; and the base is formed by lawyers serving as patent managers in such fields as modern TCM, chemical medicine and healthcare products, as well as information liaisons.

On talent development, Tasly has established a high-quality, well-structured trinity of intellectual property talent formations. The first formation consists of senior intellectual property and legal experts as the top management for intellectual property rights and legal affairs. The second formation is composed of intellectual property professionals (with patent agent certificates) and legal professionals (with lawyer certificates), who are responsible for handling concrete issues concerning intellectual property rights and legal affairs. The third formation comprises the reserves in intellectual property rights and law, who help deal with intellectual property rights related and legal affairs. The upper formation supervises and directs the lower one. The second formation is divided into specialized teams for TCM, chemical medicine and biological medicine, responsible for handling matters relating to patents, trademarks, lawsuits and contract management. The formations communicate with each other on a regular basis.

2) Integration and linkage at institutional level. On institutional design regarding intellectual property rights, Tasly stresses the strengthening of its constraint mechanisms for intellectual property to prevent the loss of such rights, the improvement of incentive mechanisms for technological innovation and intellectual property rights, and the strengthening of intellectual property inquiry systems. In recent years, it has introduced a patent performance evaluation system, which was designed to link the evaluation of patent work to that of technological innovation. According to its patent interest distribution and rewarding system, the patents and benefits brought

about thereof were evaluated regularly and the persons responsible for the patents were given due benefits and rewards. It also strengthened its incentive mechanism regarding management personnel at various levels by incorporating patent targets and patent management requirements into the annual performance evaluation of leaders of Tasly Institute and the subsidiaries (Li Xu, 2003).

On trademark management, Tasly engaged domestic and foreign experts to help formulate trademark use plans. It first built trademarks as an asset, and then evaluated them with imported advanced software. When the value of a trademark as an intangible asset rose to a certain level, it would have it evaluated by a domestic authoritative intermediary and then apply it to the group's investment development through such forms as joint venture, licensing and transferring, giving full play to the leverage of trademark assets (Yang Hong and Sheng Yuanfeng, 2000).

(5) Conclusion: TCM Internationalization

Through the analysis of the development course of Tasly, especially its experience and practice in incorporating intellectual property management into its medicinal herb cropping, production control, R&D and marketing with the aim of strengthening its competitive edge, the following conclusions can be drawn.

First, Tasly is a typical Chinese pharmaceutical enterprise built on technological innovation and new product R&D. The interaction between technological innovation (R&D, production and marketing) and intellectual property rights in the process of its development was quite obvious and such interaction featured nonlinearity (linkage between multiple elements including marketing, rather than one-to-one linkage).

Second, while applying the operation of intangible assets that combine patents with such intellectual property as trademarks and trade secrets and professional standards to promote TCM modernization, build brands and improve market competitiveness, Chinese pharmaceutical enterprises should develop an international business strategy and strive to obtain PCT patents, so as to enter international pharmaceutical markets.

Just as this book was about to be finished, Tasly made two new achievements. First, at the "The Founding of Enterprise-University-Institute Union for TCM Modernization and The Reporting Conference on FDA Phase II Clinical Trail Findings on CDDP" held in Beijing jointly by the MOH and the Tianjin Government, it found that its CDDP had already passed FDA Phase II clinical trials, and, thus, become China's first compound TCM preparation to pass the examination, showing that compound TCM could also meet the all-round challenge of modern science and technology like Western medicine. Now Tasly is doing its best to go through PDA Phase III clinical trials (Feng Guowu, 2010a). Second, in September 2010, Tasly and the Beijing Military Region's Beidaihe Sanatorium signed a transfer agreement, under which the Nephritis Relieving Tablet—a TCM recipe which had been clinically used by the sanatorium for more than 30 years—would be taken over to Tasly for re-development. Although there are many TCM clinical recipes which have been clinically used for decades and even over one century because of their evident effects, such key problems as their functional mechanisms and active constituents remain unclear. The long public use of these recipes has endangered their intellectual property rights. By applying modern scientific and technological approaches to develop these clinically verified TCM recipes into modern new drugs up to international standards, Tasly has opened up a new path for TCM internationalization (Feng Guowu, 2010b).

2. 4. 4　　From Tradition to Innovation: Fast-growing Xiuzheng Pharmaceutical Group

(1) From Traditional Products to Technological Innovation

Xiuzheng Pharmaceutical Group ("Xiuzheng") was founded in May 1995 as a small pharmaceutical factory with fixed assets only worth 250, 000 yuan. Its leapfrogging development over a dozen years has made it a large pharmaceutical enterprise group with 55 sole subsidiaries, more than 60, 000 employees and total assets of 5.7 billion yuan. It has created a miracle in the pharmaceutical industry that it has developed at a super-fast annual growth rate of 1, 876%. It had been ranked number one among the pharmaceutical enterprises in Jilin province for eight consecutive years from 2000, and in 2004 it jumped to the first place in the profit rankings of TCM enterprises in China. In July 2005, it was ranged 7th among Chinese pharmaceutical enterprises. In 2007, its sales income reached 5.7 billion yuan, up 21% over 2006. Today's Xiuzheng is a large-sized pharmaceutical enterprise that integrates scientific research, production and franchising of TCM, chemical medicine and biological medicine as well as standard herb cropping, spotted deer breeding and deep processing, and has a development framework comprising one national-level enterprise technology center, six raw material bases, eight preparation bases and ten marketing platforms.

Xiuzheng now can produce more than 800 types of products in 17 dosage forms, including four famous brands—Sidashu Capsules, Yiqi Yangxue Oral Liquid,

Naoxinshu Oral Liquid and Xiao Mi Suppositories, and national award-winning Fei Ning Granules, Gegping (Irbesartan Tablets) and Skeleto-gout Tablets. In 2006, "Xiuzheng" and "Xiuzheng Sidashu Capsules" appeared on the list of "2005 Brands Trusted and Respected by Chinese Netizen" (Table 1-9). In 2008, Xiuzheng was given the "Contribution Award for Corporate Social Responsibility. "①

Table 1-9　Chinese Top 10 Enterprises and Top 10 Stomach Drug Brands Trusted and Respected by Netizen in 2005

Brand	Enterprise	Ranking	Stomach Drug Brand
Haier	Haier Group	1	Sidashu Capsules, Xiuzheng
Xiuzheng Sidashu Capsules	Xiuzheng Pharmaceutical Group	2	Motilium, Xian-Janssen
Industrial and Commercial Bank of China	Industrial and Commercial Bank of China Limited	3	Losec, ZstraZeneca
Arawana	Yihai Kerry Investment Co. Ltd.	4	Jianwei Xiaoshi Tablet, Jiang-zhong
Sanlu	Sanlu Group	5	Cimetidine, Tianjin Smith Kline & French Laboratorles Ltd
Citroen	Dongfeng Peugeot Citroen Auto-mobile Company Ltd.	6	Wei-Tai 999 Gastro Granules
Moutai	China Kweichou Moutai Distillery (Group) Co. Ltd	7	Talcid, Bayer
Peony Card	Industrial and Commercial Bank of China	8	Bismuth Potassium Citrate Cap-sules, Livzon
King Deer	Inner Mongolia King Deer Cash-mere	9	Sunflower Weikangling
DTW	Datian W. Group Co. , Ltd.	10	HPGC biscu

Source: http://www. jschina. com. cn/gb/jschina/finance/node6358/node6359/userobject1ai1130403. html; http://www. fubusi. com/2006/2-20/134123493. html.

On intellectual property rights, Xiuzheng has in recent years applied for 152 patents, including 42 patents for invention, three utility model patents and 107 industrial design patents, and been granted 82 patents. Currently it has 420 registered

---

① Xiuzheng was given this award for its high product quality—"zero bad records on credibility" and "zero drug quality complaints" and for its donation to "5. 12" Wenchuan Earthquake-hit areas of drugs worth 35 million yuan—the biggest donation in the Chinese pharmaceutical industry.

trademarks, and the certificates of registration for over 150 trademarks such as "Xinxiu", "Shuangxiao", "Xiucheng" and "Qianxiantong" (Kang Yajuan, 2007). In 2006, the trademarks "Xiuzheng" and "Sidashu" both were chosen as Chinese Well-Known Trademarks, making Xiuzheng the sole Chinese pharmaceutical enterprise owning two well-known trademarks. In March 2005, the brand value of "Xiuzheng" was estimated at 2 billion yuan.

As a typical example of the rapid development of Chinese pharmaceutical enterprises, Xiuzheng has exhibited another development model for pharmaceutical enterprises: at the introduction stage, begin with some time-honored products that suit the market, and make efforts in process innovation and quality management to build initial brand effects; when the brand is gradually formed and enters the development stage, increase R&D investment to improve the enterprise's capacity for technological innovation and effect the shift in management mode from "production-marketing" to "R&D-production-marketing"; and when the enterprise has certain technological capacity, intellectual property begins to show its important role and gradually participates in the linkage with technological innovation. This linkage is the nonlinear interaction between R&D, production, intellectual property rights, marketing and brand (Fig. 1-16).

(2) Intellectual Property-related "Bottlenecks"

In May 1995, Xiu Laigui, who had worked in the police for 20 years, took over, from the Tonghua Municipal Detachment of Traffic Police a pharmaceutical factory affiliated to Tonghua Pharmaceutical Industrial Research Institute, a small pharmaceutical factory which was teetering on the brink of bankruptcy, with only 200, 000 yuan of fixed assets and 4 million yuan of debts. The first drug product produced after the takeover was Tianma Pills, a traditional, time-honored product. Many pharmaceutical enterprises, then, were confronted with the shortage of gastrodia tuber (or Tianma)—the most important raw material for producing Tianma Pills, but Xiu Laigui required the use of superior Tianma to produce Tianma Pills and sold the drug at a loss of 0.7 yuan per pack (Qiu Tong, 2006). Tianma Pills soon found markets for its high quality and low price. Considering the meager profit and low market access of the drug, Xiu Laigui introduced from a traditional Chinese medicine expert a recipe for liver disease therapy, called "Tianhe Shenggan", and purchased advanced production equipment with a vast investment. Taihe Shenggan soon found markets for its good quality and reputation. By the end of 1995, this small drug factory had not only paid off its four million yuan of debts but also made a profit of one million yuan.

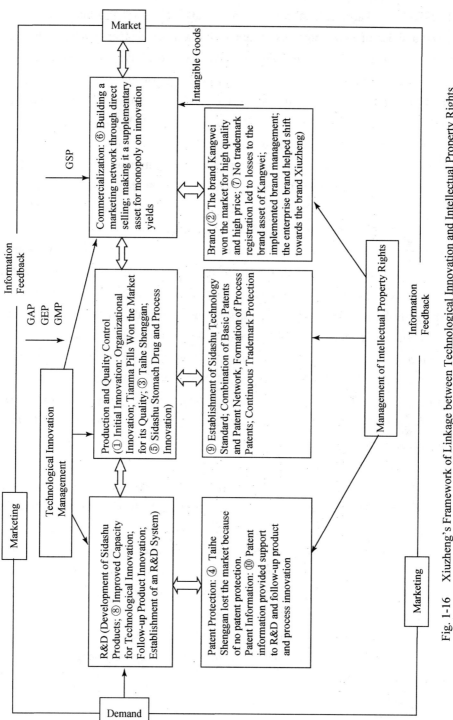

Fig. 1-16　Xiuzheng's Framework of Linkage between Technological Innovation and Intellectual Property Rights

Source:zhou Jizhong et al., 2009b.

In 1996, the pharmaceutical factory was renamed Kangwei Pharmaceutical Co., Ltd., and a series of new drugs were introduced one after another, such as "Feining Granules", "Xintai Tablets" and "Sidashu." At the end of 1996, "Taihe Shenggan Capsules" and "Feining Capsules", both produced by Kangwei, won a gold prize each at China High-tech Fair. In 1997, the sales volume of "Taihe Shenggan Capsules" exceeded 100 million yuan (Li Ruqi et al., 2006). Because no patent application was filed, the success of this drug sparked off a nationwide war on liver drugs. Kangwei had to give up this lucrative product and its markets, and shifted its focus to other products. Kangwei learned from it a lesson that without independent intellectual property rights (patent and brand), a product was liable to be followed and copied by other enterprises, however good its efficacy was.

Another brand of Kangwei was "Sidashu", a drug specially used for treating gastric diseases. When introduced in 1998, this drug was not publicized, but marketed by the company's salespersons traveling across China. Through direct selling, the company gradually developed a force of salespersons, and built a nationwide marketing network consisting of 38 provincial-level branches (two branches were set up for each big province) and 466 prefecture-level representative offices in 31 provinces (municipalities directly under the central government, and autonomous regions).

Just as the company was changing from a production enterprise to a "production-marketing" enterprise, a trademark problem arose. When the pharmaceutical factory was restructured to Kangwei Pharmaceutical Co., Ltd. in early 1996, only the business name was registered at the Tonghua Bureau for Industry and Commerce and the Jilin Administration for Industry and Commerce, but no trademark was registered at the State Administration for Industry and Commerce (SAIC). When renamed Jilin Kangwei Pharmaceutical Group Stock, Co., Ltd. in 1998, the trademark "Kangwei" was not registered either because a Shangdong-based pharmaceutical enterprise had already registered the trademark "Kangwei." The company had no choice but to once again be renamed Jilin Xiuzheng Pharmaceutical Group Stock, Co., Ltd. in May 2000, and registered the trademark "Xiuzheng" at SAIC.

By the end of 2000, "Sidashu", a drug under the trademark "Xiuzheng", had rapidly captured the stomach drug markets across the country. Xiuzheng's sales in the year registered 1.2 billion yuan.

(3) Development of Technological Innovation System

After the brand grew to a certain degree and the enterprise had certain financial strength, Xiuzheng became aware of the necessity of strengthening its technological innovation platform and capacity building. In 1999, Xiuzheng set up a technology center, and in 2000 it established a state-certified enterprise technology center with an investment of 67 million yuan, with branches in Shanghai and Shenyang. From then on, each year it would invest nearly five million yuan in lab renovation and the purchase of new lab equipment. Between 2000 and 2006, Xiuzheng's expenditure on technological innovation exceeded one billion yuan, and its R&D expenditure each year accounted for about 8.9% of its sales, far higher than the average level of less than 2% in the industry. The development of R&D base and the considerable increase in R&D expenditure gradually help the company shift from "production-marketing" to "R&D-production-marketing" integration.

Xiuzheng defined its technological innovation strategy as realizing TCM modernization, with emphasis on TCM extraction technology, biotechnology and the application of modern preparation technology in new TCM drug development and secondary TCM development. In last few years, it has retained more than 300 noted pharmaceutical experts and researchers from home and abroad; 25% of them are senior technical experts and 34% are middle-level scientific and technological personnel. In addition, it has engaged 36 visiting experts, eight doctoral tutors and three foreign experts. In the meantime, it has enhanced cooperation with universities and research institutes. For example, together with the CAS Shanghai Institute of Materia Medica and the Northeast Normal University Institute of Genetics and Gytology, it founded the National Modern TCM Research Center, carrying out cooperation in such aspects as the extraction and fermentation of active extracts of TCM; it founded the "Jilin Zhongzheng TCM Engineering Center" in collaboration with Changchun College of Traditional Chinese Medicine; its resource sharing with Jilin University, Northeast Normal University, Changchun College of Traditional Chinese Medicine, Shenyang Pharmaceutical University and the CAS Shanghai Institute of Materia Medica was to assimilate international advanced scientific and technological achievements, promote deep-level technological development for TCM modernization, create independent intellectual property and provide derivative varieties of new drugs.

During its technological innovation, Xiuzheng attached importance to the linkage between intellectual property, R&D and marketing (Fig. 1-17). In 2000, after learning from interviews with consumers that over 31.16% of women suffered from cervical and vaginal diseases, the marketing personnel realized the urgent need in the market for an effective, convenient and hygienic externally applied gynecological drug. To meet this need, Xiuzheng's pharmaceutical experts developed Xiao Mi Suppositories, which, compared with similar products in the market, was more technologically advanced, and prepared with tampons imported from the United States, which offered great convenience to women patients and enhanced their comfort. Shortly after the introduction into the market, it was well-received among consumers, and in a few years its sales reached hundreds of millions yuan.

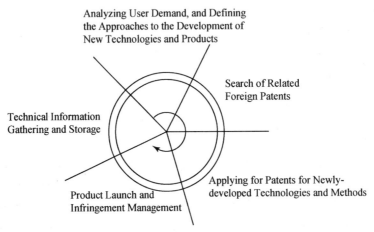

Fig. 1-17　Xiuzheng's Trinity of R&D, Intellectual Property and Market Management

Source: Zhou Jizhong et al., 2009b.

It is just based on its technological innovation system featuring "enterprise-university-research institute" cooperation that Xiuzheng has in recent years introduced a large number of new drugs, including three Category I drugs, seven Category II drugs, four Category III drugs and three Category IV drugs (Table 1-10). It has independently completed the re-development of eight types of TCM drugs.

Table 1-10　New Drugs Developed by Xiuzheng Pharmaceutical Group

Type	Name
Category I	Thymus Oral Solution, Thrombolysis, Gatifloxacin Capsules
Category II	Sidashu, Gegping (Irbesartan Tablets), Xiao Mi Suppositories, Medicines for Soothing Nervous, Fei Ning Granules, Rabeprazole Sodium, Stomach Clear Power Tablets (Itopride Hydrochloride Tables)
Exclusive Types and Protected TCM Types	Yiqi Yangxue Oral Liquid, Skeleto-gout Tablets, Naoxinshu Oral Liquid, Hepatitis B Qingrejiedu Capsules, Xiuzheng Jiangtang Capsules, Shenyanling Capsules, Wen Shen Qian Lie Capsules

Source: Based on data at http://www.china-xiuzheng.com.

In addition to product innovation, Xiuzheng also strengthened process innovation; each year it had more than 100 items of production process improvement and innovation and at least four skill contests among production technicians. For example, each year its technology center had more than 10 process improvement and innovation items regarding "Sidashu" and invested around 10 million yuan in "Sidashu" R&D and innovation. Technological innovation and process improvement made Sidashu more outstanding in healing effects. In 2003, the SFDA granted Sidashu a separate national standard, which increased Xiuzheng's market monopoly of Sidashu. Before that, Sidashu had already been included on the list of the fifth batch of OTC (Over the Counter) drugs for its definite efficacy, reliability and safety.

(4) Intellectual Property Management and Organizational Innovation

Because massive losses had been caused by improper intellectual property management in the course of its development, Xiuzheng attached great importance to intellectual property management: the technology center director and the group vice president were directly responsible for the work of intellectual property, while the board chairman himself participated in brand building and developed a 10-year brand plan. In 2006, its expenditure on patent application, routine maintenance, licensing of patented technologies, and trademark registration examination and approval amounted to 1.038 million yuan. Its emphasis on and application of intellectual property rights in return brought about great economic benefits. In 2006, the output of its four patented products, "active constituents-included, improved vitamin U belladonna aluminium capsule II (Sidashu)", "a process for refining senecio cannabifolius less granules", "an improvement method for preparing the pharmaceutical raw material of itopride" and "a Chinese materia medica preparation for rheumatism therapy", amounted to 2.14 billion yuan, and the sales income stood at 2.01 billion yuan.

Because of its marketing network, strong marketing capability and brand assets, Xiuzheng is usually able to rapidly introduce new products into the market, forming a competitive edge in time. This prompt marketing capability has also become an important means, by which Xiuzheng protects and gains profits from its innovation fruits. In addition to using intellectual property to protect its innovation fruits, it also employs administrative means to protect its new drugs. Moreover, it has also learned to use standards to create technical barriers to prevent other companies from copying its products. In recent years, it has participated in the formulation of nearly 60 standards, and it has been granted national standards for its Gatifloxacin Capsules, Wen Shen

Qian Lie Capsules, Fei Ning Granules, Jing Yao Kang Capsules, Skeleto-gout Tablets, Shenxian Zhuanggu Capsules, Fenkamamin Capsules and Itopride Hydrochloride Tables; "Sidashu" was given a separate national standard, which makes the active constituents of a single capsule more strictly controlled and more definite in efficacy and secures the leading position of "Sidashu" among Chinese stomach drug brands.

On planning for its technological innovation system, Xiuzheng also pays attention to system building. Guided by the Intellectual Property Management Measures of Xiuzheng Pharmaceutical Group, it has established three supportive sets of management measures, *Intellectual Property Secrecy Measures of Xiuzheng Pharmaceutical Group*, *Patent Application and Maintenance Measures of Xiuzheng Pharmaceutical Group* and *Intellectual Property Transfer and Incentive Measures of Xiuzheng Pharmaceutical Group*, which provide safeguards for the total process of intellectual property and technological innovation. At Xiuzheng, an employee will be rewarded 2, 000 yuan if he/she has finished a patent report, 8, 000 yuan if he/she has filed a patent application, and another 3, 000 yuan if the patent is approved. Each year the group uses innovation rewarding funds of nearly one million yuan to reward its scientific research personnel for their technological innovation achievements. It often provides intellectual property training to foster a favorable culture for intellectual property protection.

However, Xiuzheng currently doesn't have a full-time intellectual property department. The jobs of intellectual property management are scattered in related departments: the patent department is affiliated to the technology center; the marketing department is in charge of the planning and management of trademarks and brands; and the legal affairs center is responsible for patent infringement monitoring and maintenance. Patent application is primarily an internal affair and, only when necessary, an external patent agency is engaged to help complete patent application. Its patent strategy is, for the most part, a "follow-technology strategy", estimating the number of patents to be applied for as per its annual R&D objectives, rather than using patents to guide R&D. On intellectual property management, it mainly places emphasis on the roles of patents, trademarks and copyrights, but rarely employs know-how to protect its innovation results.

(5) Concluding Remarks: From Tradition to Innovation

The development of Xiuzheng is typical of what Joseph Schumpeter identified as innovation: the entrepreneurship and the innovation in organization and management modes saved a small enterprise teetering on the brink of bankruptcy. Schumpeter called "an entrepreneur as a person, whose function is to effect new combinations", he also pointed out that "an entrepreneur's function is to reform or revolutionize the mode of production through the possibilities of using a new invention or, more generally, a new method to produce new goods or old goods, though opening new sources of raw material support or new markets of products, through reorganization of an industry and so forth."① During the start-up period, Xiuzheng had no new technologies, new inventions and new products, but reorganized the enterprise by using a new production organization mode; although the products were not new, what the founder of the enterprise did first was focusing attention on the quality of the products and building the brand and reputation assets, which brought new opportunities and markets for later development of the enterprise. During the development stage, it began stressing R&D, and set the stage for its continued development through diverse modes of technological innovation; at this stage, the linkage (primarily dynamic coupling) between technological innovation and intellectual property became frequent.

This is another typical development mode of Chinese pharmaceutical enterprises.

Xiuzheng has installed—with an investment of 120 million yuan—a national-level production line for the raw material synthesis and preparation of Category I new drug "Gatifloxacin", and now is building a top-class R&D base and the largest GAP TCM production base in Jinlin province, investing 100 million yuan to set up 1, 000 GSP (Good Supply Practice) chain stores, and investing one billion yuan to build the most modern "Biomedicine Science Park" in China. And it is planned to realize a sales income of 100 billion yuan by 2015, and become one of the world's top 100 pharmaceutical enterprises in 2030.

2.4.5　NCPC's Innovation through "Enterprise-University-Research Institute" Cooperation

(1) Nearly 60-year History as a Large State-owned Pharmaceutical Enterprises

North China Pharmaceutical Company Ltd. (NCPC), founded in June 1953, is one of the largest Chinese biological and chemical pharmaceutical enterprises that focus mainly on microbiologically-fermented drugs, synthetic drugs and semi-synthetic drugs, and biotechnological drugs. The founding of NCPC ushered in an era of mass

---

① Cited from: Deng Lizhi. 2007. *A Systematic Study of Independent Brand Innovation Capacity of Chinese Enterprises*. Harbin: Harbin Institute of Technology.

production of antibiotics through microbiological fermentation in China and put an end to the history of relying on imports for penicillin and streptomycin. Through technological innovation and the continuous expansion of production and operation in the course of its development, it has extended its business from originally merely producing drugs to into a multiplicity of fields such as biology, chemical engineering, pesticides and trading, and become a sizable pharmaceutical enterprise group that owns more than 530 types of drugs and over 40 subsidiaries and invests in diverse fields.

NCPC has ranked for many years among China's top 500 industrial enterprises. The "North China" trademark was recognized as a well-known trademark by the SAIC in 1999, evaluated at 3.688 billion yuan in 2001, and chosen as one of China's five most valuable industrial brands by *Forbes* in 2004. NCPC has also won such honors as "Chinese Enterprise of Quality Control Excellence", "Trustworthy Pharmaceutical Enterprise" and one of "China Top 10 Credible Enterprises." In 2007, it was appraised as an Exemplary Enterprise in Ensuring Drug Quality, five of its products won the National Quality Product Awards, and 34 varieties were recognized as high-quality products at provincial level or above. In the same year, its sales volume stood at 5.6 billion yuan, which ranked the group 327th among China's top 500 manufacturing enterprises and 6th in the country's pharmaceutical industry (Table 1-11). It was the first Chinese pharmaceutical enterprise to be SA8000 (Social Accountability) certified; in 2008, it received the "CSR Contribution Award" as a pharmaceutical enterprise. It was also included on *Fortune's* list of China's Top 500 Listed Companies 2010.

Table 1-11　The 2007 Rankings of Large-sized Chinese Pharmaceutical
Enterprises among China's Top 500 Manufacturing Enterprises

Pharmaceutical Industry Ranking	Top 500 Manufacturing Enterprises Ranking	Enterprise Name	Business Income/ 100 million yuan
1	92	Shanghai Pharmaceutical Holding Co., Ltd.	208
2	112	Beijing Pharmaceutical Group Co., Ltd.	175
3	126	Guangzhou Pharmaceutical Holdings Limited	159
4	179	Tianjin Pharmaceutical Holdings Ltd.	115
5	313	CSPC Pharmaceutical Group Limited	59.6
6	327	North China Pharmaceutical Company Ltd.	56.1
7	388	Tasly Group	43

Source: http://news. xinhuanet. com/newscenter/2007-09/01/content_6644729. htm.

(2) NCPC Began Establishing its Technological Innovation System in 1992

Early when it was put into production, NCPC set up a dedicated scientific research body—Antibiotics Research Institute, and developed a series of new products (Lü Jiang, 1997). But on the whole, it primarily engaged in production of generic drugs before 1992. In 1992, it set up a new drug R&D center—NCPC New Drug R&D Center, the first state-recognized enterprise Technology Center in the pharmaceutical industry. In 1997, it was included in the first six pilot enterprises for technological innovation approved by the former State Economic and Trade Commission. In 2000, it was recognized as a high-tech industrialization based under the 863 Program. Years of efforts helped it form an open innovation system featuring "enterprise-university-research institute" cooperation. In 2006, it was chosen as one of the year's "Top 10 Innovative Enterprises" among large and medium-sized industrial enterprises in China.

1) Organizational design of the technological innovation strategy. To organizationally guarantee that its technological innovation could be carried out on a long-term basis, NCPC set up a science & technology committee, which was responsible for making scientific and technological policies and medium-and long-term development plans, for the justification and decision making of major scientific research and technical transformation projects and for the appraisal and rewarding of scientific and technological achievements (Wei Jiang and Wang Yi, 1999). This Science & Technology Committee, the director and deputy director posts of which were held respectively by the board chairman and the president (who also served as director of the enterprise Technology Center), together with the technical consulting, patent and engineering consulting committees, participated in the formulation of technological innovation strategies and the justification of projects, thereby forming a sound technological innovation decision-making system by which to ensure that technological innovation decisions are scientific, leading and correct and to implement them smoothly.

2) Resource expenditure and technological innovation platform building. Since the 1990s, NCPC has invested a big sum of money in R&D and built technological labs and pilot bases up to international standards. In recent years, its expenditure on R&D and technological transformation each year stood between 200 million yuan and 300 million yuan on average, over 4% of its sales income (Chang Xing, 2007). On hardware, the Technology Center currently has more than 1,700 sets of equipment, over 300 imported, including a large number of internationally advanced devices such as LC-MS (liquid chromatography-mass spectrometry), HPCE (high Performance

Capillary electrophoresis), HPLC (high-performance liquid chromatography), HPGC (high performance gas chromatography) and NMR (nuclear magnetic resonance) devices. The most highly equipped among Chinese pharmaceutical enterprises, NCPC has formed a competitive edge in terms of technological platforms for pilot experimentation and industrialization. The following three technological R&D platforms have become the important bases for the group's technological innovation.

The first is the technological platform for high-influx screening of microorganism-derived innovator drugs. This platform has China's largest microbiological culture collection and metabolite collection for the screening of microorganisms used to develop drugs, storing more than 20, 000 cultures and over 30, 000 sample metabolites, and has developed nearly 20 drug screening models. Screening over 100, 000 samples a year, the platform is domestically leading in the field of screening of microorganism-derived new drugs. It has, so far, discovered more than 50 new active compounds, some of which are ones with new structures discovered for the first time in the world and have applied for multiple national patents, involving such fields as tumor resistance, fungus resistance, metabolic regulation, immunoloregulation and antivirus. These compounds are hopeful to be developed into new drugs with independent intellectual property rights.

The second is the technological platform which uses modern biotechnology to reform the traditional industry. This platform currently has been undertaking three national-level technological innovation projects: using modern biotechnology to directly produce 7-ADCA; developing the functional genome of penicillin; and the building, screening and application of high-yield, low-oxygen consuming penicillin cultures. The first project, for which metabolic pathway engineering techniques are employed, has successfully produced the important semi-synthetic cephalosporin intermediate—7-ADCA through the fermentation of penicillium chrysogenum originally used for producing penicillin, and discovered a new metabolic pathway for which a patent application has been filed. The other two projects have also achieved significant results.

The third is the genetic drug research and industrialization platform. In the research field of genetically engineered recombinant protein drugs, NCPC has established a sound R&D technological system, had strong R&D capacity, and formed a domestically leading platform for genetic drug research and industrialization technologies including genetic recombination technology, suspension cell acclimatization and suspension culture technology, and large-scale fermentation, separation and purification technology for protein drugs.

On team building, NCPC has an engineering workforce of more than 2, 000 people. Of them, over a half hold middle-and high-level technical titles; about one third of them are researchers; three are national-level middle-aged and young experts for their outstanding contributions; and 27 are provincial-level outstanding experts. It is a modern/traditional biotechnology workforce that is able to communicate and cooperate with top-notch scientific research organizations both at home and abroad.

NCPC has also built China's first enterprise-level digital technology library for the convenience of information gathering, research, analysis and information sharing during technological innovation. In addition, its R&D bodies at various levels each have an information department staffed by professionals who gather, analyze and provide information of various sorts through multiple methods, such as market survey; salespersons also concurrently undertake the task of market information feedback. Market analysis and justification have become important part of project establishment.

3) Build a technological innovation system that allows for "enterprise-university-research institute" cooperation. Through development over years, NCPC has gradually formed an open-style technological innovation system "which is market-oriented and product-driven and which technologically connects NCPC to universities and research institutes for the purpose of together tackling difficulties involved in projects." This technological innovation system can be divided into three interconnected systems below:

The first is the in-house technological innovation system at three levels: the new drug center undertakes medium and long-term development projects in NCPC's development strategies, as well as lead research, for example, on fundamental platform technologies, developing drugs with independent intellectual property; the business units and subsidiaries conduct development of new products which can be industrialized in a short term; and the workshop labs carry out technological improvement as well as technological innovation activities with involvement of general workers.

The second is the technological innovation system designed to establish "enterprise-university-research institute" cooperation (Tian Lan, 2004). As early as the 1990s, NCPC cooperated respectively with the Chinese Academy of Medical Sciences and Peking University Schools of Basic Medical Sciences and Pharmaceutical Sciences in conducting research on genetic drugs and chemically synthesized drugs. Through project cooperation, its capacity for new drug innovation and new product development was improved rapidly, which set the stage for the research and industrialization of biotech drugs, such as genetically engineered hepatitis B vaccine, erythropoietin, GM-CSF and G-CSF. It has established a great variety of cooperation with more than 40 research institutes and universities such as the CAS, the Chinese Academy of Medical Sciences, the Chinese Academy of Preventive Medicine, the Academy of Military Medical Sciences, Peking University, Tsinghua University, Tianjin University and Yunnan University, carrying out R&D of new products and new technologies together. For example, it cooperated with former Beijing Medical University in the research on genetically engineered drugs and chemically synthesized drugs, and established a laboratory in collaboration with Yunnan University Institute of Microbiology.

The third is the technological innovation system for participating in international technological cooperation and exchange. NCPC's Technology Center has in succession established close partnership with a number of foreign organizations and enterprises, such as Kitasato Institute and Meiji in Japan, Chiron in the United States and Uppsala University in Sweden, carrying out new product R&D, technological cooperation and technology introduction in such aspects as high-flux screening of new drugs, ligand-based drug design, protein drug separation and purification technology, biologically-engineered drug industrialization technology. Its GeneTech Project, designed and built in partnership with foreign companies, is China's first GMP-conforming, largest and top-level bioengineering drug industrialization base. These technological exchange and cooperation has strengthened this Technology Center's superiority in R&D and industrialization of microorganism-derived biotech drugs.

4) Technological innovation brought intellectual property rights and increased the brand value of the enterprise. One can find from the SIPO website that NCPC has 86 patents, 66 of which are patents for invention. In recent years, the contribution of new products and new technologies to the group's development and growth has stayed at more than 30% (Chang Xing, 2007).

In the penicillin deep-processing field, NCPC has become China's largest semi-synthetic penicillin production base. In the vitamin field, it is among the global top 6 VC producers and was China's first enterprise to be able to produce all VB products listed in the pharmacopoeia; it has also introduced a series of plant-extracted products such as soybean isoflavone and lycopene, which are domestically leading in both technology and scale. On biopharmaceutics, NCPC is capable of producing four genetically-engineered products, with "North China" hepatitis B vaccine being the third largest source of supply in China. Its achievements in immunosuppressant are particularly compelling: the sales of its first immunosuppressant product "Tian Ke" (Cyclosporine Soft Capsules) have already exceeded 100 million yuan, and the successful development of follow-up products has made it a domestic enterprise with the largest number of immunosuppressant varieties, the full range of dosage forms and the best comprehensive production and R&D capacity, and the world's sole pharmaceutical enterprise which owns core technologies for the production of the five types of microorganism-derived immunosuppressant—Cyclosporine A, Rapamycin (RAPA), mycophenolate mofetil (MMF), FK506 and Mizoribine. In addition, its achievements in such fields as cardiovascular and cerebrovascular medicine, antineoplastic medicine, pesticides and veterinary medicine are fruitful, which have formed a product structure consisting of long, medium and short-term plans for product research and development. Each year it introduces new products into the market (Gao Lingyun and Wang Qing, 2007).

Continuous technological innovation also manifests in improved production processes and reduced production costs. On production, NCPC has greatly lowered energy consumption through a series of measures, such as process transformation, soft switchover of circulating water and cooling water, menstruum recovery process transformation, cascade water use, and breakdown assessment of energy targets. The implementation of various energy-saving measures, especially technology-enabled ones, has considerably lowered NCPC's comprehensive energy consumption per 10,000 yuan output value. In 2006, its aggregate water, power and gas consumption was reduced by 28%, 2% and 13% respectively compared with 2005, which led to a benefit of over 19 million yuan from energy conservation for the year. These cost-lowering measures have made the brand of NCPC more competitive in the market.

At the same time, the continued investment in technological innovation has brought NCPC a widespread reputation in the pharmaceutical field and greatly increased its brand value. In recent years, the "North China" brand was chosen as one of China's five most valuable industrial brands by Forbes; NCPC received such honors as "Chinese Enterprise of Quality Control Excellence", "Trustworthy Pharmaceutical Enterprise", one of "China Top 10 Credible Enterprises", "Exemplary Enterprise in Ensuring Drug Quality" and "CSR Contribution Award" as a pharmaceutical enterprise; five of its products won the National Quality Product Awards, and 34 varieties were recognized as high-quality products at provincial level or above.

(3) Intellectual Property Management that Serves Technological Innovation

1) Organizational design for intellectual property. At the end of 2000, NCPC officially set up an Intellectual Property Department responsible for the group's intellectual property work, showing that it took a key step towards intellectual property management. NCPC was selected as a national intellectual property pilot enterprise twice, in 2002 and 2004. This Intellectual Property Department is subordinate to the Technology Center (Fig. 1-18), for the purpose of better serving technological innovation. At the same time, NCPC equipped its Marketing Strategy Department and General Affairs Department with an office each, respectively responsible for trademark and trade secret management. Its intellectual property management power is decentralized among three related functional departments, rather than being in the hands of one general department, which is, at the present stage, conducive to the communication and interaction between Technology Center and Intellectual Property Office, Marketing Strategy Department and Trademark Management Office, and General Affairs Department and Secrecy Office and to enhancing their management efficiency.

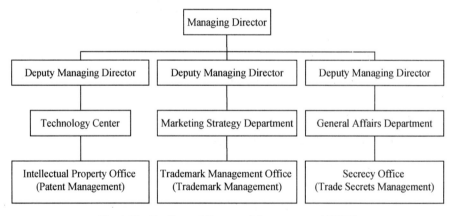

Fig. 1-18 Intellectual Property Management of NCPC

Source: Wang Yongwei, 2007.

2) Design of intellectual property management systems. To better encourage technological innovation activities, NCPC has, by considering its actual conditions and relevant national regulations, formulated a series of management measures in succession. These systems, including "*Patent Management Measures*", "*Trademark and Brand Management Measures*", "*Trade Secrets Management Measures*", "*Scientific and Technological Incentive Management Measures*", "*Technological File Management Measures*", "*Secrecy Management Measures*" and "*New Product and*

Technology R&D Management Measures", provided rules and regulations for the group's intellectual property work, and further standardized its intellectual property management, protection, application and implementation. According to its "*Patent Management Measures"*, for example, after a patent application for a "job-related invention or creation" has been accepted and approved, NCPC will give the inventor or creator a lump-sum reward higher than that specified by the state, depending on the type of the invention or creation—invention, utility model or industrial design; after application of the patent, each year it will, within the valid term of the patent, give the inventor or creator a certain percentage of after-tax profits generated by the invention or creation, depending on the extent to which the invention or creation is applied and on the nature of it—developed independently, on a commission basis or cooperatively; at the same time, the invention or creation can be submitted to apply for the group's Scientific and Technological Achievement Award as required by the "Scientific and Technological Incentive Management Measures", and if approved, it will be rewarded with a separate sum of money.

Intellectual property management also includes managing intellectual property information and inventorying intellectual property. NCPC pays attention to patent information retrieval, so that its R&D starts from a high point. Surrounding its product plans, it searches in a systematic way information and related data on foreign patents that expire within 5 ~ 6 years, involving nearly 300 varieties in a number of fields such as anti-infective drugs, cardiovascular drugs, antineoplastic drugs, diabetes drugs, gastrointestinal drugs and vitamins, including information on their manufacturers, patent status, administrative protection, and registration in China, sorts and analyzes them, and identify types of drugs which have good market prospects and accord with its development plans.

(4) R&D of "Cephalosporin" Facilitated the Transformation and Upgrading of NCPC

In October 2009, NCPC chose the transformation pathway of "cephalosporin" R&D, investing 2 billion yuan in its uppermost project of "cephalosporin" R&D. Because it owns two national-level R&D platforms—a national engineering research center of microbial medicine and a state key laboratory of antibody medicine—and has perfected its technological innovation systems for microorganism-derived and related synthetic and semi-synthetic small molecule drugs and genetically engineered recombinant protein drugs, its pharmaceutical transformation and upgrading is expected to be realized soon. Only one year later, in September 2010, the cephalosporin project was put into production in NCPC's New Park. This project is a new cephalosporin project, which currently has the largest size, most advanced equipment, highest production efficiency and best product quality in China. It is estimated that after put into full operation, each year the project will create eight billion yuan of sales and 1.3 billion yuan of taxes, just like creating another NCPC (Li Shuangfu and Hua Xuan, 2010a, 2010b). NCPC's successful transformation marked another big step towards its goal of becoming an international pharmaceutical enterprise.

(5) Conclusion: Learning from Indian Pharmaceutical Enterprises

NCPC's technological innovation system is an innovation system, in which an enterprise cooperates with universities and research institutes, and it has extended its cooperation into foreign countries to form an R&D network of international cooperation. In this process, its cooperation and exchange with research institutes and universities became frequent, entailing linkage between intellectual property and technological innovation, so that intellectual property issues involved in technological cooperation are dealt with.

However, its pace of technological innovation is not big enough, and the mind has to be further emancipated. For example, its R&D expenditure is only 4% of its sales income, which is much below Tasly's 7% and Xiuzheng's 8.9% and far lower than those of noted foreign pharmaceutical companies. Chinese pharmaceutical enterprises, including NCPC, should learn more, especially in the aspect of international development and capital operation, and become learning enterprises.

Ranbaxy Laboratories Limited (Ranbaxy) is the sole Indian private enterprise that ranks among the world's top 100 pharmaceutical businesses. Its sales income reached 1.7 billion dollars for the financial year ending in the early 2010. Founded in 1962, Ranbaxy has a history of only 38 years. Ranbaxy's (or top 15 Indian pharmaceutical enterprises') experience can be generally described as two points. The first is R&D. Ranbaxy's R&D expenditure is about 16% of its sales income (in the case of NCPC, it is only 4%), part of which is used to hire R&D and management personnel. The second is M&A and internationalization, which requires the availability of professionals in commercial and capital operation who have an international vision. Of course, the Indian government's institutional design has also played an important role, for example, following a relax policy on generic drugs, and allowing drugs approved by the FDA to come into the Indian market without re-doing the clinical trials (Pan Song, 2010).

Compared with Ranbaxy with a history of only 38 years, nearly 60-year-old NCPC has a big gap to be bridged, whether in scale, efficiency or in innovation, especially in international vision as an enterprise. It's also true with Chinese pharmaceutical enterprises including Tasly and Xiuzheng.

2. 4. 6　Innovation Management of Chinese Telecom Equipment Manufacturers

As the number of wideband users grows rapidly, the cost-free VoIP (Voice over Internet Protocol) services on wideband networks pose a challenge to telecom operators' income from traditional voice services, giving telecom operators worldwide the tremendous pressure of shifting business focus. At the same time, thanks to the congenital deficiencies in service quality and security, the increased short-term gain from fast-growing wideband services makes it difficult for operators to find a long-term profitable business model. The international telecom community is crying for a high-tech product that combines all advantages in service quality, security and cost, for the purpose of accomplishing the transition in IP networks from carrying single Internet services to carrying multiple services such as voice, data, video, private lines, 3G and NGN (Next Generation Network). As early as 2005, Huawei Technologies Co. , Ltd. (Huawei) made in Beijing and Paris the global release of its Quidway ME60 Series Multi-Service Control Gateway, the industry's first key product and solution to the IP network transition. It is thus apparent that Huawci has a strong ability to fast respond to and meet market needs through technological innovation.

(1) Huawei's Linkage between "R&D and Services"

Huawei has topped Chinese enterprises for years, both in human and financial resources for R&D. Of its employees, about 46% are R&D personnel, about 33% are service workers, and only 12% are production workers, showing that it is a typical "R&D-service" type enterprise. Its R&D expenditure has stayed at a high level, 10% of its sales income. In 2008, Huawei received the second prize of the National Scientific and Technological Progress Award in recognition of its high-efficiency "R&D-service" linkage over the years.

Although Huawei is quite successful in R&D as a telecom equipment manufacturer, it provides excellent services. On marketing and after-sales services, it has established a global marketing and service network consisting of eight regional headquarters and

55 offices and technical service centers, which are scattered in 15 developed countries in Europe and America, selling its products in more than 90 countries and regions. Its clients include the world's famous operators such as BT, Telefonica, FT, singTel, AIS, MIN and Telemar. It has also established the largest service network in China, which comprises 30 offices as well as service platforms covering more than 300 local networks throughout the country.

Precisely speaking, Huawei's R&D and services are integrated. One example is Huawei's construction of a commercial telecom network for Sunday, a Hong Kong-based telecom company. Hong Kong's geographical environment is quite complex: there are 630 buildings and 250, 000 people per square kilometer, with an average building height of 45 meters, which made the wireless environment so complex that a special scheme was needed for three-dimensional coverage. In the 5. 32-square-kilometer Tung Lo Wan (Causeway Bay), for example, to satisfy the continuous service coverage at a network transmission speed of PS384kbps, the station spacing was set at 50 ~ 350 meters. At the same time, to make Sunday able to meet the tense market competition in Hong Kong, Huawei provided it with the full-range, customized 18 types of 3G services (Portal, PTT, video telephone, video conference, visible email, etc.). Another example is its building of a commercial WCDMA (Wideband Code Division Multiple Access) network for the UAE-based telecom company Etisalat. As the first commercial network of R4 (a type of version) architecture in the world and the first commercial WCDMA network in the Middle East region, it is able to realize seamless roaming and switchover between the three operators, rapidly provide plentiful services (for example, providing monitoring services within one month) as well as networking services, and enable cutover in a week and make phone service available in a month. In the project of building as a contractor a countrywide UMTS (Universal Mobile Telecommunications System) network for Telfort, a Dutch mobile telecommunication company, Huawei provided an R4 architecture-based end-to-end solution, provided sever thousands of base stations covering the whole country, replaced the original core network with a 3G/2G-integrated one within two years, and undertook to provide 3G equipment repair services for a period of nine years (Huawei, 2009).

By the end of 2009, Huawei had joined global 123 industrial standards organizations such as 3GPP, IETF, ITU, OMA, ETSI, IEEE and 3GPP2; submitted 18, 000 proposals in all; served as board members of such authoritative organizations as OMA, IEEE, CCSA, ETSI, ATIS and WiMAX, taking 126 incumbent leadership posts. In 2009, it received the IEEE (Institute of Electrical and Electronic Engineers) Outstanding Contribution Award 2009, the only laureate of the award for the year.

In 2009, Huawei applied for 6, 770 patents, and by the year its patent applications had amounted to 42, 543, including 29, 011 Chinese patent applications, 7, 144 international patent applications and 6, 388 foreign patent applications. According to the World Intellectual Property Organization (WIPO), Huawei was ranked second in the world in 2009 for its international patent applications filed under the PCT. In the LTE/EPC field, Huawei has the world's biggest number of basic (core) patents. [1]

It was because of this that in 2008 Huawei's contract sales registered 23. 3 billion dollars, 75% of which were from overseas businesses (Fig. 1-19) (Huawei, 2009).

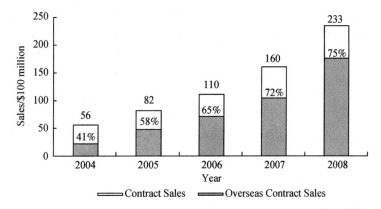

Fig. 1-19   Sales Income of Huawei (2004 ~ 2008)
Source: http://www. huawei. com.

Huawei is a multinational company with a number of R&D centers abroad. Whether an M&A strategy or alliance strategy should be adopted for its further development is a question about business organization innovation. It is also a major difficulty facing Chinese enterprises after swelling. In the telecom field, the relationship between manufacturers and operators is quite balanced in developed countries, but in China the former are usually subjected to the latter. In recent years, such telecom manufacturers as Huawei, ZTE and DTT have been expanding, so the situation has changed to a certain extent. In terms of organization innovation, these telecom companies may learn from US companies, such as Microsoft and Qualcomm.

Microsoft, though capable of purchasing any telecom operator, cooperates with

---

[1]   http://www. huawei. com.

them in the form of strategic alliance, incorporating its services into those of operators. On Microsoft TV geared towards radio & TV enterprises, Microsoft's services and products are provided in three options: first, it only provides equipment products which, after purchased, are installed by users themselves; second, it provides both products and integrated services which enable plug and play and allow users to play their own contents on their networks; and third, it provides the full range of solutions covering equipment, integration and contents, cooperates with clients in publicity and implementation, and shares profits with them. The DT-SCDMA (Time Division-Synchronous Code Division Multiple Access) standard, which has been raised by China's DTT, remains a weaker one among the three 3G international standards, because DTT could hardly control the value chain of the industry. Like Microsoft, Qualcomm, an up-and-coming young player in the US mobile market, has not only had mastery of the core technologies of CDMA (Code Division Multiple Access), but also made the CDMA standard an important part of the mobile communications value chain as mobile communications rose globally. By adopting a technological development strategy like Microsoft's, Qualcomm has built what is called BREW (Binary Runtime Environment for Wireless) and a platform for its mobile application. Like Microsoft does in wideband and radio & TV fields, Qualcomm offers the full range of solutions in the mobile communications field, ranging from technologies, services to outsourced operation. In the field of mobile games, it built a BREW-based game service platform for Verizon, the largest wireless operator in the United States, and is responsible for the operation of the platform and for cooperation with game providers and related management and promotion. Its cooperation with Verizon is exclusive and based on profit sharing; this model has, so far, been one of the most successful in the mobile game field. It is appropriate to say that Qualcomm has turned itself into half an operator and, because it owns customer resources and offers the cooperation model, is hopeful of surpassing Verizon in position (Wang Yuquan, 2005).

Although China's Huawei and ZTE have not yet extended their business into the service field as Microsoft and Qualcomm did, they have already had such strength and potentials.

(2) R&D and Marketing Services

The emerging R&D results in the telecom field in recent years have brought about a great influence and even impact on telecom markets and services, so some even believe that telecom technology has already been superfluous. The prevailing view in the telecom community, however, is that telecom technology is far from being superfluous and the problem is about changing the marketing models, making it geared towards market needs. For example, China Unicom previously technically divided its client bases by C and G networks, but now makes different marketing plans according to its client bases. Selling songs in records and the downloading of them as coloring ring back tones are two different modes of marketing; there were five million downloads in the first half of 2005 alone, the sales of which, if calculated at two yuan per download, would be 10 million yuan, equivalent to that of selling 600, 000 pieces of records (China Association of Communications Enterprises, 2005).

A new development model has thus emerged, that is, applying technological innovation results to the convergence of fixed and mobile phones. There is a symbiotic, rather than either-or, relationship between fixed and mobile phones. In July 2004, Korea Telecom, Japanese NTT, Swisscom, Brazil Telecom and Canadian Rogers Communications founded the Fixed-Mobile Convergence Alliance (FMCA), in the hope of developing a technological platform, by which to promote the convergence of fixed and mobile services. As early as 2003, as a matter of fact, "Yi Hao Tong" (All in One Number) introduced to the Chinese telecom market was just a type of "fix-mobile convergence. " With this service, a subscriber could use a bundled number as both his/her fix and mobile phone numbers and set the order of receiving calls as he/she wished. When the caller dialed this bundled number, the intelligent network could switch it to the set fixed or mobile phone, and the user could at any time choose either phone to receive the call; if the first number were not answered, the intelligent network would automatically switch it to the second or third number.

We can tell from the above analysis that China's leading telecom enterprises are not left far behind by their foreign counterparts in terms of "linkage between R&D and marketing services. "

2. 4. 7 Innovation Management of Chinese Telecom Service Enterprises

As early as the 1970s, the development of information and communications technology (ICT) changed the intension and extension of traditional service industries. In the 1980s, the development and application of Internet technologies, especially the fusion of computer, communications and Internet technologies, gave rise to revolutionary changes in service activities and industries, which led to the emergence of new service industries and modern service enterprises like "Knowledge Intensive Business Services" (KIBS) and "modern service industries."

Below is a detailed analysis of one of the features of modern service industries or KIBS: the close linkage between R&D and service activities.

(1) Close Linkage between R&D and Service Activities

"Modern service industries" are such service industries that rely on high technologies and modern management approaches, business modes and organizational forms and primarily provide producers with intermediate input with intensive application of knowledge, technology and information, as well as those developing from traditional service industries through technological and business model upgrading (Xia Jiechang et al., 2008). They are characterized by "three news" (new technology, new form and new mode) and "three highs" (high human capital, high technology and high added value) (Zhou Zhenhua, 2005). Modern service industries mainly include such industries as finance, information, telecommunications, scientific and technological services, and business services. One of the features of such industries, KIBS or "Knowledge Intensive Service Activities" (KISA) is the close linkage between their R&D and service activities.

As far as the telecom industry is concerned, the development and evolvement of the mobile communications industry is a complex process, involving many roles such as users, service providers, network operators and equipment manufacturers. Because of their different interests in the process, these roles have different stances and needs as to the development and evolvement of the mobile communications industry, and there are complex relations and cooperation between them which cannot be expressed in a simple form of interaction (Fig. 1-20). With mobile communications developing from 2G to 3G, the industrial model is becoming increasingly complex. A research on the complex relations from the linkage perspective is of great significance for understanding the development laws of the industry and helping mobile communications enterprises make their development strategies.

(2) Reorganization in the Chinese Telecom Service Market

China's telecom industry was monopolized by the former Ministry of Posts & Telecommunications until 1980 when the state relaxed its control over prices and provided financially preferential policies. As China Unicom was founded in 1994, the country's telecom industry entered a stage of competition between two telecom oligarchs—China Unicom and China Telecom. After the Ministry of Information

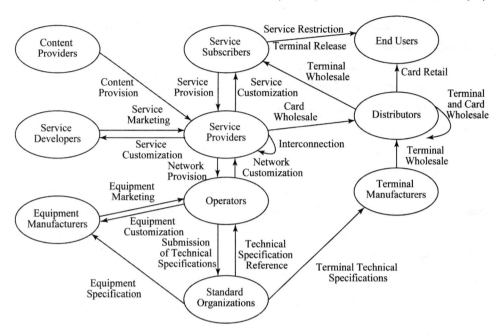

Fig. 1-20　The Complex Linkage in the Telecom Industry

Source: Liao Jianxin, 2006.

Industry was founded in 1998, China Telecom was split into four parts—fixed phone service, mobile phone service, paging service and satellite communications service, and the paging service was merged into China Unicom. In other words, the former China Telecom was broken down into three companies, China Telecom (engaging mainly in the fixed phone service), China Mobile and China Satellite Communications. In addition, to intensify competition, telecom authorities issued three telecom operation licenses, which were acquired by China Netcom, Jitong Communications and China Railcom. In 2002, a new round of market reorganizations began in the telecom industry, leading to the formation of a new China Netcom consisting the part of China Telecom north of the Yangtze River (covering 10 provinces in northern China), China Netcom and Jitong Communications, and a new China Telecom made up of the part of former China Telecom along and south of the Yangtze River (covering 21 provinces, autonomous regions, and municipalities in southern and northwest China). A "5 + 1" market pattern was thus formed: China Telecom, China Mobile, China Netcom, China Unicome, China Railcom, plus China Satellite Communications. Afterwards, to conform to the development of new technologies, telecom operators were integrated once again, forming three operators: China Telecom, China Mobile and China Unicom.

As the industrial entities were reorganized, the wide application of computer technologies and the rapid development of optical fiber communications and large scale integrated circuits brought about profound changes to the telecom industry: communication costs were greatly lowered and user demands continued to increase, leading to the change of the telecom industry from previously an industry with meager profits and even permitted policy-related losses to one with a very high input-output ratio. With increasing telecom service innovations, various new telecom services and value added services were promoted, which further stimulated market needs. On this basis, China's telecom industry saw a continued, rapid and healthy development, growing at a rate 2 ~ 3 times that of GDP over the past 10 years and the number of fixed phone subscribers has grown substantially, creating a miracle in the world. Development of the Chinese telecom market, since 2000, is shown in Table 1-12 below.

Table 1-12   China's Telecom Market between 2000 and 2008

Year \ Indicator	2000	2001	2002	2003	2004	2005	2006	2007	2008
Service income/ 100 million yuan	3 408.6	4 149.8	4 115.82	4 610	5 187.6	5 799	6 483.8	8 051.6	8 139.9
Sum of investments in fixed assets used/100 million yuan			2 034.57	2 215.2	2 136.5	2 033.4	2 186.9	2 279.9	2 953.7
Fixed phone subscribers/10,000 subscribers			21 441.9	26 330.5	31 244.3	35 043.3	36 781.2	36 545	34 080.4
Mobile phone subscribers/ 10,000 subscribers			20 661.6	26 869.3	33 482.4	39 342.8	46 108.2	54 729	64 123
Mobile Internet users/10,000 sub.							13 809.4	15 026	25 392.5
Mobile SMS/ 100 million pieces					2 177.6	3 046.5	4 296.7	5 921	6 997
Fixed phone penetration/%	20.1	25.9	33.74	21.2	24.9	27	28.1	27.8	25.8
Mobile phone penetration/%	6.77	11.44	16.19	20.9	25.9	30.3	35.3	41.6	48.5

Source: Based on 2008 data from the Ministry of Industry and Information Technology of China.

1) Mobile subscribers gradually superseded fixed line subscribers. The number of mobile phone subscribers reached a growth rate up to 30% and exceeded that of fixed phone subscribers in 2003; from 2004 to 2008, the number of mobile phone subscribers grew at 25%, 17.5%, 17.2%, 18.7% and 17.2% respectively. The substitution of mobile communications slowed down the growth of fixed-line subscribers. In fact, the growth of fixed-line subscribers tended to slow from 2000 on, particularly after 2003 when there was a rapid increase of 48.52 million subscribers. That is because the fixed phone service development tended to be saturated in urban areas and no universal service mechanism was established in rural areas, and more importantly because of the substitution of mobile phones (including the personal handy-phone system). After 2006, the penetration of fixed phones began sliding down, suggesting that the industry's focus was gradually shifting to the mobile field (Fig. 1-21).

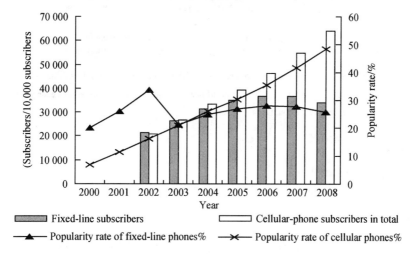

Fig. 1-21   Development of Fixed and Mobile Phone Subscribers in China between 2000 and 2008

Source: According to the data of 2008 from the Ministry of Industry and Information Technology of the People's Republic of China.

2) Internet and data service products boosted the growth of telecom income. From 2002 to 2008, the aggregate income of China's telecom industry grew-0.8%, 12.0%, 12.5%, 11.8%, 11.8%, 24.2% and 1.1% respectively. Following a brief slowdown in 2002, the industry's growth rate stayed at about 12%, which was greater than that of GDP (Fig. 1-22).

3) Service innovation increased the value per subscriber. It is noticeable from a brief estimate that the industry's income per subscriber, on average, slowly sided down

from 2000 on, until an increase in 2006 supported by SMS (short message service) and Internet service products (Fig. 1-23). In addition to voice, SMS and Internet services have grown rapidly in last few years, becoming a popular means of communications and playing an active role in improving the user value of mobile networks.

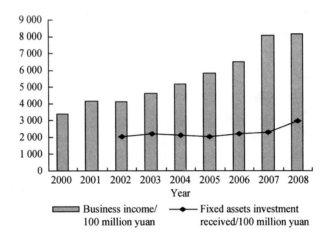

Fig. 1-22　Income and investment of the telecom industry in China

Source: According to the data of 2008 from Ministry of Industry and Information Technology of the People's Republic of China.

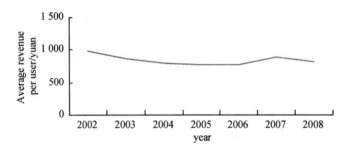

Fig. 1-23　Average revenue per user of China's telecom industry

Source: According to the data of 2008 from Ministry of Industry and Information Technology of the People's Republic of China.

Mobile communication is currently in a growth period in China and telecom business composition experiences changes, as data and multimedia services (data services for short) are rising (see Fig. 1-24). In particular, the rapid development of data services will make up for the slowing down of telephone service, which can guarantee a relatively high growth rate of China's telecom industry in quite a long time. How to lock subscribers has long been a core task for all the telecom operators in market competition, while increasing customer value via service innovation plays a crucial role in enhancing operators' competitiveness.

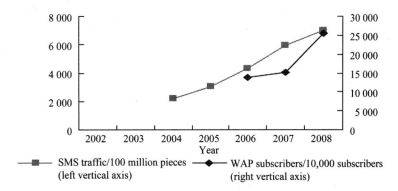

SMS traffic/100 million pieces (left vertical axis)   WAP subscribers/10,000 subscribers (right vertical axis)

Fig. 1-24   Development of SMS and WAP services of China's telecom industry

Source: According to the data of 2008 from Ministry of Industry and Information Technology of the People's Republic of China.

(3) Evolution of telecom technology and standards

Technology standards are commonly classified into statutory standards and de facto standards, while the latter are sub-classified into monopolistic model and alliance model. Monopolistic model features that enterprises do not pursue standardization sedulously and owner, director and user of the standards fall into the same one; while under alliance model, owner, director and user of the standards are separate parties. Alliance model standards are further divided into open and closed ones. Open standards can be authorized, licensed and open to those outside an alliance, an example of which is the Intelligent Grouping and Resource Sharing (IRGS) standard initiated by Lenovo, TCL, Konka, Hisense and Great Wall Computer Group, constituted by Chinese enterprises, and accessible for all qualified enterprises upon application.

TD-SCDMA (hereinafter as TD for short) standard is a 3G international standard, to which China owns the proprietary intellectual property rights. With years' research, development and experiments, a TD industry chain has taken shape and is getting mature. The development of TD plays a significant role in the independent innovation in China's telecom industry, as the patented core technology owned by Chinese enterprises provides precious opportunities for domestic enterprises to get involved at the high-end of the telecom industry chain and compete in the global market. During the development of TD technology, the Chinese telecom manufacturers contribute much more than before, as shown in Table 1-13.

Table 1-13 Patents Owned by Chinese enterprises under TD-SCDMA Standard

Name	No. of patents	Ratio/%	Name	No. of patents	Ratio/%
ZTE Corporation	116	24.9	Shanghai AGIT Communications Tech. Co. , Ltd.	18	3.9
Datang Mobile Communications Equipment Co. , Ltd.	39	8.4	Kaiming IT Co. , Ltd.	16	3.4
Comba Telecom Systems (Guangzhou) Co. , Ltd.	26	5.6	Chongqing Chongyou IT (Group) Co. , Ltd.	12	2.6
Spreadtrum Communications (Shanghai) Co. , Ltd.	20	4.3	Zhejiang Holleycomm Group Co. , Ltd.	12	2.6
Siemens China	19	4.1	Huawei	11	2.4
ST-Ericsson	19	4.1	Others	158	33.9

Source: According to Patent Database of State Intellectual Property Office (SIPO) of the People's Republic of China.

Seen from the development of international mainstream 3G standard, WCDMA and CDMA2000 systems have taken the lead of TD. By September 2007, there had been 189 WCDMA commercial networks operated in 80 countries, with 139 million subscribers, and 84 CDMA2000 Ev-Do networks with 76.73 million subscribers. In the fierce market competition, it is necessary for Chinese telecom enterprises to enhance their technological capacities, develop service innovation, speed up for marketization, and guarantee the industrialization and commercialization of TD standard.

(4) Composition of innovation system of China's telecom industry

The major elements composed of the innovation system of telecom industry, such as operators, manufacturers, government organs, research institutes, financial institutions and subscribers, keep interacting with one another to promote the optimization and upgrade of the industry, thus have clear system characteristics. Innovations are created in the linkage and interaction of the elements (see Fig. 1-25).

Chinese telecom enterprises can be roughly divided into two groups: telecom equipment manufacturers and telecom services operators. The former belongs to manufacturing industry, and the latter modern service trade.

1) Telecom equipment manufacturers. Communication equipment manufacturers include those for network equipment, switching equipment and terminal equipment, as well as for other communication equipment. Communication network equipment manufacturers are engaged in development and manufacture of wire or wireless

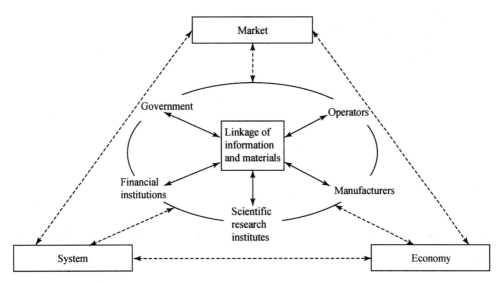

Fig. 1-25 Model of innovation system of China's telecom industry
Source: Zhou Jizhong et al. , 2009a.

transmission facilities. Switching equipment manufacturers mainly develop and produce circuit switching and interface devices, and terminal equipment manufacturers for the development and production of electrophones and radio telephones.

In one word, what equipment manufacturers do is to develop products, manufacture hardware, write software code, sell their products to operators, and provide pre-and after-sale services.

There had been 1,224 telecom manufacturers in China by 2006. As shown by data analysis, the total industrial output value of China's telecom industry had increased from 352.33 billion yuan in 2003 to 728.41 billion yuan in 2006, with an average annual growth rate as high as 27.3%. Nonetheless, the figure was still lower than the average growth rate of 29.2% for the whole manufacturing industry. As far as the product mix concerned, however, the output of China's telecom manufacture is mainly from the production of terminal devices, while the manufacture of communication switching and network equipment still remains at a relatively low level (see Fig. 1-26).

In the development of China's telecom industry, manufacturers play a major role in technological innovation. According to the statistics in *China Electronics Yearbook 2005*, the major domestic telecom equipment manufacturers had achieved a R&D intensity (i.e. the ratio of R&D expenses to sales revenue) of about 7%.

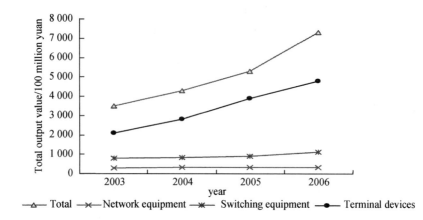

Fig. 1-26　Total industrial output value of China's telecom equipment manufacturing, 2003 ~ 2006

Source: National Bureau of Statistics of China et al. , 2007.

Nevertheless, the development of technological capacities of domestic telecom enterprises is unbalanced, with the majority having not that strong R&D capacity, except for few like Huawei and ZTE (see Table 1-14).

Table 1-14　Some technological indicators for China's telecom equipment manufacturing, 2006

Item	Percentage of R&D staff/%	R&D intensity/%	Percentage of technological transformation funds/%	Percentage of funds assimilated /%	Rate of sales of new products/%	Rate of export sales of new products/%
Hi-tech industry	2.54	1.10	0.41	14.00	19.84	40.51
Telecom equipment manufacturing	7.71	1.79	0.15	5.40	24.16	27.22
Network equipment	6.46	3.46	1.75	26.33	16.56	17.33
Switching equipment	33.85	7.19	0.06	0.92	42.60	34.39
Fixed terminals	2.93	0.77	0.28	7.56	12.83	62.89
Mobile terminals	1.56	0.43	0.07	5.15	21.19	21.58

Source: National Bureau of Statistics of China et al. , 2007.

R&D by manufacturers is an ordered process of cooperation, beginning from marketing and technological departments, both of which cooperate to fix opportunities for marketing and technology and decide based on the market analysis whether the products to be developed can meet users' demands. Afterwards, sales department will make feasibility analysis concerned, followed by product design by a development team consisting of both sales and technical staff. Finally, sales staff have direct contact with users and collect feedbacks from them to help technical staff improve the product design to users' satisfaction.

2) Telecom operators. The core task of telecom operators is to communicate with users and pass on information. Operators take responsibility for the physical transmission of information between users, including the integrity of information data transmitted.

Part of modern service trade, telecom operators feature in "3H", namely, high level of knowledge (including both technology and experience): The products of modern service enterprises are also involved in technological innovation in manufacturing enterprises, as these products are "knowledge-intensive"; high degree of linkage: Telecom operators not only often take part or are involved in innovation process of manufacturing enterprises, but also have all-channel linkage with other major elements of the innovation system, such as government departments, financial institutions, intermediaries, universities and scientific research institutes; high-level innovation: Besides the technological innovation that distinguish telecom operators from telecom manufacturers, the former also conducts system innovation, organizational innovation (e. g. the restructuring of China Telecom, China Unicom and China Mobile) and cultural innovation.

As the 3G has become the mainstream technology since 2008, a tripartite competition formed between Chinese telecom operators after series of mergers (see Fig. 1-27). The three competitors are China Telecom, China Mobile and China Unicom (New Unicom).

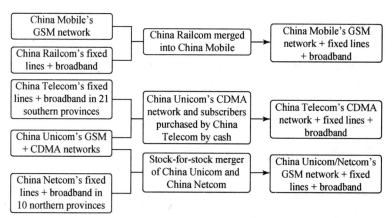

Fig. 1-27   Mergers of operators

Source: UBS, 2008.

After the merger, China Mobile is engaged in GSM network, fixed lines and broadband, and has obtained 3G TD-SCDMA license. In addition to its original fixed line business, China Telecom has taken over China Unicom's CDMA services and obtained 3G CDMA2000 license. And China Unicom was allowed to run businesses in fields of fixed lines and broadband, besides GSM network services, and has obtained 3G WCDMA license. Among the three, China Mobile takes comparatively large share of the market (see Fig. 1-28) (Zhou Jizhong et al. , 2009a).

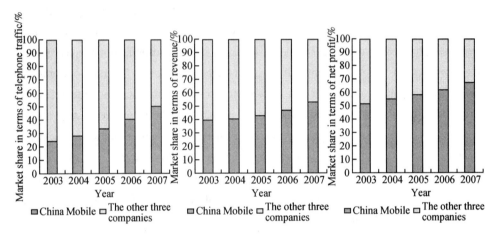

Fig. 1-28 Market share taken by China Mobile

Source: UBS, restructuring of China's telecom industry, 2008.

(5) Conclusion: learning from Indian IT enterprises

It has been less than 20 years since the foundation of India's Infosys Technologies Limited (hereinafter as Infosys for short) in 1981, which has 100,000 employees now. With a market value of over 10 billion US dollars, Infosys is the largest listed software company in India, as well as the first Indian enterprise that has been listed on NASDAQ in the United States. Its "Global Delivery Model (GDM)" enables it not only to obtain a large number of outsourcing orders, but also attract many talents both from the world. What Chinese IT enterprises shall learn from their Indian counterparts such as Infosys is to increase R&D expenses and employ high-level technical and managerial talents, as well as to work out international development strategies, so that they can make mergers in cooperation with foreign IT enterprises. As for government, it shall create a more relaxed environment for the development of domestic IT enterprises (Pan Song, 2010).

While learning from their Indian counterparts, Chinese IT enterprises shall grasp the opportunity of industrial development, namely, the "integration of three networks" (i. e. the convergence of broadcasting network, telecom network and

Internet, with Internet as the core) and "the Internet of things" (i. e. applications converging perceptive and identification technology and ubiquitous computing and network. The Internet of things is known as the third wave of development in the world's IT industry, after computers and Internet).

2.4.8   Service innovation of China's commercial banks

As information technology develops, financial service industry is getting more active in innovation. Financial institutions conducting innovation account for 58%, higher than 54% in manufacturing and the average one of 46% for modern service trade (Miles, 2000). Nonetheless, it should be noted that the innovation in banking is quite different from that in manufacturing, particularly the innovation of finance derivatives. Otherwise, these derivatives such as "mortgage-backed securities" and "subprime mortgage" that had been products of "financial innovation" in the United States finally caused the ongoing financial crisis.

Guide to Financial Innovation in Commercial Banks issued by China Banking Regulatory Commission (CBRC) on 6 December, 2006 defines the financial innovation in commercial banks, "Financial innovation refers to all innovative activities regarding strategic decisions, institutional arrangements, organizational setup, personnel preparation, management models, business process and financial products launched by commercial banks, by introducing new technology, adopting new methods, opening up new market and structuring new organizations, to adapt to economic development. The ultimate goals are to enhance risk management capabilities of commercial banks and provide customers with innovative and upgraded service products and modes." Financial innovation in a narrow sense mainly means the innovation of products such as financial instruments and services. The financial innovation in common use is in the narrow sense.

The "service innovation of commercial banks" is the same as the aforementioned concept of financial innovation in the narrow sense.

(1) Features of service innovation of commercial banks

As an integral part of modern service trade, commercial banks have some features distinguishing them from manufacturing enterprises. It is with these features that the law of service innovation activities of commercial banks can be well understood.

First of all, lots of financial innovation activities do not provide new products, but only change, add on or cut down some features of the existing financial products.

Secondly, the innovation activities in manufacturing enterprises are aimed at the maximum profits, while those of commercial banks have to give consideration to profitability, safety and liquidity, all the three of which are not necessarily positively correlated, but are substitutes to each other instead. Generally, the more profitable a financial product is, the weaker its safety and liquidity become. Therefore, the ultimate goal of a commercial bank is not the maximization of profit, but the best mix of profit, safety and liquidity, or rather, the maximum profit with secured safety and liquidity.

Thirdly, in the analysis of innovation decisions in a manufacturing enterprise, the decisions of innovation and new products are presumed to be irreversible; but in service innovation of commercial banks, a bank will not face too high "sunk cost" (retrospective cost that has already been incurred and cannot be recovered, such as time, money, etc.) if the innovation is withdrawn from or stopped in a non-profitable business area. That is the reason why innovative products and services can be fast developed in banking.

Fourthly, in quite a number of R&D competition models in manufacturing, one important assumption implied is the strong patent protection (that results in market monopolization in a rather long time, so that imitations can be rooted out). Monopolistic period long enough must be guaranteed for any innovation, to compensate for the costs of development of a new product. However, new financial products are easily imitated, which is a distinct feature of service innovation in commercial banks, therefore, there are few patent applications for such products.

Fifthly, compared with other industries, financial service industry, including commercial banks, provides the society with currencies, capitals or financial instruments, instead of ordinary products. Such special products can circulate in commodity consumption as universal equivalent or by transforming into general purchasing power quickly. Therefore, financial service industry, including commercial banks, has a special and significant influence. Moreover, the relationship between a bank and its customers is not a simple buyer-supplier one for commodities, but a credit relationship with loans as the core, which, unlike ordinary buyer-supplier relationship for commodities, is two-way communication or multi-link operation instead of the unidirectional and single-link operation in businesses, with intervals in such communication and operation, thus producting possibility of financial risks. These two features bring the financial service industry both high risks and great influence. Consequently, the regulation of this industry in many countries is often stricter than that of other industries; therefore, the threshold for entering the industry is quite high, and on the other hand, financial service provider pay major attention to government supervision when they launch innovation activities.

(2) Process of service innovation in commercial banks in China

The current bank system in China was not established until the reform and opening-up in the late 1970s. Before 1984, the People's Bank of China (PBC) had functioned as the central bank on the one hand, and operated deposit and loan businesses as well, while state-owned banks had been only subordinate institutions under the central bank. In 1983, the State Council decided to keep PBS's functions as the central bank only, and set up Industrial and Commercial Bank of China (ICBC) in 1984 to operate commercial businesses. Since then, the state-owned banks have begun to be transformed to commercial banks. It is the system innovation in China's banking since the reform and opening-up that has propelled the service innovation in commercial banks in China.

To well meet the challenge from foreign banks and enhance the competitiveness of Chinese banks after China's entry into WTO, the Chinese Government has in the new century intensified financial reform, launching shareholding reform in state-owned commercial banks, vigorously bringing in strategic investors and improving corporate governance of state-owned commercial banks, so as to enhance the independent innovation and risk resistance capabilities of these banks. With re-orientation, Chinese commercial banks have made changes in talent pooling, organizational setup and alike, giving true meanings to the development of banking services. Meanwhile, the government has also accelerated the marketization of interest rates and foreign exchange rates and unveiled regulations and policies to encourage commercial banks to speed up the innovation in financial businesses. Chinese banks have saw the material base and business opportunities for their innovative products and services in the lasting and robust economic development in China, and in the constant improvement of socialist market economy and financial market that gets maturer.

Service innovation in Chinese commercial banks has roughly gone through four stages since the 1980s (see Table 1-15) and innovative products of banking services have emerged in endless stream (see Table 1-16).

Table 1-15　Evolution of service innovation in Chinese commercial banks

Stage	Bank management system	Banking system	Evolution of banking services
Before 1984	Establishment of central bank system, financial management system	People's Bank of China	Conventional services of deposits, loans, collection and settlement; manually

Continued

Stage	Bank management system	Banking system	Evolution of banking services
1985 ~ 1995	Developing financial market, enhancing macro-control in finance, and adopting new technology	People's Bank of China Specialized banks Credit cooperatives	No significant changes in deposit and loan products; emergence of bank cards; bank drafts, cashier's cheques and bank cheques as main settlement means; more products of settlement; emergence of e-services
1995 ~ 2000	Multi-dimensional opening-up of financial market, speeding up the transformation from state-owned specialized banks to commercial banks	Establishment of three policy banks, transformation of specialized banks to commercial banks, and emergence of joint-stock commercial banks	Increase of credit products; discounting of bill and consumer credit available on market; deposits as the major liability product; launch of all-round international services; prosperous bank card business; popularized e-services; deposits and withdrawals processed at any branch bank; emergence of online banking
2000 up to now	Intensification of reform on structure of property rights in banks; loosened financial control; all-round opening-up of financial market; significant marketization of interest rates and foreign exchange rates	Coexistence of policy banks, state-controlling banks, cooperative banks, joint-stock banks and foreign banks	White-hot competition between profitable deposit-loan products; fierce competition between bank card and agent services as the services are charged; derivatives such as asset-backed securities and swap service that have become new tendencies; development of mix products such as bancassurance and bank securities, as well as of financial products; e-banking services with online banking as the representative that has become a must-have

Source: http://www.cqbanker.com/admin/uploadimages/200611131502612919.doc.

Table 1-16   Overview of major service innovations in Chinese commercial banks (1980 ~ 2007)

Product name		Year	Note to organizations and products
(Ⅰ) Savings and deposits (liability businesses)	Housing savings	1984	Industrial and Commercial Bank of China (hereinafter as ICBC for short)
	Cheque savings	1985	ICBC Shanghai Branch
	Premium savings	1985	ICBC
	Savings on durable consumer items	1985	ICBC
	Pension savings	1985	Agricultural Bank of China (hereinafter as ABC for short)
	Savings on traveller's cheque	1986	ABC

Continued

Product name	Year	Note to organizations and products
(I) Savings and deposits (liability businesses) Savings on retirement pay	1986	ABC
Savings on employees' insurance fund for collective enterprises	1986	ABC
Fixed deposits	1986	Large-denomination time deposits launched by Bank of China (hereinafter as BOC for short) in 1987
Deposits and withdrawals processed at any branch bank	1988	BOC Shenzhen Branch
Indexed deposits	1988	PBC decided on 10 September 1988 to launch indexed deposits for the 3-year-and-above fixed deposits, and announced on 17 November 1991 to stop the service; PBC decided again on 11 July 1993 to launch indexed deposits for the 3-year-and-above fixed deposits, and announced on 1 April 1996 to stop the service
Notice deposits	1988	China Merchants Bank (hereinafter as CMB for short)
Agreement savings	1988	China CITIC Bank
Deposit-to-loan savings	1993	ABC
Fixed-current account	1996	ICBC
All-in-one account for RMB and foreign currencies	1996	ICBC
Education deposits	1999	ICBC
(II) Credit businesses (asset businesses) Discount of commercial paper	1981	First trial in China for intra-city discount of commercial acceptance bill and off-site discount of bank's acceptance bill by PBC Shanghai Branch in 1981
Personal housing loans	1983	ICBC, coupled with housing savings
Outward documentary bill	1985	Outward documentary bill with L/C service launched by BOC in 1985; *Outward Documentary Bill Insurance Agreement* signed by China CITIC Bank and the People's Insurance Company (Group) of China (PICC) in July 1993, under which financing is provided for export enterprises based upon export credit insurance

Continued

	Product name	Year	Note to organizations and products
	Discount of usance bill with L/C	1985	BOC
	Mortgage loans	1985	BOC
	International syndicated loans	1986	BOC
	Collacteral loans	1986	Bank of Communications (hereinafter as BO-COM for short) ; also launched by ICBC in 1987
	Foreign exchange for RMB loans	1986	*Provisional Measures Concerning the Mortgage by Enterprises with Foreign Investment of Foreign Exchange for Renminbi Loans* issued by PBC in 1986
(II) Credit businesses (asset businesses)	Student loans	1986	ICBC
	Buyer's credit	1987	BOC
	Personal housing mortgage loan	1991	China Construction Bank (hereinafter as CCB for short)
	Time certificate of deposits for mortgage petty loans	1993	BOC
	Personal car loans	1995	CCB
	Stock collacteral loans	2000	*Regulations for Stock Collacteral Loans of Security Companies* co-issued by PBC and China Securities Regulatory Commission (CSRC) in February 2000
	Personal comprehensive loans	2000	China Everbright Bank (hereinafter as CEB for short)
	Trust and lease	1979	BOC
	Letter of Guarantee (L/G)	1980	CCB
	Acceptance/discount of commercial paper	1981	PBC
(III) Intermediary businesses	Agency service for foreign exchange trading	1982	BOC
	Agency service for bond issuance	1985	CCB
	Forward exchange trading	1985	BOC
	Agency service for forward exchange transactions	1985	BOC, agency service for forward exchange trading of the existing foreign trade contracts
	Investment consulting	1987	CCB
	Foreign exchange options/bonds/futures/options	1987	China CITIC Bank

Continued

Product name	Year	Note to organizations and products
		Currency swaps	1988	China CITIC Bank
Revolving underwriting facility (RUF)/note issuance facilities (NIFs)	1988	BOC
Forward rate agreement (FRA)	1988	BOC
Personal cheques	1985	Self-employed enterpreneurs have been allowed to use cheques only for account since 1985, and the service for settlement by savings cheque was opened for certain depositors; PBC, ICBC and ABC co-issued *Notice to Implementation and Trial Implementation of Cheque Clearance by Self-employed Enterpreneurs and Individuals* in January 1986; there was still service for domestic settlement; ICBC launched service for fixed bill and opened service for personal remittance in 1986 and ICBC cashier's cheques first came into use in 1999
Current deposits and withdrawals processed at any off-site branch bank	1986	ICBC
Intermediary services and other middleman businesses	1987	CCB began agency payment of salary in 1987; ICBC opened services such as agency payment and cash collection, agency custody, asset assessment, guarantee and attestation, consulting and advising in 1992; agency services began to expand in 1992, with cooperative services for bancassurance and bank securities opened; agreement for agency insurance signed between PICC and ICBC, ABC, BOC and CCB in May 1992 and the extensive launch of bank securities transfer service in 1999
Leveraged lease	1987	China International Trust and Investment Corporation (CITIC) started rental lease and financial leasing in 1980 and arranged for and was involved in the leveraged lease of LH 100-30 carrier for Civil Aviation Administration of China (CAAC) in December 1987
Agency management of capital	1989	China CITIC Bank

The left side of the table is labeled: (Ⅲ) Intermediary businesses

163

Continued

	Product name	Year	Note to organizations and products
	Agency cash collection	1989	ICBC Shenzhen Branch
	Offshore businesses	1992	BOC
	Repurchase agreement	1992	ICBC
	International agency accommodation line	1992	BOC
	Import L/C credit facility	1993	BOC Shanghai Branch
	Personal foreign exchange trading	1993	BOC Guangzhou Branch; telephone-commissioned trading launched by BOCOM Shanghai Branch in 1996
	International factoring	1993	BOC
	Merchant banking	1994	CMB
(Ⅲ) Intermediary businesses	Immediate payment of money gram	1994	Under the agreement for immediate payment of money gram signed by China CITIC Bank and American Express, a remittance less than 3,000 dollars can be received in 10 minutes; with BOG GLOBAL NICS, BOC opened "one-day overseas remittance" service in 1998
	Long cards/debit cards/third-party collection/all-in-one/bank-securities cards	1995	CCB
	Domestic factoring	1999	BOC, purchasing customers' receivables on open account in domestic trades
	Acceptance bill repurchase	2001	ABC
	Fixed-term-and-amount investment	2002	BOCOM
	Corporation overdraft	2002	ICBC
	Standard warehouse receipt pledge financing	2002	CCB
	Personal trust loans	2002	China Minsheng Banking Corp. Ltd (hereinafter as Minsheng for short)
	Credit asset transfers	2002	Minsheng
	Cooperation agreement for trade financing under export insurance	2003	China CITIC Bank and China Export & Credit Insurance Corporation signed a cooperation agreement for trade financing under export insurance on 29 May 2003 in Beijing
	RMB wealth management products	2004	CEB

Continued

	Product name	Year	Note to organizations and products
(Ⅲ) Intermediary businesses	Structural wealth management products	2004	Minsheng
(Ⅳ) Bank cards	RMB cards	1985	BOC Credit Card issued by BOC Zhuhai Branch in 1985 has been the first credit card issued in China
	Credit cards	1985	BOC Zhuhai Branch
	RMB debit cards	1987	BOC issued Great Wall RMB Credit Card in 1987; there emerged the centrally-controlled debit cards based on the link between banks and merchants in 1995 in China; BOC issued network-based Great Wall Debit Card in 1997
	Foreign exchange (international) cards	1986	BOC Beijing Branch issued debit-card-natured Great Wall Forex Card in 1986; BOC issued in 1998 a worldwide-accepted forex credit card, Great Wall International Card; ABC and CITI Bank co-issued in January 2000 a debit card, Visa TravelMoney (VTM card); ICBC issued in 2000 Dual Currency Credit Card and International Debit Card
	Debit cards	1991	ICBC and CCB; system of agency payment of salaries-bank giro-electronic payment opened in ICBC Zhongshan and Anshan branches in 1992; debit cards were begun to be used in consumption with the electronic payment system launched by CCB Guangzhou Branch in May 1994
	Smart cards	1994	BOC Zhongnanhai Branch in Beijing issued Great Wall Smart Card in July 1994
	Co-brand cards	1995	ICBC Shanghai Branch issued in April 1995 Peony Shanghai Airlines MasterCard (a bank-enterprise co-brand credit card), which was the first co-brand card in China; BOCOM and China Pacific Insurance (Group) Co., Ltd (CPIC) co-issued the first bank-insurance co-brand debit card, "Pacific Debit Card" in July 2010

Continued

Product name		Year	Note to organizations and products
(IV) Bank cards	IC cards	1995	BOCOM Hainan Branch
	All-in-one cards	1995	Issued by CMB in July 1995, with functions of RMB and foreign currency deposits, small financing, cash withdrawals and consumption, as well as newly-added functions of ATM cash withdrawals, toll cards and deposits and withdrawals processed nationwide since 1996
	Affinity cards	1996	First issuance of ABC Kins Charity Visa Card in December 1996 in Shanghai
(V) E-banking	ATM	1987	Automatic teller machines (ATMs) were first used in China by BOC Zhuhai Branch
	Self-service banking	1992	ICBC Shanghai and Zhongshan branches
	Telephone banking	1992	BOC Qingdao/Shenzhen branches
	Picture-phone terminal service system	1995	BOCOM Beijing Branch
	Voice-digital customer service	1996	CCB Beijing Branch
	Customer service centers	1999	ICBC Shanghai Branch, CCB Beijing and Guangzhou branches
	Online banking	1996	CMB All-in-one Net
	Mobile banking	2000	BOC
	Home banking	1999	BOC Hunan Branch
	Palm banking	2002	CMB

Source: According to data from *Almanac of China's Finance and Banking* of related years.

(3) Characteristics and problems of service innovation in China's commercial banks

In the past three decades since the reform and opening-up in China, service innovation in China's commercial banks has achieved a lot and business scope with comprehensive coverage has taken shape. The banks thus have acquired competitive capabilities to some extent. Particularly since 2004, the State Council has taken quite a number of significant policies and measures for financial reform, so that financial innovation is in full swing now. Generally, financial innovation in China's banking has presented the following characteristics and problems.

Firstly, innovation in banks is mainly boosted by financial regulatory authorities, while financial bodies lack internal driving forces on the micro level. In the West, there is mature market mechanism, under which commercial banks have greater decision-making power over and stronger intention for their financial innovation. Financial innovation is driven from bottom up, reflecting market demands and strong motivation for profits of financial institutions. Western commercial banks (European and American, as well as Japanese ones) make innovations usually for two purposes, first to make profits and second to circumvent the control for more flexible management. Based upon these two motivations, each business innovation is launched on the basis of systematic plans and research and full consideration to costs and profits, as well as necessary technical conditions, market demands and economic size of promotion.

However, almost all the financial service innovations in China have been propelled by the government. The reform and innovation of the central bank management system and managing measures has become the major external driving force for the micro-level innovation in China's banks. The financial service innovation in commercial banks follows a government supply-oriented mode of innovation in two ways. First, regulatory authorities often directly get involved in the process of financial product innovation, making decision for whether the product shall be put in the market or not. Taking consumer credit for example, regulatory authorities stopped the main consumer mortgage loan services such as housing and car loans in 1996. According to *Guidance on Granting Personal Consumer Loans* issued in 1999, Chinese commercial banks were allowed to re-open the service for consumer loans. Related implementation measures included *Administration Procedures of Automotive Loans* promulgated in 1998 and *Trial Procedures of Housing Guarantee* in 2000, all of which have given strong impetus for the development of consumer credit. Second, some financial regulations and laws have narrowed the space for financial product innovation. For instance, the current divided operation still limits the business scope of commercial banks. Such a supply-oriented mode of innovation, in fact, places financial institutions in a passive position where "(financial institutions) can develop no services, except those permitted by regulatory bodies". This strategy, in a short run, can help financial stability, but will contain the viability of financial products innovation, impede the enhancement of competitiveness of financial institutions and have other negative influences in the long run. As Chinese commercial banks have significantly enhanced the awareness of innovation in recent years, under pressure of competition in the industry at home and that from China's entry into WTO, the driving force behind the innovation has increasingly from financial enterprises, rather than the government which, however, still plays an important role.

Secondly, imitation is more than originality. An overwhelming majority of financial innovations in China's commercial banks are simulating and absorptive ones, while only very few are originally and independently developed. About 85% of China's innovative financial instruments used now have been introduced from the Western countries, and few created in China in accordance with the demands on the Chinese financial market. Despite that the experience indirectly borrowed can reduce the time and cost for innovation, the financial environment and people's demands unique to the Chinese market are likely to be ignored, causing that such imported products get "unaccustomed" to the Chinese market and are not as effective as expected. For example, CDs (negotiable certificate of deposit) created by CITI Bank in 1961 are of large denominations (usually 100,000 dollars or more) and negotiable, so that on the one hand, customers in urgent need of capitals can have funds in secondary markets, and on the other hand, banks can have stable sources for large funds. However, the two advantages of this innovative product have been abandoned after the introduction into China, so that the CDs in circulation in China are only of small denominations and hard to be transferred, and thus have become a high-cost way of sequestration, totally going against the original intention of this innovative product. Furthermore, despite absorptive innovations, innovative financial products adopted by China's commercial banks were quite limited. For instance, China has fallen far behind the West in the development of financial derivative instruments, therefore, Chinese banks have no innovative instruments that have already been traditional products in many Western commercial banks, or such instruments are still in trial as advanced products in China (see Table 1-17).

Table 1-17　Service innovations in Chinese and foreign commercial banks

Service innovations in China's state-owned commercial banks	Service innovations in foreign commercial banks
Multipurpose accounts	Negotiable certificate of deposits
Bank-securities transfers	Negotiable withdrawal accounts
Floating-rate loans	Floating-rate notes and Euro bonds
Paper financing	Futures
E-banking	E-banking
Revolving loans	Mutual funds
Network settlement	Securitized consumer loans
Consumer credit	Interest rate swaps
	SWIFT trading system

Continued

Service innovations in China's state-owned commercial banks	Service innovations in foreign commercial banks
	Options
	Financial derivative trading

Source: Deng Shimin, 2002.

Moreover, among the few original financial innovations in Chinese commercial banks, most are at low level and with low technological content, while financial products and services with high technological content and value added through independent development for specific market demands are quite scarce. It is said that the four major state-owned commercial banks in China have applied for 11 invention patents in all, which are mainly simple inventions such as RMB recognition methods and devices, anti-erasure ink and how to solve the problem of "Millenium Bug". Furthermore, some of these patents have already been expired. Other patents are mainly "practical new products" and "appearance patents" (e. g. bill counters and safes), thus cannot create the financial products with core competitiveness. Meanwhile, CITI Bank, famous for its first-rate financial services, altogether submitted 19 applications for business method patents for its financial products to the State Intellectual Property Office of the People's Republic of China (SIPO) during 1996 and 2002. The 19 patents are about financial services and systematic methods developed for the emerging network or electronic technology, and most are the invention patents with prospectiveness.

Thirdly, innovations aimed to reduce transaction costs and enhance efficiency take a large proportion in China, while the innovation in risk management is far from enough. The financial innovations aimed to reduce transaction costs and enhance efficiency in China are mainly realized in two ways: first by technologically innovative means such as bank cards, ATMs, self-banking, telephone banking, mobile banking and online banking, and second by saving costs of transactions and economies of scope through inter-bank cooperation, for example, bank-securities link, commissioned sales of insurance products, sales of funds and other fee-based agency services. This feature is quite similar to the service innovation in international banks in purposes and conducts, mainly based upon the IT revolution and the economies of scope resulting from mixed management.

However, seemingly consistent with the international financial innovations, the aforementioned ones still fall far behind both in quantity and quality. Even the fast-developing services are generally at an initial stage, and there is a wide gap between the Chinese market and foreign mature ones in terms of the market structure, profits and service development. Take bank cards for example. Its popularity rate is comparatively low in China, with only about 10% of the whole population hold bank cards. Even in economically developed cities like Beijing, Shanghai and Guangzhou, the figure is only around 50%, while the figure in the United States, Japan and Canada is 89%, 96% and 97% respectively.

In fact, an important feature of foreign financial innovation lies in the endless emergence of risk management tools. Western commercial banks have created many financial derivatives, in order to evade various risks of interest rates, foreign exchange rates and credit. Note-issuance facilities (NIFs), swap transactions, option trading and forward rate agreement (FRA), collectively known as "the four major inventions" in the global financial community, are all of significant features of risk management. However, the financial instruments such as options, swaps and FRA cannot be seen in RMB services in China, except for the foreign currency operations. This is closely related to the low marketization of China's financial industry. For example, though the marketization of interest rates has been started in China, there is still a long way to go to establish the mechanism under which interest rates are truly determined by the fund supplies on market. Therefore, interest rates currently change little in China, so that there are few demands for financial derivatives, such as FRA and rate swaps, to evade risks of interest rates. Furthermore, as the market of financial derivatives is highly speculative, Chinese regulatory authorities have been cautious about it, which also makes the market less dynamic.

Fourthly, innovation in China is mainly for grabbing market shares, which is an initial stage. Different from their Western counterparts, China's commercial banks do not take any innovative measures to circumvent control under the current interest control policy. They innovate only for taking more market shares. Western commercial banks have got to issue CDs directly or commercial bills via bank-holding companies, in order to go beyond the ceiling of deposit rates and compete with money market funds (MMFs) for more capitals. Such innovation is driven by the competitions outside the system of commercial banks. On the contrary, MMFs have not been permitted by regulatory authorities in China so far, due to the underdeveloped market for direct financing, and non-government financial agencies are under strict control. Therefore, the interest control does not threaten the survival and development of commercial banks in China; instead, state-owned commercial banks find a friendly environment within. Some joint-stock commercial banks with more flexible management have taken measures to break the interest control for more market shares. For instance, some banks increase their deposit rates or lower the loan rates in forms of giving rebates or gifts, to attract customers; facing various activities of breaking interest control in market and to retain the market shares, especially the gold customers, some banks seemingly charge customers for loan interest rates according to the official floating range of loan interest rates, but actually use general floating interest rate when taking account of interest income, and set extra management fees on account, to offset the unreceived interest income. The increase of deposit rates is directly realized with additional services, usually by adding services of various credit cards and golden cards; for example, a card holder can enjoy certain free insurance or wealth management services, if the amount (s)he has spent through the card has reached a certain level.

The innovations with the purpose of grabbing market shares, however, are likely to result in low profits and high risks for banks. Take bank cards for example. With huge manpower, material and financial resources input in bank card services by commercial banks, the number of bank cards issued has been quite considerable; nonetheless, the services are generally at a primary stage of development, where there is wide gap between Chinese markets and foreign mature ones in terms of the market structure and business development, manifested as: poor bank networks nationwide; overlapping operations and similar functions of bank cards, due to lack of coordination between commercial banks, resulting in waste of resources and curbing the fast and efficient development of bank cards. If the domestic financial institutions keep making efforts only to compete for market shares while ignoring innovations for cost-benefit accounting (including the cost-benefit of competition for market shares), they may suffer significant profit losses while basically retaining their market shares, as China's banking industry opens up and foreign financial institutions come in. China's banks can take warning from the banking industry of Taiwan. Since the 1990s, foreign banks in Taiwan have taken up 4% ~7% of all bank assets there , but their return on net assets (RONA) has been higher than that for Taiwan local banks and kept increasing to 12.9% at the lowest and 30.95% at the highest. RONA for Taiwan local banks could only reach 12.95% in 1990, and has never been over 10% since then. The figure in 2003 for local banks was merely 1.97% in 2003, a sharp contrast to that as high as 19.01% for foreign banks.

(4) Innovation ability for wealth management products in China's commercial banks is at an initial stage

1) Wealth management products have become important parts of service innovation in Chinese banks. With more innovative financial instruments, wealth management services provided in China's banks have been developed from the simple originations in a single market to the complex cross-market derivatives. The design of such products covers various aspects, including the development of RMB and forex derivatives, call trading of bonds, expansion of direct financing channels, convertibility in capital account, asset-backed securities, dynamic hedging strategy and asset configuration. Based upon the above, plus the significance of banks in China's financial system and the wide range covered by wealth management investors, wealth management services have become an important channel for financial innovation in commercial banks. The trust products co-provided by banks and trust corporations, in particular, highlight the significance of wealth management products as an important channel of all-around development of banks. The cooperation between commercial banks and trust corporations is an ideal way of financial innovation, as trust can go across capital market, money market and industrial investment, thus has system advantages in investment unmatched by any other financial services. With trust financing products produced by trust corporations, commercial banks extend their wealth management services to credit service, bond business, stock market and fund market, actually forming a "financial supermarket" with various options. It is under the trust mode that wealth management products issued by banks have connected capital from wealth management with the credit market and stock market, so that they can well work in the system framework of divided operation.

2) There is serious homogeneity in wealth management products. Although wealth management products of Chinese banks take the absolute advantage in terms of the amount issued, they mostly feature lower technology and unsustainable profits. On the contrary, those issued by foreign banks are high in technological content and with quite originality. In general, Chinese banks attach more importance to the amount of products issued, while foreign banks value product designs.

In fact, wealth management products of most Chinese banks generally have little distinctive features, as they are re-integration of existing services, or imitations of products of other banks, or modification of some wealth management products introduced from foreign banks. Consequently, most Chinese banks are largely identical only with minor differences in terms of their variety of products, structure and service functions, and there is serious homogeneity in such products. Meanwhile, low technological content and value added as well as vulnerability to imitation lead to low-cost competition with followers. Therefore, some Chinese banks take a follower strategy, waiting for new products by other banks and then developing similar ones with lower prices. Such "introductionism" harms the interests of innovation-oriented banks, and injures their enthusiasm of innovation.

Moreover, serious homogeneity of products, which implies high possibility of substitution by each other, will definitely lead to low-level market competition in the form of price competition between banks, and that is why banks banks bid against each other to increase the earning ratios of their wealth management products. According to studies on the expected earning ratios of forex wealth management products issued from 2005 to 2007, the earning ratios guaranteed by foreign banks were among the lowest, those by the five state-owned banks and joint-stock banks in China were higher, and those by regional banks such as city commercial banks the highest (Zhu Yingying, 2008). That indicates that banks had to offer higher earning ratios of their products, to consolidate and compete for more market shares (Zhou Jizhong et al. , 2009a).

(5) Conclusion: learning from Indian banks

ICICI (Industrial Credit and Investment Corporation of India), the largest private bank in India, uses advanced banking management system (e. g. , "Enterprise Content Management Solutions" provided by Interwoven, Inc.), thanks to its high-level professionals and managing staff. ICICI explores the huge business opportunities in Indian rural market, and provides various services there (which is of particular value of reference for China's commercial banks). According to the evaluation of McKinsey & Company, ICICI and other Indian banks outperform the other Asian banks, including commercial banks in China, in terms of "shareholder value enhancement", "capital allocation efficiency" and "contribution to GDP". Moreover, the bad asset ratio of ICICI is also much lower than that of China's commercial banks (Pan Song, 2010).

The reform in China's banking industry focuses on: restructuring China's financial system, giving larger development space to private banks, weakening the monopoly power of the four state-owned commercial banks, enhancing banks' core competitiveness based upon competition, and making out overall plans for the "mixed management" of financial institutions; as well as fostering top financial professionals, expanding businesses of asset management, capital lending and M&A consulting, and enhancing capabilities of cross-border financial operation and developing and using financial derivatives.

It should be emphasized that financial innovation is quite different from innovation in manufacturing. We should be particularly prudential for the innovation of financial derivatives. Products such as "mortgage-backed securities" and "subprime mortgage" must not be copied.

2.4.9　Innovation in China's enterprises

The R&D expenses totaled 461. 60 billion *yuan* in 2009 in China, 73. 3% , or 338. 17 billion *yuan* of which was for R&D in enterprises. Such a proportion is quite high even in the world, showing that Chinese enterprises have become the major player in the technological innovation in China. More importantly, there are a large number of outstanding technologically innovative enterprises in the country. In terms of industrial distribution, these enterprises are involved both in high-tech and conventional industries; as for their ownership, they may be state-owned, private or restructured; and according to their size, these enterprises can be divided into large ones, medium- and small-sized ones, as well as "monopoly" enterprises.

Shanghai Zhenhua Port Machinery Co. , Ltd. (hereinafter as ZPMC for short) only had ten-plus employees when it was founded in 1992. However, in less than 6 years, ZPMC had been ranking first in the world in terms of its market occupancy for 10 consecutive years, reaching up to 78% . By the end of 2008, its container hoisting machineries had been sold to more than 100 ports in 73 countries and areas. Its pattern of innovation is to enter the global market with "low cost plus international standards". With the advantage in lower cost of self-operated transportation and overall-unit docking, ZPMC established its superiority in technological innovation with independently developed products such as "rubber-tyred gantry cranes with GPS" (i. e. field bridges) and "dual-dan container cranes capable of hoisting two 40-feet boxes". It has also been capable of "supply of integrated equipment" and "high-efficiency automated loading and unloading system", and established its leading position in the world. Nowadays, the ZPMC container loader-unloaders can be seen in almost all important container ports around the world.

Founded in 2002, the State Grid Corporation of China (SGCC) is a super-large state-owned enterprise. The corporation decided in 2004 to develop "UHV transmission technology". However, there were various opinions from Chinese experts, when the project was under research and development. Considering its significance to the overall development of the country's energy industry, SGCC held several meetings to listen to objections, and revised the master plan and technical schemes accordingly. National Development and Reform Commission (NDRC) finally gave the official approval to "Changzhi (Shanxi Province)-Jingmen (Hubei Province) 1000kV UHV AC Transmission Demonstration Project" in August 2006. Meanwhile, SGCC made restructuring and integration of its affiliated R&D institutes, and made three technological innovations: large-capacity long-distance UHV transmission at high altitudes, controlling technology for safe and stable operation of ultra-large grids, and flexible AC transmission system technology (FACTS). By the year of 2007, the transmission capacity had been increased adding up to 110 gigawatt with "UHV transmission" projects, equal to the generation output of 6 Three Gorges Power Stations. This showed that SGCC, a large state-owned enterprise known as a monopoly one, also has the driving force and capability of technological innovation.

Zhejiang Wanxiang Group (hereinafter as Wanxiang for short) was only a blacksmith's shop when founded by Lu Guanqiu, a farmer in Zhejiang Province in 1969. However, the blacksmith's shop has been developed into a large individually-run transnational corporation in the past four decades. Its technological innovation has undergone several stages: The first one went from simple practical techniques in 1979 to specialized imitations of imported products, then to improvement of the quality of universal joints through equipment replacement and upgrading. At the second stage, Zhejiang Wanxiang Group was established at the end of 1990, representing the company's entry in a new stage of development and the forming of its technological strategy of diversified development with universal joints production as the core business. In the third stage in the late 1990s, the guideline for technical makeup was developed as input in high-level production, high quality precision equipment, top talents and high-grade products, as well as eliminating of outmode equipment and products and obsoleting of backward employees. Wanxiang has in recent years become the only manufacturer of components and parts among 120 state pilot enterprise groups and 520 state key enterprises, and listed among Enterprises Ten of Chinese engineering industry and the pilot enterprises of enterprise technological innovation demonstration project. It is from continuous innovation that Wanxiang has realized leapfrog development in the past 40 years: The company made a daily profit of 10,000 *yuan* in the 1970s, 100,000 *yuan* in the 1980s, and one million *yuan* in the 1990s, and the figure was estimated at nearly 10 million yuan in 2010. In addition to technological innovation, Wanxiang also made organizational innovation, with which it purchased several companies, including the American Schaeffler Co., Ltd. (the company that has the most universal joint patents in the world); founded 19 companies in 8 developed countries, including the United States and the UK; and cooperated with domestic and foreign institutions to make innovations in a mode of production-studies-research. By the year of 2009, Wanxiang had had over 700 patents, one world brand, and 6 top brands in China, becoming a private enterprise that has the most universal joint patents in the world.

Geely Holding Group (hereinafter as Geely for short) is a private automobile manufacturer founded by Li Shufu in 1986. It attaches special importance to talent, equipment, technological process and knowledge accumulation, the the four pillars of research and development. As a conventional automobile manufacturer, Geely benefits from its advantage in optimization of R&D resources allocation. The company inputs much in R&D. In 2008 only, for example, Geely invested as much as 990 million yuan in R&D. The yearly R&D expenses take up over 8% of the annual sales volume, and even some high-tech enterprises cannot input as much as that record high. To foster more R&D talents, Geely has invested hundreds of millions to set up Zhejiang Geely Technician College, Zhejiang Geely Automobile Industry School, Beijing Geely University and Zhejiang Automotive Engineering Institute, the first private graduate school. The total assets of Geely reached up to 13. 96 billion yuan in 2008, with a profit of 850 millions. The company has at present 12,000 employees, over 1,600 of whom are engineers and technicians. Geely is the only private one among the top ten enterprises in China's automobile industry, and won the second prize for Enterprise Technological Innovation, National Awards for Science and Technology (Editorial Board of *Report on Development of Innovation-oriented Enterprises in China*, 2009).

These enterprises, as well as the aforementioned enterprises such as Huawei, Tasly Group and North China Pharmaceutical Co., Ltd. (NCPC), plus the national innovation-oriented enterprises described in Appendix I of this book, are the backbone of the innovation-oriented enterprises in China and the hope of China's economy.

2.5　Enhancing the National Strength

There are many ways of enhancing the national strength. However, in accordance with the book's theme, this section only focuses on "how to enhance the national strength by linking the two strategies of independent innovation and intellectual property rights (IPRs)."

Answering the call on independent innovation and building an innovation-oriented country made by Hu Jintao on the National Conference on Technology in January 2006, the Ministry of Science and Technology (MOST), State-owned Assets Supervision and Administration Commission of the State Council and All China Federation of Trade Unions made a decision in the same year to launch the selection of the national innovation-oriented enterprises, to highlight the core idea that enterprises are the main bodies of self-innovation and major builders of an innovation-oriented nation, for they are not only the mainstay of independent innovation, but also the backbone of the country's economic activities.

The author took part in both processes of working out the criteria and reviewing. Ninety-one enterprises were selected in the first reviewing as the national innovation-oriented enterprises (please refer to Appendix II for the list). Altogether 356 enterprises have been selected in the past three years, and many of them are private ones.

An innovation-oriented enterprise is one that has core technology with proprietary intellectual property rights, well-known brands and sound innovation management and culture, and highly depends upon technological innovation for gaining superiorities in domestic and international markets and realizing sustainable development.

It has the following main features. Firstly, it possesses core technology with proprietary intellectual property rights, and takes a leading position in the industry in terms of its technology. It also takes a leading or active role in working out the international, national or industrial technical norms. Secondly, it is capable of continuous innovation, including a higher R&D expense-sales volume ratio in the industry, sound R&D institutes or stable long-term cooperation with domestic and foreign universities and scientific research institutes, as well as attaching importance to fostering, introducing and employing scientific and technical personnel and highly-skilled talents. Thirdly, such an enterprise has its own development strategies and culture of innovation, such as cherishing the innovation of operation and development strategy, building up and forming innovation culture of its own, and giving significance to technological innovation and innovation of self-developed brands in the operation and development strategy.

2.5.1　The backbone of independent innovation: innovation-oriented enterprises

The guideline to select innovation-oriented ones from excellent enterprises is aimed to build a technological innovation system, accurately grasp the characteristics of innovation-oriented enterprises, make comprehensive use of measures, follow the principle of "clearly-defined guides, simple and feasible operation, and objective and impair attitudes", by making overall assessment of the innovation capability, input, output, influence and management of an enterprise and systematically investigating its dependence on technological innovation for its development, so that more enterprises can be encouraged and led to take the way of independent innovation.

(1) Criteria for innovation-oriented enterprises: dependence on innovation

When an innovation-oriented enterprise is judged, it is key to evaluate the correlation between its development and its technological innovation, ie. its dependence on technological development, so as to make judgment on its "innovativeness". Considering characteristics of Chinese enterprises and related international experience, the criteria involved are divided into two groups, i. e. "basic numerical indexes" and "indexes of experts' evaluations". Basic indexes are figures for comparisons and analyses of all the enterprises and can be compared with those in related foreign studies to some extent. With figures evaluated, enterprises are assessed in the aspects related to the abovementioned basic indexes. Indexes of experts' evaluations include both qualitative and quantitative ones. The qualitative indexes are the scores made by experts in the industry based upon their analyses and judgments of an enterprise. The quantitative indexes are experts' value judgments based upon the data submitted by an enterprise. The data submitted and experts' judgments interact with each other to some extent. Indexes of experts' evaluations are used to inspect the characteristics of innovation not included in basic indexes.

(2) Enterprise grouping: for measurability

The status of enterprises is quite complicated in China. For the sake of measurability, particularly relative identity of innovation-related characteristics of enterprises of the same type, enterprises are grouped according to their size and industrial features.

As far as enterprises' lifecycle-technological innovation relationship is concerned, documents show that when an enterprise's sales income reaches one billion and 10 billion yuan, significant changes can be seen in the enterprise's R&D intensity, mode of management, etc. On this basis, enterprises are divided into three groups: medium- and small-sized enterprises with sales income below one billion yuan, large enterprises with sales income of 1 ~ 10 billion yuan, and megacorporations and company groups with sales income above 10 billion yuan.

Considering the technology intensity of an industry, an enterprise's technological innovation is closely related with the characteristics of the industry it sits in. According to a large number of studies, enterprises in industries that are similar in technology-intensity have much in common in technological innovation. On this basis, enterprises may be classified into groups that have clearly-defined boundaries and cover various industries. Accordingly, the abovementioned three types of enterprises that are grouped according to the sales volumes can be further divided as high-tech industry group, non-high-tech industry group and service industry group. In this way, enterprises are primarily divided into nine types.

(3) Operation of assessment: simple and feasible

Meeting the requirements of the national strategies and accepted by the whole society, the index system shall be highly operationable, so that government or related intermediaries can make objective assessment with the system. Indexes should be easy to be collected, quantized and compared with eath other. Indexes of the National Bureau of Statistics of China (NBS), the data that can be from an enterprise's financial accounting, and proportional indexes are more often used.

(4) Indicator structure

To define and describe the concept of "innovation-oriented", there are 5 first-grade indicators, 15 second-grade ones and 25 third-grade ones, according to an enterprise's dependence on innovation. Please see Table 1-18 for details. Among all the indicators, there are 6 "basic numerical indicators" and 19 "indicators of experts' evaluations".

Six "basic numerical indicators" include: ① ratio of R&D staff to all employees; ② ratio of expenses on independent R&D to total income; ③ the number of granted invention patents possessed by every thousand scientists and engineers; ④ average growth rate of patent applications in the recent three years; ⑤ ratio of income from new products (services) to total sales income; ⑥ pre-tax return on sales.

The 6 indicators are core indicators of innovation capability, input and output and chosen for: Firstly, according to results of surveys including documentation analysis, field surveys and discussions with enterprises, the 6 indicators are highly recognized as the quantitative ones that can well reflect an enterprise's dependence on innovation, as well as directive indicators. Secondly, most of the 6 indicators are the core indicators used worldwide for assessment of an enterprise's innovativeness. Thirdly, the 6 indicators are listed by NBS in annual statistical data of enterprises, thus easy to be collected, analyzed and compared with each other (see Table 1-18 and refer to Appendix III for details of the listed indicators).

Table 1-18 Indicator system for assessment of innovation-oriented enterprises

First-grade indicator	Second-grade indicator	Third-grade indicator
Innovation capability	Talents of innovation	Ratio of R&D staff to all employees (basic numerical indicator)
	R&D institutes	Status of R&D institutes in an enterprise (indicator of experts' evaluations)
	Assets of innovation	Ratio of fixed assets of R&D equipment to total assets (indicator of experts' evaluations)
Innovation input	R&D input	Ratio of expenses in self-funded R&D to total income (basic numerical indicator)
		Input on trust or cooperative R&D (indicator of experts' evaluations)
	Transformation input	Ratio of expenses on trial-manufacture of new products to sales income (indicator of experts' evaluations)
		Ratio of expenses in assimilation to sales income (indicator of experts' evaluations)
	Training input	Ratio of expenses on employee training to sales income (indicator of experts' evaluations)
Innovation output	Patents (copyright)	The number of granted invention patents possessed by every thousand scientists and engineers (basic numerical indicator)
		Annual growth rate of patent applications in the recent three years (basic numerical indicator)
	New products (services)	The number of new products (services) in every year (indicator of experts' evaluations)
		Ratio of income from new products (services) to total sales income (basic numerical indicator)
		Growth rate of income from new products (services) (indicator of experts' evaluations)
	Norms	Level and number of technical norms an enterprise has participated in the formulation (indicator of experts' evaluations)
	Performance	Pre-tax return on sales (basic numerical indicator)
Innovation influence	Direct influence	The number of patent-licensed projects of an enterprise (indicator of experts' evaluations)
		Income from technology transfers and licenses (indicator of experts' evaluations)

Continued

First-grade indicator	Second-grade indicator	Third-grade indicator
Innovation influence	Brands	National-or provincial-level well-known trade marks or brands (indicator of experts' evaluations)
	International influence	The number of tripartite patents possessed by an enterprise (indicator of experts' evaluations)
		Value of export of new products (services) every year (indicator of experts' evaluations)
Innovation management	Innovation culture	Entrepreneur's awareness and spirit of innovation (indicator of experts' evaluations)
		The number of rationalization proposals by every hundred employees (indicator of experts' evaluations)
	Innovation guarantee	Perfectiveness of IPR management system (indicator of experts' evaluations)
		Perfectiveness and implementation of incentive system for technological innovation (indicator of experts' evaluations)
		Strategies, programmes and plans for innovation approved by the decision-makers of an enterprise (indicator of experts' evaluations)

Source: Editorial Board of *Report on Development of Innovation-oriented Enterprises in China*, 2009.

(5) Practice of assessment

1) Initial selection. Basic requirements are determined to evaluate an enterprise's basic conditions. An enterprise meeting the following basic requirements is qualified for the indicator assessment: ① as an independent legal person, and held by the Chinese side or Chinese citizens; ② making profits for three consecutive years, with a rational asset-liability ratio; ③ possessing technology with proprietary intellectual property rights; ④ the core part of the enterprise or the group shall be certified with ISO9001, and with GMP for a pharmaceutical company; ⑤ with good credit standing and respectability (evaluated by the bank or other credit rating authorities).

2) Operation with indicators. Average values for an industry are calculated for the six basic numerical indicators. An enterprise under evaluation is considered to pass the assessment if its related indicators are higher than the corresponding average values. For the 19 indicators of experts' evaluations, experts give scores according to the analyses and judgments of an enterprise, or make value judgments referring to the

data submitted by an enterprise. The weight ratio of basic numerical indexes to indicators of experts' evaluations is about 6:4.

With years' practice, a "4 +1" index structure has gradually been constructed: 4 quantitative indicators including ratio of R&D expenses to total income from main business, the number of granted invention patents possessed by every thousand R&D workers, ratio of income from new products (including techniques and services) to total sales income, and per-capita productivity, plus one qualitative indicator of innovation management (including strategies, system, brands and culture).

3) Overall evaluation and supplementary investigation. For the enterprises that have passed the indicator assessment and been recommended by experts from the same specialized area the enterprises sit in, the Ministry of Science and Technology can entrust related intermediaries or organize experts from the same industry the enterprises sit in to examine and determine the list. For the on-list enterprises that have been challenged and outraged common sense, supplementary investigations such as field surveys and questionnaires are taken for further confirmation, and "hearings" may accordingly be held to listen to opinions from all walks of life (Editorial Board of Report on Development of Innovation-oriented Enterprises in China, 2009).

Actually, enterprises have gradually become the main force of independent innovation, since early 2006 when the state policy of independent innovation was carried out. It has been reflected not only from the 356 national innovation-oriented enterprises (most are private), but also in some authoritative ranking lists both at home and abroad. For instance, *Fortune* (China) and Pan-Pacific Management Institute (PPMI) have co-selected "2010 China's Top 25 Most Innovative Companies", in the following procedures: "2010 China Top 500 Enterprises" selected by *Fortune* (China) were taken as candidates and industry segmentation was made among them. The growth rate of main business income and the earnings before interest, taxes, depreciation and amortization (EBITDA) in the previous year (2008 ~2009) were calculated for each enterprise, and then the enterprises were ranked by scores for the two indexes respectively. Afterwards, weighted means were made from the two rankings (50% each) for each enterprise, which were ranked again by scores. One to three enterprises would be selected from each industry according to the number of candidates in an industry, so that a primary list of 60 enterprises was made. And the 25 enterprises were finally co-selected by *Fortune* (China) and PPMI from the primary list, in accordance with 8 indicators of "overall evaluation", "strategy", "marketing", "financial control", "organization and human resources", "technological R&D", "internal process" and "external cooperation".

"2010 China's Most Innovative Companies" include China Mobile, China Telecom, Suning Appliance, Li-Ning, Vanke, China Agri-Industries Holdings Limited, CYTS, Hisense, Haier, Longfor Group, FAW Car Limited Company, Belle International, Geely, Hainan Airlines, Tencent, BYD, Bank of Ningbo, Neusoft, Goldwind Science & Technology Co., Ltd., Wumart, Huadong Medicine, Yunnan Baiyao, Datang Huayin Electric Power, Ltd., Shanda and GCL-Poly Energy Holdings Limited (PPMI, 2010). The selection was conducted among listed companies, so Huawei as a non-listed company was not included.

There were three enterprises in Chinese mainland listed among Enterprises 20 in Top 100 Technology Enterprises selected by *Business Week* in May 2010. And a quarter of the first 20 ones in Top 100 Technology Enterprises are Chinese ones, if the two Taiwan-based enterprises were also considered, including: ① BYD (Chinese mainland, electronic devices); ② Apple (the United States, computers and peripheral equipment); ③ Tencent (Chinese mainland, Internet software and services); ④ Amazon. com (the United States, Internet and online retail); ⑤ Tata Consultancy Service (TCS) (India, IT services); ⑥ Priceline. com (the United States, Internet and online retail); ⑦ Centurylink (the United States, diversified telecommunications); ⑧ Cognizant (the United States, IT services); ⑨ Infosys (India, IT services); ⑩ SoftBank (Japan, wireless telecommunication services); ⑪ WPG Holdings (Taiwan, electronic devices); ⑫ Mediatek (Taiwan, semiconductors and equipment); ⑬ NTT DATA (Japan, IT services); ⑭ Rakuten. co. jp (Japan, Internet and online retail); ⑮ Nintendo (Japan, software); ⑯ Samsung (South Korea, electronic devices); ⑰ Wipro (India, IT services); ⑱ China Mobile (Chinese mainland, wireless telecommunication services); ⑲ Yahoo Japan (Japan, Internet software and services); ⑳ Oracle (the United States, software).

Evaluating 6,500 companies in the world, *Business Week* chose the ones with the market value worth no less than one billion dollars, the total income of 500 million dollars at the minimum, and the total income between 2008 and 2009 (in local currency) decreasing by no higher than 5%. With total income and operating income standardized, comparisons were made among the top 210 companies, which were graded according to the abovementioned standards, and shareholder earnings and growing rate of staff.

2.5.2 Intellectual-property strategy: with or without it

Intellectual-property strategy has become a national strategy to boost self-innovation and already been well expounded. The following cases can show how important the strategy is to enhance the competitiveness of China's enterprises and the country's national strength.

(1) The 6C case: being in a passive position without intellectual property rights (IPRs)

Quite a number of Chinese enterprises are thrown into a passive position in fierce competition on global market, as they have no products with proprietary intellectual property rights and lack core competitiveness. In recent years, there have been more cases in which China's export industries lost the advantage of lower cost, due to the protection for IPRs launched by foreign countries.

As an emerging industry, DVD player manufacturing has been fast developed. With years' development, market for DVD players gets mature, and the products are almost on a par with the world's brands in quality and brand image. According to statistics, the consumer demand of DVD players in global market was 30 millions in 2001, while about 10 millions were exported by China, equal to one third of the world's demand. About 4 million DVD players were sold in the domestic market in 2001 in China, and the figure reached up to 8 millions in 2002, taking up a quarter of the world's total production and consumption of DVD players.

However, such a promising industry in China was confronted with huge crisis, as the core DVD technology was controlled by a couple of foreign companies. Hitachi, Panasonic, Mitsubishi Electric, Time Warner Inc., Toshiba and JVC, all of which are leading developers of DVD technology and possess the core one, formed an alliance (referred to as 6C for short) in June 1999, and issued a joint statement of "DVD Patent Pool", announcing that: 6C has the proprietary rights of patents of core DVD technology, and all the manufacturers of patented DVD products all over the world must purchase from 6C patent license, before they are engaged in any production. A manufacturer, however, can make one-time purchase of 6C patent license. As for the fees, 6C rules that: a DVD manufacturer shall pay the six aforementioned enterprises 4% of net selling price or 4 dollars per DVD player/DVD-ROM player (whichever is the higher) and 4% of net selling price or one dollar per DVD decoder (whichever is the higher); furthermore, royalties for DVD discs is 7.5 cents per disc.

In November 2000, 6C announced their "Incentives of DVD Patent License" in Beijing, stating that: all the enterprises carrying out the patent license agreement within 8 months from 1 September 2000 can enjoy, for the first 6 months, a 25% discount on any production relating to patented DVD technology conducted before 30 June 2000; while the manufacturers not carrying out the patent license agreement within 8 months from 1 September 2000 shall pay the prescribed patent royalties and a 2% monthly interest for any production activities within the scope of the agreement.

Since January 2002, on request of the 3C Alliance (formed by Philips, Sony and Pioneer, three leading technology developers), the customs of some EU countries has begun to seize China's DVD products exported to EU countries, on the grounds that Chinese DVD manufacturers had acquired no intellectual property licensing.

On 9 January 2002, 3,864 DVD players exported by Shenzhen Pudi Industrial Development Corporation to the UK were under seizure of the local customs on Philips' request, on the grounds that the products had no patent granted. And on 18 and 22 January of the same year, 3,900 of all the 5,850 DVD players exported by Huizhou Desay AV Science and Technology Co., Ltd. to Germany were under seizure of the local customs, and the entry was not permitted for the rest 1,950 players.

The negotiations between China Audio Industry Association (CAIA) and 6C on DVD patent pool broke down on 10 January 2002. On 8 March 2002, 6C issued an ultimatum to over 100 Chinese DVD manufacturers under CAIA that the Chinese manufacturers must reach an agreement on patent royalties with 6C no later than 31 March 2002; otherwise, 6C will file a lawsuit. The patent royalties asked by 6C are 20% of unit-price, equal to about 20 dollars per DVD player.

The negotiations between Chinese DVD manufacturers and 6C achieved new progress on 29 March 2002. According to the memorandum, 6C will not take legal proceedings against Chinese DVD manufacturers. CAIA and 6C came to a preliminary agreement on patent license for DVD players in May, that the patent royalties were fixed as the higher of 4% of unit-price or 4 dollars per DVD player.

The disputes between 6C Alliance and Chinese DVD manufacturers had an end for the time being. However, the case well showed the importance of the products with proprietary IPRs to the development of an enterprise. An enterprise will be definitely under the control of others, if it does not possess the core technology and the core competitiveness. With years' development, market for DVD players gets mature, and the products are almost on a par with the world's brands in quality and brand image. However, the DVD products of foreign countries have been under threat from the Chinese ones, which are of lower price and keep increasing in export volumes. Therefore, foreign manufacturers laid their best card on the table, attacking Chinese DVD manufacturers with patented technology, so that Chinese enterprises were hard hit.

Actually, such a case concerning IPRs takes place not only in DVD industry. Similarly, Japanese enterprises also brought a suit against five motorcycle manufacturers in Tianjin for patent infringement. Chinese enterprises may be charged with infringement acts at any time, as quite a number of them have imitated and then assimilate advanced technologies but made no significant breakthroughs in core technology.

Chinese enterprises should learn from the 6C case that on the one hand, they shall make efforts to have and master more IPRs and enhance their own core competitiveness; on the other hand, they must have an awareness of respect and protection for IPRs. Chinese enterprises have gradually become players in the international market upon China's entry into WTO, and can take a place and develop in future competition only by acquiring the awareness of intellectual property rights, building the capability of intellectual property protection, and continuously enhancing their core competitiveness (Zhou Jizhong, 2002).

(2) "PKI": right of voice coming with IPRs

"PKI" (Public Key Infrastructure) is technology developed for the secured data transmission on Internet, guaranteeing information security with public keys and digital certificates and verifying the identity of a digital certificate holder. With PKI technology, individuals or enterprises can conduct activities and businesses well secured in privacy. For example, emails sent by a company to its customers will not be intercepted under the protection of PKI technology, and in many other cases, such as online shopping and banking, the services are provided with PKI certificates, to ensure the security of customers and consumers. "PKI mission-critical server" used to be a "sharp weapon" for some developed countries to control China, before China developed it. However, since it was successfully developed under the China's "863" Programme, foreign companies soon made a substantial price cut for the encryption card from 83,000 dollars to 12,000 dollars, and expressed their hope for all-round cooperation with China in the field of "PKI" technology and co-establishing "PKI" labs to share the technological achievements (Xu Bin, 2010).

So it can be seen why "self-innovation" is so important.

(3) Patent documentation as treasure

IPRs are as significant in patent documentation as in patent monopoly. An enterprise can get acquainted with the advances in the technology from patent documentation, so as to gain substantial benefits when it acquires and purchases patented technology and know its own and the rival's strength in technological competition. For example, a UK company charged Shanghai Yaohua Glass Factory 12.5 million pounds for the "float technique", on the grounds that there were a number of patented technologies involved in the technique and Yaohua should pay the patent royalties accordingly. Nevertheless, upon the retrieval of patent documentation concerning the technique by Shanghai Intellectual Property Administration (SIPA), it was understood that 51 of 137 patents possessed by the UK company had been or was to be invalid. The royalties were finally negotiated to be 525,000 pounds. Furthermore, according to the related patent documentation, companies in the United States and Japan were also applying for the patent of "float technique", but they had also purchased from the UK company the basic patent of the technique, indicating that the UK company's technique was more advanced. (Ma Xiushan, 2001).

2.5.3 Enhancing the national strength with the linkage between "two strategies"

The relationship between "technological innovation" and "IPRs" is actually that between process and achievements, i. e. the relationship between "the process of technological innovation through R&D and commercialization of the achievements" and "the IPRs acquired, including patents and know-how". The core of technological innovation is evidently R&D, and the essence of intellectual property management lies in services. Then what is "linkage"? As mentioned before, "linkage" in this section refers to the interaction between system elements, so that an element continuously and dynamically acts on others in the system, after it takes feedback from the interaction. Accordingly, the relationship between technological innovation and IPRs is virtually the linkage between R&D and services.

As stated above, "linkage" is the continuous cross-effect between multiple elements in a system. In accordance with systems science, functions of a system depend upon the interaction between the elements of the system. As shown in Fig. 1-29, the elements in innovation system are divided in this book into three groups: subjects (enterprise, government, university, finance unit and user), environment (system, mechanism, policy and culture) and functions (learning, opening-up, cooperation and innovation) (Zhou Jizhong, 2007). However, this grouping is simply an abstract concept model for easier understanding. In the actual operation, however, functionas (learning, cooperation, opening-up and innovation) are the content transferred in the "linkage" between subjects and between subjects and environment. The effects and efficiency of this linkage determines the performance of the whole system.

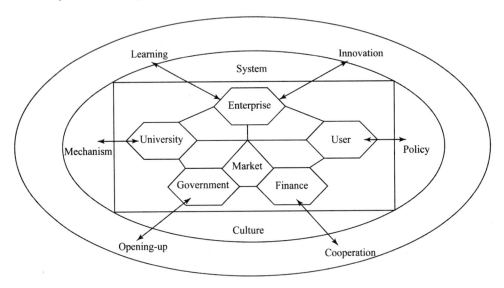

Fig. 1-29　Linkage between elements in innovation system

Accordingly, the nature of "the linkage between technological innovation strategy and intellectual property strategy", i. e. the essence of the linkage between "R&D and services", is the process in which subjects in innovation system exchange resources, information and technology through learning, opening-up, cooperation and innovation, and optimize the whole innovation system through the cycle of feedback taking-learning-feedback retaking-relearning. Though closely related, "linkage" and "interaction" are different, for linkage is the cross-effect between multiple elements in a system and features in that: First, the cross-effect between multiple elements is many-to-many instead of one-to-one in space. Secondly, the many-to-many cross-effect is continuous in time and interacts as both cause and effect. Thirdly, there exists a feedback mechanism. Systemalogically, these three features are actually nonlinear mechanism and coupling mechanism. The former ties together enterprises in an enterprise alliance, as well as an enterprise alliance and government and users. The latter·integrates the rise-and-falls and fusion of subjects resulting from nonlinear mechanism, so that enterprises make leapfrog development in performance and function of innovative activities.

An enterprise depends more and more on technological innovation, but technological innovation alone cannot guarantee exclusive possession of innovation profits or business success, for the rivals can easily imitate innovative products without protection from IPRs, and thus make manufacturer of innovative products suffer great loss. IPRs are an effective mechanism to protect technological innovation, as well as an important means of commercial competition. In other words, IPRs protect and consolidate the profits generated from technological innovation, and technological innovation and IPRs interact and link with each other; therefore, the two shall establish a strategic relationship, instead of "making single actions" separately, so that they will have much stronger power. This is an important way of enhancing the national strength (Zhou Jizhong et al. , 2009a).

From the angle of value creating and competitiveness enhancing, the linkage between technological innovation and IPRs purports to build brands, which, in turn, are another important indicator of the efficiency and effect of such a linkage.

3. Innovation Culture

Defined as a kind of "concept of value", "innovation culture" can be summed up as free exploration, democratic management, tolerance of failure and open cooperation (Zhou Jizhong, 2002). As the quintessence of innovation culture has been expounded by many, it is unnecessary to give details here again, and this books only deals with the following issues related to its subject.

3.1　Concept of Value

"Free exploration" shall be valued to and protected in process of applying for and assessing of various scientific research projects. For instance, the National Natural Science Foundation of China has worked out during application process a particular policy for "non-consensual projects" (i. e. support for and objection against a project under application have a match in the reviewing). In the author's opinion, more budget is recommended for projects of "free exploration", as they are often small-sized ones open for free application (e. g. "general projects" funded by the National Natural Science Foundation, with an outlay of 300,000 ~ 500,000 *yuan* for each project). It is particularly important to take both "free exploration" and "tolerance of failure" into consideration. "Tolerance of failure" shall be defined according to related articles in the newly-amended *Law of the People's Republic of China on Progress of Science and Technology*. Article 56 of the law regulates that "The State shall encourage scientists and technicians to carry out free exploration and dare to assume risks. Where original records prove that, although the scientists and technicians undertaking the scientific research and technological development projects, which are highly exploratory and risky, have performed their duty diligently and conscientiously, they still cannot accomplish such research and development, they shall be excused." And Article 55 rules that "Scientists and technicians shall carry forward scientific spirits, observe academic norms, abide by professional ethics, and be honest and trustworthy; and they shall not practice fraud in scientific and technological activities, or participate in or support superstition." The law creates a relaxed academic environment for scientists and technicians, and at the same time enhances professional ethics of scientists and technicians and credibility in scientific research, preventing academic misconduct.

As for "democratic management", it is worthwhile to think about how to achieve "de-administration" in universities and research institutes. The so-called "administration" here, in another word, refers to that leaders from Party committees and government and higher-level departments in-charge have final decisions over academic activities including teaching and scientific research, while teaching and scientific researching staff are basically excluded from decision-making. However, there are no immediate solutions for the issue, as education system and bureaucracy, even political system and regime are involved. As an approach to transition, "professor-ruled scholarship" is recommended at present, which is to form decision-making organizations, such as "academic boards" composed of representatives of teaching and scientific researching staff, to make decisions for teaching and scientific research issues in universities and scientific research institutes. Nevertheless, the actual implementation will be demanding, even though the approach has been written into the *National Plan for Long-term Educational Reform and Development* (2010 ~ 2020). What first needs to be defined is "principal responsibility system under the leadership of the Party committee" and the responsibilities and personnel of "academic committees".

Evidently, innovation culture provides norms for the field of science and technology, and further involves political, economic and cultural areas in a wider horizon as well. In the following sections, "freedom and democracy" and "reform and opening-up" will be discussed from political, economic and cultural angles. These two issues have actually already been touched upon in "Whole-Nation Regime" and "One-Party Rule" in Section 1 "Institutional design" of Chapter 1, particularly about the close relation between "freedom and democracy" and "Institutional design".

3.2　Freedom and Democracy

With "free exploration" and "democratic management" involved, innovation culture is naturally related to "freedom and democracy" in a wider horizon. There may be no significant differences between China and Western countries in "free exploration" and "democratic management" under innovation culture, but characteristics and expressions of "freedom and democracy" and "human rights" differ a lot in China and Western countries (including Japan), because of different environment of development such as history, society and culture in China and the West.

Freedom, put in a simple way, is that man's behaviours fit his consciousness. Within the legal rules, citizens have the right of unrestrained conscious activities, for example, freedom of speech, assembly and association. Opinions of freedom differ in various groups and from an individual to another, as freedom is a time-limited relativistic concept. Freedom is ideologically both sensible and rational, and rational and sensible choices often have differences and conflicts; therefore, it can be said that no absolute freedom actually exists. As a member of society, everyone's freedom has to be bound by self-discipline. Freedom does not mean doing as one pleases. Democracy is a series of principles and behaviours to protect human's freedom and an institutional expression of freedom. Democracy follows the principle of decision by majority and respect for rights of individuals and minority.

As China keeps enhancing its national strength, the democracy construction in China has also drawn lots of attention. The Chinese Government's stand on the issue can be seen from Premier Wen Jiabao's words in the exclusive interview with Hiroko Kuniya of NHK on the morning of June 1 2010. To the question "What do you think of the political restructuring in China, and what will China do to carry out democratization", Premier Wen Jiabao said that "China is adopting the all-round reform, including economic and political restructuring and the reform of social management system. We have known from the very beginning that there would be no success in economic restructuring without successful political restructuring, and so have we been following the principle. Political restructuring is aimed at four goals:

first to establish socialist democracy, guaranteeing citizens' rights to vote, know, participation and supervision; second to perfect socialist legal system, running state affairs according to law and building a country under the rule of law; third to ensure equity and justice; and fourth to realize the people's free and all-round development. "

As for the characteristics of "ensuring equity and justice", Premier Wen Jiabao (2010) pointed that "Equal education opportunity comes first and the most important. We have completely carried forward free nine-year compulsory eduction across the country. However, it is far from enough. We shall further develop secondary education, particularly vocational education. A scholarship and stipend system will be carried out in vocational schools. Students from rural poverty-stricken families and agricultural science students will be exempted from tuition fees. A scholarship system will also be put into practice in higher education. The enrolment ratio for higher education was 20% two years ago, with more than 20 million students in universities and colleges, but the amount for scholarship and stipend only totalled 1.8 billion yuan. The amount has been increased up to the present 35 billion yuan in the past two years, and 40% of students receiving higher education can receive scholarship and stipend. Special attention is given to rural areas, as both living and studying conditions are comparatively poor there. In addition to school sundry fees, textbook fees are also waived for students in rural areas. Subsidies are given to the rural students attending boarding schools. We shall make continuous efforts to ensure equal access to education for everyone. Another issue is medical care, which is closely related to the people's health. Therefore, we have decided to promote the reform of medical and health system. The reform of medical and health system faces many difficulties in all the countries in the world. To further promote the reform, the Central Government will invest 850 billion yuan in the coming three years into: First, the new-type rural cooperative medical service system, under which a farmer has on his/her personal account a pooling fund with 120 yuan from government and 30 yuan from the individual, so that comprehensive arrangements for serious diseases are taken and reimbursement made accordingly. With the pooling fund, it is convenient for a farmer to see a doctor in township-level clinics, county-level hospitals or hospitals in a provincial capital. The proportion of government subsidies in pooling funds will keep increasing, as government receipts increase. Second, basic medical insurance for urban residents, mainly covers "elders, children and the handicapped". In this insurance system, the insured are subsidized by the Central Government and local governments for medical service. Urban employees can enjoy the medical insurance even after they retire. Third, social security mainly include pension, unemployment insurance and medical insurance, plus work injury insurance, all of which is under gradual promotion. Take the pension system in rural areas as an example. Under this system, an insured farmer can receive a basic pension of 55 yuan per month from the age of 60. Farmers have never imagined that. Minimum living allowance has basically covered over 90% of both urban and rural residents, with more than 27 million urban residents and over 40 million rural ones. Moreover, agricultural tax has been waived, putting an end to the over 2,000-year history of agricultural tax in China. From now on, farmers in China will pay no tax or administrative charges any more, and the Central Government will give subsidies instead. However, the current social security is still at a low and basic level, and tries to cover as many people as possible. It requires time to make improvements, as China is a big country with too large a population. We shall also take various measures to alleviate income inequality. The proportion of employees' income is to be increased in first distribution, and in second distribution, government expenditure will be spent more for disadvantageous groups and on public utilities such as education and medical care. All these issues have been put in the agenda and been carried out step by step. The values of a society can be realized and its people live happily with dignity only when equality and justice is guaranteed in this society. "

Then what kind of "freedom and democracy" is pursued in China In a simple way, it is freedom and democracy aiming at "a powerful nation with prosperous people". It can also be put in the form of a mathematical expression: "a powerful nation with prosperous people" as a function, then freedom, democracy, economy, education, medical care, income, employment and management as independent variables. The integration of these variables is beneficial for the increase in function value, so that the people can enjoy substantial "freedom and democracy". In other words, what shall a country do, when people's freedom of voting, expression, demonstration as well as assembly and association results in inefficient legislation and administration, split of voters, political turbulence, stagnant and even weakening economy, miserable life and deteriorating national strength What if the nominal "freedom and democracy" actually lead to "a weak nation with poor people"?

Assumedly, there are four models of development in the world: "freedom and democracy-powerful nation with prosperous people" for developed countries, "freedom and democracy-weak nation with poor people" for developed countries, "freedom and democracy-powerful nation with prosperous people" for developing countries, and "freedom and democracy – weak nation with poor people" for developing countries. From a dynamic view of changes, should each model be given chances to full development, before a country chooses one suitable for its own development? Some hold that an important aspect of the world's development lies in more "diversities" and "options", which will disappear if there is only one model of development in the world.

The concept of "freedom and democracy-powerful nation with prosperous people" is undoubtedly a dynamic and developing one for any country, and has different characteristics and goals in different stages. For example, citizens' rights to vote and know and of participation and supervision not only reflect to what extent citizens can enjoy freedom and democracy, but also to what extent they enjoy human rights. The four aforementioned rights enjoyed by Chinese citizens differed in 1978, 1988 and 2010, and have kept progressing. The freedom and democracy in the previous stage conforms to the national condition, if it has created favourable conditions for that in the coming stage, and vice versa. As for specific indexes such as "equal education", "medical equity" and "social security" that indicate citizens' freedom and democratic right, they can be carried out in China only in 2010, but not in 1998, let alone in 1988. The development achieved in the past three decades since the reform and opening-up of China has laid a solid foundation for today's Chinese citizens to enjoy more freedom and democracy.

It can be predicted that around 2020, Chinese citizens can enjoy substantially improved freedom and democracy in new forms, for example, from the reform of electoral proceedings at all levels under "CPC's long-term reigning" to hearing system and improvements of its procedures.

It is noteworthy that the right to life takes the most important position in all human rights in any country, and it is particularly true in developing countries. Thomas Jefferson placed "the right to life" in a quite important position in his *Declaration of Independence* (Diane Ravith, 1995). Freedom and democracy must be first reflected in people's state and quality of life. This is particularly true in such a time of the global financial crisis.

3.3 Open Cooperation

Open cooperation is both the concept of value in a culture and the "soft power" of a country, thus can be taken as a fundamental national policy. It is important for both the innovation management in narrow sense, technological innovation and the innovation management in the broad sense.

We can learn from about 200 countries and areas, small or large, for their "innovation management". Furthermore, we can know more about other peoples, promote mutual friendship, clear up misunderstandings, and resolve conflicts during "open cooperation" with them, so that we can make "win-win achievements" and "multilateral benefits".

As China's political system and regime are unique in the world, the understanding from other governments and peoples in majority is of great importance, and "open cooperation" is in need accordingly. Moreover, considering great differences between China and Western countries in written language, religious identity and cuisine, therefore, China needs to intensify and deepen "open cooperation" in a long run, making all-around "open cooperation", which is generally in two forms of "going global" and "bringing in".

Deng Xiaoping proposed that "science and technology are the productive forces" in 1978, and "science and technology are the primary productive forces" in 1988. His words were as powerful as opening the ears of the deaf and the eyes of the blind, which should be attributed to his visits to the United States and Japan in the ten years and his better perceptual knowledge of the significance of science and technology in enhancing the national strength.

In scientific and technological field, China has learnt from Silicon Valley of the United States for its strategy of building high-tech industrial development zones, and from Small Business Innovation Research (SBIR) of the United States for establishing its innovation fund for technology-based firms.

In the economic field, China has learnt from and brought in advanced models of economic administration and financial instruments from abroad, such as stock market and derivative financial instruments. China has also broadly participated in the conferences and activities of international institutions such as the World Bank and International Monetary Fund (IMF), and dispatched personnel to hold important posts within. As for introduction of foreign investment, China's economic development and talents cultivation have greatly benefited from the transnational companies and their R&D centers established in China.

In the educational area, China has started to dispatch scientists and technicians and students to study and visit other countries, after Deng Xiaoping made instructions on dispatching more people to study abroad. The guideline of "supporting studying abroad, encouraging people to come back to China and free choice of going abroad and coming back" was written into the documents of the Third Plenary Session of the 14th Central Committee of the CPC in 1993. According to the statistics from the Ministry of Education, by the end of 2007, there had been altogether 1.21 million persons studying abroad since 1978, about 320,000 of whom had come back to China. The number of people studying abroad had increased by 168 times during the three decades. Master's degrees such as Master of Business Administration (MBA) and Master of Public Administration (MPA) have played an active role in the cultivation of high-level management personnel in China.

In the field of national defence, the Chinese People's Liberation Army (PLA) has had more exchanges with armies of other countries since the reform and opening-up. The Ministry of National Defence has launched its English website. Chinese peacekeeping troops have been highly valued by local peoples and the international community, for their contribution to safeguarding world peace.

As for diplomacy, China has become more and more important in the United Nations, and got actively involved in Asia-Pacific Economic Cooperation (APEC) and various activities of international and regional organizations. In the past 9 years since its foundation in June 2001, Shanghai Cooperation Organization (SCO) has been the main force of cracking down three forces, including terrorism, in the member-state regions.

In tourism, 79 overseas tourist destinations had been opened to Chinese citizens by the end of July 2009, and 28 countries are reachable for Chinese tourists.

Open cooperation in innovation culture not only includes "bringing in" and "going global", or "studying abroad", but also "teaching abroad". "Confucius Institute" is such an example of the creative idea of "teaching abroad". The Chinese Government set up the Office of Chinese Language Council International (hereinafter as "Hanban" for short) in 1987, to popularize Chinese language and culture. Planned and undertaken by "Hanban", Confucius Institute Headquarters was set up in Beijing, and was inaugurated on April 9 2007. All overseas Confucius Institutes are the branches of Confucius Institute Headquarters and Chinese-foreign cooperative ones. Confucius Institutes are non-profit public institutions that aim to promote Chinese language and culture and are often set up in foreign educational institutions like universities and research institutes. Therefore, one most important task of Confucius Institutes is to provide learners with standard and authoritative learning materials and regular channels. Particularly, Confucius Institutes have in recent years made further progress beyond Chinese teaching and been developed into a platform for promoting Chinese culture and holding cultural exchanges between China and other countries. In accordance with Confucius' ideas that "harmony is the most precious" and of "harmony with differentiation", Confucius Institutes are devoted to promoting exchanges between and harmony of Chinese culture and other cultures all over the world, and aim to build a harmonious world featuring sustained peace and common prosperity. Chinese leaders have paid much attention to the construction and development of Confucius Institutes, and many have attended the plate-giving and opening ceremonies. For example, Vice President Xi Jinping attended opening ceremonies of three Confucius Institutes in 2009. There have been nearly 300 Confucius Institutes in almost one hundred countries and areas (most located in the United States and Europe), since the foundation of the world's first Confucius Institute in November 2004 in South Korea. These Confucius Institutes have become a world-known brand of and platform for promoting Chinese language, culture and the studies of Chinese ancient civilization.

The abovementioned innovation culture and culture in the broad sense (e. g. harmonious society) are included in the "soft power".

3.4 Culture of Self Cultivation

A people's cultural attainment shall also be included in the soft power of a country, for though seemingly having nothing to do with innovation, it is supportive for innovation, and significant for the national reputation and image of a country. As the reform and opening-up policy is carried forward in depth in China, Chinese people have more contact and communication with foreigners, and their cultural attainment and quality draw attention from foreign peoples and media accordingly. For example, Expo 2010 Shanghai China has well demonstrated China's national strength and its people to visitors from all over the world. Besides, millions of Chinese go abroad every year for tourism, visits, studying and working. However, in addition to hospitality, friendliness, diligence and wisdom, there is also veiled criticism on Chinese people (though in a small number, foreigners still call these people "Chinese people" in general) for their three bad habits of queue-jumping, loud-talking and spitting, which shall be solved by education. Schools at all levels and of various kinds should attach importance to "self-cultivation", which also needs help from "the larger school of society". For an immediate improvement, institutes and organizations in charge of organizing and dealing with people going abroad, such as travel agencies and airlines, are recommended to organize training of etiquette for people going abroad, for etiquette of a people also reflects the country's soft power and should be valued.

In accordance with the Chinese Confucian school, "If there is righteousness (self-cultivation) in the heart, there will be beauty in the character. If there is beauty in the character, there will be harmony in life. If there is harmony in life, there will be order in the nation. When there is order in the nation, there will be peace in the world." "Righteousness (self-cultivation)" serves as the foundation for the other three, thus plays a crucial role in both individual and national development. Therefore, it is recommended to open a course of "self-cultivation" from primary school, separately or under "morality lessons" or "political study". Beyond school education, "self-cultivation" shall also be part of work of the aforementioned organizations and institutions in society, such as travel agencies and airlines. However, it will take quite a long time to make considerable achievements, and it may be as demanding as the economic takeoff. There must be Institutional design, innovation and creativity in the aspect as well.

"Self-cultivation" courses or culture shall include manner and etiquette on surface level (not secondary, but easy to understand), virtues of diligence, thrift and modesty on the middle level, and "credibility", "devotion", steadfastness and respect for property rights and etc. in the deep level. Chinese people have been always hardworking and thrifty. However, quite a number of people who prospered first lead an extravagant life and craze to vie with each other, making staggering waste. This can be well demonstrated simply from comparisons between "dinner gatherings" of proprietors, officials and even ordinary people in China and India. Self-cultivation "in depth" has particularly close relation with the book's topic on innovation. "Devotion to research", steadfastness and respect for property rights are all closely related to technological innovation, enterprise innovation and institutional innovation. "Self-cultivation" courses in primary and middle school and self-cultivation education in society can focus on surface and middle levels, while those for university students, graduates and cadres shall pay more attention to the middle-level content, especially "credibility", "devotion", steadfastness and respect for property rights and etc. on the deep level. As a system of self-cultivation education, specialized materials shall be prepared, and related indexes listed among assessment and taken as performance indicators for students, employees and officials.

China's intellectuals, entrepreneurs and officials shall learn from Indian intellectuals for their indifference toward fame and wealth and concentration on and devotion to studies and work, and from India's entrepreneurs for their self-esteem, self-improvement, good intention toward other people, pursuit for win-win achievements, credibility culture aiming at repaying the society, and their spirit of human orientation.

With years' effort, Chinese people will definitely show the world "a civilized land of propriety and righteousness".

4. Comments on Innovation Management and National Strength

China has been prominent in the innovativeness and continuity of the Institutional design, since it carried out the reform and opening-up in 1978. The institution innovation under the second- and third-generation leadership has been well expounded in Part I of this chapter. And "a harmonious society", "inclusive growth", "Scientific Outlook on Development" and etc. put forward by the fourth-generation leadership, as well as the Institutional design responding to the current financial crisis, such as the "4-trillion-yuan stimulus", are all system guarantees for China's ever-increasing national strength.

There is still much space for improvement in design of management, democratic and financial systems. For instance, policies for private enterprises can be more open in enterprise system design; and in university system design, whether can policies be worked out to transform "state-owned-and-run" universities, through "management buy-outs (MBO)" in enterprises, into "state-owned and individual-run" or "individual-owned-and-run" ones?

China has been strong in combinatorial innovation and technological innovation in innovation management, but is still falling far behind the United States in "meta-innovation" or "original innovation".

It is worthwhile to pay more attention to "innovation culture". In the economic and social transitional period, the cultural progress including innovation culture has been lagging behind in terms of system design and innovation management. Take "credibility culture" for example. There is still much to be improved concerning the "credibility" in application and assessment of scientific and technological research projects, brand building and IPRs. Undoubtedly, all improvements need follow-up system building by government and legislature.

The ratio of gross expenditure on R&D to gross domestic product (i. e. GERD/GDP) of China reached up to 1. 49% in 2007, ranking 23rd in the world. The indicator figure not only ranked first in developing countries, but also surpassed that of Italy among developed countries. According to *Bulletin on Major Data of the Second Check on R&D Resources* (hereinafter as *2010 Bulletin* for short) co-issued by NBS and the Ministry of Science and Technology in November 2010, China's GERD/GDP was as high as 1. 70% in 2009 (NBS et al. , 2010).

China's expenditure on R&D ranked fifth in the world, amounting to 48. 770 billion dollars in 2007, 34,321 million dollars of which was provided by enterprises, ranking fourth in the world, after the United States, Japan and Germany. Expenditure on R&D by enterprises took up 1. 05% of GDP, ranking 18th in the world. There were in China 1,736,000 persons/year (full-time equivalent) of R&D staff in 2007, ranking first in the world (there was no such an indicator submitted by the United States; otherwise, the US should rank first in the world for the number of R&D staff, China the second and the other countries were one place lowered concerning the indicator accordingly), and the number of R&D staff in enterprises 1,186,800 persons/year in 2007, ranking first in the world as well (second in fact, for the same reason as aforementioned), while the per-capita expenditure on R&D in China was only 36. 9 dollars in 2007, ranking 45th in the world and around the average. According to *2010 Bulletin*, GERD reached up to 580. 21 billion yuan in 2009 (about 84. 95 billion dollars, at an exchange rate of 1 dollar for 6. 83 yuan), and the R&D staff as many as 2,291,200 persons/year in China (NBS et al. , 2010).

China ranked 18th in *World Competitiveness Yearbook 2010* by International Institute for Management (IMD), Lausanne, Switzerland, two places forward than the previous year (IMD, 2010). China also ranked 27th in *Global Competitiveness Report 2010-2011* by the World Economic Forum (WEF), two places higher compared to the previous year (WEF, 2010) and above the average in the world.

There were altogether two Chinese Nobel Prize winners between 1950 and 2008

(i. e. Li Zhengdao and Yang Zhenning, both of whom were of Chinese nationality and living and working in the United States when winning the prizes), ranking 18th in the world.

The number of invention patents granted in China was 25,909 in 2007, ranking fifth in the world. And there were 240,192 theses by Chinese authors published on the world's top three indexes, ranking second in the world.

China's GDP reached up to 4,329. 2 billion dollars in 2008, ranking third in the world. According to the bulletin of NBS in 2010, China's GDP was expected to surpass that of Japan in 2010, climbing to the second in the world, and China would become the second largest economy in the world.

Quite a number of statistial data quoted in the book differs from one another, as they come from different sources. For instance, figures of China's expenditure on R&D were 1. 44% and 1. 54% in 2007 and 2008 respectively, according to *China Statistical Yearbook on Science and Technology 2009* co-published by NBS and the Ministry of Science and Technology, which slightly differed from that from the World Bank, IMD and WEF.

We shall pay particular attention to the proportion of the industrial output influential to the national strength in GDP. According to the report issued by the World Bank in 2010, in China's output structure in 2009, agriculture, industry and service trade took up 10% , 46% and 43% of GDP respectively. Particularly, the proportion of service trade in GDP is not only much lower than that of about 70% in European countries and the United States (77% in the US), but also lower than those of 55% in India, 58% in Russia and 66% in Brazil, and was the lowest among the 10 countries discussed in the book. It shows that China's service trade, especially modern service industry (finance, telecommunications and R&D etc.), has lagged far behind the other 9 countries. Therefore, enterprise innovation in China shall also energetically develop service trade in future. And financial service industry is the focus.

There are quite a number of problems existing in China's financial service industry at present. The industry is developing at a pace lower than the average growth rate of GDP; besides, in a irrational internal structure, the banking industry takes the leading position, while securities, insurance and trust investment services take rather low proportions, and the financial services in rural areas are seriously lagging behind in particular. China's financial service industry, therefore, shall learn more from its Indian counterpart. Despite a high degree of monopoly, banking has an unsatisfactory performance. Financial institutions lack core competitiveness, and there is a wide gap between China's financial industry and that in developed countries in services for asset management, loan, M&A consultancy and financial derivatives. And it is unable for China's financial industry to rival that of India, either. Moreover, Chinese financial institutions are comparatively weak in cross-border services (Wang Zixian, 2008). "National strength" is definitely affected by weak "financial strength", which has been well proved through the relationship between pound and the leading position taken by the UK in the past and that between dollar and the great power possessed by the US today. Therefore, the international status of Renminbi is related to that of China.

However, further study shall be done on the proportion taken by service trade in GDP. It is not necessarily the higher, the better, nor to be as high as 70%, as there must be a proper proportion of output value of manufacturing to that of service trade. If all the world's powers focus on the development of service trade, what should be the "services" traded for in international trades It is worthwhile for China to think it over by considering its current political, social and market economy systems. The author also holds that we should faithfully adhere to "the theory of development stages" and the proportion taken by service trade in GDP shall be 55% ~60% around 2020 in China. Financial derivatives shall be developed in a particularly prudent way.

If national strength is classified into "hard power" and "soft power", China shall rank among the most powerful in the world in terms of its "hard power" in economic aggregate, military power, size of population and territory and a political power as a permanent member of the United Nations Security Council. However, the per-capita "hard power" of China falls to the average in the world. For such a common view, no more details will be given here.

However, there are disputes, some of which are serious, over the "soft power" of China, for among the powers in the world, China is indeed "different from the others" in some aspects, particularly in political system, religion and language.

China is the only country without separation of power (neither "separation of the executive, legislative and judicial power", nor "separation of the executive and legislative power") in the world, and there are no "oppositions" or "bipartisanship". China has been under "the long-term leadership of the only party". The author holds that China should pursue "the combination of three rights", that is, the people's rights to vote, know and supervise shall finally come to the sustainable development of the country and society. Sustainable development is the ultimate criterion for whether a country's democratic and economic systems and social development are successful and rational or not.

China is a multi-religious country, but its religious believers, over 100 million, only take up 8% ~ 9% of the total population. Therefore, China is one of the countries with the smallest proportion of religious believers in the world. There are altogether more than 10 million Christians in China (Editorial Board of *World Affairs*, 2009). And in China's history of over five thousand years, religion has had slight influence on society, politics and people's daily life, and that is largely attributed to the prevalence of Confucianism in China's history.

Chinese characters are pictographs totally different from English letters. And Chinese cuisine is also far from the Western ones either in cookery or ingredients.

Therefore, China has left an impression of "being incomprehensible and even mysterious" on other countries. It can be said that since the foundation of the People's Republic of China in 1949, the "misleading" of some Western countries has played a rather important role in world's wrong understanding of China. As China is rising, there have been books like *When China Rules the World* (by British author Martin Jacques). The Beijing 2008 Olympic Games and Expo 2010 Shanghai China, in particular, gave opportunities to more people to know China, and more have felt intimation on China.

In other words, if "soft power" can be seen as a thought-, culture- and system generation-based capability to be accepted by others, China's "soft power" is getting stronger.

If the abovementioned "uniqueness" does not hinder the rapid economic development in China and the country's "hard power" gets stronger as time goes on, people will try to find out the reasons behind, as they are living a prosperous and happy life. In fact, different from some powers forcing others to accept their values and political system, China's social system has been gradually recognized by most developing countries, and even some people in developed countries have felt China's "soft power".

From a cognitive angle, China's "uniqueness" has its own "novel and original" aesthetic value, which will be highlighted, as "hard power" in national strength increases, and each shines more brilliantly in the other's company, for "hard power" impresses people with a corresponding "soft power" accordingly. For instance, Zhuge

Liang gained his "hard power" from his victories, for he was well versed in the art of war, and "the capability of foretelling like a prophet" became Zhuge's "soft power" accordingly, so that he could "defeat his enemies without a fight".

Nevertheless, both "hard" and "soft" power needs support from the three pillars of education, science and technology, and culture. "Science and technology and culture" have been well expounded before, and education is particularly disscussed here.

Either the "Needham Problem" that "What had happened to explain why this lead never led to 'modern' science in China?", or "Qian's Question" that "Why China's education system failed to produce world-class scientists?", the answer falls on China's education system. As the two questions have been discussed in details by many experts and scholars, this book will be only focused on a "minor problem" of "imagination". From the author's point of view, imagination is simply the ability to connect two issues that seem to be irrelevant but actually correlated with each other. But how indeed does this have anything to do with education? Quite much, in fact. Compared with those in Europe and the United States, China's kindergarten, primary, secondary and tertiary education lack ways and content to cultivate students' imagination, which is significant for the "innovative thoughts, and institution, technological and cultural innovation" discussed in this book. Isn't it out of his imagination that Deng Xiaoping could put forward so many creative ideas, such as "Shenzhen Special Economic Zone", "one country, two systems", that "Science and technology are No. 1 productive forces", and the establishment of the "Central Advisory Commission" in assistance to the transition from "the system of lifelong tenure" in "the Cultural Revolution" to "tenure system"? Therefore, it is recommended to add content and approaches to cultivate students' imagination into the curricular and teaching materials for kindergarten, primary, secondary and tertiary schools in China.

Additionally, necessary measures shall be taken, so that the ratio of expenditure on education to GDP in China can reach 4%, an objective long set in the *Law on Education* and the national education plan, as soon as possible. The GERD/GDP index of 1.5%, in the design of which the author participated, has been realized. Different from R&D input, most of which comes from enterprises, investment in education is almost all from government. With true understanding of the idea that "human resources take the first position", the goal-index of 4% can be reached not too hard. More investment in education means more children in school, like finding more mines. And if a child can study through till the graduation from university, it is as if a mine has been finally put into production long after it was first found. Japanese and Americans have seen this more clearly than we Chinese do.

The three pillars supporting China's "hard power" and "soft power" will get solid, if the expenditures on education, R&D and science and technology can take up 4%, 2% and 6% of GDP respectively.

The "soft power" unique to China is composed of economic, scientific and technological, diplomatic and military power, the efficiency in holding world super events, the capabilities of decisiveness, organization and operation in face of disasters, and the good intention toward others that scotches the "China threat" theory.

Of course, we shall be clearly aware that there is still much to be enhanced for China's "soft power", maybe more to do than for "hard power". In a simple way, we need to "open up and open more, and keep reforming".

Here the author will have a few words about "opening-up". China has made great achievements since the reform and opening-up, mainly including the establishment of 4 economic zones in Shenzhen, Zhuhai, Shantou and Xiamen in 1980; China's entry into the World Trade Organization (WTO) in December 2001; the "going global" strategy, which has encouraged enterprises to go abroad through overseas investments and economic and technological cooperation with foreign enterprises, so that China's economy has achieved sustainable development by making full use of "two markets and two resources"; the establishment of bilateral, multilateral and regional economic and trade cooperation mechanism, under which China has signed with 123 countries bilateral investment treaties (BITs), co-established over 180 multilateral and bilateral joint commissions with 129 countries and areas and 13 international organizations, set up 12 free trade zones together with 29 countries and areas in Asia, Oceania, Latin America, Europe and Africa since 2000, and signed with the Association of Southeast Asian Nations (ASEAN) and implemented accordingly free trade agreements (FTAs) for goods and services, promoting the "10 + 1" and "10 + 3" mechanisms; a large number of Chinese students studying in Europe and the United States; the establishment of strategic economic dialogue mechanism, including three Sino-US strategic economic dialogues since the mechanism was officially started on September 20 2006, as well as various forums such as "China-Europa Forum", "China-Africa Forum", "China-Caribbean Economic & Trade Cooperation Forum" and "China-Pacific Island Countries Economic Development and Cooperation Forum"; and the successful host of Beijing 2008 Olympic Games and Expo 2010 Shanghai China, and so on.

"Wider opening-up" is manifested in new measures taken and plans made in recent years, for example, regular press conferences held by Party and government organizations, the English website of the Ministry of National Defence, the construction of Hainan Island into an island for international tourism, building up a number of international metropolis, broader participation in international affairs, and more foreign students recruited in China's universities. Furthermore, we shall learn more from other countries about advanced communication system, and ideas, measures and means of Institutional design. As for "soft power", we should make efforts to enhance people's self-cultivation, by starting from improving behaviours in public places, for instance, talking in a low voice, no spitting and no queue-jumping, so as to build a civilized image of the Chinese people. It is a task more arduous than enhancing the economic strength and closely related to the national strength as well.

"Wider opening-up" is actually about how to learn to be "open" as well, for example, how to work with media. As shown in Table 1-19, China is only inferior to the United States in terms of the overall strength of media, communication infrastructures and domestic communication, but it has lagged far behind the United States, as well as the UK, Germany, Japan and Italy in international communication. No doubt it is because of the language used in communication, but it also shows that China does not regard the relationship between communication and opening up as important as to influence the national strategy and the enhancement of national strength. It is closely related with not only national interests such as foreign public relations and awareness of international crisis, but also how to solve the problems concerning the "China threat" theory and "human rights". China has launched more TV and broadcast programmes in English and other major foreign languages in recent years. Nonetheless, it is far from enough, and a larger number of more influential media tools are in need. Confucius Institutes are a good example to follow in this aspect.

Table 1-19　Media strength in major countries

Country	Ratio of communication infrastructures to that of the US/%	Ratio of domestic communication to that of the US/%	Ratio of international communication to that of the US/%	Weighted index of media strength/%
The United States	100	100	100	100
China	55.57	88.72	14.13	47.46

Continued

Country	Ratio of communication infrastructures to that of the US/%	Ratio of domestic communication to that of the US/%	Ratio of international communication to that of the US/%	Weighted index of media strength/%
Japan	36.37	65.01	19.10	39.84
The United Kingdom	25.03	21.78	37.79	27.68
India	43.59	44.01	7.06	27.07
Germany	25.70	27.40	25.20	24.95
Italy	21.01	11.13	16.94	13.91
Russia	13.68	17.29	13.80	13.90
France	14.36	14.15	14.15	13.49
Spain	11.14	6.80	12.46	9.25
Canada	11.59	9.66	8.11	8.62
Mexico	8.33	9.46	4.12	6.63
Australia	6.34	7.27	4.32	5.62
The Netherlands	5.29	4.99	4.90	4.75

Source: Hu Angang et al. , 2004.

　　Foreign experts and scholars have made many predications about China's comprehensive national strength in future. According to Goldman Sachs, the largest three economies in the world will be China, the United States and India in 2050, plus Brazil, Mexico, Russia, Indonesia, Japan, the UK and Germany as the largest ten economies. According to predictions of national economy size based upon the GDP in 2006 made by PricewaterhouseCoopers, China's GDP will reach up to 70 trillion dollars in 2050 and the United States about 40 trillion (Martin Jacques, 2010). There are opinions even more optimistic. According to Jim O'Neill, creator of the word "BRICs" and economist of Goldman Sachs, China will catch up with the United States in economic aggregate in 2027 (Ye Chuhua, 2010). No doubt China would fall far behind the United States in per-capita GDP and only around the level of moderately developed countries.

　　Moreover, China should have its own world-class or world-known brands (e. g. BYD, Huawei), films (e. g. *Aftershock*, the box-office returns of which reached up to over 600 million yuan) and music. Then which companies may build world-class brands? In addition to the "national innovation-oriented enterprises" listed in

Appendix I, "2010 China's Top 25 Innovative Companies" selected by *Fortune* (China) are also qualified candidates.

Language is power as well, so we shall make things convenient for Chinese learning. The internationalization of Renminbi is another important index for China's national strength. This process is not only to make Renminbi an international currency for price-quoting and settlement in international trades (which has been realized in Southeast Asian countries), but also to have stronger voice in the international financial circles (for which small progress has been made in the World Bank and IMF). It is unnecessary to elaborate on the significance of military power for the national strength.

It would be great contribution to the mankind and the world, if China could catch up with the United States in national strength (e. g. GDP) in 2050 when China celebrates its 100th anniversary, and surpass the United States in national strength (e. g. per-capita GDP or per-capita GNI) around 2078 when China celebrates the 100th anniversary of the reform and opening-up. Undoubtedly, all depends upon a peaceful and stable environment for further development.

However, such goals might be achieved sooner, if education, science and technology and culture could be developed in a more innovative manner, the Institutional design for government and enterprises with more creative ideas and innovation management with more vitality in China.

Appendices

Appendix I 2009 China's Top 50 Venture Capital Companies

IDG Capital Partners

SAIF Partners

TDF Capital

CDH Investments

Draper Fisher Jurveston (DFJ)

Softbank China Venture Capital

GGV Capital

Intel Capital China

3I

NewMargin Ventures/Ceyuan Ventures

Warburg Pincus

Doll Capital Management

Actis

Sequoia Capital

Luxin Venture Capital Group Co. , Ltd.

Pacific Venture Partners

Shenzhen Capital Group Co. , Ltd.

Legend Capital

WI Harper Group

DragonTech Ventures

HSBC Private Equity (Asia) Limited (HPEA)

New Enterprise Associates

AsiaVest Partners, TCW/YFY Limited

China-Singapore Suzhou Industrial Park Ventures Co. , Ltd.

Fidelity Ventures

JAIC International (Hong Kong) Co. , Ltd.

Walden International

The Carlyle Group

iD TechVentures

JAFCO Asia

Qualcomm Ventures

United Capital Investment

Shenzhen Leaguer Venture Capital Co. , Ltd.

China Merchants & Fortune Assets Management Ltd.

Infotech Pacific Ventures

Everbright Investment Management Ltd.

China Merchants Technology

Chengwei Capital

Northern Light

GSR Ventures

Accel Partners

Guangdong Technology Venture Capital Group Co. , Ltd.

Xiangtou High-tech Venture

Gobi Partners

Zhejiang Venture Capital

Canton Venture Capital Co. , Ltd.

Acorn Campus Ventures

Shenzhen Fortune Venture Capital Co. , Ltd.

Wuhan Huagong Venture Capital Co. , Ltd.

Tsing Capital

(Source: http://www. eastmoney. com)

Appendix II   List of First "National Innovation-Oriented Enterprises" (91 in Total)

China Aerospace Science and Technology Corporation

SINOPEC

State Grid Corporation of China

China Three Gorges Corporation

Shenhua Group Corporation Limited

China Netcom Group

China Electronic Information Industry Group Corporation

FAW Group Corporation

Dongfang Electric Corporation

Anshan Iron and Steel Group Corporation

Baosteel Group Corporation

China Alco

China National Chemical Engineering Co. , Ltd.

China Railway Engineering Corporation

China National Biotec Group

Datang Telecom Technology & Industry Group

China Iron & Steel Research Institute Group (former Iron & Steel Research Institute)

General Research Institute for Nonferrous Metals

China Coal Research Institute

China Textile Academy

Chinese Academy of Agricultural Modernization Sciences

China National Materials Group Corporation

China National Heavy Machinery Research Institute (former Xi'an Heavy Machinery Research Institute)

Beijing General Research Institute of Mining & Metallurgy

FiberHome Technologies Group

Lenovo (Beijing) Co. , Ltd.

Hanvon Technology Co. , Ltd.

Beijing Rechsand Science & Technology Group Co. ,Ltd

Tianjin Pipe (Group) Corporation

Tasly Group

Tangshan Railway Vehicle Co. , Ltd. (former CNR Group Tangshan Locomotive & Rolling Stock Plant)

Taiyuan Heavy Machinery Group Co. , Ltd.

Taiyuan Fenghua Information-Equipment Co. , Ltd.

Inner Mongolia Melic Sea High-Tech Group Company

Siasun Robot & Automation Co. , Ltd.

Liaoning OXIRANCHEM, Inc. (former Liaoning OXIRANCHEM Group Co. , Ltd.)

Jilin Sino-Microelectronics Co. , Ltd.

Changchun Railway Vehicles Co. , Ltd.

BOCO Inter-Telecom

Sanjing Pharmaceutical Co. , Ltd.

Shanghai Zhenhua Heavy Industries Co. , Ltd.

Shanghai Baosight Softwar Co. , Ltd.

Shanghai Electrical Apparatus Research Institute (Group) Co. , Ltd.

Linkage Technology Co. , Ltd.

Yangtze River Pharmaceutical Group

Fasten Group Corporation

SUPCON Group Co. , Ltd.

Geely Holding Group

Zhejiang HISUN Pharmaceuticals Co. , Ltd.

Chery Automobile Co. , Ltd.

Fujian Star-net Communication Co. , Ltd.

Wanlida Group Co. , Ltd.

Jiangxi Changjiu Agrochemical Co. , Ltd.

Inspur Group

Yantai Wanhua Polyurethanes Co. , Ltd.

Shandong Denghai Seeds Co. , Ltd.

XJ Group Corporation

Zhengzhou Yutong Bus Co. , Ltd.

Wuhan Huazhong Numerical Control Co. , Ltd.

Hubei New Torch Science & Technology Co. , Ltd. (formerly Xiangfan Xinghuo Auto Parts Manufacturing Co. , Ltd.)

Changsha Zoomlion Heavy Industry Science & Technology Development Co. , Ltd.

Xiangtan Ping'an Electrical Equipment Group Co. , Ltd.

Kingfa Sci. & Tech. Co. , Ltd.

Fenghua Advanced Technology Holding Co. , Ltd.

Vtron Technologies Limited (formerly Guangdong Vtron Electronics Co. , Ltd.)

Guangzhou Mechanical Engineering Research Institute

Hainan Quanxing Pharmaceutical Co. , Ltd.

Sichuan Instrument Complex Co. , Ltd.

Chongqing Communications Research and Design Institute

Holley Pharmaceuticals Co. , Ltd.

Changhong Electric Co. , Ltd.

Pangang Group Company Ltd.

Di'ao Group

Guiyang Linquan Aerospace Science & Technology Co. , Ltd.

Yunnan Baiyao Group Co. , Ltd.

Kunming Shipbuilding Equipment Co. , Ltd.

Cheezheng Tibetan Medicine Group (former Nyingchi Cheezheng Tibetan Pharmaceutical Factory)

Xi'an Haitian Antenna Technologies Co. , Ltd.

Jinchuan Group Ltd.

Spark Machine Tool Co. , Ltd.

Ningxia Orient Tantalum Industry Co. , Ltd.

Western Mining Co. , Ltd.

Xinjiang Joinworld Co. , Ltd.

Xinjiang Shihezi Zhongfa Chemical Co. , Ltd.

Haitian Plastics Machinery Group Co. , Ltd. (former Ningbo Haitian Group Co. , Ltd.)

Ningbo Powerway Alloy Materials Co. , Ltd.

Xiamen Tungsten Co. , Ltd.

Haier Group

Hisense Group

Huawei Technologies Co. , Ltd.

ZTE Corporation

（Source: Editorial Board of *Report on Development of Innovation-oriented Enterprises in China*, 2009）

Appendix Ⅲ　Interpretation of Indicators for Assessment of National Innovation-Oriented Enterprises

1. Ratio of R&D staff to all employees. R&D staff refers to all people involved in research, management and support of R&D projects, including members of project teams (research programmes), administrative personnel for science and technology in enterprises and assistants providing direct support for projects (research programmes). The ratio can be calculated by the following formula: (number of full-time R&D staff/ total number of employees) × 100%.

2. Status of R&D institutes in an enterprise (on state-, provincial- and local-level). R&D institutes in enterprises refer to comprehensive research institutes, technological development organizations and service promotion agencies set up by enterprises. The index is mainly based upon whether an enterprise has state- or provincial-level R&D centers, such as national engineering research centers, engineering technology centers, enterprise technology centers, and national engineering laboratories.

3. Ratio of fixed assets of R&D equipment to total assets. Fixed assets refer to tangible pieces of property, the uniy price of which is above 2,000 yuan and which is not expected to be consumed or converted into cash any sooner than at least one year's time, or to the major equipment in production with a unity price lower than 2,000 *yuan*. Such property shall maintain the original physical form in use. Calculating formula: (value of fixed assets of R&D equipment/value of total assets) × 100%.

4. Ratio of expenses on independent R&D to total income. Expenses in independent R&D refer to the actual expenditure by an enterprise on R&D of new technology, techniques and other innovative projects by making use of self-owned funds or loans in a year. R&D projects funded by the Central Government or government at all levels are not included in this category. Sales income refers to income from product sales, services or industrial operations provided, sales of by-

products and leftover materials, and cash pledge in industrial enterprises; income from commodity sales and other income such as extra-price income and freight charges in commercial enterprises; and service charges, consulting fees, income from technical guidance and so on in service trade and tertiary industry. Calculating formula: (input in R&D/sales income) × 100%.

5. Ratio of expenses on trial-manufacture of new products (services) to sales income. Expenses on trial-manufacture of new products (services) refer to the ones in manual work, materials, inspections, manufacturing and management in small- and medium-sized trials during the development of new products (services). Calculating formula: [expenses on trial-manufacture of new products (services)/sales income] × 100%.

6. Ratio of expenses on assimilation to sales income. Expenses on assimilation refer to the total amount spent on the assimilation of imported projects in the reporting year, including training cost, measurement cost, salaries of the staff involved, and cost of overalls, technical development, necessary auxiliary equipment and reproduction and etc. Calculating formula: (expenses on assimilation/sales income) × 100%.

7. Ratio of expenses on employee training to sales income. Expenses in employee training refer to the amount spent for employees on learning of advanced technology and on improvements of their cultural level, mainly including official business fees, operating expenses, payment to part-time teachers, expenses on studies and research, equipment cost, commissions paid to the organizations entrusted for contracted training, and other petty expenses. Calculating formula: (expenses on employee training/sales income) × 100%.

8. The number of granted invention patents (proprietary technology) possessed by every thousand scientists and engineers. Scientists and engineers refer to the employees with bachelor's degree and above, as well as the ones without the abovementioned degrees but with middle or high titles.

According to the *Patent Law of the People's Republic of China*, inventions refer to new production programmes targeting products, approaches or related improvements. Proprietary technology, also known as confidential technology, refers to all the know-how, experience and skills concerning production, management and finance in compliance with rules and laws, including process flows, formulae, ingredients, technical regulations, and skills and experience of management and sales etc.

9. Annual growth rate of patent applications in the recent three years refers to The average value of patent application growth rates in adjacent months.

10. The number of new products (services) every year. New products (services) refer to the industrial products trial-produced or produced with new domestic or foreign designs, and structure, materials or techniques involved are much improved compared to the previous products, so that product performance is enhanced or functions increased. Such new products (services) feature in: ① new mechanism, structure or improvements in the structure of previous products; ② new materials and components; ③ new characteristics of performance; ④ new uses or market demands. New products (services) are usually developed with new product development assignments (signed by legal representative and clarifying goals).

11. Ratio of income from new products (services) to total sales income. Calculating formula: [sales income from new products (services)/sales income] × 100%.

12. Growth rate of income from new products (services). Calculating formula: {[sales income from new products (services) in the reporting period – sales income from new products (services) in the previous year]/sales income from new products (services) in the previous year} × 100%.

13. Level and number of technical norms formulated by enterprise means the number of industrial, national and international norms worked out, partially or mainly, by an enterprise every year.

14. Pre-tax return on sales refers to ratio of profits and taxes to net sales revenue, reflecting the profitability and contribution degree of an enterprise's sales income. Pre-tax return on sales reflects the situation of a year. Annual profits and taxes are the average value of five years, calculated in 10,000 yuan, and annual sales income the average value of three years, calculated in 10,000 yuan. Profits and taxes include turnover tax, income tax and after-tax profits. Net sales revenue refers to the net sales deducting sales allowances, discounts and returns. Calculating formula: pre-tax return on sales = (annual profits and taxes/annual sales income of products) × 100%.

15. The number of patent-licensed projects of an enterprise. Patent-licensed trades refer to the trade practice, under which a patentee signs with the licensee a license contract for patent exploitation in compliance with the patent law and other rules of law, permitting the licensee to exploit the patented technology within the conditions and scope set in the contract.

16. Income from technology transfers and licenses. Income from technology transfers and licenses refers to the income an enterprise gains by transferring the technology possessed to another party to use.

17. The number of tripartite patents possessed by an enterprise. Tripartite patents are the ones granted by all the three countries (parties) of the United States, Japan and Europe.

18. The number of rationalization proposals by every hundred employees. A rationalization proposal refers to any operational improved method and measure proposed by one or more employees for the enterprise's production, operation or management, which is beyond his/her/their responsibilities. Calculating formula: (total number of rationalization proposals by employees/total number of employees) × 100%.

(Source: *Survey Report by the Evaluation Team of National Innovation-oriented Enterprise*)

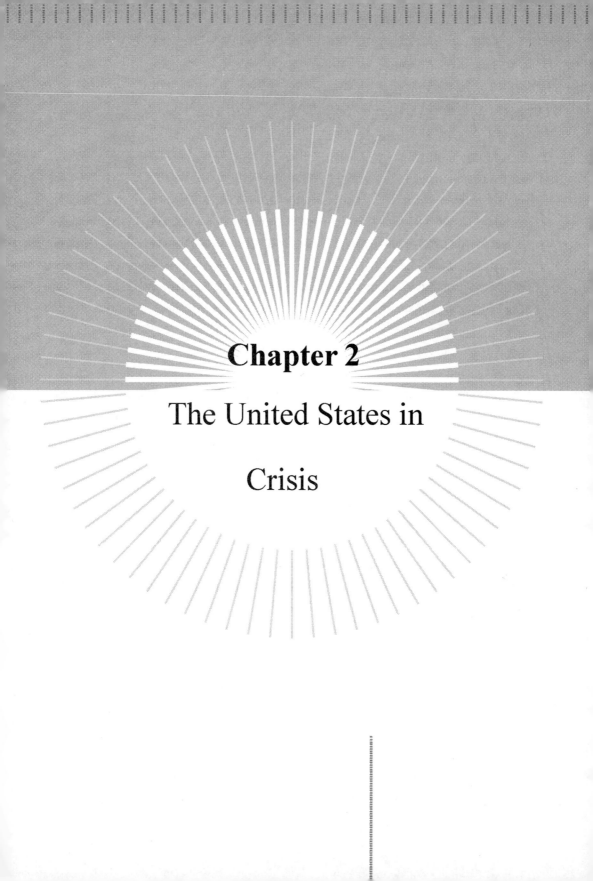

Chapter 2

The United States in

Crisis

The topic of this chapter indicates that the United States is experiencing the most serious financial and economic crises since "the Great Depression" in the 1930s, as well as the second "dollar crisis" (the first one refers to the collapse of "gold standard" in the 1970s) (Ye Chuhua, 2010). Therefore, it is no exaggeration to say that the United States in crisis.

The United States is a short term for the United States of America, with a territory of 9,629,000 square kilometers (the land area of which is 9,159,000 square kilometers) and 308 million people (statistical data in 2008). The United States is rich in natural resources, ranking among the top in terms of its reserves of coal, petroleum, natural gas and iron ore. The forest coverage reaches up to 33%. 56% of the whole population are Protestants (i.e. Puritans), 28% Catholics, 2% Judaists and 10% are non-religious people (Editorial Board of *World Affairs*, 2009). Puritanism has played a crucial role in the development of the States, which is undoubtedly the youngest one of the world's powers today. The US has a relatively short history of 234 years since its foundation in 1776, in which time China has experienced radical changes from the late Qianlong's Reign of the Qing Dynasty till present day. During the one century after its independence, the US expanded its territory through the Westward Movement, with the immigration progress reaching to climax and agriculture developed. The American Civil War during 1861 and 1865 eliminated slavery and cleared away the obstacles to the development of capitalism. Boosted by technological revolution, the US completed its industrialization at a fast pace in the late 19th century, and developed from a small country with 890,000 square miles and 3.93 million people (in 1790) in the beginning of its independence to a large nation of 45 states with a population of over 70 million people. In 1890, the US took up 31% of the world's industries, leaping into the first position in the world by surpassing the UK's 22%, and became the world's richest and most developed country (Tang Jin, 2006). In other words, it only took 114 years for the US to develop from a small and weak country at the independence to the richest and most developed one in the world.

Following France and Germany, the United States has become the world's center of science and technology since the end of 1930s. Its leading position in science can be well proved by over 200 American Nobel Prize-winning scientists. And Edison and Bell were the most prominent representatives of technological innovation. Moreover, there are in the US also enterprise management talents such as Taylor, Ford and Steve Jobs, incumbent CEO of Apple Inc, as well as masters of science and technology management like Vannervar Bush.

The United States has enjoyed its strong national strength and leading position in the world for 120 years. Nevertheless, its national strength has also seen a trend of decreasing since the 1990s. To maintain its leading position, the US places the hope on the military hegemony, but has to retreat from time to time, due to its slumping economy.

There are so many books on the reasons for the prosperity of the US. This chapter, therefore, only discusses about "innovation management" from angles of Institutional design, innovation management and innovation culture.

1. Institutional Design

The United States has national conditions quite different from those of China: a young country and an old one with histories of over 200 years and 5,000 years respectively; different cultures of Puritanism and Confucianism; different political systems of separation of powers and the leadership under one party; different market systems with private ownership and public ownership as the mainstay respectively, and so on. Therefore, the US "focuses on the legal system" and "stresses separation of powers" in system innovation, while China is characterized with "the national system" and "planned management". Briefly, China and the US have quite different characteristics in institution innovation, as the political systems they adopt are two typical ones in the world. The differences in the political system have not only formed the diversified political setup of the world today, but also given innovation management various models and methods, so that countries can have more choices for their development. And diversity of choices is a sign of the world's progress.

1.1　National Institutional Design

The United States worked out constitutional document, the *Articles of Confederation* in July 1776, and promulgated the world's first written constitution for a unified nation in 1787. The Congress made quite a number of revisions to the Constitution after 1787.

The US' political system is typical in the West, featuring separation of powers (separation of the legislative, executive and judicial power), two-party system (the Democratic Party and the Republican Party leading elections), and federal system (separation powers of the Federal Government and state governments) (see Fig. 2-1). Some hold that the modern "federal system has been one of the greatest contributions made by the United States to the government art" (Almond et al., 2010). Federal system can be seen as a perfect one, if there are no other political systems challenging it. However, people begin to think about defects of federal system, as the US faces declining political and economic strength, national prestige and reputation. Particularly, as China shows in "the period of rising" that it has achieved prosperity with a political system totally different from the US', people are trying to find out one, two or more political systems ideal for future development.

The system of "separation of powers" has been adopted for years. Historically, the founders of the United States like Jefferson and Franklin had been deeply influenced by the ancient Greek philosopher Aristotle's idea of "discussion, executive and judicial functions" of poleis, the English philosopher Locke's thought of "separation of the legislative, executive and federative powers", and Montesquier's, a French philosopher during Enlightment, view that a nation has "the legislative, executive and judicial powers separated from and dependent upon each other" in his *The Spirit of Laws*, and they wrote the thought of "separation of powers" into *Declaration of Independence* and the *Constitution of the United States of America*, as the fundamental system of the US (Dong Xiuli, 2010). The advocates of federal system maintain that the system can make the legislative, judicial and executive powers checked and balanced. Objectively, the system does indeed check and balance the three powers to some extent. However, the defects in the system are also evident. According to a report from the US Congress, there are over 100 steps and procedures before a bill may be rectified by the Congress as a law. During the process, a bill can be delayed, rejected or revised at any time. Congressmen often bargain for a bill in three ways of flattering, compromising and giving favors (Cultural Office under Embassy of the United States to China, 1984). Such "bargain" has shed a light on the effect of a bill passed. The situation in developed countries is so disappointing, let alone that in less-developed countries which follow suit.

Many heads of state and government at the time of the foundation of the United States were interested in and even master hands of science and technology, such as George Washington and Thomas Jefferson (one of the drafters of *Declaration of Independence*), the former of whom was the first US President and devoted to improving agricultural technology, holding that technological improvements in agriculture, animal

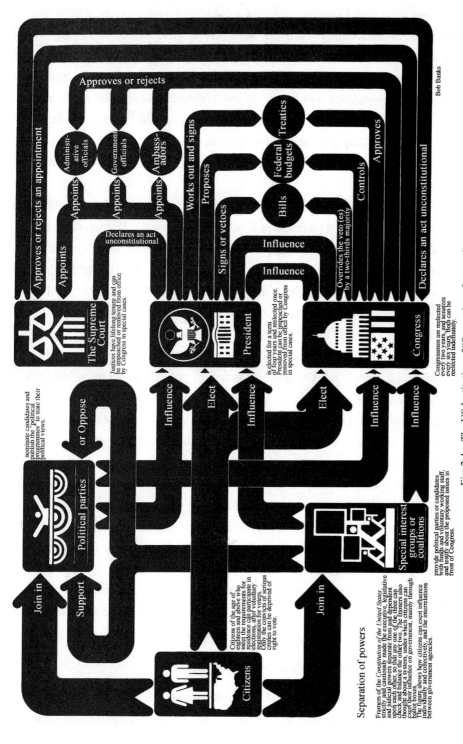

Fig. 2-1   The US Institution of "Separation of powers"

Source: *Steering the Course: Policy-making in the United States* by Cultural Office under Embassy of the United States to China

Separation of powers

Framers of the *Constitution of the United States* strictly and cautiously made the executive, legislative and judicial powers separate from and dependent upon each other, so that any one of the three can check and balance the other two. The framers also thought about a system, under which citizens can exert their influence on government, mainly through ballot boxes.
The figure shows how citizens can exert influence individually and collectively, and the interrelations between government agencies.

husbandry and agricultural sidelines were the most important and practical work that he could do to serve the country, and the latter the third President, inventing swivel chair, revolving stand for food and a new moldboard. Of course, we shall not forget the inventor of lightning rod, Benjamin Franklin, who was also one of the drafters of *Declaration of Independence* and envoy to the UK and France. All of them were designers of political system in early time of the US. Franklin founded the first anti-slavery society in the US, and Jefferson was famous for his words that "I have sworn upon the altar of God, eternal hostility against every form of tyranny over the mind of man." (Zhou Jizhong, 1991)

The early US system designers have had profound influence on their successors in system design and design of science and technology system. However, it is also because of the Institutional design that the US has turned from the largest creditor nation to the largest debtor in the world at the beginning of the 21st century. Upon various considerations, including that "the salaries are much higher in the US than in developing countries" and that "the industries unfavourable, even harmful to the domestic environment and resources shall be moved out of the US", most of manufacturing enterprises have been moved out from the United States (mainly to Asian countries). Under the industrial restructuring, the US government has worked out the industrial development system and related policies on modern service trade, which takes finance, R&D and designing as its mainstay, encouraging people to lend from banks and use tomorrow's money today. Consequently, on the one hand, output value of service trade took up 77% of GDP in the country (in 2007), while on the other hand, the country became the world's largest deficit country in foreign trade, owing trillions of dollars to other countries, including China. The US is "an actually bankrupt country" (or rather, a technically-bankrupt country), due to insolvency. The ongoing financial, economic and dollar crises hitting all the countries in the world are basically the evil consequences of the abovementioned Institutional design of the US.

Evidently in the national financial system, the United States adopts a "market-oriented" one based upon capital market. Stock assets take a proportion in GDP larger than that of banks' assets.

1.2 National Sci-Tech Decision-Making System

Though both the White House and the Congress play significant roles in the sci-tech decision-making, the former is the core of the system, including the Office of

Science and Technology Policy (OSTP), President's Council of Advisors on Science and Technology (PCAST) and the National Science and Technology Council (NSTC). Among the three, OSTP functions as an administrative and coordinating body, the director of which is also one of President's advisors on science and technology, providing suggestions on science and technology concerning federal policies and plans. The other two bodies are both councils of consultation and coordination. The three bodies are all in the responsibility of the Assistant to the President for Science and Technology (only Bill Clinton used to hold the concurrent post of Director during his terms). Science and technology committees are set up under both the House of Representatives and the Senate. Those in the House of Representatives are Committee on Science, Space and Technology and Committee on Natural Resources, and the one in the Senate is the Committee on Commerce, Science, & Transportation. There are subcommittees under these committees. Besides, there are three supporting bodies under Congress, including Congressional Budget Office (CBO), General Accounting Office (GAO) and Congressional Research Service (CRS).

However, there has been never such an organization like "the department of science and technology" in the United States. NSTC was just established in 1993 during the terms of President Bill Clinton and functioned as a tool for President Clinton to coordinate federal policies on science, space exploration and technology. Under President George W. Bush, NSTC worked as a high-level body for macro coordination, making national R&D budgets on a macro level, while the managing powers over scientific and technological issues and resources are specifically down to the Department of Defense (DoD), the Department of Health and Human Services (HHS), the Department of Energy (DOE), the Department of Agriculture (USDA), the Department of Commerce, the National Aeronautics and Space Administration (NASA) and the National Science Foundation (NSF), and coordinated by Assistant to the President for Science and Technology and OSTP for such as policy-making and budget allocation. In Congress, the committees or subcommittees on science and technology under the Senate and the House of Representatives work both as the legislative and supervisory bodies charged with supervision over the working-out and implementation of Government's policies on science and technology and R&D budget plans. Such a "seemingly loose organized" sci-tech management system actually conforms with the US' concept of value that science and technology shall have least government intervention, as scientific and technological activities need most freedom and creativity. Politicians often know little about highly-specialized scientific and technological activities, and there is consultation on high-level decision-making provided by official and non-government authorities, such as PCAST, the National Academy of Sciences (NAS) and the American Association for the Advancement of Science (AAAS). Such a "seemingly loose organized" sci-tech management system is supported by the Federal Government, enterprises, universities and colleges, and scientific and technological research institutes. With separation of powers between the Federal and State governments, the Federal Government is in charge of management of the national scientific and technological issues, and competent departments in the Federal Government are the seven mentioned above including the Department of Defense.

Table 2-1 shows R&D budgets and capability of resource allocation in the US departments in FY2011.

Table 2-1   R&D budgets in the US federal departments in FY2011 (Unit: 1 million dollars)

	Actual value in FY2009	Appropriation in FY2009	Estimated value in FY2010	Budget in FY2011	Amount changes in FY2010~2011	Percentage of change in FY2010~2011/%
DoD	80,821	300	81,090	77,548	-3,542	-4.4
HHS	30,595	11,063	31,177	32,156	979	3.1
NIH	29,289	10,363	30,442	31,398	956	3.1
NASA	10,887	790	9,286	10,986	1,700	18.3
DOE	10,301	2,967	10,693	11,219	526	4.9
NSF	5,379	2,197	5,092	5,571	479	9.4
USDA	2,437	176	2,591	248	-143	-5.5
Dept. of Commerce	1,393	576	1,516	1,727	211	13.9
NIST	552	411	580	706	126	21.7
Dept. of Homeland Security (DHS)	1,096	0	1,150	1,046	-106	-9.0
R&D in total	147,318	18,153	147,353	147,696	343	0.2
R&D for national defense	84,646	300	85,038	81,695	-3,343	-3.9
Non-national defense R&D	62,672	17,853	62,315	66,001	3,686	5.9
Basic research	29,583	7,794	20,002	31,341	1,339	4.5
Applied research	29,054	5,385	28,327	30,276	1,949	6.9
Research in total	58,637	13,179	58,329	61,617	3,288	5.6
Development in total	83,866	1,482	84,373	81,455	-2,918	-3.5
R&D equipment	4,815	3,492	4,651	4,624	-27	-0.6

Source: According to the data published by OSTP of the White House on 1 February 2010.

Every fiscal year begins in October in the United States. From Table 2-1, we can see how the US Federal Government budget for science and technology is allocated.

Compared to that in FY 2010, the US Federal R&D budget only increases by 0.2% in FY2011, basically the same with the previous year. And R&D budget for national defense even decreases compared to that in the previous fiscal year. During the terms of President Reagan, the expenditure on R&D for national defense took up 70% ~ 80% of Government's total expenditure on R&D. However, since President Clinton took office, the US policies on science and technology have shifted the focus from national defense and military R&D to R&D for civil uses, so that the percentage kept decreasing and the gap between expenditure on R&D for national defense and that on non-national defense R&D was narrowed year by year. In 2009, the former took up 57.5% and the latter 42.5%, with a difference of 15 percentage points. And the figures in 2010 were estimated the same as the previous year. In the FY2011 Budget, the ratio of expenditure on national defense to non-national defense R&D stands at 55. 3∶44.7, with the gap between the two further narrowed. The change is actually a reflection of the change in the world's political structure in the US sci-tech system, after the USSR-Eastern Bloc disintegrated and the Cold War came to an end.

Seen from types of research, the expenditure on basic research and that on applied research were basically the same in 2009, taking up 20% each of the total expenditure on R&D. The expenditure on experiments and development took up about 57% of the total R&D expenses, and that on R&D equipment 3%. The proportions of budget for basic research, applied research, and experiments and development are 21.2%, 20.5% and 55.2% respectively in FY2011. The US government has a stable allocation for the three.

There are 4 government departments with the FY2011 R&D budget over 10 billion dollars, including DoD with 77.548 billion dollars, HHS with 32.156 billion dollars, the National Institutes of Health (NIH) under HHS with 31.398 billion dollars, DOE with 11.219 billion dollars and NASA with 10.986 billion dollars, followed by NSF with 5.571 billion dollars, USDA with 2.448 billion dollars, Dept. of Commerce with 1.727 billion dollars and the National Institute of Standards and Technology (NIST) under Dept. of Commerce with 706 million dollars. The seven federal departments have received the most R&D budget for years and been the ones most closely related to scientific and technological issues in the United States, showing that issues concerning science and technology are dealt with by only a few departments in the US Federal Government. That

NIH can gain a budget of 31.398 billion dollars and the amount approved by Congress are often larger than that has been asked by Government indicates a common view among Government, Congress and the people in the United States, that life, health and medical research are given much attention to. This common view is a concept of value and culture values, as well as years' tradition that has been the focus of the US governments, congressional policies and laws in the past, at present and in future.

The FY2011 American Federal budget for R&D indicates that the Obama Administration has been fully aware of the significance and irreplaceability of technological innovation for the United States to maintain its national strength, economy and leading position as a world's power.

It should also be seen that the American governments have continuously and stably input more in science and technology since the ending of the Second World War. Taking the expenditure on R&D for example, as an indicator for a country's input intensity in science and technology, GERD/GDP means the ratio of expenditure on R&D to a country's gross domestic product. The indicator figures have been around 2.0% ~2.8% in the United States for decades, which can be seen as an important reason why the United States can keep strong national power and competitiveness.

1.3　The Sci-Tech System Design in the Early 20th Century

It is basically referred to as the sci-tech system design in the 1940s and 1950s in the United States. Since then on, scientific and technological undertakings have become a national course of the United States, which was to some extent because of the WWII. It was during this time that the US replaced the UK to be the world's great power, after the *Bretton Woods Agreement* and its gold-dollar standard replaced the previous gold-pound standard, and the United States launched the Marshall Plan, which was officially the European Recovery Programme (ERP).

1.3.1　"System of contracted appropriations" during the wartime

In the United States, science and technology have become the national resources, the achievements of which can be turned into "productive forces" and "combat effectiveness", since the Second World War. There has never been a ministry-level institution in the American Federal Government in charge of scientific and technological affairs (i. e. no Department of Science and Technology under the Federal Government). However, the Office of Scientific Research and Development (OSRD), a wartime provisional agency, made exceptional contributions to the transformation of science and technology into military equipment, weapons and medical commodities (e. g. development of atomic bombs and commercialization of radars and penicillin). The "system of contracted appropriations" created by OSRD in wartime was actually a system innovation. OSRD signed with universities, scientific research institutes and enterprises contracts, prescribing salaries, management fees, responsibilities, patents and asset allocation and etc. These contracts for scientific and technological achievements were boosts to R&D and managerial staff, for responsibilities and rights were clarified, so that the efficiency of research and development and the transformation of R&D achievements was enhanced. For example, 150,000 people were involved and two billion dollars input in the Manhattan Project of research and development of atomic bombs, and it had taken just 3 years for the successful test explosion of the first atomic bomb, which owed much to the "system of contracted appropriations".

The enterprises and universities that received the largest number of such contracts from Government during the Second World War, such as DuPont, General Electric Company (GE), Kodak, Radio Corporation of America (RCA), Massachusetts Institute of Technology (MIT), University of California, California Institute of Technology , Harvard University and Columbia University, have all enjoyed rapid development after the war, which is to some extent attributed to the "system of contracted appropriations".

Such a system became the model of the postwar sci-tech appropriation system in the US and the embryo of today's "system of industry-university-government transactions (IUGT)".

1.3.2　Science: the endless frontier

(1) Background

Either the abovementioned "system of contracted appropriations" and NSF, or *Science: The Endless Frontier* is related to Vannevar Bush, who took the lead in writing the report titled *Science: The Endless Frontier* that drew a blueprint for the US' postwar development of science and technology.

During the Second World War, all the belligerent countries made use of all resources, including both existing and potential sci-tech resources, the core of which was to transform scientific and technological achievements into operational equipment, weapons and medicines. Out of the special relationship with wars, science and technology (especially the latter) always developed in an unprecedented way during the wartime, from battles between the ancient Greek and Rome, through the Spring and Autumn Period and the Period of Warring States in China, to the Gulf Wars more recently. In the early stage of the Second World War, many victories of Germany were attributed to the country's advantages in military science and technology. "In order to transform scientific and technological achievements into operational equipment, weapons and medicines as soon as possible", the US Federal Government decided to establish a provisional agency OSRD directed by Vannevar Bush, an inventor, professor and vice-president in Massachusetts Institute of Technology (MIT) and director of the Carnegie Institution. A great number of advanced weapons and military supplies were soon produced, after OSRD had successfully applied the "system of contracted appropriations" among governments, universities and enterprises and the chain of innovation between institutional and product innovation started to work. The well-known ones include radars, commercialization of penicillin, and atomic bombs, which played important roles in the war. The then-President Franklin Roosevelt was deeply impressed and influenced by these achievements (Zachary, 1999).

(2) Problems

Right before the defeat of Germany and Japan in the Second World War, in his letter to Vannevar Bush, Director of the Office of Scientific Research and Development on 17 November 1944, President Roosevelt talked about how to employ the experience in "coordinating scientific research and in applying existing scientific knowledge to the solution of the technical problems paramount in war" in peace time ahead. Roosevelt raised the following four questions in this letter.

"First, what can be done, consistent with military security and upon the approval of the military authorities, to make known to the world as soon as possible the contributions of efforts in the war time to scientific knowledge? The diffusion of such knowledge should help us stimulate new enterprises, provide jobs for veterans and other workers, and significantly improve people's well-being.

Second, with particular reference to the war of science against disease, what can be done now to organize a program to continue efforts on medicine and related sciences? The fact that the annual deaths in this country from one or two diseases alone are far more than the total number of lives claimed by this war reminds us of our duty to the future generations.

Third, what can and will the Government do to aid research activities by public and private organizations? The proper roles of public and of private research, and their interrelation, should be carefully considered.

Fourth, can an effective program be proposed for discovering and developing young scientific talent to ensure scientific research in this country to reach a level comparable to what has been done during the war?

We are not faced with new fields for which we should make full use of our talent. If we pioneer in these fields with the same vision, boldness, and drive as we did this war, we can provide more jobs and creat a more fruitful life.

I hope that, after such consultation as you may deem advisable with your associates and others, you can let me have your considered judgment on these matters as soon as possible——reporting on each whenever you are ready, rather than waiting for completion of your studies in all. " (Bush, 1960; V. Bush et al. , 2006)

(3) Organization

On receiving President Roosevelt's letter, Vannevar Bush, then Director of the Office of Scientific Research and Development, promptly invited distinguished American experts and scholars to form four expert consulting committees on the issues concerning the four questions raised by the President. The experts and scholars invited included Nobel Prize winners and presidents of distinguished universities. For instance, in the committee targeting the President's first question, there were K. Compton, President of the MIT and Chairman of the National Security Council (NSC), and J. Conant, President of Harvard University and Chairman of the National Defense Research Committee. Dr. E. Doisy, Chairman of Department of Biochemistry, St. Louis University and winner of the Nobel Prize in Physiology or Medicine, worked for the committee charged with consultation for the second question. O. Barclay, Director of Bell Labs and I. Rabi, Winner of Nobel Prize in Physics in 1944 were among those working for the third question. And members of the fourth committee included Dr. H. Moe, Secretary General of John Simon Guggenheim Memorial Foundation and Dr. H. Bethe, President of the American Physical Society (APS). The participation of world-class experts is essential for qualified research reports. Bush submitted his report titled *Science: The Endless Frontier* on July 25, 1945, and attached a letter as reply to President Roosevelt on 17 November 1944. Dr. Vannevar Bush wrote at the end of this letter, "The pioneer spirit is still vigorous within this nation. Science offers a largely unexplored hinterland for the pioneer who has the tools for his task. The rewards of such exploration both for the nation and the individual are great. Scientific progress is one essential factor to the national security, better health, more jobs, a higher standard of living, and our cultural progress. " (Bush, 1960; V. Bush et al. , 2006)

(4) Programs

Science: The Endless Frontier, an answer to President Roosevelt's four questions, actually drew a blueprint for the US' postwar scientific and technological development. The report has six parts, as outlined below:

Introduction——Scientific progress is essential: science should be a proper concern of the government; and freedom of exploration must be guaranteed.

Fight against disease: Basic research in medicine and the underlying sciences are essential to progress in the fight against disease. Government should extend financial support to basic medical research in the medical schools and universities. An independent national medical research foundation should be established.

Science and the public welfare: Enterprises should conduct industrial research. A permanent Science Advisory Board should be established as the bridge linking up scientific bureaus and the government. International exchange of scientific information should be further promoted. Federal R&D budget is necessary. More shall be input in scientific research in universities and research institutes. A National Research Foundation should be set up, to ensure the development of the national basic research.

Renewal of scientific talent: People's intelligence is the greatest resource of a national. Basic educational policy will determine the future of the country's scientific development. Talents are badly in need due to the war. A programme would provide 24,000 undergraduate scholarships and 900 graduate allowances.

Scientific rejuvenation: Our ability to overcome potential enemies depends upon scientific advances; we shall provide to veterans with access to education, and lift restrictions on scientific development in the war time.

The means to the end: We should work out the principle of government's funding scientific research—funds that are provided stably and sustainedly; establish institutions that manage and fund basic research, and organize a National Research Foundation (purpose, organization, functions, and budget).

(5) Elements of *Science: The Endless Frontier*

A significant plan for scientific and technological development, *Science: The Endless Frontier* has the following two features:

1) Prospectiveness. When the Second World War was about to end, there were hundreds of things for a state leader like the US President to do. The four abovementioned questions picked up from thousands and the intention to find ways of development through promoting scientific progress and fostering scientific talents show

the vision and prospectiveness of the decision maker. The report writers' thoughts are shown in the general report and the four sub-reports. For example,

"(But) without scientific progress no amount of achievement in other directions can insure our health, prosperity, and security as a nation in the modern world."

"A nation which depends upon others for its new basic scientific knowledge will be slow in its industrial progress and weak in its competitive position in world trade, regardless of its mechanical skill."

"It is my judgment that the national interest in scientific research and scientific education can best be promoted by the creation of a National Research Foundation."

"The greatest resource of a nation (is) the intelligence of its citizens, more important than any other natural one."

"The future of science in this country will be determined by our basic educational policy."

"Most future leaders of science and technology in US are serving in the army now. We should have recruited and trained the talent in uniform prior to the end of war. Otherwise we would find it severely hinder the leadership of science and technology in this country. Such hindrance, in peacetime or war, would be fatally destructive to our standard and ways of living." (Bush, 1960; V. Bush et al., 2006)

As the above ideas were already written in *Science: The Endless Frontier* 65 years ago, and are still influential even today, there is no doubt why "planning and policy-making" occupy such important positions and have so much significance in management sciences (Penick, 1972).

Perspectiveness is the most exceptional feature of *Science: The Endless Frontier*. If management is seen as designing of environment, in which people can make full exploration of their potential to achieve an organization's objectives, *Science: The Endless Frontier* has actually designed the environment for the US' postwar scientific and technological development, so that scientific and technological personnel can make innovations within and achieve the national goals of promoting scientific and technological, economic and social progress.

2) Feasibility. The large-scale scientific and technological plan of *Science: The Endless Frontier* has been feasible, as it has employed various management functions, such as planning, organizing, controlling and budget (a numerical plan), and combined theories and practice, which makes it proudly influential.

The plan for the establishment of a National Science Foundation (NSF) proposed in the report was of feasibility. The purpose of this foundation is to fund basic research and applied research in the US and bridge university education and scientific research.

As for its organizational structure, the Foundation would have a council composed of 15 members and divisions of medical research, natural sciences, national defense, scientific personnel and education etc. Based upon the estimate of the input in scientific research from the Government and universities and research institutes, a budge was made for the operation of the Foundation: 33.5 million dollars for the first year and 122.5 million dollars for the fifth year. Due to its theoretical significance and feasibility, the law of establishment of the National Science Foundation (NSF) was passed by Congress in 1950. Since then, NSF has played a crucial role in promoting basic research and education on science and technology in the US. The NSF FY2011 Budget is as large as over 5 billion dollars.

Report of the Committee on Science and the Public Welfare expounds the issue of establishing "the national research budget". The report explains with tables the relationship between scientific research expenditures and national income, proportions of national scientific research funds from enterprises, government, universities and non-profit organizations, and the ratio of expenditures on basic research to those on applied research. These designs have formed the framework of the American federal R&D budget after the Second World War.

Report of the Committee on Discovery and Development of Scientific Talent proposes a programme providing 6,000 four-year undergraduate scholarships (which can support 24,000 students) and 300 three-year allowances (900 receivers) and costing 29 million dollars annually. The report also advises to make revisions to *Servicemen's Readjustment Act*, making detailed provisions of arrangements and funds for veterans' education after the war. These plans have been all implemented after the war. Many veterans recruited for further education war have become experts and scholars active in science and technology, and economic and educational fields in the US. Therefore, the country has taken the preemptive opportunities in the "war" of salvaging and fostering talent after the Second World War, thanks to the elaborate designs in *Science: The Endless Frontier*.

1.3.3 Organizational design: the National Science Foundation (NSF)

After the Second World War, in order to continue the effective long-range support for basic research in peacetime, and the US Government and the Congress was to discuss the establishment of a "National Research Foundation" proposed in the report *Science: The Endless Frontier* submitted by Vannevar Bush, Director of the Office of Scientific Research and Development (OSRD). The Congress passed a bill establishing such an organization. However, after two years of debate, President Truman vetoed the bill, for reason that such a foundation would transfer the decision-making power of major national policies, the Government's major administrative functions and the power of allocating huge public funds to an actual non-governmental organization. That means the foundation will not under the public supervision, indicating the lack of trust in the democratic procedures. Another two years later, the Congress finally passed the *National Science Foundation Act of 1950*, after having made revisions according to President Truman's suggestions. It had been five years since the bill was first drafted in 1945. It is true that it may take longer to pass a bill. However, five years' time is still too long for such an issue on whether the director of a foundation is elected by people or appointed by the President.

The NSF celebrates its 60th anniversary this year. As a federal agency in charge of scientific and technological management, it has played an ever-important role in promoting scientific and technological development in the US in the past 60 years. NSF's mission is to promote the US' scientific development by funding basic research programmes, improving science education, enhancing scientific information and strengthening international cooperation in sciences. NSF's policy-making body is the National Science Board (NSB), the leadership of which includes one chairman, one vice-chairman and 5 assistants to the chairman. NSB members are all appointed by the US President. NSB's mission is to establish the overall policies of NSF. There are many committees on various disciplines, as well as *ad hoc* committees on specific issues. Since 1968, NSF has submitted every two years a report on the development of sciences and disciplines in the country through NSB to the President (and transmitted to the Congress). The report is titled *Science and Engineering Indicators*. NSF functions in the five categories of programmes for basic research, science education, applied research, science policy and international cooperation.

The National Natural Science Foundation of China (NSFC) founded in 1986 was to some extent modeled on the US' NSF in terms of structure and functions.

1.3.4   Responding to crises with science, technology and education

Another concept of the US' Institutional designers (or rather a tradition in Institutional design) is to consciously turn to science, technology and education for solutions once the country is hit by crises. Such a concept was most evident in 1944 and 1958 when President Roosevelt and President Eisenhower were in office (the Second

World War was about to end and the Soviet Union launched the first artificial satellite).

It's been tradition for the Americans to pursue natural sciences and knowledge of technology, since they have long been under an invisible influence of the Protestant culture value of "believing in God through the touch and understanding of Nature". This concept of value was reflected not only by the founding-fathers of the United States, such as President Washington and President Jefferson, who were interested in science and technology, but also by President Roosevelt ruling during the Second World War and the President Eisenhower who were not that interested in science and technology themselves. As abovementioned, President Roosevelt's question that "With particular reference to the fight against disease through science, what can be done now to organize a program to continue our efforts on medicine and other related efforts?" hastened the birth of *Science: The Endless Frontier*, and that may be because of Roosevelt's suffering of infantile paralysis, and the President paid special attention to the development of medical research. And President Eisenhower turned to science and technology for solutions that could make the US prepared after the Soviet Union had launched the world's first artificial satellite.

Thanks to his victories in the Second World War, General Eisenhower took office as the 34th President of the United States in March 1953. During his two terms, President Eisenhower was confronted with the biggest challenge from abroad after the Second World War, when the Soviet Union, the rival of the United States, launched the world's first artificial satellite. The whole country was greatly shocked. On the press conference on 9 October 1957, President Eisenhower said that the US had planned for the launch of an artificial satellite during the International Geophysical Year between June 1957 and December 1958. The programme had been approved and funded with 22 million dollars by NSF, which was later added up to 110 million dollars. The US Government and Congress took significant measures to counter this crisis. First, the National Aeronautics and Space Administration (NASA) was established. Secondly, the President's Advisors on Science and Technology were appointed. And thirdly, new laws were passed to cultivate scientific and technological talent.

Half a year after the abovementioned press conference, President Eisenhower submitted a special report to Congress, asking to establish a civilian space research and coordinating body. The Congress passed in July 1958 the *National Aeronautics and Space Act*, after hearings and discussions. Three months later, NASA was officially established. The Act specifies three missions of NASA: researching on flights in the outer space;

researching on, manufacturing, testing and operating aerospace crafts for the purpose of scientific research; and making scientific research related to space exploration. The amendment to the Act passed in 1960 stresses the power and responsibilities of NASA, clarifying national programmes for space exploration charged by NASA, to avoid redundant research and development by the DoD. Besides, the National Advisory Committee on Aeronautics (NACA) chaired by the President has been cancelled since then. Table 2-1 shows that NASA is among the four federal agencies, of which the FY2011 R&D budget is higher than 10 billion dollars. With a budget of about 11 billion dollars, NASA is only after DoD and IIHS and roughly the same as DOE.

Another measure taken by President Eisenhower was to appoint an Assistant to the President for Science and Technology, PAST for short. The position was first taken by Dr. James Killian, then President of MIT.

A third measure was the *National Defense Education Act* (NDEA) passed in 1958. The guideline of the Act lies in: For the national security, the whole nation must try the best to develop the intelligence and skills of youth, which requires programmes ensuring the talented students to afford higher education, and the proportion of professionals with the knowledge of basic sciences and receiving technical training in the whole population shall rise. In the second year after the Act had been passed, 65% of the American universities and 80% of full-time undergraduates received student loans. In FY1960 alone, the Federal Government provided 90% of the total loans, equaling 61.5 million dollars, and the rest 10% was provided by the universities participating in the student loan programmes. Thanks to NDEA, the American universities saw substantial changes in teaching staff, instruments and equipment, and books and data quantitatively and qualitatively, and the higher education and universities have been greatly improved in the United States.

In the over-two-hundred-year history of America, there have been three milestones in the educational development. The first was the *Morrill Act of 1862* passed during the Civil War. Under the Act, the Federal Government would give 11 million acres (about 67 million *mu*[①]) of land for free, to establish a college in each state, for education on agriculture and mechanical skills. These colleges are known as "land-grant colleges". The second milestone was the fourth part "Renewal of Our Scientific Talent" in the abovementioned report *Science: The Endless Frontier*. And the

---

①　One *mu* equals about 667 square meters.

third one was the *National Defense Education Act* issued to deal with the external challenges. Educational development has provided the US' scientific and technological innovation with human resources, the most precious of the kind (Zhou Jizhong, 1991).

That the US Government has always turned to science, technology and education for long-range solutions responding to crises, in 1945, or in 1957 ~ 1958, or at any time when the country was confronted with crises. That is because of its concept of cultural value, traditions and systems in this country.

1.4　The Sci-Tech System Design in the Late 20th Century

It is basically referred to the sci-tech system design in the US in the 1980s and 1990s, when the country had already been a "super power" in the world, so that we can see the characteristics of sci-tech system design of such a super power at that time.

The US Congress passed the *Small Business Innovation Development Act* in 1982, and made amendments to the Act in 1992. The Federal Government worked out "Small Business Innovation Research (SBIR)" programmes under the Act, on the grounds that though important for the economic development and particularly in the technological innovation, the small businesses in the US could not exclusively enjoy benefits from R&D input, due to the spillover of R&D achievements, so that the income on R&D investment in small businesses is always lower than the maximum income as expected. Furthermore, small businesses have various worries in R&D input, as they cannot find financing as easily as large enterprises do. Therefore, the government shall give support for technological innovation, particularly early-stage research and development, in small businesses. According to the US Small Business Administration (SBA), any enterprise with fewer than 500 employees is regarded as a small business. Small businesses are in a disadvantageous position in the allocation of national R&D budget and resources, and usually receive no R&D funding from the government. Therefore, re-distribution of R&D resources is necessary for the sake of fairness. As ruled in SBIR, the 11 agencies (DoD, DOE, HHS, USDA, Dept. of Commerce, NASA and NSF etc.) whose surplus of annual R&D budget is higher than 100 million dollars must allot certain proportion of funds from the budget to the SBIR reserve. Up to now, the American small businesses have received about 10 billion dollars as the R&D funds from SBIR.

The OSTP worked out the first programme for "National Critical Technologies" in April 1991, listing "22 technologies essential for the US national security AND economic prosperity of the United States", which fall in five categories of materials, manufacturing technology, information and communications, bioengineering and life science, and aerospace and ground transportation. The *National Critical Technologies*" report has been published every two years since then.

As a programme, the Policy Report by President Clinton and Vice President Gore in February 1993, *Technology for America's Economic Growth: A New Direction to Build Economic Strength* discusses issues of "making the research and experimentation tax-credit permanent, investing in a national information infrastructure, promoting advanced manufacturing technology (AMT), facilitating private sector development of a new generation of automobiles, and improving technology for education and training".

The "National Information Infrastructure (NII)" programme, worked out by OSTP in September 1993 and commonly known as the "Information Super Highway", purports to build an information network for two-way transmission of text, audio and video, converging networks of computer, telephone, television and cable television into a huge high-speed communications network. The US Congress approved an act to allot 1.5 billion dollars to the programme over the following 5 years.

The National Institutes of Health (NIH) worked out in 1998 *New Goals for the U. S. Human Genome Project (HGP): 1998 ~ 2003*, setting to develop the improved DNA sequencing technology and complete human DNA sequencing.

The National Science and Technology Council (NSTC) worked out in June 1999 the IT2, and the four basic research areas in information technology were included. High-speed computer (HSC) (the computing speed of which is $100 \sim 1,000$ times higher than that of the then-fastest computer) and computing tools were under research and development. The leading team was chaired by Assistant to the President for Science and Technology, and the members included the heads of NSF, NASA, NIH and persons in-charge of DOE and DoD (Zhou Jizhong, 2002).

1.5 The Sci-Tech System Design in the Early 21st Century

It is basically referred to as the US' sci-tech system design in the first decade of the 21st century, when the US was hard hit by the 9/11 attacks, plus the Iraq War and the War in Afghanistan under the administration of President George W. Bush. Furthermore, the financial, economic and dollar crises triggered by "mortgage-backed securities (MBS)" and "subprime mortgage" have weakened the country's national strength and even got the whole world into trouble.

1.5.1 Two bills on innovation and the *America Competes Act*

"Innovation" has been the goal pursued by the US' Institutional designers and a "sharp weapon" for solving various problems, since the late 20th century when the country's national strength began to go downhill.

The OSTP, the President's Council of Advisors on Science and Technology (PCAST) and the National Science and Technology Council (NSTC) are the US' core agencies of top policy-making for science and technology. Since the beginning of the 21st centuries, these agencies have written various reports, creating an atmosphere for new laws, or working out "detailed rules and regulations" of implementation to translate legal language into "operational procedures". Such reports included *A New Generation of American Innovation* by the White House (2004), *Science for the 21st Century* by NSTC (2004), and *Assessing the US R&D Investment: Findings and Proposed Actions* (2002) and *Sustaining the Nation's Innovation Ecosystem: Maintaining the Strength of Our Science and Engineering Capabilities* (2004) by PCAST, etc.

"A new generation of innovation" proposed in the repot *A New Generation of American Innovation* by the White House (2004) is basically referred to as the innovation encouraging clean and reliable energy, ensuring better delivery of health care, and expanding access to high-speed Internet in the US. Specifically, the Department of Energy will fund new hydrogen research projects totaling 350 million dollars, to bring hydrogen and fuel cell technology from the laboratory to the showroom. The new hydrogen projects address four key areas: creating effective hydrogen storage, conducting hydrogen vehicle and infrastructure "learning demonstrations", developing affordable and durable hydrogen fuel cells with lower cost, and launching a Hydrogen Education Campaign.

The health care reform was promoted through health information technology. The project has four goals as below: adopting health information standards, doubling funding to 100 million dollars for demonstration projects on health information technology, fostering the adoption of health information technology, and creating a new, sub-cabinet level position of national health information technology coordinator.

The country shall promote innovation and enhance the national economic competitiveness and security through broadband technology, aiming at: making access to broadband permanently tax-free through legislation, developing new technology of access to broadband, and removing obstacles hindering the approval and administrative examination of rights of way for the access to the broadband.

According to *Assessing the US R&D Investment: Findings and Proposed Actions* by PCAST (2002), there have been shifts in the US R&D budget allocations, which may lead to imbalance. First of all, in FY2000, private sector R&D was 67% of the total, much higher than federal funding. Secondly, it is reasonable that enterprises focus more on the trail and development while government on basic and applied research, but whether the balanced is kept is also a concern. Thirdly, federal R&D funding is mainly on life sciences and technology (including biology, medical science and agronomy), but the proportion for physical sciences and technology (including physics and chemistry), math, and engineering sciences and technology is comparatively low. The imbalance resulted from the changing proportion has impact on not only research achievements, but also the balance of research personnel in different areas. More importantly, it has affected the efficiency of investment, i. e. the efficiency and effect of resource allocation.

Therefore, the report addresses the R&D investment and the effectiveness of the R&D effort from the following more detailed perspectives: R&D investment and economic impact investment, R&D infrastructure, human resource development, R&D investment and anti-terrorism and defense, R&D investment and people's well-being and R&D investment and knowledge generation.

The report calls on the Office of Management and Budget (OMB) and OSTP to evaluate the issues mentioned above before PCAST can make an overall review of the evaluations (Zhao Zhongjian, 2007).

Sustaining the Nation's Innovation Ecosystem: Maintaining the Strength of Our Science and Engineering Capabilities by PCAST (2004) creates the concept of "innovation ecosystem" consisting of entrepreneurs, inventors, a skilled workforce, research universities, R&D centers and venture capital, and basic research projects.

The report is particularly concerned about poor science and math capabilities of the US students. Twenty years ago, the National Committee on Excellence in Education talked in their report *A Nation at Risk* (1983) about the crisis in the American primary and secondary schools, where student's capabilities were declining. Yet, the problems have not been solved in the past 20 years. The report concerns about and devotes a lot of space to comparing capabilities, interest and degree-holding of students in the US and other countries.

From the perspective of leading the national science and technology enterprise,

Science for the 21st Century by NSTC (2004) clarifies four major responsibilities of the scientific and technological undertakings supported by the Federal Government: sustaining the leading position of the nation's science and technology, responding to the nation's challenges with timely, innovative approaches, accelerating the transformation of science into national benefits, and developing science and technology education and forstering excellent workforce. As quoted in this report the words of a 2003 Nobel Prize Winner for physiology or medicine that "All science is interdisciplinary", the report holds that interdisciplinary research is highly efficient. The report cites examples such as how the discovery of dark energy has driven physics and astronomy research, the significance of social, behavioral and economic sciences to social and economic development (that is why NSTC established a Subcommittee on Social, Behavioral, Economic Sciences in 2003), how mathematics can animate scientific and technological discoveries, and the relationship between game theory as the basic science and auction markets and public policy.

In such an atmosphere, the US Congress proposed two bills in 2005 and 2006 respectively, namely the *National Innovation Act of 2005* and the *National Innovation Education Act*, both of which laid a foundation for the *America Competes Act* approved in 2007. The two acts are outlined as below, as the *America Competes Act* is a US system design most directly related to the book's topic.

The *National Innovation Act of 2005* is composed of five chapters in three sections. Below are excerpts from or abstracts of some sections from the Act.

Title I Innovation Promotion

Sec. 101. President's Council on Innovation. The Council's duties includes monitoring implementation of legislative proposals and initiatives for promoting innovation, including policies related to research funding, taxation, immigration, trade, and education, as these policies have influence on the American innovation capabilities.

Sec. 102. Innovation Acceleration Grants Program. Priority in the awarding of grants shall be given to projects that meet fundamental technology challenges and that involve multidisciplinary work and a high degree of novelty.

Sec. 103. A national commitment to basic research. Such a plan shall be developed with a focus on utilizing basic research in physical science and engineering to optimize the United States economy as a global competitor and leader in productive innovation.

Sec. 104. Regional economic development. Priority should be given to projects that emphasize private sector cooperation with State and local governments and non-profit organizations. *Guide to Developing Successful Regional Innovation Hot Spots* shall be prepared.

Sec. 105. Development of advanced manufacturing systems. The National Institute of Standards and Technology shall coordinate the activities of the Small Business Innovation Research Program, the Small Business Technology Transfer Program, and the Manufacturing Technology Program of the Department of Defense, develop and test standards, and support pilot test beds of excellence.

Sec. 106. Study on service science. In order to strengthen the competitiveness of the US enterprises and institutions, the Federal Government should pay special attention to the emerging discipline known as service science, and support it through research, education, and training.

Title II Modernization of Science, Education, and Healthcare Programs, including "Graduate fellowships and graduate traineeships", "Professional science master degree programs", and "Innovation-based experiential learning", under which the National Science Foundation shall award grants to local educational agencies to enable the local educational agencies to implement innovation-based experiential learning in a total of 500 secondary schools and 500 elementary or middle schools in the United States.

Title III Incentives for Encouraging Innovation. This chapter is mainly about the permanent extension of research credit. The amendments to the *Internal Revenue Code of 1986* include opening "Lifelong Learning Accounts" and regulation relating to valuation of intangibles and to private foundation support of innovation, in order to make an exempt of taxes.

Title IV Department of Defense Matters.

Sec. 401. Revitalization of frontier and multidisciplinary research. It shall be the goal of the Department of Defense to allocate at least 3% of its total budget to science and technology. Of this amount, at least 20% shall go for the basic research.

Title V Judiciary and Other Matters.

Sec. 501. The Congress realizes the importance of retaining high tech talent in the US. Comprehensive immigration reform should be adopted.

Sec. 502. Study on barriers to innovation. Particular attention should be paid to practices that may be significant deterrents to the US businesses engaged in innovation risk-taking compared to foreign competitors, including tort litigation (Zhao Zhongjian, 2007).

The *National Innovation Education Act* is composed of twenty sections in four chapters. Below are excerpts from or abstracts of some sections from the Act.

Title I Improving Pre-kindergarten through Grade 16 Education. It refers to the educational system from kindergarten to bachelor's degree. This title may be cited as the *College Pathway Act of 2006*.

Title II National Science Foundation Magnet Schools and Innovation-based Learning. "Magnet schools" are public schools with specialized courses or curricula, targeting the problems of high absence and dropout rates. Such schools provide cross-district schooling. It is reiterated in this chapter that the Director of the National Science Foundation shall award grants to local educational agencies to enable the local educational agencies to implement innovation-based experiential learning in a total of 500 secondary schools and 500 elementary or middle schools in the United States.

Title III Teacher Training and Professional Development. Federal assistance should be given to support to establish Teachers Professional Development Institutes that mean a partnership or joint venture between or among one or more institutions of higher education, and one or more local educational agencies serving a significant low-income population, to improve the quality of teaching and learning through collaborative seminars designed to enhance both the subject matter and the pedagogical resources of the seminar participants.

Title IV STEM (Science, Technology, Engineering and Mathematics) Education and Research. More support should be given to science education through the National Science Foundation (Zhao Zhongjian, 2007).

One year before the *America Competes Act* was passed, George W. Bush, the then US President, first proposed the *American Competitiveness Initiatives* (ACI) in his *State of the Union Message* on 31 January 2006. The report maintains that basic research, innovation and reform are fundamental elements to ensure the American sustainable competitiveness. More details about the report are revealed below, as it has been one of the most important federal policies on science and technology in the United States since the beginning of the 21st century, through which we can better understand the American sci-tech system design and direction of policy on science and technology in the 21st century.

The document officially published by the Domestic Policy Council (DPC) and OSTP in February 2006 was titled the *American Competitiveness Initiatives*, proposing the actions of promoting R&D, innovation and education to enhance the national competitiveness in the following ten years (2007 ~ 2016). This medium- and long-term plan aims to enhance the US national strength by increasing R&D investments and promoting innovation, and will have profound influence on the US' scientific and technologic development, in the following ten years and even longer. The report focuses on research, innovation and education, and is designed to sustain the US leadership in science and technology through keeping its leadership in innovation, so as to maintain its power and security in the world.

According to the report, the US Government will allot 136 billion dollars in total over the following ten years for R&D, education, start-ups and innovation. It has been the largest investment plan for science and technology, since the Apollo Project launched in the 1960s.

Quantitative goals: ① 300 grants for schools to implement research-based math curricula; ② 10,000 more scientists, students, post-doctoral fellows, and technicians with opportunities to enter innovation enterprise; ③ 100,000 highly qualified math and science teachers by 2015; ④ advanced placement tests passed by 700,000 students from low-income families; and ⑤ 800,000 workers with skills needed for the jobs of the 21st century.

Qualitative measures: ① Doubling, over 10 years, funding for innovation-enabling research at key Federal agencies that support high-leverage fields of physical science and engineering: the National Science Foundation, the Department of Energy's Office of Science, and the National Institute for Standards and Technology within the Department of Commerce; ② Modernizing the Research and Experimentation (R&E) tax credit by making it permanent and working with Congress to update its provisions to encourage additional private sector investment in innovation; ③ Strengthening K-12 math and science education by enhancing our understanding of how students learn and applying that knowledge to train highly qualified teachers, develop effective curricular materials, and improve student learning; and ④ Increasing our ability to compete for and retain the best and brightest high-skilled workers from around the world by supporting comprehensive immigration reform that meets the needs of a growing economy.

Policy environment: Sustained scientific advancement and innovation are key to maintaining the national competitive edge, and should be supported by a pattern of related investments and policies, including: ① Private sector investment in research and development that enables the translation of fundamental discoveries into the production of useful and marketable technologies, processes, and techniques; ② An efficient system that protects the intellectual property resulting from public and private sector investments in research; and ③ A business environment that stimulates and encourages entrepreneurship through free and flexible labor, capital, and product markets that rapidly diffuse new productive technologies. (Zhao Zhongjian, 2007)

Upon the two acts and the Federal Government's *American Competitiveness Initiatives* mentioned above, the Congress passed *America Creating Opportunities to Meaningfully Promote Excellence in Technology, Education, and Science Act* in April 2007. The act was signed into law by the President on 9 August, 2007 and known as the *America Competes Act*, as the title is abbreviated to COMPETES.

The abovementioned two acts, the *America Competes Act* and the Federal Government's *American Competitiveness Initiatives* indicate that the US Government and Congress have attached great importance to innovation and issued quite a number of acts and plans concerning innovation. First, the number of laws on science and technology issued by China has been much smaller than that in the US in the 20th century alone. Laws on science and technology in China only include *Law of the People's Republic of China on Science and Technology Progresses*, *Law of the People's Republic of China on Promoting the Transformation of Scientific and Technological Achievements*, and *Patent Law of the People's Republic of China*. Secondly, science and technology and education, and innovation and education are seen in the American acts as indivisible, which reflect the US' concept of value and cultural traditions. Therefore, the *National Innovation Act of 2005* and the *National Innovation Education Act* are interrelated. Furthermore, the essence of the two acts are not only reflected in the Federal Government's *American Competitiveness Initiatives* of 2006, but also integrated into the *America Competes Act* of 2007. For instance, the ideas of "training science and innovation talent", "retaining the best and brightest high-skilled workers from around the world", "increasing investments in research and development", and "the Research and Experimentation (R&E) tax credit", etc.

The Obama Administration has developed the related policies on science, technology and innovation in the following aspects, since President Obama took office in January 2009.

1) Appointing the President's Advisors on Science and Technology (PASTs). Shortly after taking office, President Obama restored the PAST posts, enhancing the significance of science and technology in the government's policy-making process.

2) A substantial increase in investment in science and technology. The *American Recovery and Reinvestment Act* signed by President Obama in February 2009 rules that

supplementary appropriations of 18. 3 billion dollars be invested in research and development in FY2009 ~ 2010, which have been the largest annual increase in R&D funding in the US. At the 146th annual meeting of the National Academy of Sciences (NAS), President Obama shared his plans to give the largest commitment to scientific research in American history—devoting 3% of the US GDP to research and development, and to substantially increase over 10 years the R&D funding for physical sciences, mathematics and engineering that have been not sufficiently valued in the past, by doubling, over 10 years, the fund for basic research of the agencies in charge of funding for these disciplines, including the National Science Foundation, the Department of Energy's Office of Science, and the National Institute for Standards and Technology under the Department of Commerce.

3) Stimulating enterprises to invest in R&D. A total of 75 billion dollars of the economic stimulus package will be used to make the Research and Experimentation (R&E) tax credit permanent. Government procurement of high-tech products will also be enlarged.

4) Taking new energy industry as the pillar industry for the US economic recovery. President Obama calls the New Energy for America Plan "a great plan at the present age". The budget plan includes: a Government input of 43. 35 billion dollars for the development of clean energy, equaling about 10% of the total disposable government funds under the *American Recovery and Reinvestment Act*; 150 billion dollars over 10 years for R&D and demonstrations of clean energy; as announced by the US Government in 2009, 777 million dollars over 5 years invested by the Department of Energy's Office of Science in setting up 46 energy frontier research centers (EFRCs); 11 billion dollars by the government under the *American Recovery and Reinvestment Act* for R&D of smart grid, and 3. 4 billion dollars by the government in October 2009 to set up the Smart Grid Investment Grant Programme.

5) Specific measures for developing advanced automobile technology, next-generation biofuels and advanced information technology, including broadband, information and communications technology and network technology, as well as for lifting restrictions on stem cell research (Obama signed the president's executive order in March 2009 to lift the former administration's restriction on stem cell research), and for supporting the National Nanotechnology Initiative (NNI) and space development programmes (Ministry of Science and Technology of the People's Republic of China, 2010).

In brief, the new Obama Administration has showcased its governing philosophy of attaching great importance to science and technology in the national economic and social development.

1.6 The Legislative and Executive Efficiency and Effect

The legislative procedure in the US Congress shows another side of the American Institutional design, concerning "efficiency and effect" in management science. Despite good effect that may result from the "seesaw battles" between Congress and the President, the efficiency of the legislative procedure is rather low. It would be contrary to the expected, if neither efficiency nor effect was satisfactory. The section briefly introduces the legislative procedure in the United States (see Fig. 2-2).

The bill establishing the "National Research Foundation" proposed in Vannevar Bush's report *Science: The Endless Frontier* written by some members of Congress was a "proposal" in Fig. 2-2. The discussions, hearings, debates and consulting in both chambers of Congress correspond to the phases of "introduction", "review", "debate", and "conference committee". Approved by both the House and Senate, a bill will be sent to the President to be signed into law or vetoed, or the President can take a "pocket veto" on the bill. The Congress can attempt to "override" a presidential veto of a bill and force it into law, if a 2/3 vote by a quorum of members in both the House and Senate is secured. Otherwise (Congress usually cannot override a presidential veto of a bill, as the Congressmen and Congresswomen from the same Party as the President usually support the President, and the required "2/3 vote by a quorum of members in both the House and Senate" cannot be reached), a bill will be revised in accordance with the President's suggestions and sent to the President again to be signed into law; otherwise a bill cannot become law. The "seesaw battles" between Parties, the President and Congressmen and Congresswomen, and the efforts of lobbies and interest groups may prolong the legislative procedure, during which a bill may die at any time.

A concern here is the low efficiency, in spite of a satisfactory result. And it would be more disappointing, if the final result was not that satisfactory due to compromises (not uncommon) and both effect and efficiency were poor. That is why countries cannot efficiently make policies and laws by following the abovementioned "democratic procedure", or even have unsatisfactory result and efficiency. Even the Americans think that policy-making is impaired by the cumbersome legislative procedure in Congress. For example, the *Civil Rights Act* that plays a significant role in the Americans' life had not been approved by Congress for decades, as the Senators from the South killed the bill by manipulating rules and procedures adopted in Congress.

Fig.2-2　The US legislative procedure

Source: *Steering the Course: Policy-making in the United States* by Cultural Office under Embassy of the United States to China.

Members of Congress can delay any bill they have no intention to approve by various procedural means. A proposal may be effectively vetoed in a single procedural vote (Cultural Office under Embassy of the United States to China, 1984).

Evidence was also found in a piece of news. The House of Representatives vetoed a proposal by an overwhelming majority of 292 votes against and 126 for in May 2010. The proposal of bill was introduced by M. H. P. Bart Gordon, the former Chairman of the House Committee on Science and Technology. The bill asked to fulfill the goals set in the *America Competes Act*, namely to double, over 10 years, the budget for scientific research and education projects of the agencies, including the National Science Foundation (NSF), the National Institute of Standards and Technology (NIST) and the Department of Energy's Office of Science (SC of DOE), and to enhance the American competitiveness by strengthening the basic research in physical sciences (including physics and chemistry) and the research of energy.

The issue came against the abovementioned process of innovation bill drafting and related legislative procedure. As early as at the end of 2005, two Senators, one a Republican and the other a Democratic, co-introduced a bill titled the *National Innovation Act of 2005*, aiming to sustain the US' leadership in innovation, R&D and training scientists and engineers. The bill of the *National Innovation Education Act* proposed in June 2006 was designed to enhance the national competitiveness by improving its educational system, including improving pre-kindergarten through to Grade 16 education, developing magnet schools and innovation-based learning, promoting teacher training and professional development, and strengthening STEM (science, technology, engineering and mathematics) education and research. More than 270 leaders from the American business circles and higher education signed an *Innovation Manifesto* in Washington D. C. in March 2007, calling on the Congress to take immediate actions to ensure the innovation agenda for the American sustainable competitiveness and urging the Congress to enhance by legislation the country's competitiveness and sustain the US' leadership in innovation. And the Congress finally approved the *America Creating Opportunities to Meaningfully Promote Excellence in Technology, Education, and Science Act* (i. e. the *America Competes Act*) in April 2007, which reflects the major concerns in the US scientific, technological and educational reform.

Gordon hoped, before his retirement, to realize his long-cherished wish to enhance the country's Competitiveness by significantly increasing funding for scientific research and education, through his proposal of "fulfilling the goals set in the *America*

Competes Act". However, the proposal was opposed by a Democratic M. H. R. Ralph Hall, who proposed to freeze in the coming three years the funds of the three agencies mentioned above (NSF, NIST and SC of DOE) so that they could not pay salaries to employees watching, downloading and exchanging pornographic images on government computers or in the office. Another Democratic member of Congress pointed that there were such workers in NSF, which was confirmed by the leader of NSF, who estimated that there were about 12 workers who had severely violated the rules in NSF (*Science Times*, 2010). The government officers who visit pornographic websites on office computers violate related rules and should be penalized. However, it was ridiculous for this reason to veto in Congress a bill aiming to increasing the funding for scientific research and education. People would not help doubting whether the Democratic Party tried to launch an attack on the Republican Party on this occasion.

Then comes a reasonable question: Since the Congress can be operated in such a "democratic" manner, is there any other system that can challenge or rival the existing system for policy- and law-making?

Some conclusions can be drawn here, based upon the above discussions on the American Institutional design and policy-making for science and technology.

The US Government and Congress have attached great importance to science and technology in the country's development, either at the very beginning of the Independence, or since the Second World War. It is shown in the fact that the American top policy-makers can reach an agreement on turning to science, technology and education for solutions to counter challenges and crises (including the ongoing financial crisis). Particularly, they always link science, technology and education with each other, and attach great importance to talents. Even today both quantity and quanlity of scientific and technological talents in US rank first in the world. However, top policy-makers are still worried that the American students are not as good as the foreign students in the US. They believe that the American national strength can be well sustained, as long as these foreign talents can be retained in the country and serve the country in various trades. That is the bottom line of the US competitiveness and of the the sci-tech system design and administration of the US Government and Congress.

2. Innovation Management

Research and development activities have been grouped into basic, applied and development research for the first time in the second part "nature of scientific research" in Vannevar Bush's report *Science: The Endless Frontier* (1945). He then named the three as "pure scientific research" and "applied research and development". According to the report, "pure scientific research" was funded at first neither by the US Government nor Congress, but an Englisher named James Smithson in the 19th century instead, who donated a legacy of 500,000 pounds to the US. After ten years' debate, the US Congress finally decided to establish the Smithsonian Institution with the donation, which was designed to be engaged in basic research and non-profit technology services. Later on, the Carnegie Institution and the Rockefeller Institute funded by the Carnegie Corporation of New York and the Rockfeller Foundation respectively became institutions engaged in basic research early in the US. A number of industrial laboratories, including those named after Bell and Edison, have been set up since 1890, when technological and industrial revolutions took place in the US. These laboratories have been engaged in applied research and experimentation and development (Bush, 1960).

The process of research and development can be explored from various angles, one of which is to investigate innovation process from the angle of time series of R&D or technological innovation.

With time series, innovation process can be investigated from its stability (or from the life cycle of products), which is a regular correlation between technological innovation frequency and innovation stability, set up by Professor N. Abernathy in the Harvard University and Professor J. Utterback in MIT. This correlation is thus also known as the A-U Model of Innovation. In the unstable initial stage of innovation, product innovation is of high frequency. Over time of transitional and stable stages, innovation frequency declines. The situation differs in the case of technical innovation, which is of low frequency at the unstable initial stage, as in technical processes, innovation and improvements in equipment, facilities, modes and methods are only possible with product innovation developing to a certain level. Therefore, technical innovation accelerates from the unstable stage through the transitional one, and usually reaches a climax before the stable stage, while in the stage stage, both product innovation and technical innovation are almost in stagnation. That can be seen as the preparation stage for next innovation (Zhou Jizhong, 2002).

2.1　R&D Organizing and Management

The US scientific research institutes can be grouped into four categories of federal laboratories, scientific research institutes in universities, company research institutes, and non-profit research institutes.

There are altogether more than 700 federal laboratories in the United States, of various sizes of from thousands of workers to as few as ten-plus people. The R&D funding for these laboratories take up about 30% of the government's annual R&D budget. The government-owned and government-operated (GOGO) ones are basically engaged in basic research, the government-owned and contract-operated (GOCO) in applied research, and the federally-funded R&D centers (FFRDCs) are the ones equipped with large-scale facilities or operated with particular functions. Funded by the Federal Government, FFRDCs are entrusted to universities, enterprises or non-profit organizations for daily operation. The largest ten federal laboratories are also known as the national laboratories and under the command of the Department of Energy. For example, the Brookhaven National Laboratory has 4 winners of Nobel Prize in Physics, 3,100 research personnel and around 4,000 visiting scholars. It has achieved a lot in the transformation of scientific and technological achievements.

There are 150 ~ 200 research universities in the United States. According to the definition by the Carnegie Corporation of New York, a research university receives an annual federal R&D funding no less than 15.5 million dollars and confers at least 50 doctor's degrees every year. And research universities are further grouped into Type I and Type II based upon the size of R&D funding. Twenty first-class universities, such as MIT, Harvard University and Stanford University, take up about 50% of research work done in all US universities. Research universities are mainly engaged in basic research, taking up about 60% of basic research in the US.

The expenditures on R&D in company laboratories take up about 75% of total R&D funding in the United States. These laboratories are basically engaged in applied and development research. General Mobiles Corporation (GM) alone spends as much as 8 ~ 9 billion dollars on research and development every year.

2.1.1   Company R&D institutes and their management

(1) Bell Laboratories

Founded in 1925, Bell Laboratories was previously the research and development subsidiary of the American Telephone & Telegraph Company (AT&T). The Lucent-Bell Laboratories became a R&D institute separated from AT&T in 1996, and was changed to Lucent Technologies-Bell Labs Innovation, to highlight the close relationship between Lucent Technologies and Bell Laboratories. Lucent Technologies spends 11% ~ 12% of its annual sales income on research and development launched in Bell Labs, totaling 4 billion dollars a year. Alcatel and Lucent Technologies merged into Alcatel-Lucent in 2006.

Bell Laboratories is mainly engaged in basic research, advanced technology and product development. Ten percent of the total 28,000 researchers all over the world are engaged in basic research, 10% in advanced applied research and 80% in product development. Eleven scientists of Bell Laboratories have won Nobel Prizes. Among them, W. Shockley, W. Brattain and J. Bardeen invented transistor, for which they won 1956 Nobel Prize for Physics. And Bell Laboratories has obtained more than 27,000 patents since 1985.

As for the organization, Bell Laboratories has been benefited from its leadership, talent and teamwork. Upon the commercialization of scientific and technological achievements, Bell Laboratories has also been a pioneer in adopting the organizational form of "incubator", which is also known as "venture corporate".

As early as in May 1997, Bell Laboratories established in Beijing and Shanghai Bell Labs (China), and recruited first 12 Chinese research fellows. Bell Laboratories Asia Pacific and China founded in 1999 and headquartered in Beijing has more than 700 researchers, 90% of whom hold master's or doctor's degrees and 50% are fresh graduates. The headquarter trains about 200 Chinese researchers every year, with training fees of 10 million dollars. One of the focuses of training lies in how to foster team spirit. Nowadays, Bell Labs (China) is even stronger than Bell Laboratories in the United States in product development. According to Bell Laboratories (US), it only takes one year for Bell Labs (China) to get success in some development projects, while the Labs in the United States have to use 2 years. In March 2000 when Bell Laboratories celebrated its 75th anniversary, Bell Labs Research China (BLRC) was founded. It is the first basic research laboratory Bell Labs established outside the United States (Xu Jun, 2001).

(2) 3M Company

Research and development may have an organizational form different from that for ordinary activities, as R&D involves creative processes. 3M Company is picked up here as an example.

Founded in 1902 and formally known as the Minnesota Mining and Manufacturing Company, 3M Company is an American multinational conglomerate corporation based in St. Paul, Minnesota. Over the past 100-plus years, 3M Company, "a smoothly running engine of innovation", has produced about 60, 000 products, including household and medical products, transportation products, building products, commercial products, educational products, electronic products and communications products, which have enriched people's life and work.

As for the organizational structure, the innovation unit in 3M Company is the New Business Exploration Team, which is an innovation working team. Such a team composed of voluntary professionals is constantly engaged in research. It usually consists of personnel specialized in engineering and technology, production and manufacturing, marketing and sales, and even finance. Once approved by 3M Company, the members of an innovation working team work as full-time, which encourages the passion for and dedication to innovation among the members.

Furthermore, 3M's "15 Percent Time" Programme allows employees to use 15% of their paid time to pursue their own ideas, so long as what they do is about research on new products. And these employees are known as "intrapreneurs". And the system of "flexitime" has been naturally formed. Moreover, 3M Company also rules that 25% of sales income in each division should come from the sales of new products developed in the previous 5 years, and the figure "25%" is linked to bonuses.

3M's "Innovation Funnel" is the innovation model of the company's R&D (Fig. 2-3). The process of technological innovation consists of three phases: the "doodling" phase, the "design" phase, and the "direction" phase. So many new ideas generated during the "doodling" phase are screened to come to the "design" phase, and the selected go into the "direction" phase. There are factors of "constraint" and "support" in each phase. "Innovation Funnel" is named so, as the number of innovations in each phase declines, forming a shape of funnel (Gundling, 2001).

2.1.2　Non-profit research institutes in the US

Non-profit research institutes are integral parts of the American research and development organizations. These organizations are mainly engaged in research for public welfare and are non-governmental ones with independent legal personality. They can enjoy government's preferential measures, but have to be under related departments' audit for being non-profit. The council is the policy-making body of a non-profit research organization. The US non-profit research institutes can be classified as below:

Independent non-profit research institutes: The major form of the US non-profit

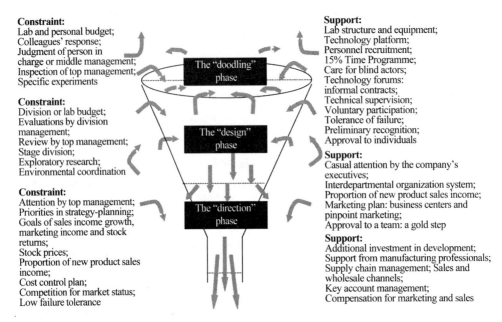

Constraint:
Lab and personal budget;
Colleagues' response;
Judgment of person in
charge or middle management;
Inspection of top management;
Specific experiments

Constraint:
Division or lab budget;
Evaluations by division
management;
Review by top management;
Stage division;
Exploratory research;
Environmental coordination

Constraint:
Attention by top management;
Priorities in strategy-planning;
Goals of sales income growth,
marketing income and stock
returns;
Stock prices;
Proportion of new product sales
income;
Cost control plan;
Competition for market status;
Low failure tolerance

The "doodling" phase

The "design" phase

The "direction" phase

Support:
Lab structure and equipment;
Technology platform;
Personnel recruitment;
15% Time Programme;
Care for blind actors;
Technology forums:
informal contracts;
Technical supervision;
Voluntary participation;
Tolerance of failure;
Preliminary recognition;
Approval to individuals

Support:
Casual attention by the company's
executives;
Interdepartmental organization system;
Proportion of new product sales income;
Marketing plan: business centers and
pinpoint marketing;
Approval to a team: a gold step

Support:
Additional investment in development;
Support from manufacturing professionals;
Supply chain management; Sales and
wholesale channels;
Key account management;
Compensation for marketing and sales

Fig. 2-3   3M's Innovation Funnel
Source: Ernest Gundling, 2001.

research organizations. There are about 100 such institutes, such as Stanford Research Institute International and Bettelle Memorial Institute, which are mostly funded by government through grants or contracts.

Federally-funded R&D centers (FFRDCs) managed by non-profit organizations, such as the FFRDC managed by RAND Corporation.

Voluntary health organizations engaged in scientific research. Most are members of the non-profit organizations under the American Medical Association (AMA).

Associations for science and technology and chambers of commerce engaged in scientific research, such as the American Chemical Society (ACS), the American Dental Association (ADA), and the American Society for Testing and Materials (ASTM).

Private scientific research foundations: About 1, 000 out of over 30, 000 American private foundations fund scientific research, such as the Ford Foundation, the Rockefeller Foundan, Doris Duke Charitable Foundation, and the M? bius Foundation. Private foundations can provide scientific research with funds in a more flexible way and usually fund the projects that cannot receive funding from government or enterprises, or the ones that cannot be conveniently funded by government or enterprises. Such scientific research projects mostly fall in life sciences.

A case of non-profit consulting organizations: RAND Corporation

RAND Corporation is a non-profit consulting company in the US and a world-known think tank. A wide range of scientists and academics used science and technology on the battlefield of the Second World War. In 1944, Commanding General of the Army Air Force H. H. "Hap" Arnold wrote a memorandum concerning the American research and development after the Second World War and in new possible wars, asking to organize these scientists and academics to establish "an independent half-private and half-official research institute to give objective analysis". Responding to the suggestion, the United States Army Air Force (USAAF) signed with the Douglas Aircraft Company a research and development project worth 10 million dollars (known as the Project RAND) at the end of 1945. With a funding of 1 million dollars from the Ford Foundation, the Project RAND was separated from the Douglas Aircraft Company in 1948 and became an independent consulting organization, headquartered in Santa Monic, California. A council composed of 21 members from academic and business circles and the public sector is in charge of policy-making of the company. Approximately 1,600 people work at RAND, around 800 of whom are professional researchers. Besides, RAND also engages about 600 distinguished professors and senior experts outside the company as consultants and contract researchers. RAND provides services in fields of national defense, science and technology, education, health, energy and transportation, and is engaged in contract research projects entrusted by government or other organizations. The company adopts matrix management and groups its research entities into "discipline divisions" and "planning divisions". The former are further divided into 6 disciplines of natural sciences, economics, engineering, information sciences, management sciences and social sciences, and the director of each discipline is responsible for selecting research personnel and organizing review of research results. The latter ones include International Programme, National Security Research Division and Project Air Force, as well as Institute for Civil Justice, and project teams are set up under each division. According to the entrusted research projects, the planning divisions establish project teams composed of personnel selected from different disciplines and manage the funding. In the past decades, about 90% funding of RAND has come from research contracts signed with the US Army, government and enterprises. For the staff management, RAND features in a high degree of decentralization and full respect for the researchers' work (Zhou Jizhong, 2002).

2.1.3 Science parks

(1) Silicon Valley

"Silicon Valley" was developed out of Stanford Research Park established on the Stanford campus in 1951. A science park may by differently named around the world, such as science and technology industrial park, incubator or science city, and it is known in China as hi-tech development zone. The world-known science parks include the American Boston Route 128 High-Tech Region, the Research Triangle Park in North Carolina, the Cambridge Science Park in the UK, the Tsukuba Science City in Japan, the Singapore Science Park and the Zhongguancun Science Park in Beijing. Generally, a science park may be established in a well-facilitated city area with a population of tens of thousand people, convenient transportation and at least one famous university that can provide R&D resources. An important function of a science park is to realize technological innovation and make the achievements commercialized. Usually, an enterprise based in a science park can require and enjoy various preferential measures by government. A science park is actually a large incubator, in which high technology and high-tech products, enterprises and industry get developed.

Thousands of high-tech companies have been set up in Silicon Vallye in the past decades, and hundreds of billion dollars generated from here. The huge success has been naturally inseparable from Stanford University. F. Terman, former Dean of Stanford School of Engineering and "the father of Silicon Valley", designed the Stanford Industrial Park (now Stanford Research Park), following his teacher Vannevar Bush's idea of establishing "a Bosten high-tech industrial park". As early as in 1939, Terman helped to establish Hewlett-Packard that had significant and profound influence on the development of Silicon Valley later. With support of the Californian government, the original science park went beyond the boundaries of Stanford University and was developed into Silicon Valley.

As for the organizational structure, Silicon Valley has made its great success out of its development and organizational structure of in the enterprises within. "The development system invites new-comers and encourages experimentation by spurring manufacturers to produce various products to compete under the common criteria recognized in an industry. This makes it possible for companies to be only engaged in the production with specialized technology and purchase other parts from other manufacturers. With first successful trials in some Silicon Valley enterprises, this development-oriented production structure fast dominated in the area and actually has been a source of the powerful competitiveness of Silicon Valley high-tech industry. " (Tang Genghua et al. , 2002) On the contrary, under the " vertically integrated production structure" adopted in Bostern Route 128 High-Tech Region, customers are tied to the full services for software and hardware provided by a fixed manufacturer, so that the competition can keep stable inside an industry.

We can better understand the two models through comparisons between Hewlett-Packard in Silicon Valley and Digital Equipment Corporation (DEC) in Boston Route 128 High-Tech Region. In mid 1980's, both companies adopted the vertically integrated production structure. However, Hewlett-Packard realized in the late 1980s that it was unnecessary to manufacture all the parts needed, and began to sign outsourcing contracts with other companies to purchase some parts, thus formed a production alliance. During the process, Hewlett-Packard had to make adjustments to its power structure, which was transformed from a centralization system to a democratically-operated network of powers. Then an operational model of decentralized organization came into being. Furthermore, Hewlett-Packard established good enterprise-community relationships. On the other hand, DEC was a centralized company that had strong control over the economic development in Route 128 High-Tech Region.

Silicon Valley was structurally developed in higher production efficiency and stable regional economy resulting from network production structure and high specialization.

Cluster structure is another structural advantage promoting the fast development of Silicon Valley. Silicon Valley enterprises have enjoyed strong competitiveness thanks to the cluster structure and high production efficiency and low transaction cost in particular. The cluster structure has been developed from the defense and military technology in the 1950s, through semiconductor and computer hardware to software technology, till today's diversified development. There are 6 clusters in the Silicon Valley intermediary services alone, namely venture capital, commercial banks, law firms, accounting firms, head-hunting companies and consulting services, which are highly specialized and concentrated. For instance, venture capital companies cluster together around the Menlo Park, law firms in Palo Alto and accounting firms in San Josey. High-tech companies also cluster together. In this way, professionals in the same field can communicate with each other frequently and closely, and it is easier for customers to find what they want in a more economical manner.

(2) Science Park of University of Utah

Different from Silicon Valley, Science Park of University of Utah is located in Utah, a less-developed state in the United States. Moreover, University of Utah is at present no rival to Stanford University. It has currently 2,100 teachers engaged in scientific and technological research in 90 research laboratories and institutes. With over 300 million dollars R&D funding from government and private companies in recent years, University of Utah is strong in research on human genes, bioengineering, chemical and fuel engineering, and computer graphic design. Organizationally, the university promotes the economic development and commercialization of technological achievements in Utah, by establishing research foundation and the technology transfer office (TTO) and by co-establishing the state improvement center.

Science Park of University of Utah is the "intermediary" between university, government and private enterprises. The University receives research funding from government and enjoys preferential policies, while the State Government of Utah receives scientific and technological talent, high technology and high-tech products trained and produced by the university. The donations from private enterprises are the main source of the university's research foundation, while the university provides these enterprises with talented graduates. In addition to the local government, the Federal Government and related departments are as well fund the university's research, including the Department of Energy, the National Science Foundation and the National Institutes of Health. For example, a Myriad Genetics private company adopted the university's research achievements in human genes for its new product development and market services, and University of Utah has in the past years received three million dollars for cardiovascular research, 1. 5 million dollars for obesity-related research and 75, 000 dollars for hypertension studies, by means of holding the company's stocks and receiving royalty fees and research funding from the company.

Science Park of University of Utah was founded in the 1970s on a piece of 600-acre land granted by the State Congress from the land that had been originally for military bases and returned to Utah by the Federal Government. The Science Park has in the past decades had more than 40 enterprise tenants and over 6,000 employees.

The Science Park is designed to intensify the University's scientific research, find scientific research projects, improve the scientific research infrastructure in the Park, develop the regional economy, and accelerate the transformation of scientific and technological achievements. An enterprise tenant in the Science Park must be engaged in technology- or business-oriented substantive research, have support from foundation (s), put restrictions on assembled high-tech products or related research, make pollution-free, noiseless business operations in buildings in the Park, and keep disconnectable links with University of Utah.

The enterprise tenants are engaged in biotechnology, biomedicine and computer software and hope to benefit from University of Utah and its scientific researchers. The university has enjoyed the benefits from the Science Park at the beginning of the 21st century: 1,400 employees from 48 departments of the university have established offices in the Park. Eighteen companies have signed with the university contracts for cooperative research. Twenty companies have financially aided University of Utah. Employees from 15 companies have taught in the University. Seventy-five percent of the enterprise tenants have invited the university teaching and administrative personnel as their consultants. Most tenant companies use the university's libraries. Sixty-six percent of the enterprise tenants have cooperated with the university in research projects. And the university can receive an annual research funding of about four million dollars (Espin, 2002).

2.1.4　Venture capital companies

Venture capital is actually a kind of financial system design.

(1) Supermicro

In 1957, Bill Congleton from Supermicro made a tour to Massachusetts Institute of Technology (MIT) for potential projects. He found the research on computer by Ken Olsen and Harlan Anderson, two engineers from MIT Lincoln Laboratory quite interesting. Olsen and Anderson wrote a 4-year business plan with the help of Congleton. Supermicro invested 70,000 dollars in Digital Equipment Corporation (DEC) founded by Olsen and Anderson to exchange for 77% of DEC's share. Most of DEC's directors at the time were from Supermicro, participating in DEC's management and financing issues. Fourteen years later, the market value of DEC's stocks was over 5,000 times that at the very beginning. By the 1980s, DEC had realized a sales income of up to 13 billion dollars and ranked 30th in the Fortune Global 500. Through its development, DEC has kept good relationship with MIT, teachers and graduates of which have worked in DEC, including the computer genius Chester Gordon Bell. It was because of Bell's designs that DEC could finally become a rival to IBM. Actually, the early venture capital companies in the United States, including American Research and Development Corporation (ARD) and Supermicro, were frequent visitors to MIT and "Boston Route 128" Science Park, looking for investment projects with business potentials and for project managers. It is not uncommon to see successful cases of cooperation between venture capitalists and MIT teachers, students and graduates. In the case of DEC, Congleton is the venture capitalist, and Olsen and Anderson the inventors and venture entrepreneurs.

(2) Gene-tech

Gene-tech was born out of the "linkage" between the late venture capitalist Robert Swanson and the biochemist Herbert Boyer at the University of California, San Francisco. Swanson used to be an employee in Kleiner Perkins company and was interested in biotechnological projects with commercial potential. Upon learning about a technology developed by Boyer, Swanson paid a visit to Boyer in 1976, talking about the commercial potential of Boyer's recombinant DNA technology. At the end of their meeting, Genetech was born. The new-born Genetech gained 100,000 dollars venture capital by giving 25% of its share to Swanson's employer Kleiner Perkins. Swanson raised funds for Genetech in this way for a couple of times. Shortening its original lead time from 10 years to 7 months, Genetech saw the market value of its stocks rocket from 400,000 dollars to 11 million dollars. The high returns on high risks were closely related to the linkage between the venture capitalist Swanson and the inventor Boyer. Swanson was actually playing multiple roles in the process, including the angel investor for Boyer's project, Kleiner Perkins' general partner and the manager of the venture firm Genetech. As the angel investor, Swanson had enthusiasm for Boyer's new technology and faith in its commercial potential, recognized Boyer's technology and his capabilities, and participated in the development of Genetech from the very beginning, disregarding others' opinion that it would take 10 ~ 20 years for Boyer to produce microbacteria from the human hormones. It was the venture capital raised from Kleiner Perkins by Swanson that made significant contribution to the success of Gene-tech. Therefore, a successful venture capitalist should at least be capable of recognizing a technology and the abilities of its project manager, and having faith in the commercial potential of the technology and being capable of financing in capital market. It can be put in this way, that the role of a venture capitalist, an angel investor in particular, is irreplaceable.

(3) Mike Markkula

Mike Markkula was a retired venture capitalist of Intel. Hewlett-Packard and Atanasoff-Berry Computer (ABC) had refused to provide funding to manufacture the

Apple II personal computer developed by S. Jobs and S. Wozniak, before Mike Markkula was introduced to the two inventors. With his sharp vision, Markkula saw the huge commercial potential in Jobs and Wozniak and their Apple II personal computer. Therefore, Markkula invested 391,000 dollars, applied for a credit loan from Bank of America, wrote a business plan and found a venture capital of 600,000 dollars for the Apple II personal computer project. With his critical funding and support, the Apple II personal computer went on the market in 1977 and Apple Computer, Inc. became among the Fortune Global 500 companies in 1982 (Liu Manhong, 1998).

2.2　Innovative Management Methods

There are a huge number of innovative management methods adopted in the United Sates, all of which have played crucial roles in the US economic, scientific and technological, and social development, and made significant contributions to the advancement of the world's economy and science and technology. The innovative management methods include "the Ford system", "the TOWS Matrix", "Michael Porter's Five Forces Model", "value chain analysis", "the Fifth Discipline", "model (s) of bounded rationality", "departmental organizational structure", "brainstorming techniques", "the Delphi method", "total quality management (TQM)", "agile manufacturing", "supply chain management", "enterprise resource planning (ERP)", "customer relationship management (CRM)", "critical path", "analysis of competency", "balanced scorecard", "product life cycle", "franchising", "chainstore operation", etc., all of which seem to form a course list for management method studies. This book only touches a few innovative methods as examples to illustrate how innovation of management methods contributes to economic and social development.

The "Ford system" combines Adam Smith's (the author of *An Inquiry into the Nature and Causes of the Wealth of Nations*) idea of division of labour and Frederick Winslow Taylor's (the author of *The Principles of Scientific Management*) "scientific management" for standardized production, and uses the combination in mass production. Specifically, in flow process involving conveyer belts, raw materials are first mechanically processed and assembled into parts and components, which are then sent to various process steps on the general assembly line that runs at a certain speed. The parts and components will be assembled into automobiles. In this way, labour productivity has been greatly enhanced and huge profits generated for the company. Therefore, "the Ford system" has been actually similar to an industrial revolution.

Based upon his studies and surveys of over 4,000 American enterprises, the MIT Professor Peter Senge made a conclusion quite different from the idea of "reductionism" that breaks a unity into parts. According to Senge, people have lost their systems thinking, since they are accustomed to breaking a problem into parts for understanding. That is to say, there are "barriers to organization"——an organization or team has barriers to learn and think. To solve the problem, Senge has proposed "five disciplines", namely "personal mastery", "mental models", "building shared vision", and "team learning" that finally form into "systems thinking". The "Fifth Discipline" refers to "systems thinking" that integrates the other four to gain a better integrated result as a whole. It is evidently a thinking model of universal relevance and has been successfully adopted in many American enterprises and in some other countries.

"Franchising" was a business model created by Singer Sewing Company in 1865. In the franchising, a franchisor signs contracts with franchisees to give special permission to the franchisees to use one, some or all of the franchisor's intellectual properties, including trademark (s), corporate name, patented technology (technologies) and business model. The franchisees operate under the franchisor's business model and pay franchise fees. This business model is also known as franchise chain. According to franchise types, franchising is classified as product/trademark franchising and as franchise stores. With the latter, the franchisees should provide products and services of the quality under the operating principles required by the franchisor. As for the form of franchise stores, the franchisor provides the franchisees with support in training, advertising and research and development, and the franchisees have to pay royalties in addition to franchise fees. Parties involved in franchising can be manufacturers and wholesalers (e.g. Coca-Cola and its bottling factories), manufacturers and retailers (e.g. automobile manufacturers and distributors, petroleum companies and gas stations), wholesalers and retailers (e.g. suppliers and supermarkets), and retailers and retailers (e.g. fast food stores). Franchising is particularly suitable for service trade, for which a famous example is McDonald's Corporation (GEC Program, 2003).

The reform in business model can not be overlooked, as it has introduced a revolution to the organizational structure of service trade all around the world, benefiting both enterprises and consumers. We can have a better understanding of the abovementioned innovative management methods, by making comparisons between McDonald's and Chinese fast food restaurants, and between Starbucks and Chinese teahouses, in their operating models, sizes and economic profits.

As described above, the economic benefits generated from innovative management methods can promote social development in a way similar to technological innovation does. The United States has made significant contributions to the world in innovation of management methods.

2.3   Commercialization of R&D Achievements: Marketing Innovation

2.3.1   Institutional design for commercialization of R&D achievements: the Federal Technology Transfer Act

The *Federal Technology Transfer Act of 1986* is an amendment to the *Stevenson-Wydler Technology Innovation Act of 1980*. The 1986 Act encourages Government-operated laboratories to co-establish scientific research conglomerates with enterprises to promote technology transfer, and clarifies that technology transfer is one official task of government-operated federal laboratories, each of which shall spend 0.5% of its budget on technology transfer. The government will provide funds to facilitate communications between federal laboratories. Technology transfer fees will not be turned in to the national treasury; instead, they belong to the laboratories. Individual inventors can obtain about 15% of technology transfer fees for compensation. Upon the issuance of the Act, technology transfer organizations were gradually established, including the National Center for Aerospace Applications, the Federal Laboratory Consortium (FLC) Intelligence Agency, and Institute for Management and Technology. Even Brookhaven National Laboratory, a large-scale energy laboratory engaged in basic research, has gained considerable income from technology transfer.

2.3.2   From basic research to high-tech commodities

Logically, basic research is the foundation and source of both R&D and innovation, and high-tech commodities. Achievements of basic research play a significant role in and have profound influence on scientific and technological activities, and economic and social development. Fig. 2-4 illustrates an example.

On the top of Fig. 2-4 is MP3, a well-known product that has produced huge economic and social benefits, and below it are R&D achievements. Such a piece of high-tech commodity closely related to a nation's economy and people's life as MP3 actually comes out of basic research. The figure illustrates from left to right 5 basic research sources for MP3: First on the left is MP3's micro hardware memory, which

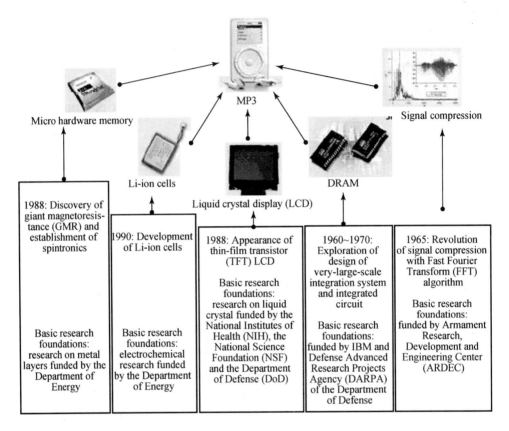

Fig. 2-4   How basic research influences innovation

Source: Domestic Policy Council and Office of S&T Policy, White House, 2006.

came from the discovery of giant magnetoresistance in 1988. The discovery of magnetoresistance and the establishment of spintronics had benefits from the basic research on "metal layers" funded by the Department of Energy. Second on the left is a piece of Li-ion cell, power source of an MP3. Li-ion cell came from the "electrochemical" research in 1990 funded by the Department of Energy. In the middle is MP3's FFT-LCD from the basic research on "liquid crystal" in 1988 funded by NIH, NSF and DoD. Second on the right is MP3's dynamic random-access memory (DRAM), an achievement of basic research on "design of very-large-scale integration system and integrated circuit" in the 1960s and 1970s funded by IBM and DARPA. Top on the right is signal compression technology that was achieved in the basic research project of "revolution of signal compression with Fast Fourier Transform (FFT) algorithm" in 1965 funded by Armament Research, Development and Engineering Center (ARDEC). Every major technology involved in MP3 has actually come from related basic research (Domestic Policy Council in Office of Science and Technology Policy, 2006).

There are many other examples, for instance, the relationship between the theory of relativity in physics and atomic energy, and that between the double helix model of DNA in biology and genetic engineering and genetically modified foods (GMF), etc. Of course, it is a systematic engineering to transform basic research achievements into new commodities, during which applied research, experimentation and development, and commercialization of achievements (marketing) are involved and integrated. Nonetheless, basic research plays a decisive role as the source of the whole process.

2.3.3　A case of marketing innovation for high-tech commodities: Dell

Dell was founded by Michael Dell in 1984. From the very beginning, Dell has chosen direct sales via Internet. This marketing policy is based upon quite simple calculation: In direct sales, Dell can save 25% ~45% intermediary fees and consumers can have direct impressions upon Dell products and enjoy lower prices. Internet is evidently a tool most ideal for direct sales. However, in the mid 1980s, many people held doubt for and even opposed against this unconventional model. Salesmen at that time were the fiercest opponents of this model, for they were worried about losing jobs.

According to Dell's annual financial statement, the daily revenue at the end of the fourth quarter in FY1999 was 14 million dollars, roughly 25% of the whole quarter's tax. Dell's goal is to do all its businesses on Internet. According to studies of Direct Marketing Association, the e-commerce in computer and electronics industries developed by Dell and Cisco made the taxes from e-commerce reach up to 395.3 billion dollars in 2003 alone.

As early as in the mid 1980s, customers were able to download software from Internet to know about or purchase Dell products. Dell technical support staff would give customers instructions on how to update their software. Dell's official website was launched in 1995. In the autumn of the same year, Dell installed its first interactive application——order-making software, with which a customer was able to choose ideal configurations and receive a corresponding price list. Afterwards, Dell showed enterprises and scientific research institutes how purchasing procedures could be simplified via online purchasing. Meanwhile, Dell enhanced its services (after-sales services in particular), which is crucial for online direct sales. "Mass customization" is an important link in Dell's direct sales system. Mass customization can be realized in four ways: Cooperation: Dell and customers cooperate in products. Adjustments: Dell makes adjustments to product functions, for example. Packaging: Dell provides different products for different customers. Transparency: Dell provides products or services unique to customers. Mass customization has been proved to be an effective way to reduce inventory and lower costs.

As for the management, Dell has embraced the famous "three principles of gold" since its foundation in 1984: direct sales, understanding of customers' needs and reducing inventory. Online direct sales can effectively improve the relationship between a company and its suppliers and customers, to further form a "virtual entity", which can build a larger company faster.

Dell had a deeper understanding of the "three principles of gold" in an unexpected event in 1989 when it bought chips more than needed, with the hope that it could realize the expected sales volume. Unfortunately, chip capacity was upgraded from 256K to 1M, just after Dell had bought chips, and chips became much cheaper than before. Dell thus suffered severe losses. The significance of reducing inventory was well proved again. Dell has since then stopped manufacturing parts and components all by itself, and signed outsourcing contracts with reputable suppliers (Sanders, 2002). For better communication with customers, Dell holds "platinum seminars" twice a year around the world.

Direct sales model has been adopted through Dell's global development. For example, in the late 1990s, the sales income of Dell Asia Pacific increased by 79% during 1997 and 1998, and by 37% during 1998 and 1999. The company's net income from its European market also increased by 50% in FY1998 ~ 1999. Dell has set up its own market for direct sales in over ten Asia-Pacific countries. The company announced in February 1998 that it would establish in Xiamen, China, a 12,500-square-meter customer center as the base for production, sales, services and technical support for Dell computer systems in China. The "Dell China Customer Center" was expanded into a facility of 32,500 square meters in November 2000.

In addition to direct sales model and "mass customization", Dell has also introduced some other advanced business management models, including "Just In Time" (JIT), "agile manufacturing", "supply chain management", and "e-logistics", with which the company has become the second largest computer manufacturer in the world. With the revenue of 57.4 billion dollars, Dell ranks 25th in the Fortune Global 500. Approximately 75,100 employees are working at Dell around the globe.

Dell's marketing model can be summarized as: Individual and company customers can make direct orders from Dell through the company's global information and communications network, so that Dell can configure products in accordance with customers' requirements, known as customization, and provide services. Dell has greatly enhanced its competitiveness with this model, under which costs at links of manufacturers, distributors and retailers have been effectively lowered, and efficiency enhanced and inventory reduced.

Dell's core competitiveness lies in its capabilities of hardware and software customization, establish personalized customer relationship for mass customization at a higher level, and have more advanced management and sustainable product logistics (Zhou Jizhong, 2002).

2.3.4　The role of intermediaries in R&D achievement transformation

The outstanding American intermediaries have contributed a lot to the high transformation rate of R&D achievements in the United States. The abovementioned Silicon Valley and Science Park of University of Utah are both science and technology intermediaries in nature. Such intermediaries also include various technology transfer offices (TTOs), improvement centers, incubators and research foundations, etc. Following are some cases.

Case 1: The role of science and Technology (S&T) intermediaries in R&D achievement transformation in Utah

In addition to Science Park of University of Utah, there are also University of Utah Research Foundation (UURF), Utah State Improvement Center, and Technology Transform Office (TTO).

The University of Utah Research Foundation (UURF) is a non-profit S&T intermediary under University of Utah, and is responsible for the administration of Science Park of University of Utah and the collection of royalty and licensing fees. The operating cost of the Foundation comes from rental from enterprise tenants, royalty and licensing fees. One of the Foundation's important tasks is to manage the funding and operation of technology commercialization projects. The projects provide a two-year funding of 35,000 dollars at maximum per year. The total funding provided by the Foundation every year is five million dollars. License(s) can be applied as the two-year funding comes to an end. The projects are designed to financially aid university researchers in developing technologies with commercial potential, so that they can collect data for the projects, support the early-stage development and the building of product prototype, and work together with the potential license-owners. Only tenured professors can submit competitive applications for funding from UURF. Applications are evaluated by business consultants for the feasibility of commercialization and for the economic relevance. Successful applicants will receive consultation on market.

Utah State Improvement Center is an S&T intermediary of another type. It provides services after technology transformation, further develops the transformed technology, evaluates the possibility of technology transformation and funding obtaining, and helps with funding. Only teaching and administrative staff of University of Utah can apply for technology commercialization projects founded by the Center. Whether an application is approved depends upon possibility of commercialization, proportion of matching funds (at the minimum 2 : 1), an applicant's qualification and possibility of financing for commercialization.

Technology Transform Office (TTO) is an S&T intermediary as well. It was first founded out of a bill approved by the US Congress in 1980. The funds of TTO come from the royalty fees for research of University of Utah. TTO is dedicated to promoting economic development and creating jobs through technology commercialization, and gains income from sharing royalty fees with investors and research institutes. In this way, it can also protect intellectual properties of University of Utah, and helps technology owners with finding market and customers, and inventors with license application.

TTO's responsibilities include: organizing evaluation of inventions; meeting with inventors; patent searching; determining whether an invention is qualified for patent or commercialization; helping with defining market and potential license-owners; preparing materials for improvement; establishing perspective application connection; coordinating conferences, shows and demonstrations; helping inventors with license application, etc. It takes about one year for TTO to help completing a license application, including preparation for payment of royalty fees and other charges, agreement drafting, project negotiations and aid in striking a bargain. In protecting rights and interest of the university's teaching and administrative staff, TTO defines new potential sources of cooperative research, helps the university working staff with gaining shares in newly-established companies, and creates jobs for graduates, by means of collecting 30% of net income from royalty fees and enhancing the satisfaction degree of product development by the university's staff.

The abovementioned S&T intermediaries, including the Science Park, had achieved as described below in 2001 alone.

In FY2001, Science Park of University of Utah gained four million dollars from rental income and 3.2 million dollars from royalty fees, license agreements and stock profits. Among the rental income of four million dollars, 350,000 dollars was for administrative work and another 1.5 million dollars for university research (seed fund and technology commercialization fund) and the lump-sum investment in infrastructure. As for the income of 3.2 million dollar from royalty fees, license agreements and stock profits, 25% of gross income was used for patent maintenance, and nearly 50% of net income went to supporting TTO's operation, 30% for payment to inventors of the patented technologies, and the rest for the departments and divisions the inventors were working for. In a year, TTO tracked 25 ~ 40 patents, signed 30 ~ 40 license agreements and more than 200 material transfer agreements. By the year of 2001, there had been 93 state improvement centers in Utah, which produced altogether more than 1,000 patents, over 2,000 licenses and over 2,000 jobs.

Drawing experience from the successful cases, the University of Utah made a conclusion on the link between technological inventions and market: Only approximately 2% technological inventions can be used to found a new company, and only 10% of the newly-founded companies may succeed. 1 ~ 200 million dollars are needed for the development of a new product. It takes 5 ~ 10 years to put a new product on market (Espin, 2002).

Incubators are another type of S&T intermediaries. In the North America where incubators have been developed at a highest speed, there had been 731 incubators by 2000, serving more than 20,000 incubated enterprises, which usually get mature within 2 ~ 3 years. The "incubated" and "grown" enterprises have together created 250,000 jobs in the United States. Various incubators take different proportions in the United States: 43% for comprehensive operations, 25% for technology, 10% for manufacturing, 9% for emerging industries, 6% for services and 5% for low-income enterprises.

Incubators for technology businesses were created for: the needs of technology commercialization, the appearance of emerging industries and the high return on investment pursued by investors.

As an intermediary, an incubator functions as the creator of new entrepreneurs, companies and jobs.

The US Department of Commerce allotted 300,000 dollars to a sample survey on incubators for technology businesses, low-income enterprises and comprehensive operations. The respondents included 50 projects, 125 companies and 107 shareholders of enterprise groups and incubator managers. All the enterprises joining incubators during 1990 and 1996 were included in the survey. According to the survey, an incubator had on average created 468 posts and 234 derivative posts, with the subsidy cost estimated at 1,109 dollars per post. In a macroeconomic model, every dollar public investment (subsidy) could receive a return of 4 dollars from local taxes. The return of investment was as high as 4 times, which was a considerably ideal result. On average, an incubated enterprise realized an increase of 240,000 dollars in annual sales income and had 3.7 posts more annually (including full-time and part-time jobs). The survival rate of the surveyed incubated enterprises reached up to 87%, higher than the average 50% for all the American enterprises. As for the average income of the surveyed incubators in 1996, those for technology businesses gained 21.9 million dollars and comprehensive operations 5.9 million dollars. Taking incubators for technology businesses for example, the total sales income of "incubated" and "grown" enterprises was only 168,500 dollars in 1993, but increased to 1,144,300 dollars in 1996. The average total employment in technology incubators was in 1996 calculated 256.7 persons and 79.9 persons in those for comprehensive operations. Evidently, technology incubators stand out among all the incubators.

Case 2: Austin technology incubator (ATI): an intermediary for the american high-tech businesses

Founded in June 1989, the Austin Technology Incubator (ATI) is a programme of the IC^2 Institute of the University of Texas (UT) at Austin. ATI is a community-based intermediary for technology businesses, funded by the University of Texas, the Greater Austin Chamber of Commerce, the Austin municipal government and private enterprises and aimed to boost the regional economic development. With its success, ATI has attracted enterprises from countries such as the US, Canada, Brazil and Australia to join in, which is known as "the Austin model".

"The Austin model" includes: the community market-oriented development of enterprise; an environment for innovation in which UT, scientific research institutes, enterprises and government have close cooperation; and innovation resources making full use of professional talent, technology, funds and intelligence. All the above three have formed an innovation system of ATI.

ATI looks for and admits any enterprise that: has at least one special technology-supported product or service, an aggressive and excellent management team, the potential to create more jobs, products that have been on market for at least one year, and funding sources.

The process of review and evaluation may take about 45 working days in 5 stages:

Stage I: Submission of the business plan;

Stage II: Internal review: by one Review Supervisor and 2-3 ATI staff;

Stage III: Discussions between Executive Director and Review Supervisor on the admission details;

Stage IV: Meeting with the entrepreneur to talk about the business plan and evaluate the entrepreneur's capabilities;

Stage V: External evaluation (usually including 3 outside reviewers from market, finance and technology circles).

An enterprise accepted into ATI can gain from ATI both tangible and intangible resources.

The tangible resources include: conference facilities and services of an e-strategy center; online services for capitals and venture capital; Austin Software services; and office equipment and facilities.

The intangible resources include: connection with UT, the Greater Austin Chamber of Commerce, the Austin municipal government and private enterprises; support from community business organizations, for example, support for venture capitals provided by the website "know-how"; academic resources; indoor consultation from ATI professionals; visits to ATI successful projects and participation in symposiums; participation in UT's internship programmes; international market and related key contracts obtained via the global network.

As a technology intermediary, ATI has become the innovation center of the American innovation system in the Austin area, and created large numbers of jobs for communities. During the ten years from 1989 to 1999, ATI had attracted 100 companies to join in, and 55 had been well grown. By 1998, the "grown" and "incubated" enterprises in ATI had created nearly 2,500 high-salaried posts, each of which had produced 3 ~ 5 derivative posts in service as well. The output value of the ATI "incubated" enterprises was approximate 200 million dollars, and four "grown" enterprises were listed on NASDAQ with the total market value of 385 million dollars. ATI has also incubated quite a number of innovation companies, the revenue of which during 1992 and 1999 reached up to 100 million dollars. These innovation companies possess numerous patents. The time for commercialization of laboratory achievements averages 18 months and the cash cycle has been shortened to less than 6 months.

Moreover, ATI has contributed a great deal to the economic development in the Austin region. There was not a single incubator in Austin in 1989 when ATI was founded and the regional economy was in depression. However, business opportunities in Austin ranked first on *Fortune* in 1999 and third in 2000. Austin has thus become one of the cities with the most business opportunities in the world. Furthermore, Austin has also been one of the world's best cities for living and working (Zhou Jizhong, 2002). Patent is one of the best indicators for Austin, as it is a city full of creation, innovation and invention. According to the analysis of areas of patent-related activities in the 1990s made by the United States Patent and Trademark Office, Austin was more active than larger cities that had economic diversities, such as Phoenix City, Seattle and Denver. Austin was called the American third most innovative city by *The Wall Street Journal* in 2006, in the year of which there were 2,306 patents in the city (see Fig. 2-5).

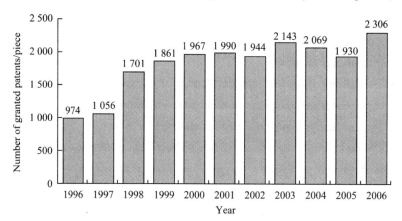

Fig. 2-5　The number of granted patents in Austin (1996 ~ 2006)

Source: Data from the United States Patent and Trademark Office, sorted out by Locke Liddell & Sapp, Austin, Texas.

2.4　Controlling and Incentives in Research and Development

Planning and controlling among the four functions of management are actually two aspects of an issue. Or rather to say, controlling is operated to the content and indicators in planning. Proactive controlling has to be made together with incentives. Controlling and incentives in science and technology include research and development, and evaluation of and appropriate reward for R&D projects.

2.4.1　Selection of the national critical technologies

The United States national critical technologies are taken here as an example. Under the *National Defense Authorization Act for Fiscal Year (FY) 1990*, the Executive Office of the President set up the National Critical Technologies Panel (NCTP), which has since then on submitted a report on the "National Critical Technologies" to the US President and Congress every two years, reviewing and selecting over 20 national critical technologies according to the criteria listed in Table 2-2.

Table 2-2　Selection criteria for the US national critical technologies

	Criteria	Notes
National needs	Industrial competitiveness	Technologies that can enhance the American competitiveness on the global market by putting new products on market and improving the existing products in cost-saving, quality and performance
	National defense	Technologies that have significant influence on the American national defense by improving the performance, cost-saving, reliability or production capacity of weaponry and equipment
	Energy guarantee	Technologies that can cut dependence on imported energy, reduce energy costs or enhance energy efficiency
	Quality of life	Capabilities to contribute to the national or the world's health, human well-being and environment
Significance/ being critical	Market leadership	Capabilities to sustain the American leadership in technologies that are crucial to national economy or defense
	Improvement of performance/quality/ production capacity	Capabilities to generate economic or military benefit through revolutionary or progressive improvements in the existing products and techniques
	Leverage	Potential of government R&D investment to spur private enterprises to invest in technology commercialization, or possibilities of a technology to lead to success of other technologies, products or market
Market size/diversity	Vulnerability	The US may suffer severe damage if a technology is monopolized by some other countries
	Diffusion/promotion	A technology that lays a foundation for many other technologies, or is closely related with sectors of the national economy
	Market size expansion	Capabilities to lay significant influence on economy by expanding the existing market, creating new industries, generating capitals or creating jobs

Source: *Gaining New Ground: Technology Priorities for America's Future*, The US Council on Competitiveness.

According to the above criteria, 22 critical technologies in 6 fields were evaluated in the United States in 1991. The 6 fields include materials, manufacturing, information and communications, bioengineering and life sciences, aerospace and ground transportation, and energy and environment.

2.4.2 Evaluation of scientific research achievements

Scientific research achievements generally refer to those of basic research and applied basic research. The evaluation principles include creativity and innovativeness of scientific discovery, advance nature and progressiveness of scientific theories, and applicability and spillover of scientific research achievements (social and economic benefit). Peer review is adopted in such evaluation, as scientific research is the mental work involving highly-specialized knowledge. Peers are selected according to disciplinary divisions to form various "science communities". Evaluation may be conducted by means of correspondence review and conference review, as well as of qualitative and quantitative assessment. In quantitative assessment, citation frequency is a commonly-used criterion.

Since scientific research is engaged in exploring the laws of the unknown world and its phenomena, research achievements need to be published, and the ownership of achievements is prioritized according to the publication time of theses, which is the issue of priorities in scientific discovery. The problem of priorities can be dated back as early as to the times of Newton. The best-known examples include the priority dispute between Newton and Hooke over credit for gravitation, and the Newton-Leibniz controversy over the invention of the calculus in the 17th century, as well as the war between Darwin and Wallace for the priority over the biological evolution in the 19th century. As science advances, academic journals have got more and more important in determining priorities in scientific discovery.

SCI, i. e. Science Citation Index, thus cannot be ignored here. It has been half a century since SCI was first published in 1961 by Institute for Scientific Information (ISI) that had been founded by Eugene Garfield. SCI is an international multidisciplinary citation index, including natural sciences and many other disciplines. According to sourcing journals, SCI is grouped into SCI and SCI-E. The former includes about 3,500 journals, and the latter, SCI-Expanded is a larger version of SCI and has around 5,300 journals. Both SCI and SCI-E can be searched through international online retrieval and Internet. There are three types of paper SCI journals, including bimonthly, annual and bound volume. SCI contains five parts: citation index, patent citation index, source index, corporate index and permuterm subject index.

The "impact factor" (IF) created by Eugene Garfield in 1972 measures the importance of scientific journals and is calculated as: IF = the number of articles published in the previous two years that were cited by indexed journals in the current year/the total number of "citable items" published by the journal under evaluation in the same previous two years.

According to the above indicators and method, the top three citation index systems that are known as the international authoritative statistical systems, namely SCI, EI (Engineering Index) and ISTP (Index to Scientific and Technical Proceedings), publish the total number of articles published on the three indexes and citation frequency of a country every year.

The evaluation of technological achievements, however, is more complicated than that of scientific research achievements. The evaluation indicators include technological advance of achievements, and economic and social values of the applications, etc. The criteria for the US national critical technologies in Table 2-2 can be seen as macroscopic first-grade indicators for the evaluation of civil technological achievements, disregarding the content for national defense within.

2.4.3 Reward for scientific and technological achievements

Functionally, management controls through both evaluation and reward, and the latter should be based upon the former.

Briefly, such reward is recognition of scientific and technological research fellows and their achievements, and made by scientific and technological circles and subcommunities of various disciplines and specialties.

The reward made by specialized science and technology communities can take various forms, including nomenclature, citation and awards.

1) Nomenclature. For example, the time Newton was living in and mechanics and physics at the time were named after Newton, as "the Newton times" and "Newton mechanics". Cuvier has been known as "the father of paleontology", Faraday "the father of electronics", and Jenner "the father of immunology". A discipline may be named after a scientist, such as "Euclidean geometry" and "Keynesian economics". A unit or concept can be named after a scientist, for instance, "Planck constant", "Brownian motion" and "Zeeman effect". Or a unit can be named after the scientist, such as ampere, volt, ohm, Joule, watt, oersted, etc.

2) Citation, eg., citation frequency according to SCI.

3) Awards are more direct compared with nomenclature and citation.

Jonathan Cole and his brother, both of whom are American scholars, made a survey on notability and reputation of prizes in physics among the community of physics. Ninety-eight out of over 150 prizes were selected. Reputation was assessed in a five-grade system, with 5 as the highest and 1 the lowest. Reputation value of each prize was the average of scores from all the physicists participating in the survey. Notability of each prize was assessed according to the total number of winners of the prize who were physicists in grades 1-6. Table 2-3 only takes 40 prizes from the survey.

Table 2-3 Notability and reputation of prizes in physics

Prize	Notability/point	Reputation/point
1. Nobel Prize in Physics	100	4.98
2. Member, the US National Academy of Sciences	95	4.22
3. Fulbright scholarship or lectureship	94	2.58
4. Research Fellow, the National Science Foundation	93	2.43
5. Guggenheim Research Fellow	92	3.14
6. Enrico Fermi Award	92	4.31
7. Rhodes Scholarships	91	3.20
8. Member, the Royal Society	86	4.01
9. Research Fellow, the Sloan Foundation	83	3.18
10. Honorary degrees, Harvard University	81	3.70
11. Oersted Medal	80	3.31
12. Honorary degrees, the University of Berkeley	78	3.10
13. Research Fellow, the Ford Foundation	72	2.69
14. Barkley Award	68	3.65
15. Fellow, the US National Research Council	68	2.97
16. Heinemann Award	66	3.80
17. Honorary degrees, Johns Hopkins University	65	3.00
18. London Awards	65	4.03
19. Honorary degrees, the University of North Carolina	64	2.20
20. Research Fellow, the Rockefeller Foundation	61	2.90
21. The Laurens Prize	57	3.80
22. Research Fellow, the US Atomic Energy Commission	59	2.30
23. Member, the French Academy of Sciences	56	4.10
24. The Presidential Citizens Medal	56	3.40
25. American Physical Society Awards	54	3.40

Continued

Prize	Notability/point	Reputation/point
26. Medal of Honor	53	3.70
27. Atoms for Peace Awards	51	3.80
28. The NIH Research Grants	49	1.80
29. Honorary degrees, Vanderbilt University	49	2.30
30. Westinghouse Science Talent Search	49	2.10
31. Compton Gold Medal	48	3.70
32. Einstein Gold Medal	47	4.20
33. Max Planck Medal	47	4.00
34. Research fellow, Carnegie Institution	43	2.50
35. Presidential Medal of Freedom	43	3.90
36. Franklin Medal	41	3.43
37. Rumford Medal	43	3.27
38. National Medal of Science	38	4.02
39. Corporate Research Awards	38	2.59
40. Lorentz Medal	36	4.00

Source: Quoted from *Awards for Science and Technology: Mechanism and Functions of Awards for Science and Technology*, 33-34.

There are national and non-governmental awards for science and technology in the United States. The National Medal of Science Award is a high-level one for outstanding scientists in physics, chemistry, biology, mathematics, engineering and social sciences. The number of winners is no more than 20 every year. The Award is also known as the Presidential Science Award, as it is conferred by the United States President. However, the Award is not selected from science awards of states, and there is no such a science award in a state corresponding to the National Medal of Science Award. Neither a corporate science award nor a society/association one is subordinate to the other.

The ones conferred by scientific and technological societies and associations are important non-governmental awards. For example, there are over 40 awards under the American Chemical Society (ACS), such as Award for Creative Invention, Award for Fuel Chemistry, and Langnuir Award for Chemical Physics. And also, there are numerous corporate awards for science and technology, the most distinguished ones of which include Westinghouse Science Talent Search by Westinghouse Electrics, Innovation Awards, New Talent Awards, Software Awards and Hardware Awards by IBM, and Quality Awards by Ford.

Functions of awards for science and technology include: guiding the development of scientific and technological personnel; bringing into play scientific and technological personnel's creativity; discovering and training scientific and technological talent; creating an ideal environment for scientific and technological development; setting objective criteria for the evaluation of scientific research institutes and personnel; protecting the rights and interest of owners of scientific and technological achievements and encouraging technological innovation; promoting scientific and technological achievements known to the public and sharing scientific and technological resources.

2.5 R&D Human Resources

2.5.1 Incremental returns

Theodore W. Schultz, the winner of the Nobel Memorial Prize in Economic Sciences, wrote in his book *Origins of Increasing Returns*: To a large extent, R&D investment falls into the category. In a broad sense, research and development is the main origin of technological progress, which comes from basic and applied research that needs specialized human capital. The application of production technology created by R&D scientists should bring increasing returns. For example, the worldwide organized agricultural research has become a secondary sector of considerable size in economy. The annual expenditure on the organized agricultural research was about eight billion dollars calculated at the constant price in 1985. Then let's carefully observe the scientific work of top gene specialists dedicated to increasing plant (crop) yields. The scientific work is important part of the organized agricultural research and greatly increases food-producing capacity of agriculture. This important source of increasing agricultural productivity has far from being exhausted. Therefore, it is quite necessary to sustain and increase investment in the specialized human capital.

Another human capital investment that can realize increasing returns in human life cycle is basic education. It is critical to master a language with good reading and writing skills. In the aspect, many low-income countries have also made evident progress since the Second World War. The progress can be measured with the improving basic education. With abundant evidence, we can see that the return on investment in basic education for farmers has remained high in agricultural countries marching toward modernization. However, the investment in education training specialized human capital is still seriously inadequate. The high returns on basic education shows that basic education is an origin of increasing returns that result in economic growth (Schultz, 2001).

Schultz's "incremental returns" are a relative concept to "the law of diminishing marginal returns" in economics. The law refers to progressive decrease in the marginal output of a production process as the amount of a single factor of production is increased, while holding the given technology and the amounts of all other factors of production constant. Here, diminishing marginal returns are on the premises of changing a single factor of production while holding the given technology and all other factors of production constant. Schultz's "incremental returns", however, take place when the two premises in the law of diminishing marginal returns have both changed.

In economic accounting, the difference between the growth rate of national income and that of national resource input is known as residual growth rate. Under the law of diminishing marginal returns, the growth rate of output shall be lower than that of input, with all other conditions held constant. However, residual growth rate has been proved positive in practice. It is agreed by the academic circles that this has resulted from the law of increasing returns on human capital.

2.5.2   Intellectual capital

Different from the factors of production defined in economics, namely land, labor force and financial capital, human capital highlights mental assets. Intellectual capital has a larger extension than human capital, including organizations' "mental" assets, in addition to human ones. Therefore, intellectual capital is the sum of human, customer, shareholders, and cultural and structural capital.

As early as in January 1995, a couple of entrepreneurs and specialists enthusiastic about guiding corporate knowledge management with intellectual capital concept called a symposium to discuss intellectual capital-related issues. The participating companies included the Dow Chemical Company, DuPont, Hoffman, Skandia, Hewlett-Packard, Hughes and legal and economic consulting groups. A Conference on Intellectual Management was founded by the above companies in 1999.

Intellectual capital is mainly composed of human capital and intellectual assets, which are external existing knowledge hierarchy. When an intellectual expresses his/her knowledge in a perceptible manner, his/her embrained knowledge is transformed into intellectual assets. What intellectual properties protect is intellectual assets.

Specifically, human capital includes experience, know-how, skills, creativity, etc. ; intellectual assets refer to inventions, methods, drawings, designs, database and so on; and intellectual properties are patent rights, copyright, trademark rights, trade secrets, etc. A company shall try its best to transform employees' human capital into the company's intellectual assets; or rather to say, to transform employees' implicit "tacit" knowledge into explicit "specifiable" knowledge.

Case study: patent management in the Dow Chemical Company

The Dow Chemical Company was founded by Herbert Dow in Midland, Michigan in 1897. It is a bit younger than DuPont that has a history of over 200 years. The Dow Chemical Company realized sales of 58 billion dollars in 2008 and its 46,000 employees working around the world provide thousands of products and services to customers in about 160 countries and areas. The company has taken sustainability as a principle for chemical industry and innovation.

Dow, the founder of the Dow Company, was a pioneer in chemical industry and gained the patent of the electrolytic method of bromine extracting from brine. Therefore, the Dow Company has actually followed its founder's path in technological inventions. Since the company spends tens of millions of dollars on its tens of thousand patents every year, management of the company's huge intangible assets is a particular value-added operation. Patent management is an investment in intangible assets. The intangible asset management of the Dow Company includes planning, competitiveness, evaluation, classification, valuation, investment and portfolio. The procedure goes like this: a patent is evaluated for its validity before the classification of being out of use, in use and to be used. According to valuation and competitiveness assessment, the company abandons or gives out the out-of-use patents, so that no more patent tax is paid and tens of million dollars can be saved. The Dow Chemical Company and a consulting company co-developed a technology factor method, special for intangible asset evaluation in calculating the proportion intangible assets take in the company's total net assets. In this way, the Company has gained returns of 200 ~ 300 million dollars from patent royalties.

2.5.3   Global allocation of R&D human resources in the American R&D companies

Distribution of R&D human resources reflects the allocation of R&D human resources in a company. According a recent Business R&D and Innovation Survey

(BRDIS) in the United States, the American R&D companies employed globally 27.1 million people in 2008, 1. 91 million of whom are R&D personnel. Table 2-4 illustrates the distribution of employees and R&D personnel and the per capita R&D budget in the American R&D companies.

Table 2-4　Global distribution of employees and R&D personnel and budget allocation in the American R&D companies in 2008

| Industry | Number of employees/1,000 persons | | | | | | R&D budget/100 million dollars | | |
| | Total number of employees | | | Number of R&D personnel | | | | | |
	Global	US	Overseas	Global	US	Overseas	Global	US	Overseas
All	27,066	18,258	8,538	1,909	1,461	448	3,457.4	2,832.4	625.0
Manufacturing	16,364	9,912	6,452	1,129	835	294	2,369.8	1,900.5	469.4
Chemicals	2,258	1,271	986	205	155	50	659.6	524.5	135.1
Pharmacy	1,053	630	423	148	114	34	559.6	451.3	108.6
Computer/electronics	2,455	1,222	1,234	380	268	112	748.4	590.4	158.1
Transporting equip-ment	3,159	1,808	1,350	233	169	65	523.8	420.9	102.9
Aerospace	1,210	893	317	105	85	19	292.2	275.7	16.5
Information	2,855	1,962	892	299	221	78	447.9	370.7	77.2
Finance/insurance	1,361	1,278	83	10	9	1	12.4	11.6	0.7
Professional/scientif-ic/technical services	1,594	1,234	360	366	302	6644	464.1	400.1	64.1

Note: The data has been processed with rounding.

Source: *Overview of Global R&D Investment*, 3-4, Vol. 14 ~ 15, 2010, Institute of Scientific & Technical Information of China. Translated from *2008 Business R&D and Innovation Survey* from *NSF Annual Report 2010*.

"R&D personnel" in Table 2-4 refer to the employees provide direct support for research and development, including scientists and engineers engaged in R&D, and R&D-related administrative and technical personnel. As shown in the table, the US enterprises have recruited top R&D personnel around the globe. The overseas R&D personnel take up 23. 5% of the total employees, equaling about one quarter. The global average of R&D budget is about 181,000 dollars, and 194,000 dollars per domestic R&D person and 140,000 dollars /overseas R&D person. The per capita R&D budget in manufacturing is 210,000 dollars, higher than that of 139,000 dollars in the other industries. Pharmacy has a highest per capita R&D budget of 378,000 dollars (Institute of Scientific & Technical Information of China, 2010).

2.6 Case Study of Industrial Research and Development: R&D in the American Pharmacy

Pharmaceutical industry is crucial to people's life and health. With an ever-increasing population and people's higher demands on health, the industry is seen as a pillar industry in all the countries. Moreover, all countries are facing a problem of aging population, and pharmaceutical industry thus draws more attention from both government and the public. For example, medicare reforms launched in both the US and China in 2010 have received great attention. The ratio of population of 65 years and over to the total population in 2007 was 12% in the US, 8% in China, 16% in the UK, and 20% in Germany (World Bank, 2009), and the figures may be 15% in the US, 13% in China, 22% in the UK, and 22.5% in Germany in 2020 (see Fig. 2-6). Since medicine concerns people's health and life, pharmaceutical industry has been ahead of the other industries in the world in the past 60 years since the Second World War.

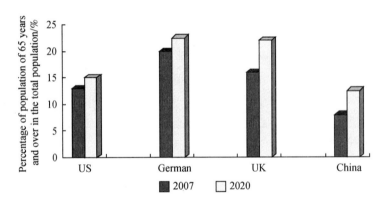

Fig. 2-6　Trend of aging in China, US, UK and Germany

Pharmaceutical industry is a high-tech industry, and the ratio of R&D input to sales is about 10%. The figures in the world-known pharmaceutical companies are even as high as 15% ~ 20%. Among Top 50 Pharmaceutical Companies (Global), there are as many as 20 American companies, including Pfizer, Merck, AstraZeneca, Johnson & Johnson, Bristol-Myers Squibb and Eli Lilly, all of which are operated with high R&D intensity.

Different from other high-tech industries (such as aerospace, telecommunications, computer, office automation, etc.), pharmaceutical industry is comparatively dependent upon basic research; or rather to say, there in no distinguishable boundary between basic research, applied research, and experimentation and development in pharmaceutical R&D. Additionally, compared with the other high-tech industries, pharmaceutical industry has four unique and distinct characteristics, namely high input, long period, high risks, and high returns.

As for high input calculated with constant price, the input between the completion of a synthetic compound and the product on-market was tens of million dollars in the 1960s and 1970s, while a new drug needs on average 300 ~ 500 million dollars nowadays. R&D input into a new drug has got larger than marketing input. According to statistics, the R&D budget in pharmaceutical industry is the largest in America, as five times high as that in defense and aerospace and twice as that in computer industry. Pfizer Inc. as today's largest pharmaceutical company in the world has had an annual R&D budget of about 8 billion dollars in recent years, equaling 20% of its annual sales.

The period between submission of the patent application of a new compound and the approval to the compound to be a new drug on-market has been lengthened from the averaged 6 ~ 8 years in the 1960s to today's 12 ~ 15 years.

High risks in pharmaceutical industry mainly sit in the following three aspects.

First, high input does not necessarily have high returns. As early as in 1991, the Pharmaceutical Research Center of America made a global survey on 49 R&D- and innovation-centered pharmaceutical companies. According to the survey, the ratio of new pharmaceuticals on-market to compounds synthesized and screened was on average 2,271:1 in Japan, 4,317:1 in Europe, and 6155:1 in the US. The PhRMA statistics in 1995 showed that the ratio had increased to 5,000 ~ 10,000:1 by the year, and the new drug recalled after the approval to go on market had not been included, such as Pfizer's Trovafloxacin, a fourth-generation quinolones drug in 2000, and Bayer's Lipobay, an antilipemic drug in 2001. According to statistics, one out of five new drugs on average can make profits, and one out of 23 can be financially successful with an annual sale of over 100 million dollars. In other words, every new drug costs 300 ~ 500 million dollars on average, and the risks are quite high. What is worse, if a new drug that has been developed with huge investment is kicked out of the market by a cheaper "substitute", the company will definitely suffer severe losses. Therefore, it is crucial for pharmaceutical companies to pay close attention to R&D trends and business information on "potential rivals".

Secondly, the actual duration of patent right protection for a new drug has been shortened. The patent length of a new drug refers to the period from the completion of a compound to the approval to the new drug to be on market. However, the lengthened patent length results inevitably in a shortened actual duration of patent right protection. For a 20-year duration of patent right protection for drugs set by WTO's *Agreement on Trade-related Aspects of Intellectual Property Rights* (TRIPs), the 10-plus years from the completion of a compound to FDA's approval to the new drug to be on market are counted in. Therefore, the actual duration of patent right protection for a new drug has been shortened to 6 ~ 8 years nowadays (see Fig. 2-7). Upon the end of duration of patent right protection for a drug, imitations of the drug will definitely bring immense negative impacts on the profits of the original one.

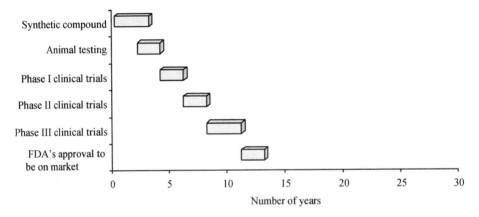

Fig. 2-7　Period of time for pharmaceutical R&D at different stages in the United States

Thirdly, the ever-increasing medical expenses push most countries, including China, to review and make reforms on the existing medical and social welfare systems, and put strict restrictions on medicine prices, which brings pharmaceutical companies under dual pressure: ① of increasing R&D expenses; and ② that R&D investment cannot be compensated on market through free pricing. Such pressure will undoubtedly have negative impacts on further R&D in pharmaceutical companies.

However, once a pharmaceutical company has succeeded in manufacturing a new drug that has significant effects on a certain disease, the company will have surprisingly huge commercial returns. As early as in 2000, each of top 10 pharmaceutical companies in sales market had at least one "heavyweight" drug from which the company could gain sales of over one billion dollars a year. Pfizer at the time had 7 such "heavyweight" products, with the total sales of 16, 507 million dollars; six for Merck, with total sales of 13, 295 million dollars; and four for Squibb, with the sales of 5. 1 billion dollars. Losec MUPS of AstraZeneca headed the sales market in 2000, alone with the sales as high as 6. 3 billion dollars. High risks and returns in the industry push large pharmaceutical companies to cooperate and make alliances with each other, for globalized businesses. Pfizer and Merck have both purchased some large-scale pharmaceutical companies in recent years.

The long period includes both time for new drug R&D (Fig. 2-7) and process of drug research and development (Table 2-5) (Zhou Jizhong, 2002).

Table 2-5　Process of drug research and development in the United States

1. Discovery of curative effect: Biological/physiological research on curative effect	12. Pre-clinical new drug confirmation
2. High-throughput screening	13. Pre-clinical new drug application
3. Lead discovery	14. Clinical new drug confirmation (5,000:1)
4. Structural characteristic: lead compound	15. Phase I clinical trials: safety and biological verification (20-80 healthy volunteers)
5. Lead optimization: rational structural modifications	16. Phase II clinical trials: evaluation of efficacy and side effects (10-300 volunteers)
6. Auxiliary experiments: verifying specificity and/or efficacy	17. Phase III clinical trials: long-term curative effect and adverse effects (1,000 ~3,000 volunteers)
7. Pharmacodynamics	18. Preparation for new drug application
8. Pre-clinical development: safety, bioactivity and animal testing	19. FDA review
9. Patent preparation for compound/application	20. FDA approval to be on market
10. Analytical method: pharmacodynamics, pharmaceutics, and process chemistry	21. Marketing and sale
11. Pharmacokinetic and toxicologic studies	

According to *2008 Report on R&D Strategy in the US Pharmaceutical Businesses*, the total income of the US pharmaceutical industry reached up to 315 billion dollars in 2007, ranking first in the world. There were approximately 3. 2 million direct and indirect employees in the industry. The US pharmaceutical industry spent as much as 65. 2 billion dollars on research and development in 2008, increasing by 3. 16% compared with the previous year. More than 2, 900 pharmaceuticals were under research and development in the United States in 2008. The sales volume was expected to increase by 1% ~2% in 2009 compared with that in 2008.

3. Innovation Culture

The American innovation culture has long closely interrelated with the Protestant culture in the country. The cultural orientations of independence and progress, pioneering spirit and innovation, freedom and equality, and pragmatism in the Protestant doctrines have all profoundly influenced the American innovation culture (Dong Xiuli, 2010).

If "free exploration" attached more importance to individuals in innovation, then "democratic management", including democratic leadership, organizational structure and faculty governance, is crucial for groups in innovation. No doubt democratic management is needed in all fields, industries and organizations, and particularly important for science and technology, scientific research institutes and universities, as creativity in science and technology requires more for free exploration and democratic management. For the fields in need of free exploration, democratic management plays a role of guarantee; and for educational institutes, it is necessity. Faculty governance in higher education is actually a sort of democratic management. Compared with that in the United States, quite a portion of administrative work in Chinese scientific, technological and educational institutes is still heavily "executive-oriented", which is to great extent closely related to the long-existing negative impacts of China's feudal past, the sluggishness resulting from decades' planned economy and the comparatively lagging political restructuring in China. The following cases show what China can learn from the United States.

Case 1: Faculty governance in MIT

MIT is a comprehensive private university located in Boston, Massachusetts, and was founded by the distinguished natural scientist William Barton Rogers in 1861. However, MIT had not recruited any students until 1865, due to the Civil War. By 2009, there had been 78 Nobel Prize winners studying or working at MIT. With generations' efforts, MIT has been known as "the world's best university of sciences and engineering", and the shrine of sciences in heart of students around the world. MIT's natural sciences and engineering enjoy high repuution in the world, and the university is also known for its excellence in management sciences, economics, philosophy, political science and linguistics. Additionally, MIT has precious assets such as Lincoln Laboratory, the world-class Computer Science and Artificial Intelligence Laboratory (MIT CSAIL), the top-grade Media Lab, and Sloan School of Management where many top CEOs have come from. To place more stress on the New Energy Plan for America, a national policy to sustain the American economy and deal with the ongoing financial crisis, President Obama visited MIT for an inspection and made a speech there, immediately after he had received the Noble Prize in Peace in October 2009, which highlighted again the leading position MIT takes in the US and world's new technological revolution. President Obama hopes to build MIT into a free university to serve a fast-developing America.

MIT established a governing body known as "Academic Senate" as early as it was under the president James Killian (Special Assistant for Science and Technology to President Eisenhower in 1958, the first Presidential Science Advisor), to invite the faculty to participate in the university management. Some schools under MIT established their own "Academic Senate" later.

By the 1980s, there had been over 10 faculty governing bodies with various functions in MIT, such as Committee on Educational Policy, Committee on Graduate School Policy, Faculty Policy Committee, Committee on Industrial Liaison Programme, Committee on Outside Professional Activities, Committee on Undergraduate Admissions and Financial Aid, Committee on Student Affairs, Committee on the Library System, Committee on Academic Performance, Committee on Discipline, Committee on Curricula, Committee on Nominations, James R. Killian, Jr. , Achievement Award Selection Committee, and Herold E. Edgerton Faculty Achievement Award Selection Committee, etc. Faculty governance has been in almost all the academic aspects in the university.

In addition to the abovementioned standing committees, the president and directors at various levels may create some ad hoc faculty committees to address particular issues when necessary. For instance, some schools and departments may set up faculty committees for particular ceremonies or to write outlook reports on future strategic development and tackle academic problems. Committee on Educational Survey was a typical one of the latter. As early as in August 1946, MIT decided to set up an ad hoc faculty committee to reexamine the quality, plans, methods and objectives of the Institute's undergraduate education. Killian, who was MIT's vice president at the time, made in-depth studies on the issue and suggested that a faculty committee be created with deans and professors from various units included, but excluding administrative personnel. Deans of schools under MIT (e. g. schools of sciences, engineering, medical sciences and architecture, etc.) could give their support to the Committee through suggestions and aids. The Institute gave full authority to Committee on Educational Survey, so that it could review and reexamine the undergraduate education plan and its objectives, organization and implementation in a manner as comprehensive as possible. The survey covered some basic issues: whether undergraduate admission criteria needed to be revised; whether the undergraduate education plan that had been worked out before were too specialized; the effect of curricular; whether the existing education plan was rather theoretical than practical or the other way round; whether the teaching hours for elective humanities by science and engineering students could be guaranteed; whether students had lost initiative in studying due to over-tight timetable; whether the faculty for undergraduate education was strong enough; and whether school directors gave effective guidance on implementation of the undergraduate education plan, etc.

Killian made a suggestion to the president Compton that the chemical engineering professor Warren K. Lewis be pointed as the chair of the committee. After two years' survey, MIT Committee on Educational Survey chaired by Professor Lewis submitted the well-known "Lewis Report", which not only answered the questions raised by Killian, but also put forward some outline-natured propositions for future educational development. For example, the undergraduate education plan should be revised according to social and industrial development in the United States, while giving consideration of the interrelationship between science and technology and society.

The academic activity plans proposed by some faculty committees, for instance, "Independent Activity Plan" (IAP), have been carried on in MIT, as they were highly practicable and popular with students. There is a 4 ~ 5 week vacation from Christmas to the coming February in MIT every year, during which time the Institute and students co-organize a series of teaching activities, including various lectures, speeches, experiments, and visits and practices, to enrich the students' vacation life and make up the deficiency in classroom teaching. To have better effects, professors, teachers and students co-established an IAP Committee, under which there are a subcommittee on management, one on planning, and a coordinating office. The IAP Committee issues every year "the IAP Programme Guidance" on hundreds of activities one or two months before the IAP period. Students and teachers can choose activities they would like to participate in, as audience or speakers or hosts. Teachers and students have a better communication through the process. Professors can in these activities receive strong feedback to the information they have given (students can raise any questions in a free, even rather straightforward manner), so that they can draw ideas from within when revising teaching plans for a new semester, and submit through various faculty committees strategic proposals on the development of MIT. Killian once said, "Education is not only acquired in classroom or experiment, but also through daily intercourse. Of course, it's the intercourse that can stimulate intelligence and foster a sense of social responsibility. What we shall do is to create such an environment in MIT for education in the broadest sense. This education shall play its role proactively and lively, rather than in a passive manner." The author of this book felt in person what Killian meant, by participating in IAP during 1987 ~ 1988 when the author was a visiting scholar in MIT (Zhou Jizhong, 2002).

Case 2: Human-oriented corporate culture in Hewlett-Packard

Hewlett-Packard was founded in 1939, headquartered in Palo Alto, Silicon Valley, California. "The HP Way", the management model adopted in Hewlett-Packard has been known for its focus on and respect for employees and teamwork. "The HP Way" is generally summarized as "attaching importance to the increase in profit instead of total income, encouraging teamwork, adopting open management, full employment, equal emolument and flexible working hours" (Michael Beer et al., 2007). Human-oriented culture has been actually a distinct feature of Hewlett-Packard and even the whole Silicon Valley. Briefly, it is a culture under which scientific and technological personnel in high-tech businesses enjoy a high degree of autonomy. As a representative of Silicon Valley culture, Hewlett-Packard is just like a home to scientific and technological personnel where they are fully trusted and highly specialized and enjoy a high degree of autonomy and splendid salaries and benefits.

The senior administrators of HP adopt the "management by walking around" (MBWA). Bill Hewlett and Dave Packard, founders of Hewlett-Packard attached importance to communication with employees, and walked around the canteen, talking with them during lunchtime. To create an environment for communication, the company provides free coffee and doughnuts twice a day, and holds irregular beer get-togethers in the afternoon. The whole company is filled with friendliness and trust.

The open bins and storerooms are a symbol of trust in "The HP Way". Engineers in Hewlett-Packard can freely take and use the materials and spare parts from the open bins and storerooms, and can take these spare parts back to home for use, as a kind of aid to innovation made by engineers. Such a policy will be definitely beneficial to innovation in and benefits of Hewlett-Packard itself.

Organizationally, Hewlett-Packard adopts a decentralized organizational structure.

Business departments are built into semi-autonomous commercial units, the heads of which have full powers over product development, planning, production and marketing. Furthermore, Hewlett-Packard has been one of the first companies that adopt "flexible working hours", under the flexible organizational structure of which employees have more freedom for innovation. Decentralization and authorization are main ways of redistribution of power. They are not only a way of organizational management, but also reflect a company's corporate culture.

All the employees can participate in the company's management. All the above management measures finally come to democratic management, which is reflected not only in production and business, but also in daily life and leisure and entertainment in the company. The company tries its best to play down the internal hierarchy and create an equal and harmonious environment for teamwork, for example, in aspects of parking lots, executive suites and executive restaurants.

Hewlett talks about "The HP Way" like this, "Generally speaking, all the policies and measures in the HP Way have come from a belief that all our men and women want to work well and create something out. They can do it, as long as there is an appropriate environment provided. The HP Way is the tradition to care for and respect all the individuals and recognize their personal achievements. It sounds like a cliché, but Dave (Packard, another founder of Hewlett-Packard) and I sincerely believe in it… Therefore, individual dignity and value are elements extremely important to the HP Way. " (Yuan Zhengguang, 1993)

Introduction in Hewlett-Packard's objective statement reads, "Hewlett-Packard shall not take a tight military organizational structure… All the employees shall enjoy full freedom, so that every one can take the way he/she thinks the best to accomplish the work, and contribute to the company's objectives. " (Yuan Zhengguang, 1993)

Hewlett-Packard's corporate culture has been reflected not only on the success of co-founders Hewlett and Packard, but also on the failure due to the deviation from "The HP Way" after the company had new executives (e. g. HP's purchase of Compaq in the early 21st century), and on the company's back to "The HP Way" after the executives have been turned over again.

4. Comments on Innovation Management and National Strength

Two years ago, US President Barack Obama made his victory speech titled

Change Has Come to America, saying that "Change is coming to America". However, the Obama Administration has no significant new ideas in the national system design in the past two years, neither in economic, financial, monetary policies, nor in those on environmental protection or on science and technology. Even the "HealthCare Reform" Obama has pushed forward still needs to be further tested by practice. Innovation management and culture are barely satisfactory, either.

America has been long in a leading position for its input-output ratio for science and technology. The United States spent 368. 8 billion dollars on research and development in 2007 and its R&D budget ranked first in the world, equaling the sum of those in the five countries following (Japan, Germany, France, China and the UK). The expenditure on R&D took up 2. 67% in GDP (i. e. national R&D intensity), ranking 7th in the world, after Israel (4. 68%), Sweden (3. 64%), Finland (3. 47%), and Japan (3. 40%). The US enterprises spent 265. 193 billion dollars in 2007, ranking first in the world.

The US ranked third in *World Competitiveness Yearbook 2010* by International Institute for Management (IMD), Lausanne, Switzerland, two places lower than the previous year (IMD, 2010). America also ranked fourth in *Global Competitiveness Report 2010 ~ 2011* by the World Economic Forum (WEF), two places lower compared to the previous year (WEF, 2010).

There were altogether 249 person-time of American citizens winning Nobel Prizes between 1950 and 2008, ranking first in the world. The number of American Nobel Prize winners has been much bigger than the sum of those in the other countries.

The number of invention patents granted in America was 81,329 in 2007, second only to Japan.

And there were 625,090 theses by American authors published on the world's top three indexes, ranking first in the world and taking up 26. 59% of the total.

The America's GDP reached up to 14,264. 6 billion dollars in 2008, ranking first in the world and higher than the sum of those of Japan (second), China (third) and Germany (fourth) (Ministry of Science and Technology of the People's Republic of China, 2010). The US economic aggregate still ranks first in the world, much larger than that of China that ranked second in 2010.

What the US has achieved in innovation of management methods has proved America a country full of innovativeness. The US has taken the lead in thought, system, management and technological innovation in the past over 200 years. America is still having the leadership in science and a world power that attaches great importance to education and science and technology (another one is Japan).

The American innovation culture, including the "melting-pot", lays rich soil and creates environment for the above innovations, which have laid a solid foundation for the US to develop into the strongest country in the world after the Second World War. "Soft power" cannot be ignored when we talk about the US national strength. The American "soft power" based upon its "hard power" has played a significant role in enhancing the US national strength. The American "soft power", including McDonald's, Coca-Cola, Hollywood movies, and even the American English, as well as the world's current money the US dollar and "the American democracy" "the separation of powers", has had profound influence on all the countries in the world.

An immense number of books have been written on "the American democracy", and there is no need to repeat it again. Here only two paragraphs are quoted from Tocqueville's *Democracy in America*. "I have already observed that universal suffrage has been adopted in all the States of the Union ··· The most able men in the United States are very rarely placed at the head of affairs···On my arrival in the United States I was surprised to find so much distinguished talent among the subjects, and so little among the heads of the Government··· It must be acknowledged that such has been the result in proportion as democracy has outstepped all its former limits"; "I have already spoken of the natural defects of democratic institutions, and they all of them increase at the exact ratio of the power of the majority. To begin with the most evident of them all; the mutability of the laws is an evil inherent in democratic government, because it is natural to democracies to raise men to power in very rapid succession. But this evil is more or less sensible in proportion to the authority and the means of action which the legislature possesses ··· The unlimited power of majority in America pushes the instability of democracy to the extreme." (Tocqueville, 2007).

Alexis-Charles-Henri Clérel de Tocqueville, born in 1805, was a French political thinker, sociologist and historian. The 25-year-old Tocqueville made a 9-month tour to America for in-depth inspection of the American society in 1831. Back to France, he published his best-known work *Democracy in America Volume I* in 1835. Giving his fulsome compliments to the early democracy in America in his book, Tocqueville also clearly points out the defects in it. What is more important is that people today have more diversified understanding of democracy, as conditions in America and the world have greatly changed compared to those 175 years ago. Comments on this will be given in "Conclusions" of this book.

As a matter of fact, the US national strength has been problematic since the American foreign trade showed in 1971 the first deficit in the 20th century. However, different from the other developed countries, the US has had no weak industries and can maintain its average industrial productivity at a comparatively high level (Porter, 2007). Nonetheless, America has changed from the world's Number One lender to the largest debtor in the globe. Some maintain that it has been due to economic depression, over-large war spending and tax-cutting policy involving huge amount of money. The author holds that compared to that during 1950s and 1990s, the US national strength has evidently got weakened from the mid and late 1990s till today, for reasons that: First, developing countries such as China, India, Brazil, Indonesia, Mexico, Turkey and South Africa have been on rise, and the situation keeps going on. Secondly, from the angle of management innovation that is stressed in this book, the American Government and Congress have been less innovative in the Nation's system design in recent years. The Bush Administration got stuck in wars, and the economic policy got lapsed. In the meantime, there were quite a number of loopholes in financial supervision, due to the lack of appropriate industrial policy. The "HealthCare Reform" and "Financial Reform" pushed forward by the Obama Administration are still under controversy, and whether they can work needs to be examined in practice. Thirdly, America has spent too much on the Iraq War, the War in Afghanistan and national defense, as well as on the outer space development. There are contradictions in the American education particularly. The US has the largest number of first-class universities in the world; however, the American students are not as good as students from the other countries. The American students have a relatively-low level in mathematics and few are willing to study sciences or engineering. High-level talent prefers areas of finance, law, management and medicare, which leads to ever-increasing training expenditure in American companies. Even like this, the American local labor force is inferior to that in Japan and Germany in knowledge and skills. This may be because that Americans have lost the driving force for competition and innovation, since the per-capita national income has risen to the level of "being affluent".

More importantly, the US Government has been in trouble in system design. At the cost of its sovereign credit, the US Government internally encourages its people to consume on credit and borrows heavily around the globe, spending tomorrow's money today. In the system design for industrial restructuring, on the one hand, manufacturing businesses with low added-values have been moved out of America to the other countries, upon the consideration of higher salaries required by the American employees and of protection to the environment and resources in the United States; while on the other hand, modern service trade, including finance and R&D design, has been attached much importance to. These systems have finally resulted in today's financial and economic crises, and a probable dollar crisis in future, which may be hundreds of times more serious than the ongoing Greece debt crisis and bring disaster to all the other countries, including China.

According to the American authorities and the experts from the UK, "The long-term debts held by the US Government had been 52.7 trillion dollars by 1 October 2007, calculated by the United States Government Accountability Office (US GAO). For a better understanding, GAO divided the figure as below: a debt of 175,000 dollars per American citizen (the per-capita GDP in the United States was 46,280 dollars in 2007), 410,000 dollars per full-time employee and 455,000 dollars per household. To deal with the existing debts, the US Government has to pay for a new debt of 1.86 billion dollars every day now. According to Rob Arnott in his essay published on the UK *Financial Times* on 4 November 2008, the debts of the US Government, social security, enterprises, individuals and non-profit organizations are summed up to as eight times the US GDP. Calculated with a GDP of 14 trillion dollars in 2007, America has debts of over 100 trillion dollars. " (Liu Lina, 2009).

That the US Government can develop credit economy and policy of "printing money to buy" (Ye Chuhua, 2010) on purchasing foreign commodities relies on that: First, the US dollar is the currency for valuation and settlement in international trade. Secondly, America has high GDP and production capacity in high-tech industry, agriculture and service trade. Thirdly, the US has very strong soft power. And fourthly, the country has powerful backing in defense and military strength. At present, the world is watching how the Federal Reserve's quantitative easing monetary policy to buy 600 billion dollars government bonds works.

Nevertheless, America's financial strength is still the powerful backing of the country's national strength, as the US is still the No.1 in the world's financial circles, with New York as the largest financial center and the US dollar the current money in the world, and a huge number of financial innovations come from America.

The US has the strongest defense and military power in the world. 1.379 million military personnel on active service, 522,000 of whom are army men, 524,000 in navy and US Marine Corps (USMC), and 333,000 in air force. The whole US armies are equipped with 5,163 strategic nuclear warheads plus nearly 4,800 inactive ones in reserve, 4,282 military planes, 2,161 cruise missiles, and 580 intercontinental missiles. The US Navy has 5 fleets and 11 aircraft carriers. In addition, there are 826,000 people in reserve force (Editorial Board of *World Affairs*, 2009). The military spending took up 4.2% of the US GDP in 2007 (and as high as 4.6% in 2008), with the value of export of 7.454 billion and 587 million dollars for import in arms transactions (World Bank, 2009).

Undoubtedly, "prosperity of a nation" is actually a relative and dynamic concept. With its economic aggregate, scientific and technological strength, military power and soft power, particularly its tradition in attaching importance to education, science and technology, and its capabilities to attract and maintain the brightest talent from all over the world, America may regain its declining national strength, so long as it makes innovation in the system design. Additionally, different from China, America has advantages in import in the businesses with natural resources as raw materials, for instance, agroforestry products such as cottonseed oil, logs, corn, soybean, fish and peanuts, and mineral products like petroleum coke and coal, as the country is rich in natural resources.

Finally, the example of DuPont will be taken to draw an end to this chapter, as the company has had a course of development similar to that of America.

Founded in 1802, DuPont has been a company focusing on chemistry and chemical engineering and had a long history of giving research and development priorities. The company has set up more than 60 R&D laboratories in over 10 R&D divisions. By 1988, the R&D spending had been as much as 1.32 billion dollars. The company has adopted the "farm to fork" strategy since the early 20th century. DuPont invented synthetic rubber in 1925. After the first nylon stockings were produced in 1940, the company has continued to develop over 1,000 nylon products. By the 1990s, DuPont had taken up one quarter of the production capacity in polyester, acrylic and polyamide in the United States and over one fifteenth of the world. DuPont had been a synonym of the kingdom of plastics, since its first plastic products (pyroxylin) in 1925 till the best plastic products, polytetrafluoroethene (PTFE) in 1945. Materials such as synthetic rubber, ethylene, nylon, Dacron and plastics have changed modes of production in many enterprises and of living of people. DuPont spent 200 million dollars on development of Freon in 1991, which has been widely used as refrigerant in refrigerator production.

DuPont used to focus on the American national defense and be a military manufacturer. It was called "death dealer", due to its involvement in the "Manhattan Project", participating in the research and development of the first atomic bomb.

DuPont has been excellent in management innovation as well. In the first 70 years of the 20th century, "the DuPont Way" meant high efficiency and fat profit. As for system innovation, flexitime has long been adopted in DuPont, so that the DuPont R&D personnel are allowed to take 5% ~ 15% of their paid time for research and development they are interested in. These people are known as "intrapreneurs". As the first group company in the United States, DuPont has made significant changes in its managerial system. The "executive committee" set up in 1918 was the "shadow board of directors" in DuPont, and held weekly meetings to review investments and make decisions. In this way, the previous individual decision-making process had been replaced by group decision making. DuPont launched the organizational restructuring in 1962, forming a decentralized "troika" management system composed of general manager, chief financial officer and president (Yuan Zhengguang, 1993).

However, as time flies, DuPont's position has declined from the 10th in the first "Fortune Global 500" published in 1955 to today's 86th. The company has fallen behind other chemical companies, such as 3M and P&G, which indicates a decline of the company's strength. Nonetheless, DuPont is still a transnational company that has annual revenue of 27 billion dollars, 1.8 billion dollars annual profit and many well-known brands.

Different from the previous preference to "pure science", DuPont's incumbent CEO has adopted the policy of "market-driven science". She has predicted a substantial increase in DuPont's profit (Carol, 2010).

With a history of 208 years, similar to that of the US, DuPont has undergone a similar course of development to that of the country. It had been the most prosperous company in the world during the 19th century and the 1990s, and saw a decline in the following 10 ~ 20 years, when other companies have gained their strength. DuPont, in its ups and downs, however, has well controlled the development direction and resorted to scientific and technological advancement the past over two centuries. And quite different from the US credit economy and policy of "printing money to buy", DuPont has maintained a chemical manufacturing entity.

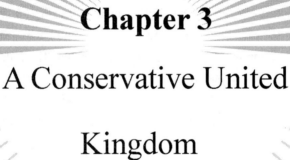

Chapter 3

A Conservative United

Kingdom

The United Kingdom ("UK") has a territorial area of 244, 100 square kilometers (including inland waters) and a population of 60. 587 million (2006 est.). The UK has the most plentiful energy resources among EU countries, but only has forest coverage of 12%. Most of the citizens have faith in Protestantism. The full name of the UK is the "United Kingdom of Great Britain and Northern Ireland". Great Britain consists of England, Scotland and Wales, which together with Northern Ireland form the four parts that comprise the UK. In December 1999 the UK handed over the administration power of local affairs to Northern Ireland which thus established an autonomous government with legislative and administrative power but not the power of defense, diplomacy and taxation (World Affairs Editorial Board,2009). Though being an island country, the UK is connected to the rest of the world through its accession to a great many international organizations; for example, the Commonwealth of Nations links it to other 53 member states, and the EU connects it with 24 European countries. From the mid-17th century to the mid-and late-18th century the UK was the world's scientific center, and the representative figure was Newton. The Industrial Revolution began in the UK in the second half of the 18th century, because, in addition to scientific and technological factors, ①on the institutional design, the UK formed a relatively stable constitutional monarchy, ②the intermediate classes and wage earners emerged in its social structure, and ③the specialized division of labor led to the national industry and values thereof (Tang Jin, 2006). Around the First World War more than 100 years later, the UK had already possessed a cluster of colonies of 12. 7 million square miles in land and 431 million in population, each one fourth of the world's total area and population then, claiming to be "the empire on which the sun never sets". It was in the same period, in the 1920s, however, that the UK was being overtaken in national power by the rising United States and Germany. A main reason is that due to strategic and financial problems, the UK was at a standstill in the industrial restructuring, leading to the gradual disappearance of its industrial superiority which was confined to traditional fields such as textile, steel, coal and shipbuilding. In emerging industries such as power, chemical engineering, petroleum, electric apparatuses and automobiles, German had already outstripped the UK; besides, the world scientific center had shifted from the UK to France and Germany in succession. In over 60 years after the First World War, despite the decline in national power, the UK has remained among developed countries.

Not only were such great scientists as Isaac Newton, Charles Robert Darwin,

Michael Faraday, James Clerk Maxwell and Alan Turing born in the UK, but during the Industrial Revolution of the 18th century a great number of inventors—represented by James Watt—also came to the fore there. The year 2009 marked the 200th anniversary of the birth of Charles Robert Darwin, the founder of the "theory of evolution", and the 150th anniversary of his masterpiece *On the Origin of Species*. The UK is a multi-ethnic and multi-religious country, a point which must not be ignored when the UK is studied. From the mid-20th century to the present, the UK has largely impressed people as a "conservative" country, which might be attributed to the reminiscence about the prosperity of the two centuries from the 18th century to the early 20th century.

1. Institutional Design

1.1　National Institutional Design

The UK's constitution is an unwritten constitution which comprises a number of documents including the *Magna Carta* (Latin for "Great Charter", 1215), the *Bill of Rights* (1689) and the *Parliament Act* (1949).

In the UK, the rule of law was established in the 17th century, the separation of powers between the government and the parliament was established in the 18th century, and the party government was established in the 19th century. The UK's political system is roughly as follows. Nominally, the country's head of state is the queen, and the head of government is the prime minister. The Parliament consists of two houses. The members of the lower house (House of Commons) are elected by the electorate, and because the party or parties winning the majority of seats from the cabinet, the lower house generally supports the government; important legislative powers rest with the lower house. The upper house (House of Lords) consists of peers (or nobles), either hereditary or knighted for various reasons, rather than ones elected. This political system design and operation have had a history of more than 200 years. Since the Second World War, though the UK follows a multi-party system, it has been the Labour Party and the Conservative Party who reign in rotation (now the Liberal Democrats have become the third largest political party to run in elections (Almond et al. ,2010).

The "New Public Management" and "privatization" reforms introduced after Margaret Thatcher came to power in 1979 were a large-scale and far-reaching institutional design by the UK government since the Second World War. The privatization wave which took place in the UK during the 1980s also mainly originated in the institutional design of "New Public Management." In 1979, the UK government set up an Efficiency Board within the Cabinet Office, to study how to improve the management of civil service and as well as the working efficiency and expenditure efficiency. The method proposed was to set up an executing body by which to accomplish the government's executive functions under government policies and under the energy use framework. The early privatization reform paid attention to the privatization of national industries, while the "Next Steps Initiative" focused on the reform of government departments.

On national scientific and technological system design, the UK cabinet didn't set up a special department, and from 1964 onwards, the responsibility for trade, industry, science and technology first rested with the Board of Trade and the Ministry of Technology and later with the Department of Trade and Industry ("DTI").

On national financial system design, the UK is a financially developed country, with London being one of the world's financial centers. Similar to the United States', the UK's financial system is usually described as "market-oriented", which is a capital market-based financial system. To GDP, stock market assets play a greater role than banking assets.

1.2 Scientific and Technological System Design

When science becomes a national cause, it also becomes an organic part of national social and economic activities. A country's economic system reform will also entail the reform of its scientific and technological system. Even the UK, a country that has a long tradition of science and attaches great importance to academic freedom, also has continuously adjusted its strategy for scientific and technological development and reformed its original mechanisms – and even systems – for research institutions, so that its resource allocation could suit strategic objectives as well as R&D closely related to economic competition. In the UK, the department responsible for government administration and funding public research institutions is the seven Research Councils founded in the 1920s, which are subordinate to the Office of Science and Technology under the DTI.

The UK government usually announces its scientific and technological policies and institutional design by publishing a White Paper. For example, it published the famous

White Paper, *Our Competitive Future: Building the Knowledge Driven Economy* in 1998, and *Digital Briton* in 2009 which stated that communications technologies and industries and creative industries should be vigorously developed. In addition, in 2009 alone, UK's government departments published in succession planning reports such as *Building Britain's Future: New Industry, New Jobs, Life Sciences Blueprint and Investing in a Low-carbon Britain*. In *Building Britain's Future: New Industry, New Jobs*, the life sciences, low carbon, digital technology and advanced manufacturing are viewed as four emerging industries for the future development of the UK.

On the innovation system design, the UK's then Prime Minister announced the "UK Innovation Investment Fund" in June 2009, which will invest in a small number of technology funds that have the expertise and track record to invest directly in innovative small businesses in the abovementioned four industries. This Fund plans to raise funds jointly by the government, businesses and private investors, with the aim to make it worth up to one billion pounds in 10 years (MOST of China, 2010).

On scientific innovation investment design, the DTI's *Science and Innovation Investment Framework 2004 ~ 2014* gives plans, with the objectives of building the UK an important knowledge center of the world economy, continuing to keep a scientific research level next only to that of the United States, building enough research centers of excellence, reacting more actively to the needs of national economy and public service, increasing the percentage of enterprise R&D investments to GDP from 1.25% in 2004 to 1.70% in 2014, and increasing the percentage of national R&D investments to GDP from 1.90% in 2004 to 2.5% in 2014 (DTI, 2005).

On institutional design for the reform of scientific and technological organizations, the UK carried out what could be said to be an institutional innovation in the 1980s and 1990s, and that was the privatization of national laboratories.

1.3   Privatization of National Laboratories

As early as the mid-19th century, as the world science center then, the UK began setting up research institutions. Through development over one century, the UK formed a sizable system of Public Sector Research Establishments (PSREs), the main part of which is the national laboratories subordinate to government departments and the laboratories subordinate to the Research Councils (RCs). The RCs, subordinate to the DTI, are the main bodies in the UK that fund and govern the basic research and strategic research at higher-education institutions. Before 1994 the RCs included the

Agricultural and Food Research Council, the Science and Engineering Research Council, the Natural Environment Research Council, the Medical Research Council and the Economic and Social Research Council. Since 1994, there have been seven RCs, and they are: Biotechnology and Biological Sciences Research Council (BBSRC), Engineering and Physical Sciences Research Council (EPSRC), Medical Research Council (MRC), Natural Environment Research Council (NERC), Particle Physics and Astronomy Research Council (PPARC), Council for the Central Laboratory of the Research Councils (CCLRC) and Economic and Social Research Council (ESRC). The CCLRC only provides the RCs with instruments and equipment but does not fund projects, while other RCs all have disciplinary project teams. For example, for the EPSRC founded in 1994, one important component of its funding of research is to determine on the basis of peer review whether or not to approve the application for funding of research projects (The British Council, 1998).

Because of its declining international competitiveness, in scientific and technological fields, the UK government had a pressing need to change key fields and adjust strategic objectives to enhance its national and economic competitiveness. Under this context, most national laboratories could only rely on more restricted support from the government for continuing their operation within the government department framework, such reliance would lead to narrowed room for their development because of government restrictions. Compared with private research institutions with flexible mechanisms, the national laboratories showed less competitiveness in such aspects as capital accumulation and use as well as research findings development. Confronted with reducing assignments and the plight of inadequate funds, some of them were even hard to continue their operation.

From the 1970s onwards, the UK government began reforming public sector research establishments, but because of substantial controversies among the government, the scientific community and the public on the reform objectives and measures, the reform was progressing slowly until the 1990s, when there was a surging call for privatization of public sector research establishments as John Major's administration obviously stepped up the reform. Thereafter, the UK government took active actions to adjust its scientific and technological policies and funding system; particularly, following the 1993 publication of the White Paper, *Realizing Our Potential: A Strategy for Science, Engineering and Technology*, the government's scientific and technological policies apparently inclined to be "market-driven", encouraging scientific research institutions to conduct research of commercial value. On the one hand, the UK government took measures to encourage businesses to increase investment in R&D, but on the other, it reduced year by year the proportion of government financial allocations to science and technology. The proportion of the government R&D expenditure to the total was lowered from 35.0% in 1991 to 18.6% in 1995. In 1995, the privatization scheme was officially implemented. This process could be divided broadly into three stages.

(1) Stage 1: From the early 1970s to the mid-1980s

The UK government's reform on public sector research establishments was closely linked to the general context of the government function transfer. As a matter of fact, the "New Public Management" movement already began in the UK as early as the late 1960s, with emphasis placed on narrowing the administrative scope, cutting the public expenditure and increasing market orientation and competition. It was just in this context that the UK government began pondering once again over the relationship between government departments and the subordinate research institutions. The primary objective of reforming public sector research establishments then was to boost the pertinence of government departments' scientific research investment and the accountability of research institutions subordinate to the government. The main means of the reform was fund management to intensify competition and improving efficiency. The original idea was to get most R&D activities controlled by unified central financing, with the aim to improve the government's efficiency of scientific and technological management. It was suggested in the government green book of 1970 that a central R&D agency, namely the UK R&D Council, be founded to serve government organizations and the private sector, and that a planning, analysis and appraisal procedure be introduced to straighten up government objectives and appraisal results. However, this idea wasn't put into action.

In 1970, the UK's government sector was restructured: the functions of the former Department of Science, Technology and Education were split and assigned to related government departments or RCs. In 1971, the Central Policy Appraisal Panel submitted a report which introduced into the government's applied research the "Customer-Contractor Principle", i.e., a customer pays a contractor for what it is commissioned to do. According to this principle, the government invests in science and technology like a customer who purchases what he/she wants. To fund research therefore, the government must, first of all, define what research the government departments need to support its policies, and then identify proper customers to commission research from research councils, with the aim to change the previous relationship in administrative appropriation between government departments and their research bodies and increase R&D expenditures from the non-government sector. This report produced a far-reaching effect on the UK government's scientific and technological management.

In 1972, the "Customer-Contractor Principle", which began manifesting in management activities, directly led to changes in the government's research funding management. Government departments more rigorously enhanced the planning and management on research funding, and established the ROAME (Rationale, Objectives, Appraisal, Monitoring and Evaluation) model. In addition, competitive bidding for research funding was carried out. Of the total research funds, the proportion of funds subjected to competitive bidding increased continuously, and by the FY 1997 ~ 1998, this indicator was 50% for funds managed by the RCs, and more than 80% for those by government departments.

It was also proposed in the abovementioned report that each department involving scientific and technological research appoint a Chief Scientist to make their R&D policies, and that such policies be implemented by another office, namely the R&D management office. The purpose was to distinguish the duties within government departments and distinguish the duties of government departments from those of their research institutions in support of the implementation of the "Customer-Contractor Principle". Though most departments didn't make such functional division, they all could carry out funding management by means of bidding. Government departments and research institutions remained within the same sector, but their roles were separated. On the whole, there were no substantive reforms that were put into action: most laboratories continued to be subordinate to government departments, no rigorous control was imposed on research funding, and most of jobs of laboratories were, for the most part, decided by laboratories themselves. After Margaret Thatcher came to power in 1979, the Conservative Party-led government attempted to reduce the size of the public sector, stress budgetary accountability and shift the focus to funding management. The ROAME model was further enhanced and became a rule for relevant research funding decisions.

(2) Stage 2: From the mid-1980s to the early 1990s

In this stage, Margaret Thatcher's administration slashed R&D funding, bringing surging pressures to research institutions. The main reform then was to re-define the functions of research institutions to weaken the connection between government departments and research institutions and strengthen the self-determination of research institutions. The government's research institutions were no longer subordinate to government departments, but sought R&D funding themselves as Executive Agencies. In 1987, the "Next Steps Initiative" was put into action, appraising the government departments' research institutions and choosing appropriate research institutions as Executive Agencies (Table 3-1). All government departments, especially the DTI and the Ministry of Defence (MOD), actively implemented this initiative. From 1989 to 1995, about 63% of civil research institutions were turned into Executive Agencies.

Table 3-1 Public Research Institutions Changed to Executive Agencies before April 1992

Executive Agency	Department	Time
Central Science Laboratory	Ministry of Agriculture Fisheries and Food (MAFF)	April 1992
Central Veterinary Laboratory	MAFF	April 1990
Agricultural Development and Advisory Service	MAFF/Welsh Office	April 1992
Scottish Agricultural Science Agency	Scottish Office	April 1992
Transport Research Laboratory	Department of Transport	April 1992
Defence Research Agency	Ministry of Defence (MOD)	April 1991
Chemical and Biological Defence Establishment	MOD	April 1991
Meteorological Office	MOD	April 1990
Building Research Establishment	Department of the Environment	April 1990
Forensic Science Service	Home Office	April 1991
Natural Resources Institute	Overseas Development Administration	April 1990
National Engineering Laboratory	DTI	October 1990
National Physical Laboratory	DTI	July 1990
Laboratory of the Government Chemist	DTI	October 1989
Warren Spring Laboratory	DTI	April 1989

Source: quoted in *Scientific and Technological Innovation Management*, p74.

In 1988, the UK Government Chief Scientific Advisor Sir John Fairclough raised a principle regarding public R&D expenditure: public R&D funding should be used for research relatively far from the market, research close to market should be left to businesses, and government funding should be confined to the fields where the market makes them unable to produce maximum benefit to the economy as a whole. Fairclough reaffirmed the "Customer-Contractor Principle", encouraging the development of inside market by which to intensify the competition for public R&D funding in the public research sector. The government adopted this principle, and reduced R&D support to businesses close to the market except for the aviation industry.

(3) Stage 3: From the early 1990s to the early 21st century

In this stage, the reform on public research institutions shifted its focus to the institutional framework and surmounted the restrictions which property-related issues had on the reform, and the principle of privatization of public sector research establishments was established and put into action. This was closely related to the privatization wave throughout the UK since the 1980s. During the privatization wave, some argued that the private sector could offer more efficient services, and that even in fields where privatization was not appropriate, the public institutions should be separated in management from the central government. In 1992 the Conservative Party once again came to power, and in 1993 ~ 1995 published substantial reports, including *An Assessment of the Allocation*, *Management and Application of Government Funding for Science and Technology*, a reported completed by a panel organized by the UK Government Chief Scientific Adviser (GCSA). This report reviewed the course of the UK's reform on public research institutions since the 1980s, stating that since 1980 the scientific and technological management had been driven towards market orientation but progressed slowly and that most research institutions had become more commercially conscious after turned into Executive Agencies. It held that competition was the key to improving efficiency but the property arrangement hindered competition, and concluded that the property arrangement should be separated from obtaining of powers. It found that the contractual relationship between government departments as customers and their laboratories as Executive Agencies could guarantee the continuity of work, and that cooperation in making plans reduced the overlapping of departmental bodies. Such relationship was similar to that between the government and the private sector, unlike what some said private establishments were inappropriate for scientific and technological research. This report also provided specific suggestions about privatization.

Such idea was also reflected in the UK's 1993 White Book, *Realizing Our Potential: A Strategy for Science, Engineering and Technology*, which highlighted the country's requirement of reforming research institutions. According to this White Book, many services provided by the government's research institutions could also be provided by private establishments; privatization meant the development prospects for private establishments but should proceed not too fast; and market orientation should be first encouraged before privatization.

The pivot of the privatization of public sector research establishments in the UK during the 1990s was Michael Heseltine, President of the Board of Trade and Secretary of State for Trade and Industry, who accepted the idea of privatization, proposed that several options be considered by KPMC (UK) and engaged PA Consulting Group for studying together. Heseltine announced the appraisal of public sector research establishments one by one, the study of their future positions and the discussion of their privatization, rationalization and different property options, and that the appraisal would begin with the institutes subordinate to the DTI, requiring that the DTI's laboratories must have a cultural transition to suit the possibilities of thorough privatization. Different from the views given in the abovementioned White Book, Heseltine was unwilling to adopt a mild approach but advocated selling these laboratories directly and rapidly. The appraisal panel began working in December 1993, and submitted a report in March 1994, concluding that most government-sponsored research institutions should be privatized, especially for agricultural R&D and consultancy ones which didn't provide government departments with frontier services. The report recommended that the remainder be reformed in their existing models. Soon afterwards, the House of Commons Science and Technology Committee also introduced a report giving its opinions: ① the appraisal was too brash; ② the selection of sample institutes was fairly random; and ③ whether privatization was a good choice was doubted. This report also raised opinions about the appraisal panel: ① privatization was only feasible when it was not to lower the country's scientific knowledge base; ② the continued inspection reduced these jobs' reputation among the institutions; and ③ the appraisal panel had no knowledge of the difference between government departments' laboratories and the RCs' ones. In November 1995, under the leadership of Heseltine, the "Priorities Programme" started, which was to promote within the DTI the privatization of the National Engineering Laboratory and the Laboratory of the Government Chemist, as well as the GOCO (Government-Owned, Contractor-Operated) reform of the National Physical Laboratory. In addition, the Department of Transport tended to privatize the Transport Research Laboratory, and the MAFF included the ADAS (Agricultural Development and Advisory Service) in the scope of privatization.

1. 3. 1   The Reform Process and Privatization Model of National Laboratories

In advancing the reform of national laboratories, the UK was very prudent, first experimenting in part and summarizing experience, then making progress step by step and in orderly ways. The UK government actively promoted the process of merging, shutting down and privatizing research institutions. It had a complete set of procedure for the privatization of national laboratories, which began with scrutiny followed by review and appraisal for every five years. The key in the initial stage was to resolve two issues: the formulation of criteria for "merging, changing to other business and retaining" of national laboratories, and the demarcation in property of national laboratories after incorporated into businesses and of their own economic entities. The process of scrutiny was primarily divided into two stages: scrutinizing reform schemes which comprised five main options, namely shutdown, merger with other laboratories in related fields, privatization, changing to Executive Agencies, and returning to the central government; and conducting forward-looking analysis as to how these institutes could offer services more efficiently.

The policy of the government was only to fund the national laboratories which had great significance for national interest as a whole, and to transform the operating mechanisms of the remainder so that they were market-oriented. In developed countries, there are mainly four types of government-operated national laboratories: GOGO (Government-Owned, Government-Operated); GOCO (Government-Owned, Contractor-Operated), COCO (Contractor-Owned, Contractor-Operated), and POGO (Privately-Owned, Government-Operated). Different types of laboratories differ greatly in the approach and final form of privatization. Discriminative treatment is needed as many factors are involved. For example, a scheme for complete privatization can only be considered when an appropriate buyer has been identified and the requirements of government departments satisfied.

On the privatization model of national laboratories, from the UK's practice, there are three variations of privatization: trade sale, converting to nonprofit organizations, and GOCO. In 1995 the UK government finalized a list of national laboratories to be privatized, including the Transport Research Laboratory (TRL), the Building Research Establishment (BRE), the National Engineering Laboratory (NEL), the Laboratory of the Government Chemist (LGC), the National Resources Institute (NRI) and the United Kingdom Atomic Energy Authority, as well as the national laboratories to be contractor-operated—the National Physical Laboratory (NPL) and the A-Weapons Laboratory.

Trade sale: One type was to transform a national laboratory to a private company through a contract, for example, in the case of the NEL; another was to resell a national laboratory to an consortium formed by businesses or other social organizations, for example in the case of the LGC; and the third type was what is called management buy-out (MBO), i. e. purchasing a research institution by its management and employees, for example, the privatization of the BRE.

Companies Limited by Guarantee: Some national laboratories weren't sold to general businesses, but to businesses of a special type, namely companies limited by guarantee, or guarantee companies. A guarantee company has no shareholders, and its members are accountable for the company's debts as guarantors. A form of nonprofit organization, it involves no profit distribution because it has no shareholders. It keeps a corporate status for the purpose of getting financing for other projects. Generally speaking, this form of organization can guarantee more public interest than usual businesses. An example is the reform of the TRL.

GOCO: The GOCO model has been practiced in the United States for many years. All national laboratories (for example, Los Alamos, Sandia, Lawrence-Livermore and Argonne National Laboratories) of the U. S. Department of Energy are managed by private organizations or private universities as commissioned by the government. In the UK, this model only previously existed at the A-Weapons Authority and the Royal School of Naval Architecture. There are many GOCO variations, and the key is that the government owns most assets and has the power of transferring these assets (sometimes also include staff, for example in the case of the NPL) to different contractors. The NPL is a perfect example of this model (Table 3-2).

Table 3-2 Organizational Forms and Examples of Technological Products Providers in the UK

Form of Organization	Feature	Example
Next Step Initiative Agencies	Originally not but later became a trading fund	Defence Evaluation and Research Agency (DERA); Meteorological Office
GOCO	A private contractor operates a national laboratory; essentially government-owned, privately-operated	NPL
Companies Limited by Guarantee	Private companies, which have quasi-legislative functions for protecting the public interest or guaranteeing standard integrity, with behavior restricted to some extent	BRE; TRL
Completely privatized businesses		LGC; ADAS; NEL

Source: quoted in *Scientific and Technological Innovation Management*, p78.

1.3.2 The Operation of Reformed National Laboratories

There were 50 research institutions subordinate to the UK's government departments and RCs in December 1993, and by the end of 1995 only 37 of them were left as a result of mergers and privatization. In 1997, after a review for selection, the government announced that only 28 research institutions were reserved. After the Labour Party came to power in 1997, though not inclined to privatization in policy, the ruling party still approved the implementation of the scheme for partly privatizing the DERA, the UK's largest national laboratory, which aroused the objection from the Labor Party camp. The debate over the reform shifted to what role the national laboratories ought to play in economy. On 10 February 1999 the Minister of State for Science and Technology and the Secretary-general of Finance submitted to the HM Treasury a research report with suggestions about technology transfer and commercialization. This report received a positive response, and in July 2000 the UK government promulgated measures for intellectual property management and some departments introduced incentive schemes for technology commercialization (Table 3-3).

Table 3-3 The Incentive Scheme of the BBSRC

Income from commercialization		Proportion of receipts paid to relevant staff involved in the commercialization process, %
Gross receipts	Below 1,000 pounds	100
	1,000 pounds to 50,000 pounds	20
Net receipts	50,000 pounds to 500,000 pounds	10
	500,000 pounds to 1 million pounds	5
	Above 1 million pounds	2.5

Source: Office of Science and Technology, Good Practice for Public Sector Research Establishment on Staff Incentives and the Management of Conflict of Interests. July 2000.

1.3.3 The UK's National Laboratories in the Reform

(1) National Physical Laboratory(NPL)

The National Physical Laboratory (NPL), founded in 1900, is the UK's metrological research center and shoulders the task of maintaining the country's basic measurement standards. As the national standard laboratory managed by the DTI, the

NPL primarily serves the DTI, but also offers services to other government departments, industries, the private sector and the Europe Union (EU). The maintenance of measurement standards is an important element of ensuring the UK's competitiveness and public security. In the past, the NPL was funded by the DTI, but as the DTI continued to reduce its budgets on standard measurement research, the NPL was confronted with new difficulties and challenges. In June 1990 it was turned into an Executive Agency of the DTI. This reform gave the NPL more decision-making power and accountability, effectively lowered its costs and improved its efficiency. In the meanwhile, however, the UK government slashed the funding for science and technology and altered funding priorities, with considerable reductions in investment in the national measurement system, even by 30% in some fields, which led the NPL to struggle hard for survival. After 1992, Heseltine began advancing the privatization process of national laboratories, and the government engaged in the investigation and analysis of the NPL's operational model. MPMG provided the government with four reform schemes: ① still leaving the NPL managed by the DTI as before, as an Executive Agency of it; ② converting it into a nonprofit organization on the basis of guarantee; ③ making it a GOCO laboratory; and ④ privatizing it completely by selling it to the private sector. After an evaluation of minimum costs necessary for these solutions and of possible benefits, KPMG recommended the GOCO scheme on grounds of the following points.

1) Complete privatization (for example, trade sale) would not bring tremendous commercial appeal, and the DTI's needs for the research work of the NPL were in decline (such trend might change little in the future), producing a negative effect on research prospects of the NPL; at the same time, the NPL's potential for obtaining research projects and funds from other customers would be more limited, which would lower the laboratory's interest in seeking potential commercial benefits. Therefore, the NPL needed a stable and considerable fund necessary to guarantee research funding.

2) The UK would still need a national standard laboratory in the future, and to ensure that the laboratory could be incorporated into the government department as needed in the future, or when the original contractor had financial problems or the laboratory was taken over by an inappropriate company, the government department had the power to transfer the laboratory to another appropriate company.

3) The NPL's international partners (including other national laboratories) might be unwilling to come into contact with a completely privatized establishment.

4) The ownership of the NPL premises and some other complex lease-related issues made it very difficult to sell the NPL directly.

5) The DTI would always be the primary customer of the NPL, making it necessary to keep the right to raise requirements on the NPL.

If the GOCO model was to be adopted, the NPL would have the fairly flexible independent business management power.

Therefore, the DTI decided not to make the NPL completely privatized, but to convert it into a GOCO establishment, mainly considering that: ① the land the NPL occupied was part of a Loyal Park, which had restrictions on commercial purposes, so the privatization of it would give rise to complex legal problems; ② the NPL should be independent from industrial businesses it served, with a view of preventing monopoly; ③ because the NPL's potential for the growth of income from the non-government sector was relatively small, a private company would be unwilling to take any property-related risk; ④ due to the need for the national standard laboratory, the government was willing to control and supervise it by virtue of the ownership of public property, in order to protect the laboratory from failure; and ⑤ if the NPL were made completely privatized, its international partners would be unwilling to continue their cooperation with it. In April 1994 the DTI accepted the advisory company's suggestion, setting about the restructuring of the NPL. Some 50 organizations showed an interest in it, and after screening, five conglomerates (some in partnership with universities) had the opportunity to offer their bids. The DTI chose two of them for the final round of selection, and finally awarded the contract to the grouping led by Serco in partnership with AEA Technology and Loughborough University. Serco, an international outsourcing public company, offers a wide range of services to public and private sector customers, including supportive services to the European Space Agency's laboratories and the European Organization for Nuclear Research (CERN), as well as astronomical observatories in southern Europe. On October 1, 1995, Serco and the DTI signed a contract to found NPL Management Ltd for the purpose of managing the laboratory.

The contract between Serco and the DTI set out the main obligations between the partners, the aims and objectives of contractorisation and the monitoring arrangements. The key features of the contract were: the 5-year term of contract; that the NPL would continue to perform the DTI's research programmes; a guarantee that DTI would place at least 30 million pounds of research at the NPL each year for the period of the contract, which was about 80% of the overall expected DTI income each year, with the remainder obtained in competition with other contractors; that the government would continue to own the physical assets at the NPL – buildings, land, major equipment etc. but that the staff would be transferred to and provided with a pension scheme by NPL Management Ltd; that NPL Management Ltd. could use the laboratory's physical assets to compete for other commercial opportunities (within the government, EU and the private sector) so long as its behavior would not conflict with the functions of the national standard laboratory and guarantee its capacity to work for the DTI; that the commercial services of NPL Management Ltd. would be restricted to prevent monopoly, and its profits, if above a certain level, would be shared with the DTI, but both parties would re-invest these shred profits in work at the NPL. This gave the NPL an incentive to become more efficient, making long-term planning far easier; a portion (about 1. 5 million pounds) of the research funding guaranteed by the DTI would be used as funding for "strategic research", the content of which was determined by the NPL subject to approval from the DTI.

After the NPL became a GOCO, its management was substantially restructured: the president of Serco and 5 executive managers and 4 non-executive managers from Serco and University of Cambridge formed a new laboratory council; a loose management committee was formed by personnel including technology department directors; 4 Serco managers took up the posts of financial manager, market and communication manager and support service manager, forming the main management framework. Executives were greatly reduced in number and expenditure decreased. And the adoption of enterprise-type management led to an easier accounting system, more prompt and efficient procurement and more flexible funding management. After four years of practice, by 1999, the GOCO model had contributed remarkably to the development of the NPL: reduced bureaucratic management and streamlined operational procedure; acquaintance with private enterprise management skills; freedom from interference of political changes; a 20% reduction in daily expenditure, and an increase of 150 researchers; research continuity and smooth transition; growth of income from outside sources, but 80‰ ~ 85‰ of annual income coming from the public sector, without occurrence of short-term behavior originally feared to happen. According to a report submitted to the government minister by the Royal Society, the NPL had not only maintained but also improved its research level, seen an enhanced sense of mission, increased its income through technology transfer and research in partnership with businesses, and had the great satisfaction of seeing the industrial application and customer recognition of its measurement technologies. The successful transformation of the NPL led the government to plan for NPL reconstruction by way of private financing, including the construction of office buildings and laboratories of 40, 000 square meters by an consortium formed by banks, a building company and a human resources management company. Private businesses would also benefit from the practice: acceptable financial returns, risk sharing, appropriate incentive and security mechanisms, technology compositeness of laboratories after privatized and trust from the government and customers.

The contract between the DTI and Serco was renewed in 2002. The success in the contractor-based management of the NPL has aroused worldwide interests in the GOCO model.

(2) Defense Evaluation and Research Agency

The UK government intervened and participated in the defense research reform early. After two major rounds of splitting and amalgamation directed by the UK Ministry of Defense in 1991 and 1995, the Defense Evaluation and Research Agency (DERA) became the largest national laboratory inside the Ministry of Defense, except for scientific and technological research resources. In the FY 1999 ~ 2000, the DERA hired 11, 656 researchers, and its turnover amounted to 1. 0415 billion pounds. At the beginning, the DERA had not been considered an object of privatization because security issues were considered to be too complex to solve. Later it was given the status of a trading fund, making it possible to realize commercialization of its research findings, and then the DERA began playing the dual role of researcher and R&D funder. Each year the DERA outsourced to businesses and research establishments its work of research worth about 30% ~ 35% of the total research funding; in 1996 ~ 1997 such outsourcing cost 162 million pounds. Subcontracting was also considered an important technology transfer mechanism.

(3) Laboratory of Government Chemist

The Laboratory of Government Chemist (LGC), the earliest laboratory of the DTI, was founded in 1842 to mainly detect adulteration of tobacco. It provides analytical, investigatory services, advisory services and policy support to government departments, public institutions, local authorities and other organizations (principally those concerned with consumer protection, revenue protection and public health). In 1989, it became a part of the DTI. There was consideration of reforming the LGC to a nonprofit institution, but the reform was eventually rejected because of capital structure problems. In November 1995, the LGC was sold to a management-led consortium also comprising the Royal Society of Chemistry and venture capitalists 3I plc. The laboratory reserved its name and continued to carry out its statutory responsibilities. Because of this statutory role, it was necessary to find an ownership arrangement necessary to guarantee the impartiality of the LGC, which made the involvement of the Royal Society of Chemistry very important. Any future transfer of share ownership could result in the government exercising its reserved rights under the sale agreement to terminate the guaranteed work programme. On 31 March , 1996, the consortium bought the LGC for a payment of 360, 000 pounds to the government, and at the same time, the DTI made a payment to the consortium of 19, 600 pounds.

(4) Transport Research Laboratory

The Transport Research Laboratory (TRL) was founded in 1933, and became a part of the DTI in the 1960s and an Executive Agency of it in 1992. The TRL principally serves the DTI, providing it with technical services that help improve the safety and efficiency of the UK's transport system. In March 1995 the Secretary of State for Transport announced the government's intention of transforming the TRL into a private institution. But when a consortium consisting of the Royal Autmobile Club (RAC) and the Automobile Association (AA) etc. was prepared to acquire the TRL, controversy was raised. In January 1996 the government announced the transfer of the TRL to the Transport Research Foundation, a company limited by guarantee founded by the former senior management of the TRL. On 31 March, 1996, the Transport Research Foundation made a payment of 6 million pounds to the government and obtained from the latter a research contract worth 32 million pounds. The TRL, now called TRL Limited, is a wholly owned subsidiary of the Transport Research Foundation with 86 transport sector members and 25 employee members.

(5) National Engineering Laboratory

The National Engineering Laboratory (NEL), situated in East Kilbridge, Scotland, provides engineering technology services to a wide range of UK and international public and private sector clients such as oil and gas, energy, transport and defence. The NEL has substantial testing facilities, many of which are not replicated elsewhere in the UK. The largest customer of the NEL was and still is the DTI. Though advantageous in many ways, it was in a stage of decline in the late 1980s. In 1988 the government attempted to sell it to a French company but the sale did not proceed because of its poor commercial position. In 1990 the NEL became an

Executive Agency of the DTI. Despite its efforts made to reduce its costs and deficit, the NEL still failed to meet the DTI's requirements. In 1993 a decision was made to sell it. This decision aroused great controversy at the beginning over whether a privatized laboratory would be capable of providing the public with impartial advisory services, and the staff of the NEL voted against a proposed management buy-out. The opponents argued that the selling of the laboratory was a dogmatic policy, an indifference to the public property, abandonment of the government's accountability to science and technology. On 31 October 1995 the NEL was officially transferred to Assessment Services Ltd. , a subsidiary of the Germany electronics group Siemens. Because the NEL had a deficit of 216, 000 pounds, the DTI paid Siemens 1. 95 million pounds to take over the laboratory. In addition, the DTI undertook to give the NEL a work contract for the following five years worth 30 million pounds. Soon after the sale, Assessment Services Ltd. became a division of a Siemens group called the National Engineering Assessment Group.

(6) Building Research Establishment

The Building Research Establishment (BRE) is a primary institution providing the UK government and other clients with research, consultancy and technical support in such aspects as construction and other forms of construction, fire protection and environmental protection. The BRE also directs an information transformation programme for the Office of Energy Efficiency of the UK Department of the Environment. By March 1996 the BRE's annual business volume was more than 40 million pounds, including over 30 million pounds from the Department of the Environment. The BRE also has such massive facilities as wind tunnel. It was funded by the Parliament before 1988, but later reforms required it to earn 10% ~ 15% of its annual income from the private sector. In 1990 the BRE became an Executive Agency. After 1992 general election, it was proposed that the BRE be transferred to the DTI, but the idea was opposed by the building community, which was worried that the building industry would lose its special position if the BRE were transferred to the DTI. From then on the BRE remained an Executive Agency of the Department of the Environment until November 1995, when the government announced the likelihood of privatizing the BRE after assessment. In April 1996, two privatization schemes were proposed. The first scheme was selling the BRE to a nonprofit institution incorporated by the building sector – the National Construction Center (NCC), which was to be controlled jointly by five industrial entities forming the Department of the

Environment's Building Advisory Council and to control or own other seven or eight building research organizations. The second scheme was directly selling the BRE. Because the building community failed to raise a scheme to the government's satisfaction, the government announced the selling of the BRE in October 1996. In January 1997 the BRE was sold to a management-led team.

The following works by English scholars provided raw data for the study of the abovementioned privatization reforms of the national laboratories in the UK: *Administrative Reform of United Kingdom Government Research Establishments: Case Studies of New Organizational Forms* by Rebecca Boden, Deborah Cox, Luke Georghiou and Katharine Barker; *Successful Contractorisation: The Experience of the National Physical Laboratory* by Andrew Wallard; and *Government Laboratories: Transition and Transformation* published In 2001 by IOS Press.

1.3.4　Comments on the Reform of National Laboratories in the UK

The privatization of national laboratories in the UK is divided into three types: selling to the private sector, transformation into nonprofit institutions, and GOCO (essentially, "government-owned, privately operated"). Currently, the reform of the GOCO type is fairly successful; the experience from the NPL is likely to become an example for national laboratories that need to be privatized (not all national laboratories need be privatized). Because the GOCO model has been practiced in national and federal laboratories in the United States, a look at this country may help better understand the privatization of national laboratories in the UK.

The United States' national laboratories and federal laboratories are government-funded high-level scientific research facilities, and the primary management models of them are GOGO (Government-Owned, Government-Operated) and GOCO (Government-Owned, Contractor-Operated). GOGO can also be described as "government-owned, government-operated". Of more than 700 national and federal laboratories in the United States, over 40 (mostly large laboratories in such research fields as defense, space and energy) practice the GOCO (or "government-owned, privately-operated") model. Considering that after the Cold War, the aforesaid national and federal laboratories in defense, space and energy (primarily nuclear energy and nuclear weapons) were facing great problems in the aspects of mission orientation, management structure and research performance, the US. Congress intended to close and merge some laboratories for the purpose of simplifying the administrative structure and cutting down expenditure. In 1994, the US. Department of Energy set up a non-government independent panel consisting of 23 industrial, academic and public representatives, headed by Bob Galvin, the incumbent president of Motorola. The panel investigated the national laboratories under the Department of Energy and finally submitted what was known as "Galvin Report". In March 1995 the Congress held a hearing over the "Galvin Report". This report pointed out the flaws in the GOCO model for the Department of Energy national laboratories: because the Department of Energy still had de facto control over all of its laboratories by virtue of its rules and regulations, the GOCO model was essentially "government-owned, government-operated"; these laboratories had altered their research direction for many times in their development, making the direction of missions ambiguous, and because of the excessive structure, there were many rebuilt fields and bases; and there were many other problems such as excessive management hierarchy, excessive plans and directives and excessive audit and evaluation. To truly carry out the GOCO model therefore, the report recommended that the national laboratories be corporatized, owned by the government but managed by nonprofit companies. The Department of Energy would fund the laboratories and become their main customers, but would not have a hand in specific affairs of them. Because the Department of Energy national laboratories, such as the Argonne National Laboratory, the Brookhaven National Laboratory and the Los Alamos National Laboratory, are the largest and most powerful not only in the United States but also in the world, the reform produced a tremendous effect on developed countries like the UK, France, Germany and Japan, especially the UK which is closely linked to the United States in politics, economy, science and technology and culture. It is not hard to see the relationship between the two countries if we notice that the privatization reform of the UK's national laboratories was also actually carried out in 1994 and 1995: in April 1994 the DTI accepted KPMG's advice of making the NPL a GOCO facility, and in October 1995 Serco and the DTI signed the contract to found NPL Management Ltd. for management of the NPL. To put it another way, the privatization of national laboratories in the United States and the UK was not isolated but one of symbols of the times. This also has a value of reference for China's reform on government-owned research institutions.

Advantages of the GOCO model are that: there is no loss in ownership of national research establishments, and private firms play a role of revitalizing assets; private firms' management ideas, approaches and skills help restructure and improve the management of research establishments; research activities inside research establishments will become more efficient without administrative command from government departments; government departments will purchase from research establishments a portion of products they need, and provide them with funds as contracts require, which not only makes research establishments' activities fairly stable but also increases their income. For example, technology transfer at such large laboratories as the Argonne National Laboratory and the Brookhaven National Laboratory is very successful (Zhou Jizhong, 2002).

Such a detailed description of the UK's course of science and technology restructuring is to help understand that such an old-line empire also has the motive power for institutional reform; on the other hand, the reform, especially the institutional design and reform on the NPL, is inspiring for the institutional transformation of Chinese government-owned research institutions. Is there possibly a GOCO model besides the three models (namely, restructured into enterprises, transformation into intermediaries and merged into companies)? More choices, more flexibility, anyway.

2. Innovation Management

2. 1   The Cultural and Institutional Superiority of Cavendish Laboratory

The outstanding scientific research organizations founded by the UK-a big power with a long tradition of science-are a major contribution to the world's scientific development. The Cavendish Laboratory is one of them. Its founding marked that laboratories had evolved from scientists' personal activities into social and specialized scientific laboratories.

The construction of the Cavendish Laboratory started in 1871 with a donation of 8,450 pounds from William Cavendish, the incumbent Chancellor of Cambridge University. The prominent physicist James Clerk Maxwell was in charge of the building and development of the laboratory and, after the laboratory was opened in 1874, became the first Cavendish Professor of Physics and named the laboratory after Cavendish. Five years later, 28-year-old Joseph John Thomson became the Cavendish Professor of Physics, who would hold the post for 35 years.

Thomson's great contribution to the Cavendish Laboratory manifested not merely in his research findings (he discovered electrons in his research on cathode rays and was awarded the 1906 Nobel Prize in Physics for the discovery), but more importantly, he created an "open collaboration" innovation culture for the laboratory and passed it down by means of institutional design. From 1895 onwards, the laboratory began allowing students from outside Cambridge to study as postgraduates there, resulting in generations of young scholars coming and studying under the direction of Thomson. The laboratory established a complete set of management systems for postgraduate training which led to a top-notch type of study. Among Thomson's students, Ernest Rutherford, William Lawrence Bragg, C. Wilson, Owen Richardson, Charles Barkla and many others won the Nobel Prizes. This is an innovation culture-empowered academic development chain handed down from generation to generation.

In 1919, Thomson was succeeded by Ernest Rutherford, a scholar from New Zealand, who carried forward the innovation culture of "open collaboration" and led the laboratory to great achievements. For example, James Chadwich discovered the neutron, and Patrick Blackett improved the Wilson cloud chamber and made great achievements in nuclear physics and cosmic rays.

Under the leadership of Thomson and Rutherford, the Cavendish laboratory became the shrine of physics, whose superb institutional design and innovation culture attracted worldwide physicists and was then worldwide spread to create more excellent laboratories.

Following Rutherford's death in 1937, William Lawrence Bragg succeeded him as the Cavendish Professor, who proceeded to shift the focus of the laboratory from nuclear physics to crystal physics, biophysics and astrophysics. The culmination of these studies was the discovery of the double-helix structure of the DNA molecule in 1953 by James Watson and Francis Crick, both of whom were awarded the Nobel Prize for Physiology or Medicine in 1962.

Over 115 years from the founding of the laboratory to 1989, 28 scientists were awarded Nobel Prizes, with the laboratory hailed as the "cradle of Nobel Prizes". Put it in a way related to the subject of this book, the Cavendish Laboratory is a good example of integrating innovation culture, institutional design and innovation management together.

2.2　Review and Incentive for Scientific Research

Review and incentive fall under the controlling function of the management science. The rationale for scientific research projects, publication of papers and the level of research findings are all subject to expert review. And scientific research review differs from technological development review both in form and content.

2. 2. 1   Peer Review at the Engineering and Physical Sciences Research Council, UK

In the UK, institutions responsible for funding and managing basic research and applied research are the RCs, whose role is similar to the United States' NSF and China's NSFC. The UK has 7 RCs, and the Engineering and Physical Sciences Research Council (EPSRC) is one of them. Founded in 1994, the EPSRC determines, as an important part of its research funding work, whether or not to approve application for funding of research projects.

The largest of the 7 RCs, the EPSRC is responsible for funding the research and training in eight scientific and engineering programmes: mathematics, physics and chemistry; materials, information and computer technology; general engineering, manufacturing engineering, infrastructure and environmental and healthcare engineering.

For easier assessment, the EPSRC has created the systematic form of "societies" whose members are recommended by persons in the same industrial and academic fields. A society typically consists of 40 ~ 150 members, who will work with the society for at least 3 years. Currently the EPSRC has 17 societies involved in assessment of its projects.

A research applicant can submit his/her application for EPSRC funding at any time, which should contain a two-page summary of his/her achievements over previous years and a six-page detailed description of his/her planned research project. After receipt of the application, the APM will first check the application to see if it is eligible for funding, and then chooses review experts to assess it. At least three review experts will be chosen, one nominated by the applicant and other two chosen from related societies. If the application has passed the review, the ESRC will forward the application to a prioritization panel which prioritizes applications according to review results. This panel generally consists of 8 ~ 12 members from societies, which meets about four times a year. Finally, whether or not funding is approved, the project manager will, 26 weeks after receipt of the application, inform the applicant of review opinion in an anonymous way.

In fact, the peer review system at China's NSFC has also continuously improved. Currently, applications are reviewed at two levels. The seven (now eight) NSFC departments first check the eligibility of applications they receive, and then send them to 5 peer experts for online review (this is similar to the EPSRC's three-person review panel, and the difference is that the 5 review experts are chosen randomly from the expert bank by disciplinary principals and kept secret from the applicant). Applications which have passed the communication review will be sorted out pro rata and then forwarded to the second round of expert meetings for final judgment (similar to the EPSRC's prioritization panel). Review results will also be made known to the applicant (Zhou Jizhong, 2002).

2.2.2   Scientific and Technological Awards

The UK was the world's first country to create a science award. In 1731, the Copley Medal was created upon a donation by Sir Godfrey Gopley, which has been given every year from then on by the Royal Society to reward physical science researchers. Famous science awards created later include the Bakerian Lecture established in 1775 through a bequest by Henry Baker and granted by the Royal Society to outstanding scientists in natural history and experimental philosophy; and the Rumford Medal, founded in 1800 and awarded by the Royal Society in recognition of important scientific discoveries and important technological inventions. In addition, there are also the Darwin Medal, the Thomas Henry Huxley Award etc. in the UK.

Such awards are time-honored and primarily given to individuals, cover a wide range of disciplines, focus more on physical sciences than on technological inventions, and are generally low in amount of reward (Zhou Jizhong and Wu Zuoming, 1993).

Since the Nobel Prizes were first awarded in 1901, 76 person-time of laureates came from the UK, and in nearly 60 years from 1950 to 2008, the UK had 53 person-time of laureates, both next only to the United States in the world.

In July 2009, the Science and Innovation Minister Lord Drayson announced the creation of the innovation awards, in recognition of the country's most outstanding innovation activities and figures. Such awards are given in 13 categories, which can be applied for by all organizations and research teams across the country (MOST of China, 2010). The creation of the awards delivered an important message: the UK, a big science power, began emphasizing technological innovation.

2.3   Transformation of Scientific and Technological Achievements

Since the UK began learning the successful experience of Japan in transformation of scientific and technological achievements in the 1980s, the UK has made various attempts to promote the cooperation between universities and businesses in transforming scientific and technological achievements, for example institutional design and creating foundations. In 1998, the DTI, the Department for Education and Employment and the Higher Education Funding Council for England jointly created a foundation, to which was added 200 million pounds every year for encouraging cooperation between universities and businesses. In addition, the UK government decided to invest 25 million pounds to build 8 enterprise centers at famous universities for training scientists, engineers or entrepreneurs into innovative entrepreneurs. The DTI also doubled its funding for the Teaching Company Scheme, which was to be used for funding about 200 research projects a year, and provided 10 million pounds for establishing partnerships between universities and businesses.

The UK Innovation Investment Fund was launched in June 2009 with the aim to promote small businesses' innovation and technological achievement transformation. The UK government announced the same year that small businesses would be allowed to enter free the government procurement network seeking public procurement contracts up to 100,000 pounds, with a view of promoting their innovation activities.

On the whole, however, the UK's technological transformation level is inferior to its scientific achievements.

2.4   Science and Technology Input and Output

2.4.1   National R&D Input and Output

According to the statistical report in March 2009 by the UK Office of National Statistics, the UK's gross expenditure on research and development (GERD) for 2007 was 25.4 billion pounds, of which 63% was allocated to businesses, 26% to universities, 5% to government research bodies, 4% to the RCs, and 2% to nonprofit organizations; the GERD/GDP ratio was 1.79% (MOST of China, 2010), which was much lower than its previously 2.5% and than that of the United States, Japan, Germany and North European countries, and only 0.1 percentage point higher than China's 1.7% (2009).

In 2007, the UK's business enterprise R&D expenditure stood at 26.345 billion dollars, ranking 6th in the world, next to that in the United States, Japan, Germany, China and France. The same year, 2,929 patents for invention were granted in the

UK, coming in 10th in the world. The UK was much outstripped by the United States, Japan and Germany in business enterprise R&D expenditure and granted patents for invention, which suggested that the scientific and technological output of the UK's enterprises was low. And for the year, the UK's R&D personnel in 10, 000 person-year were 334, 700 (full-time equivalent, FTE), coming in 7th in the world.

From 1950 to 2008, the UK had 53 person-time of Nobel Prize laureates, ranking 2nd in the world.

In 2008, the UK had 163, 194 papers published on the world's three major index journals (SCI, EI and ISTP), coming in 3rd in the world (next to the United States and China).

In the IMD *World Competitiveness Yearbook 2010* the UK ranked only 22nd, one place lower from the previous year (IMD, 2010). And it was ranked 12th in the World Economic Forum's *Global Competitiveness Report 2010-2011*, up one place from the previous year (WEF, 2010). The UK's lower positions suggested its falling national competitiveness.

Nevertheless, the UK's scientific and technological output and efficiency were extraordinary. According to its own report —*International Comparative Performance of the UK Research Base* published in September 2009 by the UK Department for Business, Innovation and Skills, in 2008, the UK's share of world publications was 7.9%, next only to the United States and China; its share of indexed articles was 12% of world total and it was ranked 2nd behind the United States; it had the highest output rate of articles per unit of R&D input; its articles co-authored with other countries increased and were fairly highly indexed, and especially papers with the United States, Germany and France had impact 50% higher than the UK research base average (MOST of China, 2010).

2.4.2 Input and Output of Enterprises

The 2008 R&D performance assessment report by the UK Department for Innovation, Universities and Skills (DIUS) provided a statistical analysis of global top 1,400 companies and UK's top 850 companies in research and development. Among the UK's top 850 companies, 88 pharmaceutical and aerospace companies were included among the global top 1, 400 companies. Between 2007 and 2008, the top 850 companies increased their investment in R&D by 9. 5% from the previous year, and the UK's 88 largest R&D investors increased their spending on R&D by 10. 3%.

These top 850 companies are mainly in five sectors: pharmaceuticals & biotechnology; aerospace & defense; software & computer services; fixed and mobile communications; and automobiles & parts. For the 850 companies, the R&D expenditure in these five sectors was 60% of their total R&D expenditure, and pharmaceutical and biotechnological companies' R&D expenditure accounted for 37% of the 850 companies' total. It is thus obvious that pharmaceutical and biotechnological companies are not only the leading force of the UK's enterprise research and development but also the cornerstones of its economy.

The following seven companies are the most important of UK enterprises. Of the global top 25 companies in research investment in 2008, the UK had two pharmaceutical and biotechnology comanies: GlaxoSmithKline (GSK) was ranked 13th for its R&D investment of 3. 246 billion pounds, with annual growth of – 6. 1%, which in 2007 was ranked 7th; and AstraZeneca, which was ranked 19th for its R&D investment of 2. 533 billion pounds, with annual growth of 29. 8%. Rolls-Royce and Airbus are the largest R&D investment companies in the UK's aerospace and defense sector, ranked 8th and 7th respectively among the top 850 companies; their R&D investment together accounted for 64% of the sector's total. In the fixed and mobile communications sector, British Telecom (BT) ranked 3rd, Vodafone 14th and Telefonica 24th among the top 850 companies, whose R&D investment together accounted for 95% of the sector's total.

It can be concluded from above statistics that enterprise R&D activities and investment in the UK highly converge. The abovementioned seven companies are quite prominent in the UK's R&D activities (DIUS, 2008).

3. Innovation Culture

The UK was the first science center in modern times. During 90 years from 1770 to 1860, it possessed 30% of the world's momentous scientific discoveries and 57% of technological inventions; its labor productivity rose twenty-fold, and its industrial output value was 39% of the world's total.

From Newton and Hooke of the 17th century, Dalton of the 18th century, to Darwin, Faraday and Maxwell of the 19th century, the UK's tradition of scientific innovation came down in a continuous line, leading the UK to retain until now powerful scientific research capacity and strength. This is closely linked to the UK's tradition of innovation culture (Zhou Jizhong, 1993).

Compared with Japan's "combinatorial innovation culture", the UK's innovation culture can be described as a "radical innovation" culture, in which scientists and engineers pursue the essential laws of nature and explore unprecedented discoveries and inventions, rather than finding new ideas through combination of existing research findings. When the two innovation cultures are compared, it is justifiable to say that combinatorial innovation can faster and more pertinently apply the combination of available findings (typically applied research findings or experimental development findings) to the commercial development of technological achievements and thus obtain economic benefits, while radical innovation leads more to basic research findings with much more far-reaching effects on scientific, technological and social development and economic activities, which can only produce tremendous benefits through future applied research and experimental development. Examples are Newton's law of universal gravitation, Darwin's theory on the origin of species, Turing's "automatic machine", and Crick's double-helix model of DNA structure (in collaboration with U. S. scientist James Watson. Of course, this is only a brief generalization, intended to show that the UK's scientific and technological workers are more efficient and effective in radical innovation while Japan's are more efficient and effective in combinatorial innovation.

The problem of the UK's innovation culture is the strong traditional awareness which, in present terms, stresses form and procedure more than innovation. A "gentlemanly" style still exists in the UK, which leads avoidance of intense competition to have become a mostly recognized value.

4. Comments on Innovation Management and National Strength

To sum up, the UK has its own characteristics and tradition in innovation management. But the UK, the world's most powerful nation in science and economy at one time or another, has been in a state of decline in national strength since the 1950s. It was only ranked 22nd in the IMD *World Competitiveness Yearbook 2010*, and only 12th in the World Economic Forum's *Global Competitiveness Report 2010-2011*. It has been no longer in the camp of world top powers in terms of national competitiveness.

Important factors affecting the UK's national strength include: on political system design, the country's political system and institutional design had flaws, leading to the low government operation efficiency and increasing scandals among governmental and parliamentary officials; on science and technology system design, the efficiency of scientific and technological achievement commercialization and industrialization was low, and though it sent people to learn Japan's experience in the 1980s, little effectiveness was achieved. If it is appropriate to say that environments do change things, then it is reasonable to tell that today's UK lacks a favorable environment for commercialization of technological achievements.

From the industrial competition perspective, the UK is only competitive in consumable commodities, finance and insurance, for example in such sectors as food, cosmetics, finance, insurance, auction, international law and merchandise control. Manufacturing, a cornerstone of national economy, is less commendable in the UK. The UK's industry agglomeration is low, leading to high production and transport costs. In a word, in manufacturing fields, the UK has a low share in worldwide markets.

Like the United States, the UK has many first-class universities, but domestic students are more enthusiastic about such disciplines as finance, management and law than about engineering science and technological disciplines. And because of unsound enterprise training systems and flaws in social education systems, the UK is behind Japan and Germany in terms of talent training (Porter, 2007).

But the UK still is one of the world's financial powers, and London still is one of the world's financial centers. This is a sort of support to the UK's national strength.

The UK has regular armed forces of 186, 900 people, including 106, 200 for the army, 35, 500 for the navy and 45, 000 for the air force, and it has three-four nuclear submarines and some 160 ~ 200 nuclear warheads (World Affairs Editorial Board, 2009). In 2007 the UK's military expenditure was 2. 5% of the GDP (it was up to 2. 7% in 2008), weapon exports amounted to 1. 15 billion dollars and weapon imports to 698 million dollars (The World Bank, 2009).

Chapter 4

A Hovering Germany

Germany, officially the Federal Republic of Germany, covers an area of 357,000 square kilometers and has a population of 82. 218 million (estimated at the end of 2007). Its natural resources are less abundant, but forests cover about one third of the territory. Germans make up the majority of the population, and 31.4% of the residents have faith in Roman Catholicism and 30. 8% in Protestantism (Editorial Board of *World Affairs*, 2009). From the 1830s to the late 1930s, Germany was the world science center, with representatives including mathematician Carl Friedrich Gauss of the 19th century and Albert Einstein and Max Planck of the 20th century. Almost in the same period, Germany became the center of the world economy. It had great national power during the First and Second World War. Since the Second World War ended with its defeat, though not as great as before, Germany has remained top in the world in economic, scientific and technological power. Different from other developed European and American countries, Germany has been and still is a big exporter in the world. Following Greece's debt crisis this year particularly, Germany's position, attitude and performance were so eye-catching in the European economy that other European countries could not compare with it.

But as to how to deal with "Germany reunification" and "European unification", though both were already unified de facto, tons of problems existed, making Germany hesitant, hovering at a crossroads.

1. Institutional Design

1.1　National Institutional Design

The *Basic Law for the Federal Republic of Germany* (namely the constitutional law of Germany; "Basic Law" below), which came into force after the Second World War in May 1949, established five institutions of Germany: republicanism, democracy, federalism, rule of law and welfarism. Therefore, some also describe the market economy of Germany as "social market economy", namely a "market economy with high welfare." Germany's federalism is fairly decentralized, with the federal government little intervening in economy.

The Basic Law was amended as appropriate after East and West Germany were reunified in 1990. The parliament consists of the Bundestag which exercises legislative powers, supervises law enforcement and elects the President of the Bundestag; and the

Bundesrat which participates in legislation and has its members elected by and represent the governments of the 16 federal states (10 of former West Germany and 6 of former East Germany). Germany carries out the multi-party system, with main parties including the Christian Democratic Union (CDU), the Christian Social Union (CSU) and the Social Democratic Party of Germany.

When addressing the founding ceremony the German Academy of Engineering, in Octorber 2008, German Chancellor Angela Merkel stressed that: education, scientific research and innovation had become crucial for the successful development of Germany; the GERC/GDP ratio would reach 3% by 2010; Germany's "high-tech strategy" was very correct, and high technologies should be employed to solve problems about resources, climate change, energy, food etc. ; and a liberal innovation environment should be created·by virtue of the "Scientific Freedom Act" (Merkel, 2009).

One year later, in October 2009, Germany's coalition government officially signed the coalition agreement Growth, Education, Unity, which consisted of five parts: Prosperity for all, Sustainable economy, Germany the Republic of Education: Good education and strong research, Social progress: Through cohesion and solidarity; Freedom and security: Civil rights and a strong state; and Securing peace: Through partnership and common responsibility in Europe and the world.

This agreement stressed that Germany's prosperity should be underpinned by innovation, research and new technology.

In May 2009, the Federal Ministry of Education and Research (BMBF) issued the Eight-point Plan for Innovation and Growth, proposing that scientific and technological innovation should be relied on to respond to the current economic crisis. The content of this plan included: strengthening the education and training system; advancing the high-tech strategy; assisting innovation in eastern Germany; making and implementing tax systems and policies conducive to innovation; training and importing skilled workers; creating a liberal environment for research and creation; and actively participating in international cooperation in science and technology. This plan was made against the background that in 2009 the country's exports dropped by 14. 4% and its economy grew negatively at a rate of 5% year on year-a severe situation to such a big exporter. In addition, the federal government also initiated such plans as the Plan for Innovation of SMEs and the Plan for Integration of Economy, Science and Technology (MOST of China, 2010).

Similar to that of France and Japan, Germany's financial system is, briefly, a "bank-led" : banks and enterprises are closely connected, bank loans are the primary source of financing for enterprises, and banking assets take a bigger share than the market value of shares in the GDP. Dominant banks in Germany include Deutsche Bank and Dresdner Bank. But Germany's securities market is less developed than those of the United States and the UK.

Like France, Germany's institutional designers made great contributions to the institutional building of the European Union (EU) and its scientific and technological system building. In 1950 after discussions with France, Germany officially put forward a plan of sharing coal and steel resources among European countries. In 1951, promoted by Germany and France, the *Treaty Establishing the European Coal and Steel Community* was signed between the six European countries (France, West Germany, Italy and the three Benelux countries-Belgium, Luxembourg, and the Netherlands). In 1965, the European Community (EC) was established. In 1991, the EC members signed the *Treaty of Maastricht*, marking the formation of the EU. In 2002, the euro came into circulation as the uniform currency of the EU. During the 60-year development of the EU, Germany and France have always played key roles.

1.2　Institutional and System Design on Science and Technology

The Basic Law states that in Germany "subjective initiative takes precedence over government intervention in terms of science, technology and economy".

In early 1995, the federal government set up a "Council for Research, Technology and Innovation" chaired by the Chancellor, as the highest science and technology decision-making and coordinating body of Germany. The German Council of Science and Humanities (Wissenschaftsrat), co-founded by the federal and state governments, is the most important advisory agency within the federal government.

Different from the United States, the German federal government is also equipped with the Federal Ministry of Education and Research that is in charge of national scientific, technological and educational affairs. Bot' 'he Federal-Länder Commission for Educational Planning and Research Promotion (BLK) and the Science Council are the federal government's advisory bodies in the fields of science, technology and education.

1.2.1　Government R&D Institutions and the R&D System of Universities

Germany's R&D organization system, though not as big as that of the United

States, is quite complete.

(1) Research institutions of the German federal government

The German federal government's research institutions mainly include the Helmholtz Association of German Research Centres (HGF), Max Planck Society (MPG), "Blue List" institutions (BLE), and other R&D institutions that belong to the federal government. The federal government also supports the aforesaid institutions, colleges and universities, and enterprise R&D institutions. The Länder (state governments) also allocates funds to HGF, MPG, BLE, colleges and universities, and their respective R&D institutions.

HGF is Germany's most important and largest basic research organization, under the leadership of which the 16 research centres, large basic research bases built with government investments, hire a total of about 24, 000 staff and each year receive some 7, 000 visiting scholars from both home and abroad. In September 2001, HGF became a registered association, with main bodies also including the Committee of Financing Partners and the Senate. Founded in 1948, MPG, Germany's large research organization that funds and manages basic research, consists of more than 80 institutes, hiring more than 11, 000 people-including some 2, 800 scientists and 6, 500 visiting scientists, doctoral students and postdoctoral students; it is similar to the Chinese Academy of Sciences (CAS) in structure and function.

The German Research Foundation (DFG) is a German research funding organization, whose structure and function are similar to those of the National Natural Science Foundation of China (NSFC).

(2) R&D Institutes at universities

Germany has some 350 universities, including over 90 comprehensive universities and about 180 specialized ones. Because German universities practice the principle of "unity of scientific research and teaching" which was raised during "Humboldt's reform" in the early 19th century, most of them keep R&D institutions.

1.2.2 Scientific and Technological System Formed by Enterprises and Nonprofit Organizations

(1) R&D establishments at enterprises

Large enterprises such as Siemens and Daimler have R&D establishments of their own. At the same time, the industrial community also funds laboratories co-founded by universities and enterprises, and financially aids HGF, MPG and BLE through projects. In addition, some private foundations in Germany fund various research establishments by way of projects.

(2) Nonprofit R&D Organization—Fraunhofer Society

The Fraunhofer Society (FhG), founded in 1949, is a non-profit organization in the form of a registered association. It carries out market-oriented R&D activities as commissioned by enterprise, by signing contracts on high-tech applied research and experimental development. It employs a staff of more than 9, 000-including 5, 500 researchers, working in 60 institutions in 37 cities throughout Germany.

1.2.3　The EU's International Research Institutions in Germany

Because Germany is a mainstay of the EU and its science and technology programmes, there are also some research institutions built in Germany as required by the EU or its science and technology programmes. For example, the Institute for Transuranium Elements (ITU), the German Heidelberg Laboratory and the Hamburg Laboratory of the European Molecular Biology Laboratory (EMBL) are all EU's international research institutions built in Germany, which also receive funding from the German federal government (Jin Zhonghua, 2005). To promote the EU's Seventh Framework Programme for research and technological development, the German federal government had by 2009 invested 19.6% of the total funding in this programme (MOST of China, 2010).

2. Innovation Management

2.1　Technology Innovation Management at Enterprises

Generally speaking, German enterprises have the competitive advantages of a high degree of industry, agglomeration, emphasis on R&D, and high-quality and plentiful human resources, and Germany therefore has a great number of advantageous industries in world's export markets, especially chemical engineering and precision instruments.

(1) Siemens: Representative of Enterprise Innovation Management in Germany

Though large enterprises in Germany are outnumbered by those in the United States, nearly all of them are excellent ones in technological innovation. This is related to the tradition among German enterprises of valuing technological development. Siemens AG is a good example. Siemens & Halske, the predecessor of Siemens AG, was founded by the inventor Werner Siemens in 1847 and was renamed as such in 1966.

Siemens has the following advantages in innovation management.

1) Top management in the capacity of technical experts. Siemens is an internationally renowned high-tech company which has been in the control of technical experts since its founding. In 1842, 26-year-old Werner Siemens obtained his first patent for his invention of an electroplating process; in 1845 he invented the pointer telegraph of self-interruption; in 1846, he developed gutta-percha cables, which earned his company a great fortune, and the next year he used such cables to lay an underground telegraph line from Berlin to Gross Bayle; in 1866 he invented the self-excited generator by replacing permanent magnet with electromagnet, and at the same year he invented the alcohol batchmeter. Werner Siemens' substantial inventions and discoveries not only brought Siemens physical wealth and brand effects, but in an intangible way set the tradition for the company that the corporate executive should have mastery of technology. His two younger brothers were electric experts, and his three sons were all management experts; his offspring continued to control Siemens AG until 1981, when the Siemens family for the first time relinquished day-to-day control over the company, but the tradition of managing the company by an expert has remained till today.

2) Talent training system. As early as in 1922, Siemens founded an "apprenticeship fund" used for training workers. It established one after another Werner Siemens College, Siemens Technical Academy and more than 60 training bases. By the 1990s, all leaders at Siemens at workshop director level and above were engineers, managers qualified as engineers and technicians accounted for one fourth of the company's total managers, and skilled workers were over a half of all the workers. At its famous R&D base, the Siemens City, there are world top-notch continuous training schools and customer training courses.

3) High transformation rate of R&D results. Some of the well-known examples of Siemens transforming R&D results into goods are: the use of X-rays discovered in 1895 by scientist Roentgen to make X-ray machines; the successful operation of a 50MW nuclear reactor developed by Siemens in 1965; the development in the 1970s of the telephone signaling system capable of transmitting 10, 800 telephone signals at one time, which led to the automation of all telephones in West Germany; and the capability of producing 4M-bit memory chips in the late 1980s, only years after its

entry in 1984 of the computer and electronics field.

4) Quality control systems. To ensure the quality of process design, contour design, technical documents, delivery, installation and maintenance, Siemens established quality control systems and standards for all stages including product planning, design, R&D, manufacturing, installation and maintenance, reflective of the world-famous "Quality First" demeanor of German enterprises.

5) Intensive R&D input. During the 1990s, Siemens' R&D intensity (ratio of its R&D investment to its sales) already reached up to 10%, and its R&D personnel accounted in number for 11% of its total employees. It was just because of such highly intensive R&D resource allocation that Siemens could introduce new products from year to year, making 90% of its products available on the market for only four years (Yuan Zhengguan, 1993).

Today, Siemens operate in more than 190 countries all over the world, owning about 600 plants, R&D centers and representative offices worldwide. It has 6 key business areas: information & communication, automation & control, power, transportation, medical, and lighting. Its global operations are undertaken by 13 business groups, including Siemens Financial Services and Siemens Real Estate. For FY 2005, Siemens employed about 461, 000 people worldwide, and reported global revenue of 75. 445 billion euros and a net income of 3. 058 billion euros, with 80% of the revenue coming from outside Germany. In 2005, it invested 5. 2 billion euros in research and development, to keep its leadership in technology. In FY 2004, Siemens saw some 8,800 inventions by its R&D personnel, an increase of 7% from the previous year, two thirds of them applied for patents (www. siemens. com).

Siemens' successful experience was also shared by other high-tech corporations in Germany such as Bayer AG and Robert Bosch GmbH.

(2) Bayer AG

Bayer AG was founded in 1863 with primary business of chemical engineering. In 1862, Friedrich Bayer, the founder of Bayer AG, successfully experimented with production of the dye fuchsine form the raw material of tar. Next year, in 1863, he founded Bayer AG. On 6 March 1899, Bayer's trademark Aspirin was registered, which would become the most widely-used and most famous drug brand in the world, hailed as the "drug of the century." Bayer's business management experience is: diversity of product and production line; market and customer diversity; and intensive worldwide R&D to guarantee competitiveness.

With regard to R&D investment, early in the 1990s, Bayer's R&D expenditure reached 3 billion Deutsche Marks, 7% of its sales. On employee training, Bayer provides the courses of 40 disciplines in scientific, technological and management fields for training of technical personnel and international management personnel, each year with thousands of employees receiving training. It owns Europe's largest chemical literature library with a collection of more than 650, 000 books. It also practices an "Employee Suggestion Scheme" to reward those employees who have made rationalization proposals (Yuan Zhengguang, 1993).

Today Bayer is one of the global top 500 businesses, employing 120, 000 people working in 350 branches and 750 plants at 200 locations throughout the world. With four pillar business sectors-polymers, pharmaceuticals & healthcare, chemistry and agriculture, it produces more than 10, 000 types of products. It is one of the largest industrial groups in Germany (www. baier. com).

(3) Robert Bosch GmbH

In 1886, Robert Bosch, who had worked for noted inventor and businessman Thomas Edison for a time, founded the "Workshop for Precision Mechanics and Electrical Engineering", the predecessor of Robert Bosch GmbH. He directed the invention of the spark plug and magneto, and developed such automobile devices as headlights, auto horns and oil pumps. In 1928, Robert Bosch GmbH produced the world's first electric tool. Therefore, Robert Bosch GmbH has the tradition of research and development alike. During 1990s the company's R&D intensity reached about 6%. Of course, it also has the tradition of staff training. Early in 1913, Robert Bosch opened a technician training school for the company, and developed continuous education schemes for workers and managers (Yuan Zhengguan, 1993).

Today, Bosch Group has already become a leading technology and service provider in the world. It has about 275, 000 employees in the fields of automotive technology, industrial technology, consumer goods and intelligent building technology. For FY 2009 it reported sales of about 38. 2 billion euros. Bosch Group comprises Robert Bosch GmbH and its more than 300 subsidiaries and regional companies in over 60 countries. If its sales and service partners are included, then Bosch is represented in roughly 150 countries. This worldwide development, manufacturing and sales network is the foundation for further growth. It spent more than 3. 5 billion euros on research and development for each of recent years, and applied for over 3, 800 patents worldwide (www. bosch. com).

2.2　Science and Technology Intermediary: Steinbeis Foundation

The main component of Germany's industrial and economic framework is small and medium-sized enterprises (SMEs), and technology intermediaries serve as the bridge to promote technological innovation of SMEs. German technology intermediaries not only come in large numbers but also operate in a compliant way. The Steinbeis Foundation is a good example of them.

The Steinbeis Foundation, founded in 1971, is an organization headquartered in Stuttgart, Germany dedicated to services for the transfer of knowledge and technology. Only a regional technical consulting firm at its inception, it has become a powerful global technology transfer organization through efforts over 40 years.

Three decades its founding, in 2001, its business revenue totaled 89. 9 million euros, 91.4% (82.2 million euros) of which came from its four key business areas-consulting, research and development, evaluation and expert reports, and training and employee development. For the year, its contract-based projects amounted to 21,253, including 8,464 consulting projects, 6,721 R&D projects, 2,399 evaluation projects and 3,669 training and employee development projects. It had 470 technology transfer centers in 40 countries worldwide: 108 transfer centers at universities and research institutions, 192 at universities of applied sciences, 119 established with its partners, 26 at cooperative universities. Steinbeis GmbH, an independent subsidiary of the Steinbeis Foundation, encompasses almost all Steinbeis Transfer Centers, subsidiaries, and a variety of other Seinbeis enterprises, serving as the mainstay of the entire Seinbeis network.

In 1998, the Steinbeis Foundation founded the Steinbeis University Berlin, a small private university in Berlin, Germany. By 2006, the university had 18 professors, 537 faculties, 65 research institutions, and 1,608 students-some of them from China. At the same time, the university provides a wide variety of lectures and seminars for enterprises. Each year the foundation organizes training and symposia for over 100, 000 people, most of whom wish to obtain a master's degree. Most training courses are on e-commerce, computer, network, knowledge management, quality control and human resource development.

In 2006, the Steinbeis Foundation's clients totaled over 10, 000 in more than 40 countries including China, and 70% of them were SMEs. The foundation employed 4,661 people, including 796 professors, 1, 185 permanent personnel and 2, 680 project personnel; of these employees, 92.7% were professors and experts in science, engineering technology and economy, and the remainder were management personnel. Its revenue totaled 94.9 million euros for 2006, and 124 million euros for 2008.

The Steinbeis Foundation's institutional design is the customer-driven contract system and the formation of a global network of over 700 technology transfer centers.

At the core of its four major service fields are consulting services. Clients dominantly are SMEs. Its consulting services encompass: consultancy provided by an expert at most for 5 hours; marketing, technical and commercial evaluation and report submission by an expert in relevant field for enterprises and financial institutions, especially start-ups and spin-offs; design for enterprises of diverse development strategies; consultancy on total quality control, corporate image and product design; demonstration, consultancy or report submission for regional development and business promotion activities, and so on. Over 6,700 R&D projects nearly cover operations of all sizes and in all sectors, including the optimization of products, processes and systems. Priority fields of its R&D and consulting services are information, communications, micro-electronics, systems engineering, life sciences, processes and manufacturing technology. Its interdisciplinary R&D projects have increased in recent years. Most of its evaluation projects are about market, technological, enterprise and performance evaluation. Its Training and employee development projects have increasing importance. The foundation's slogan is "We Accelerate Innovation".

In 1998, the author visited the Steinbeis Foundation at its headquarters in Stuttgart, and in 2006 visited the Steinbeis University Berlin, feeling the foundation's contribution to German in talent development. In the meanwhile, the author wished Chinese foundations of the same trade could learn the plentiful experience from the Steinbeis Foundation in institutional design and operating mechanisms in the field of technology transfer.

2.3　Science and Technology Input and Output

Among the EU countries, Germany's scientific contribution is up to 21% — synthesized by publication of papers. Germany's advantageous scientific fields are: aviation and aerospace, chemistry and chemical engineering, precision instruments, astronomy and physics, mathematics etc. (Jin Zhonghua, 2005).

In 2009, Germany's GERD/GDP ratio reached 2.9%, suggesting that it could achieve a 3% GERD/GDP ratio by 2010 as required by the Lisbon Strategy.

In 2007, Germany's R&D expenditure stood at 83. 822 billion dollars, ranking 3rd in the world. Its enterprise R&D expenditure totaled 58. 637 billion dollars, next only to the United States and Japan (China ranked 4th for its 34. 321 billion dollars), and its ratio to GDP was 1. 77% , ranking 10th in the world. The same year, its R&D personnel in 10, 000 person-year were 498, 000 (FTE), coming in 4th in the world, and enterprise R&D personnel in 10, 000 person-year were 320, 000, ranking 4th in the world too; its per-capita R&D expenditure was 1,019 dollar, ranking 11th in the world.

Germany ranked 16th in the IMD *World Competitiveness Yearbook 2010*, down 3 places from one year ago (IMD, 2010), and 5th in the World Economic Forum's *Global Competitiveness Report 2010 ~ 2011*, up 2 spots from one year ago (WEF, 2010).

From 1950 to 2008, Germany had 30 person-time of Nobel Prize laureates, ranking 3rd in the world.

In 2007, 13, 839 patents for invention were granted in Germany, coming in 7th in the world. In 2008, Germany published 161, 107 papers on the world's three major index journals, ranking 4th in the world.

From the economic aggregate perspective, Germany's GDP reached 3, 650. 2 billion dollars in 2007, coming in 4th in the world (MOST of China, 2010).

From above indicators, Germany remains a big power in the world in economy, science and technology, but its competitiveness has declined.

3. Innovation Culture

The Germans are highly cultured and good at rational thinking. A great number of noted poets, litterateurs, philosophers and scientists are Germans, such as Goethe, chiller, Hegel, Einstein and Planck, as well as Marx and Engels. It is these people who fostered the fertile soil and foundation for the present-day innovation culture of Germany. And it is not hard to find the cultural tradition of imagination of Germans.

The cultural values of German enterprises are: conscientiousness, meticulousness and quality first. For example, the Fraunhofer Society's idea of product development is to: continuously introduce new technologies appealing to industrial enterprises, developing high-level prototypes, specimens and sample pieces; carry out pre-experimental research and development first, and then identify the sources of funds according to the nature of assignments. During its development of industrial robots, the society first carried out pre-experimental research and development, and when it became aware that robots would be bound to draw strong interests from industry, it first developed robot prototypes such as "automobile engine smartly installed with rubber sleeves" and "assembly system of high flexibility" and finally was awarded contracts by many enterprises. After obtaining these contracts, on the one hand it conducted the development of new products, and on the other it carried out market analysis and economic feasibility study, with the aim to allow industry to realize mass production of new products. Because the society's pre-experimental research, prototype development, market analysis and economic feasibility study were always customer needs-oriented and for industrial application, its development of new technologies and new products was well in step with industrial development, leading to the increased fame and influence among industrial enterprises (Zhou Jizhong, 1993).

To develop jobholders into talents with above-described qualities entails education (education in the broad sense encompasses social education and lifelong education). In addition to attaching importance to research universities, German establishes professional colleges and technical training systems. By so doing, technical education and technical training become a part of innovation culture. This is because, from the perspective of technical talent composition, not only are professional colleges needed to develop engineers, but also the vocational schools to train a large number of skilled workers. In Germany's education system therefore, greater importance is given to professional colleges and vocational schools (than those in China), and there are many such schools which provide high-quality education. At the 1968 higher-education restructuring conference among state governors, Germany made the decision to establish three-year colleges. It was stated in German's higher education framework law of 1976 that the diplomas of college students and those of traditional university graduates were equally authentic. German colleges were very popular because of higher employment rates for college graduates and of free schooling (Zhou Jizhong et al. , 1993). As a result, at German enterprises, scientists and engineers take a higher proportion of executives than those in other countries, and there are more and high-quality skilled frontline workers. This is the human resource guarantee for the high quality of German products. This point can be roughly understood from the above-described cases of Siemens, Bayer and Bosch.

Loosely speaking, risk evasion is also part of German values, and the idea and practice of "starting from scratch" is not praised in the country.

4. Comments on Innovation Management and National Strength

Germany used to be the world science center and is still a big power in science, technology and economy, which together with China constitute the world's two largest exporters. The "Germany-France Axis" is the mainstay of the EU.

Germany's innovation management pays great attention to: research and development, especially industrialization and commercialization of research results; human resource development, especially the development of professional colleges and vocational schools and various training schools (Germany is counted as one of the best in this regard); and quality control and system building, leading German products to enjoy worldwide reputation for their high quality up to the present.

Personally speaking, Germany's soft power is, first of all, its awareness and spirit of "cooperation and openness". This is noticeable in scientific and technological innovation. Not only is Germany a vigorous supporter of the EU and its R&D programmes, but Germany also actively carries out scientific and technological cooperation with developing countries including China. For example, the Max Planck Society has been for years in cooperation with the Chinese Academy of Sciences, and the cooperation between Germany and China in such aspects as environmental protection has also produced plentiful results.

Constrained by its defeat during the Second World War, Germany only has armed forces of 247,700 people, including 101,700 for the army, about 18,500 for the navy and 45,200 for the air force (Editorial Board of World Affairs, 2009). In 2007, Germany's military expenditure was 1.3% of the GDP (it was up to 1.4% in 2008), its weapon exports amounted to some 3.4 billion dollars and weapon imports to 85 million dollars (The World Bank, 2009).

Compared with the 1960s, 1970s and 1980s, Germany's national strength was, for the first 10 years of the 21st century, in a state of decline. This was manifested in such aspects as national competitiveness, industrial competitiveness, innovation capacity and economic strength. In the IMD *World Competitiveness Yearbook 2010*, Germany was only ranked 16th, which was unimaginable in the past. That was concerned not only with the development of emerging countries such as China, India and Brazil but also with the present-day financial crisis and the stagnant European market.

Germany's institutional designers currently are confronted with two "unification difficulties". The first is "reunification of West and East Germany. " Over the past 20 years, the forcible use of the systems and institutions of the former Federal Republic of German to "reunify" former East Germany not only failed to produce desired economic results but also gave rise to social problems in both parts of Germany, and the originally designed "reunification of powerful countries" (former East Germany was a "powerful" country in the Soviet-East European bloc, while the former Federal Republic of Germany was also a "powerful" country in the Western camp) didn't produce remarkable effects. The second is "European unification". Though the creation of the EU and euro was innovative and Germany has done much to it, the EU countries differ greatly from each other, and on the occasion of crisis, problems are hard to tackle; for example, Greece's debt crisis made Germany stand at a nonplus.

From the pillar industry perspective, Germany's advantage lies in its expertise in complex chemical engineering, precise instrument manufacturing and electric industry, and its disadvantage is the lack of competitive emerging industries such as semiconductor, software and computer industry, biotechnology, and modern service industries like finance and telecommunications. Moreover, German universities give inadequate importance to management sciences. Compared with the United States, the UK and France, there is almost no famous business or management school in Germany. The majority of noted German entrepreneurs are technical experts. For example, corporate strategy management talent and modern marketing talent are fewer in Germany than in other Western powers.

On the whole, Germany stresses tradition and the standard operation of flows, which ensures the high quality of its products. But overemphasis also means stiffness and lack of creativity.

From German's innovation culture tradition and overall strength, especially the fact that it is the world's second largest exporter only behind China, if it can make innovations in institutional design and get out of the above-described plights, it still has the potential for rejuvenating.

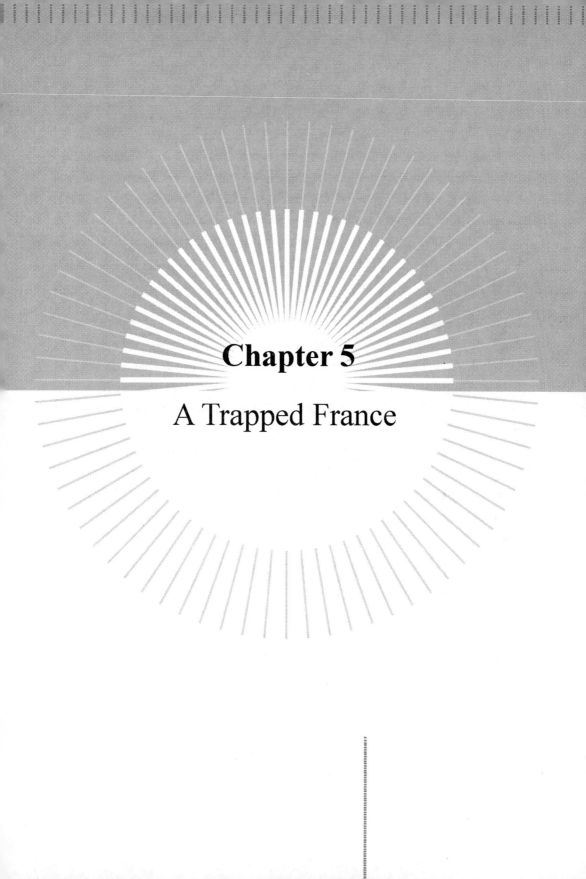

Chapter 5

A Trapped France

France, officially the French Republic, covers an area of 551,600 square kilometers and has a population of 64.47 million (2008 est.). Its natural resources are less abundant, and its forest coverage is 27.4%. Among the whole population, 64% have faith in Catholicism, 3% in Islam and 27% nonreligious (Editorial Board of World Affairs, 2009). Historically, the French Enlightenment of the 18th century set the stage for the development of science, and the representative figures were, among other Enlightenment thinkers, Denis Diderot and Jean-Jacques Rousseau. The theory "separation of powers", which was raised by Enlightenment thinker and jurist Montesquieu in his masterwork, *The Spirit of Laws*, was very influential for the political system design of Western countries.

From the mid and late 18th century to the mid-19th century, France became another science center after the UK, with the representative figures of chemist Antoine Laurent de Lavoisier of the 18th century and microbiologist and chemist Louis Pasteur of the 19th century. Both the French Revolution which broke out on July 14, 1789 (later established as the French national holiday), and the Paris Commune founded in March 1871, are shining parts of history. Today, France is the advocate of the European integration and the leader of the EU—the unitary political organization of Europe. In 2008, with its GDP of 2,861.2 billion dollars, France became the world's fifth largest economy (behind the United States, Japan, Germany and China). In countering the financial crisis and European predicament lasting from 2009 to the present, France is currently less charismatic than Germany in Europe. The present national power of France seems some insufficient in relation to its ambition to command the EU. The institutional designers and executors of the French governments since the de Gaulle's administration could hardly get out of the predicament in a fairly long time.

1. Institutional Design

1.1 National Institutional Design

According to the current *Constitution of the Fifth Republic* (which took effect in 1958), the President, the head of the state, is elected by direct universal suffrage, appoints the Prime Minister, presides over the Council of Ministers, and has the right to dissolve the Parliament. The Parliament consists of the National Assembly whose members are elected by direct suffrage, and the Senate whose members are elected indirectly by an electoral college consisting of members of the National Assembly and local assemblies. France carried out the multi-party system, with main parties including the right-wing Union for a People's Movement, the left-wing Socialist Party and the centre-right Union for French Democracy.

Since 1986, the French government has been in a disharmonious period of "left-right cohabitation", with the President and the Prime Minister or the Parliament belonging to two political blocs. Currently, on the whole, it is the government, not the legislature, that controls the two houses of the Parliament.

Compared with the United States, the UK and Germany, the French government has a greater degree of intervention in national economy, and its market economy is described as "government-dominated market economy". Politically, France, different from the UK and Germany, frequently seems to stand up to the United States as an equal. This was particularly apparent during de Gaulle's reign. Its retreat from the NATO (North Atlantic Treaty Organization) and the creation of the EU are two examples-the former was negative and the latter positive.

Like Germany, in its institutional design France wished to play the leading role in the integration of Europe. The most prominent achievement of France lies in its contribution to the development of the EU. On May 9,1950, French foreign minister Robert Schuman proposed his plan for the creation of the European Coal and Steel Community (namely "Schuman Plan"). On April 18,1951,the six countries-France, Italy, West German, Netherlands, Belgium and Luxemburg signed the *Treaty Establishing the European Coal and Steel Community* (also known as "Treaty of Paris") which would be effective for 50 years. On April 8,1965, the aforesaid six countries signed the *Brussels Treaty*, deciding to combine the European Coal and Steel Community, the European Atomic Energy Community and the European Economic Community into what later became known collectively as the European Communities (EC). The *Brussels Treaty* came into force on July 1,1967 and the EC were officially established. On December 11, 1991, the EC meeting in Maastricht of the heads of state adopted the *Treaty on European Union* (commonly known as "Maastricht Treaty") for establishing the "European Economic and Monetary Union" and the "European Political Union". The *Maastricht Treaty* was officially signed by the EC members on February 1, 1992, and came into force on November 1, 1993, replacing the EC with the EU. The unitary currency of the EU, the euro, began to be officially in use from January 1,1999 in 11 EU countries-Austria, Belgium, France, Germany,

Finland, Netherlands, Luxemburg, Ireland, Italy, Portugal and Spain, replaced the national currencies of these countries on January 1, 2002. Both the EC and the subsequent EU were headquartered in the capital of Belgium, Brussels.

In 2010, the membership of the EU with "France-German Axis" being its mainstay swelled to 27 countries. Now the EU is a cross-border political and economic union covering 4.322 million square kilometers and with a population of 500 million and GDP of 14.5 trillion euros, and a "country-like" multinational organization with its own constitution, institutions such as parliament, court of justice and court of auditors, and positions such as chairman and foreign ministers.

On the design and development of the EU Constitution, the designers (including those from France) showed their capabilities of management innovation. For example, on voting mechanism design, the former weighted voting system was changed to the double majority voting system under which the Council of Ministers (namely Council of the European Union), when making decisions, need to obtain support both by 55% of the member countries and by regions representing 65% of the EU population; the EU has legal personality in both internal and international law (Jin Zhonghua, 2005), and so on.

Some of the important international organizations, such as UNESCO and OECD, are headquartered in France, allowing France to exert its capability of institutional design.

On national financial system design, similar to Germany, France has a "bank-led" financial system: banks and enterprises are closely connected, bank loans are the primary source of financing for enterprises, and banking assets take a bigger share than the market value of shares in the GDP. Dominant banks in France include Crédit Agricole and Crédit Lyonnais. But France' securities market is less developed than those of the United States and the UK.

1.2　System Design on Science and Technology

France officially promulgated the *Law on Innovation and Research* in 1999, with main contents including: establishing technology transfer mechanisms and strengthening cooperation between enterprises and universities; encouraging research personnel to engage in transformation of research results and found science and technology enterprises; providing preferential policies for innovative enterprises; reforming tax policies and systems in support of enterprise innovation (research tax and credit funds for the year reached a size of 3 billion francs); and founding innovation enterprise incubators and start-up funds.

In response to a downward slide in its level of science and technology, the French government promulgated the *Law for Research Planning* in February 2006, instituting the science and technology reform to tackle the adverse situation. Soon afterwards, in September 2006, the "High Council for Science and Technology" was created to "advise the President and the Government on any issue concerning national guidelines for policy on scientific research, technology transfer and innovation", whose Chairman was to be appointed by the President and serve for four years. In January 2007, the "French National Research Agency (ANR)" was used as the government's administrative body governing the bid invitation for and peer review and funding of projects from public research institutions and enterprise R&D institutions. The three main government departments responsible for the funding of scientific and technological innovation are: the ANR, the "French Agency for Industrial Innovation" (founded in January 2005) dedicated to funding the innovation activities of large enterprises and the technological innovation projects of enterprises, and the "French Agency for Innovation (ANVAR)" which supports the industrialization and commercialization of technological innovation findings of SMEs.

At the same time, in response to the new situation, France adjusted its priority areas in science and technology. The first two priority areas were: life sciences, with priority research programmes including the "Human Genome Project" and AIDS and healthcare technology programmes, to be implemented by such research institutions as universities, the French National Center for Scientific Research (CNRS) and the French National Institute of Health and Medical Research (INSERM); and space science & technology, with priority research programmes as on earth and meteorological observation, space communications, satellite positioning and navigation, to be implemented by such institutions as universities, the National Centre for Space Studies (CNES) and the CNRS. The abovementioned priority areas were followed by: energy, environment & sustainability, information & communications technology, land & air transportation and equipment, mathematics, physics and chemistry, and human and social sciences.

During 2006 ~ 2008, the French government allocated 1. 5 billion euros to its "Competitiveness Clusters" initiative (designed to bring together regional enterprises and research institutions to co-develop innovation projects) introduced in 2005, establishing 71 competitiveness clusters-17 of them were international competitiveness clusters involving such fields as nanotechnology and aviation & aerospace technology and 54 were national competitiveness clusters. In September 2007, the French Prime Minister announced that the reduction of tax on research credits would increase to 100% from previously 50% (this means that an enterprise pays tax after deducting all its R&D investment from its business turnover).

After Nicolas Sarkozy took office as the President of France in May 2007, his administration formulated a new policy on science and technology. In July 2009, the French Ministry of Higher Education and Research published the *National Research and Innovation Strategy* ("*Strategy*" below). The *Strategy* begins with a rationale statement that "research and innovation represent the first steps to be undertaken to come out of the current economic downturn and the country has no choice but to invest in the future through the development of research and innovation".

Then it gives an account of the current situation of science and technology in France: France is the world's 5th scientific power and excels in several areas-mathematics, physics, nuclear, space, agronomy and archaeology.

But the problem confronting France is this: since the beginning of the 21st century, France's share in European industry has been on the decline due to inadequate investment in research and innovation, especially the private sector's inadequate investment in R&D; its ranking both in the European patents system and the US patent system has been dropping since 1994; the relationship between public research institutions, universities and enterprises is not close enough; and there is inadequate mobility of researchers.

The *Strategy's* five guiding principles are: fundamental research as a political choice; research geared towards society and the economy; better consideration of the risks and the need for security; importance of human and social sciences within the strategy; and multidisciplinarity-an essential part of modern research.

France's research and innovation system has three functions: policy making-formulation and implementation of the national policy; programming-defining priorities and allocating resources as planned; and research and innovation—the production, distribution and value appreciation of knowledge. To make the research and innovation system become an innovation ecosystem, there is the need to evaluate this system, intensify the development of tax exemption plans and venture capital channels for enterprise R&D, encourage the opening of innovation infrastructure and strengthen cooperation.

The *Strategy* lays particular emphasis on "priority areas", which is in fact an institutional design on scientific and technological development. The priority areas include both areas of excellence and emerging areas. The *Strategy's* definition of the three priority areas is very creative. They are a group of scientific and technological subject clusters, which not only include advantageous subjects but also reflect the main directions of national development.

(1) Health, welfare, food and biotechnology

Health, covering prolonged life expectancy, disease treatment and healthcare, is of top concern of society and its citizens. With one European in every four aged over 60 in 2010, the growth rate of this age category already stands at 7% per year. Particularly, as France's research findings in the field of health technology are seldom adopted by enterprises, making it difficult to extend research findings, and the cooperation between enterprises, universities and research institutions is insufficient, it is necessary to further develop various existing clusters (for example, research and higher education clusters, and integrated science parks) and develop interdisciplinarity (for example, mathematical and digital modeling of biological processes).

(2) Environmental urgency and eco-technology

This includes such issues as climate change, the depletion of resources and the erosion of biodiversity. These aspects concern such vital issues as human survival environments and food production, and if scientific and technological problems in these fields are well addressed, there will be tremendous economic potential and development opportunity. At the same time, this also involves France's traditional research fields such as energy research (nuclear energy and hydrocarbons) and agricultural research, which entails interdisciplinarity. For example, building an integrated mode of various types of resources requires the provision of various data models by research in water, soil, terrestrial, aquatic, marine and coastal fields. France's key research areas for the current stage are nuclear, photovoltaic solar energy, second-generation bio-fuels and ocean energy.

(3) Information, communication and nanotechnology

This area is the source of changes in modern society. For example, the high-speed Web 2.0 has already played a significant role in the production and distribution of knowledge. This area is vital for the development of France in aviation and aerospace, defense, health and energy. France's key development directions in this area are: the Internet of Things, hardware and software integration, nanotechnology and software. This is because France has already felt the pressures from India and China in the field of software. At the same time, the cooperation in research between France's two main research organizations—the National Centre for Scientific Research and the National Institute for Information and Automation Research (French Ministry of Higher Education and Research, 2009).

At the same time, France has also actively participated in the formulation of the EU's scientific and technological institutions, for example, the EU's research programmes which covered five-year periods, Joint Research Centre and European Research Area. In April 1985, the then French President Francois Mittererand proposed promoting technology cooperation between European countries, which led to the creation of the "EUREKA". The EU's research programs which covered five-year periods were what later became known as "Framework Programmes for Research and Technological Development" ("Framework Programmes"); the ongoing Framework Programme is the seventh of its type. Generally speaking, the Framework Programmes have been designed to: gain leadership in key scientific and technology areas through collaboration of laboratories; stimulate the creativity and excellence of European research; enhance the creativity of fundamental research; make Europe most attractive to top-notch talents; build a research foundation in the interest of Europe; and coordinate national research programmes.

2. Innovation Management

2.1 R&D Management at Research Institutions and Enterprises

2.1.1 French National Center for Scientific Research and Carnot Institutes

French National Center for Scientific Research (CNRS) is similar to the China's CAS in function, structure and status, and it can be classified as a "quasi-academy of sciences."

The CNRS, founded in 1939, is the largest governmental research organization in France, under the administration of the French Ministry of Higher Education and Research. The highest authority of the CNRS is the Board of Trustees, consisting of 20 persons in all—including the Chairman of the Board, three government representatives (two from the French Ministry of Higher Education and Research and one from the French Ministry of Finance), four science and technology representatives, four industry and business representatives, four labor representatives, and four otherwise elected persons. The Chairman of the Board is appointed by the French government, and the Director General is the head of the CNRS.

Through reform over years, the CNRS currently encompasses ten research institutes. Three of them are national institutes, including National Institute for Mathematical Sciences, National Institute of Nuclear and Particle Physics, and National Institute for Earth Sciences and Astronomy; and the other seven are: Institute of Biological Sciences, Institute of Chemistry, Institute of Ecology and Environment, Institute for Humanities and Social Sciences, Institute for Computer Sciences, Institute for Engineering and Systems Sciences, and Institute of Physics. The CNRS also carries out interdisciplinary research in the following domains: life and its social implications; information, communication and knowledge; environment, energy and sustainable development; nanosciences, nanotechnologies and materials; and astroparticles: from particles to the Universe.

The CNRS currently has 1,074 laboratories or research units, 90% of which are operated in partnership with universities and industry. These laboratories have a greater degree of openness than the institutes and laboratories of China's CAS. The CNRS has also a Strategy & Planning Department, an Office of Director General, and 19 Regional Offices.

In 2010, the CNRS employed 33,300 people, including: 25,700 CNRS tenured employees, 11,500 researchers, 14,200 engineers and support staff, 5,000 foreign researchers (including doctors and post-doctors), and 1,714 guest researchers (1,205 from European countries). Its budget for 2010 was 3.116 billion euros, of which 60 million euros came from the CNRS itself and the remainder was provided by the government. In 2009, it was awarded 3,765 patents and 1,663 contracts (www. cnrs. fr).

The French National Institute of Health and Medical Research (INSERM) is also an influential government-funded research organization in France.

From 2009 onwards, France created cross-field research coordination organizations such as the French National Alliance for Life Sciences and Health and the French National Alliance for Energy Research Coordination, in order to implement the *National Research and Innovation Strategy* with respect to the priority areas.

In 2006, France created a network of "Carnot institutes" engaging in technology transfer and promoting the collaboration between governmental institutes and enterprises. The "Carnot institutes" are administered by the French National Research Agency. Each year the French government invests 60 million euros in the "Carnot institutes" initiative. At present, the 33 "Carnot institutes" employ 13,000 researchers, and their research contracts signed with enterprises account for 45% of the country's total contracts signed between enterprises and governmental research institutions, up to 1.3 billion euros in value (MOST of China, 2010).

2.1.2   R&D at French enterprises and "competitiveness clusters"

Total, headquartered in Paris, is one of France's largest corporations. It experienced two mergers: in November 1998 it took over Belgian Petrofina to form Total Fina which in March 2000 acquired French Elf Aquitaine, and was later renamed back to Total.

As the fifth largest publicly-traded integrated international oil and gas company in the world, Total employs 96,950 people and operates in more than 130 countries throughout the world. Its sales in 2007 reached 158.7 billion euros; but according to its 2009 annual report, its sales for 2009 declined to 131.327 billion euros. The primary decision-making body of Total is the Executive Committee which has three management departments, Strategy & Risk Assessment, Finance, and Human Resources. Total engages in all aspects of the petroleum industry, including upstream operations (oil & gas exploration, development and production, LNG) and downstream operations (refining, marketing and the trading and shipping of crude oil and petroleum products).

Total also produces base chemicals (petrochemicals and fertilizers) and specialty chemicals for the industrial and consumer markets. In addition, it engages in coal mining and power generation operations. Now it is helping to secure the future of energy by progressively expanding its energy offerings and developing complementary next generation energy activities (solar, biomass and nuclear).

Nevertheless, Total's R&D investment in recent years has been unsatisfactory. As a matter of fact, most French enterprises are unsatisfactory in terms of their R&D investment positions in Europe. According to statistical analysis by the 2009 EU Industrial R&D Investment Scoreboard, in 2009, the average R&D growth rate of EU companies was 8.1%, while that of French companies was only 0.7% —far from the former. Among large companies in France, only PSA Peugeot Citroën had two-digit R&D growth—14% , with R&D investment reaching 2. 37 billion euros.

In 2005, the French government decided to build "competitiveness clusters" with the aim to promote the cooperation between governmental research institutions and enterprises and the commercialization and industrialization of enterprise R&D achievements. The French Agency for Innovation is currently responsible for organization and management of competitiveness clusters. Five years later, 71 competitiveness clusters were built throughout the country, including 7 world class competitiveness clusters, 10 world class purpose competitiveness clusters and 54 national competitiveness clusters. These competitiveness clusters have received a gross investment of 4. 3 billion euros, of which one billion euros came from national finance and 570 million euros from local government finance.

A competitiveness cluster refers to an association of the enterprises, training centers and public or private research institutions within a particular region, formed through partnership for the purpose of developing together innovation projects. Such cooperation, which is generally based on shared markets or research fields, seeks maximum complementarity of advantages necessary to improve competitiveness, in expectation of producing certain international influence. From their form and content, competitiveness clusters is similar to "high-tech development zones" in China. Currently, these French competitiveness clusters house a total of 5,000 enterprises— mostly innovative SMES plus over 500 foreign enterprises, have more than 10,000 researchers, and carried out 2,000 planned innovation projects (Fig. 5-1).

In fact, early in the 1980s and 1990s, France established four forms of regional technology transfer system: regional innovation and technology transfer centers, regional advisory network, regional technology-intensive zones and regional research and technology institutes. The then largest regional technology-intensive zone was the Sophia Antipolis Science & Technology Park (Zhou Jizhong, 1993), the predecessor of today's competitiveness clusters. This indicates the continuity and development of France's strategy and policy for scientific and technological innovation.

Like China's high-tech development zones, France's competitiveness clusters differ in level of development from region to region. According to an evaluation conducted at the end of 2008 by The Boston Consulting Group (BCG) and CM International with regard to the competitiveness clusters in France, of the 71 competitiveness clusters, only 39 had realized their development objectives, and 13 weakest ones were still far away

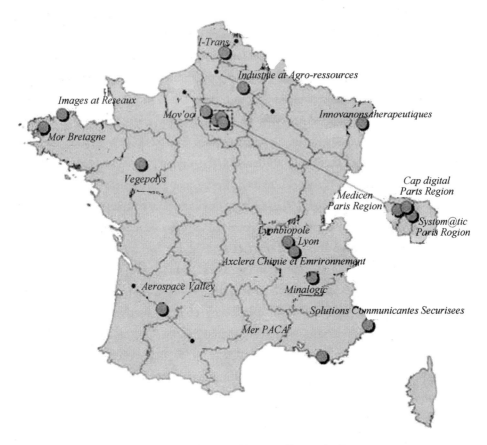

Fig. 5-1　Map of Competitiveness Clusters in France.

Source: Website of the Consulate General of France in Shanghai: Map of Competitiveness Clusters in France.

from their objectives. The French Court of Audit conducted an audit of the competitiveness clusters in June 2009, and in its audit report suggested reducing the number of competitiveness clusters to increase their efficiency. Feeling intangible pressures from the French government's adjustment measures, all these competitiveness clusters are actively seeking ways of improving their management efficiency and technology transfer rates (MOST of China, 2010; Shi Liping, 2010).

2.1.3　International Thermonuclear Experimental Reactor

There are also some international scientific and technological organizations and projects established or built in France. The International Thermonuclear Experimental Reactor (ITER) is an example.

ITER is a massive science and technology project estimated to last 35 years and cost four billion euros (of which 20% is used for construction and 80% for R&D, equipment manufacturing and experimental operation. Currently the participants of this project are: the EU, China, India, Russia, Japan, South Korea, Canada and the United States. The site of ITER is at Cadarache, a small town 70 kilometers northeast of Marseilles, France. Hailed as the "artificial minisun", this international scientific research cooperation project will make technological and engineering preparations for future demonstration and commercial nuclear fusion reactors, and finally realize the goal of providing humans with endless clean energy through controlled nuclear fusion ways. In August 2007, China's National People's Congress Standing Committee ratified the *Agreement on the Establishment of the ITER International Fusion Energy Organization for the Joint Implementation of the ITER Project* signed by the Chinese government. As an important participant of this project, China has undertaken much central work of the project. The Tokamak complex groundbreaking ceremony was held in late July 2010, and the poloidal field coil winding complex is about to be constructued. It is estimated to realize the first plasma in 2019 and officially start deuterium-tritium operation in 2027.

2.2   Science and Technology Input and Output

In 2008, France's R&D expenditure was 42.7 billion euros, of which 20.6 billion euros (48.2%) came from the government and 22.1 billion euros (51.8%) from enterprises, with the ratio of R&D expenditure to GDP standing at 2.16%. To achieve the "Europe 2020" strategy proposed by the European Commission, France's ratio of R&D expenditure to GDP ought to meet the target of 3%. In fact, however, France's indicator currently only ranks 14th in Europe, and it is quite difficult for France to achieve the objective (this indicator is 2.9% in Germany, which is much nearer to the objective). In 2007, France's ratio of R&D expenditure to GDP was only 2.08%, ranking 14th in the world, and its enterprises' ratio of R&D expenditure to GDP was 1.31%, ranking 14th, too.

The French Agency for Innovation has 5.5 billion euros in supporting technological innovation activities of SMEs since September 2008, and plans to invest 60 million euros each year in support of the 33 "Carnot Institutes" aiming at technology transfer.

In 2008, France had 363,900 researchers (FTE), ranking 5th in the world.

France comes in 13th in the Economist Intelligence Unit's (EIU's) ranking of the world's "Most Innovative Countries".

France is only ranked 24th in the IMD *World Competitiveness yearbook 2010*, up 4 places from one year ago (IMD, 2010), and 15th in the World Economic Forum's *Global Competitiveness Report 2010 ~ 2011*, up 1 place from one year ago (WEF, 2010).

From 1950 to 2008, France had 17 person-time of Nobel Prize laureates, ranking 4th in the world.

In 2005 France's share of global patents for invention was 4.5%. In 2007 France had 9,642 patents for invention, ranking 8th in the world. In 2008, it published 116,233 papers on the world's three major index journals, ranking 6th in the world. In 2008, its GDP stood at 2,861.2 billion dollars, ranking 5th in the world (MOST of China, 2010). The above data shows that France, though still a scientific power, has been on the decline in terms of its status. Particularly, its national competitiveness ranks quite behind.

3. Innovation Culture

France is a country with a tradition of innovation culture. The French Enlightenment of the 18th century provided powerful ideological weapons for the later political, economic, cultural and scientific and technological development of Western countries and even countries all over the world. For example, Diderot, chief editor of *Encyclopédie*, thought highly of science and technology education, and he proposed cutting down classical subjects and giving prominence to the disciplines of mathematics, physics and chemistry. Other two representative figures of the Enlightenment were Helvetius who maintained that "men owe everything to education", and Rousseau who believed that "nature education is at the heart of science and technology education". The abovementioned figures and their treatises were instrumental in the 19th-and 20th-century development of education, culture, science and technology in France and even in Europe and the world as a whole, and still play a very much inspiring role in the present-day development of innovation culture. This also represents the French culture's contribution to the world.

Compared with other ethnic groups in the world, the French is more romantic. Therefore, "doing things unconventionally" is acclaimed in France. French apparel, cosmetics and architecture are not only fashionable but also of great individuality.

French enterprises have strong brand awareness and attach great importance to brand strategies, which enables France to set trends in these fields. Standing amid the bizarre and motley buildings in La Defense—a new district of Paris, one can have a good understanding of how strong the French innovation culture is: the perfect integration of French modern architectural styles and processes is so impressive to visitors from all over the world.

4. Comments on Innovation Management and National Strength

France used to be the world science center and has been one of the five permanent members of the UN Security Council since the founding of the UN. From its overall national strengthen in politics, economy, science and technology and military, France is still one of the world's big powers now. In Europe, the "France-Germany Axis"— supported EU makes its position in Europe instrumental. During the reign of the former President de Gaulle, the policy of administering the country independently from the United States made France characteristic in the world stage.

The French, famous for its romance, has innovation awareness and capacity, which can be seen from the Concorde developed in partnership with the UK, the Airbus aircrafts and Ariane rockets developed in cooperation with other European countries.

Nevertheless, France's national strength has been on the decline since the beginning of the 21st century due, on the one hand to the rise of developing countries such as China, India and Brazil, and on the other to its decline in R&D and innovation input and output, plus the French government's lack in institutional design of new ideas. This is noticeable from France's international rankings: its R&D expenditure/ GDP ratio only ranks 14th in Europe, and it ranks 24th in the IMD World *Competitiveness yearbook 2010*, 15th in the World Economic Forum's Global *Competitiveness Report 2010 ~ 2011*, and 13th in the Economist Intelligence Unit's (EIU's) ranking of the world's "Most Innovative Countries".

Militarily, France has armed forces of 348,000 people, including 135,000 for the army, 58,000 for the air force and 42,000 for the navy. It owns independent strategic nuclear forces-one nuclear—powered aircraft carrier and four ballistic missile submarines, as well as more than 600 military aircrafts. In 2007, France's military expenditure/GDP ratio was 2.3% (which reached 2.4% in 2008), its weapon exports amounted to 2.69 billion dollars and weapon imports to 63 million dollars (The World Bank, 2009).

Because of the politically persistent "left-right cohabitation", policy makers could hardly give full play to administration policies designed during elections and the several consecutive French governments failed to introduce ambitious policies or plans. Moreover, as the France-dominated EU and euro suffered grossly during the financial crisis and Greece's debt crisis, the country's national competitiveness has been fluctuating at a moderately high level in the world in recent years.

Chapter 6
A Stagnating Japan

Japan covers a land area of 378,000 square kilometers and has a population of 127.8 million people (2007 est.). Lacking natural resources, Japan relies on imports for nearly all important resources and energy sources. In Japan, Shintoists and Buddhists account for 49.6% and 44.8% of the religious population, respectively (Editorial Board of World Affairs, 2009). Because of lacking natural resources, Japan has a fine tradition of cherishing education, science and technology, in order to develop human resources. Vigorously developing education, science and technology has been the primary task of all governments since the Meiji Restoration. Japan's economy and national strength began growing in the 1950s—only years after its defeat in the Second World War, thrived in the 1960s, and reached its peak in the 1970s and 1980s.

In Japan, technology is more advanced than science, and business management is more developed than science and technology. It boasts a large number of noted innovation entrepreneurs, such as Konosuke Matsushita, Soichiro Honda, Masaru Ibuka, Akio Morita and Koji Kobayashi-their business management approaches and corporate cultures have benefited both Japan and the world as a whole.

From the 1990s to the present, Japan has been in an economic downturn. Nevertheless, it is the third largest economy in the present-day world (in 2010 China overtook Japan as the world's second largest economy). Japanese citizens are long-lived and enjoy a high income per capita, which however has brought about the problem of population aging. The Japanese government's prediction shows that by 2025, people aged over 65 will account for 25% of the country's total population. This, coupled with low birth rates, means a considerable reduction in Japanese labor forces, a big headache to Japan. Over the past 10 years, therefore, Japan seemed to be in a standstill compared with its previous pace of development.

1. Institutional Design

1.1　National Institutional Design

The current constitution of Japan is the *Constitution of the State of Japan* enacted in May 1947 after the Second World War. Article 9 of this constitution provides that "···the Japanese people forever renounce war as a sovereign right of the nation and the threat or use of force as means of setting international disputes. In order to accomplish the aim of the preceding paragraph, land, sea, and air forces, as well as other war potential, will never be maintained. The right of belligerency of the state will not be recognized" (Editorial Board *of World Affairs*,2009).

Japan maintains a parliamentary system with the Emperor as the symbol of the state. The Japanese constitution provides that the Emperor is the symbol of Japan, but the Emperor only has pro forma power. Japan's national political system and structure follows a parliamentary system based on the separation of legislative, judicial and executive powers. The Diet consists of two houses—the House of Councilors and the House of Representatives, both consisting of elected members. The House of Representatives plays a greater role than the House of Councilors in selecting the Prime Minister and in voting for important bills as on budget.

The Cabinet, the national highest administrative organ of Japan, is formed by the majority party with a majority of seats in the Diet. By convention, the head of the majority party in the Diet is generally the matter-of-course candidate for the Prime Minister. If no party has secured a majority of the seats in the Diet, two or more parties with the most seats will form the Cabinet, and the leader of the party with most seats will serve as the Prime Minister. The Prime Minister has the power to dissolve the House of Representatives and require general elections to be held ahead of schedule.

Japan practices a multi-party system, with political parties including the Liberal Democratic Party (LDP), Social Democratic Party (SDP), New Komeito, Democratic Socialist Party, Communist Party, Japan Renewal Party and Japan New Party. In recent years, the political ecology that the LDP had long been in the saddle changed, with the Japanese governments reigned either by the LDP together with other party or by the SDP alone, but all the Cabinets were "short-lived". One of the main reasons was "power-of-money politics". The first condition for becoming the LDP chairman was "the ability to raise money", and only by obtaining "political donations" from the financial circles could the party win the general election, be in power and repay the financial circles. This brought money and politics together closely, leading to a series of scandals. For example, in the 1970s, Lockheed Corporation bribery scandal led Prime Minister Kakuei Tanaka to fall from power; in the 1980s, the Recruit bribery scandal ruined Prime Ministers Yasuhiro Nakasone and Tanaka Kakuei; and in the 1990s, the Sagawa Kyubin corruption scandal led to the arrest of Shin Kanemaru, Vice President of the LDP.

Courts are the judicial bodies of Japan exercising the judicial powers. Seemingly, all judicial officers exercise their powers independently, who are subject only to the Japanese constitution and laws, but the long-ruling LDP often exerts its influence on the judicial bodies (Almond et al. , 2010).

In the Cabinet of Japan, the Ministry of Education, Culture, Sports, Science and Technology (MEXT) is in charge of affairs about education, science and technology.

It is generally accepted that Japan's "economic miracle" after the Second World War is attributed to the Japanese government's institutional design of moderate and effective intervention in economy (especially industry policies introduced by the former Ministry of International Trade and Industry). Some attribute it to three reasons: the Japanese government's rigorous control over the domestic market, which can be described as "strategic capitalism"; well-educated and low-cost labor forces; and open world markets (Almond et al. , 2010). Others hold that Japan obtained a great many big orders from the United States during the latter's invasion of North Korea in the 1950s, which helped Japan get out of its decline in national strength after the Second World War.

During the Cabinet restructuring when Koizumi was in power, seven restructuring programs produced great effects on scientific and technological fields: the privatization reform; establishment of asocial system to encourage individual initiative; enhanced welfare and insurance to help people enjoy security and stability; development of human capital by strengthening individual choice; social conditions that allow people to work and live at their discretion, as well as a revolution that influences lifestyles; authorization of local governments to maximally support local autonomy; and financial reforms to make the government streamlined and efficient. The effects on the educational, scientific and technological fields were: the introduction of free market mechanisms into education; the introduction of private business management models into the operation of Japanese national universities; and the increase of scholarships to students (OECD, 2006).

But the Japanese Cabinet governments were largely short-lived. Prime Minister Kakuei Tanaka (who took office in July 1972) was in power only for two years, and most of his successors ruled for two years or one year or even several months. Because of the frequent change of the Prime Minister and national elections, Japan's institutional design always lacked long-term objectives. Therefore, most of the country's institutional design lacked new ideas.

On national financial system design, similar to France and Germany, Japan has a "bank-led" financial system: banks and enterprises are closely connected, bank loans are the primary source of financing for enterprises, and banking assets take a bigger share than the market value of shares in the GDP. To improve strength, a number of Japanese banks were reorganized into four main financial groups: Mitsubishi Tokyo Financial Group (MTFG) consisting of Bank of Tokyo-Mitsubishi, Mitsubishi Trust and Banking Corporation and Nippon Trust Bank Limited; UFJ Holdings, Inc. consisting of Sanwa Bank, Tokai Bank, and Toyo Trust and Banking; Sumitomo Mitsui Financial Group (SMFG) formed with the merger of Sakura Bank and Sumitomo Bank; and Mizuho Financial Group (Mizuho) consisting of the Dai-Ichi Kangyo Bank, Fuji Bank, and Industrial Bank of Japan. But Japan's securities market is less developed than those of the United States and the UK.

1.2　System Design on Science and Technology

In 1995, the Diet of Japan enacted the *Science and Technology Basic Law*, the fundamental law providing guidelines for the Cabinet's development every five years of national science and technology policies and plans. The Japanese Council for Science and Technology Policy (CSTP) is responsible for coordinating the ministries of the Cabinet to develop the "*Science and Technology Basic Plan*" ("*Basic Plan*" below). The first *Basic Plan* was made in 1996. The CSTP is the top decision-making body in Japan for science and technology, which consists of the Prime Minister, six cabinet members heading Ministries closely related to science and technology policy, five members from academia and two from industry. The basic principles of developing the *Basic Plan* are: optimization of resource allocation to improve R&D capacity; improvement of R&D infrastructure; repayment of R&D investment to society and industry; and scientific and technological contribution to world knowledge. Japan's priority areas for science and technology development are: life sciences, information and telecommunications, environmental sciences, nanotechnology, and materials science and technology.

In 2007, the Japanese government published two strategic reports. One is "*Innovation 2025*" published in February, which selected a range of policy study subjects, such as "pulling out of the economic crisis and initiating the powerhouse of world economy growth", "doubling investment in information technology", "promoting the reform of universities", and "promoting the scientific and technological restructuring for national prosperity". Another is "*Strategic Technology Roadmap*

2007" published in April by the Ministry of Economy, Trade and Industry and other relevant ministries, which selected 25 sub-sectors of 5 main areas-information and communications, life sciences, energy and environment, nanotechnology and materials, and manufacturing.

Ministries closely related to science and technology policy are: Ministry of Education, Culture, Sports, Science and Technology (MEXT; with a 64% share of government R&D investment), Ministry of Economy, Trade and Industry (METI, the former Ministry of International Trade and Industry; with a 16.9% share of government R&D investment), Ministry of Defence (with a 4.1% share of government R&D investment), Ministry of Health, Labour and Welfare (MHLW; with a 3.6% share of government R&D investment), Ministry of Agriculture, Forestry and Fisheries (MAFF; with a 3.5% share of government R&D investment), and Ministry of Land, Infrastructure, Transport and Tourism (MLIT; with a 2.3% share of government R&D investment).

The Japan Science and Technology Agency (JST) and the Japan Society for the Promotion of Science (JSPS) are primary academic funding organizations in Japan.

2. Innovation Management

2.1 Science & Technology Development Strategies at Enterprises

Japan's market economy is also known as "corporation market economy", indicating private enterprises play a dominant role in Japan's economic development. From the science and technology strategy perspective, it means that Japan's private enterprises play a leading role in the country's R&D. In Japan, private enterprises are responsible for some 80% of the country's R&D funding. Most Japanese enterprises attach importance to R&D. On the whole, Japanese high-tech enterprises are world leaders both in R&D expenditure and patents for invention. Representative Japanese companies are Panasonic, Sony, Hitachi, Sharp, Toyota, Honda, NEC, and Canon, etc.

Case: The patent development strategy of Sony

After the he Second World War, Japanese industrialist Masaru Ibuka founded Tokyo Tsushin Kogyo K. K. (Tokyo Telecommunications Engineering Corporation) in Tokyo, Japan in 1946, which was renamed as Sony Corporation in 1958.

As early as in the late 1940s, Sony began developing tape recorders, and purchased the JPO (Japanese Patent Office)-granted patent for the method of high-cycle AC bias voltage which had been invented by Japanese experts in 1940. With this patented technology, Sony successfully developed tape recorders in 1950. Its then tape recorder production was one third of Japan's total. Nearly at the same time, Americans invented this method, too, and had it patented in the United States. After learning that a US company was to export tape recorders to Japan, Sony, on the grounds that "if first awarded in Japan, a Japanese patent has the right to prohibit the import of foreign taper recorders", requested the Japanese court to ban the US company from exporting to, selling, using, exhibiting or transporting US-made tape recorders in Japan. On September 15, 1952, the court consented to Sony's request and banned the import of American tape recorders. But this US company had obtained from the Japanese government an import permit before which was confined to such general supplies as stationery and automatic parts to foreigners in Japan, rather than an import permit for electric products, its tape recorders finally entered the Japanese market. Sony brought an action to the US military headquarters in Japan on the grounds that Sony had first registered the patent and American tape recorders were beyond the scope of business, and finally won the case.

In 1947, scientist John Bardeen et al. at Bell laboratories-then a division of Western Electric Company—invented the transistor whose patent was held by Western Electric Company. Four years later, Ibuka visited the United States and decided to purchase the monopoly right of the transistor. In 1953, as instructed by Ibuka, Akio Morita went to the United States and signed the deal with Western Electric Company buying the patent for 100,000 dollars. In the subsequent development, Ibuka came up with the concept of "micromation" (core competitiveness of Sony), and in 1955 Sony produced Japan's first pocket-sized transistor radio, TR- 63, and created the record of 500,000 units exported to foreign countries. In the meanwhile, when an agency of a famous US brand wanted to make a deal with Sony on the condition of labeling the latter's products with a US company's trademark, Sony refused on the grounds that if Sony gave up its own trademark in exchange for temporary profits there would never be a future Sony.

Sony didn't enter the field of color televisions until the 1960s, when it purchased through patent license trade a patent (without prototype) for a new type of color television. Through research and development, Sony produced a new type of color television by changing the single electron gun in the patent to three guns. Sony used this improvement to compete with Radio Corporation of America (RCA). In 1968,

Sony released its KV-1310B Trinitron color televisions and defeated RCA (Ma Xiushan, 2001).

In early 21st century, Nobuyuki Idei, then Chairman of Sony, changed Sony's independent R&D strategy set by Ibuka and Morita, and instead pursued his "bringing strategy" that "it is more efficient to buy technologies from other companies than to spend time developing technologies". Sony has been seeing decline, because on the one hand Sony expanded its motion picture and game business, while on the other it slashed its R&D investment. In 2002, Sony fell behind Canon in digital appliances; Apple's iPod took the lead in portable music players; on such fronts as SED displays, Sony lacked core technologies, too; on LED displays, Sony could only accept supplies by Samsung. The primary reason for these was the fall of capabilities of technological innovation and innovative product manufacturing.

From Sony's case we can see how important an R&D strategy is to a high-tech company.

2.2 Science and Technology Development Strategies at Universities and Research Institutions

Japan has 649 universities, including 99 national universities, 72 local public universities and 478 private universities. There are a small number of scientific research academies and institutes that belong to the central government of Japan, and they employ some 16,000 researchers in all. The most influential are the Institute of Physical and Chemical Research (RIKEN) which operates as a Special Public Research Corporate, and the Japan Atomic Energy Agency (JAEA). The scientific research academies and institutes which belong to local Japanese governments have some 15,000 researchers in all, about 50% of whom engage in agricultural research.

Part of the Japanese governmental organization reform started in 2001 was to convert government-funded research institutions and universities into "Independent Administrative Institutions (IAIs)" and "National University Corporations", and to slash administrative personnel with the remainder no longer serving as civil servants. A portion of national universities will become research universities.

Compared with the United States and Germany, the university-industry cooperation in Japan is not close.

RIKEN is the largest natural sciences research institution in Japan. It conducts research in many areas of science, including physics, chemistry, biology, engineering, medical science, life sciences, material science, nanotechnology and information science, covering the entire range from basic research to practical application. Founded in March 1917 as a private foundation, RIKEN is the earliest of its kind, funded by a combination of the Imperial Household, the government and industry. It is now an IAI. Similar to GOCO research establishments in the United States and the UK, an IAI is funded primarily by the government but manages its operations at its discretion.

With some 3,000 researchers, each year RIKEN has a budget of about 6.2 billion yuan and publishes about 2,300 papers. Similar to China's CAS in some ways, RIKEN has no educational organization like CAS Graduate University, but conducts high-end research intensively.

2.3   Innovation Management at Enterprises

(1) Management innovation and R&D of Toyota

The Japanese economy took off in the 1960s but suffered heavily from the oil crisis in the 1970s. Japanese enterprises' "crisis management" emerged in this context, with the countermeasures of carrying out management innovation and introducing a series of creative management methods which would be welcomed worldwide. Below is an account of two management methods introduced by Toyota.

One is "Just-in-time" (JIT), introduced by Toyota Motor Corporation. Driven by orders, JIT combines the processes of supply, production and distribution closely through Kanban (client requirements) to considerably reduce material reserves, inventories and finished products, lower costs, improve productivity and increase profits. To achieve JIT, an enterprise needs to carry out three reforms.

The first is organizational reform. For this purpose, it is necessary to organize work units into flexible teams; establish efficient acceptance processes and shorten processes for work in progress; re-formulate quality control standards; and re-establish the transportation system.

The second is interaction with suppliers. To ensure that suppliers' materials or goods arrive at the production line at the right time, the enterprise needs not only to precisely formulate its production processes, procurement schedules and transportation processes, but also to have knowledge of the suppliers' production plans, so that there is close long-term cooperation between the buyer and the suppliers.

The third is the availability of a punctual transportation system. For this purpose, the buyer and the suppliers must agree on shipment, transportation, delivery and acceptance. The enterprise should adjust its organizational structure in support of the transportation system, and have a controlled number of freight forwarders which employ automatic packing equipment.

The three reforms all rely on computer-based management. JIT enables zero inventory, cost reduction, and the maximal reduction of waste.

JIT is appropriate for both manufacturing and logistics sectors.

The other is "Lean production" (LP), an innovative management achievement developed by Toyota and summarized by a professor at Massachusetts Institute Technology (MIT). The LP philosophy is to get ride of all those enterprise activities which waste human, material and financial resources or add no value, and to maintain high-level quality by which to improve competitiveness. Therefore, an enterprise' LP system is built on three pillars-JIT, TQM (total quality management) and GT (group technology), which runs under support of a computer network and relying on concurrent working and grouping. Different from mass production, LP stresses continuous price reduction, zero defects, zero inventories and varieties of products. To achieve this, it is necessary to: improve the flow of production, eliminate multitudinous quality testing processes and reworking phenomena, and eliminate from the product design stage the quality problems which later might happen (namely, concurrent working); eliminate unnecessary movements of parts and components, and consider each process of production layout from the very beginning, with the aim to save production time; eliminate inventories, and change "batch production and queuing supply" to "one-piece flow" i. e. , only one work piece moves between working procedures; improve production activities, reduce the time for production preparation, eliminate stop time, and carry out overall productive maintenance (routine maintenance, predictive maintenance, preventive maintenance and immediate maintenance) to reduce waste; and improve labor productivity, including direct labor productivity and indirect labor productivity.

JIT and LP can be applied in any manufacturing enterprise and in some service enterprises (for example, in e-commerce, JIT is used to reduce logistics costs) (GEC Program, 2003).

Toyota not only stresses management innovation, but also invests tremendously in R&D. In 1984 ~ 1989, its R&D expenditure increased from 750 million dollars to 2. 2 billion dollars, up to 5% of its sales-slightly higher than that of GM and Ford at the time.

In the 1980s and 1990s, Toyota generally only took 3 ~ 4 years to develop a new model of cars, while it took about seven years and ten years for Volkswagen and Mercedes-Benz respectively to do the same. During this period, to manufacture more automobile dies, Toyota developed an automatic die manufacturing procedure, in which the computer-operated machine tool could produce high-precision dies rapidly. The body panels produced by Toyota's punches were so precise in contour that parts and components could generally be placed in due positions just right without the help of a welding gun. According to a survey by researchers at University of Michigan, Toyota's costs for designing and manufacturing dies and punches were a half and even two thirds lower than those at GM, Ford and DaimlerChrysler.

Toyota's R&D capacity and management innovation brought out the best in each other, which improved the company's competitiveness greatly. For example, the above-described JIT approach entailed the in-time delivery of parts and components to the production line, while Toyota's technological development division already designed a great variety of automobile models of various sizes, with each specification including several variations such as double, three, four and five-door fast back cars and hatchback cars.

In addition, Toyota pays great attention to employee training. Its employee training time generally doubles that of a European automaker, but the employees have a lower error rate and make more rationalization proposals. According to statistics, it would only take 19 hours for Toyota to make a limousine, while Mercedes-Benz would spend the same time correcting errors on the assembly line. The workers of Toyota made about 60 rationalization proposals a year on average, while the workers of its European counterparts only made one piece of improvement advice a year on the average (Zhou Jizhong, 1993).

Toyota's technological innovation methods in those years are summarized by some as below: frequent business trips and video conferences combined Toyota's R&D systems into one whole; the satellite-structured new product development system gave concurrent consideration to technological development and project management, linked specialization and skill distribution together, and identified the sources of defects through every complaint of customers; training and job rotation confronted every engineer to customers (Sigvald Harryson, 2004).

(2) Core technological competitiveness of NEC

NEC was founded in 1899 in Tokyo. By 1967, integrated circuits had become one of the main operations of NEC whose sales ranked number one in Japan and ahead worldwide. Kunihiko Iwadare, the founder of NEC, was an entrepreneur of innovation spirit. In 1964, Kobayashi Koji who had joined NEC in 1929 immediately after his graduation from Tokyo Imperial University Department of Electric Engineering, became President of NEC. The same year, after reading *The Production and Distribution of Knowledge in the United States*, a book by Fritz Machlup at Princeton University, Koji conceived the thought that knowledge is the foundation of an enterprise's technological competitiveness. In 1966, at a meeting of the Institute of Electrical Engineers of Japan, Koji gave a reported titled "The Position of Japan's Knowledge Industry and Electronic Industry", which described NEC's three lines of business: communication-transmitting information, computer-processing information, semiconductor-underpinning communication and semiconductor. This "knowledge industry" thought was quite advanced at the time, 30 years ahead of *The Knowledge-based Economy*, a noted book written and published by OECD in 1996. In 1977, at the INTELCOM' 77 in Atlanta, Koji put forward his concept of "C&C" or "integration of computer and communications technologies". C&C (computer and communication) represented not only the technological innovation strategy of NEC but also its core competitiveness. C&C represented NEC's innovation culture, too, conveying such a message: communication technologies eliminated the time and space restrictions on human abilities of information transmission, while computer technologies eliminated restrictions on abilities of information generation, processing and storage; the integration of both greatly broadened human capacities for creation of knowledge and thus ushered in the information age.

From the 1980s, NEC had a C&C Committee consisting of executives which was responsible for integration and coordination of communication and computer operations and for research and development. On communication technologies, NEC focused on digital switching systems, optical fiber communication and mobile communication; on computer technologies, it focused on supercomputers, microcomputers, software and system integration, industrial electronic systems and multimedia; on electronics, it focused on memories, integrated circuits, electronic parts and components, and semiconductors (Fig. 6-1). NEC's technological competitiveness enhanced its corporate competitiveness. In nearly 20 years, NEC's sales grew from 3. 8 billion dollars in 1980 to 41. 1 billion dollars in 1996, and its R&D expenditure reached 6. 8% of its sales (Zhou Jizhong, 2002).

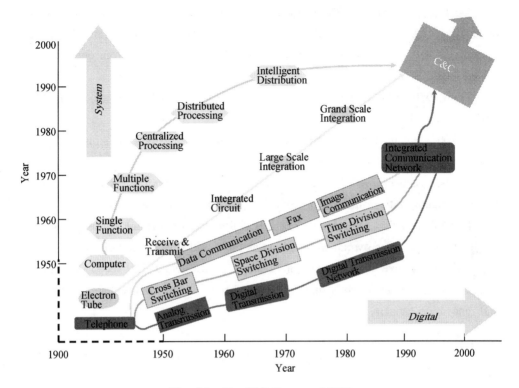

Fig. 6-1　The C&C Strategy of NEC

Source: *Computer and Communication*, Koji Kobashi.

Today's new concepts of NEC such as C&C Foundation, C&C Research Laboratories and C&C Cloud are all an extension of Koji's strategic thought of C&C.

2.4　Science and Technology Input and Output

In Japan, enterprises are the primary body of R&D funding, and they have contributed to 70% ~ 80% of the country's total R&D funding for consecutive many years. This is the resource guarantee of Japan's high transformation rate of scientific & technological achievements.

In 2007, Japan's R&D expenditure was 148.4 billion dollars (ranking 2nd in the world, behind only the United States' 368.8 billion dollars), 3.40% of the GDP (ranking 4th in the world, behind Israel's 4.68%, Sweden's 3.64% and Finland's 3.47%). Enterprise R&D expenditure reached 114.496 billion dollars, ranking 2nd in the world. The same year, Japan had 935,200 reseachers (FIE), behind only China (1.736 million person-years).

Japan is only ranked 27th in the IMD *World Competitiveness Yearbook 2010*, down 10 places from one year ago (IMD, 2010), and 6th in the World Economic Forum's *Global Competitiveness Report 2010 ~ 2011*, up 2 places from one year ago (WEF, 2010).

From 1950 to 2008, Japan had 9 person-time of Nobel Prize laureates, ranking 6th in the world.

In 2007, Japan had 127,644 patents for invention awarded, ranking 1st in the world.

In 2008, Japan published 154,739 papers on the world's three major index journals, ranking 5th in the world (MOST of China, 2010).

In 2008, Japan's GDP reached 4,906.9 billion dollars, ranking 2nd in the world, but in 2010 Japan was overtaken by China as the world's 3rd largest economy.

From the above data, though in a stage of economic decline, Japan still is counted as one of the world's most powerful for its science and technology strength and innovation capacity.

3. Innovation Culture

Japan has a quite plentiful innovation culture. Below is an account of only several aspects of it.

The first is "daring to take risks, and tolerance for failure". This is an important part of the Japanese innovation culture, and a spirit, too, which the Chinese culture lacks and in dire need of. A question deserving of deep consideration is how far we are away from this point in our work, in our teaching and in our project review.

Japan has made a deserving innovative step towards developing people's quality of "daring to take risks, and tolerance for failure". In July 2000, the Japan Science and Technology Agency founded the Association for the Study of Failure. It is stated in a June 2000 report by the "Symposium on Science and Technology in the 21st Century" that much of new knowledge, new discoveries and new technologies are built on repeated failures, that knowledge can be gained for sure from accidents and failures, and that viewing lessons thus learned as the shared property of society will be an effective means to improve technological reliability. The report suggests gathering various cases of accidents and failures to build a teaching database, and applying them to such aspects as R&D and production management, thus building a "science of failure". The mission of the Association for the Study of Failure is to build a "science of failure", and gather accidents and failures in the field of science and technology together to form a "resource of knowledge" from which to learn valuable experience. It will engage experts and scholars in such fields as science and technology, psychology, law and enterprise quality management as members of it carry out failure research. The teaching database was initially created in 2002, covering such fields as machinery, materials, chemistry and civil engineering (Zhou Jizhong, 2002).

The golden saying "Failure is the mother of success" is both qualitative and quantitative. Rough statistics reveal that only 2 ~ 3 out of 10 venture business projects which venture capital firms invested in were successful, with a failure rate of up to 70% ~ 80%. Therefore, venture capital investment can also be described as willing to take risks. It is just because of this that many firms in Silicon Valley provides in their articles of association that carping comments on new thoughts and new ideas are not allowed. In fields and industries where there is tense competition, most venture businesses are bound to fail. To put it another way, the order that "failure will not be tolerated" not only goes against the laws of development, but also fails to have a good understanding of what "failure" is.

The second is "combinational innovation", including combinational technologies and approaches. The above-described Toyota's LP approach is just a system management approach which first combines three methods-JIT, TQM and GT and then combines computer network, concurrent working and grouping. NEC's C&C is also an approach of combination of computer and communication. The combination of technologies can be found everywhere. As combinational technologies and approaches can better promote the commercialization and industrialization of products both in content and form, they can be used to explain why Japan's scientific and technological innovation could greatly boost its economic and national strength.

The third is "field management". Japanese enterprises' notion of "viewing the plant as a laboratory" is another reflection of their innovation culture, i. e. so-called "field operation". Enterprise R&D and field operation are closely linked. Field management also includes "Management by Walking Around." at HP.

The fourth is "eagerness to learn and ask". The Japanese do well in learning from foreigners. Japanese enterprises are willing to invest human and financial resources in learning opportunities such as making visits and participating in conferences. Even enterprises and universities are willing to learn from each other. In

Japan, for example, technical and intelligence personnel are enthusiastic about browsing patent documents, so Japanese enterprises do very well in R&D and commercial intelligence. In this regard, Japan keeps ahead of other countries and has already formed a good tradition of innovation culture.

4. Comments on Innovation Management and National Strength

Japan is an island nation with meager natural resources. It has had the tradition of attaching importance to education, science and technology since the Meiji Restoration. Early in 1910, Japan's educational investment already accounted for 3% of its national income. By the 1950s, this ratio had reached 8.4% (Zhou Jizhong, 1993). Its R&D expenditure/GDP ratio has been over 3% in recent years. These indicators come out top worldwide. It is thus obvious that Japan not only has a long tradition of attaching importance to education, science and technology but also willingly invest in them. These are the two major pillars of Japan's "economic miracle", the source of management innovation and science and technology innovation in Japan. The series of management innovation Japan created in the 1980s astonished and benefited the world. Japan takes pride in its innovation entrepreneurs such as Konosuke Matsushita, Koji Kobayashi, Soichiro Honda, Masaru Ibuka and Akio Morita-whose achievements have not only been written in MBA textbooks but also the spiritual wealth of human civilization.

Due to shortage of natural resources, Japan has relied on foreign trade for national development all through the ages. In 2009, Japan's exports amounted to 580.79 billion dollars and imports to 552.25 billion dollars, with foreign trade totaling 1,133.04 billion dollars. Its foreign trade with China totaled 228.85 billion dollars, 20.2%, about 1/5 of its total foreign trade; its exports to China amounted to 97.9 billion dollars, 16.9% of its total exports, and its imports from China amounted to 130.94 billion dollars, 23.7% (about 1/4) of its total imports (Li Wei, 2010). It is obvious that Japan's trade with China or Sino-Japan trade has great significance for both Japanese and Chinese economy.

Constrained by its defeat during the Second World War, Japan's military is currently organized by the Japanese Self-Defense Forces (JSDF). The JSDF, with a fixed number of 257,000 solders, actually numbers 242,000 with 149,000 in the Ground Self-Defense Force, 45,700 in the Maritime Self-Defense Force and 47,000 in the Air Self-Defense Force (Editorial Board *of World Affairs*, 2009). In 2007, Japan's military expenditure/GDP ratio was 0.9% (it was up to 1.0% in 2008), and its weapon imports amounted to 519 million dollars (The World Bank, 2009).

Entering the 21st century, Japan has seen political turbulence and economic recession, leading to a decline in its national strength. This is attributed partly to Japan's export-dominated economic structure, which makes it vulnerable to global economic crises. The ongoing financial crisis has made Japan's exports shrink. Flaws in Japan's political system design have also contributed to the consequence. Some of Japanese policies inhibit competition (Porter, 2007). For example, among other things, the "basically lifetime employment system" that some Japanese enterprises adopt for their employees, and excessive protection policies towards medical care and other industries, have made Japan unable to compete with advanced countries.

In 2010, Japan was overtaken by China to become the world's third largest economy. With its tradition of attaching importance to education, science and technology and of innovation spirit, Japan still has the conditions for reversing its decline.

Chapter 7

A Declining Italy

Italy, officially the Italian Republic, covers an area of 301,200 square kilometers, and has a population of 59.13 million-most of the citizens are Italian speaking the language of Italian. Lacking natural resources, Italy relies on import for much of natural resources and energy sources. Most of the citizens have faith in Roman Catholicism (Editorial Board of World Affairs,2009). Italy has an admirable history. The ancient Roman Empire lasted nearly a millennium. The Renaissance, which spanned the 14th to the 17th century, originated in Italy and spread throughout Europe, producing worldwide influence. During this period, representative Italian figures in literature and arts included the poet Dante, the painters Michelangelo and Raphael, and the writer Boccaccio, who are acclaimed as the pacesetters. In the period from the 14th to the 17th century, the Italian scientists, notably Vinci and Galileo, inaugurated a brand-new era of experimental science, and the world's first modern science center came into being in Italy.

Italy became industrialized in the 1950s and 1960s and realized an economic takeoff in the 1970s, with economy and national strength at levels of developed countries. It boasts many world famous brands in such fields as fashion, furniture and leather, and takes pride in renowned fashion designers as Giorgio Armani and Gianni Versace. The Italian tourism and agriculture are also quite developed. In the field of science and technology, Italy has had 19 Nobel Prize laureates, including the radio telegraph system inventor Guglielmo Marconi and the physicist Enrico Fermi. Italy also enjoys worldwide recognition in such fields as silk dyeing and finishing, leather bating, machining and robot manufacturing.

Since the 1990s, however, Italy has been on the decline in economy, science and technology, thanks to the severe brain drain, especially its R&D investment remaining low for years in a row. Italy is a typical developed country that has changed from rise to fall.

1. Institutional Design

1.1　National Institutional Design

The current constitution of Italy was enacted by the Constituent Assembly in December 1947 after the Second World War, and promulgated in 1948.

French is a parliamentary republic. The head of government is the prime minister elected by the political part with most seats in the parliament or by the parties that form the Council of Ministers together, who has the real power. The Chamber of Deputies and the Senate have equal powers, with members elected by universal and direct suffrage. Italy has a multi-party system, with main parties including The People of Freedom, Democratic Party, Northern League, and Union of the Center.

Within the Italian government, the Inter-ministerial Committee for Economic Planning (CIPE), founded in 1967, has the primary function of formulating national economic development plans; CIPE also has some other functions, for example, participating in the formulation of national scientific and technological development plans and in the auditing of annual budgets for science and technology. The Ministry of Education, University and Research (MIUR) of Italy, which was established in 2001, administers the country's educational, scientific and technological affairs and formulates national research plans and national development strategies.

1.2 System Design on Science and Technology

In Italy, government departments for institutional design on science and technology are the CIPE and the MIUR, with participation of the National Research Council (CNR), the Italian National Agency for New Technologies, Energy and the Environment (ENEA), the Lincean Academy (Accademia Nazionale dei Lincei), etc.

The Italian government has developed a series of scientific and technological development plans over the first decade of the 21st century. In 2002, the Italian government announced the National Science and Technology Policy Guidelines, and raised the national science and technology development strategy by which to vigorously strengthen the building of a knowledge-based economy and a national innovation system, enhance the capacity for industrial innovation and promote the close connection between science and technology and the market, thereby contributing to economic growth and employment growth. In 2004, the MIUR submitted the National Research Plan for 2004 ~ 2006 in which the basic research, R&D of key technologies, industrial R&D and high-tech enterprise clusters are used as axes to improve the country's competitiveness and innovation capacity.

Italy's science and technology development plans include national research plans, CNR plans, aerospace plans, big science plans, action plans for sustainable development and for an information society, etc.

In Italy, SMEs dominate in its industrial pattern. On institutional design on science and technology, the Italian government has promulgated a series of policies and laws to promote innovation at SMEs, mainly including: the national applied research fund law enacted in 1968 to support technology import and innovation in national traditional industries (such as textile, apparel, leather, and marble processing), to which the law No. 67 of 1998 added that 10% of applied research funding could be used for technical training; the economic invention law enacted in 1982 to established a revolving fund for technological innovation in support of the transfer of innovative technologies of SMEs and an industrial research center in support of industrialization and commercialization of research findings; the laws No. 140 and 449 on R&D activities and tax credit enacted in 1997 to adopt a "tax credit" policy towards enterprise R&D activities, i. e. deducting enterprise R&D expenditure pro rata from payable tax, notably for small enterprises; the decree No. 593 on R&D support issued in 2000 to fund projects to be supported as a result of evaluation or negotiation or automatically; and the law No. 326 on enterprise R&D support enacted in 2003 to give a government subsidy up to 10% of enterprise R&D expenditure.

Italy's economic policy has been described as "state capitalism" or "government-intervened market economy" by Western scholars. As a defeated country of the Second World War, the Italian government reorganized the so-called four national industrial groups after the war: ENI based on oil and energy, IRI based on manufacturing, EFIM based on finance, and ENEL based on power.

On building an environment for scientific and technological innovation, the Italian government founded a business development promotion company SPI which develops, implements and manages innovation plans for industrial promotion and helps build enterprise innovation centers. In 2000, SPI and 6 state-owned enterprises formed a national development company SI with the aim to further promote technological innovation at enterprises.

Since the Trieste AREA Science Park-Italy's first science park—was established under the President Order No. 102 of 1978, more than 30 science parks have been built throughout the country, whose main functions are to incubate high-tech enterprises and strengthen enterprises' technological competitiveness, the connection of technologies with markets, and the combination of universities and enterprises (Han Jun, 2005).

2. Innovation Management

2.1 Scientific Research Organizations

The most important scientific research organization in Italy is the National Research Council (CNR). The CNR is the largest comprehensive research organization of Italy, which also undertakes the duty of science and technology management. It was founded in 1923 and was transformed into a public body in 1945. Since the MIUR created in 1979 became the government department responsible for the country's science and technology affairs, CNR has been a comprehensive research organization which focuses on academic research and is in charge of science and technology management. The CNR originally had 314 institutes which were later reorganized into 108 institutes. These institutes conduct research in five areas: basic research, life sciences, earth and environment sciences, social and human sciences and technologies, and engineering and information sciences. The CNR employs more than 8,000 people, including over 4,000 researchers, nearly 3,000 technical staff and more than 1,000 management personnel. Similar to China's CAS in structure and function, the CNR can be classified as a "quasi-academy of sciences". In fact, there are other "quasi-academies" in the world, for example, the Max Planck Society (MPG) in Germany, the French National Center for Scientific Research (CNRS), the Commonwealth Scientific and Industrial Research Organisation (CSIRO) in Australia, and the Russian Academy of Sciences (PAH). Therefore, China's CAS is not a copy of the former USSR Academy of Sciences, and currently there are many typical "quasi-academies" in the world. Currently, the CNR has signed cooperation agreements with China's CAS, Chinese Academy of Agricultural Sciences (CAAS), Chinese Academy of Forestry (CAF), Chinese Academy of Social Sciences (CASS) and National Natural Science Foundation of China (NSFC).

Other research institutions in Italy include: the Italian National Agency for New Technologies, Energy and the Environment (ENEA), National Institute of Health of Italy, National Institute for Nuclear Physics, National Institute of Material Physics, and Italian Space Agency. The noted Lincean Academy, one of the world's oldest science academies, was founded in 1601. Encompassing no institutes itself, it is of the highest academic honor and is a consulting organization, with a membership of more than 500 people.

In addition to research institutions subordinate to the government, examples of enterprise-level research centers include: ENI Research Center, Fiat Research Center (CRF), Ansaldo Research Center (AR), Thales Alenia Space (AS), and some other large enterprise research centers and high-tech companies. ENI Research Center, on the of the largest enterprise R&D centers in Italy, engages in oil and gas research, with more than 650 researchers based in four places including Rome and Milan. Founded in 1976, CRF, of Fiat Group, employs nearly 1,000 people, with an output value exceeding 100 million euros; it conducts research and development on automobiles and engines, electronics, information systems etc. Employing nearly 3,000 people, AS conducts research and manufactures products in four high-tech fields-communications, remote sensing, space infrastructure and scientific satellites. AR, of Finmeccanica Group, has some 200 employees conducting research on energy including nuclear fusion, industry and transportation. Compared with the research centers at large enterprises (for example, Huawei, ZTE and Haier) in China, these enterprise research centers of Italy are much smaller (Han Jun, 2005).

2.2   Innovative Management of Enterprises

The most typical characteristic of Italy's SMEs management innovation is the model of "one industry for one region"-a cluster of enterprises within one region engage in one industry. This manifests mainly in traditional industries such as apparel and furniture. In the furniture industry district of the Italian province of Udine, there is a "wood and furniture triangle" used specially for production of wooden tables and chairs. On a land of less than 70 square kilometers, there are 786 SMEs which produce wooden tables and chairs. They employ more than 6,000 people in all, about eight persons per enterprise. Though largely family businesses, these SMEs produce 30 million tables and chairs a year, 80% of the national market, 50% of the European market and 32% of the world market, whose gross sales in 2002 ~ 2005 exceeded 1.2 billion dollars. Because most of these family businesses have their own land for supply of wood used for production, they can be called combinations of agriculture, industry and commerce, and they thus have stronger abilities to resist risks. A traditional industry in the province of Udine, the wooden tables and chairs production industry have experienced ups and downs from its inception in the 18th century to the present. Its scale today is attributed to the wood and furniture technical service center CATAS founded in 1969 and to Promosedia founded in 1983 to promote the products of these enterprises, both of which brought technological innovations to the district. From the 1970s onwards, these SMEs strengthened technological innovation both in design and quality, increased investment in technologies, integrated traditional to new technologies, and employed such tools as computer-aided design, leading to higher level of technology and enhanced competitiveness. The abovementioned CATAS provide enterprises with free testing, quality inspection and technical training, and organizes meetings and seminars for enterprises to communicate experience and share information, with the aim to improve their technological competitiveness and enterprise competitiveness. And it provides consulting services for about 800 enterprises every year. Promosedia was created by the regional chamber of commerce (with a 30% share in it) as an association of consisting of 96 enterprises (with a 70% share in it); each year, it organizes an international table & chair exhibition, exhibiting the district's enterprises to the world in various forms.

Such a model can also be seen in other regions of Italy, for example Como (for silk), Carpi and Prato (textile and apparel), Sassuolo (ceramic tiles), Merano (glass), and Carrara (marble processing). This enterprise innovation management, which is connected with small and medium-sized family enterprises, has formed a competitive and vigorous enterprise development model through technological innovation (Han Jun, 2005).

2.3　Science and Technology Input and Output

In 2007, Italy's GERD was 21. 116 billion dollars (ranking 9th in the world), and its GERD/GDP ratio was only 1. 13% (ranking 29th in the world; from statistics in 2003 ~ 2007, this ratio stably stood at around 1. 1%); its BERD was 11. 668 billion dollars, ranking 10th in the world, and its BERD/GDP ratio was 0. 55%, ranking 28th in the world. The same year, Italy had 192,000 researchers (FTE), ranking 10th in the world, and its enterprise researchers were 82,000 (FTE), ranking 12th in the world.

Italy only ranks 40th in the IMD *World Competitiveness Yearbook 2010*, up 10 places from one year ago (IMD, 2010), and 48th in the World Economic Forum's *Global Competitiveness Report 2010 ~ 2011*, remaining the same as in the previous year (WEF, 2010). Its national competitiveness has declined to a world medium level.

From 1950 to 2008 Italy had 5 person-time of Nobel Prize laureates, ranking 13th in the world.

In 2008, Italy published 98,332 papers (with a global share of 4.18%) on the world's three major index journals (SCI, EI and ISTP), ranking 7th in the world, behind the United States, China, the UK, Germany, Japan and France.

In 2007, Italy had 5,257 patents for invention awarded, ranking 9th in the world (MOST of China, 2010).

From above indicators, Italy's scientific and technological strength, innovation capacity and national competitiveness have all declined considerably. It is an undisputed fact that Italy has been in a state of decline.

Because there are less statistics on science and technology in Italy, the three tables below (Table 7-1 to Table 7-3) give a detailed account of science and technology indicators in Italy.

Table 7-1　Statistics on R&D Expenditure in Italy 2003 ~ 2007

Year	Sector	Expenditure/1 Million Euros	% Up or Down from Previous Year	% of GERD
2003	Public institutions	2,582	0.7	17.5
	Private nonprofit institutes	208	11.8	1.4
	Enterprises	6,979	−1.1	47.3
	Subtotal	9,769	−0.4	66.1
	Universities	5,000	4.3	33.9
	Total	14,769	1.2	100.0
2004	Public institutions	2,722	5.4	17.9
	Private nonprofit institutes	233	12.0	1.5
	Enterprises	7,293	4.5	47.8
	Subtotal	10,248	4.9	67.2
	Universities	5,004	0.1	32.6
	Total	15,252	3.3	100.0
2005	Public institutions	2,701	−0.8	17.3
	Private nonprofit institutes	330	41.6	2.1
	Enterprises	7,856	7.7	50.4
	Subtotal	10,887	6.2	69.8
	Universities	4,712	−5.8	30.2
	Total	15,599	2.3	100.0

Continued

Year	Sector	Expenditure/1 Million Euros	% Up or Down from Previous Year	% of GERD
2006	Public institutions	2,835	5.0	—
	Private nonprofit institutes	331	0.3	—
	Enterprises	7,975	1.5	—
	Subtotal	11,141	2.3	—
2007	Public institutions	2,814	-0.7	—
	Private nonprofit institutes	357	7.9	—
	Enterprises	8,381	5.1	—
	Subtotal	11,552	3.7	—

Note: Data for 2006 and 2007 were estimated values due to absence of data on universities.

Source: Italian National Institute of Statistics (Istat); cited from *Report of International Science and Technology Development 2010*.

Table 7-2 Statistics on Different Types of R&D Expenditure in Italy 2003 ~ 2005

Year	Sector	Expenditure/1 Million Euros				Composition/%			
		Basic research	Applied research	Experimental development	Total	Basic research	Applied research	Experimental development	Total
2003	Public institutions	1,139	1,232	212	2,582	44.1	47.7	8.2	100.0
	Private nonprofit institutes	99	104	5	208	47.7	49.9	2.4	100.0
	Enterprises	337	3,398	3,245	6,979	4.8	48.7	46.5	100.0
	Subtotal	1,575	4,733	3,461	9,769	16.1	48.5	35.4	100.0
	Universities	—	—	—	5,000	—	—	—	—
	Total	—	—	—	14,769	—	—	—	—
2004	Public institutions	1,080	1,427	215	2,722	39.7	52.4	7.9	100.0
	Private nonprofit institutes	100	124	9	233	42.9	52.3	3.9	100.0
	Enterprises	432	3,453	3,408	7,293	5.9	47.3	46.7	100.0
	Subtotal	1,612	5,351	3,884	10,887	15.2	49.2	35.7	100.0
	Universities	—	—	—	5,004	—	—	—	—
	Total	—	—	—	15,252	—	—	—	—

Continued

Year	Sector	Expenditure/1 Million Euros				Composition/%			
		Basic research	Applied research	Experimental development	Total	Basic research	Applied research	Experimental development	Total
2005	Public institutions	1,067	1,454	180	2,701	39.5	53.8	6.7	100.0
	Private nonprofit institutes	143	175	12	330	43.3	53.0	3.6	100.0
	Enterprises	442	3,722	3,692	7,856	5.6	47.4	47.0	100.0
	Subtotal	1,652	5,251	3,884	10,887	15.2	49.2	35.7	100.0
	Universities	—	—	—	4,712	56.7	33.4	9.9	100.0
	Total	4,322	6,926	4,351	15,599	27.7	44.4	27.9	100.0

Note: Statistics on some universities is lacked as per then classification.

Source: Italian National Institute of Statistics (Istat); cited from *Report of International Science and Technology Development 2010* .

Table 7-3   Statistics on Researchers in Italy 2003 ~ 2005

Year	Sector	Researchers		Technical Personnel and Other		Total	
		Qty	Qty (FTE)	Qty	Qty (FTE)	Qty	Qty (FTE)
2003	Public institutions	17,389	13,976.0	25,221	17,487.0	42,610	31,463.0
	Private nonprofit institutes	3,085	1,716.0	2,269	1,285.0	5,354	3,001.0
	Enterprises	30,500	26,866.3	50,689	41,091.5	81,189	67,957.8
	Subtotal	50,974	42,558.3	78,719	59,863.5	129,153	102,421.8
	Universities	56,480	27,774.0	64,256	31,632.0	120,736	59,406.0
	Total	107,454	70,332.3	142,435	91,495.5	249,889	161,827.8
2004	Public institutions	17,817	14,237.0	26,244	18,164.0	44,061	21,401.0
	Private nonprofit institutes	3,701	1,955.0	2,685	1,457.0	6,386	3,412.0
	Enterprises	31,676	27,594.1	50,146	39,925.2	81,822	67,519.3
	Subtotal	53,194	43,786.1	79,075	59,546.2	132,269	103,332.8
	Universities	47,401	28,266.0	65,865	32,468.0	123,266	60,694.0
	Total	110,595	72,012.1	144,940	92,014.2	255,535	164,026.3

Continued

Year	Sector	Researchers		Technical Personnel and Other		Total	
		Qty	Qty (FTE)	Qty	Qty (FTE)	Qty	Qty (FTE)
2005	Public institutions	18,818	14,454.0	26,734	18,230.0	45,552	32,684.0
	Private nonprofit institutes	5,044	3,023,0	3,547	1,840.0	8,591	4,863.0
	Enterprises	31,485	27,938.6	55,124	42,786.3	86,609	70,724.9
	Subtotal	55,347	45,415.6	85,405	62,856.3	140,752	108,271.9
	Universities	70,187	37,073.3	66,431	29,902.4	136,618	66,975.7
	Total	125,534	82,488.9	151,836	92,758.7	277,370	175,247.6

Source: Italian National Institute of Statistics (Istat); cited from *Report of International Science and Technology Development 2010*.

3. Innovation Culture

The essence of Italy's innovation culture is the brand culture. There are famous fashion brands such as Versace, Gucci and Valentino, famous shoe brands like Costume National, Tod's, D&G and Gucci, as well as well-known brands for handbags, ceramic tiles, leather goods and furniture. Italian enterprises valuing brand building is closely associated with Italian family businesses valuing marketing.

A brand culture refers to the establishment-by giving a brand rich cultural implications—of definite brand positioning, the formation of consumers' identity with the brand through effective marketing communication ways, and the ultimate establishment of strong brand loyalty. Specifically, it is the unity of spiritual symbols a brand has about values, life attitude, aesthetics and personality and the material embodiments such as product quality, level of technology and after-sales services. A brand culture makes customers more satisfactory by creating the high-level unity of material utility and brand spirit. Italy's brand culture is closely related to the nation's pursuit of taste and style and passion for design and arts, and has its origin in the Renaissance.

In Italy, the industrial cluster culture has its tradition and is linked to the development of family businesses in Italy. Main industrial clusters include textile, apparel, home appliances, lighting and related machines and equipment (such as marble cutters), as well as personal articles (such as jewelry and sanitary ware). Nearly all industrial clusters in Italy are dominated by SMEs and family businesses, featuring high geographic concentration and low production and transport costs.

4. Comments on Innovation Management and National Strength

Though Italy only has a history of 150 years from the Kingdom of Italy (1861 ~ 1964) through the founding of the Italian Republic (in 1946) to the present, its historical tradition dates back to the ancient Roman Empire. Italy began industrialization in the early 20th century, but it didn't see great development until the 1950s. From the 1950s to the late 1960s, the Italian economy grew rapidly, with the annual growth rate of Gross National Product (GNP) increasing from about 6% to about 9%. Italy thus became a developed country and a member of the Group of Seven (G-7). In 1986, Italy's global share of exports exceeded 5.2%, and its overall growth rate was only behind that of Japan, ranking 2nd among developed countries (Porter, 2007). It thus can be said that the 1980 saw the fast growth of Italy in both economic strength and national strength. With decades of accumulation, in 2003, Italy's GDP stood at 1,300.9 billion euros, and its per capita GDP was 22,823 euros (Han Jun, 2005).

Nevertheless, SMEs remain the mainstay of the Italian economy; the above-described "one industry for one region" clusters of SMEs, particularly, have played a tremendous role. In Italy, family businesses, about one fourth of the country's total enterprises, are willing to adopt advanced business organization and management models such as the divisional system, for they are afraid that decentralization would cause them to lose control over their businesses (Chandler, 2004).

Though a developed country, Italy has been far behind other developed countries like the United States, Japan, the UK, France and Germany in terms of national strength. Since the 1990s, its national strengthen has been on the decline. There are mainly three reasons as below.

Over the past 20 years, such developing countries as China, India and Brazil were growing rapidly economically and in national strength. This led to the slowdown and even decline of Italy in such indicators as its global share of foreign trade and GDP growth rate, because Italy lacks natural resources and relies on import.

The alternation of the Italian government has been frequent. The present Italian government is already the 62nd session of it in 65 years since the end of the Second World War in 1945. The short-lived government ruling led to the inconsistency of national development strategies and policies, and the governments or coalition governments formed by different political parties were typically "opposite rather than complementary to each other". We can imagine that how much time and energy there would be for political parties to study and make national policies since they are all busy with elections. "Short-term effects" and "short-term political performance" thus usually become the development goal of the government. This also shows that "institutional designers" are shortsighted.

Italy's investment in education, science and technology is inadequate because of lacking inadequate understanding of what strategic position the education, science and technology should have in national development. In this point, Italy has a gap to be narrowed in relation to China and India, not to mention the United States, Japan and Germany. It thus seems to have inadequate staying power, which can be clearly seen from the data given in the preceding section "Science and Technology Input and Output". Hundreds of years have passed since Italy became the world's first modern science center thanks to Italian scientists-most notably Leonardo da Vinci and Galileo, and from 1950 to the present the number of its Nobel Prize laureates was only one fourth of that before 1950 (Italy has 19 person-time of Nobel Prize laureates in all, only 5 of them were laurelled after 1950).

Favorable factors for national development of Italy: the flexible commercial structure and production system with the mainstay of SMEs have created many world famous brands in such sectors as textile, apparel, leather, furniture and marble processing; and Italy is at an advanced level in Europe or the world in such high-tech fields as mechanical equipment, robots, micro-electronics and biopharmaceuticals.

Unfavorable factors include: lacking effective institutional design on the long-term development of education, science and technology (as a result, with a population which accounts for 5.26% of OECD countries' total population, Italy's R&D investment is only 2.4% of OECD countries' total, and Italy is the country with least R&D investment among the countries with per capita GDP at 20,000 dollars to 25,000 dollars) (Han Jun, 2005); severe brain drain and shortage of human resources; lacking high-tech large enterprises which underpin the national economy.

Due to its defeat in the Second World War, Italy only has armed forces of

301,000. In 2007, its military expenditure/GDP ratio was 1.8%, its weapon exports amounted to 562 million dollars and its weapon imports to 176 million dollars (The World Bank, 2009).

In the final analysis, Italy, as a developed country, has been obviously on the decline in terms of its national strength since the 1990s, and it is a typical example of "changing from rise to decline".

Chapter 8
An Anxious Russia

Russia, officially the Russian Federation, is the largest country in the world, with a territorial area of 17.0754 million square kilometers. It has a population of 142 million (2008 est.), of which ethnic Russians comprise 79.8%. In total, more than 180 ethnic groups live within Russia. Russia abounds with natural resources, and forests cover 51% of its territory. Its natural gas reserves account for 35% of the world's total proven reserves, ranking 1st in the world, and its oil reserves compose 13% of the world's total proven reserves. It has the world's largest iron ore reserves and the second largest coal reserves. In Russia, 50% ~53% of the residents believe in Orthodox Church, and 10% believe in Islam. Historically, the October Revolution which broke out on 7 November 1917 gave birth to the first socialist country in the world, the Russian Soviet Federative Socialist Republic. The Union of Soviet Socialist Republics (Soviet Union) was founded in 1922, and later expanded into a union of 15 republics. The Soviet Union was dissolved on December 26, 1991. Soon later, the Russian Federation was founded as an independent state, the sole successor state of the former Soviet Union (Editorial Board of World Affairs, 2009).

In history, Russia had many famous persons, for example, the revolutionary leader Lenin, the chemists Lomonosov and Mendeleev, the biologist Pavlov, the astronautic scientist Tsiolkovsky, the litterateurs Tolstoy and Gorky, and the poet Pushkin.

Since the dissolution of the Soviet Union, however, Russia has been staggering on the political, economic, scientific and technological fronts. Today's Russia is in great bewilderment as it couldn't go back to the old road of the former Soviet Union and its "shock therapy" was little effective. In recent years, the Russian institutional designers have frequently hesitated over whether to learn the experience of rising China, return to the old road of the former Soviet Union or to develop Russia in Western ways.

1. Institutional Design

1.1 National Institutional Design

The Russian Federation is the sole successor of the former Soviet Union, and its institutional design follows that of the former Soviet Union in many ways. Therefore, it is necessary to first give a brief account of the institutional design of the form Soviet Union. In 1957, Nikita Khrushchev, then the General Secretary of the Central

Committee of the Communist Party of the Soviet Union, carried out the "regional national economy committee reform" which gave some of the power of the central government to local governments. But the reform failed, leading to his removal from power. Alexei Kosygin then came to power as Premier, who initiated a reform mainly aimed to "relax control over economic planning, increase economic independence of enterprises and carry out the 'completely economic accounting system'". This reform failed, too, because of the worsened economic situation and economic chaos. During the 1970s and 1980s, though several sessions of government also introduced such policies as "transforming the mode of economic growth" and "accelerating technology import and enterprise equipment updating", no great results were obtained. The former Soviet Union's "total-factor productivity" was always in decline during the periods from 1971 to 1975, from 1976 to 1980 and from 1981 to 1984 (Wu Jinglian, 2010). It was not until mid-1989 that Mikhail Gorbachev-the last head of state of the Soviet Union-proposed transition towards some type of market economy, but it was too late, and the across-the-board failure of his political system design led directly to the dissolution of the Soviet Union in 1990.

The Constitution of the Russian Federation adopted in December 1993 following its founding states that Russia is a democratic federal law-governed state with a republican form of government. On political system design, Russia follows the system of separation of powers: the President and the Government of the Russian Federation exercise the executive power; the Federal Assembly, which consists of the Federation Council (Upper House) and the State Duma (Lower House), exercises the legislative power, with the State Duma having greater power than the Federation Council; and the Supreme Court and the Constitutional Court exercise the judicial power. Russia follows a multi-party system, with main political parties including the United Russia, Communist Party of Russian Federation, A Just Russia, and Liberal Democratic Party of Russia.

The privatization of state-owned enterprises has been one of the main institutional designs in Russia as a country in economic transition since Putin's assumption of president and prime minister. In July 2010, the Russian government decided to sell a portion of shares (worth 29 billion dollars in total) of 10 large state-owned corporations including Rosneft Oil, Bank for Foreign Trade (Rosvneshtorgbank) and Russian Railways. It is estimated that this will relax control over large state-owned enterprises, attract capital and technology from private and foreign investors, and bring an income in tens of billions to the Russian government.

On September 10, 2009, in an article titled "Go Russia!", Russian President Dmitry Medvedev pointed out the severe problems in Russia, with "poor economic performance" at the top. Two months later, he stressed in his "union message" that "only by developing an innovation-based economy can we ensure that Russia be in a world leading position and this concerns the survival of the nation" (MOST of China, 2010).

1.2   System Design on Science and Technology

In 1999, the Russian government decided to set up the "Federal Government Scientific Innovation Committee".

In 2000, the Russian government decided to set up the "Ministry of Education and Science of the Russian Federation". In the current framework of the Russian government, departments concerned with scientific and technological affairs include: the Ministry of Education and Science and the Federal Agency for Science and Innovation under it, the Ministry of Economic Development and Trade, the Ministry of Information Technologies and Telecommunications, the Ministry of Industry and Energy, the Russian Federal Space Agency, and the Russian Academy of Sciences (RAS). The main executive bodies of government R&D budgets include: the Russian Academy of Sciences, the Russian Federal Space Agency, the Federal Agency on Industry, and the Federal Agency for Science and Innovation. The three main national foundations are: the Russian Foundation for Basic Research (RFBR), the Russian Foundation for Humanities (RFH), and the Foundation for Assistance to Small Innovative Enterprises (FASIE).

In March 2002, Russian President Putin approved the *Basic Policy of the Russian Federation in Science and Technology for 2010 and beyond*. In August 2005, the Russian government approved the *Basic Directions of the Policy of the Russian Federation on Innovation System Development until 2010*, which raised the three objectives of building the Russian innovation system: creating economic and legal environments conducive to innovation, building innovation infrastructure, and establishing a national innovation system for industrialization of knowledge results. In March 2006, the federal government approved the *State Program for Establishment of High-Technology Parks in the Russian Federation*, planning to set up seven high-technology parks in Moscow and other places which would focus on nanotechnology, biotechnology and information technology.

In early 2006, the Interdepartmental Commission for Science and Innovation Policy of the Russian Federation adopted the *Strategy for the Development of Science and Innovation in the Russian Federation until 2015*, in which it is stated that Russia's R&D investment/GDP ratio should reach 2% in 2010 and 2.5% in 2015.

In addition, Russia promulgated in succession intellectual property laws such as the *Patent Law* (2003) and the *Trademark Law*. Since 1994, Russia has established some 40 venture capital funds (National Innovation Capacity Evaluation and Research Panel, Development Research Center of China Association for Science and Technology, 2009).

In the subsequent science and technology reforms, the Russian government decided to strengthen basic research, keep a stable force of researchers, and build national innovation bases including "Technological Innovation Centers" and "Industrial Innovation Consortiums".

The abovementioned *Basic Policy of the Russian Federation in Science and Technology for 2010 and beyond* ("*Basic Policy*" below) is a comprehensive, systematic programmatic document, which comprises five parts: "General provisions", "The purpose and objectives of state policy on science and technology development", "The major directions of state policy on science and technology development, and the ways of their implementation", "The main measures of state stimulation of scientific, technological and innovative activities", and "The basic mechanisms and stages of implementation of the *Basic Policy*".

Part II of the Basic Policy, "The purpose and objectives of state policy on science and technology development", raised the tasks which should be accomplished to achieve the goal of the state policy on science and technology, for example, the adaptation of scientific research institutions to a market economy, providing both public and private capital for development of science and technology, and a rational combination of regulatory and market mechanisms and measures of direct and indirect incentives in pursuit of priority directions of science and technology. It is worth noting that four out of the 11 tasks in all are about defense and military: "strengthening the knowledge and technology transfer between the defense and civilian sectors of the economy, developing and promoting the use of civilian and military technologies"; "accelerating the transfer of scientific and technological achievements that contribute to the prevention of military conflicts and some other purposes"; and particularly, "the development and modernization of armament, military and special equipment, promoting the military-industrial complex"—this is the strong point of Russia by which it can not only enhance its defense and military resources but also expand its arms trade, and "improvement of technical means, forms and methods of combating terrorism, including international terrorism"—this is out of consideration for domestic security.

In part III of the Basic Policy, "The major directions of state policy on science and technology development, and the ways of their implementation", seven most important areas of public policy in the field of science and technology were defined.

1) The development of fundamental science and, the most important, applied research and development. This is an important factor which determines the status of Russia in the modern world. Here, particular attention is given to the objective of "preserving and promoting scientific and technological schools, ensuring the continuity of scientific knowledge".

2) Improvement of state regulation in the field of science and technology development. This includes, among other things, developing a national innovation program and mustering resources for the purpose of it, and determining priority technologies at all levels; the state procurement of developed products; creating modern incorporations, and exploiting the world market of knowledge-intensive products; introducing competition mechanisms and improving the public sector financing of science and high technology. Emphasis is once again placed on the objective of "maintaining the necessary level of financing of the development and modernization of armament, military and special equipment so as to strengthen Russia' position in the world market of arms and military technology".

3) Establishing a national innovation system, including creating a favorable legal environment, constructing innovation infrastructure, developing mechanisms for commercialization of scientific and technological achievements as well as science and technology intermediaries, coordinating the relationship between the participants in the innovation system and giving them policy support.

4) Improving the utilization of scientific and technological achievements, with attention paid to forging close relations between intellectual property and the results of scientific and technological activities.

5) Preserving and developing the human resource capacity of the scientific and technological sector. This includes, among other things, "creating conditions for the

return and employment of leading Russian scientists and professionals working abroad", and "forming a system for the training of highly qualified personnel in the field of innovative entrepreneurship".

6) The integration of science and education, mainly for the purpose of creating scientific-educational production centers (innovation centers) to consolidate efforts and resources needed for the training of highly qualified personnel in science, technology and innovation.

7) Development of international scientific cooperation, including establishing a legal and regulatory framework that encourages foreign investment in domestic fields of science, technology and innovation, and improving the systems for the export, customers control and transfer of scientific and technological achievements, including technologies both for civil and military use.

Part IV of the Basic Policy, "The main measures of state stimulation of scientific, technological and innovative activities", raised the main measures which include: "changing the system of compensation of the employees of budgetary research institutions, including giving the heads of state scientific research institutions the right to determine salaries, without ceilings, to the employees who make significant contributions to Russia's development of science and research and development of knowledge-intensive technologies"; "using 3% of the federal budget directed towards 'basic research and for promoting scientific and technological progress' for the funding of scientific schools"; "improving the guarantee of pensions for researchers of higher qualification (doctoral candidates and doctors)"; "giving financial aid to veteran scientists who have made outstanding contributions to the development of priority research directions or to creating new techniques and technologies"; and "improving the current system of accreditation of academic institutions through gradual transition to their qualification and certification in accordance international quality standard".

Part V of the *Basic Policy*, "The basic mechanisms and stages of implementation of the Basic Policy", raised the objectives by two stages. The objectives of the first stage (2002 ~ 2006) are to: clarify the legal basis of scientific, technological and innovation activities including intellectual property; establish systems and mechanisms for the order of the state for scientific and technological products; establish mechanisms for multi-channel financing of R&D activities and programs with the use of budgets at all levels, as well as extra-budgetary sources; develop draft concepts of scientific and technological security of the Russian Federation and the fundamental principles of the innovation policy of the Russian Federation from 2002 ~ 2006; develop mechanisms to improve the economic interest in the use of scientific and technological developments in addressing the socioeconomic problems, restructuring and technical upgrading of production, in order to enhance the competitiveness of domestic products and services; and establish a national system for management of scientific, technological and innovation activities.

The objectives of the second stage (until 2010) are to: complete the formation of a national innovation system and the whole structure of scientific and technological complex, capable of functioning effectively in a market economy; and ensure a stable position of the Russian Federation in the sphere of science and high technology (Ministry of Education and Science of the Russian Federation, 2003).

From the *Basic Policy* described above, on development of science and technology policies and systems, not only is Russia ahead of other countries in economic transition, but it is not inferior to developed countries. Some of its efforts are worth learning.

It is apparent that the Russian government's institutional design on science and technology is already greatly different from that of the former Soviet Union. That is consistent with the country's national institutional design and economic development strategy. But the deficiency is that the execution to this institutional design on science and technology has been not determined and effective enough. For example, the objective of "Russia's R&D investment/GDP ratio reaching 2% in 2010" cannot be achieved for sure, not to mention "2.5% in 2015". Of course, this is also related to Russia's national institutional design, economic strength and political environment. To put it another way, this is closely linked to the Russian government's institutional design, for example, the so-called "shock therapy" and "privatization".

In May 2009, President Dmitry Medvedev chaired a session of Commission on Economic Modernization and Technological Development, saying that Russia's problems about scientific and technological innovation occurred not only in the technological R&D stage but also in the promotion and industrialization stages and that 90% of enterprises in Russia needed to be modernized through scientific and technological innovation. Afterwards, he presided over 6 sessions of the commission, and listed energy, information, nuclear energy, space and healthcare as the top five priority areas of Russia in the sphere of science and technology.

In May 2009, too, the Russian President approved the *National Security Strategy of the Russian Federation Until 2020*. This strategy clarified the status and role of science and technology in the national security strategy, and raised the objectives to be achieved: establishing national scientific research organizations which are economically competitive and meet defense needs; creating a national innovation system; viewing the fundamental science, applied science and education as top priorities for development of an innovation-based economy. It also set the long-term tasks for science, technology and education in the interest of national security: creating a research system of fundamental and applied sciences, and building a network of federal universities and research universities in order to develop human resources necessary for the development of science, technology, education and high-tech industries.

In August of the same year, the Russian President approved the *Amendment to certain Russian Federation's Laws related to the Creation of Entities by federally-funded scientific and educational institutions for the Translation of Scientific and Technological Research Achivements*, which are considered the legal basis for addressing the dissociation between scientific research and production.

In 2009, Russia implemented the *Federal Law on the Transfer of the Rights to Unified Technologies*, which provided for the conditions and contractual articles for technology transfer, and for principles of benefit distribution. The same year, in order to join the Organisation for Economic Co-operation and Development (OECD), the Russian Ministry of Education and Science developed a report titled *National Innovation System and State Innovation Policy of the Russian Federation*. This report proposed that the following must be achieved to improve the national competitiveness: development of labor resources in science and technology; economic restructuring; implementation and consolidation of the available competitiveness of Russia in such sectors as energy and raw materials, transport infrastructure as well as creation of new competitive advantages related to diversification of economics and improvement of the research and technological complex (MOST of China, 2010)

In 2009 alone, the Russian government, under the leadership of the President, introduced so many laws and policies directly or indirectly relating to scientific and technological innovation. It is therefore apparent that a mainstay of Russian President Dmitry Medvedev's "new deal" is the reliance on scientific and technological innovation for national prosperity.

2. Innovation Management

2.1　Innovation Approach: TRIZ

The sphere of technological innovation management is almost dominated by American and Japanese theories, doctrines and approaches. Few speak of the innovation management or innovation approaches of the former Soviet Union or Russia. The TRIZ approach, which was introduced into China a few years ago, has changed the view of people, because it was developed by a Soviet inventor, Genrich Altshuller who was born in 1926 in Tashkent, the former Soviet Union and in 1990 moved to Petrozavodsk, Russia. TRIZ, the acronym of Teoriya Resheniya Izobreatatelskikh Zadatch, the English transliteration for Russian т еории решения изобрет ат ельских задач, is translated as the Theory of the Solution of Inventive Problems. In China, TRIZ is transliterated as "Cuizhi" which means "the extraction of wisdom". Because Altshuller created TRIZ in the era of the former Soviet Union and published the theory in Russian, he could be counted as a native of the former Soviet Union. And since the Russian Federation is the sole successor of the former Soviet Union, TRIZ could be considered a research finding of the former Soviet Union or Russia.

The first basic concept of TRIZ is "Technical System", namely a system capable of executing a particular function which consists of one or more subsystems. For example, the technical system of an automobile comprises the power train, braking, heating, operating and other subsystems. The "evolution of technical systems" has the following eight patterns: ① S-shaped evolution; ② increasing ideality; ③ uneven development of subsystems; ④ increasing dynamism and controllability; ⑤ increasing complexity followed by simplicity through integration; ⑥ harmonizing the rhythms of parts of the system; ⑦ transition from macro to micro levels and increasing field application; and ⑧ decreasing human involvement with increasing automation.

The second basic concept is "Level of Invention". There are five levels of invention: Level 1, a simple improvement of a particular technical system; Level 2, an invention containing a solution to a technical contradiction; Level 3, an invention containing a solution to physical contradictions; Level 4, development of radically new technologies; and Level 5, discovery of the previously unknown.

The third basic concept is "Law of Ideality", which means that in the process of evolution any technical system tends to be increasingly reliable, simple and effective, i. e. increasing ideality.

The fourth basic concept is "Contradiction", which means that the improvement of a particular characteristic or parameter of a technical system is to bring change and even degradation of another characteristic or parameter of the system. Contradiction exists widely in design of various products. In traditional design, a compromise approach doesn't solve conflicts thoroughly, but reaches a compromise between conflicts, or a reduced degree of conflict. The TRIZ theory considers that the symbol of product innovation is producing a new, competitive solution by solving or removing the conflicts in design. A design can drive the evolution of a product only by identifying and solving conflicts continuously.

A technical contradiction or conflict refers to the co-existence of both useful and harmful results as a result of an action, or the deterioration of one or several systems or subsystems due to the import of a useful action or removal of a harmful action. A technical conflict typically appears as a conflict between two subsystems of one system.

TRIZ has 40 inventive principles for problem solving. A problem is solved by nine steps: analysis of the problem; analysis of the problem's model; formulation of the Ideal Final Result; utilization of outside substances and field resources; utilization of informational data bank; change or reformulation of the problem; analysis of the method that removes physical contradiction; utilization of found solution; and analysis of steps that lead to the solution.

The inventive principles are: segmentation, extraction, local quality, asymmetry, combining, universality, nesting, counterweight, prior counter-action, prior action, cushion in advance, equipotentiality, inversion, spheroidality, dynamicity, partial or overdone action, moving to a new dimension, mechanical vibration, periodic action, continuity of a useful action, rushing through, converting harm into benefit, feedback, mediator, self-service, copying, inexpensive substitute, replacement of a mechanical system, pneumatic or hydraulic construction, flexible membrances or thin film, use of porous material, changing the color, homogeneity, rejecting and regenerating parts, transformation of the physical and chemical states of an object, phase transformation, thermal expansion, using strong oxidizers, inert environment, and composite materials.

　　Contradictions or conflicts in reality differ tremendously, and without induction it is impossible to create stable solutions. The TRIZ theory contains 39 generic conflicting parameters (the latest research findings have already increased the number to 48 and put forwards 31 commercial parameters in all). Altshuller developed a contradiction matrix (a table of pairings) which contains these 39 generic property parameters (for example weight, length, area, volume, velocity, force, pressure, shape, stability, temperature, brightness, waste of energy, energy consumption, power, loss of information, accuracy, level of automation, productivity etc.) and abovementioned 40 inventive principles. In practice, at least two out of the 39 parameters is used to represent a conflict between two factors before finding in the contradiction matrix the inventive principles for solving the conflict. In so doing, more than 1,500 technical contradictions can be solved (Altshuller, 2008).

　　Altshuller (who had obtained a patent for invention at the age of 14) initially raised the TRIZ theory in 1946 after a study of more than 1,000 patents, and later on together his colleagues sorted out 40,000 from 200,000 patents for the purpose of seeking best solutions to various inventive problems. By using these most effective solutions, they further improved the basic methods used in TRIZ for the resolution of inventive problems. These methods in return could be used to help obtain the most effective solutions to newly emerging inventive problems. Obscurely, Altshuller was arrested and jailed because of his TRIZ. He was freed in 1954, and was finally recognized in the 1980s by the government and society of the former Soviet Union. In 1989 the Russian TRIZ Association was formed, with Altshuller chosen as the first president of it. In September 1999, a couple of days before the founding of the Altshuller Institute for TRIZ Studies in the United States, Altshuller died. Today, TRIZ training courses of various types are held throughout the world (including China), and a great many organizations for TRIZ studies have been established, including the international Altshuller Institute for TRIZ Studies (www. aitriz. org). More than 2.5 million patents have been studied, leading to the enriched theory and methodology of TRIZ. Some companies have developed computer-aided innovation systems based on TRIZ and patent databases. TRIZ, however, still more remains an innovation thought or approach.

　　It took over 40 years from the formulation to the actual use and spread of TRIZ, and the creator was jailed forI creating it and suffered frustrations before gaining recognition. This is unimaginable and is a tragedy in world history of invention. It is thus apparent that national institutional design is on top of the institutional design on science and technology and scientific and technological innovation, as well as the decisive factor for the development of a country and for its scientific and technological advancement.

2.2 Science and Technology Input and Output

In 2007, Russia's GERD was 14.506 billion dollars, ranking 14th in the world; its GERD/GDP ratio was only 1.12%, ranking 29th in the world, which was lower than not only China's 1.49% but also Russia's previous data. In 2008, Russia's financial revenues grew considerably as a result of the great surge in international gas and oil prices, but the country's funding for science and technology stood only at some 5.3 billion dollars, only accounting for 1.74% of the country's total central financing budget and 0.30% of GDP. It is obvious that Russia attached importance to science, technology and innovation merely verbally.

In 2007, Russia had 912,300 researchers (FTE), ranking 3rd in the world, only behind China and Japan. That was mainly a legacy of vast human resources in science and technology that the former Soviet Union had left over.

Russia is only ranked 51st in the IMD *World Competitiveness Yearbook 2010*, down 2 places from one year ago (IMD, 2010), and 63rd in the World Economic Forum's *Global Competitiveness Report 2010 ~ 2011*, without change form one year ago (WEF, 2010). Its national competitiveness has declined to a moderately low level.

From 1950 to 2008 Russia had 9 person-time of Nobel Prize laureates, ranking 6th in the world.

In 2008, Russia had 29,903 patents for invention awarded, of which 22,668 patents were awarded at home and 7,235 awarded abroad. This indicator ranked 6th in the world in recent years (MOST of China, 2010).

In 2008 Russia's GDP reached 1,674.3 billion dollars, ranking 8th in the world.

From the above, Russia's scientific and technological strength, innovation capacity, and especially national competitiveness have all declined considerably. It is already an undisputed fact that Russia has been in a state of decline as compared with the former Soviet Union.

3. Innovation Culture

Russia used to be famous for a host of scientists. Noted Russian scientists are, among others, the chemist Mikhail Lomonosov, who developed an atomic and molecular theory; Dmitri Mendeleev, the creator of the periodic table of elements whereby he revealed the inner law of elements; the famous physiologist Ivan Pavlov, who discovered the conditioned reflex and in 1904 was awarded the Nobel Prize in Physiology or Medicine for his classical theories on blood circulation and digestive physiology; the famous biologist and pathologist Ilya Ilyich Mechnikov, who received the Nobel Prize in Medicine in 1908, shared with Germany scientist Paul Ehrlich, for his work on phagocytosis; the physicist Pavel Cherenkov, who shared the 1958 Nobel Prize in Physics with Ilya Frank and Igor Tamm for the discovery of Cherenkov radiation; The prominent physicist Lev Landau, who received the 1962 Nobel Prize in Physics for his research into condensed matters, especially liquid helium; Leonid Kantorovich, prominent mathematician and economist and one of the founders of modern computational mathematics, who laid the foundation for the theory of linear programming and shared the 1975 Nobel Prize in Economics with US economist Tjalling Koopmans for their contribution to the theory of optimum allocation of resources; the physicist Pyotr Kapitsa, who received the Nobel Prize in Physics in 1978, shared with US scientists Arno Allan Penzias and Robert Woodrow Wilson, for his basic inventions and discoveries in the area of low-temperature physics; and Sergei Korolev, the prominent Soviet rocket and aerospace designer. From 1904 to the present, Russia and the former Soviet Union had a total of 16 Nobel Prize laureates.

There is a person worthy of special mention, and he is Konstantin Tsiolkovsky, the Russian preeminent scientist and pioneer of the astronautic theory. In 1903, Tsiolkovsky published his work, *Exploration of Cosmic Space by Means of Reaction Devices*, which dealt with the feasibility of space travel by means of jet apparatus and derived his famous rocket equation. The creation of this formula provided a theoretical basis for space travel. In his work he raised, for the first time, the idea of using a liquid rocket, thinking that solid rocket propellants produced less energy and was hard to control while a liquid rocket could overcome such weaknesses. He also dealt with the use of a multistage rocket to overcome terrestrial attraction for the first time. In his science fictions he mentioned space suit, state of weightlessness, moon lander, and so on, which thoroughly coincide with modern space technology.

Why were these Russian scientists that preeminent? It should be noted that these scientists were not conducting research alone, but around each of them there was a scientific community, or scientific school of thought. Whether in big countries such as the United States and Germany or in small ones like Denmark, there are scientific schools of thought, for example, the Copenhagen school centered on the theories developed by Danish physicist and Nobel Prize laureate Niels Bohr. But Russian schools of thought are particularly out of the common: they cover a wide span of disciplines and are quite preeminent. Examples include the Pavlovian school of thought, the Cherenkov school of thought, the Landau school of thought, and the Tsiolkovsky school of thought.

Russia is practically the only country in the world in which accreditation of scientific schools of thought is carried out. In recent years, some 1,500 groups of a certain size have participated in the national accreditation of scientific schools, 650 of them recognized (Yu Minduo, 2009).

The Lebedev Physics Institute (LPI) at which Russian physicist Pavel Cherenkov worked is also worth special mention. This institute has so far had 7 Nobel Prize laureates (Pavel Cherenkov, Igor Tamm, Ilya Frank, Nikolay Basov, Alexander Prokhorov, Andrei Sakharov, and Vitaly Ginzburg), 6 of them in physics and 1 winning a Peace Prize. A great number of physicists at the LPI have received the most prestigious domestic prizes and awards. The names of these scientists are associated with a great many momentous scientific discoveries, for example, Mandelshtam-Brillouin scattering, Vavilov's law, Levshin-Perren formula, Tamm levels, Hartree-Fock method, Vavilov-Cherenkov effect, Franz-Keldysh effect, Veksler-McMillan principle of phase stability, Ginzburg-Landau superconductivity theory, supersymmetric theory, and controlled thermonuclear fusion. Research work at the LPI laid the bases of radio engineering and nonlinear theory of vibrations, semiconductor electronics, radioastronomy, high-energy physics and many other trends of modern physics. The internationally well-known Large Hadron Collider project in Europe is built on the theories developed by two Soviet scientists (Vladimir Veksler and Gersh Budker), with the theory of the Vavilov-Cherenkov effect and Ginzburg's theory of transition radiation used as primary testing methods. The LPI, the world leader to the present in the fields of laser, nanoelectronics, strong electronics as well as medical and scientific equipment research and development, remains Russia's most powerful institute of physics with a combination of scientific research, teaching, information and culture. Currently, the LPI has a research force of 1,600 people at an average age of 53, including 22 academicians, 200 doctors and over 400 doctoral candidates. Within its framework, there are the Astro Space Center, Division of Quantum Radiophysics, Division of

Optics, Division of Theoretical Physics, Department of Physical Electronics, Division of Solid State Physics, Division of Nuclear Physics and Astrophysics, Department of Neutron Physics, as well as some other subordinate departments, and branches scattered in other cities in Russia. Each year, the LPI publishes more than 20 types of physical treatise and more than 1,500 research papers at domestic and foreign magazines, with paper citations ahead of all other research institutions in Russia. A dozen RAS research institutions have been derived from the LPI. During the 1990s, though Russia's socioeconomic development encountered certain difficulties, the LPI remained the flagship of basic research in Russia, not shifting to make money nor swaying its faith in science, because of a still firm base of science-the powerful school of science. The scientists there engages in basic research and applied technology development as they always did, regardless of what happens outside, of whether there are homes to be allocated to them, and of research funding-adequate and inadequate (Yu Minduo, 2009).

It is justifiable to describe them as the "PLI School of Thought".

Scientific schools of thought are a type of scientific communities, and their formation and development embodies the formation and development of an innovation culture. The formation of a school of thought, according to the "paradigm theory" of American historian and philosopher of science Thomas Kuhn, is usually based on a paradigm comprising the theories and methods shared by a group of researchers. With the shared scientific language and professional rules (such as theorems, laws and algorithm), the members of a scientific school can communicate with each other fairly sufficiently, making it easy to solve a divergence of opinion by means of debate. A scientific school typically has the values all of its members share, the members encourage each other in pursuit of and dedication to their comm. Goals and their similar way of thinking and shared terminology allow them to benefit from, inspire and complement each other in discussions. These roles, which outsiders can hardly play, enable faster development of disciplines and subjects (Zhou Jizhong, 1987). At the same time, academic debates between scientific schools can produce the mighty power which promotes further development of science.

Scientific schools are just like a particular fertile soil that grows bizarre flowers and grass. In the Russian government's fundamental policies such as the *Basic Policy of the Russian Federation in Science and Technology for 2010 and beyond*, there are contents support and develop scientific schools, showing that the Russian government is determined to foster scientific schools as an innovation culture and innovation organizations. Russia's innovation culture is certainly not merely the scientific school culture, but the latter is the most splendid part of the former.

Compared with Russia's scientific schools as an innovation culture, scientific schools of thought seem to be something of a rarity in China. In the sphere of science before the Cultural Revolution, it seems to me that there were only Li Siguang's "school of geomechanics" and Chen Guoda's "school of Diwa (geodepression) tectonics", with both persons known together as "Li in the North and Chen in the South". There were academic debates between the two schools, which helped to promote academic prosperity. But during the "anti-rightist struggle" in the 1950s, the "*Babaiqi*" (uproot negative examples) movement and, especially, the 10-year-long Cultural Revolution, the term "school of thought" became a byword for the base camp of reactionary academic authority and even for the counterrevolutionary clique. There were rare schools of thought both in science and art. Both the "four greatest female impersonators" and the "four greatest *laosheng* actors" of Peking opera were established before 1949. From 1949 to the present no "school" has been heard. From the perspective of Russia's scientific achievements in portion to scientific schools, does China exceptionally lack the soil for innovation culture? If yes, how to cultivate this soil? And can this provide a way of thinking to resolve the "Needham Question" and the "Qian Xuesen's Question"?

If we say that the above-described scientific achievements and scientific schools all were before the 21st century, then what is the force that makes Russia still keep the vigor of scientific invention and discovery in the 21st century when its national strength has been on the decline? One of the reasons is that Russia's scientific school culture highlights the spirit of dedication to science. Below is a piece of news in 2003, eight years from now:

The Russian Science & Technology News Center published a list of top ten scientific and technological achievements in Russia for the year of 2003. From the scope of these achievements, basic research remains the priority of Russia in scientific development, and operative technologies and developments are underway.

1) The Joint Institute for Nuclear Research in Dubna successfully synthesized the elements 115 and 113 on the periodic table of elements, which reconfirmed the assumption of "island of stability". Since the first artificial synthesis of the elements plutonium and neptunium in the 1940s, research into the properties of transuranic

elements and their applications has become the new research direction of nuclear physics and chemistry. An important issue in this basic research is whether there is an upper limit for Dmitri Mendeleev's periodic table of elements. A total of 17 new elements including the element 112 have so far been synthesized.

2) Scientist Vitaly Ginzburg at the Lebedev Physical Institute of the Russian Academy of Sciences, and Russian scientist Alexei Alexeyevich Abrikosov in the United States, were awarded the 2003 Nobel Prize in Physics for their outstanding contributions to the theory of superconductors and superfluids.

3) The first Russian power system (1kW) based on a solid oxide fuel cell has been successfully tested in the All-Russia Research institute of Technical Physics, at the Russian Federal Nuclear Centre in Snezhinsk. This is the first technology which Russia has developed to convert chemical energy into electrical energy by using a fuel cell.

4) Scientist Vladimir Nazarov, at the Sternberg State Astronomical Institute, built a new model of earth axis vibration which increased the accuracy of calculating the direction of earth axis vibration from previously $2 \sim 3m$ to $0.02m$. This achievement provides great possibilities for increasing the accuracy of GPS and will be widely used in global transportation, communications, terrestrial, marine and cosmic navigation. Vladimir Nazarov received the 2003 Descartes Prize for the achievement.

5) Professor Lev Revtovsky, at Institute of Cytology and Genetics, Siberian Branch of the Russian Academy of Sciences, published an articled titled "An Analysis of Genetic Difference between Individuals of Global Different Races", on *Science* magazine, earning him The *Lance* magazine prize. This article is acclaimed as the best published on global biological and medical magazines in 2003. By using the method proposed by this article, what race an individual belongs to can be determined simply through an analysis of his/her biological samples (blood or other tissue and organ), without the presence of the person and his archive. This achievement will play an important role in genetic diseases research and medicolegal expertise.

6) The RAS Institute of Physical Chemistry for the first time synthesized a compound of xenon and acetylene, four months after an international panel of scientists theoretically believed in the existence of compounds with the carbon chain constituent of inert atoms. This achievement is acclaimed as a revolution in organic chemistry.

7) The first genetically engineered insulin production line in Russia has been built.

Totally computer controlled, it comprises the cultivation, separation and cleaning of cells, the separation and cleaning of regenerated protein, and the crystallization and drying of the medicine.

8) The cancer vaccine developed by the RAS Institute of Gene Biology in Moscow has entered phase II clinical trials. The vaccine is a type of cells with an altered structure cytokinesis gene-a protein that promotes the immune system.

9) The RAS Paleontological Institute discovered the vertebral column of a mammoth penetrate by some ancient lethal weapon, in the Khanty-Mansi Autonomous District, proving for the first time the fact of fights between man and mammoths. This discovery shows that there were human beings living in Northern Siberia 14,000 years ago.

10) Russia has built the country's first synthetic oil production line with technologies developed by the RAS Institute of Problems of Chemical Physics. Experiments by multiple parties have proved that the quality of synthetic oil complies thoroughly with the European standard" (Dong Yingbi, 2004).

4. Comments on Innovation Management and National Strength

Obscurely, why has Russia been on the decline since the dissolution of the former Soviet Union in 1990, despite its powerful science and technology? Didn't the judgment that "Science and technology are primary productive forces" work in Russia?

The problem lies not in science and technology, but in institutional design. The dissolution of the former Soviet Union was associated with the so-called ideological "innovation" of Mikhail Gorbachev and related institutional design. Of course, the direct institutional design came from the Russian government led by then Russian President Boris Yeltsin. There has been a brief account in section one "Institutional Design" of the institutional design over the decade since Putin's first inauguration of the Russian President (2000 ~ 2010).

We may have a basic understanding of the Russian government's "institutional design on science and technology" from the "*Basic Policy of the Russian Federation in Science and Technology for 2010 and beyond*" described in section one of this chapter, "Institutional Design". The level of Russia's institutional design on science and technology is advanced among countries in economic transition, and is not inferior to developed countries. The problem lies in the Russian government's "national institutional design". From the national institutional design in the early years of the 21st century, if it is said to be a "progressive reform" in China, then in Russia it is largely a "leap-forward reform" which has left Russian economy and society in great fluctuation. Another problem is the execution of "national institutional design" by governments at various levels and enterprises of various types. Russia has a multi-party system in which the political parties are largely for elections and can hardly perform the function of "national institutional design". This is quite different from China's Communist Party. The decision makers and institutional designers differ from executors in understanding and interest relationship. It is thus not difficult to understand why there are wide discrepancies between explicit specifications (such as R&D indicators) in Russian policies and their implementation results. This can be explained by previously described Russian R&D expenditure and international rankings. What's more, Russia is behind China both in papers published on the world's three major index journals and in patents for invention. All these suggest that Russia's national strengthen has been in decline as compared with the former Soviet Union.

Russia is one of the world's largest military powers, and a big weapon exporter. It has armed forces of 1.134 million, including 370,000 for Ground Forces, 200,000 for Air Force, 170,000 for Navy, 100,000 for Strategic Rocket Forces, 70,000 for Military Space Forces, and 36,000 for Airborne Troops (Editorial Board of World Affairs, 2009). In 2007, Russia's military expenditure/GDP ratio was 3.6% (up to 4.3% in 2008), its weapon exports amounted to 4.59 billion dollars and its weapon imports amounted only to 4 million dollars (The World Bank, 2009).

But the "rise and fall" is dynamic and relative. It is dynamic, as a country may change from rise to fall or from fall to rise, which only denotes a particular development stage or period in history. It is relative, the rise or fall of a country is a result of vertically comparing with the country itself and horizontally comparing with other countries. To sum up, from the overall perspective of Russia's scientific tradition and preeminent achievements, institutional design on science and technology, abundant resources, framework as a big country (the territorially largest country in the world, and one of the permanent members of the United Nations Security Council), it is possible for Russia to resurge. In conclusion, the inclusion of Russia into "BRICs" is reasonable, so is its current ranking as "the last of BRICs". In other words, Russia is currently behind Chin and India in innovation management on institutional design.

Chapter 9

A Quickening India

India, officially the Republic of India, has an area of about 2. 98 million square kilometers (excluding the Indian-occupied areas along the Sino-Indian border and that part of the Kashmir region actually controlled by India), and a population of 1. 112 billion (2006 est.)—the second largest in the world. India has abundant natural resources, with coal reserves ranking 3rd in the world; forests cover 20. 6% of the territory. India is a multiethnic society, with Hindustani—the dominant ethnic group in the country—accounting for 46. 3% of the population. It is also a multi-religious country, with major religions including Hinduism (80. 5% of the population), Islam (13. 4%), Christianity (2. 3), Sikhism (1. 9%), and Buddhism (0. 8%) (Editorial Board of World Affairs, 2009). India is one of the world's "four great ancient civilizations". Both Mahatma Gandhi and poet Rabindranath Tagore were Indian. Indian scientist C. V. Raman received the Noel Prize in Physics for his work on the scatting of light and for the discovery of the effect named after him.

India gained independence form the UK in 1947 after more than 30 years of colonial history.

As an agricultural country, India has an irrigated area of 59 million hectares-the largest one in the world. Its "Green Revolution" in the 1960s brought about food self-support. Like China, coal is the primary energy source in India, which accounts for 55% of India's total energy demand. Statistics in 2005 showed that India has coal reserves of 247. 8 billion tons, 10% of the world's total coal reserves (Chang Qing, 2006). Known as one of BRICs, India has developed rapidly since the 1990s in terms of its economic, scientific and technological strength and national strength. Most Western countries are bullish about the future of India, and India itself also has confidence to outperform China. The development of India, I think, can also be called the "rise of India". Of course India has its own problems, for example the "caste system" which still exists today (Almond et al. , 2010).

Broadly speaking, the strengths for the "rise of India" are as follows: influenced by the UK in terms of political and economic systems, India experienced less resistance than in other developing countries in the formation of its market economy system, making it easier to learn and practice the experience of market operation (for example, in acquisitions and mergers); India's modern service industries (finance, software, telecom, outsourcing etc.) are developing so rapidly that no other development countries compare to it and, particularly, India outstrips China in private banking efficiency; some of its high-end manufacturing industries (such as the pharmaceutical industry) are also fairly competitive; its human resources have greater potential advantages because of its swelling of young labor forces, high percentage of English-speaking talent, and lower labor costs, and India has a great number of successful businessmen in Western countries (about 20 million Indians live abroad, including five million of Indian nationality), which is favorable for socioeconomic development of India; in recent years India's GDP has been growing fast, at some 8%.

The weaknesses of the "rise of India" are as follows: the parliament and the federal government, and the federal government and the states handicap each other, leading to low working efficiency; the infrastructure (such as transport, roads, bridges etc.) is poor; most manufacturing industries and basic industries are not well-established; India's economy is less developed, with 2005 GDP per-capita only at 720 dollars, and one fourth of the population live below the poverty line; its female illiteracy rate stands at 46% and its male at 25%; 70% of India's population live in rural areas and 60% of its labor forces engage in agriculture, suggesting that India remains a low-income agricultural country (Dutz, 2009); in India, the population of so-called "untouchables" excluded from the four castes is over 135 million, about 10% of India's total population, and the "caste system" is interwoven with religious institutions, which, coupled with the low social position of women and the conflict of interest between the states, leads to sharpened social contradictions and thus handicaps economic and social development.

India is not only rising, but also catching up, currently with China in four to five years as shown its timetable, and then with the United States roughly by the mid-21st century as estimated by the Indian side.

1. Institutional Design

1.1 National Institutional Design

The current constitution of India came into force in January 1950.

India is a federation with a parliamentary system, with the council of ministers headed by the Prime Minister. The parliament consists of two houses, the Council of States (upper house) and the House of People (lower house). India's political structure and system is largely a copy of that of the UK. But different from the UK and the United States, the legislature of India has smaller powers, which is subjected to the federal government in law making and the function of supervision. India has a multi-party system which consists of a variety of parties, mainly the Indian National Congress, the Bharatiya Janata Party, and the Communist Party of India.

The department in charge of scientific and technological affairs, of the council of ministers within the federal government of India, is the Ministry of Science and Technology. India invests much in defense science and technology. It has carried out many international cooperation programs and projects in this regard, for example, in collaboration with Russia in developing the fifth-generation fighter plane.

In 1958 the Indian parliament adopted the *Scientific Policy Resolution*, which can be considered the fundamental law of India in the sphere of science and technology. In 1970, the parliament enacted the first Indian patent law after its independence, the *Patents Act 1970* (during the UK's reign of India, a Patents Law was promulgated in 1859), which was later amended and improved many times.

In 1991 India began economic reforms (some scholars view India's economic reforms as 13 years later than China's, calculated based on China's economic reforms in 1978). From then on, India's economic reforms promoted the country's reform on science and technology, both supplementing each other. India's economic reforms are similar to China's in form.

The most successful aspect of India's institutional design lies in its market economy reform, which offered a favorable development environment for internationalization of private enterprises in India. For example, India's annulment of the licensing system in 1991 provided a good opportunity for Indian private enterprises to develop overseas. A dozen years later, in India's IT, pharmaceutical and banking industries there appeared world-famous enterprises, most of them private enterprises, whose development benefited from India's institutional design on economic reforms.

Among the current social, political and economic systems in India, in addition to the abovementioned parliamentary electoral system, there are other systems inherited from the feudal society, including: the caste system, under which there are four Hindu classes-Brahman (priests), Kshatriya (bureaucrats), Vaishya (traders and urban craftsmen), and Sudra (peasants and tenants), below them the untouchables (currently India has more than 100 million untouchables) who are de facto slaves; and the system of non-segregation of urban and rural areas inherited from the British institution, under which Indian farmers can enter cities freely-that's why there are extended slums in Indian cities.

Therefore, India's social, political and economic systems manifest themselves in the pluralism of colonial, feudal and modern social systems.

The strength of the Indian political system lies in its likeliness to gain recognition from Western countries, but its weakness is low government efficiency. According to data published by PRS Legislative Research, a New Delhi-based think tank, during the 170-hour "quarterly meeting" of the House of People for July to August 2010, 100 hours was wasted by the members for wrangling and fighting and, immediately before the end of the meeting, they adopted a multiplicity of bills in a short time as if they were obliged to do so.

1.2　Institutional Design on Science and Technology

The Scientific Advisory Council to the Prime Minister (SAC-PM) and the Scientific Advisory Committee to the Union Cabinet are merely advisory bodies, but due to their broad representation, the macro programs, plans and policies on science and technology that the two bodies made represent the country's top design or planning blueprints in the sphere of science and technology. The Ministry of Science and Technology is the Indian government ministry charged with formulation and administration of the rules and regulations and laws relating to science and technology in India, under the leadership of which are the Department of Scientific and Industrial Research, Department of Biotechnology and Department of Ocean Development. In addition, the Office of the Inter-ministerial Scientific Advisory Council is also housed at the Ministry of Science and Technology.

The *Technology Policy Statement* of 1983 and the *Science and Technology Policy* of 2003 are government policies for the purpose of implementing the *Scientific Policy Resolution* adopted by the parliament.

In 1999, the Prime Minister of India proposed the idea of making India a knowledge power in 2010. The next year, a task force formed by heads from such bodies as the Scientific Advisory Committee to the Union Cabinet submitted the report *India as Knowledge Superpower: Strategy for Transformation*, which focuses on the development of science, technology and education, especially on the effective transformation of scientific and technological results into commodities and competitiveness.

In 2009, India approved a program called "Innovation in Science Pursuit for Inspired Research (INSPIRE)", for the purpose of making talent interested in science at an early stage and providing them with opportunities for experiencing innovation, offering scholarships for higher education, and providing doctors and post-doctors in basic and applied research with scholarships.

However, the most successful of all of India's institutional designs on science and technologies is India's requirement enunciated in *India as Knowledge Superpower*: *Strategy for Transformation*, i. e. the countrywide social transformation from an agricultural society to a knowledge society. In this "transformation strategy", the development of modern service industries, primarily software, telecom, finance and outsourcing, is no doubt the highlight of the strategy, and has been proved a correct transformation strategy by later practice. In less than a decade, this strategy has played a significant role in India's social transformation and even in the process of its rise.

2. Innovation Management

2.1　Organizational Framework for Science and Technology

2.1.1　Organizational framework of government departments for science and technology

India founded the Scientific Advisory Council to the Prime Minister (SAC-PM) in January 2005, with members coming from government departments, universities, research institutions and enterprises. The Scientific Advisory Committee to the Union Cabinet propose specific schemes for implementation of the policies, laws and regulations developed by the SAC-PM. The Planning Commission of India, similar in position and functions to China's National Development and Reform Commission, develops science and technology plans while making India's Five-Year Plans. The Ministry of Science and Technology of India, founded in 1971, has a position and functions similar to China's Ministry of Science and Technology. The Department of Scientific and Industrial Research, under the Ministry of Science and Technology, is in charge of scientific and technological affairs relating to enterprises. Under the leadership of the Department of Scientific and Industrial Research, the Council of Scientific and Industrial Research (CSIR), which was modeled on the UK's Department of Scientific and Industrial Research, was founded in 1942 and is charged with industrial R&D administration. The CSIR currently has 40 national laboratories, and employs some 21,000 people, about 15,000 of them scientists and engineers; it receives a budget of approx. 400 million dollars from the Indian government, about one fifth of its revenues. The Department of Biotechnology and the Department of Ocean Development, both under the Ministry of Science and Technology, have research institutions of their own. The Ministry of Defense (under it a Defense Research and Development Organization), the Ministry of Commerce and Industry, the Ministry of Agriculture (under it an Indian Council of Agricultural Research), and the Ministry of Health & Family Welfare (under it an Indian Council of Medical Research) are Indian government branches relating more to scientific and technological affairs, and the Ministry of Human Resource Development is in charge of affairs relating to human resources in science and technology (Fig. 9-1).

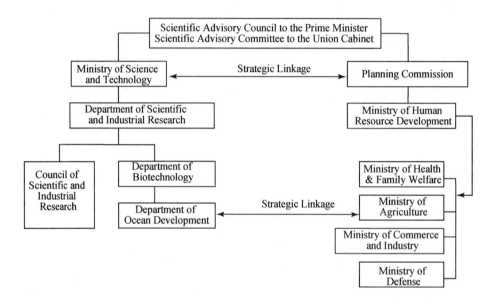

Fig. 9-1   Linkage between Public R&D Institutions in India

Source: Based on *Unleashing India's Innovation: Toward Sustainable And Inclusive Growth* (2009).

2.1.2   Organizational framework of universities

India has 342 universities and institutions of higher education, 18 of them Central Universities (founded under central legislation) and 211 of them State universities (founded under state legislation). The Indian Institutes of Technology (IITs), founded in 1961, are a group of seven engineering and technology-oriented institutes of higher education. They are top-notch institutions of higher education, the cradle of high-level talent in science and technology. It is reported that 40% of the 2,000 enterprises in the Silicon Valley are led by India entrepreneurs, a half of them from the IITs (Chang Qing, 2006). But compared with demand in India for talent, high-level universities are in a small number, so are masters and doctors trained each year. Statistics show that some 7,000 persons receive a doctor's degree in science and technology a year in India. It is estimated that by 2010, to maintain its market share in global modern service industries, India will need 2.3 million professionals, presenting a gap of some 500,000 to be met (Dutz, 2009).

2.2　Industrial Scientific & Technological Innovation and Results Transformation

A 2006 survey about innovation of Indian enterprises drew the following conclusions.

In India, enterprises engaged in innovation are largely larger, export-oriented and ISO-certified, and they are eager to absorb knowledge. Innovation-oriented enterprises are concentrated mainly in drugs and pharmaceuticals, auto components, and garments, and they have higher labor productivity. Garment enterprises are most likely to acquire new technology, while drug and pharmaceutical firms are most likely to pay royalties, use e-mail and computers, and subcontract R&D (Dutz, 2009).

2.2.1　Information technology and outsourcing

The software and information service industry has a quite prominent position not only in India but also in developing countries as a whole. In India, information industry-driven outsourcing has won contracts from many enterprises in developed countries. Because the Indian government has many favorable policies towards the country's information industry, plus low-cost yet qualified human resources in information technology and their proficiency in English, and enterprise leaders' familiarity with market prediction and operational rules, Indian enterprises are fairly capable of process management and quality control, which has made information technology the fast growing and most lucrative of Indian industries.

Early in 1986, the Indian government promulgated a Policy on Computer Software Export, Development and Training. In 1989 the Indian government launched the country's first Software Technology Park (STP) Scheme. In 1991, the Software Technology Parks of India (STPI) was established under the Ministry of Communications and Information Technology, which is charged with organization and implementation of the STP Scheme. STPI Bangalore, which was established in 1992 inside Electronics City in Bangalore, Karnataka, is the earliest and fastest growing of its kind in India. STPI initiated comprehensive data communication services under the name of "SoftNET", with the aim to offer high-speed reliable data communication connectivity between software enterprises and their overseas R&D facilities and their partners abroad. Then the largest microwave radio network in India, SoftNET was the first to offer commercial Internet services in India in 1993. The Network Operation Center-Bangalore guarantees network connectivity across the whole city by way of microwave radio. In addition to provision of private data communications, STPI also do front-end jobs on behalf of the Indian government, i. e. communicating about behavior and feedback between the government and enterprises, helping foreign-funded software companies to go through approvals in a one-stop manner, and providing customs bond and export certificates. The incorporation of a software company within STPI framework enjoys a great many favorable policies, for example, duty-free import of hardware and software, corporate income tax exemption (up to 90%) until 2010, permission to set up wholly foreign-funded companies, exemption of excise tax on purchase of domestic capital goods, and tax reimbursement on paid central sales tax.

In FY2008 ~ 2009, India's software output value was about 87 billion dollars, and its software exports amounted to about 50 billion dollars.

Due to economic globalization, international outsourcing may use global time difference to lower costs for not working at night. For example, there is a time difference of 10 hours between the United States and India, and if at the end of the day an American company delivers its data for processing to an Indian outsourcing company which is working in the morning, the American company will receive processed data next morning, which represents good efficiency and results. Thus, over 80% of American companies choose Indian companies as their top choice for outsourcing services.

The financial crisis led to a shrunk market share of India in the United States. Indian outsourcing companies in time considered developing into the markets of Europe and Japan. But there were two obstacles ahead, language and culture. Therefore, Indian outsourcing companies quickened training of their employees in language and culture. For example, according to Indian companies' culture, once projects are signed, Indian companies will complete the projects as required by contracts, not wishing frequent client involvement. But Japanese clients wish they can be informed of project progress at all times, and wish their involvement in projects. The Chinese culture is similar to that of Japan, so Chinese companies are more likely to obtain Japanese contracts and become rivals of Indian companies. Training efforts of Indian outsourcing companies have led to their rapid progress in European and Japanese markets. Tata Consultancy Services Limited (TCS) hopes to provide quality services in the languages of Germany and French to companies in Germany and France. In the FY2008 ~ 2009, the three largest outsourcing companies in India, TCS, Infosys and Wipro, earned 30%, 30% and 25% of their global income from the European market, respectively (Yin Xiaoshan, 2009).

Tata Consultancy Service Limited (TCS), founded in 1968, is a subsidiary of Tata Group, a prominent conglomerate company in India. After over 40 years of development, TCS has become the flagship of the Indian software industry. It focuses on investment in software projects and standards, software quality assurance, software project management, software processing, software engineering R&D, etc. TCS attributes its success to its close relationship with academia, workplace specialization, and emphasis on internal training and research. The primary business of TCS is providing software and consultancy services to enterprises of various types and sizes (in finance and banking, insurance, telecom, transport, retailing, manufacturing, drugs and pharmaceuticals, etc.). TCS is India's largest IT enterprise and largest software services exporter, and it is the largest independent provider of software and services in Asia. Currently it has more than 100 branches in over 30 countries worldwide, offering software services to 55 countries. Employing more than 40,000 people and with a client base of nearly 1,000, TCS provides IT and business consultancy services to domestic and foreign governments, enterprises and other organizations. In 2002, TCS established Tata Information Technology (Shanghai) Company Limited in Shanghai, and set up an R&D center in Hangzhou, China.

Infosys, officially Infosys Technologies Limited, was founded in 1981, and now has become a large-sized global company with an annual income from consultancy services exceeding 4.8 billion dollars, with products and services including technology consultancy, application services, system integration, product design, independent testing and certification, IT infrastructure services, and outsourcing. Infosys pioneered the Global Delivery Model (GDM). Infosys has more than 50 offices and R&D centers in India, China, Australia, Czech Republic, Poland, the UK, Canada, Japan and many other countries. Infosys and its subsidiaries had 11,3796 employees by March 2010. A 2006 survey of the Asia-Pacific region by Technology Review published by the Massachusetts Institute of Technology showed that the Indian company Infosys is among the world's 10 most innovative companies (Dutz,2009). Some summarized Infosys' core competitiveness as democratic management, brand effect, global delivery, global talent and crisis management, and held that its corporate culture is "free of sexual discrimination" (female employees already account for 26% ~27%, which is expected to reach 50%) and has an atmosphere of humane management-"proper treatment of employees" (Pan Song,2010). Infosys also has offices in Beijing and Shanghai, China.

Promoted by above-described companies, the main operations of Indian outsourcing companies are now shifting from the low ends of the value chain such as call center, data entry and after-sales services to the high ends of the chain like market analysis, engineering design, legal consultancy and patent application.

India has more than 3,000 software companies with some 500,000 employees all together, and the top ten software companies each employ more than 10,000 people, with a rate of return above 20%. Early in 2006, the Indian outsourcing industry employed 1,050,000 software engineers and skilled workers, and indirectly created 2.5 million jobs in traditional service industries such as transport and catering. At that time, Indian companies charged only 18 dollars to 26 dollars per hour for their software development services, which was far lower than 55 dollars to 66 dollars in Western countries. Therefore, each year, there were more than 660 multinational companies outsourcing related jobs (worth more than 1 million dollars for each of these multinationals) to Indian companies.

The National Association of Software and Services Companies (NASSCOM) of India estimated that by 2008, India's share of global software and back office service outsourcing would reach 51% (the figure would be only 4.9% for China), with annual sales estimated to reach $ 48 billion. According to the latest industrial research findings published by New Delhi, India will change from currently a BPO (Business Process Outsourcing) center to a KPO (Knowledge Process Outsourcing) base worth 17 billion dollars by 2010.

India's software outsourcing industry is expert at module design-designing and producing software in a short time as clients requires. By using the fastest supercomputer in India, Intel India developed engineering software with the same degree of difficulty as that in the United States. Intel India develops microprocessors and chips for Intel, and, on the basis of this, develops next-generation Ethernet switching silicon, network processors and enterprise software. In 2006 alone, Intel India filed applications for 63 patents.

Outsourcing will not always be passive. After years of successful outsourcing, Indian enterprises considerably increased their strength and thus expanded outwards. According to a 2007 joint research report by the Federation of Indian Chambers of Commerce & Industry and Ernst & Young, In FY2006 Indian enterprises completed 48 acquisitions and mergers in the United States, for a combined investment of more than 2 billion dollars, of them 48% in IT and related industries, followed by pharmaceuticals, hotels, agricultural products and automobiles (Liu Linsen,2007).

The following two tables (Tables 9-1 and 9-2) show the outsourcing capability of India.

Table 9-1　Share of Global Offshore Outsourcing by Countries in 2006, %

	India	China	Philippines	Canada	Mexico	Other Latin American Countries	Other Asian Countries	East Europe	Australia
Share of global offshore outsourcing	43	12	8	6	4	9	8	7	2

Source: Quoted from *Annual Report on China's Service Industry 2007* (2009), p107.

Table 9-2　Income Levels (hourly pay) of Service Sectors in the United States and India in 2002 ~ 2003 (Unit: Dollar)

Occupation	United States	India
Telephone operator	12.57	Below 1.00
Medical information recorder	13.17	1.50 ~ 2.00
Payroll manager	15.17	1.50 ~ 2.00
Law clerk	17.86	6.00 ~ 8.00
Accountant	23.35	6.00 ~ 15.00
Financial researcher	33.00 – 35.00	6.00 ~ 15.00

Source: Quoted from *Annual Report on China's Service Industry 2007* (2009), p114.

Data shows that one third of Fortune 500 companies outsource some of their operations to Indian companies. Since the beginning of the 21st century, India's output value of service outsourcing has kept at over 30%, whose income is more than one fourth of the country's income from exports, contributing 6% to its GDP (Pan Song, 2010). The service outsourcing industry has become one of the pillar industries in India.

2.2.2 Biotechnology and pharmaceutical industry

In 1986 the Indian government established the Department of Biotechnology under the Ministry of Science and Technology. It is estimated by the Department of Biotechnology that India's sales of biotechnological products will reach 4. 27 billion dollar in 2010.

Ranbaxy Laboratories Ltd. , founded in 1961, is the largest pharmaceutical company in India. At its inception, Ranbaxy mainly produced active pharmaceutical ingredients by modeling innovative drugs of Western countries. Five years later it was owned by Delhi businessmen Bhai Mohan Singh. Afterwards, Bhai Mohan Singh. 's son Parvinder Singh, who had received a doctor's degree in chemistry from University of Michigan, took over Ranbaxy.

After 20 years of development, in 1988, a plant of Ranbaxy got USFDA approval, obtaining the opportunity of exporting active pharmaceutical ingredients to the United States. 10 years later, Ranbaxy once again obtained the FDA approval to introduce into the United States its first product with independent patents for processes, the antibiotic cefaclor. Today, North America has become the largest market for Ranbaxy. In 2009, the company's gross income was 1. 34 billion dollars, 29% (391 million dollars) of it coming from North America. Ranbaxy has plants in 7 countries as well as branches in 46 countries, selling its products to more than 100 countries and regions. Ranbaxy is noted for its rapid pace of replication, excellent level of technology, original preparation technologies, new drug delivery system (NDDS), four leading technical platforms, R&D of new compounds, and 28 global brands. It ranks 6th among global pharmaceutical companies for its obtaining 44 patents a year on average, thanks to its extraordinary drug R&D capacity with R&D intensity (ratio of R&D spending to sales) up to internationally advanced 15%. Ranbaxy's fruitful R&D achievements come from its 1,200 researchers (167 of them holding doctor's degrees and 291 holding master's degrees), who conduct research mainly in anti-infective drugs, cardiovascular drugs, central nervous system drugs, urinary tract drugs, tumor drugs, and diabetic drugs.

Ranbaxy's core competitiveness lies in its capabilities of independent R&D and overseas market development. In the early 2010 its sales already reached 1. 7 billion dollars, making it India's sole company among the global top 100 pharmaceutical companies. Ranbaxy has its own marketing teams in global 49 countries, distributes its drugs in more than 125 countries, and owns production bases in 11 countries which employ people from more than 50 countries, all of these revealing that Ranbaxy has become the largest multinational pharmaceutical company in India. Ranbaxy operates worldwide in accordance with international team standards. Another advantage of globalization is that its worldwide operations can effectively help it to avoid risks which may come from excessive dependence on a particular region. The United States remains to be the largest market of Ranbaxy, but its rapid development in emerging markets can well balance the possibility of reliance on global economic powers (Pan Song, 2010).

The immediate objective of Ranbaxy is to become one of global top five enterprises of generic drugs and over 5 billion dollars in annual sales by 2012.

There are other biopharmaceutical companies in India, such as Biocon and Panacea Biocon. India's biopharmaceutical companies have a much greater tendency than those in any other development country to enter the US market. In 2003, Indian pharmaceutical companies accounted for the most Drug Master Files applications (126) with USFDA, more than China, Israel and Spain combined (Dutz, 2009).

The rise of Indian pharmaceutical companies is closely linked to India's institutional design. Among other things, the 1991 abolishment of the licensing system (in favor of pharmaceutical companies' overseas expansion), the 2000 announcement of the "New Millennium Biotechnology Policy" (for strengthening R&D at pharmaceutical companies) and the 2009 revised *Patents Act* (prohibiting replication of Western patent drugs) created an environment conducive to the development of Indian pharmaceutical companies.

2.2.3   Acquisitions and mergers of Indian enterprises

Acquisitions and mergers (M&As) are a type of enterprise development route, a normal form of operation, regardless of whether there is innovation. It is roughly estimated that unsuccessful M&As outnumbers successful ones. But Indian enterprises' M&As have nearly become an advantage, a royal road to their rapid development. Table 9-3 shows top ten M&As by Indian private enterprises, from which we can see the internationalization strategy of Indian private enterprises and how they are confident in it. They firmly believe that they have a vision of international operation and have the ability to choose and use such assets of companies to be acquired as brands and trademarks, patented technologies, talent and human resources, dedicated equipment and facilities, marketing channels and networks, clients and organizational capital. Through more than 1,500 international M&As, Indian private enterprises not only obtained experience in international business operation but also quickly improved their own popularity, reputation, scale and value, leading them to rapidly become international large enterprises. Official Indian statistics show that the average size of overseas acquisition by Indian enterprises have risen from 10 million dollars per M&A case to 60 million dollars per M&A case. For example, through international M&As, the Indian steel magnate Lakshmi Mittal not only made his steel enterprises able to produce iron and steel of 116 million tons a year, but also gained control over 60% of iron ore his enterprises needed. Following Mittal's model, Tata Steel also saw robust development through international M&As, overtaking China's Baosteel in 2005 to become the world's most competitive steel company (Pan Song, 2010). Indian enterprises have advantages to carry out M&As: they enjoy a relaxed environment created by the government's institutional design; and India has a large number of outstanding entrepreneurs experienced in international business operation.

Table 9-3   Top 10 International M&As by Indian Private Companies

No.	Indian Private Enterprise	Company Acquired	Sector	M&A Volume / $ 100 million
1	Tata Steel	Corus, UK	Steel	121
2	Bharti Airtel	Zain, Kuwait	Telecom	107
3	Hindalco	Novelis, US	Aluminum	33.31
4	Essar Group	Algoma Steel, Canada	Steel	16
5	United Spirits	Whyte and Mackay, Scotland, UK	Beer	12
6	GMR Energy	A 50% stake in Intergen, UK	Power	11
7	Sterlite Industries	Asarco, US	Copper	26
8	Suzlon	Hansen Transmissions, Belgium	Wind power	5.65
9	Sun Pharmaceutical	Taro Pharmaceuticals, Israel	Pharmaceutical	4.5
10	Wipro	Infocrossing Inc., US	Software	5.57

Source: Pan Song, 2010.

2.3   Science and Technology Input and Output

In 1990 ~ 2008, India's GERD increased year by year, but its GERD/GDP ratio fluctuated between 0.8% and 0.9% (Fig. 9-2).

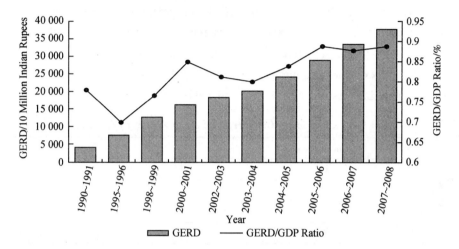

Fig. 9-2   GERD/GDP Ratios of India (1990 ~ 2008)

Source: Quoted from a compilation of Statistical Repots on Research and Development in India 2007 ~ 2008,
published in A General Survey of Global Scientific and Technological Investment (Issue 182),
Institute of Scientific and Technical Information of China.

The low statistical values of India's GERD are, some scholars think, probably because of their exclusion of multinational companies in India. If multinational companies in India were included, India's GERD/GDP ratio would stand between 1.0% and 1.1%, and, some scholars believe, were likely to near or top 2% (MOST of China, 2010). GERD statistics is an difficult part of science and technology statistics. I thus visited and consulted UNESCO and OCED experts in R&D statistics, and learned that it is not easy for a developing country to solve difficulties involved in this regard. For example, China's ratio of basic research expenditure to GERD is very low, between 5% and 6%, which is incredible. But to ensure measurement consistency between countries in science and technology statistics, international authoritative statistics prevail in this book.

In 2007, India's GERD was 4.775 billion dollars (ranking 24th in the world), and its GERD/GPD ratio only stood at 0.75% (ranking 38th in the world)-much lower than China's 1.49% and India's previous data (up to 0.8% ~ 1.0%).

India is ranked 31st in the IMD *World Competitiveness Yearbook 2010*, down one place from one year ago (IMD, 2010), and 51st in the World Economic Forum's *Global Competitiveness Report 2010 ~ 2011*, down two places from one year ago (WEF, 2010).

From 1950 to 2008 India had one Nobel Prize laureate, ranking 20th in the world.

In 2007, India had 954 patents for invention awarded, ranking 21st in the world (MOST of China, 2010). In 2008, India published 64,869 papers on the world's three major index journals, ranking 11th in the world (MOST of China, 2010). But in some disciplines, both the number of papers by Indian scholars and their rate of citation are quite impressive. (Table 9-4 and Table 9-5)

Table 9-4 Citations of Bio-energy Research Papers by Countries

Indicator	United States	India	China	Japan
Qty. of papers	895	844	641	254
Total citations	12,357	10,946	4,863	3,174
Citations per paper	13.81	12.97	7.59	12.5
H index	50	42	26	28

Note: The *h* index means that a scientist has index *h* if *h* of his/her *N* papers have at least *h* citations each, and the other (*N-h*) papers have at most h citations each.

Source: Liu Bin et al., 2010.

Table 9-5 Citations of Bio-energy Research Papers by Institutions

Indicator	Indian Institutes of Technology (IITs)	Chinese Academy of Sciences (CAS)	Agricultural Research Service of United States Department of Agriculture
Qty. of papers	132	84	72
Total citations	1,942	632	1,060
Citations per paper	14.71	7.52	14.72
H index	24	14	20

Source: Liu Bin et al., 2010.

As far as cost effectiveness of science and technology input and output is concerned, data shows that India has lower costs for R&D achievements. For example, according to statistics by The World Bank, in 2004, the R&D expenditure per each research paper (not expenditure for paper publication) calculated by dividing GERD by the total number of research papers was 460,000 dollars for India, 953,000 dollars for China, 431,000 dollars for Russia, and 682,000 dollars for Brazil; when GERD was divided by the number of patents approved by the United States Patent and Trademark Office (USPTO), the R&D expenditure per patent (not expenditure for patent development) approved by the USPTO was 16 million dollars for India, 47 million dollars for China, 39 million dollars for Russia, and 377 million dollars for Brazil. This was probably because of India's lower wages for researchers. 2006 data showed that the total annual payroll cost of an Indian scientist or engineer was roughly 22,600 dollars a year, compared with 90,000 dollars in the United States (Dutz, 2009). This also suggests that India has higher cost performance of researchers among BRICs. Global firms are very willing to locate innovation centers in India, which perhaps is one of the main reasons. Between 1998 and 2003, more than 300 multinational companies (50% of them from the United States) set up their R&D centers in India, and they employed over 80,000 scientists and engineers and spend about four billion dollars a year (72% of it from the United States) (Dutz, 2009).

3. Innovation Culture

India is a religious country. Buddhism spread into China from India and had a great influence on the Chinese ancient culture. But the religion in India with the largest number of followers is not Buddhism, but Hinduism, with 80. 5% of the population recording it as their religion; only 0. 8% of the population has faith in Buddhism. Other religious groups in India include Muslims (13. 4%), Christians (2. 3%) and Sikhs (1. 9%). A religious culture has an influence not only on social development and people's life, but also on innovators' innovation behavior and management in a subtle manner. For example, faiths have moral restrictions on human beings and commercial activities. For another example, religious activities require mind peace and concentration, which intersects somewhere with " free inquiry" and " pursuit of truth" required in scientific and technological activities.

In a knowledge economy-based society, " good faith" as part of religion helps shape social culture and the " good faith culture" as part of corporate culture, while the " good faith culture" is helpful for people to understand that " piracy is illegitimate". " When installing computer software, an Indian employee would insist on installing one suite of software only for a computer, viewing the installation of one suite of software for two or more computers as piratical, tortuous and illegitimate. If his employer disagreed, the employee would usually refuse, or otherwise resign. Why are there basically no pirated discs, software and books, no fake famous-brand products, in India?" (Yuan Nansheng, 2007). This provides an explanation for the connection between religion and "good faith culture". If justifiable, this explanation can be linked with innovation culture.

Below is an excerpt from *Know India*, a book by Yuan Nansheng who served as Consul General of China to Mumbai in India (later Chinese Ambassador to the Republic of Zimbabwe, and currently Chinese Ambassador to Republic of Suriname).

"Most impressively, Indian intellectuals work in earnest, not eager for quick success and instant benefit. They do whatever you want them to do, and persist with great patience, thinking nothing about 'job-hopping' or 'risking their fortune in doing business'. Huawei established its R&D centre in Bangalore, India, which employs nearly 600 Indian software experts who are all meticulous and cooperative, never regarding themselves as infallible. I accompanied delegations from Chinese to visit this center many times, and each visit gave me more impression of the Indian workers at the center. If you let an Indian expert do a job, director of the center Yuan Ziwen says, he will document your requirements and ask for your confirmation before he begins the job. After an interim task has been finished, he will once again request your confirmation of his work already done and of next-step requirements, and then proceed with the job until completion of it. As over one hundred global software companies including Intel were establishing their R&D centers in Bangalore and indigenous software development firms were growing fast, software talent were increasingly in dire need in Bangalore and the rest of India. But at Huawei's R&D center, there was rare job-hopping among its Indian software experts, though Huawei was not superior to other similar institutes in working conditions and remuneration. This shows that Indian intellectuals pay more attention to working environment and career development than to how much they earn. Indian universities and research institutions are places of doing scholarship and research, rather than government offices. At such eminent universities as University of Mumbai and Bangalore University, there are no rows of office buildings, no concepts of officials of complex rank. Intellectuals at these institutions largely basically work for work's sake, very few choosing to get rich wrongfully, and no university has been heard of running for the profit purpose what is called on-the-job postgraduate courses. As long as you have a certain knowledge of Indian intellectuals, you cannot help but admire them for their attitudes towards fame and wealth and for persistence and perseverance in whatever they do" (Yuan Nansheng, 2007).

This lengthy citation is very convincing because it was written by a Chinese diplomat with a deep insight into India's society and intellectuals. Not only can it let us spontaneously have respect for India's intellectuals and innovation culture, but also make it easy to understand "rise of India".

Indian enterprises' innovation culture can be described as good faith culture, and human-centered culture which highlights self-esteem, kindness to others, pursuit of win-win, and repaying the society.

India's innovation culture has these features: research with great concentration, not seeking quick success and instant benefit; respect for intellectual property, protecting and encouraging creative work; and emphasis on teamwork.

In a broader sense, innovation culture not only refers to innovation-generating culture, but also includes the culture of creating an innovation environment. As far as the latter is concerned, the spirit of Mahatma Gandhi and the Indian traditional culture have far-reaching influences which manifest in self-control, bearing no ill will against any body, paying attention to moral uplift, hardworking and self-cultivation, dedication to truth, and patriotism.

Much of the Indian culture and innovation culture is worth learning by present-day Chinese intellectuals, enterprises and officials.

4. Comments on Innovation Management and National Strength

As one of the world's "four great ancient civilizations" and one of the two big countries with rising economy and national strength, India has the tradition of innovation culture and the ability of innovation management. A clear proof is that India is the leading developing country in modern service industries such as software, finance and outsourcing. A total of 33 Indian private enterprises have become world-class international corporations. In 2009, India's service industry contributed 55% to its GDP (a percentage far greater than China's 43% in the same year). Young Indians account for a big proportion in the country's labor forces, suggesting that there will be no aging problem (50% of the population is aged below 35) in a long period to come. Some predict that India's economic growth rate is likely to reach 10% in 2012 and surpass China's in 2014 (Pan Song, 2010). It is worth a special mention that: India is more experienced than China in market economy operation, and its financial system and market order is one of the best among developing countries; India's banking system and stock market each have a history of more than 100 years; India's commercial banks outstrip China's in main performance indicators; and India's capital market is more transparent and efficient than China's.

Compared with China, India has another favorable condition, and that is its international development space that makes it able to achieve success one way or another. Largely influenced by the UK, India is roughly the same as Western countries in political system and ideology, making it barrier-free in such aspects as international relations, foreign trade, flow of personnel, and cultural exchange. The author participated in a September 2007 conference titled "The Dragon and the Elephant: Understanding the Development of Innovation Capacity In China and India", organized by the Board on Science, Technology, and Economic Policy of the United States National Academy of Sciences, which gave me a certain knowledge of this point. In present-day Western countries' strategies with restrictions on China, India is usually taken good care of for its special position. On the other hand, India has unusual relations with Russia, and both countries have close cooperation in economy and military. All these are favorable conditions for the rise of India. On M&A, for example, India not only has experience in market operation, but also imposes no political barriers as in China to its enterprises. That's why India's overseas M&A volume accounts for 98% of its FDI (Foreign Direct Investment) (Pan Song, 2010).

But compared with China, too, India still has troubles for the rise of it. First, politically, as a developing country India has the multi-party system and other Western democratic systems, the maladies are evident: low government efficiency, frequent "power for money deals" arising from elections, and "corruption" which involves not only government departments and enterprises but also military and police. Second, guerilla revolts exist in both northern and southern India, there is turbulence in Kashmir, and there are social problems such as "the class of untouchables". Third, India's infrastructure, manufacturing and transportation, such as highways, airports and ports, are backward. In my eye, the rise of either China or India is conducive to global social and economic development, but the prediction or estimate that India can overtake China in a short term is perhaps over-optimistic.

Table 9-6 is a brief comparison in current national strength of India and China based on statistic data by The World Bank.

Table 9-6   A Brief Comparison of India and China

Indicator	India	China
Gross national income (GNI) per-capita (dollars, 2009)	1,180	3,590
Growth of GDP per capita (%, 2006 ~ 2007)	7.6	12.4
Average annual population growth (%, 2007 ~ 2015)	1.3	0.5
Population aged 15 ~ 64 (%, 2009)	64	72
Average annual growth of labor force aged 15 and older (%, 1990 ~ 2007)	1.9	1.1
Labor force participation rate of population aged 15 and older (%, 2007)	55	73
Labor productivity (%, 2008)	5.4	8.6
Gini index (%, 2005)	36.8	41.5
Gross enrollment ratio, preprimary, primary, secondary, tertiary (%, 2007)	40, 112, 55, 12	39, 111, 76, 22
Hospital beds (per 1,000 people, 2002 ~ 2007)	0.9	2.2
Survival to age 65, male and female (% of cohort, 2007)	60, 69	75, 83
Gross savings and net national savings (% of GNI, 2007)	38.8, 29.2	54.4, 43.7
Average GDP growth (%, 2007, 2009)	9.0, 7.7	11.9, 9.1
Average annual growth of imports and exports of goods and services (%, 2007)	7.5, 7.7	19.9, 13.9
GDP, and ratios of agriculture, industry and services to GDP 100 million dollars, %, 2009)	13,101.7, 17, 28, 55	49,847.3, 10, 46, 43
Mobile phone subscribers per 100 people (2008)	30	48
Personal computers per 100 people (2007)	3.3	5.7
Internet subscribers per 100 people (2008)	4.5	22.5
ICT spending/GDP (%, 2008)	4.0	5.8
Households with television (%, 2006)	53	89
R&D personnel per million people (2000 ~ 2006, 2007)	111, —	926, 1,071
R&D expenditure/GDP (%, 2000 ~ 2006, 2007)	0.69, 0.80	1.42, 1.49
Exports of high-tech goods, and their ratio to manufactured goods (100 million dollars, %, 2007)	49.4, 5	3,369.9, 30

Continued

Indicator	India	China
Patent applications by residents (2007, 2008)	(4,521), —	(153,060), (194,579)
Trade in merchandises and services (% of GDP, 2007)	30.8, 15.2	67.8, 7.9
FDI net inflows and outflows (% of GDP, 2007)	2.0, 1.1	4.3, 0.5
Military expenditures (% of GDP, 2009)	3.0	2.0
Weapon imports and exports (100 million dollars, 2007)	0.08, 4.75	3.55, 14.24

Source: The World Bank, 2009; The World Bank, 2010

With 28 indicators covering national development, economy, science and technology, education, health, military etc., Table 9-6 can roughly reflects the national strength of the two big developing countries in recent years. The table has great reference value now that the statistical data contained are relative objective and most of them are about the years 2007, 2008 and 2009.

China outperformed India in the following indicators: GNI, two times more than India's; GDP, more than 2 time that of India; average annual GDP growth and GDP growth per capita, three-four percentage points higher than India's; labor productivity, 3.2 percentage points higher than India's; labor force participation rate of population aged 15 and older, 18 percentage points higher than India's; gross enrollment ratio of secondary and tertiary school, 20 and 10 percentage points higher than India's respectively; hospital beds, more than twice that of India's; ratio of gross savings and net national savings to GNI, 15 and 14 percentage points higher than India's respectively; ratio of survial to age 65, male and female, 15 and 14 percentage points higher than India's respectively; ratio of FDI net inflows to GDP, more than twice that of India (China's ratio of FDI net outflows to GDP was only half that of India's); average annual growth rate of exports and imports of goods and services, 12 and 6 percentage points higher than India's; mobile phone subscribers, personal computers and Internet subscribers per 100 people, all much higher than India's; R&D personnel per 100 people (2000 ~ 2006), nine times that of India; R&D/GDP (2000 ~ 2006), with China already up to the level of developed countries, comparing with the moderately high level of developing countries; exports of high-tech goods and their ratio to manufactured goods, and patent applications by residents, dozens of times that of India.

India outperformed China in: average annual growth of labor force aged 15 and older, 0.8 percentage points higher than China's; ratio of services to GDP, 12 percentage points higher than China's; and ratio of service trade to GDP,7 percentage points higher than China's.

The above comparison suggests that India has superiority over China in services and labor force growth, while China has superiority in national development, economy, science and technology, education, health etc.

As to soft power, advantages of India are as follows: due to political and language reasons, India has superiority in diplomacy, with far better relations than China with Western countries and dealing well with Russia, Brazil, South Africa and Japan; international M&A has rapidly increased India's presence in the world; as one of the "four great ancient civilizations", India has a long history, whose religious culture and successful Bollywood are influential in the world.

Advantages of China are as follows: China has produced a far-reaching influence in the world as a fast growing big country; its unique political system, economic system and mechanisms not only have a "differentiation" influence on Western countries, but also are exceptionally appealing to developing countries; as one of the "four great ancient civilizations" too, China has a long history and its Confucianism and "Confucius Institutes" are influential in the world.

Militarily, India has armed forces of 1. 27 million, ranking 4th in the world, including 1. 035 million for the army (equipped with intermediate and long-range missiles), 70,000 for the navy (equipped with aircraft carrier), and 170,000 for the air force (equipped with advanced fighter planes purchased from Russia and France (Editorial Board of World Affairs, 2009). In 2007, India's military expenditure/ GDP ratio was 2. 5% (up to 3. 0% in 2008), its weapon exports amounted to 14 million dollars and weapon imports to 1. 32 billion dollars (The World Bank, 2009). In recent years, India has increased its expenditures to purchase weapons from the United States, Russia and European countries and cooperated with Russia and the United States in developing advanced weapons, attempting to become a military power in Asia and even in the world.

It should be noted that this is only the situation in 2007 ~ 2008. If India gains further strength in services, finance and human resources, then there will be ups and downs when China and India are compared in strength. Some Indians and Americans predict that India will catch up with China in 2012 or 2015 and overtake China around 2020. The prediction is perhaps over optimistic, but the rise of India is the fact.

Chapter 10

An Ambitious Brazil

Brazil, officially the Federative Republic of Brazil, covers 8.5149 million square kilometers, and has a population of 184 million (2007 est.), 53.74% of them whites and 38.45% of color. The official language of Brazil is Portuguese. A total of 73.8% of the population have faith in Roman Catholicism. Historically Brazil was the sole colony of Portugal in Latin America. From the 1950s onwards, Brazil began transition from an agrarian country to an industrial country. Over the past decade, Brazil has been one of a group of four emerging economies called the BRIC countries for its rapid economic growth. Brazil has abundant natural resources, with iron ore reserves, production and exports all coming in first in the world. It also had abundant oil and natural gas proven in recent years. With forests covering 57% of the area, Brazil has timber reserves of 65.8 billion cubic meters. Brazil abounds with waterpower resources; it has 18% of the world's freshwater, with an amount of freshwater per-capita of 29,000 cubic meters, and its waterpower reserves reach 143 million kilowatts. With an economic structure similar to developed countries', Brazil is the largest economy in Latin America; it has developed agriculture, and its service industry output value tops 50% of GDP. Between 1967 and 1974, Brazil's annual economic growth rate stood at 10.1%, hailed as "Brazil miracle" (Editorial Board of World Affairs, 2009). But from the global financial crisis which struck in 2008, the Brazilian economy suffered heavily. Its GDP continued to decline in 2009 following a 3.6% drop from the previous quarter for the 4th quarter of 2008. From November 2008 to January 2009, Brazil had 800,000 unemployed people throughout the country (MOST of China, 2010).

Brazil has been chosen to host the 2014 FIFA World Cult and the 2016 Olympic Games. It seems to Brazil, as the largest country of Latin America, that all happen as it wishes. Now it is in the prime of its development, endeavoring to get stronger.

1. Institutional Design

1.1　National Institutional Design

The first constitution of Brazil was promulgated in 1882. The current constitution is the eighth constitution of Brazil promulgated in October 1988 which was amended in 1994 and 1999 by the National Congress of Brazil.

In politics, Brazil is a federal presidential republic, with the bicameral Congress-both houses of which have legislative powers and budgetary scrutiny powers. Brazil has a multi-party system, with main political parties including the Workers' Party, Brazilian Labour Party, Brazilian Democratic Movement Party, Socialist People's Party and Brazilian Communist Party.

Brazil has a federal system with a greater degree of separation of powers. Its spheres of government comprise three levels: the Union (federal government), state governments and local governments.

Within the cabinet there is the Ministry of Science and Technology charged with administration of science and technology.

During the 2002 election, the former President of Brazil Luiz Inácio Lula raised the goal of "helping poor Brazilians realize three meals a day", elevating the right of survival for poor Brazilians to one of priority objectives of government policy. In 8 years that followed, the Lula administration implemented a series of social policies, notably the "Zero Hunger" and "Family Allowance" programs; in five years from 2003 to 2008, the income of poor people increased by 22%, while that of rich people only rose 4.9%; the minimum salaries of workers also increased from 200 reals[①] in early 2003 to 465 reals in early 2009, the record high over the past two decades. According to statistics by the Brazilian Institute of Geography and Statistics (IBGE), Brazil's Gini coefficient was on the decline for ten consecutive years, down to 0.515 in 2008 from 0.567 in 1998. As to the "rise of Brazil", a Brazilian view is that a big-power position of Brazil is manifested more as a "regional big power" and that currently Brazil has no conditions to become one of the world's big powers like China and the United States. But in some international affairs, especially some regional ones, the important role of Brazil has been increasingly evident and gradually won worldwide recognition. This also reveals that Brazil is in some state of rise. Therefore, it is suitable to say that Brazil now is in the best stage of development in its history (Zhou Zhiwei, 2009).

Following its economic takeoff, Brazil has gradually adjusted its foreign policy and increased its involvement in international affairs, trying to from a "regional big power" to a "global big power". First, while seeking to become a permanent member of the United Nations Security Council, Brazil actively participated in activities of the International Monetary Fund (IMF) and the United Nations as well as related work on international coordination, and spoke at major international conferences and forums

---

① Present-day currency of Brazil. 1 real is equal to some 4 yuan.

over issues such as climate change, trade, finance, peace and security. As a part of its national institutional design, Brazil seeks to build a new type of union beyond union and conventional relations. Just as the former Foreign Minister of Brazil, the foundation of Brazilian foreign policy still is the integration of South America, with particular attention given to enhancing the close relations between Brazil and Argentina, both of them big powers in South America. Second, Brazil played an important role within such non-binding organizations as "BRIC", "G-20" and "IBAS" (India, Brazil and South Africa). In the meanwhile, Brazil's concurrent trade and political efforts further broadened the country's international activity space and capacity. In 7 years, Brazil saw rapid growth in its trade with developing countries, with a four- and five-fold increase in its trade with Arabian countries and with African countries, respectively. Great changes have happened to the image of Brazil in the world (Amorim, 2010).

To promote the country's science and technology and economic development, the National Congress of Brazil promulgated one after another some laws intended to promote scientific, technological and innovative development, for example, the *Information Industry Law*, the *Law on Tax Incentives for Private Investment in Science and Technology*, the *Law on Government Procurement of High-tech Products*, and the *Innovation Law*.

Brazil enacted a range of laws and regulations to develop its information industry. In 1984, the National Congress of Brazil adopted the *Information Industry Law*. According to this law, any enterprise whose investment in scientific and technological innovation reaches 5% of its output value will enjoy a 50% reduction in income tax as well as exemption of industrial product tax, and the government will also enterprises with low-interest loans and give financial and credit support to enterprises' technological innovation projects and research equipment they are to purchase.

In the 1990s, to promote the export of software products, the Brazilian government introduced the "Brazilian Program for Software Export" (SOFTEX 2000), with the aim to make Brazil one of the world's five largest software developers and exporters. This program was co-launched and initially funded by the National Council for Scientific and Technological Development (CNPq) of Brazil and the United Nations. Designed to foster high-level Brazilian software enterprises and world-class software products, the program required the assistance by Brazilian bodies in foreign countries of software companies in participating in international or domestic major computer & software exhibitions and fairs, the regular provision of forums within Brazil, the announcement of latest developments on management, science and technology, and markets, and the formulation of preferential policies to encourage export of software products.

In the end of January 2007, the Lula administration incorporated into the *Growth Acceleration Program* (PAC) the development of the information industry, with the view of considerably lowering tax directed towards the information industry. In the first half of 2007, 4.3 million computers were sold in Brazil, of which notebooks, up 156% from the same period in 2006, amounted to 365,000; the sales volume of notebooks for 2007 reached 2.1 million units, 211% of that for 2006.

In December 2004, Brazil promulgated the *Innovation Law* by which to encourage the establishment of cooperative links between research institutions, universities and enterprises, shorten periods for transformation of scientific and technological results, develop and improve enterprises' competitiveness, change the passive situation in which the transformation of scientific and technological results lags behind, and finally promote sustainable social and economic development (MOST of China, 2010).

Directed towards the problem of disconnection between the previous research models of public research institutions and enterprises' demand for technological results, the *Innovation law* provided the legal framework needed to improve technological development and commercialize technologies. According to the Innovation Law, only by publishing a previous "request for licencees" can public scientific and technological institutions be able to accelerate the process of licensing and selecting the best partners. This law requires public scientific and technological institutions to create "Offices of Technological Innovation" which, among other duties, are responsible for the management of the technology generated by researchers, with special attention to decisions regarding intellectual property and licensing.

1.2 Institutional Design on Science and Technology

The Brazilian Ministry of Science and Technology launched a *Strategic Program* with main objectives to: achieve the best integration of scientific and technological innovation and strengthen regional development, with the federal government supporting scientific and technological activities of state or regional research and development centers; accelerate the production sector's investment in scientific and technological development, diversify national funding of scientific research and development, and financially support scientific research at national enterprises; increase technological independence, develop and promote original technologies appropriate for national conditions; create new scientific and technological fields geared towards requirements of scientific development, and develop export-oriented and internationally competitive technologies.

In the early 21st century, the Brazilian government introduced scientific and technological programs regarding several fields in support of the above Strategic Program, including, among others, the "Scientific and Technological Program for 2000 ~ 2003", "New Millennium Institute Program", "Fund Program for Research and Development in Ten Industries", "Green-and-Yellow Fund Program", and "Action Plan 2007 ~ 2010: Science, Technology and Innovation for National Development". With its capable biotechnology researchers, Brazil has vigorously implemented its genome project, ranking only behind the United States in the world in human cancer genome cracking and mapping. On biomedical technology, Brazil has made significant achievements in immunity research and pharmaceutical development about tropical diseases, with biomedical products possessing a 80% share in the domestic market. In addition, in order to quickening the development of nanotechnology, the Brazilian Ministry of Science and Technology and the CNPq developed a nanotechnology program in 2001, funding projects in three fields-nanomaterials, nanobiotechnology and chemistry, and nanomachines.

In July 2009 the Brazilian government conducted an evaluation of the "Action Plan 2007 ~ 2010: Science, Technology and Innovation for National Development", concluding that the main problem was about how to improve enterprises' innovation efficiency and effectiveness.

2. Innovation Management

2.1   Organizational Framework for Science and Technology and Innovation System

In 1951, Brazil founded the National Research Council (later renamed National Council for Scientific and Technological Development, namely CNPq) responsible for administering national affairs regarding scientific and technological research and the development of human resources in science and technology. Afterwards, the National Fund for Scientific and Technological Development was founded in 1964, and the National Fund for Technology Support was created in 1969. In 1985, Brazil established the Ministry of Science and Technology under the federal government. Within the federal government, the body that directs scientific and technological policy consultancy is the CNPq, while the Ministry of Science and Technology is charged with scientific and technological administration at national level, funding planning, organization and financial allocation regarding R&D projects (National Innovation Capacity Evaluation and Research Panel, Development Research Center of China Association for Science and Technology, 2009). The Agronomical Institute of Campinas and University of Campinas are prominent representatives of government research institutions and research universities in Brazil, respectively. Large Brazilian enterprises with strong R&D capacity include, among others, Embraer S. A. , Vale S. A. -the world's third largest mining company, and Petrobras.

2.2   Research Results Commercialization and Enterprise Innovation Management

Early in 1981, the CNPq and related research institutions launched a "National Alcohol Program", replacing gasoline with alcohol produced form sugar cane as automobile fuels, for the purpose of solving the then oil shortage of the country. Costing billions of dollars, this project finally succeeded with vigorous support from the Brazilian government, relying mainly on Western developed countries' multinational corporations in Brazil and their R&D centers. By the mid-1980s, two million Brazilian automobiles used pure alcohol as fuel and 8 million ones used gasoline containing 20% alcohol as fuel, resulting in a 50% reduction in Brazil's oil exports. Because the "Alcohol Program" was largely carried out by R&D centers of multinational corporations including Germany's Volkswagen, the United States' GM and Ford and Italy's Fiat, it didn't improve the country's R&D capacity substantially.

Benefiting from the Brazilian government's policies and laws regarding technological innovation, Brazilian enterprises also made their own achievements in the first several years of the 21st century. For example, the Flex-Fuel Engines technology, which was developed and introduced in 2004 by Brazil, allows automobiles to use fuels of mixed gasoline and alcohol, which not only made alcohol produced from sugar cane a major export of Brazil but also lowered the country's dependence on fossil fuels.

Embraer S. A. , Petrobras and Vale S. A. are leading Brazilian enterprises in innovation management.

Embraer is the fourth-largest civil aircraft company in the world and one of the largest exporters in Brazil. It is a world leader in development and manufacturing of feederliners with 120 seats and below. After its successful use of ethanol as aircraft fuel, Embraer retrofitted an old model into the world's first aircraft using ethanol as fuel in 2004.

Petrobras, founded in 1953, is the largest state-owned enterprise of Brazil. Its success in its technology for deep-water exploration has contributed to its position as a world leader in oil and gas production over the past decade. Upon its completion of global largest share offering in history, Petrobras will become the fourth largest company in the world and the second largest company in America by market value. Its financing plan aims to raise 66. 9 billion dollars, used mainly for oil exploration in ultra-deep waters near Brazil.

Vale S. A. , founded in 1942, is the largest producer of iron ore and pellets in the world, and the third largest mining conglomerate in the world. In recent years it obtained the patent for its water-free ore treatment technology which allows a considerable reduction in costs for operation and slag treatment. Vale ahs also successfully developed the world's first natural gas-powered train used specially for transport of iron ore.

On agricultural research, Agronomical Institute of Campinas and University of Campinas conducted fruitful research (Zhou Jizhong,1993). The *"Action Plan 2007 ~ 2010: Science, Technology and Innovation for National Development"* , which has been implemented in recent years, proposed plans to strengthen the domestic research, production and distribution network of biodiesel. In 2008 ~ 2009, the Brazilian Ministry of Science and Technology launched a "Biodiesel Research and Development Program, which included the extraction of biodiesel from cash crops such as oil palm and cassava, and invested 40 million reals (about 160 million yuan) in development of biodiesel.

As the 21st century arrived, it was the time for Brazil to tackle technical difficulties on its own strength. This first happened in the field of energy. Increased investment in energy science and technology led to the discovery of large oil fields one after another in Brazil in 2008 and 2009, making Brazil a big oil producer in the world.

The Brazilian government has developed a range of preferential policies with the aim to strengthen the transformation of scientific and technological achievements, but similar to China, Brazil is confronted with the complex problem of how to improve the transformation rate of scientific and technological achievements.

2.3 Science and Technology Input and Output

In 2007, Brazil's GERD was 14.651 billion dollars (ranking 13th in the world), and its GERD/GDP ratio was only 1.10% (ranking 31st in the world). Its enterprise R&D expenditure was 6.89 billion dollars, ranking 17th in the world, and its enterprise R&D expenditure/GDP ratio was 0.52%, ranking 31st in the world. 60% of Brazil's gross R&D investment came from the government and 40% from enterprises. In the same year, Brazil had 354,100 researchers (FTE), ranking 6th in the world.

Brazil is only ranked 38th in the IMD *World Competitiveness Yearbook 2010*, up two places from one year ago (IMD, 2010), and 58th in the World Economic Forum's *Global Competitiveness Report 2010 ~ 2011*, down two places form one year ago (WEF, 2010).

In 2007, Brazil had 24,074 applications for patents for invention, ranking 12th in the world, 241 of which were awarded, only ranking 32nd in the world.

In 2008, Brazil published 47,636 papers on the world's three major index journals, ranking 15th in the world (MOST of China, 2010).

Due to continuously increased investment in scientific research and development, Brazil has already been in a leading position among Latin American countries in terms of scientific and technological innovation. Currently, Brazil has fairly high levels in such fields as information technology, small-sized aircraft manufacturing, automobile production, hydropower engineering and technology, mining, bioengineering and new materials.

In Brazil, 80 of more than 800 institutions of higher education have R&D centers, with nearly 7,000 doctoral students in 2003.

Compared with developed countries, main problems facing scientific and technological innovation in Brazil, according to the Brazilian business circles, are: insufficient utilization of R&D resources, inadequate channels by which enterprises obtain R&D funding, lack of venture capital support and of mechanisms for organic combination of venture capital and research institutions, low transformation rate of scientific and technological results and inadequate importance given to it.

3. Innovation Culture

Brazil is a nation pregnant with passion and romance, comparing to France. Therefore, the Brazilian people are imaginative, capable of shaping an innovation culture.

The feature of Brazil's innovation culture is pragmatism and taking into consideration national conditions, as manifested by the above-described three large Brazilian enterprises, the Agronomical Institute of Campinas and University of Campinas in their scientific and technological innovation and management innovation.

From the implementation of its "Alcohol Program" mentioned above, Brazil depended to some extent on developed countries' multinational corporations and their R&D centers in the development and transformation of scientific and technological achievements. The situation has improved in recent years, but it is still foreign research institutions and individuals that applied for and obtained the majority of patents for invention. It still takes time for Brazil to foster its own innovation culture. Compared with other nine countries covered in this book, Brazil still has a long way to go in terms of its development of an innovation culture.

4. Comments on Innovation Management and National Strength

The former Lula administrative was fruitful in national institutional design. The Brazilian people have many expectations of the new administration.

On innovation management, Brazil vigorously implemented national programs such as "Alcohol Program" and "Biodiesel Program" on the basis of institutional design on science and technology, taking into consideration the features of national resources (large varieties and high yields of cash crops) and economic development. This led to remarkable achievements. Problems are inadequate importance to basic research, low transformation efficiency of technological results, and certain dependence on research institutions and capital of developed countries, especially the United States.

The data below came from statistics by The World Bank, from which we may have a knowledge of the national strength of Brazil in 2007 ~ 2009.

In 2009, Brazil's GNI (Gross National Income) was 1,557. 24 billion dollars, ranking 10th in the world, with GNI per-capita standing at 8,040 dollars-behind the top 80 in the world; its GDP was1,571.98 billion dollars, 7% of it for agriculture, 27% for industry, and 66% for services, with average annual GDP growth at −0.2%.

In 2007, Brazil's labor force participation rate of population aged 15 and older was 65%.

In 2007, its gross enrollment ratio of preprimary, primary, secondary and tertiary education (% of cohort) was 69%, 137%, 105% and 25%, respectively.

Its hospital beds per 1,000 people were 9. 7 (in 2002 ~ 2007), its ratio of population with improved water supply to the country's total population was 91% (in 2006), and its ratio of population with improved health facilities to the country's total population was 77% (in 2006).

In 2008, its labor production (namely GDP growth rate per capita of the employed population) was 3.8%.

In 2007, its Gini coefficient (an important indicator used to measure a country's or society's gap between rich and poor; it is the per cent of that part of income for unequal distribution to the total income of all residents) was 55.0%.

In 2007, its rate of gross savings (per cent of savings to GNI) was 17.0%, and its rate of net national savings was 4.4%.

In 2007, its average annual growth of exports of goods and services was at 6.6%, and its average annual growth of imports of goods and services was at 20.7%.

In 2007, in Brazil, for every 100 people, 63 were mobile phone subscribers and 35. 2 were Internet subscribers; mobile networks covered 91% of the population; there were 36 daily newspapers per 1, 000 people (2000 ~ 2007); households with television were 91% of the total households (2006); personal computers per 100 people were 16. 1; the ratio of information and communications technology (ICT) expenditures to GDP was 5.8%; exports of ICT goods were 3. 2% of gross exports, imports of ICT goods were 14. 5% of gross imports, and exports of ICT services were 1. 8% of gross exports of services.

In Brazil, the number of researchers in R&D per million people was 461 (2000 ~ 2006); the ratio of R&D expenditures to GDP was 0. 82% (2000 ~ 2006); Ratio of high-technology exports was 12% to manufactured exports (2007); the number of patent applications filed by residents was 3,810, and that by non-residents was 20,264

(2007).

In 2007, Brazil's merchandise trade accounted for 21.9% of GDP, and service trade for 4.7%.

In 2007, Brazil had 5.026 million inbound tourists and 5.141 million outbound tourists; the country's inbound tourism expenditure accounted for 2.9% of exports, and its outbound tourism expenditure accounted for 6.6% of imports.

In 2007, Brazil had armed forces of 293,000, including 190,000 for the army, 48,000 for the navy and 55,000 for the air force. Its military expenditures were 1.6% of GDP, its weapon exports were 24 million dollars and weapon imports were 175 million dollars (The World Bank, 2009).

From the above data, Brazil is one of the most powerful developing countries and ranks first in Latin America, but still has a gap to developed countries.

Though Brazil is an agricultural country, its agriculture accounts for only 7% of GDP, its industry accounts for 27%, and its services account for 66%, revealing a sound industrial structure. Brazil has a 65% employment rate, slightly lower than China's 73%, but higher than that of the UK, France, Germany, Italy, Japan, the United States, Russia and India, ranking 2nd among the 10 countries treated in this book. But Brazil's Gini coefficient is as high as 55%, already at the dangerous brim. This suggests that inequality still exist in income distribution among the Brazilian people, and Brazil ranks last in this regard among the ten countries.

Brazil outstrips China in the four gross enrollment indicators. On health conditions, Brazil outstrips China and India in hospital beds per 1,000 people and the ratio of population with improved water supply health facilities. But on R&D, Brazil's GERD/GDP ratio is only 0.82%, suggesting that though Brazil endeavored to improve its own R&D capacity, it failed to break away with reliance on developed countries, for example, the United States, in the sphere of scientific and technological innovation.

In capital terms, Brazil's ratio of gross savings is greatly lower than China's, but higher than those of the UK and the United States.

Among the BRIC countries, Brazil has the lowest average annual GPD growth rate and the lowest average annual growth rates of goods and service exports, but it has the highest average annual growth rates of goods and service imports; in the sphere of ICT, Brazil is ahead of China, India and Russia in such indicators as mobile phone subscribers and Internet subscribers per 100 people, mobile network coverage, daily newspapers per 1,000 people, households with telephone, and personal computers per 100 people.

Abundant natural resources represent a big advantage that Brazil has to improve its national strength. Brazil's iron ore production, reserves and exports rank first in the world, and its iron ore has very high grades, largely over 60%, and are opencast and easy to exploit; it has bauxite reserves of 500 million tons, with aluminum smelting capabilities second to none in the world; it has uranium reserves of 240,000 tons, ranking 6th in the world; it has the world's largest niobium (a superconducting material) reserves-4.559 million tons in proven reserves, with niobium production accounting for 88% of the world's total; Brazil has abundant waterpower resources, with the combined installed capacity of the country's two largest hydraulic power stations alone reaching some 20 million kilowatts; a big agricultural country, Brazil has arable land of 3.7 million square kilometers, 43.3% of the territory; it is the world's largest producer of both coffee and sugar cane, and the third largest produce of soybean, cocoa and corn; its tropical rain forest in the Amazon Basin, the largest of its type in the world, covers 240 million hectares, and its countrywide forests cover 57% of the territory; Brazil has the largest offshore oilfield so far in the world, which is expected to produce more than 50 billion barrels, probably making Brazil one of the world's top ten oil producers (Editorial Board of World Affairs, 2009; Zhou Jizhong, 1993). Only the United States and Russia in the world can compare with Brazil in terms of natural resources. As long as Brazil has correct institutional design and is determined to execute, its national strength still has great room to improve, and its inclusion into the rank of world powers can be expected soon.

In conclusion, Brazil is second to none in Latin America in level of science and technology, economic strength and national competitiveness, and has vigor and potential for development as one of the BRIC countries. Brazil is on the rise.

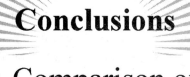

Conclusions

A Comparison of
Ten Countries

To show the rise or decay of the world's ten big countries in a book with a length of some 450,000 words, omissions are unavoidable. What's more, these countries were merely looked at from the innovation management perspective with brief accounts-rather than detailed analysis-of their economy, politics, culture and international relations. As for the ten countries, more detailed analysis was given to China, in nearly half the length of the book, which is followed by the United States, in some one fifth of book's length.

There are many ways that can be used to measure how powerful a country is. The International Institute for Management Development's (IMD's) "World Competitiveness Yearbook" and the World Economic Forum's (WEF's) "Global Competitiveness Report" are currently international authoritative publications which survey countries from the competitiveness perspective and make rankings of them. But the two evaluation indicator systems both stress quantitative indicators and data analysis thereof which though very important, can hardly accurately measure the rise or decline in national strength of a country, regardless of how precise they are. And what's more a country's competitiveness is not wholly the same as its national strength. To "national strength" as an exceptionally broad research subject, quantitative data can only reflect part of national conditions of a country. Therefore, this book was treated in a broad-brush way from its framework, chapters and sections to paragraphs. The conclusions of it of course can only be "for your information".

What is called "national rise or decay" in this book is of course the evolvement of national strength. Different from the framework and evaluation methods of the WEF and IMD which mainly use quantitative indicators for measurement of "national competitiveness", it is a comprehensive approach which views "institutional design", "innovation management" and "innovation culture" as three pillars of national strength measurement and makes reference to statistical analysis of various quantitative indicators including the WEF's and IMD's "competitiveness rankings" and The World Bank's development indicator statistics. Each of the countries covered in this book was treated in a broad-brush manner.

The national strength of a country is a relative and dynamic concept, a point repeatedly stressed in the book. On the basis of this, it is concluded from analysis that of the 10 big countries, China, India and Brazil are currently in a state of rise, while the United States, Japan, Germany, the UK, France, Italy and Russia are in a state of relative decline.

Of the three rising countries, China is rising on a large scale, India on a medium scale and Brazil on a small scale; of the 7 declining countries, Italy and the UK are in decline on a large scale, Russia on a medium scale, and the United States, Japan, Germany and France on a small scale.

The decisive factor governing a country's national strength and competitiveness is its capability of institutional design. In other words, the capability of institutional design and execution decides everything. Systems of a country, including its political, economic and scientific and technological systems, serve as the country's "outlines" which decide what measures to take and what effects they have. The execution of systems and their design are an organic whole, which is self-evident. The abilities to design systems is closely connected with the abilities of the ruling party, the abilities of party and political leaders at various levels and the abilities for institutional innovation, the execution of systems depends on the country's stability, consistency of systems and policies, and abilities of control over situations and crises. Apparently, today's China has advantages in this regard.

As far as selection of government officials is concerned, China's one-party rule and whole-nation regime enable countrywide selection of outstanding talent, while in a country where "two or more parties rule in rotation", talent are basically only selected within the ruling party, and after the expiry of its tenure (four or eight years), this ruling party is replaced by another ruling party which will select talent within its own party. In the latter case, it is almost impossible that "people work to the best of their abilities" on the one hand; on the other, with political parties ruling in rotation, systems and policies are frequently changed, making it difficult to implement systems stably and continuously, and making "sustainable development" almost impossible.

At the core of administration is the synthetic effect of efficiency and effectiveness. At this point, China is noted for the efficiency and effectiveness of its administration. Western "separation of powers", though to a certain extent able to restrict powers, leads to mutual buck passing, impediment and even condemnation and deliberate obstruction, making systems or policies greatly discounted or die on the vine.

But everything has its two sides. China's current institutional design on "one-party rule" and "whole-nation regime" also has problems which have to be solved. Some problems have come to the fore in practice, while others are in a state of latency. For example, "one-party rule" and "whole-nation regime" are likely to cause centralization of powers, and especially after significant achievements are made, there is likely to be monopoly of powers as a result of "power expansion", leading people to no longer have faith in government. Only eight years after the Kuomintang's regime was overthrown in 1949, a spate of false events took place, including the "anti-rightist struggle of 1957", "Great Leap Forward of 1958" and "Lushan Conference of 1959", which were followed by the ten-year-long catastrophic "Cultural Revolution". That was an extremely profound lesson. To prevent such occurrences, the first thing to do still is "institutional building", followed by "open-style learning", learning successful experience from the rest of the world, including the United States, Japan and India.

But learning from foreign countries must not happen before standing firm on one's foothold; otherwise it is useless. Chapter 1 "China in a Century" mentioned the promotion of the democratic system of "unity of the three rights" on the basis of sticking to the institutional design of "one-party rule" and "whole-nation regime", i. e. guaranteeing the sustainable development of the country and society with the institutional design of gradually broadening the right to supervise, to know and to vote. This experience and practice is worth learning by other countries.

As far as institutional design and execution is concerned, India and Brazil introduced a series of fundamental policies in support of national development. For example, India's policies such as "revitalizing the manufacturing industry on the basis of the fast growing service industry" and "promoting the second green revolution" not only brought into play India's advantages in modern service industries and agricultural field, but also identified the connection between economic development and scientific revolution. On international relations, India has kept fruitful relations with the United States, Europe and Russia, which is worth learning by China. Brazil's development strategy which gives priority to employment is also worth learning. At the same time, both India and Brazil are big countries with relatively stable political situations. India's Singh administration and Brazil's Lula government not only reigned for a long period but also secured the steady development of the countries, contributing much to the rise of them.

In contrast, the situation of Italy is not that optimistic. In history, Italy has ranked behind among developed countries since the 19th and 20th centuries. Among G7 countries, Italy has also ranked first or second backwards. After The Second World War, Italy thrived in several decades and reached a high level in the 1980s.

But since then, the government changed frequently and political parties were busy with elections, without any big moves in terms of national institutional design. Following the circulation of a uniform currency across EU, the Italian economy was continuously on the decline. In fact, for quite a long period, there have been no big improvements in Italy, whether in institutional design and execution, or in management innovation and cultural innovation.

Though Russia is in the same rank as Italy, the situation of it is different. Before the dissolution of the former Soviet Union, Russia, though confronted with many problems, was only behind the United States in combined political, military, economic, scientific and technological strength, and was recognized as a superpower. But after the dissolution of the Soviet Union, Russia was not that awe-inspiring. The biggest problem facing Russia still is about institutional design. The rulers hesitated between Western systems and Chinese systems, but finally chose to follow Western political systems. Therefore, Russia's current institutional design, which has not yet found a scheme appropriate for the national conditions, is reflective both of Western systems and of those of the former Soviet Union. The country's reform has neither a definite direction nor a clear picture. But different from Italy, Russia inherited much from the former Soviet Union and is a permanent member of the United Nations Security Council; its people are creative, and its natural resources are in great abundance; it is the present-day world's sole match for the United States in military strength, and it is one of the largest weapon exporters in the world. Though ranked last among the BRIC countries, Russia still has prospects for revitalization. From the dynamic perspective, Russia is most likely to "change from decline to rise" one day, as long as its institutional design is innovative enough.

The national strength of the UK—"the empire on which the sun never sets" in its prime—already began declining around The Second World War. It is because of Western political structure too that the UK has achieved little in national institutional design. The ruling parties were low-efficient, nor were they determined enough to execute their policies. On scientific and technological achievement commercialization, for example, the UK sent officials to learn Japan's experience in the 1980s when the Japanese economy was fast growing, and some institutional reforms (which can be seen from its White Papers) were carried out, but little effectiveness was resulted in. And when the financial crisis and Greece's debt crisis struck, the UK found it hard to move even a step ahead, unable to make ends meet. But fortunately, the legacy from the old-time empire, together its scientific and technological strength and soft power (such as the English language and the Commonwealth of Nations), will hold the UK from falling too fast.

From its international position, Germany has seen a decline in its national strength, compared with that whether in the 1930s or in the 1960s. The "Germany reunification" in 1990 didn't produce desired effects but turned out to be an encumbrance. But the Germans are creative, and Germany currently still is an economic power and big exporter in the world, and the backbone of EU. From the extent of decline in national strength, Germany is doing better than the UK and France.

France's situation is similar to that of Germany. Since the de Gaulle administration, France's national strength has been in decline, though not greatly, because of the politically long "left-right cohabitation" which led to no significant achievements in institutional design, innovation management and innovation culture. Whether or not France can "change from decline to rise" depends largely on the situation of Europe or EU. From the current situation, it is not very likely that France is to resurge.

Japan seemed out of control from its economic takeoff in the 1950s, "economic miracle" in the 1960s to its position as the world's second largest economy behind only the United States in the 1970s and 1980s. But because of its economic depression which has lasted from the late 1990s to the present, plus political turbulence, frequent government replacement, gross corruption of officials, and aggravated population ageing, Japan has been obviously in a state of decline. But Japan has the tradition of attaching importance to education and science and technology, which usually made it able to turn the corner through reforms on educational, scientific and technological systems. Thus, it is possible for Japan to "change from decline to rise", as long as the international economic environment improves and the country does better in institutional design.

The national strength of the United States has been analyzed in Chapter 2. Compared with its unrivaled national strength following the dissolution of the Soviet Union and Eastern Europe block, the national strength of today's United States is of course in decline. This decline has both relative and absolute aspects. Because of side effects of "separation of powers" and "two parties ruling in rotation" in American democracy, there is no "new deal" like that introduced by Roosevelt, and the struggle for power between the White House and the Congress and between the Republican Party and the Democratic Party frequently leads to the loss of development opportunities. This worldwide financial crisis originated in the maladies in American systems and mechanisms and signaled the critical situation that the United States was already "nationally bankrupt". The United State is now in debt worldwide, and if it is unable to repay in the future, the result would be disastrous. But the United States also has advantages in systems. The United States has the tradition of attaching importance to science, technology and education, and always has big moves that "turn the corner" in scientific, technological and educational systems. It is second to none in strength, tradition and practice of attracting talent, and it excels in "using people to the best of their abilities". This is particularly worth learning. Of course, the United States is still behind none in the world in terms of its economic strength, military strength and soft power, making it most likely to "change from decline to rise" as it surpassed the former Soviet Union in 1958 and Japan in the 1980s. Therefore, the United States is in the rank of those in slight decline.

Now, many are comparing China and the United States. As long as there are favorable international and national environments, I think, China is most likely to catch up with the United States between 2030 and 2050 (optimists think it is around 2030), and surpass the United States between the 2060s and the 2070s. There is a time span for the prediction because this involves factors which can hardly be predicted, such as the exchange rate between Chinese Renminbi and the US dollar, and Taiwan's return to China. But in either case, innovation is vital. Ideological, institutional, management, scientific and technological and cultural innovation underpins national strength. In this regard, the United States is still worth learning in many aspects. For example, the United States is exemplary in how to create and bring into play soft power. But the contents which are inconsistent with socialist values, such as "cultural aggregation" and "cultural hegemony", should be eliminated. Of course, if the United States' national strength declines rapidly, China's catch-up process would be accelerated now that speed is relative. Consideration should also be given to China's reunification with Taiwan, because the reunification of China will advance the realization of above predictions.

The table below shows statistics on 41 indicators given in The World Bank's *World Development Indicators 2009 and 2010*, including GDP and human development indicators. From this table, the ten countries' national strength can be measured from multiple aspects.

Table A Comparison of ten Countries in 41 Indicators

Country / Indicator	China	India	Russia	Brazil	United States	Japan	Germany	UK	France	Italy
GDP/ $ 100 million (2007, 2009)	32,055.1 49,847.3	11,768.9 13.101.7	12,900.8 12,307.3	13,133.6 15,719.8	137,514.0 142,563.0	43,842.6 50,675.3	33,173.7 33,467.0	27,720.2 21,745.3	25,898.4 26,493.9	21,016.4 21,127.8
Average annual GDP growth/% (2000 ~ 2007, 2009)	10.3 9.1	7.8 7.7	6.6 -7.9	3.3 -0.2	2.6 -2.4	1.7 -5.2	1.0 -4.9	2.6 -4.9	1.8 -2.6	1.0 -5.0
GNI/ $ 1 billion (2007,2009)	31,260 47,782.7	10,710 13,687.1	10,698 13,296.7	11,221 15,752.4	138,864 145,026.0	48,289 48,303.1	32,073 34,846.9	24,643 25,674.8	24,666 27,546.1	19,882 21,124.9
GNI per capita/ $ (2007, 2009)	2,370 3,590	950 1,180	7,530 9,370	5,860 8,040	46,040 47,240	37,790 37,870	38,990 42,560	40,660 41,520	38,810 42,680	33,490 35,080
Average annual population growth/% (2007 ~ 2015)	0.5	1.3	-0.6	1.1	0.9	-0.3	-0.2	0.3	0.3	-0.2
Average annual growth of labor force aged 15 and older/% (1990 ~2007)	1.1	1.9	-0.1	2.9	1.1	0.2	0.3	0.4	0.7	0.3
Labor force participation rate of population aged 15 and older/% (2007, 2009)	73 72	55 64	59 72	65 67	62 67	57 65	54 66	59 66	51 65	46 66
Labor productivity/% (2008)	8.6	5.4	6.3	3.8	3.0	0.4	-0.7	1.0	0.5	-0.4
Gini index/%	41.8 (2005)	36.8 (2004 – 2005)	37.5 (2005)	55.0 (2007)	40.8 (2000)	24.9 (1993)	28.3 (2000)	36.0 (1999)	32.7 (1995)	36.0 (2000)
Gross enrollment ratio of university/% (2007, 2008)	22, 23	12	70, 77	25, 34	82, 83	57, 58	—	59, 57	56, 55	67
Life expectancy(2007)	73	65	68	72	78	83	80	79	81	81
Hospital beds per 1,000 people (2002 ~ 2007)	2.2	0.9	9.7	2.4	3.1	14	8.3	3.9	7.3	3.9

Continued

Country \ Indicator	China	India	Russia	Brazil	United States	Japan	Germany	UK	France	Italy
Gross savings/GNI ratio/% (2007, 2009)	54.4 52.0	38.8 34.0	31.3 30.0	17.0 15.0	14.0 —	31.0 —	24.9 26.0	15.7 16.0 (2008)	19.2 20.0	19.8 18.0 (2008)
Net national savings/GNI ratio/% (2007)	43.7	29.2	18.4	4.4	-0.8	17.0	10.4	1.0	5.9	5.2
Average annual growth of exports of goods and services/% (2007)	19.9	7.5	8.1	6.6	—	—	—	—	—	—
Average annual growth of imports of goods and services/% (2007)	13.9	7.7	6.4	20.7	—	—	—	—	—	—
Average annual growth of agriculture/% (2007)	4.2	3.1	3.9	4.0	3.2	-1.7	-0.4	1.4	-0.3	-0.2
Average annual growth of industry/% (2000 ~ 2007)	11.6	8.6	5.8	3.1	1.3	1.7	1.5	0.1	1.4	0.3
Average annual growth of services/% (2000 ~ 2007)	10.6	9.3	7.2	3.4	2.9	1.6	1.1	3.4	2.0	1.4
Average annual growth of manufacturing/% (2000 ~ 2007)	10.9	8.0	—	3.2	2.1	1.9	1.6	-0.4	1.2	-1.2
Agriculture/GDP ratio/% (2007, 2009)	11 10	18 17	5 5 (2008)	6 7	1 —	1 —	1 1 (2008)	1 1 (2008)	2 2 (2008)	2 2 (2008)
Industry/GDP ratio/% (2007, 2009)	49 46	30 28	38 37 (2008)	29 27	22 —	30 —	30 30 (2008)	23 24 (2008)	21 20 (2008)	27 27 (2008)
Services/GDP ratio/% (2007, 2009)	40 43	52 55	57 58 (2008)	66 66	77 —	68 —	69 69 (2008)	76 76 (2008)	77 78 (2008)	71 71 (2008)
Manufacturing/GDP ratio/% (2007)	32	16	19	18	14	21	23	14	12	18

Continued

Indicator \ Country	China	India	Russia	Brazil	United States	Japan	Germany	UK	France	Italy
Military expenditures/ GDP ratio/% (2007, 2009)	2.0 2.0	2.5 3.0	3.6 4.3	1.6 1.7	4.2 4.6	0.9 1.0	1.3 1.4	2.5 2.7	2.3 2.4	1.8 1.7
Mobile phone subscribers per 100 people (2007, 2008)	42 48	21 30	115 141	63 78	85 89	84 86	118 129	118 126	90 93	152 151
Daily newspapers per 1,000 people (2000 ~ 2007)	74	71	92	36	193	551	267	290	164	137
Households with television/% (2006)	89	53	98	91	95	99	94	98	97	98
Personal computers per 100 people (2007)	5.7	3.3	13.3	16.1	80.5	—	65.6	80.2	65.2	36.7
Internet subscribers per 100 people (2007, 2008)	16.1 22.5	7.1 4.5	21.1 31.9	35.2 37.5	73.5 75.8	69.0 75.2	72.3 75.5	71.7 76.0	51.2 67.9	53.9 41.8
ICT expenditures/GDP ratio/% (2007, 2009)	7.9 5.8 (2008)	5.6 4.0	4.1 4.1	5.8 4.6	7.5 7.0	7.2 6.9	6.2 5.4	6.7 7.0	5.7 5.1	5.8 4.9
Ratio of ICT goods exports to total goods exports/% (2007, 2008)	30.9 27.5	1.3 1.3	0.5 0.4	3.2 1.8	16.3 12.8	19.3 14.3	9.6 6.9	20.5 7.7	8.0 5.4	3.7 2.8
Ratio of ICT service exports to total service exports/% (2007, 2009)	4.5 5.3 (2008)	41.6 50.3 (2008)	6.0 6.3	1.8 2.0	4.3 4.4	1.2 1.2	7.8 8.4 (2008)	7.8 8.3 (2008)	4.1 4.3	3.5 2.4
Researchers in R&D per million people (2000 ~2006, 2007)	926 1,071	111 —	3,255 3,305	461 —	4,651 —	5,546 5,573	3,386 —	3,033 2,881	3,353 —	1,407 —
R&D expenditures/ GDP/% (2000 ~ 2006, 2007)	1.42 1.49	0.69 0.80	1.08 1.12	0.82 —	2.61 2.67	3.40 3.45	2.52 2.55	1.80 1.84	2.12 2.10	1.10 —
High-technology exports/ $ 1 million(2007)	3,369.9	49.4	41.4	93.0	2,286.6	1,214.3	1,559.2	630.7	804.7	278.2

Continued

Indicator \\ Country	China	India	Russia	Brazil	United States	Japan	Germany	UK	France	Italy
High-technology exports/manufactured exports/% (2007, 2009)	30 29	5 6	7 7	12 12	28 27	19 18	14 14	19 19	19 20	7 7
Patent applications filed by residents(2007, 2008)	153,060 194,579	4,521 —	27,505 27,712	3,810 —	241,347 231,588	333,498 330,110	47,853 49,240	17,375 16,523	14,722 14,743	9,255 —
Merchandise trade/GDP ratio/% (2007)	67.8	30.8	44.8	21.9	23.1	30.4	71.9	38.1	45.1	47.4
Service trade/GDP ratio/% (2007, 2009)	7.9 6.8	15.2 15.7	7.6 8.4 (2008)	4.7 4.8	6.3 6.1	6.4 —	14.4 14.5	17.5 18.5	10.7 10.2	11.1 10.4
FDI net inflows/GDP ratio/% (2007)	4.3	2.0	4.3	2.6	1.7	0.5	1.6	7.1	6.2	1.9

Source: The World Bank, 2009; The World Bank, 2010.

Above indicator data can be analyzed from several levels.

The first level is a comparison of BRIC countries, the second level is a comparison of BRIC countries with developed countries, and the third level is a comparison of the ten countries.

China, India, Russia and Brazil are representative of emerging countries in the world, and they are likely to be world powers in the future. The 8 years from 2000 to 2007 marked the most robust economic growth of emerging countries. The average annual GDP growth rate of each of the BRIC countries was higher than that of developed countries, with China and India leading the BRIC countries. But as far as the absolute value of GDP and GNI are concerned, China was much higher than three other countries, whose GDP and GNI already topped the total sum of three other countries. In 2010 China overtook Japan to become the world's second largest economy, with GDP probably exceeding the total sum of three other BRIC countries. But in GNI per capita, Russia and Brazil are much ahead of China and India. In population, China, India and Brazil outstrip Russia in population growth and labor force growth. As for employment rate, China leads the 10 countries. But in national income distribution, Brazil's Gini coefficient is already at the edge of danger (if Gini coefficient is greater than 45% ~55%, inequality in income distribution will increase fast), while those of China, India and Russia differ not much. Labor productivity, the GDP growth rate per capita of employed population, comes from the combination of industrial capital, labor and skills. China leads the 10 countries in labor productivity, and the BRIC countries outperform developed countries in this indicator. Germany and Italy have negative labor productivity.

On university enrollment ratio, Russia stands out in the group of ten countries, ahead of other countries at a ratio as high as 77%. As for life expectancy, the BRIC countries are lower than developed ones. On the indicator of hospital beds per 1,000 people, China and India are lower than other countries, suggesting that the two big developing countries till have a long way to go in the sphere of health.

In capital terms, China is much ahead of other countries in gross savings ratio and net national savings ratio; the three Asian countries—China, India and Japan each have high figures in this regard, which is probably connected with Asian culture and values. The United States has a negative net national savings ratio, which is of course related to its values and institutional design such as "credit consumption". On foreign direct investment (FDI), the UK and France have obviously higher FDI net inflows than other countries, showing that within the statistical period the two developed countries performed well in attracting foreign capital.

Only the emerging countries were compared on the indicator of average annual growth ratios of goods and service imports and exports. China has a quite outstanding export growth ratio, while Brazil has the largest imports. China is only behind Germany in goods trade's share of GDP, and India is only behind the UK in service trade's share of GDP.

On industrial structure, India has a sounder industrial structure than China, whose services' share of GDP is 12 percentage points higher than China's. But China's manufacturing's share of GDP not only doubles that of India, but also is higher than those of other 9 countries.

In developed countries, agriculture's share of GDP is very low, but services' share of GDP is quite high. China needs to increase its services' share of GDP, which is the direction in which China adjusts its industrial structure in the future, giving special priority to modern service industries including finance, telecommunications and R&D. Pleasingly, China outstrips nine other countries in growth rates of agriculture, industry, manufacturing and services.

On information indicators regarding national development, developed countries lead developing countries in mobile phone subscribers per 100 people, daily newspapers per 1,000 people, households with television, computers per 100 people and Internet subscribers per 100 people, which is something that is expected. But among the BRIC countries, Russia outperforms three other countries, and India lags behind. It seems that India's leading advantages in the IT field have not yet benefit the common people. China is ahead of other countries in ICT (information and Communications Technology) expenditures' share of GDP and ICT goods exports' share of total goods exports, but India is far ahead of nine other countries in ICT service exports' share of total service exports.

On GERD/GDP ratio, namely R&D intensity, Japan ranks first for its 3.45% (2007), immediately followed by the United States and Germany. China's R&D intensity is 1.49% (up to 1.70% in 2009), which is the highest among developing countries and higher than that of Italy as a developed country. On R&D researchers per million people, developed countries generally lead developing countries (in fact, Russia cannot be counted as a developing country, but an industrialized country). On high-technology exports and high-technology exports' share of manufactured exports, China is far ahead of 9 other countries; though this represents China's strength, multinational corporations within China contribute a lot in this regard. As for the indicator of patent applications filed by residents, with 194,579 (2008) China is only behind the United States and Japan and far ahead of 7 other countries. According to the *Bulletin of the Second Investigation of Scientific Research and Experimental Development Resources* co-published in November 2010 by China's National Bureau of Statistics and Ministry of Science and Technology, in 2009, China's GERD/GDP already reached 1.70%, its GERD arrived at 580,210 million yuan (about 84.95 billion dollars), and its R&D researchers reached 2.2912 million person-year (NBS of China, 2010).

As to the sensitive indicator of military expenditures/GDP ratio, the United States and Russia are far ahead of other countries, with China ranking 6th. It should be noted that The World Bank's data on China is higher than what is published by China itself. Undoubtedly, in addition to the big figures, the United States and Russia have much higher military strength, especially in nuclear weapons, than other eight countries.

In addition, The World Bank's *World Development Indicators 2009* also shows that between 2005 and 2007, economies with current account surpluses were China

(26% of all surplus economies), Germany (18% of all surplus economies), Japan (15 of all surplus economies) and Russia (5% of all surplus economies), and current account deficit economies were the United States (57% of all deficit economies), the UK (6% of all deficit economies) and Italy (3% of all deficit economies).

In addition to the indicators given in The World Bank's *World Development Indicators 2009*, the institutional design, innovation management and innovation culture, which this book has tried to explore, are more important aspects that form the national strength of a country. Or in other words, it is the combined action of the three aspects that impel the generation of abovementioned indicator data. What's more, the vitality of private enterprises, including their capabilities of international business operation, is an important part of national strength. India has more advantages than China in this aspect.

With respect to financial strength, China is far behind Western developed countries. But even for the most financially powerful United States, its delight equals worry: it has the world's most developed capital market and securities market as well as an international currency, but it is also the largest debtor nation in the world.

To consider varieties of indicators, aspects, fields and contents described above, the rise or decline of a country can only be a relative and dynamic concept and cannot be described briefly.

Because there are many uncertainties about the change of international situation and factors responsible for change in national strength of countries are in a constant flux, the actual rise or decay of other countries might be different from above accounts. But China's development will be wholly contrary to such views as "China Collapse" and "China Threat", and is bound to stride on the road of "sustainable development".

References

Alexis de Tocqueville. 2007. *Democracy in America.* Translated and edited by Zhang Xiaoming. Beijing: Beijing Publishing Group, 53, 70-71.

Alfred D. Chandler. 2004. *Big Business and the Wealth of Nations.* Translated by Liu Xielin et al. Beijing: Peking University Press, 260-280.

Angela Merkel. 2009. A speech by German Chancellor Angela Merkel at the founding ceremony of the German Academy of Science and Technology. Translated by Huang Qun. *Scientific and Technological Policy and Development Strategy,* (5): 11-15.

Bao Guozhi, Li Xian. 2008. *Tasly Strengthens Independent Innovation for Great Health Industry.* http://www. tasly. com/news. aspx. [March 17, 2008].

Bush V. 1960. *Science—The Endless Frontier.* Washington D. C. : National Science Foundation.

Business Week. May 30, 2010. Top 100 Scientific and Technological Companies. *Business Week.*

Carol L. 2010. Can Ellen Kullman make DuPont great again? *Fortune China,* (7): 114, 121.

Celso Amorim. 2010. September 2, 2010. *Brazil Will Play an Ambitious Role in the New Balance of the World.* Originally published on Le Monde, August 31. Reference News, 3.

Chang Qing. 2006. *A Survey of Science and Technology in India.* Beijing: Science Press, 5-7, 14-17, 35-36, 40-49, 115-123, 164.

Chang Wenzuo. 2007. *Administer according to Law to Ensure Administrative Protection of Drugs.* Beijing: A speech at 2007 Pharmaceutical Intellectual Property Forum.

Chang Xing. 2007. North China Pharmaceutical Group Corp. : An Innovative Mindset towards International Competition. *Chinese Journal of Medical Guide,* (5): 225-227.

Cheng Liru. 2007. *Strategy for Value Innovation and Enterprise Technology Innovation: A Study of the Chinese Pharmaceutical Industry.* Beijing: University of International Business and Economics Press, 71.

Cheng Zhendeng et al. 1992. *On Investment in Science and Technology: A Study of Unified Investment in Science and Technology and Investment System in China.* Beijing: Scientific and Technological Literature Publishing House, 7-15.

Chen Jin, Zheng Gang. 2009. *Innovation Management.* Beijing: Peking University Press, 1-21.

Chen Yanbing, He Wuxing. 2008. *Why China Is So Successful: A Record of Top Decisions Leading China to Success.* Beijing: CITIC Press, 11-12.

Chen Zhengliang. 2008. *China "Soft Power" Development Strategy Research.* Beijing: People's Publishing House, 299.

China Association of Communications Enterprises. 2005. *China's Communications Industry Development Summit.* http//tech. qq. com[July 8, 2005].

China Innovative Enterprises Development Report Editorial Board. 2009. *China Innovative Enterprises Development Report 2009.* Beijing: Economy & Management Publishing House, 149-154, 190-194, 210-220, 233-262.

Department for Innovation, Universities & Skills of the UK. 2008. *The 2008 R&D Scoreboard.* Quoted from Institute of Scientific and Technical Information of China. 2009. A Survey of Global

Investment in Science and Technology.

Department of Trade and Industry of the UK. 2005. Science and Innovation Investment Framework 2004-2014. *Scientific and Technological Policy and Development Strategy*, (1): 9-11.

Diane Ravitch. 1995. *The American Reader: Words that Moved a Nation*. Beijing: SDX Joint Publishing Company, 49.

DiMasi J A. 1995. Success rates for new drugs entering clinical trial testing in the united states. *Clinical Pharmacology and Therapeutics*, (58): 1-14.

Domestic Policy Council and Office of Science and Technology Policy, White House, USA. 2006. *The American Competitiveness Initiative-Leading the World in Innovation*. http://www. whitehouse. gov/state of the union/2006/aci/[2006-11-27].

Dong Biying. 2004. *Top Ten Pieces of Scientific and Technological News in Russia in 2003*. www. people. com. cn. [August 1, 2004].

Dong Xiuli. 2010. *Political Basis of the United States*. Beijing: Peking University Press, 44-45, 78-80.

Editorial Board of World Affairs. 2009. *World Affairs Almanac 2008/2009*. Beijing: World Affairs Press, 149, 154, 237-241, 583, 590- 600, 606, 744-748, 751, 754-758, 797-801, 881-883, 886.

Ernest Gundling. 2001. *The 3M Way to Innovation*. Translated by Chen Xuesong et al. Beijing: Huaxia Publishing House, 204-205.

EU report. The 2009 EU Industrial R&D Investment Scoreboard. Compiled by Institute of Scientific and Technical Information of China. *A Survey of Global Investment in Science and Technology*, (23-24): 1-7.

Feng Guowu. 2010a-8-8. A Historical Chapter That Opened CTM Internationalization: How Tasly Went Through FDA Approvals. *Science and Technology Daily*, 1-2.

Feng Guowu. 2010-b-9-16. Let CTM Compounds Soar: Tasly's Journey of CTM Discovery. *Science and Technology Daily*, 8.

Financial Innovation and Science & Technology Forum. http://www. bomed. net: 8080/tepic. jsp [June 18, 2008].

Fred E. January 31, 2002. How the University of Utah Promotes Industry-University-Research institution Integration: Partnership between Public and Private Sectors for the Promotion of Economic Growth. *Science Times*.

Gabriel A. Almond et al. 2010. *Comparative Politics Today : A World View, Updated Edition (8 th Edition)*. Translated by Yang Hongwei et al. Shanghai: Shanghai People's Publishing House, 175-188, 362, 368-369, 371, 380, 834-838.

Gao Lingyun, Wang Qing. 2007. North China Pharmaceutical Group Corp: A New Journey of Scientific Development. *Hebei Enterprises*, (4): 46-47.

Gareth Jones and Jennifer George. 2005. *Contemporary Management (3rd Edition)*. Translated by Zheng Fengtian and Zhao Shufang. Beijing: Posts & Telecom Press, 6-8.

GEC program. 2003. *Management Tools Analysis.* Guangzhou: Guangzhou Economic press, 39-43, 145-149,381-382.

Genrich Altshuller. 2008. *40 Principles-TRIZ Keys to Technical Innovation.* Translated by Lin Yue et al. Harbin: Heilongjiang Science and Technology Press, 1-13, 119-126.

G. Pascal Zachary. 1999. *Endless Frontier: Vannevar Bush, Engineer of the American Century.* Translated by Zhou Huimin et al. Shanghai: Shanghai Scientific and Technological Education Publishing House, 3, 285-312.

Han Jun. 2005. *A Survey of Science and Technology in Italy.* Beijing: Science Press, 16-25, 58, 42-44, 120, 160-180, 5, 33.

Han Shide. September 8, 2010. Innovation Relay Center: Build a Bridge for Technology Transfer. *Science and Technology Daily,* 6.

Hartmann G C, Myers B M. 2000. *Technical Risk, Product specifications, and Market Risk.* Washington D. C. : National Institute of Standards and Technology of US Department of Commerce[2010-12-30].

Heinz Weihrich and Harold Koontz. 2004. *Management: A Global Perspetive.* Translated by Ma Chunguang. Beijing: Economic Science Press, 4.

Hu Angang et al. 2004. An Empirical Analysis of the Rapid Rise of Media in China. *Strategy and Management,* (2). Quoted from: Chen Zhengliang. 2008. *China "Soft Power" Development Strategy Research.* Beijing: People's Publishing House, 299.

Huang Shuofeng. 2006. *Rivalries between Major Powers: A Comparison of World Powers' Overall Natonal Strength.* Beijing: World Affairs Press, 11-13, 17-26, 76-105.

Huawei Technologies Co. Ltd.. www. huawei. com [February 9, 2009].

Hu Jintao. January 10, 2006. Stick to the Independent Innovation Road with Chinese Characteristics and Endeavor to Build an Innovation-oriented Country. *Guangming Daily,* 1.

IMD. 2010. *World Competitiveness Yearbook Results 2010.* http://imd. org.

Institute of Scientific and Technical Information of China. 2010. U. S. R&D Companies Employed 27 Million People Worldwide in 2008. *A Survey of Global Investment in Science and Technology,* (14-15): 1-4.

J. Carl Hsu 2001. *The Way We Do It—Bell Labs And Other Innovative Stories.* Beijing: China Commercial Press, 46-50.

Jiang Zemin. 2006. *A Collection of Works by Jiang Zemin (3rd Volume).* Beijing: People's Publishing House, 34-41, 64-68, 101-106.

Jin Zhonghua et al. 2005. *A Survey of Science and Technology in EU.* Beijing: Science Press, 17-18, 207-213.

Joe Tidd, John Bessant and Keith Pavitt. 2008. *Managing Innovation: Integrating Technological, Market and Organizational Change (3rd Edition).* Translated by Wang Yuehong and Li Weili. Beijing: Tsinghua University Press, 3-31.

John E. Ettlie. 2008. *Managing Innovation: New Technology, New Products, and New Services in a*

Global Economy. Translated by Wang Lihua et al. Shanghai: Shanghai University of Finance & Economics Press, 3-41.

Jolly V K. 2001. Commercializing New Technologies: Getting from Mind to Market. Translated by Zhang Zuoyi et al. Beijing: Tsinghua University Press, 20.

Joseph E. Stiglitz. August 19, 2010. How Does China Build an Innovation System. *Social Sciences Weekly*, 1.

Lee H, Choi B. 2003. Knowledge management enablers, processes, and organizational performance: an integrative view and empirical examination. *Journal of Management Information System*, (20/1): 179-228.

Liao Jianxin. 2006. An Analysis of China Mobile's Industry Model. *China New Telecommunications*, (9): 8.

Li Ruqi, Li Xiaodong and Ge Dongsheng. 2006. *The Power of Xiuzheng*. Beijing: Peking University Press, 8.

Li Shuangfu, Hua Xuan. 2010a-10-15. NCPC Accelerates Industrial Transformation and Upgrading by Force of Cephalosporin. *Science and Technology Daily*, 3.

Li Shuangfu, Hua Xuan. 2010b-10-16. R&D "Acceleration" Brings about Endless Power. *Science and Technology Daily*, 3.

Liu Bin et al. October 18, 2010. Bibliometrics Shows Fruitful Global Bioenergy Research Findings. *Science Times*, B2.

Liu Chuanshu. August 26, 2010. Scientific and Technological Innovation: Shenzhen Special Economic Zone over Past Three Decades. *Science and Technology Daily*, 4.

Liu Lina, February 11, 2009. A Paper-to-Money Game: The Real Truth of U. S. Debts. *Global View*, March 3, 2009. Quoted from China Reading Weekly.

Liu Linsen. 2007. India's Strategic Transition from BPO to KPO. *Economic Herald*, (9): 61-64.

Liu Manhong. 1998. *Venture Capital: Innovation and Finance*. Beijing: China Renmin University Press, 179-196.

Liu Qiusheng. 2001. New Product Development. Beijing: Tsinghua University Press, 62.

Liu Wei, Tong Xiaohui and Yao Yunhua. 2007. An Analysis of Tasly's "Patent Network" Surrounding Danshen Products. *Journal of Traditional Chinese Medicine Management*, 15(10): 727-729.

Liu Xielin. 1999. Strengths and Weaknesses of Diversified Operation from the Core Competitiveness Point of View. *China Soft Science Magazine*, (7): 104-107.

Liu Xielin, Ma Chi and Tang Shiguo. 1999. What Is a National Innovation System. *The Journal of Quantitative & Technical Economics*, 16(5): 20-22.

Liu Xielin, Zhao Jie. 1999. An Evaluation of Interaction in China's Innovation System. *Scientific Research Management*, 20(6): 1-7.

Liu Yuexuan. 2006. *A Study of Tasly's Competition Strategy*. Chengdu: a master thesis from Southwest Jiaotong University, 31.

Li Wei. 2010. *Japan Development Report* (2010). Beijing: Social Sciences Academic Press (China), 412-414.

Li Wenjian, Chen Yang and Xie Gang. 2007. Company IPR Management Based on Resource Competitive Views: An Example of Tasly Pharmaceutical Co. , Ltd. *Intellectual Property*, (4): 45-49.

Li Wenjian, Li Chuncheng. 2008. Developing Autonomous Brands: Interaction between Technology, Market and Intellectual Property. *Studies in Science of Science*, 26(1): 119-123.

Li Xiangping, Wang Ying. 2010. Track Latest Research Findings in Social Scientific Study of Religion: The 7th Annual Conference of the Social Scientific Study of Religion in China Held in Beijing. *Social Sciences Weekly*, 4.

Li Xu. 2003. Tasly's Development and Protection of Independent Intellectual Property. *Tianjin Science & Technology*, 30(2): 11-12.

Lu Yongxiang. 1998. *Innovation and the Future: National Innovation System Geared Towards the Age of Knowledge Economy*. Beijing: Science Press, 7-10.

Lü Jiang. 1997. The Basic Characteristic of NCPC's Corporate Culture. *Economy and Management*, (6): 21.

Mark Dutz. 2009. *Unleashing India's Innovation: Toward Sustainable And Inclusive Growth*. Translated by Zhang Chuanliang. Beijing: CITIC Press, 21-35, 50-58, 60-63, 84-88, 90-91, 108, 148.

Martin Jacques. 2010. *When China Rules the World: the Rise of the Middle Kingdom and the End of the Western World*. Translated by Liu Qu. Beijing: CITIC Press, 3.

Ma Xiushan. 2001. *Innovation and Protection: A Revelation of Patent Management*. Beijing: Science Press, 62, 79-81, 84-85, 109.

Ma Yan. 2007. *An Integrated Study of Biomedical Value China*. Shanghai: a doctor thesis from Fudan University, 125.

Ma Youshong, Wang Na. 2007. CSPC Pharmaceutical Group Spots a "New Domain" of Scientific and Technological Innovation. *China Venture Capital*, (6): 36-38.

Michael Beer et al. 2007. Hewlett-Packard: Culture in Changing Times. Translated by Zhu Chunling. *Harvard Business School Case* (II): *Organizational Behavior*. Beijing: China Renmin University Press: 94.

Michael Porter. 1997. *Competitive Advantage*. Translated by Chen Xiaoyue. Beijing: Huaxia Publishing House, 241.

Michael Porter. 2007. *The Competitive Advantage of Nations*. Translated by Qiu Ruyun. Beijing: CITIC Press, 17-18, 65, 241, 324-347, 661-664, 350-385, 386-417, 446-468, 469-493.

Miles I, Boden M. 2000. Services, knowledge and intellectual property// Andersen B, Howells J R, Hull I Miles, Roberts J. *Knowledge and innovation in the new service economy*. Cheltenham: Edward Elgar.

Ministry of Education and Science of the Russian Federation. 2003. Basic Directions of the Policy of the Russian Federation on Innovation System Development until 2010. Translated by Ye Xiaoling. *Scientific and Technological Policy and Development Strategy*, (4): 10-20.

Ministry of Higher Education and Research of France. 2009. National Research and Innovation Strategy. Translated by Zhou Xiaofang. *Scientific and Technological Policy and Development Strategy*, (11): 6-19; (12): 5-15.

Ministry of Science and Technology. 2007. *China Science and Technology Indicators 2006*. Beijing: Scientific and Technological Literature Publishing House, 210.

Ministry of Science and Technology of China. 2010. *Report on International Scientific and Technological Development 2010*. Beijing: Science Press, 136-144, 153-155, 158-162, 164-168, 170-176, 177-182, 281-301, 308-311.

National Bureau of Statistics of China, Ministry of Science and Technology etc. November 24, 2010. Bulletin of the Second Investigation of Scientific Research and Experimental Development Resources. *Science and Technology Daily*, 5-7.

National Innovation Capacity Evaluation Taskforce of the Development Research Center of China Association for Science and Technology. 2009. *Evaluation Report on National Innovation Capacity*. Beijing: Science Press, 117-120, 123-127.

OECD. 1994. *Frascati Manual 1993*. Paris: OECD, 17-37.

OECD. 2006. *Governance of Public Research: Toward Better Practices*. Translated by Fan Lihong et al. Beijing: Scientific and Technological Literature Publishing House, 106-108.

Pan-Pacific Management Institute, Fortune China. 2010. Most Innovative Chinese Companies in 2010. *Fortune China*, (168): 56-58, 60, 62, 70, 72-76.

Pan Song. 2010. *We Should We Learn from India: The Rise of Super-class Enterprises in India and Revelations*. Beijing: China Machine Press, 9, 2-22, 38-44, 54-70.

Paul Trott. 2005. *Innovation Management and New Product Development* (2nd Edition). Translated by Wu Dong et al. Beijing: China Renmin University Press, 1-29.

Penick J C, Pursell M, Sherwood D, et al. 1972. *The Politics of American Science 1939 to the Present*. Boston: MIT Press, 101-188.

Project Management Institute. 2000. *A Guide to the Project Management Body of Knowledge*. Newtown Square, Pennsylvania, USA.

Public Affairs Office of the Embassy of the United States in China. 1984. *Steering the Course: Policymaking in the United States*. Public Affairs Office of the Embassy of the United States in China, 6-8, 45-46.

Publicity Division of Administrative Committee of Zhongguancun Science Park. June 28, 2010. Action Plan for Building the Zhongguancun National Innovation Demonstration Zone (2010 ~ 2012). *Science and Technology Daily*, 7.

Qiu Liangju. 2007. France Tries to Reform and Improve its Scientific and Technological Innovation System. *Scientific and Technological Policy and Development Strategy*, (11): 27-31.

Qiu Tong. 2006. *Xiu Laigui and Xiuzheng Philosohpy*. Changchun: Jilin People's Publishing

House, 30.

Rebecca Saunders. 2002. *Business the Dell Way*. Translated by Zhou Yueping. Beijing: China Machine Press, 25, 27-30, 57-58.

Research Group on Development and Strategy of Science and Technology of China. 2002. *Research Report on Development of Science and Technology of China* (2001). Beijing: CPC Central Party School Press, 124, 165-167.

Science Times. June 3, 2010. The U. S. House of Representatives Votes Down a Bill of Increasing Research and Education Funding. *Science Times*, A4.

Shi Liping. 2010. *France Competitiveness Clusters Entered a Stage of Adjustment and Improvement*. http://www. fr. china embassy. org [April, 15, 2010].

Shi Wenjun, Zhu Changhui. 2007. A New Exploration into How Domestic Pharmaceutical Enterprises Compete with Foreign Counterparts. *Modern Preventive Medicine*, 34 (17): 3293-3294.

Shi Yigogn, Rao Yi. 2010. A Discussion of Problems about the Present Research Fund Allocation System and Research Culture in China. *E-Magazine at ScienceNet. cn*, (172): 9-13.

Sigvald Harryson. 2004. *Japanese Technology and Innovation Management: From Know-how to Know-who*. Translated by Hua Hongci et al. Beijing: Peking University Press, 194-198.

Song Luzheng. March 14, 2010. How is China's political system superior to Western one. *Reference News*, 14.

Tait J, Williams R. 1999. Policy approaches to research and development: foresight, framework and competitiveness. *Science and Public Policy*, 26(2): 101-112.

Tang Genghua et al. 2002. *Top 10 Ideas about High-technology Industrialization in Silicon Valley*. Beijing: Haitian Publishing House, 43.

Tang Jin. 2006. *The Rise of the Big Power*. Beijing: People's Publishing House, 152-154, 171-173, 408.

Tasly Newsgroup. 2006. *Tasly Builds a Modern CTM Industry China through Independent Innovation*. http://www. tasly. com [January 10, 2006].

The British Council. 1998. *A guide to the organization of science and technology in Britain*. London: The British Council.

Theodore W. Schultz. 2001. *Origins of Increasing Returns*. Translated by Yao Zhiyong and Liu Qunyi. Beijing: Peking University Press, 26.

The World Bank. 2009. *World Development Indicators 2009*. Translated under the direction of China Financial & Economic Publishing House. Beijing: China Financial & Economic Publishing House, 14, 22, 40, 52, 64, 72, 84, 122, 192, 202, 208, 294, 295, 296, 307, 314, 328, 390.

The World Bank. 2010. *World Development Indicators 2010*. http://data. worldbank. org[2010-12-20].

Tian Lan. 2004. NCPC's Road to Technological Innovation. *China Venture Capital & High-Tech*, (10): 60-62.

UNESCO. 1990. *Guide to Statistics on Science and Technology*. Translated by Tian Qingwen. Beijing: Scientific and Technological Literature Publishing House, 1-30.

V. Bush et al. 2004. *Science: The Endless Frontier*. Translated by Fan Dainian et al. Beijing: The Commercial Press, 1-64.

Wang Weigang. 2007. *A Study of Characteristics and Mechanism of Pharmaceutical Growth in China*. Shanghai: A doctor thesis from Tongji University, 48.

Wang Yongwei. 2007. *Implement Intellectual Property Strategy to Promote Enterprise Development*. A speech at 2007 Pharmaceutical Intellectual Property Forum, Beijing.

Wang Yumei. 2007. *Obstacles to the Growth of Pharmaceutical Industry in China*. Shanghai: Shanghai People's Publishing House, 47-48.

Wang Yuquan. 2005. *The Spring of Telecommunications*. www. tech-ex. com [July 7, 2005].

Wang Zhongyu. July 30, 2009. Get out of the Frog of "Overall National Strength". *Science Times*, A3.

Wang Zixian. 2008. *A Report on Productive Service Development in China* in 2007. Beijing: Economy & Management Publishing House, 107-114, 360-361.

WEF. 2010. *The Global Competitiveness Report 2010 ~ 2011*. http://weforum. org[2010-12-20].

Wei Jiang, Wang Yi. 1999. Enterprise Innovation System: A Case Study of NCPC's Technological Innovation System. *Chemical Enterprise Management*, (7): 26.

Wen Jiabao. June 2, 2010. *Speech by China Premier Wen Jiabao when interviewed afternoon on June 1 by NHK announcer Hiroko Kuniya*. http://news. ifeng. com [June 2, 2010].

Wu Guisheng. 2000. *Technological Innovation Management*. Beijing: Tsinghua University Press, 31, 138-140.

Wu Hongyue. November 26, 2007. CSPC Pharmaceutical Group Puzzled by Industrialization of New Drugs. *Science and Technology Daily*, 7.

Wu Jinglian. 2010. *The Course of Economic Reform in Contemporary China*. Shanghai: Shanghai Far East Publishers, 22-25.

Xia Jiechang et al. 2008. *A Study of Integrated Development of High Technology and Modern Services*. Beijing: Economy & Management Publishing House, 2-3.

Xu Bin. September 16, 2010. *Independent Innovation as a National Policy: An Interview with MOST Policy and Regulation Office Director Mei Yonghong*, 3.

Xu Qingrui. 2007. *Overall Innovation Management: Theory and Practice*. Beijing: Science Press, 3-13.

Xu Zhi, Zhou Jizhong. 2008. Enigma of Chinese basic research intensity: An explanation based on the AH model. *Scientific Research Management*, (1): 63-69.

Yan Aoshuang. August 26, 2010. The Exploration and Practice of "Beijing Model" for Transformation of Scientific and Technological Results. *Science and Technology Daily*, 8.

Yang Hong, Sheng Yuanfeng. 2000. New Brands for Traditional Medicine. *China Trademark*, (12): 15-16.

Yang Shizhang. January 10, 2007. A Revelation of Tasly's Defense against Patent Infringement. *China Consumer News*, 6.

Yang Zhenyin, Deng Ning and Liu Xin. 2003. Reflections on Present-day Science and Technology Reform in China. *Strategy and Management*, (3): 29-36.

Yao Weibao. 2005. China's Biotechnology and New Pharmaceuticals Patent Protection: The Present Situation, Problems and Sustainable Innovation Strategy. *Science and Technology Management Research*, 25(9): 22.

Yao Wenping, Wang Weiwei and Xiao Feng. July 27, 2005. Tasly's Way to an International Brand. *China Intellectual Property News*, 4.

Ye Chuhua. 2010. *When Will China Surpasses the United States*. Taiyuan: Shanxi Publishing Group and Shanxi Economic Publisher, 117, 119-127.

Yin Xiaoshan. 2009. India's Outsourcing Bypasses Europe and Japan. *CEOCIO China*, (18): 20.

Yuan Hongmei, Yu Shuangli. 2007. International Intellectual Property Protection and Development Right Study: Drugs as Study Samples. *Journal of Liaoning University (Philosophy and Social Sciences Edition)*, 35(3): 143-146.

Yuan Nansheng. 2007. *Know India*. Beijing: China Social Sciences Press, 29-33, 239-240.

Yuan Zhengguang. 1993. *Giants in a Global Economy: Global Top 100 Conglomerates*. Beijing: Encyclopedia of China Publishing House, 143-154, 192, 332-341, 406-411, 530.

Yu Minduo. 2009. *Feel the Dedication Spirit of Russian Scientists*. Http://www. gkong. com [August 20, 2009]. A contribution by Expert Consultative Committee of Chinese Association of Automation.

Zeng Peiyan. 2010. *An Overview of Decision Making for West China Development*. Beijing: Chinese Communist Party History Publishing House and Xinhua Publishing House, 4-21, 39-40, 84-87.

Zhang Jing. 2005. Tasly: Core Competitiveness Equals to Marketing plus R&D. *Stock Market Trend Analysis Weekly*, (7-8): 27-28.

Zhang Xueying. 2009. Corporate Culture and Human Resource Management in India. *China Petrochemical Industry*, (4).

Zhang Zhengmin, Duan Ziyuan. August 19, 2010. Western China Likely to Become a New Barn in China. *Science Times*, A3.

Zhao Zhongjian. 2007. *Innovation Leads the World: Innovation and Competitiveness Strategy of the United States*. Shanghai: East China Normal University Press, 1-31, 39-55, 64-76, 78, 158-167, 202-258.

Zhou Jizhong. 1987. *Communities in the Domain of Science*. Beijing: People's Publishing House, 13-14, 41-42.

Zhou Jizhong. 1991. *The United States as a Scientific and Technological Power: Decision-making Trends*. Beijing: Science Press, 3-5, 22-25.

Zhou Jizhong. 1993. *International Scientific, Technological and Economic Cooperation*. Beijing:

Science Press, 39-40, 47-49, 64-65, 71-72, 82, 92-94, 111-112.

Zhou Jizhong. 2002. *Scientific and Technological Innovation Management*. Beijing: Economic Science Press, 3-9, 46, 47-48, 49-62, 71-86, 111-113, 136, 148-149, 154-155, 158-159, 195-200, 217-218, 374-376, 379-382, 390, 406-407, 446-449, 451-452.

Zhou Jizhong et al. 1993. *A Discussion of Science, Technology and Education*. Beijing: Science Press, 146.

Zhou Jizhong et al. 2009. *The Basis and Source of Innovation: Basic Research Investment, Evaluation and Coordination*. Beijing: Science Press, 1-4, 371-402.

Zhou Jizhong, Wu Zuoming. 1993. *The Science of Scientific and Technological Incentives: The Mechanism and Functions of a Scientific Incentive System*. Hangzhou: Zhejiang Science & Technology Press, 33-34, 111-112.

Zhou Jizhong, Xu Zhi and Hou Liang. 2009a. *Research, Development and Service in Innovation System Engineering*. Beijing: Economic Science Press, 1-10, 102-136, 203-242.

Zhou Jizhong, Zhao Yuanliang and Ye Zhimin. 2009b. *Linkage between Technological Innovation and Intellectual Property*. Beijing: Science Press, 1-11, 99-127.

Zhou Jizhong, Zhang Guilin and Hou Liang. 2007. "R&D and Service" Linkage at Both Ends of Industry Chain: The Core of Value Innovation. *China Soft Science Magazine*, (2): 49-52.

Zhou Shangang et al. 1993. *Potential for Development: An Analysis of Basic and Applied Research Resources in China*. Wuhan: Huazhong University of Science & Technology Press.

Zhou Yawei. 2007. *Puzzles and Breakthroughs in CTM Intellectual Property*. 2007 Pharmaceutical Intellectual Property Forum.

Zhou Zhiwei. 2009. From "a Persistent Potential Power" to "a Rising BRIC Country": On Transition of the Brazilian Development Model. *The Contemporary World*, (11).

Zhuang Wu. 2007. Pharmaceutical Innovation: A Long Way Ahead. *Shanghai Medical & Pharmaceutical Journal*, 28(1): 27-31.

Zhu Min, Sun Ruihua. 2007. A Unique View on Breakthrough in Pharmaceutical Innovation System. *New Economy Weekly*, (11): 13-27.

Zhu Yingying, Li Ping and Zhu Xiaolin. 2008. *An Insight into Financial Innovation of Chinese Banks: Financial Product-based Research*. 3rd Financial Innovation and Science & Technology Forum. http://www.borneol.net:8080/topic.jsp [June 18, 2008].